Pipedreams

A Freak Tale

Stephen Hartford
Michael Harmon

PIPEDREAMS

A Freak Tale

RETROBATE BOOKS
Barrington, NH

Published by Retrobate Books (USA)
www.retrobatebooks.com

First published in May 2012

Pipedreams – A Freak Tale is purely a work of fiction, whose sole purpose is to entertain. All references to persons living, dead, or yet to be born are completely fabricated, unless you are a time-traveling hippie from 2468 and can prove otherwise.

Pipedreams – A Freak Tale is intended to reflect the culture of a particular time and place, and is not meant to serve as a template on how to live one's life. No one should use drugs or associate with communists. Drugs aren't particularly good for you and communists are really boring.

Printed in the United States of America.

Dedications

Steve would like to dedicate this book to his sister Rebecca Carson, his nephews Dean and Dana Murdo, his grandniece Echo Howes and his grandnephew Shane Savage, and would be remiss if he failed to include the boys of Eastside: Weeksie Bird, Haremoan and Tinkerbell.

Mike's dedications go to his wife Wendy, his three children, Jodi, Tim and Emily, and the rest of his family for their love and support, with a special thanks to Lark Weimar and Robyn Walonski for their enthusiasm and encouragement.

Most importantly, we dedicate this book to all the denizens of Woodstock Nation.

Acknowledgements

We would like to acknowledge the contributions of

❧ Bill Milanese, for the words to his song, "Barney McDougal III"

❧ Michael Weeks for his herblore

❧ John Lucas for his help with Greaser lore and dialogue, and for the "hot car" references in the Greaser litany at Overhaul

❧ Dave Harrington for his technical expertise

❧ Tim and Emily Harmon for their help with graphic design

❧ Wendy Harmon for her editing, and without whose help we would still be thinking about getting published

Introduction

Pipedreams – A Freak Tale is a really long book that took a really long time to write. So long, in fact, that I can't actually remember when we began it, though its roots are in the mystical time of the late 1960s.

I was in the Air Force in those days, serving as a military intelligence analyst attached to the 7th Air Force Headquarters at Tan Son Nhut, just outside of Saigon—a position neither as exotic nor as interesting as it sounds.

On occasion an Army friend (let's call him Free Will) would go AWOL from his unit and stay with me for a few days. Since Free had an anti-authoritarian attitude even greater than my own and habitually traveled with an ammo can full of excellent weed, I was always glad to see him.

One evening we were torching up some of Free's Cambodian Red (not to be confused with Cambodian Reds—primo pot, not Pol Pot) when the conversation turned to what was going on in "The World"—that part of the universe that was not 'Nam. The years of 1968-69 were a time of dramatic social change—some of it good, some bad, but all of it fascinating. It was the age of merriment and marijuana, to be sure, but also the age of Manson and My Lai. Considering all of the heavy shit going on in the streets of Amerika, Free and I had to ask ourselves if maybe we weren't in the wrong war.

It was our considered opinion that the world would be a far better place when the "good guys" (by which we meant hippies and lefties) were finally in charge. We had no idea what that world would be like, but we knew it would have to be an improvement.

Several years later I mustered out of the service. It was now 1971 and I did all the things a young guy did in those days: I grew my hair long, altered my consciousness at every given opportunity, and bummed about for the better part of a year. In time I attended college (briefly), met a girl and got married (again, briefly), and embarked on a career of looking for a career. In all that time, though, I couldn't get the notion of a hippie-centric universe out of my mind. What would it really be like? For some reason I saw it as part *Lord of the Rings*, part *Road Warrior* and a lot of *The Fabulous Furry Freak Brothers*, with just a touch of H.P. Lovecraft.

Over the years I worked out a cast of characters, complete with backstories, a series of unique cultures and a five-hundred-year history. I also had a lot of "what ifs," bad jokes, obscure cultural references and even a rudimentary plot. What I didn't have was a great sense of organization. For that I turned to my old friend Mike who, being a solid citizen, married with kids and a real job, knew all about…

"Structure" is the word that Steve was looking for. And since I've completed that sentence for him, I might as well finish the introduction.

Allow me to set the stage. I was also a child of the sixties, though not as early sixties as Steve. I heard plenty about events going down during that time—stuff like Woodstock, Chicago, and Kent State. And yes, I am aware that the Kent State Massacre happened in 1970, but almost everyone in my era thought of it as the sixties. In fact, I believe that most people of my generation see the sixties starting around 1963-64 when The Beatles were first introduced to America—by album in 1963 and on *The Ed Sullivan Show* in 1964—and ending in 1973 with the signing of the Paris Peace Accords, ostensibly ending the conflict in Vietnam.

Steve and I met in the sixties when I was in high school and he was home from Vietnam on leave. When he came back for good, a group of us hung out, mostly having fun and questioning the establishment. As we grew older, Steve and I remained friends. Both of us went on to higher education and both of us got married—neither endeavor was successful for either of us, on our first attempts. Over the years Steve and I always found time to get together, to drink copious amounts of coffee and share stories and ideas.

During that time Steve and I, along with another writer friend, had our own informal writing group. We met each week and read and critiqued each other's work. Sometimes we held our writing sessions at local restaurants, guzzling cups of joe and discussing great philosophical truths, often expounding on observations and extrapolating them into fictitious theories and conspiracies. It was a time of imagination and oo-a-gation. (For the uninitiated, "oo-a-gating" should be classified as interactive people-watching.)

By then, the novel already had a truly unique and entertaining concept. It also had a few great characters and wonderful descriptions mixed with liberal doses of purple prose. But it was short on plot and did not fulfill the promise of its naissance. So one day over coffee (it's a theme in our lives), I shared some ideas I had about developing the plot, adding flesh to some minor characters, and expanding what was already there into as much cool and outrageous stuff as possible. The wheel of fortune spun upward and a collaboration was born.

For my part I redesigned plotlines, scenes, and characters in detailed outline form. Steve would take the outlines I gave him and bring them to life with description and dialogue. Sometimes I wrote specific sections myself. When we were done, we had reread, reinvented and rewritten over and over and over. After thirty years of dissecting and nitpicking, we came to the realization that if we kept going, we might not finish before the next "sixties."

From the beginning, Steve and I shared a belief that writing a novel should be about characters and storytelling. Perhaps it's overstating the obvious, but to us reading a novel should be fun, not work. Steve was a fan of underground comix and expressed his desire that the book should have a similar feel, meaning that the more outrageous things we could pack into the novel, the better.

Although we may not have articulated them as such, we had five goals. The first was to write a story about the sixties—its people, its politics and its music. The second was to have real characters—ones that people could relate to. The third was to have elements of mythological tales: heroes, villains, immortals, the usual stuff. The fourth goal was to cram as many jokes, subtle references and crazy stuff as possible between the covers. The fifth goal… Seriously, we didn't have a fifth goal, unless it was for you, the reader, to have as much fun as possible reading our story.

Enjoy.

Steve and Mike
May 1, 2012

NORTHERN REACHES

MOLOCH

GREAT WHITE LANDS

PITSTOP

KRAKKERTON KHAMSHAFT

TINKER'S DAM

DOWNEAST

SMUDGEPORT

KLAVEN'S KEEP HIMMLERBURG

LUBEJOB

GREAT EAST LAKE

PURPLE MTS

DAMNATION ISLES

PIGGIE POINT

DARKENWOOD

PLAINS OF DRAGSTRIP

SWETSHOP

HILLCOMMUNE

SMOKEY WATERS

RIPOFF PASS

OZONE

INDIAN STREAM

COVENSTEAD

FAIR

ZAPPATOWN

PARANOIA FLATS

GU

THE FREAKLANDS

OWSLEYBURG

CAMP HOFFMAN

SATIVA FIELDS

RUINS

EASTSIDE

GULLEY OVEN

SUMMER LUV

FETID BOG

LEFTOPIA

GONIC

SLUDG

SHAMBULLAH

FAT CITY

JUKIN CITY

BURNOUT POINT

FUNKYTON

RIVERTOWN

SHOAL ISLANDS

ISLINGTON

SATURDAY NIGHT

NUKEPLANT

FROGGY BOTTOM

WHISKEY RIVER

DREGLANDS

BAHSTON

CUTTYSUNK MARSHES

N

W E

S

MAP OF STREET-CORNER EARTH

Prologue

Highway 61 Revisited

Late afternoon shadows were already growing long when the Dark Man reined his great black warhorse to a halt along Highway 61. Within the depths of his cowl he smiled, recalling ancient times when this stretch of road had been called US 1. Only he knew that now.

In the centuries that had passed since he last came this way, almost everything had vanished. Dank cellar holes, hidden in the underbrush, held the crumbled remains of houses and buildings that had succumbed to the passage of time. Where lush fields once waved in cool shore breezes, dark, brooding twisted pines now stood. The road, reduced to little more than a wagon path, revealed broken black shards of asphalt pushing up through half a millennium of dirt and rotted vegetation.

The Dark Man sniffed the air; it was heavy with salt and scents of the sea. Through a clearing on his right he could see the coast and a vast expanse of ocean spreading out to the horizon. Behind him the setting sun blazed red, illuminating two huge, domed structures that rose above the shoreline. This was the only remaining landmark to indicate that he was about to enter Street-Corner Earth, a loosely united group of nation-states also known as The Freaklands.

The silent domes stood menacingly, as if they were about to disgorge a frightening, eldritch secret. Over the years many ghastly tales arose about this place, now called Nukeplant. Locals had long since forgotten its real name, or function, but still they hurried past it like frightened children walking by a graveyard at night. Even the Dark Man could not remember this place's original name, but he was well aware of its purpose. He was the only one alive who still knew such things, and inside of his hood, his grin broadened in self-satisfaction. He was the Dark Man. Or, as he preferred to be known for the time being, Sweet Billy Bejeezuz.

As the sunlight faded, it shaded the domes a bright pink. The color reminded him of the sunburned buttocks of a young lad whose favors he'd enjoyed once on a beach not far from here. Part way up the side of one of the domes was a bold emblem carved in the likeness of a pair of crossed hammers. This was the symbol of the long-extinct Neo-Luddite Party, whose soldiers had aimed their wrath at places like this when they brought down Helter-Skelter. The compounds surrounding the domes had been razed during the decades-long revolt that murdered civilization and sank mankind into a new Dark Age, but even the Neo-Luddites stopped short of breaching the domes. Though zealous, they were not stupid.

Bejeezuz dismounted and rested on a patch of moss beside the road. A chance passer-by would have seen only his eyes beneath the cowl of his cloak, but that would have been enough to send him scurrying on his way. The Dark Man's eyes were timeless, without soul, like the eyes of a reptile. They were eyes that never knew sleep, or love.

As he rested, Bejeezuz thought about his kingdom in the west, Yewtah, with its shining tabernacle by the Great Brine Lake. There he was known as Garlock, or more commonly, Mister Man, though over the years he'd had innumerable names in a myriad of diverse places. But even the Dark Man himself did not know his real, given name. His failure to remember was not because it was hidden behind a multitude of other guises, but was evidence of the memory loss he'd suffered at the hands of Freaks, the inhabitants of Street-Corner Earth. To be precise, his memory loss was caused by their ancestors, but as to where, or when, or even how it occurred, he hadn't a clue. Regardless, he did remember that the Freaks, then and now, were his sworn enemies.

To the Freaks he was little more than a creature of fable, a night-gaunt. The Bad Dude they called him, or Old Charlie, having confused him with Charles Manson over the years. In Hillcommune, the spiritual center of the Freaks, he was known as The Evil Weed, the weed with its roots in hell.

Others knew him as well. The Indians of the plains called him Big Slicky Boy, and spat at the mention of his name. In Dixieland he was Slitherin' Jim to the Whites and De Jiveman to the Blacks. To the Fascists of the Great Whitelands, just north of Street-Corner Earth, he was remembered in legend as Big Brother John Birch. To their neighbors, the degenerate, inbred Greasers of Khamshaft, he was Lord Flatbush.

Bejeezuz lingered until well after dusk. Stealth was necessary if he were to find The Book and become, without question, the most powerful being in existence. He didn't mind being seen at night by a few who might regard him as a curious traveler, but it wouldn't be wise to have everyone in Street-

Corner Earth see him passing in the daylight. At least, not yet.

A ghostly silver moon rose with him as he prepared to mount his stallion, Apocalypse. Checking the straps of the battered guitar case tied behind his saddle, he laughed aloud, exulting in the sound of his own voice, modulating it until his laughter sounded like the cry of a foul bird of prey.

"I'm the Midnight Rambler, babies," he said to the evening shadows creeping up to touch the hem of his long black cloak, "and I've come to rock you some heavy roll."

He cackled to the night and spurred Apocalypse on. Except for the long deep shadows cast across the road by tall pines, Highway 61 was bathed in an unholy pale glow. Apocalypse stormed from shadow to light and back again as horse and rider thundered toward The Freaklands.

It was not long before the Dark Man came to a crossroads where he veered east on the Froggy Bottom Road, along the seacoast of what had once been southern New Hampshire and Maine. As he rode, he fingered the time-blackened spearhead hanging on a gold chain around his neck. It was a powerful talisman given to him a very long time ago, by a fan in Cleveland, Ohio.

The fan was the head of a local quasi-Nazi cult that revered the spear and used it in its blasphemous rites. He had claimed that the spear was the Heilige Lance, the so-called Spear of Longinus—the very spear that had pierced the side of Christ. Constantine, Charlemagne, and even Hitler were all said to have possessed it in their times. At first Bejeezuz doubted the claim, but once he touched the cold ancient metal he knew. It was real, all right. And now, here in the land of his enemies, he would use the magic of the spear and The Book against them.

Bejeezuz stopped when he saw the lights of Saturday Night glowing in the distance. The border town's only tavern, Ruby Tuesday's, was accustomed to many strange visitors, so he shouldn't arouse any undue attention. It was the perfect place for a hot meal and a few discreet questions. The answers, in a town this far from the centers of trade, should give him a good idea of how his plan was working.

He laughed again and rode towards the lights. As he passed isolated houses on the outskirts of town, toddlers awoke in their cribs screaming that the bogeyman was about. In other houses the occupants tossed fitfully in their sleep and grabbed for their covers to keep out an eerie chill.

Bejeezuz reined Apocalypse to an abrupt halt. There was a strange, vaguely familiar scent on the night air, a scent not of forest or sea, but more like a warm, fetid breeze off a peat bog. It was a smell that he did not completely recognize, but that his instincts told him to fear. His hand grasped the smooth butt of the flintlock pistol hidden under his robes and didn't let go until he arrived at the tavern. Dismounting, he sniffed the air again, but the scent was almost gone, mixing with the aromas of cooking food wafting from inside. His inability to place the peat scent bothered him, but for now a warm repast was his prime consideration.

Inside the tavern his worn, black boots with their six-inch soles pounded on the oak floor, raising small clouds of dust. There were a few local Freaks sitting at a heavy table near the fireplace. They were joking when he entered, but quieted at the appearance of the tall, gaunt stranger. He glared at them from beneath his cowl. The Freaks cringed and turned to their ale, buzzing for a minute before resuming their local chatter.

Bejeezuz selected a dark booth away from the fire where he could observe the goings-on and listen for any news. Not long after he sat down a young, long-haired lad came to take his order.

"May I help you?" the boy asked, averting his eyes, not quite brave enough to investigate the darkness under the hood.

"Certainly," Bejeezuz replied in a controlled, friendly voice. "I'd like a fine cut of venison cooked almost enough to be called rare, and a couple of jugs of Tree Frog." He smiled to himself. One of his scouts had reported that the local beer served here was an excellent brew.

As the waiter walked off, Bejeezuz eyed his firm buttocks lustfully and licked his lips with his long pale tongue. "There'll be time enough for that later," he told himself.

His thoughts turned to a strange young Freak who had been visiting his dreams recently. The images were brief and vague, but somehow haunting, as if harbingers of a yet untold story.

He extracted a twisted black cigar from his cloak and lit it with the candle on his table. He settled back and blew smoke rings out of his hood while silently checking out the other customers. Smoking long black stogies had become his passion, and his trademark, back when he first gained control of Westcommune. Westcommune... That was it! He remembered now. Westcommune had been his, and the thieving ancestors of the Freak-scum in Street-Corner Earth had taken it from him. The peat bog scent had been there, at the very end, when he was forced to escape naked into the desert. He was enraged that whoever or whatever that odor was should surface now, and he vowed that he would erase it from the face of the earth before he finished conquering The Freaklands.

When the waiter returned with his food, Bejeezuz put his angry thoughts aside and asked the young lad a question that would tell him how well his men were carrying out their mission.

"Tell me, boy," the Dark Man queried, as the waiter set a large plate of meat and vegetables on the table. "How much would it be for a bowl of Hillcommune Red to go along with the Tree Frog?"

"I'm sorry, sir," the young waiter replied, "but we're out of the Red temporarily. We do have some Sativa Fields Beige, but that has doubled in price the last couple of months."

Bejeezuz grinned. "Really? What has caused such a sorry state of affairs?"

"Our supplier, Ernie Mungweasle, claims that the Greasers and Fashies keep ambushing the weedwagons. Personally, I think he's just trying to drive up his prices."

"How interesting," Bejeezuz grunted. He began to wolf down his food, ignoring the waiter. At least this time his men were doing their job.

The waiter left and returned with the Dark Man's beer, placing it on the table next to his plate. Bejeezuz gulped down some of the brew and noticed that the waiter didn't seem quite ready to leave. He was staring at Bejeezuz's cigar smoldering on the edge of the table.

"Is there something I can help you with, boy?"

"Uh, I just couldn't help wondering why you were interested in purchasing some weed when you have such a large number right there. I must admit it's the strangest one I've ever seen. Not that I've seen that many, you know. Even here, most people frown on that method.... Oh, I'm sorry, that's none of my business."

Bejeezuz laughed, causing the waiter to jump back. He'd forgotten that tobacco was unknown to these Freaks, and that smoking weed in a rolled fashion was considered a vulgar act practiced only by the crudest louts, or in times of extreme desperation.

"I've been traveling a long time," he explained. "This is just some terrible ragweed I was forced to rely on after a highwayman accosted me on the road and stole my pipes and stash."

"I find it hard to believe that *you* would be the target of a common thief," the waiter said suspiciously.

"Oh, he was no common thief, boy. A good five inches taller than me, he was, smelling of a swamp. He was desperate for weed and I did not dare deny him."

"And he left you your money?"

"I said he was desperate for smokeables, didn't I?"

"But certainly money would buy him whatever he wanted."

"You calling me a liar, boy?" Bejeezuz sneered.

"Oh, no sir."

"Good, then get your tight little ass out of here before it gets you in trouble."

The lad hurried off and Bejeezuz returned to his meal. He'd been on the road for two days, leaving behind the insanity that was coming down in the tottering shitpile that used to be called Boston. It was a bad scene all around in Beantown. He and his boys had come all the way from Yewtah to investigate a cache of ancient weapons and machinery found there. It turned out that the cache was guarded by a bunch of crazy niggers who killed two of his men before they could salvage much of any value. One thing they did find, however, were some documents containing information concerning the whereabouts of The Book, the same one he'd been seeking for years. The information was not specific, but it was promising. At first he'd sent some of his men ahead to pave the way for him in Khamshaft and the Great Whitelands. Then, as things started to get hairy in the crumbling ruins of the Hub, he left a lieutenant in charge and headed north to search for The Book. With it and his spearhead, Boston and everything north would be his.

He guzzled the last bit of Tree Frog and headed out the door. Apocalypse greeted him nervously, straining at the reins tying him to the hitching post. In one effortless motion, Bejeezuz swung onto his back. Gathering the reins, he was about to ride off when the young waiter burst through the door.

"Sir, you haven't paid…"

"I know, Freakling," Bejeezuz smiled, leaning forward until his cowled face almost touched the waiter, "and you're lucky I don't have time to leave you a proper tip, Sweetcheeks." The boy's mouth remained open, but he couldn't utter a syllable. He stood like stone, terrified by the Dark Man's visage.

Apocalypse carried Bejeezuz's crowing laughter into the night, leaving the boy to wander back into the tavern with a vacant look in his eyes.

Chapter One

The brightly painted caravan wagon rattled through the streets of Rivertown. It swayed as it rolled over the cobbles, its high, iron-shod wheels throwing out occasional sparks.

Josiah Toad lay rolled up in a shabby, patchwork quilt on the narrow cot inside. As he twitched in fitful slumber, his mind churned out fragments of dreams. Many were pleasant: scenes of his hilltop home on Smuttynose Island, where he plied his dual trade of pipesmith and amateur historian; Toker Jones' headshop in Islington, where he'd consumed many a mug of good Stumpwater Ale; even the Rusty Roachclip Tavern, up the street from the Rivertown docks, where he and Ernie Mungweasle had encountered the traveling musician, Tambourine.

There were darker visions as well—hellish visions, bits and pieces of nightmares that had been ruining his sleep since Suzie had left him. A crackling wall of flame stretched into the sky, drowning out the screams of the dying. It faded and was replaced by an ominous horseman on a great black stallion, riding out of the west. Like a dark river, the dream rider flowed through primeval forests and down ruined roads in strange, lonely places. He stopped briefly at the edge of an expanse of ancient towers whose broken spires rose high into a filthy gray sky. Slinking through the twisted, rubble-strewn streets like a prophet of deceit, the dark-robed figure made his way to the tallest ruin. Once inside he began to climb slowly, seeking.

Toad awoke with a start. Late afternoon sunlight filtered through the tiny window over his head. He sat up and peered out of it just as the wagon clattered past Lennon Park. The sun was dipping behind the maple trees that fringed the park, their leaves still brilliant reds and golds despite the late October chill. The sun's rays silhouetted the Summer of Love Memorial at the center of the green, which stood in sharp contrast against the burning sky. The monument depicted a Freak man and woman holding aloft a huge peace symbol. It had been as bright and shiny as a new copper Abbie when it was first erected fifty years ago, in 2418, but the years had tarnished the memorial to a dull dark green, and generations of surly pigeons had frosted it liberally with their droppings.

The park went out of view as the wagon rolled up Bleeker Street toward the Burnout Point Road. Toad turned from the window and dully regarded himself in the cracked mirror hanging over a trunk at the back of the wagon. He sat for some time looking at the squarish, bearded face in the glass, taking note of the shaggy, shoulder-length hair and deep-set green eyes as if they were the features of a stranger. The Toad in the mirror appeared older than his own twenty-seven years. Satisfied that he was still himself and his dreams were just dreams, Toad reached into the pocket of his faded mariner's coat and extracted a small, half-filled wooden weedpipe.

Lighting the pipe with his tinderbox, Toad sat back on the cot, toking methodically until the murmur of voices coming from the front of the wagon drew his attention. Beyond the canvas partition he could hear Ernie and Tambourine discussing previous journeys to Covenstead Fair.

The pair laughed over stories of past fairs, each trying to top the other with tales of wild revelry and extraordinary good fortune. Every account seemed to involve overindulgences in weed, liquor or women, leading to one outlandish adventure after another. Obviously, there was a world of things Toad had never experienced.

As entertaining as the stories were, they also revealed a special camaraderie between Ernie and Tam, a bond that Toad and Ernie did not share. It caused the pipesmith to speculate about what else his friend may not have shared. Although somewhat secretive by nature and profession, it seemed that lately Ernie had been more mysterious than usual. What other secrets did he hold under his worn top hat? Toad wondered if he would regret letting the older Freak talk him into this trip to the mainland.

Ernie, a traveling herbalist, was unlike anyone Toad had ever known. They had first met five years ago, shortly after Toad's father died, leaving him the family weedpipe business along with an impressive collection of rare and ancient books. Toad happened to be in Islington the very morning that Ernie made his first visit to Smuttynose Island. From his vantage point at a booth in Toker Jones', the pipesmith was the first to see the tall stranger in the dark frock coat and top hat disembarking from Captain Chives' ferry at the wharf across the street. In a town where visitors were rare, the mysterious-looking Freak with waist-length black hair and pendulous mustache stood out like a crow in a flock of sea gulls. The newcomer got off the ferry and loped across the street, entering Toker's place like it was his own, and announced his profession. Before you could say "Jumpin' Jack Flash," he sauntered up to the counter and pulled choice lids of mainland Honkweeds from his bulging backpack. Toad bought a kilo of Hillcommune Red from Ernie that day, and after the herbalist sold out all of his supply, he took Toad aside to propose a business arrangement.

As it turned out, Ernie had heard of Toad before. This was not entirely surprising since the Toad family had been producing fine weedpipes for generations. It came to light during their conversation that selling Honkweed was only the most obvious of the lanky stranger's endeavors. For a few Rubins he could procure just about anything a customer might desire. In Toad's case that turned out to be old and exotic books, which Ernie delivered whenever he came to the island, in exchange for money or pipes.

Over the years the two Freaks developed a mutually beneficial friendship. Toad was a scholar; Ernie was a traveling man. Between the two of them, they probably knew more about the history of Street-Corner Earth than some of the learned elders at Shambullah University, although Toad had never been far from home in his life and Ernie hated to read anything more demanding than the occasional comic almanack.

Ernie's visits to the island, though infrequent, were always quite regular—at least until the last six months. In the early spring Ernie had breezed in for a couple of days and left with a consignment of pipes. He returned several weeks later but refused to take any more pipes, saying he was going on a long trip for some friends and didn't know when he would come back to Smuttynose.

Months passed and there was no word from Ernie. During his extended absence the supply of weed on Smuttynose began to dry up. Toker Jones and some of the others in town searched for a new source of supply in Rivertown, but gave up when they found that nothing was available except inferior homegrown, selling at inflated prices. Rumors began to circulate that brigands were attacking and burning the weedwagons coming out of Sativa Fields and Hillcommune. Soon everyone in Street-Corner Earth would be down to sticks and seeds.

Then, just a few nights ago, Toad was sitting in his study, nursing a crock of Stumpwater Ale and going through a pile of old books that had been in his family for generations. A knock came on the door, just as he was about to examine the *Necronomicon,* a worn manuscript that was hardly more than a sheath of moldy, indecipherable handwritten pages. With a grunt of surprise he tossed the pages into his desk drawer and went to see who was there. On the step stood Ernie Mungweasle, his hair slightly streaked with gray and walking with a stoop that brought his six-foot-four frame down to Toad's level.

"Ernie!" Toad exclaimed, almost tripping over himself in his eagerness to embrace his friend. "I'd damn near given you up for lost."

The herbalist replied with a smile that lit up his odd, angular features. "No fear, man. Like a bad Abbie, I always return."

Walking past Toad, he entered the living room where he paced back and forth like a caged cat, as he always did when he returned from a long journey with stories to tell.

Toad signaled his teenage apprentice, Gary Goober, to prepare coffee, then sprawled in his chair by the fireplace and eyed his friend with curiosity.

"You seem a bit travel-worn," Toad commented. "Can I offer you something to eat?"

"I'm set."

"You sure? You look thin, even for you."

Ernie stopped his pacing and leaned against the bookcase at the far end of the room, desultorily searching the titles of Toad's collection. He drummed his fingers on the spine of Zoab Pedanticus's *History of the Western Communes* as if deep in thought. "You know how it is," he said at last. "Life is strife, they say. I've been on the road a lot lately. Maybe it shows."

"It does. You ought to settle down, Ernie. It isn't healthy to spend all your time running around with Dylan-only-knows-what kind of riffraff."

The herbalist shrugged at the advice, selected a small book from the shelf and began to leaf through it. By the light of the fireplace Toad saw that it was *Cruickshank's History of Firearms*. Ernie riffled through it for several seconds, then closed it with a snap.

"I was born to be wild," he said. "I'd wither and die if I lived like you do, cooped up in a house on a rock pile in the middle of the ocean. That, to me, would be more wearing than a life on the road."

Toad wanted to make some kind of sarcastic reply to Ernie's dig, but his brain failed to yield one. Gary's timely return with a coffeepot and a pair of mugs saved him the effort. Wordlessly, the young apprentice placed them on the slate-topped coffee table and retreated, leaving the older Freaks to their discussion.

Ernie watched until Gary shut the door, then laid the book back down on the shelf and turned to Toad.

"A minute ago you said I looked worn," he remarked. "Well, perhaps I do. But when was the last time you took a good look at yourself? You're so hollow-eyed and unkempt you'd scare a Rowdie up a back road."

"Rowdies," Toad mumbled. "They're the least of my worries. While you've been out bopping around the countryside, I've been working overtime to keep my business above water."

Ernie nodded knowingly at this. "Yeah, I understand. The way things are going, it won't be too long before you have no business to worry about."

Toad poured a cup of coffee for Ernie, then one for himself. He waited for the herbalist to sit down in the chair opposite him before continuing the discussion.

"You know," he confessed, "in a way I'd been blaming you for my business failure, even though I knew it was just my lousy management skills. Poor Gary, I've even blamed him."

"Your business difficulties have nothing to do with my absence, or Gary, or you. Greaser brigands are raiding the weedwagons coming out of Owsleyburg and Hillcommune. What they don't take, they burn. Consequently, the weed supply is low and there's no demand for pipes or paraphernalia. If this continues, there may be no Honkweed crop this year to speak of."

"So, the rumors are true. But I've never heard of Greasers caring about weed."

Ernie shrugged, taking a sip of coffee. "Maybe the brigands aren't Greasers. Nobody's really sure. These weed robbers make sure not to leave any survivors."

"That's terrible. What's being done?"

"The Weedgrowers Guild has hired Leftopian mercenaries to guard the roads. It's hoped that will solve the problem, but Radiclib soldier-boys don't work cheap and they're having problems of their own with an onslaught of Fascist raiding parties back home."

"It's good something is being done, though. We need the weed."

The herbalist nodded, taking another sip from his cup and setting it to one side. "Not to mention coffee, spices, medicinal teas, and all the other supplies that Hillcommune exports to the lowlands."

"So, Ernie, where have you been all these months, while all this was going on?"

"There'll be time for my tales later, Toad. Why don't you tell me what's really been bothering you. I suspect business concerns are only part of it."

"I'd really rather not get into *my* problems," Toad replied.

Ernie laughed, slyly. "Tell you what," he said. "If you'll tell me what's bugging you, I'll tell you where I've been these last few months, and turn you on to some really high-test Honkweed at the same time."

"Weed? You've got weed?"

"An herbalist without weed can hardly be doing his job, can he? I have my sources. Now, do we have a deal or not?"

With little struggle, Toad relented. "Okay, get out your stash."

"Your story first."

"All right. Do you remember those two books you brought me on your last visit?"

"Sure do. Harriman's *Tales of Street-Corner Earth* and Enos Articulatus's *Origins of the Freak and Radiclib Peoples*. I had a hell of a time getting my hands on those babies."

"Those are the ones. They taught me that books, ignorant women, and a failing business don't mix."

"I'm not sure that I follow you," Ernie replied, cocking an eyebrow. "But I should have figured there was a woman involved in this somehow."

"Yes... well... Just after you left last spring, Suzie Creamjeans moved in with me. Remember her? She used to work as a waitress at Toker's."

"The little brunette with huge gazongas? I've seen sweeter dispositions on a rabid dog. You've done better, Toad."

"I know, but she was great in bed. You know how things are on Smuttynose; all the good women are either taken or looking for Mr. Natural. The few I've managed to hook onto have dropped me as soon as a more enterprising Freak showed them the least interest."

"Women are like that everywhere, Toad. I don't know what to tell you."

"I know. Still, I was hoping things would be different with Suzie."

"Cosmically optimistic, Toad."

"Cosmically horny, more'n likely. I must have been desperate, even though I didn't think so at the time."

Ernie nodded, fingering his long, drooping mustache. "Had I been around I would have advised against you getting involved with Suzie. Rumor has it that she used to hang out at Desolation Row."

"That was more than rumor, Ernie. But I wouldn't have listened to you anyway. Once I nibbled Suzie's bait, she set the hook and reeled me in. I was such an idiot."

"More than one man has fallen that way, Toad. I've been in the same situation more times than I care to admit."

Surprised, Toad glanced up at Ernie over the rim of his mug. "You? I always thought you were a real lady-killer."

"I've had my good spells along with my bad, as does every man. Still, I don't see what any of this has to do with those histories I brought you."

"Well, as I said, Suzie moved in soon after you left. The first month or so went well. I still had lots of orders to fill. I was happy; between making pipes by day with Gary and keeping late hours with Suzie, my life was pretty full. Then the orders started dropping off. I hoped for things to pick up, but they didn't. Soon, I left Gary to produce what few pipes I needed while I spent more and more time in my library, losing myself in reading. I dug into Harriman and Articulatus, and then I started re-reading sections of Pedanticus' *History*. That was my downfall."

Ernie drained his cup, refilled it from the pot, and fixed Toad with a quizzical stare. "Pedanticus was pretty bad, but how did a dead scholar get between you and Suzie?" he asked.

"Not him specifically—historians in general. I've always been interested in history, but I've never fully agreed with many of the accounts of the origins of our people. After reading those three books, I went on to reading some of Kermit Badmoon's poetry and stuff like the *Luddite Manifesto* of Simon Doomsayer. I was hooked; I wanted to write my own history of Street-Corner Earth."

"A worthy endeavor."

"I thought so. I was getting bored with the pipe business anyway. There are just so many variations in design and that's that. The need to expand my intellectual horizons grew stronger daily, so I compiled notes from my books and started writing."

"I take it Suzie didn't like that idea."

Toad chuckled bitterly. "Worse than that, she thought I was a fool from the very start. She couldn't see me expending effort towards something that wouldn't keep her in weed and parties. We began to argue, often viciously. I tried explaining to her that I didn't want to be known as just a pipesmith, and that my research was part of an important and meaningful project. She cursed me and said I was too much of a thinker to be a real man. Before long, she ran off with Gumma Lout, leader of the Rowdie clan at Desolation Row. She took with her the last of my stash and some money I'd been saving."

"A terrible state of affairs," Ernie sympathized. "You know, I'm surprised that you islanders ever allowed Rowdies to migrate here in the first place. On the mainland they're considered degenerate scum, half Greaser and half Freak, with no good characteristics of either race. They've been run out of almost every town they've tried to settle in."

Toad nodded wearily at this. "We found that out too late. We all told Bomber Crabtoe that he was a fool to sell his farm to off-islanders. They probably stole the money to pay for it, and they've turned decent cropland into a squalid shanty town where vice and crime run rampant."

"You could still run them off the island."

"I doubt it. They're too firmly entrenched. It would take a mass uprising to root them out. As long as they keep to themselves and don't get out of hand, I don't see that happening."

"I suppose not. Well, on with your story then."

"There's not much left to tell," Toad replied, shrugging. "After Suzie left I immersed myself in writing while Gary took care of the house and business. It didn't take me long to discover I had the same luck with writing that I did with women. I got really bummed out.

"Now I'm obsessed with my failures. The more I dwell on them, the more depressed I get. To tell you the truth, my life is beginning to look hopeless."

Unnoticed by either Toad or Ernie, Gary Goober had entered the room and was standing quietly by the door. "Mr. Toad's been drinkin' a lot lately," the apprentice blurted out. "He stays in his study all hours of the night, but he hasn't written anything in weeks. He just broods, starin' at his papers and drinkin' until he passes out. When he ain't out cold, he wanders around the place like a ghost, sighin' to himself. It ain't my place to say anything, I know, but I worry about him."

Startled, Toad turned in his chair and fixed Gary with a hard stare.

"I see," Ernie remarked, tugging at his mustache. "You are evidently a good friend as well as a loyal apprentice. Leave me alone with your master, Gary. I wish to speak to him in private."

"Sorry, Mr. Mungweasle, I didn't mean to…"

"You've caused no trouble, son. Now, please."

After Gary left the room, closing the door behind him, Ernie moved to the bookcase again and resumed leafing through Toad's copy of *Cruickshank's*. He glanced at Toad from time to time, but the pipesmith found it hard to meet his gaze.

"The kid's impertinent," Toad said weakly. "There's no excuse for what he just did."

"Nor is there for wallowing in self-pity, Toad. You're in a rut, man. And it's high time we do something about it. You can start by loading up a pipe with some of this."

Ernie tossed a small leather pouch in Toad's direction, then flipped through a few pages in the book and silently began reading a passage. As Toad fumbled with the drawstrings of the weedsack, the herbalist turned to the bookcase, perused a few volumes from the top shelf, and then returned to his chair.

"This stuff's guaranteed to put the color back in your cheeks," he remarked, grinning so that his angular, long-nosed face looked lopsided.

The pipesmith nodded as he removed the cover of his clay stash jar and emptied the contents of the weedsack into it, letting the finely manicured weed sift through his fingers. It was dry and strangely cool to the touch, and so pale that it seemed to shimmer like foxfire in the dancing light from the hearth. With a mixture of wonder and reverence, Toad studied the few sparkling particles clinging to his fingertips. Slowly, he raised them to his nose and sniffed. They smelled of must and age, like time itself.

"Light up a bowl and we'll talk," Ernie said, folding his hands behind his head as he sprawled in the chair.

There was a carved wooden churchwarden lying on the table. Toad picked it up and filled it from the jar. Packing it tightly, he lit it with a splint from the fire and took several quick tokes before passing it to Ernie. His lungs were filled to bursting as he sat back to savor the first effects.

Before his shoulders hit the chair a tingling sensation rushed over him, as if he'd been immersed in a mineral spring. Then, without warning, the high exploded and hit him like a blow from a Rowdie's fist. He blacked out briefly, and when he came back he found himself staring at Ernie's face. It seemed different somehow—older, wiser. The herbalist caught the stare and grinned knowingly.

The room, too, seemed to have altered, as if it now existed in different dimensions of time and space. The fire on the hearth had drawn in on itself, burning with a brilliance that sent sharp black shadows cavorting around the room. Deep within the shadows flashing pinpricks of light appeared, like stars in a winter sky. The surrounding air was filled with the mad buzzings and dronings of an invisible insect chorus.

Finally, Toad exhaled. He gazed in wonder as the smoke wreathed about his head. He'd smoked many a fine weed in his life, but nothing like this.

"Dylan's Bones," he gasped, giggling foolishly. "What is this wondrous shit?"

Ernie wiggled his eyebrows and leaned forward in his chair. "It's called Thirdworld White. It's a rare albino strain that grows only in the dank, sunless tunnels under the city of Bahston. I pinched this from a kilo I had shipped ahead to Hillcommune."

"Thirdworld? I thought that was only a legend, like Haight-Ashbury or Woodstock."

"It's no legend. Certain acquaintances of mine have been visiting the underground settlements of the Blackfolk for several years now. Surely, it's mentioned often enough in those old books of yours."

The pipesmith nodded, scratching his badly trimmed beard thoughtfully. "Well, in *Destinies*, Kermit Badmoon predicted the rise of something called the Thirdworld before the year 2500, but Badmoon was a lunatic who died raving in the Jukin City Healery years ago. I've also heard it said that the Oldhips possess a true history of the world, the *Book of Love*, which speaks of an underground race of dark-skinned people. Actually, little is known of these things."

Ernie grinned at him. "Little is known by stay-at-homes and adventure-shunners. Myself, I've been there."

Toad cocked an eyebrow, but the look on his friend's face convinced him. "How? Why?"

"As a favor for a friend of a friend. I couldn't believe this guy when I first met him. He was a short, scruffy little dude who jabbered in an outrageous dialect and kept his face hidden behind weird mirrored spectacles. His name was as strange as his looks. He went by the handle Beatnik Maynard."

"Why did he want you to go to Bahston?"

"For weed, and for certain artifacts which I'm not at liberty to talk about. Enough of that, though. We have more important matters to discuss."

The pipesmith disagreed vehemently. "What important matters? Damn, Ernie, with what you could tell me about the Thirdworld, I could write a book that would be a guaranteed success."

The herbalist countered back. "You could never do it."

"Ha! With your help, I could have a good first draft done in a month."

"You'll never produce anything of worth until you change your approach."

"What's wrong with my methods? You've never even studied them."

Ernie clasped his hands behind his head and leaned back, pausing a moment before continuing. "You can't write a true history of the world and its peoples without having been out among them. You could use accounts of my travels, but the finished product just wouldn't ring true."

"What am I supposed to do, run all over hell-and-gone like you?"

"Why not?" Ernie replied. "At least once, anyway. I'm headed up to Covenstead Fair for a few days, and I could use the company."

Toad felt slightly cold at the suggestion, though he didn't know why. "Well... uh..."

"No 'well-uhs' about it. You've been cooped up too long. A short road trip will give you the new perspective you need."

Maybe it was the weed, or maybe it was Ernie's persuasive manner, but Toad found himself warming to the proposal, ever so slightly.

"What about my business?"

"Gary can run it. He has been already. You said so yourself."

"I suppose so. But, Halloween is coming up and I was planning a party for my friends in Islington."

Ernie smiled knowingly then, as if sensing that the conversation was drifting in his favor. "An Island Halloween can't hold a candle to the one they have at Covenstead."

"I'm sure that's very true, but I'd just about promised Toker and Eddie Irvwhip and Mister Poetryman..."

"Almost promised isn't actually promised, Toad. I've seen some of these backwoods Halloweens in my time. They're okay for your local hilltop caperings, but even the party they throw in Rivertown Square is nothing compared to the Fair."

"I don't know..."

"Partyin's not even the half of it," he'd said cheerfully. "Even in hard times there will be more weed in Covenstead than you can imagine. I'll be helping with that. I've got some stashed in my wagon back on the mainland. There'll be all sorts of people there too. You can sell your pipes

16

and see a little piece of the world at the same time."

Feeling his resolve crumbling like spring ice, Toad shook his head.

"Stop talking," he blurted. "Give me a minute to think."

It didn't take much more than that for him to make up his mind. The promise of weed and adventure was just too strong to resist. Rising early the next morning he packed his knapsack and handed the house keys over to Gary. Then, looking back only once, he and Ernie set off down the hill toward the docks.

Ernie and Tambourine had ceased their chatter. The wagon was no longer on the cobble streets of Rivertown but on the rutted woods road that led out of town to the ferry landing at Burnout Point. The only sound that came from beyond the canvas flap at the head of Toad's cot was the soft playing of Tambourine's guitar. Toad recognized the tune of *Blowin' in the Wind*, the same ancient ballad the skinny, curly-haired musician had been playing the night before in the Rusty Roachclip Tavern.

Toad poked his nose out of the canvas as the last houses of Rivertown disappeared behind the maples, glowing with the day's last rays of sunlight. For a moment he watched, enthralled, as Tambourine picked out the chords on his battered old instrument. He had to admit that the musician played guitar better than anyone he'd ever heard.

The young mainlander, with his scruffy leather jacket and odd nasal accent was easygoing and instantly likeable, but there was something strange about him as well, a vague quality that Toad could not quite articulate. He'd noticed it last night when Ernie had invited the musician to join them at their fireside table, and he was noticing it now as he watched Tambourine's long fingers slide along the neck of his guitar. It was as if the younger man carried some great secret with him, tucked away in his jacket pocket along with his weedpipe and guitar picks.

The playing stopped. Tambourine slipped his pick into his jacket pocket and set his guitar down on the seat beside him.

"Few living Freaks can play the git-fiddle like you can, Tam," Ernie remarked admiringly. "I'll never understand why you gave up playing professionally."

"I got tired of all the hassle, Ernie. Juggling all those concert dates got to be a real pain. I was losing my identity as well, becoming what my audiences wanted me to be instead of my real self. I'm happier now just playing for room and board."

"That doesn't seem like much."

Tambourine grinned as he stuffed his guitar into his fringed leather carry-sack. "It's enough. Sometimes my talent gets me laid as well."

"If you're so down on the concert scene, why are you traveling all the way to Covenstead to catch someone else's act?"

"'Cause you never know what you can learn from these newcomers, Ern."

"Newcomer? Isn't this guy the same one that used to be lead singer for Meadow Muffin when they played out of Zappatown?"

Tambourine chuckled knowingly. "You may be many things, Ernie, but you're no expert on contemporary music. B.B. Jism retired from Meadow Muffin back in '66. This guy, Sweet Billy Bejeezuz, never played with Meadow Muffin; he's new. Didn't you see the posters for his concert plastered all over Rivertown? Why don't you and Toad catch his show with me when we hit Covenstead?"

"Maybe we will, if the meeting doesn't run late."

Taking mention of his name as a cue, Toad made his presence known. "How'm I expected to sleep with all this yakking going on?" he asked, affecting an exaggerated yawn.

"Welcome back to the land of the living," Ernie said, offering him a hand forward. "Can you light the wagon lamps before you sit down? The sun's fading fast, and it's still quite a way to the ferry."

With the town more than a half-mile behind them the caravan was entering the deep woods. As the last bit of twilight ebbed from the narrow strip of sky overhead, Toad took his tinderbox from his pocket and, after a few tries, managed to light the candles mounted in lanterns on either side of the plank seat. From here on, the wagon's lanterns would provide the only illumination. His task complete, he sat down between Ernie and Tambourine. The musician, at six feet even, was only slightly taller than Toad, but Ernie, augmented by his stovepipe hat, seemed to loom up into the evening shadows.

"I trust you slept well, Brother Toad," Tambourine said, using the Oldhip form of address.

"I'm afraid not. I guess I'm not yet used to life on the road."

"You will be," Ernie offered. "In time you may even come to like it."

Toad laughed. "That remains to be seen."

"Ernie has a point," Tambourine drawled. "Wayfaring has a way of getting into your blood. Every new horizon draws you, like a lodestone draws iron."

"There's no iron in my blood, I assure you. I'm quite content to leave Thirdworld jaunts and all that to the likes of friend Mungweasle here."

Tambourine exploded with sudden laughter. "Thirdworld indeed! Is that the kind of stuff Ernie's been filling you with? The Thirdworld is only an old story to amuse children with, nothing more."

Ernie turned towards Tam. "It might amuse you, Brother Musician, to know that not only have I been to the Thirdworld, but I stayed there for

18

many weeks."

The musician arched his eyebrows. "Then, it really exists?"

"Didn't I just say that?"

Tambourine stared off into the distance for a moment, his long fingers kneading through his curly thicket of hair. "Wow," he breathed. "If the Thirdworld exists, then other places might as well."

"What places?" Toad asked.

"Motown, my friends! The City of the Golden Disks. In ancient times, those skilled in music-craft were more powerful than they are today. It is said that their power is still locked in the golden disks of Motown. According to an old Musician's tradition, the Thirdworlders hold the key to its location."

Ernie shook his head. "They didn't mention Motown or any other place."

"They wouldn't. You're not a Musician, Ernie."

"Musician or not, the Thirdworlders were pretty tight-lipped about everything. There was no mention of Motown. Sorry."

Tambourine's blue eyes studied Ernie. "Still, you've been to the Thirdworld. Tell me about it."

"You might as well forget about that," Toad interjected. "He's as close-mouthed as a quahog on the subject."

"Is that so, Ernie?"

"I'm silent for good reasons—reasons that will become apparent all too soon."

Tambourine shrugged, undaunted. "I find it intriguing that a member of the Clear Light Society would seek out the Thirdworld. I've never known you Diggers to do something like that without good cause."

Ernie shook his head angrily, scowling at his companions. "Am I surrounded by blabbermouths? It seems I've been too free with things I've told both of you."

"One should be truthful with one's friends," Tambourine said.

"Oh, indeed? And if it gets back to Skulk that I've been talking, I'm out of a job."

"We won't say anything," Toad offered, though his mind was spinning. He'd encountered references to the Clear Light Society in several of his books, but he had no idea that the ancient order of mystics and scholars still existed, or that Ernie was a member. Perhaps mainlanders were worldlier and knew of such things, but somehow the lanky herbalist didn't seem to be the type to be tied in with such an arcane organization. Ernie was an adventurer, certainly, but hardly a scholar. Toad wanted to question him further, but decided to let Tambourine continue.

"So, tell me," Tam said, sitting back comfortably on the wagon seat.

"Does your Thirdworld trip have anything to do with this meeting you're going to at Covenstead?"

"I can't say any more."

"Why not? The cat's out of the bag anyway. Toad and I are your friends; we won't say anything."

Ernie paused. He seemed to be choosing his words carefully. "We need good weed connections. Things are drying up around here. At Covenstead I'll be meeting with representatives of the Weedgrowers Guild."

"By which you mean, Oldhips?"

"They make up a large part of it. There's a potent variety of albino Honkweed that grows in the Thirdworld. I've already sent a quantity of it ahead to them for their aggie experts to experiment on. Considering the current crisis, it might be worth our while to import it, or find a way to crossbreed it with say, Red—to make an even stronger strain. A more potent weed means that smaller quantities would need to be transported. Thus smaller, more easily guarded shipments."

"Clever, though I don't know if I could abide pink weed."

"Very funny. Trust me, you could live with it. Anyway, I've been a member of the Street-Corner Earth Herbalists' Association most of my life, so I'd be a natural go-between."

"I see," Tambourine remarked, lapsing into silence.

Toad had listened to the exchange between the two with interest. The herbalist's explanation seemed too blithe, too contrived. In Toad's experience real explanations of things had loose ends; Ernie's story had none. The pipesmith studied Tam's face as he gazed ahead into the darkness. Toad decided that, if he read Tambourine correctly, then he and the musician now had something in common—neither of them believed their friend.

It was highly unusual for Ernie, at least the Ernie Toad knew, to be close-mouthed about his adventures. In the past he'd always related his tales by flapping his arms wildly for emphasis and tumbling into extrapolations of extrapolations, usually intended to highlight his role in the saga. Eventually, he would wander back to the point of his story. But this story had been different, short and to the point, and obviously thought out in advance. Then there was the matter of Ernie concealing his membership in the Clear Light Society. Ernie's insistence that Toad accompany him to Covenstead was beginning to feel a bit sinister. Maybe he was overreacting, but as soon as he could get Ernie alone he wanted to get to the bottom of this little mystery.

"We're almost there," the herbalist remarked, breaking the silence. "Unless I miss my guess, those lights I see shining through the trees are from the ferry landing."

Tambourine chuckled dryly. "And hardly a moment too soon. My backsides can't take too much more of this wagon seat. If I ever travel with you again, Mungweasle, I'm going to bring along a pillow."

Ernie gave a sudden snap of the reins and his horse quickened its pace. Soon they were through the last stand of trees and crossing a small clearing to where a torchlit pier extended out into the slow-moving waters of the Sludge River. At the end of the pier stood a dilapidated shack; a blue and white peace symbol banner fluttered from the pole beside it.

As the herbalist's wagon clattered up the pier a short, burly figure brandishing a crossbow leaped out of the shadows and into their path.

"Halt! Who goes there?" the figure demanded.

"It's me, Seth. Ernie Mungweasle. Can't you see the logo painted on the side of my wagon, for Dylan's sake? What's got you slipping around in the shadows like a Radiclib commando? You having the DTs again, or something?"

"I should be so lucky," Seth said, obviously relieved to see a friendly face. He lowered his crossbow and stepped into the light, revealing himself to be a Freak in his early fifties with thinning hair and a great red nose that resembled a lump of putty. "I'll have you know that I've been off the jug for a coupla months now. But if some of the shit that's been going down around here continues, I'll be back on it as soon as a cat can flick its whiskers."

Ernie leaned forward in his seat. "Problems, eh?"

"Yeah, you might say. I'm getting too old for this job, Ernie. Things are bothering me that didn't used to bother me. Outlanders, I mean."

"It's getting close to Halloween, Seth. You've got to expect odd travelers heading in and out of Covenstead this time of year."

The ferryman shook his head. "Not like the ones I've seen lately. I'm used to Raddyclibs and Hunters, Rowdies, and all that. But lately I've been getting Greasers, and I've been hearing stories of Whiteriders traveling the Owsleyburg Road late at night. And, none of that prepared me for the like of the passenger I had a couple of nights back."

"Oh yeah?"

"Holy Bob, what a scary bastard. A big, black-cloaked dude. Rode in here on a huge warhorse. I couldn't see none of his face, but he was puffing on a burning stick that looked like an oversized joint and smelled like a dump fire. He just sat there, arrogant as you please, and demanded that I take him across to Fat City."

Toad felt the flesh on his back crawl. Was it possible? Could the dark horseman Seth described be the same creature that had been haunting his dreams?

The ferryman gave a nervous glance from side to side before continuing.

"I was about to protest the lateness of the hour, but there was something in his manner that suggested I'd do well not to refuse him. He didn't say much to me on the trip across, but several times I heard him whispering to that great black beast of his. It's eerie, but I'll swear that horse understood his every word.

"'Two Rubins for the trip,' I says to him, after we'd docked at Fat City, and he'd mounted his horse again.

"'Here's one,' he cackles, shooting me the finger, 'and you can fry in Hell for the other, ferryman,' he says, wheeling his horse around and thundering off into the night. Weird laugh he had, too. It chills me to the marrow, just to think of it."

By this time Ernie was leaning far forward in his seat, fascinated with Seth's story. "So, you saw nothing of this stranger's face?"

"No, his cowl covered it. I just saw his eyes. They were pale blue, and they never blinked. Not once."

"Interesting."

Seth looked at Ernie as if expecting further comment, but the herbalist just shrugged as he got down off the seat and began leading his horse toward the ferry.

Silently, Toad followed the others to the end of the pier. Seth's story troubled him deeply. He paused, opened his mouth for a second, then closed it again. Though the ferryman's dark stranger resembled the specter that haunted his sleep, maybe it was best not to inquire too closely, lest he discover that his nightmares might not be just dreams after all.

Toad hurried to help the others as they strained to move Ernie's wagon into place on the barge-like ferryboat. Soon the lumbering craft was pushed away from the pier and drifted quietly on the waters of the Sludge. Toad stood at the stern, watching the brightly lit ferry landing disappear in the distance, wondering just what he was getting into. Then slowly and with a forced smile, he wandered toward the bow to await the landing at Fat City. After a while Seth joined him, leaving Ernie and Tam to man the tiller.

"Mungweasle tells me this is your first trip across the Sludge," the ferryman said.

"That's true," Toad replied.

"He also tells me you're a bit of a historian."

Toad nodded.

"Good, good. Fat City'll interest you, then. It's a ghost town now; everyone abandoned it after the '23 plague and never returned. You being interested in history, I guess you already know all about it."

"You mean the 'Bum Trip'? Sure, I know a little about it. That's what people called the Plague of 2423," Toad stated in his most scholarly voice. "They say it ravaged towns all along the east bank of the Sludge, claiming several thousand lives before subsiding as mysteriously as it had begun." The Bum Trip was just an event from his parents' time; it didn't interest Toad as much as events that had transpired centuries before.

Seth picked at his teeth with one yellowed fingernail. "What most people don't know is that the word 'Tripp', in this case, is spelled with two p's. There's quite a story to it, if you'd like to hear it." Then, without waiting for Toad's reply he began his tale. "My uncle was living in Fat City at the time the plague started. He turned out to become a bit of a historian himself. Surely you've heard of him—Simon Garfunkel, the younger."

Toad hadn't, but he was too polite to say so. He just smiled and stared off into the darkness.

"According to Uncle Simon," Seth continued, "the hell of it was, the day the plague started was one of the finest days of the year, a beautiful late June morning so warm you could swim in it. Trees, green with the fullness of their new canopies, swayed gently in the soft breezes. Up and down the main street flower boxes, adorning the houses and shops, blazed with the yellow and orange of marigolds, their brilliance softened by the varying colors of pansies that peered out around them like mischievous children playing hide and seek. The cloudless sky, blue as a robin's egg, arched over a tidy village bustling with activity."

"Apparently, Uncle Simon was a somewhat garish historian," Toad interrupted.

"Well... uh... he was a little odd, but I wouldn't go so far as to call him gayrish. I know what people said, and he wasn't like that at all. Least ways, no one ever proved it," Seth replied, confused and a little annoyed. He gazed back toward the stern for a moment, as if deciding what he should say next, and then continued. "As I was saying, that day was a day so fine that shopkeepers were bringing their merchandise outside to sell without really caring if it sold or not. Workers and loafers alike swarmed about the wharves like ants.

"Nobody knew how or where the news started, but a rumor quickly circulated that a Downeast ship was sailing upriver, towards town. This was an unheard-of event. Other than barges, gundalows, and pleasure craft, few ships came this far upriver, certainly never Downeast craft. Downeasters are a coastal people, proud and arrogant about their seagoing heritage. They'd sooner ride out a Nor'easter in one of their fishing boats than travel brownwater.

"Turns out, this boat was a small sloop, the *John B.*, out of Tinker's Dam. Its main sail was emblazoned with the likeness of a pine tree. As it approached, it listed heavily to port and began moving erratically in the current. Clearly, it was in trouble.

"Some of the hardier townsfreaks rowed out in their skiffs and attached ropes to the floundering craft. Took them some doin', but eventually they got her to shore.

"Of the four crewmen, only the captain remained alive, and just barely. His skin was bluish-gray and cold to look at, although he was burning up with fever and he stank of sickish-sweet bile. The locals cared for him as best they could, but he lived only long enough to tell his name, Tripp, and some of what had happened to his crew.

"They had visited many ports among the far-flung islands, so they could have contracted the disease anywhere. But the sickness started when the *John B.* was a day out of the Penobscot Archipelago. It hit fast. The crew succumbed quickly—in a matter of days. It was horrible: high fever, hallucinations, shakes so bad it seemed as though their bodies would fall apart. But the worst was the blood that oozed from their eyes and the pores of their skin as they breathed their last. Captain Tripp's final words were that he'd be grateful to be dead.

"The captain was right about the disease; it was fast. Within a day it had infected the town. By the end of the week over half of those infected had succumbed. Uncle Simon was one of the very few who remained uninfected. It was he who called the plague 'The Bum Tripp' to memorialize Captain Tripp. By the middle of July the 'Bum Tripp' was boogeying up and down the eastern bank of the Sludge. Fortunately, none of my family ever got it."

Toad continued to stare out into the darkness. The story of the plague had made him feel vaguely uncomfortable. "It sounds awful," he said, "but they say that the disease disappeared as quickly as it arrived. It makes an interesting story, but what's the point?"

"Point? I dunno, I guess I thought *you* of all people, bein' a historian and all, would be interested in a little local lore," Seth replied. "But if you're looking for a point, I suppose it goes to show you, no matter how wonderful things seem, evil can creep in unseen, bringing death, destruction and a whole boatload of misery."

"I see."

The ferryman leaned close. "You do, do you? Well here's one more thing. I haven't thought about the plague in years, but ever since I ferried that black-robed fella across the Sludge the other night, I can't *stop* thinking about it." With that, he wandered back to the stern, leaving Toad to ponder his words.

Chapter Two

Gully Oven was a bowl-shaped depression at the end of a small glen that sloped down from the main road. Over the millennia the face wall had eroded, forming a large concave overhang, reminiscent of a huge, half-buried clamshell rising out of the beach.

On one side of the Gully, hidden deep in the shadows beneath the wagon, Tambourine snored soundly. On the other side, a small campfire crackled in front of the overhang, where the pipesmith sat propped against his knapsack and bedroll. Heat from the modest fire collected under the smooth rock shell, forcing Toad to remove his scarf and heavy woolen mariner's coat. No wonder the ancients called this rock formation an oven, he thought, as he wiped his sweaty palms on the knees of his patched and faded jeans. Leaning back, Toad stared into the darkness under the wagon as the musician's snoring faded. It didn't seem fair that Tam could sleep so soundly, while Toad was left awake with a multitude of jumbled thoughts churning around in his head.

A twig snapped, shattering the silence of the moonlit gully. Ernie's elongated form emerged from the forest, staggering under a load of firewood. The herbalist moved slowly, weary from the river crossing and the long ride north from the deserted town of Fat City. Loading and unloading the wagon from the ferryboat had been harder than Toad had expected and the road out of the deserted town, though still used, had been narrow and rutted, slowly falling apart along with the town it once serviced. Bouncing around on that wagon seat was like riding a rocking chair in a landslide. After a few hours they had become exhausted and needed to stop for the night.

Shuffling to his feet, the pipesmith left his comfortable spot by the fire and walked over to help Ernie with the firewood.

"We gotta talk," he announced, taking several chunks of wood and heading back toward the overhang.

"Right now?" Ernie replied blankly. "It's getting late, you know."

Toad stirred the fire with a stick. After tossing a few pieces of wood into the blaze, he returned to his seat. "Yeah, I know it's late, but this can't wait."

The older Freak dropped his load of firewood and dusted the chips from his frock coat. "Okay, let's have it."

"Ernie, we've been friends for years, and I never thought you were the type to deceive a friend."

"I don't know what you're talking about, Toad."

Toad nodded as the herbalist took a seat across the fire from him. "I think you do. There's a bunch of questions bouncing around in my head that are crying out for answers."

"Let's take them one at a time, then."

"Why didn't you tell me you were a Digger? Why'd you hold that from me all these years?"

"That's easy," Ernie replied, with a smile that the flickering firelight made seem sinister. "I couldn't tell you."

"You told Tambourine."

"That was an accident. We were drinking together one night and in the general course of the conversation it just slipped out."

"Just like that, huh?"

Ernie hunched forward, a vaguely hurt expression on his face. "Yeah, just like that. Let me tell you something about Tambourine Dill, Toad. If you've got something to hide, don't hang around the devious Mr. Dill. He got me drunk and bragging about my exploits, then goaded me into telling more than I should have. Tam's a crafty one, he is. But he's a trustworthy friend."

"That doesn't answer my question."

"No, it just explains how I slipped. You see, Toad, the Society demands complete secrecy. I took the blood oath years ago. Tam has known, but until today he was the only one who knew. Besides, my being a Digger has nothing to do with you."

"It doesn't?"

"Of course not. I don't even know why you think it should."

Toad sat up straighter, staring across the flames into Ernie's eyes. "Okay, another thing. You seem quite unwilling to talk about your Thirdworld exploits. Have you forgotten that hearing them was part of my reason for coming along with you?"

"You'll hear them in time."

"Will I? By the way Tambourine acts, I get the impression that either he thinks you're making things up or that there's more to your story than you're letting on. He's known you longer and better than I have, so he must have reasons for feeling that way, especially since you're a Digger."

Ernie steepled his fingers and rested his chin on them. "I told you, my membership in the Society has nothing to do with you."

"Well, I'm not convinced. Ernie, you've never invited me along on one of your other trips, so why was it so important that I come along on this one? It's all too coincidental."

The herbalist shook his head. "You're getting hyped up over nothing. This has nothing to do with the Clear Light Society. I'm simply going to Covenstead for a Weedgrowers' Guild meeting. The reason I haven't said much about the Thirdworld to you and Tam is because I'm worried that whoever is knocking off the weedwagons will get wind of it. If you think there is more to it, then you've got an overactive imagination."

Toad wasn't placated. "I suppose the Dark Man is a just a product of my imagination as well."

"Dark Man?"

"The one Seth spoke of."

Ernie's right eyebrow jittered, a revealing tic that the herbalist displayed when he was nervous. "C'mon, Toad. Seth's a boozer. He just let some wandering weirdo get the best of him, that's all."

"I wish I could believe that, Ernie. But I got a strange feeling when I heard Seth's story. His passenger sounds an awful lot like a creature I've been having nightmares about the past few weeks."

"That's just a coincidence, Toad. A very interesting one, I'll grant you, but a coincidence just the same. Dreams are strange things, but most of the time they don't mean anything."

"And sometimes they do."

Ernie stifled a yawn. "Most likely your dreams are caused by PSS, Post Suzie Syndrome, also generically known as the Ball-Busting Broad Disorder. Quite common, really. Anyway, it's late. Let's talk about this some other time."

Toad wanted to keep talking, but by now Ernie's yawns were coming in quick succession, each more pronounced than the last.

"I told you, my dreams are not about Suzie. I think you know exactly what I'm talking about. I think you know more about this Dark Man than you're letting on."

"Relax, Toad. I know nothing. I swear."

"There's too damn many coincidences popping up on this trip. I don't like it, and I've got half a mind to pack my bags and head for home."

"You've got less than half a mind if you do," Ernie replied. "There's over twenty-five miles of river, woods, and ocean between you and home, not to mention a few Rowdies and maybe a Greaser or two."

"You're saying I should stick with you?"

"I'm saying, shut up and go to sleep. You're overreacting to being out in the world for the first time. We'll be in Covenstead tomorrow. Once you get there and you start checking out the crowds and exhibits, your attitude will change."

"Maybe."

Ernie spread his hands expansively. "Toad, you'll love the place. It'll be fun. Trust me."

"We'll see." Toad wasn't totally convinced, but he had little choice. Beyond the circle of firelight, Gully Oven was dark and foreboding. Even thinking of turning back was madness.

Ernie shuffled to his feet to throw a few more sticks on the fire. As he rose clumsily on one leg, a small leather-bound book tumbled out of his pocket and landed at Toad's feet.

"What's this?" the pipesmith cried, snatching the book away from Ernie's grasping fingers. As he examined the battered volume, anger flared up inside him like a brush fire. "Hey, this is one of my books!"

Ernie nodded sadly, looking suddenly old and worn. "Yes, I'm afraid it is."

"You stole it from me! How could you?"

"Hear me out, Toad. I can explain."

"So can I, very easily. You're a lousy thief."

"Hey, cool it. I just…"

"You just nothing, man. Dammit, Ernie, how could you do this to me? I thought we were friends."

"We are."

Toad rose to his feet, with the book clenched tightly against his chest.

"Sit down and give me a chance to explain," Ernie mumbled, looking up at Toad. "And be quiet; we don't want to wake Tambourine."

Toad sneered, and then stuffed the book roughly into the front of his shirt. "I can't believe it," he snarled. "Dylan's Bones, Ernie, this is my copy of *Cruickshank's!* It's well over six hundred years old, probably the only book of its type in existence."

"I know."

"No, you don't! Simon Doomsayer and his Luddites burned books by the millions back in 2047, during the Night of a Thousand Fires. This one book may be the only record of the terrible weapons of the ancients."

Ernie lowered his hands. "It's not the only record we have of their weapons, nor is it the most revealing, but it is unique. That's why I had to borrow it."

"Borrow? Dammit, you stole it."

"I gave it to you, remember?"

Toad's jaw dropped. "Yes, I do, but what's that got to do with it?"

"This precious book of yours came from the collection of my employer, Theophilus Skulk. You, nor he, can ever really own an antique. You can only be its steward. History calls, time moves on, and that stewardship must end."

The pipesmith shook his head. "Say what you will, you still had no right to take it without permission. What possible use is it to you? You don't even like to read."

Ernie poked at the fire with his stick. "Look, you were right earlier, when you said I wasn't being honest with you. But there are important reasons for my actions."

"They'd better be good ones, Ernie. "

"I said they were important. The security of all Street-Corner Earth may depend on what I do. I couldn't take the chance that you wouldn't let me bring it. Tomorrow at the meeting there will be a delegation of Radiclibs from Leftopia, personal envoys representing Mizjoan herself. They'll be there to discuss beefing up security on the weedwagons. Their help'll be expensive—thousands of Rubins."

Toad crossed his arms across his chest. He could feel the hard cover of the little book against his skin. "I already know most of that. What's this got to do with you stealing a book?"

"A lot. The Guild will have a hard time meeting the Radiclibs' price. I was hoping to use *Cruickshank's* to sweeten the pot a bit. When I confiscated it, I wasn't sure you'd be coming with me, and you'd never have let me take it myself."

Toad mulled this over. "Ernie, that's unspeakable. First, you take something that doesn't belong to you, and then you want to turn its dangerous secrets over to a nation of professional warmongers. I'd rather burn *Cruickshank's* in that fire than see it put to such foul uses."

"See? That's where your naiveté leads you astray. That would be insane."

"You're the one who's insane. I refuse to be part of your scheme."

Ernie removed his top hat and ran his fingers through his waist-length hair. For the first time Toad noticed just how gray it was becoming, the strands of near-white twisting through the black like threads in a tapestry.

"Toad, Toad, Toad," the herbalist said in exasperation. "It's no longer a matter of what you or I want to be a part of, it's a matter of what must be. If the weedwagons don't get through, the entire economic structure of Street-Corner Earth will collapse. It'd be a tragedy that'd make the Plague of '23 look like a family picnic. We need the Radiclibs' help, regardless of what we think of their politics. *Cruickshank's* will give us the necessary bargaining edge."

"I'm still not convinced."

"Consider this, then; if you threw that book into the fire, you'd be little better than an old-time Luddite."

"You've taken a hell of a chance with our friendship," Toad said gruffly.

"I know that, but the future of our people is more important than either one of us. I'm sorry if I've been dishonest to you, but I'd do it again if I had to. Can I have the book back now?"

"I'll hold onto it, Ernie. That is, until I've decided what to do with it, or whether I'm even going to continue on with you."

"Whatever you want," Ernie replied, fighting back a yawn. "I'm not going to take it away from you, though it's not yours to hold onto forever." He rose to his feet and started to untie his bedroll. "Still, I'd like you to consider seeing this through, for the good of Street-Corner Earth. Even if you don't trust me."

"I'll sleep on it."

"Do that. We'll have a busy day in Covenstead tomorrow."

Ernie rolled out his sleeping bag and got into it fully clothed. Before long, his snores were echoing faintly off the overhang. Toad sat gazing into the fire, his fingers softly rubbing the book under his shirt. Hours later, when he did retire, sleep came slowly. When it finally rolled over him, it was deep and dreamless.

Chapter Three

The narrow trail out of Gully Oven slowly widened as it wound past low, brush-covered hillocks, becoming a broad roadway as the wagon entered a deep oak forest. The oaks, reluctant to give up their russet leaves, towered above the travelers. The air was crisp and pungent with the musty scent of moss and fallen foliage. Toad breathed deeply and lay back against the wagon seat, watching the occasional leaf flutter to the forest floor, joining a sea of others that had already taken the plunge. He closed his eyes and listened to the dried leaves crunching beneath the wagon's wheels, amazed at how they managed to keep time with the light plinking of Tambourine's guitar.

Eventually, the half-naked oaks gave way to stands of pine and the pines to stubbled fields surrounding the infrequent farmhouse or cabin. By the time the sun was at its zenith houses were closer together and the road was a broad, almost-smooth highway joined by smaller wagon paths. Other travelers appeared, some on foot, others crowded into high, swaying wagons. As the numbers of travelers increased, Toad's eagerness to see Covenstead grew in proportion until the events of the night before were gently pushed aside.

The herbalist's wagon rumbled uphill past a knot of young Freaks with walking sticks and backpacks. The wayfarers leaned heavily on their staffs as they trudged up the grade.

The wagon crested the top of the hill and Toad gasped in amazement as he looked down on the rich patchwork of fields in the valley below. The fields extended as far as the eye could see, from the Sludge River in the west to the foggy downs of the east. Covenstead Hill rose like a fist from the blanket of varicolored fields. The ruins of an old fortress crowned the top of the hill, their gray battlements looking strangely out of place among the brightly colored tents and buildings of Covenstead Fair.

The old fort fascinated Toad. He recalled reading once that it had been built by Whitelander Fashies just before the beginning of the twenty-third century, when they controlled much of what was now central Street-Corner Earth. In 2307, it fell to Radiclib raiders under the command of Maxwell "The Hammer" Berkeley, and the Fascists were driven north beyond the Purple Mountains. During the years of peace that followed, the fort had developed into a trade center, due to its proximity to the Sludge. It now housed the offices and stables of the Fair Commission.

As Covenstead grew and spread, large frame structures like the Exhibition and Concert Halls were built, looming up over the colorful confusion of tents, shops, and outdoor markets as the Fair became a permanent city. Only the old fort seemed out of place now, dominating the hilltop like a gray skull tossed atop a pile of bright Yule wrappings. From a distance, the jostling throngs in the streets looked like crazed insects going about bug business.

Toad let out a low whistle of appreciation.

"Kinda grabs you, don't it?" Ernie commented.

Toad nodded as his attention turned to a flatbed wagon rumbling by. On it a pair of old gray-haired Freaks sawed away on fiddles, while a youth in green and brown motley juggled balls and tenpins.

"This is one of the great benefits of life on the road, Toad," the herbalist continued, indicating the whole valley with a sweep of his hand. "You never know what you'll see over the next hill or around the next bend. There's always something to astound or amuse you."

"I've been astounded several times already on this trip," he said, turning to Ernie, "but I can't say as I've been amused."

"I can dig that," Tambourine said, setting aside his guitar. "This is the first you two have spoken all day. Been fighting or something?"

Toad glanced at Ernie but the herbalist stared straight ahead, as if he hadn't heard the question.

"I had trouble sleeping last night," Toad replied glumly.

"Oh. Well, Covenstead'll make you feel better. I can't think of a better place to be on Halloween."

Toad smiled, neither agreeing nor disagreeing, and watched the crowd thronging the road with interest. He saw Freaks from all walks and stations of life: some in the rude garb of farmers or tradesmen, others in the elegant finery of the city. More than a few had already foregone regular clothing and were dressed in bright and outlandish Halloween costumes, though it was barely noontime and the traditional parties and celebrations were hours away.

There were almost as many outlanders in the crowd as Freaks. Toad saw several dozen Radiclibs in tight gray uniforms riding through the crowd on proud warhorses. Not far behind them was a small group of Yipp tribesmen, complete with bushy black hair and scowling, war-painted faces. Almost wild men, the leather-clad Yipps were distant cousins of the Radiclibs, though the two groups had little to do with one another. The Yipps lived in small nomadic clans on the border territories of Leftopia and generally avoided their cousins and other races completely. When they did decide to mingle, they were shown every consideration, for their ferocity in battle was legendary.

Tambourine pointed out some Hunters—woodland Freaks who made their living trapping and shooting, supplying the city centers with game and furs. They lumbered along the streets, dressed alike in leather caps and heavy coats printed in red-and-black check. Huge, wicked-looking skinning knives swung at their belts while short, heavy crossbows were strapped tightly on their backs.

There were others in the crowd that needed no explanation— Downeasters, who inhabited the coastal lands east of Sativa Fields, dressed in their distinctive sou'wester hats and long oilskin coats; Oldhips, in flowers and beads; and the occasional sneering Rowdie. Though the swirling mixture of humanity delighted Toad, it apparently made no impression on Tambourine or Ernie. Only when a pair of Greasers rumbled by in a flame-painted chariot, the sun reflecting off their leather jackets and oiled hair, did either offer any comment.

"Greasies," Ernie muttered. "Just what we need to see."

Tambourine shrugged. "It's Halloween; they have as much right to be here as anyone else, Ernie. Though, to tell the truth, I don't like them any better than you do."

"They're trouble. In Leftopia, they'd be killed just for crossing the border. I'm surprised we allow them to come and go as they damn well please. Might as well invite the Fascists too."

"Fascists have always been our enemies, Ernie. Greasers, at least, are related to us Freaks, even though the connection is far in the past. Besides, they're only trouble in large groups."

"I'd consider one Greaser too many."

As the wagon approached the ancient earthworks that encircled Covenstead Hill, Ernie pulled back on the reins. He eased past a haywagon full of drunken, costumed celebrants that had run off the road into a ditch. Toad watched in amusement as the revelers stumbled out of the back, soiling their finery with dust and chaff as they tried to roll the wagon back onto the roadway.

"Looks like you're going to have a hard time finding a place to park this rig," Toad observed, as Ernie piloted their course through a street crowded with wagons, surreys and carts of all types.

Ernie shrugged. "There's a travelers' commons about halfway up the hill, Toad. I should be able to find a space there."

"I wouldn't count on it," Tambourine interjected. "I've never seen this place so crowded."

People and livestock were everywhere, taking up the roadways and sidewalks. Somehow, Ernie's wagon got through it all. As it inched through Covenstead's teeming streets, Toad observed signs of the coming celebration all around. Black and orange God's eyes, multicolored streamers, and talismans of all descriptions stirred in the breezes above every window and doorway. Above the streets, colorful ropes decorated with paper lanterns stretched between housetops, while carved pumpkins lay in disorganized piles on the porches of shops and taverns. When the Fire Ceremony began at midnight, costumed revelers would carry the glowering jack-o'-lanterns to the great bonfire that would be lit in the courtyard of the old fortress. The lighting of the fire signaled the beginning of the harvest feast that would last for the next three days.

The road grew steeper and the crowd seemed to thicken and change. Besides Freaks, there were more and more Oldhips and Rowdies, and greater numbers of uniformed Radiclibs than Toad would have imagined possible. Once again, he spotted a knot of surly Greasers shoving their way through the crowd. There was even a band of shaven-headed Born-Agains, banging on drums and haranguing a disinterested group of Freaks sitting on the steps of the Weeping Guitar Hotel.

The commons Ernie had spoken of was People's Turf, a large dusty field across from the Exhibition Hall. It was crowded with wagons and buggies of every possible type. Ernie managed to find an open spot on the far side, across from a row of shops and tents. Cook fires burned in the spaces between the wagons. The smells of food simmering in heavy cast iron pots mixed headily with the odors of animals, incense, and burning Honkweed.

Soft music drifted from a dozen quarters. Groups of older Freaks sat joking and gossiping around the fires while their rambunctious offspring played noisily in the middle of the field. As Ernie unhitched his horse, Toad noticed several teenage girls in long, printed skirts eyeing Tambourine. He envied the musician.

Ernie had parked the wagon so that its back faced the street. As Tambourine and Toad began settling in, Ernie took his horse by the reins and began leading it toward the public stables at the far end of the commons.

"Want me to go with you?" Toad offered. He needed a chance to chat with Ernie. He wasn't entirely ready to forgive him for the theft of the book and wanted to get him alone to work on his conscience some more.

The herbalist shook his head. "Thanks for offering, but I've got to go and see some people. Be back later."

"Uh-huh."

"Seriously. I haven't told anyone that I'm bringing a friend. I have to explain your presence before we get there. They're nervous types."

Toad shrugged. "I guess I'm not the only one you lie to, then."

"Not fair, Toad. Everything's cool. I'll be back in a bit."

"Whatever." Shaking his head again, Toad returned to the wagon as Ernie headed off toward the stables.

Tambourine was sitting on the tailgate of the wagon tuning his guitar. He didn't even look up when Toad approached.

"How about a song?" Toad asked. "I could use one."

Tambourine stood up and left his guitar leaning inside the wagon. "Not just now, Brother Toad. I've got to check on tickets for that concert tonight."

"Have you got a meeting, too?"

"No, but I feel the need to be alone. Why don't you try selling some of your pipes while Ernie and I are gone? You may learn more about Covenstead that way than any other."

Pushing aside feelings of distrust and abandonment, Toad took up Tambourine's seat on the wagon's tailgate, opened his sample case and laid out pipes on Ernie's old quilt. Watching the crowds pass by would soothe his uneasiness, he thought; the wide variety of fairgoers fascinated him. As he arranged his pipes, he felt himself relax. Ernie could do and say what he wanted, but Toad still possessed *Cruickshank's* and wouldn't give it up without a fight. After the meeting he and Ernie would have a talk. By then, Toad would have figured out exactly what to say. If the outcome wasn't to his liking, he would return to Smuttynose, taking the priceless old book with him. In the meantime, he planned to sell his wares in peace and contemplate the Fair around him.

While he waited for people to notice his array of pipes and paraphernalia, Toad took his best churchwarden, a full two feet long with a bowl of polished antler, and stuffed it with the last of his meager supply of weed. Instead of verbally haranguing potential customers as the other merchants were doing from tents and wagons up and down the street, Toad just sat back and toked away, confident that his pipe would be advertisement enough.

Seeds crackled and popped as Toad toked deeply and settled into observing the passing parade of fairgoers. He'd seen more Rowdies in his life than he'd cared to, and plenty of Downeasters, since Islington was one of the stopovers for their sleek, high-masted schooners. However, Radiclibs and Oldhips were new sights for him. Radiclibs seemed grim and somehow dangerous, but the Flower Folk had a light in their eyes that drew Toad to them. About twenty of them were gathered around a brightly painted caravan, about five wagons down; Toad gawked at them with unabashed curiosity. He enjoyed the sight of the women in their long dresses and the men in their embroidered shirts and beads.

A pair of Greasers walked by, sneering at him. He kept an eye on them as they slouched off across the street and entered The Bongwater Tavern. He was so intent on tracing their path that it took a moment for him to notice a pretty Oldhip girl as she fingered one of his simple one-hitters.

"Would you like that one?" Toad asked, cheerfully.

The girl replied with a smile that lit up her delicate features. "Very much, brother, but I have no money. All I have is this bag of sunflower seeds." She held the leather sack up for Toad's inspection.

The pipesmith found the girl's idyllic smile irresistible. "You've caught me at a weak moment. It just so happens that I'm famished. One of my one-hitters for your seeds seems an even trade. Done?"

"Done!" she squealed, picking up the tube and admiring it before handing him the bag. He smiled at her again, but she was off like a shot, showing her new acquisition to her friends.

No sooner had the girl disappeared into the crowd than a farmer with a wispy billy-goat beard bought a pair of clay pipes for twenty Abbies, the heavy copper coins handed out one by one. As the farmer walked away, testing the draw on one of the pipes, Toad smiled to himself. Coming to Covenstead may have been a good decision after all.

Over the next two hours Toad sold most of his pipes and accessories, making special deals with those he thought couldn't afford them, and extracting a few extra Abbies from those who could. There was something about Covenstead that was beginning to work on him. Its smells and sounds and bustling throngs assailed his senses like fine weed. He loved being in a strange, exotic city far from home, selling his pipes and talking to customers. What fascinated him most was the endless kaleidoscope of humanity: the farmers and Oldhips, the Radiclibs and Freaks, the wealthy in their finery, and the drifters in their rags.

From his spot on the Turf, Toad observed many odd-looking people whom he would have snubbed on Smuttynose. As he held his tinderbox to his pipe, trying to draw out one last resin hit, he saw by far the most peculiar fellow yet, approaching the wagon.

Though quietly dressed by Covenstead standards, the man was not one that would pass unnoticed in a crowd. He was barely five feet tall and his blue-black hair and small, pointy goatee were cut much shorter than was the fashion. His jeans, turtleneck sweater and sandals were moldy with age, and the black beret he wore tipped rakishly low on his forehead was riddled with moth holes. The oddest thing about him, though, was his spectacles. They were large and round with mirrored lenses that Toad thought must be impossible to see through. As extraordinary as the little man appeared, Toad somehow felt that he should know him.

The stranger stopped to examine the logo painted on the side of the wagon in flowing frisconouveau script. Toad noticed that the man's skin was dark and smooth, like tanned leather. Although he appeared little older than Toad himself, something about the odd little fellow suggested great age. When the man finished inspecting the wagon, he turned toward Toad and smiled. The pipesmith felt his skin quiver. The man's teeth were numerous and small, and seemed far too white.

"Hey, man," the stranger said in a low, gritty voice. "These are Brother Mungweasle's wheels. Is he, like, around?"

Toad found the man's voice oddly soothing. His former tension faded and he smiled back. "He's got business on the other side of town. I don't know when to expect him back."

"Man, that cat's always off somewhere."

"Cat?" Toad had never heard the term before, though he considered himself an expert on colloquialisms.

"You know, a hipster. Like, a cool and groovy dude."

"Oh. You know Ernie, then?"

"We've met. Like I said, Brother Mungweasle gets around."

"Are you a friend of his?"

"Hey, are you?"

"Sometimes I wonder," Toad replied, realizing that the man was gazing past him at something inside the wagon.

"I see you and Brother Mungweasle, like, aren't traveling alone."

"Huh? What makes you think that?"

"If I'm not mistaken, that guitar behind you belongs to a cat named Tambourine Dill."

Toad was becoming alarmed at how much the little stranger seemed to know. "W-what makes you say that?"

"Check out the words scratched onto the body of that git-box, and you'll see, man."

Picking up the instrument, Toad noticed for the first time the crude, uneven letters scrawled across its front: THIS MACHINE KILLS FASCISTS.

"Interesting sentiment, but what does it mean?"

"Hey, it could mean a little or it could mean a lot, but for now just say it means this is Tam Dill's git-box."

The stranger was starting to get on Toad's nerves. "Yeah, it's Tambourine's. What's the big deal about an old guitar?"

The stranger's grin widened, irritating Toad all the more because he couldn't see the eyes behind the heavy mirrored glasses. "The 'deal', man, depends on who wields it, as it is with the tools you use to carve your pipes. In another's hands those same tools might only make sweepings."

"Look, who are you anyway?"

The man shrugged, sunlight flashing off his outlandish spectacles as he started to walk away. "I am who I am."

"That's no answer."

There was a flash of reflected sunlight; then a voice drifted out of the shadows between the wagons as the stranger disappeared. "It's the only answer, man."

Toad hurried to get another glimpse of the mysterious character, but he was nowhere to be seen; he had vanished as if he'd never existed. "Weird little dude... but this *is* Covenstead Fair," he muttered to himself as he went back to pitching his wares.

By the time Toad saw Ernie and Tambourine returning from the far side of the commons his pipes were all sold, thanks to some imaginative dickering. The encounter with the shabby little stranger was all but forgotten.

"Good news," Ernie yelled as soon as he was in earshot. "Tam's got tickets for the concert tonight. We can all go after the meeting."

"I've wanted to discuss that meeting of yours all day, Ernie. Where have you been?"

"I'll have to tell you that on the way, pal. We only have a couple of minutes. We've gotta hurry to get there on time."

Toad gathered up his sample case and Ernie's quilt and stowed them in the wagon.

"It's a wonder you remembered to come back for me at all," he remarked.

Ernie clapped a reassuring hand on the pipesmith's shoulder. "I know you're a little upset now, Toad, but after the concert you'll be in a better mood. Hurry and grab your coat. These people don't like to wait."

Dusk was settling in as they made their way through the streets of Covenstead. Costumed revelers scurried from house to house, to the series of small parties and get-togethers that would continue on until the Fire Ceremony. Hearing the laughter and music spilling from a thousand well-lighted windows and doorways, Toad silently hoped Ernie's meeting wouldn't take too long. The evening was just beginning; his purse was bulging with coins and he wanted to experience as much of Covenstead nightlife as possible.

"You seem in a better mood already," Ernie remarked, as he led Toad through a confusing maze of tents, alleyways, and side streets. "Can I assume that you've changed your mind about continuing on with me?"

The pipesmith shook his head. "That's the problem with you, Ernie, you assume everything and tell nothing."

"Slow down, pal. I've told you everything."

"That remains to be seen. If I don't like what I hear at this meeting of yours, I'm leaving, even if I have to walk all the way back to Smuttynose. I better get more answers there than I've gotten from you."

"Your questions will be answered momentarily," Ernie replied, nodding toward a dilapidated two-story structure across a narrow street. Its windows were boarded shut and paint was peeling from the walls in long strips. A faded sign over the door read WILLY'S FUN ARCADE, but the old building looked anything but fun; it wore a lonely, deserted air. Toad hesitated as he approached the steep outside staircase leading to the second story. It was only through Ernie's urging that he began the long climb to the scarred door at the head of the stairs.

Chapter Four

The meeting was already in progress by the time Toad and Ernie reached the shabby, second-floor door. Toad could hear strident voices arguing inside, but could make out little of what was being said. Ernie knocked furtively and the voices fell silent. Soon the door creaked open and a scowling black-bearded face peered out at them. The fierce man wore the tight gray uniform of a Radiclib officer.

"Greetings, Rudy," Ernie said cheerfully. "Sorry we're late."

The scowl deepened. "As well you should be, Comrade Mungweasle. Tardiness is counter-revolutionary."

"I'll remember that, Rudy."

"The name is Comrade Major Rudy, comrade. And, you still haven't given me the password."

"Can the protocol," a woman's voice demanded from behind the Radiclib. "Let the man in so we can get on with this meeting."

Rudy glowered but did as the woman suggested, grudgingly swinging the door open to admit the two Freaks. Toad nodded nervously as he squeezed past the powerfully built Radiclib. Something in the way the soldier looked at him made him cringe. When he noticed the short, broad-bladed sword at Rudy's belt his stomach did a slow turn. What in hell had Ernie gotten him into?

The meeting room did nothing to heighten Toad's spirits. It was small and windowless, illuminated only by a pair of tallow candles at the center of a round oak table. Mismatched chairs huddled around the soft light; the apparent remains of a pool table lurked in a dark corner and a flyspecked peace symbol banner loitered on the far wall.

Besides the Radiclib called Rudy there were three other people in the room: a tall, slender, dark-haired woman in green fatigues emblazoned with the red star and Honkweed leaf patch of the elite Weatherman Forces, an elderly bewhiskered Oldhip in a tattered brown robe, and a thin, clean-shaven man with chest-length blond hair whose open-throated white meditation shirt and double strand of wooden beads denoted him as an Oldhip Tribechief. Toad's eyes widened as he regarded the members of the contrasting groups. It didn't seem possible that they could coexist in the same space.

The young Oldhip spoke first, rising from his chair to shake hands with Ernie and Toad. "Welcome, my brothers," he said softly. "We've been awaiting your arrival."

Ernie grinned broadly. "Greetings, Wheatstraw, son of Bambu. It's been a long time."

"Too long, Brother Mungweasle. We miss you in Hillcommune. Is this your friend we've heard of?" The Oldhip turned to Toad and smiled, his eyes flashing peace and goodwill. The pipesmith took his hand and found it callused, yet gentle to the touch.

"Wheatstraw, this is Josiah Toad, pipesmith of Smuttynose."

The Oldhip's smile broadened as he released his grip. "Peace be with you, Brother Toad. I own several of your pipes and consider them as fine as those of our own craftsmen."

Toad blushed. "I'm honored," he said.

"Let me introduce you to the others. Comrade Rudy you've met. This lady is his mate, Comrade Major Kentstate. The venerable fellow beside me is my trusted friend and advisor, Brother Foreseein' Franklin."

The elderly Oldhip nodded and offered a firm, surprisingly strong handshake. "Peace," he rasped.

"And flowers," Rudy growled. "Really, Comrade Kentstate and I don't have time for these polite amenities."

"What I have to say won't take long," Ernie interjected. "But I'm sure it'll be of interest to our Radiclib friends."

Rudy took a seat next to Toad, instinctively causing the pipesmith to wiggle away. "Get on with it then," he grumbled.

"Perhaps it would be best if we first bring Comrades Mungweasle and Toad up to date on what we've been discussing," Kentstate remarked, throwing her mate an irritated glance. Rudy turned away, disgusted.

She stood up and stared directly at Ernie, then at Toad. "Our Oldhip comrades have made a generous financial offer to us in exchange for guarding their weed shipments from Hillcommune and Owsleyburg. Sadly, we must refuse this offer."

"Why?" Ernie inquired, leaning forward in his seat. "Does Joannie have so much cash that she wouldn't be interested in collecting a few more Rubins?"

The Radiclib bristled. "Her name is Comrade Leader Mizjoan," Kentstate said flatly. "And, as you know, the Leftopian People's Republic is not a rich nation. We could surely use the money, but we simply don't have the manpower to spare."

"None at all?"

"None. Fascist patrols have been giving us a lot of trouble along our northern reaches these past few months. We fear they're building up for a full-scale invasion. As much as we'd like to, we can't spare the men or weapons."

"Perhaps we could make better arrangements on price," Wheatstraw suggested.

The lovely brunette shook her head. "Money isn't the issue here, Comrade Wheatstraw. If the troop build-up along the northern provinces of Freelandia and Weatherlandia becomes much heavier, Leftopia could be overrun. If we go, the rest of Street-Corner Earth will follow. Is that worth risking just so the Guild and you Oldhips can reap high profits?"

"These high profits you speak of aren't so high," Foreseein' Franklin rasped, his wispy chin whiskers bobbling as he spoke. "The whole economy of Street-Corner Earth *and* Leftopia is based on the Honkweed crop. If the caravans can't pass safely through Sativa Fields, our nations will die from within. We need your help."

Rudy shook his head and drummed his fingers noisily on the tabletop. "It can't be done. Your people will have to learn to defend themselves against these Greaser brigands."

"We have no proof the brigands are Greasers," Wheatstraw remarked. "None have been reported taking part in the attacks. The degree of violence employed makes us believe that it's been Fascists, whipped into a frenzy by their Brotherhood of Whiteriders."

"Believe what you will, Oldhip," Rudy said. "But Greasers are as violent as any other pig race. And, I see that the Freaks allow them to wander around their cities at will."

"Only in small groups, Brother Rudy."

"They shouldn't be allowed at all. They may be easier to stomach than Fascists, but I'd have nothing to do with either race."

"There is no proof that Greasers are involved with any of our troubles," Wheatstraw remarked.

"There's truth in what Rudy says," Ernie interrupted. "The Fascists are the only problem now, but Greasers could be in on it soon enough."

Rudy snorted. "Could be! Dylan's Bones, no wonder you let Rowdies live among you. You're so naive. Before you come to your senses, Rowdies will be partying over your graves with their buddies, the Fascists and Greasers."

"I hardly think so," Ernie said. "Nevertheless, I have the solution to our problems right in my pocket."

The room grew still. The herbalist offered everyone a knowing wink and, from inside his voluminous coat, slowly extracted a long object wrapped in heavy cloth. Toad wondered what he was up to. He looked around and saw the same question mirrored in four other pairs of eyes.

Ernie gently unwrapped the object and placed it on the table. Toad felt his jaw drop as if it were on oiled hinges. Though the others stared at the artifact with intense curiosity, only the pipesmith made a motion to reach out and touch it. Nervously, he ran his fingers along the bizarre creation of wood and metal, examining the object's pitted tube and flint-and-steel mechanism attached to one side.

"Ernie, this can't be. It's a flintlock pistol!"

"It is, Toad, just like the ones you've seen illustrated in *Cruickshank's*."

Rudy glowered at the weapon with disgust. "Big deal," he snorted. "Some fool makes a bong with a built-in tinderbox and you idiots treat it like it was made of gold."

Foreseein' Franklin regarded the pistol closely, a look of dismay gathering in his rheumy old eyes. "I have read of such things, years ago in the *Book of Love*. It's a gun—a weapon the ancients used to kill each other in great numbers."

"That's right," Ernie said and grinned. "With enough of these, I'm sure neither Greasers nor Fascists would pose a serious threat."

Rudy started to say something, but Kentstate motioned him to silence. "You have more of these things?"

"They can be obtained."

"And you can make them work?"

"That should present no great problem."

"The damn thing doesn't look very dangerous to me," Rudy said, grunting, in spite of his mate's hard stare.

"Guns could kill at great distances, even greater than that of the best longbow," Foreseein' Franklin said. "It is written that they issued forth thunder and lighting that could pierce a man like an arrow. Simon Doomsayer's Luddites destroyed them all many years ago and their evil magick passed from the world."

Ernie's grin widened and grew more wolfish. "Apparently old Simon's boys missed a few. There's hundreds more where this baby came from."

Toad felt the tension rising in the room. Rudy and Kentstate leaned forward and regarded the old pistol with open awe, though neither had quite enough courage to touch it. Franklin looked worried, as did Wheatstraw.

"Somehow you wish to use this—gun—to bargain with us?" Wheatstraw asked.

Rudy shook his head. "Not with you Oldhips, with us Radiclibs. And you think this ancient toy will buy our services, Mungweasle?"

"Believe me, comrade, it is an offer you can't refuse."

Toad wondered what kind of game Ernie was playing with these people. Shifting uncomfortably in his seat, the pipesmith felt the weight of the book hidden under his shirt and began to understand.

Kentstate regarded Ernie with a fixed stare, her dark eyes flashing. "What's your offer, comrade?"

"Imagine weapons like this in the hands of Radiclib soldiers. You could defend the weed shipments *and* protect yourselves against the Fascists."

"Tempting," Kentstate replied, "but where did you get this thing, anyway?"

Ernie straightened up in his chair and tipped his hat a little lower on his forehead. Toad knew the gesture. It meant that a story was about to ensue—a long, complicated story. He'd seen it many nights in his own living room back on Smuttynose.

"I got it in the Thirdworld," Ernie began. "It was a gift from Muhammud JP-4 Umamma, chief of the Blackmen."

"I'm wearing my riding boots, Comrade Mungweasle, but I doubt they are *that* tall," Rudy growled. "Thirdworld. Blackmen. I didn't come all the way from Camp Hoffman to hear silly old legends."

Wheatstraw cocked his head. Something flickered in his clear blue eyes like an awakened memory. "I once heard that long ago a race of dark-skinned people lived underground near some of the ancient cities. They were thought to have died out centuries ago. What do you know of such things?"

"It's all in a tale," Ernie chuckled.

Rudy grumbled and shook his head. "Mungweasle's tales exist only to inform us of his prowess."

Ernie chose to ignore the Radiclib. "About six months ago Theophilus Skulk, present head of the Clear Light Society, summoned me to his headquarters at Froggy Bottom. I had some business going down in Saturday Night at the time, so I was able to get to Froggy Bottom within hours of receiving his message.

"It was late in the afternoon, almost dusk, when I arrived at Skulk's, where I found him sitting on his porch, talking to the shabbiest little vagabond I've ever seen—and I've seen a few. Skulk hailed me as I was coming up the steps and introduced me to the stranger, who went by the handle of Beatnik Maynard. From the way Skulk treated the dude, I guessed that he must be someone of great importance.

"Maynard did most of the talking, as Skulk and I listened. He gave away very little about himself, but he did say that he'd long had an interest in the Clear Light Society and shared our passion for history and archaeology. His interests ranged far afield, and he needed our help in one of those distant places. In return, he said he'd turn us on to the archaeological find of the century.

"Now, this all sounded like prime bullshit to me, but Skulk seemed to be groovin' with it, so I went along. Life is easier if I agree with the boss from time to time.

"Maynard produced some maps and handed them to me to look over. One was a map of the coastal region south of Saturday Night, all the way to Bahston. The other was a street plan of a place called Churlston which, it turned out, was part of Greater Bahston. There was a place on the Churlston map marked with a red X. It was there, Maynard said, that I would find the entrance to the Thirdworld and the treasures it contained."

Rudy's scowl disappeared, replaced by a look of greedy interest. "Treasure?"

"Yeah. Rich treasure—though he declined to tell me more about it. He said that everything would become clear when I got there and that I'd probably thank him some day for the opportunity I was being given.

"I set out for Bahston the next day, taking the necessary supplies and the maps Maynard had given me. Traveling by day, I got just south of Nukeplant. After that I traveled by night, paralleling Highway 61 and sleeping in the forest while the sun was up. This is an area little frequented by Freaks, and the maps I carried would be damning if I were caught by any of the Whipmasters that patrolled the region near Bahston. Beatnik Maynard said that they were quite hostile towards outsiders, particularly Freaks. If captured, I'd have been taken to the high towers of the Massas, as the rulers of Bahston are called. From there, no man returns.

"After four days' journey, I came within sight of Bahston—a great tumbled pile of ruins surrounded by swamp and woodland. Daylight was still a few hours off, but in the center of the city lights burned in the highest towers. In the shanties along the river's edge and in the tottering brick tenements half buried in the forest, lights were starting to come on as the inhabitants awoke. I hurried across the old wooden bridge that spanned the river and made towards the docks of Churlston.

"Keeping to the shadows and deserted alleyways, I kept moving, cautiously. One of Maynard's maps led me to an abandoned weed-infested court within sight of a huge granite obelisk that marked one of the highest hills. It didn't look promising; I only found a small dark hole concealed under a pile of bricks. Not wanting to be seen by the ragged figures that were beginning to fill the streets, I crept into the opening and began inching my way forward. When I had crawled maybe twenty feet, I stopped and lit a candle with my tinderbox. My heart was beating like a drum. In the light I noticed that the passage was becoming wider and deeper. Before long I found that I could stand upright, as the tunnel pitched sharply downward.

"Suddenly, I was surrounded. Several figures loomed out of the shadows. Their skin was as dark as pitch, so I couldn't see their faces clearly, but their eyes and grinning teeth glared at me like jack-o'-lanterns. Light from my candle reflected off the long-bladed knives they held in their hands. One huge Blackman leveled a crossbow straight at my face. 'Don't move a muscle, white boy,' he advised, 'cause if you do, you can sho 'nuff kiss your ass goodbye.'

"I stood stock still while the big Blackman's companions checked me over.

"'This whigger's different from others we've seen, Mamba,' one of them said. 'Look at his clothes. Look at his hair.'

"'Where you from, whitey?' the one called Mamba asked. 'You sure ain't from around here.'

"Without saying too much, I told them where I was from and what I was doing in Bahston. Mamba seemed to recognize Maynard's name. 'Come with me,' he said, taking me firmly by the arm.

"The Blackmen took me through a complicated series of airy tunnels, well lit by rows of guttering torches. It seemed that we must be miles underground. We ended up in the Blackmen's village. I have never seen anything so strange. Their houses were long, one-story buildings that appeared to be made out of metal. They vaguely reminded me of my caravan, only much longer and with many glass windows. They even had metal wheels, but they were so large that it would take a dozen workhorses just to make them budge. Around each house were patches of carefully tended albino Honkweed. I was taken to the best kept of the metal houses and, with great ceremony, ushered inside. In the center, sprawled on a pile of pillows was an enormous Blackman. He was an older, somewhat heavier version of Mamba. He was smoking from a tall water pipe and seemed only slightly surprised to see me.

"'We caught this white boy sneaking in the entrance of the Red Line, Papa,' Mamba reported. 'He claims to be a friend of Beatnik Maynard's.'

"The older Blackman heaved himself up off the pillows and stood regarding me with quiet curiosity. He towered over me. I knew he could snap me in two if he felt like it. I got to tell you, I was pretty nervous.

"'I'm called Umamma—Muhammud JP-4 Umamma,' he said, engulfing my hand in his meaty fist. 'Sit down, friend of Maynard, and we'll smoke some herb and rap.'

"That was my first exposure to the albino Honkweed. And, as Brother Toad can attest, it kicks ass. Before I knew it I was telling Muhammud about my mission—how Maynard wanted me to see the treasure that the Blackmen guarded. A smile spread across his face that reminded me of sunrise. 'Kind of a pushy request for a white boy,' he said. 'Usually, I'd cut your balls off and have them for lunch for axin' such a thing. But you're in luck; I'm not very hungry today. Besides, that funky lil' Beatnik is a cool dude, cool enough to be a Brother. I can't off a Brother's buddy, not today anyway. You'll see what you want to—when the time's right.'"

Forseein' Franklin reached out and tapped the old flintlock with one gnarled finger. "And that treasure was this gun?"

"Not only the gun. There was much, much more. The Blacks were sitting on a gold mine of pre-Luddite artifacts. Incredible stuff. Stuff you couldn't even begin to imagine, never mind put a price on."

By now everyone was listening to Ernie's story with rapt attention. Toad had seen Ernie hold audiences spellbound before, but never as well as now.

"There's one thing I don't understand," Kentstate interjected. "With all their wealth and weapons, why do these Blackfolk choose to live underground?"

"Centuries ago, Comrade Kentstate, during the chaos that was Helter-Skelter, they were driven underground by their enemies. When the mighty crimelords who were the ancestors of the Massas put down the Neo-Luddites and seized control of the cities, conditions grew so bad on the surface that the Blacks elected to stay underground, where they were well hidden and fortified against attack."

"What manner of men are these Massas?"

"Nobody really knows. They never leave their high towers at the heart of the old city. Only their Whipmasters are seen abroad, and of course the thousands of Prole slaves who mine the ruins for metals and a rare substance called plastic. Evidently, plastic is the basis of their currency."

"Still, it sounds as if the Blacks are well armed. Why don't they just rise up and overthrow the Massas?"

"Because they're outnumbered by Proles and Massas at least a hundred to one. Fighting does occur, though, when Prole miners break through into their tunnels. Besides, guns take a special exploding powder to operate, and supplies of it are limited. Getting the components for its manufacture required sending scouts above ground. Often their scouts never returned. These missions were always quite dangerous, and after the appearance of the one the Blacks called The Jiveman, they became impossible."

"Sounds like more old legends to me," Rudy grumbled. "Isn't The Jiveman just another name for Old Charlie?"

"To some, I guess. Regardless, he and a band of black-robed companions rode into Bahston about a week after I arrived in the Thirdworld. Mamba and I watched the whole thing from a hidden observation post on Beekan Hill. The Whipmasters were out in full force that day, and the Proles were even more subdued than usual. The whole mob parted like water as The Jiveman rode alone to the highest of the Massas' towers. It was like he was expected."

Toad's mouth flopped open, but no words came out. He felt his skin tighten as a chill raced up his spine. Ernie's words echoed in his ears. The herbalist had known all along that the Dark Man was real, and not just a product of Toad's imagination.

The pipesmith wanted to speak out, to denounce the lying, mind-gaming Mungweasle to the world. His jaws started to move but clamped shut as, underneath the table, a heavy boot heel crunched down on his toes. It bore down, lightened up momentarily, but then came down harder. Ernie's gray eyes glared, conveying a clear message: this was neither the time nor the place. Toad winced, but kept his mouth shut.

"Jiveman or not, this all concerns us very little," Wheatstraw remarked, spreading his hands. "Bahston and the Thirdworld are a long way from here, through thick forests and treacherous swamps. Its people never come here and, usually, ours never go there. I fear your story is straying, Brother Mungweasle."

"My story runs in many directions. Believe me when I say it concerns us more than you might know."

"Continue, then," Wheatstraw replied, "though the connection between us and this Jiveman, or whoever, is not clear to me."

"The connection will be clear enough shortly. Soon after the stranger arrived, there was a concerted effort to roust the Blackfolk from their tunnels, the first purge of its kind in decades. It seemed as if The Jiveman wanted something in those tunnels, something important. He must have known about the Blackmen's treasure. The Blackfolk called it the Sunken Museum."

"A museum? Underground?"

Ernie nodded. "All three stories of it. I think it might be the existing undercellars of a much larger structure that once stood above ground. More than likely, it was one of the many buildings that the Neo-Luddites razed during Helter-Skelter. Maynard hadn't lied; it *was* the archaeological find of the century. Unfortunately, it turned out that the black-cloaked stranger knew of it too, and was willing to forfeit countless Prole lives to get to it."

"Amazing," said Wheatstraw.

The herbalist's eyes seemed to flash sparks. "I've never seen anything like it. Thousands of years' worth of pre-Helter-Skelter artifacts, all neatly preserved and labeled. From what we could learn there, we could rewrite history. There would be no more legends, only facts."

"That's a bold statement," rasped Foreseein' Franklin.

"It was meant to be bold, Brother Franklin. However, even as we speak, the museum may be in the hands of the enemy. They actually held it for several days after their first assault, when they got the Proles to mine in through the roof. They brought in great winches and started stripping the upper stories. It was only at the cost of many Black lives at the Battle of Green Line that the invaders were driven back above ground. Though hundreds of Proles died, they took as much as they could with them—guns and items far more horrible. Even now these things may be heading north."

Thinking about his dreams, Toad shivered. There *was* a Dark Man, and he was headed this way. He tried to move his foot, but it didn't get far before Ernie's boot heel was back in place and pressing down.

"Why do you think this Jiveman is heading to Street-Corner Earth?" Wheatstraw asked. "What would we have that a man like him would value?"

"You'd have to ask him that. All I know is that one of Muhammud's spies saw some of his black-cloaked henchmen directing the loading of an ocean barge at Churlston. There were uniformed Fascists among the barge's crew. I don't have to remind you that the Sludge can accommodate barges all the way north to Great East Lake. Believe me when I say you'll need the weapons that the Society can provide, and you'll need them soon."

Rudy looked grimmer than usual. He nodded his head with heavy deliberation. "Our agents have seen huge barges running the river late at night, displaying no insignia or lights."

"If these are the barges from Bahston, what could be on them?" Kentstate wondered.

Ernie shrugged. "Guns, probably, or worse."

"Worse?"

"When the Proles retreated, they took several massive machines with them. Steam tractors were what they were called—great iron beasts said to be able to move under their own power. If The Jiveman gets them working, well..." He spread his hands and shrugged sadly.

"This is grave indeed," Wheatstraw stated. "But what proof...?"

"Proof! We don't have time for proof. When I left the Thirdworld, battles were still going on. There was no way to tell who the victor would be. Perhaps The Jiveman has already won and is even now heading north, spreading his evil before him. "We've enjoyed peace for decades, and now suddenly there's trouble with brigands, trouble with Fashies, and unmarked barges going up the Sludge at odd hours. Something evil is afoot in Street-Corner Earth."

Wheatstraw got to his feet. He looked deeply troubled. "I believe you have convinced us all of our peril, Brother Mungweasle. Our present problems look insignificant, compared to what you've told us."

"What can be done?" Foreseein' Franklin asked. "It seems that more than the weedwagons need protection now."

"We have this gun," Ernie stated, holding it for everyone to see. "The Society is working to get more, Dylan willing. Beyond that, Toad has a book on gunlore. Using it, we might be able to manufacture our own. First, however, he and I have to go to Camp Hoffman and see Mizjoan, personally."

Toad shot Ernie a disparaging glance, but did not say anything, fearing another heel would be stomped onto his foot.

"But, what of the weedwagons?" Franklin continued.

"Yet another reason to see Mizjoan," replied Ernie.

"*If* she'll see you, Comrade Mungweasle," Rudy growled. "She's become more discriminating than when last you met."

Ernie grunted as he slipped the pistol into his belt. "She'll see me," he said, patting the bulge under his coat. "Now, if there's nothing more to discuss, my friend and I have a concert to attend. The tickets were five Rubins apiece, and we don't want to be late."

"You paid to get in?" Rudy laughed. "Guess you haven't got the right connections after all, comrade. The rest of us were sent freebies."

Kentstate drummed her fingers nervously on the tabletop. She looked deeply troubled. "On the way here I saw a pair of black-cloaked characters like the ones you mentioned, hanging around the entrance to the Concert Hall. At the time I thought they were just some Freaks getting a jump on Halloween, but now I'm not so sure."

Toad groaned, but Ernie gave him a quick unseen jab to the ribs.

"It's possible that The Jiveman may already be here," Ernie said, stepping out onto the landing, shoving Toad ahead of him. "Maybe you should all skip the concert tonight. If the black-cloaks are here to cause trouble, Toad and I will keep an eye on them."

Toad tried to whimper out some feeble protest, but Ernie took him firmly by the arm and led him down the stairs. Below them the torchlit midway spread out in all directions, like the spokes of a glowing wheel.

"Quit dragging your feet," Ernie said. "The night's still young, and so are we."

"Ernie, I *am not* going to Camp Hoffman…"

"I know, I know. We'll talk about it later. You came to Covenstead to have fun and tonight's the night. Just let the old master show you how."

Soon they were winding their way toward People's Turf through streets crowded with masked and costumed celebrants. Toad's brain felt as confused and jumbled as the sights and sounds surrounding him. He told himself that in the morning he would definitely head for home. But for tonight, he ceased resisting and let himself be propelled toward whatever the night would bring.

Chapter Five

The first stars of evening were blinking on overhead as Sweet Billy Bejeezuz leaned against a post on the Concert Hall's back dock, chewing on the end of one of his long black cigars and gazing down on the brightly lit streets of Covenstead. Inside the envelope of his cowl he was smiling. He almost felt happy.

A few Freaks were beginning to drift into the hall, and within an hour swarms of them would be piling in to see his show. It pleased him to think of them paying to see him, then screaming and writhing in ecstasy while his music cast its spell.

By itself his music could incite the masses, but it did not possess the power that allowed him to command them. Long ago, Bejeezuz learned that the ancient spearhead he wore around his neck could focus the power of his music to bind people to his will. The spell wasn't permanent, however, nor did it work on everyone. The combination of the spearhead and The Book would cure that. Together they would make him invincible. In the meantime, the chaos caused by his concert would allow the combined force of Fascists and Greasers he had waiting, twenty miles to the north, to walk in and take Covenstead without too much trouble. Once he had Covenstead, with its fortified hill, he could launch an attack on Rivertown and gain a stranglehold on the entire region.

Bejeezuz licked his lips in anticipation as he waited for the hall to fill. His plan was proceeding nicely. Free tickets to his concert had been sent to dignitaries from Leftopia, Hillcommune, and other important districts of Street-Corner Earth. His spies had informed him that some of those so honored were in town. Wheatstraw, Tribechief of Hillcommune was one, along with his friend and mentor, Foreseein' Franklin. Unfortunately Mizjoan Berkeley, leader of the Radiclibs, was still at Camp Hoffman; it was too much to hope that she would make the trip in these troubled times.

But luckily two of her most trusted advisors had been spotted on the midway, carrying tickets.

The back door of the Concert Hall creaked open, breaking Bejeezuz's concentration. He turned to see Jack Rabid, his second in command, approaching. Jack, like Bejeezuz's entire inner circle, wore the same black cloak and thick-soled boots as he did, but only Jack could come close to the sinister look that Billy had perfected. Bejeezuz knew that to some, Jack seemed even more ruthless than himself, but that was only because Jack lacked subtlety. Bejeezuz had never been able to teach the younger man that it was easier to catch flies with honey than vinegar. Jack always wanted to crush the little bastards, right on the spot. It was for this reason that Bejeezuz had left The Other in charge in Yewtah. The Other was more like himself, more trustworthy, less likely to screw things up. Jack, on the other hand, needed almost constant supervision.

Several inches shorter than Billy, but broader and more heavily built, Jack looked the part of the perfect henchman. Standing next to his boss on the platform, he pushed back the hood of his cloak to reveal his square-jawed profile and short blond hair. As a prelude to speaking, he spat on the worn planks and rubbed it in with the heel of his boot.

"Everything's set up the way you wanted it, Boss."

Bejeezuz pondered the colorful rows of tents and shops a moment longer, savoring the victory at hand, purposely keeping Jack waiting.

"Very good, Jack," he replied at last. "Very good, indeed."

Jack nodded happily, like an oversized mutt that had just been given a pat on the head.

"Yes," Bejeezuz cackled. "We have these fog-brained Freaks right where we want them, right by the ol' weedsack. Next we're gonna squeeze until they're on their knees and begging for mercy."

The younger man chortled approvingly. "Why don't we just let the Fascists and Greasers loose on them, Boss?"

"Because this is *my* plan, Jack. Besides, we don't want our friends getting the idea that they don't need us. That could cause unnecessary trouble. Once Street-Corner Earth is under my control, then let our allies try and get uppity. I'll be able to locate The Book by then, and no one will be able to stop me—not the Freaks, not the Fascists, not anybody."

Jack considered this. "When you gonna get that book, Boss?"

"Soon, Jack. I've got agents out looking for it now. Those manuscripts we found in Bahston didn't reveal the exact location, but they gave me some leads. For now, I want you to go and get the boys together. I want them ready to go on."

Jack nodded and started toward the door.

Before following, Bejeezuz flicked his cigar over the side, watching it spark as it hit the cobbles below. Grinning, he inhaled deeply to savor the refreshing night air. He abruptly stopped, clutching at his throat as if choking, then quickly sniffed again, two or three times. It was there—the scent of peat bog that he'd smelled at Saturday Night, and before, long before, at the fall of Westcommune. It wasn't close yet, but it was near enough to envelop him with fear.

"JACK!" he bellowed, as his assistant was reaching for the door.

The thick soles of his boots pounding on the deck, Jack hurried back to Bejeezuz's side. "What's the matter?" he asked.

"Smell the air!" Bejeezuz commanded.

"What?"

"The air!" Bejeezuz shrieked, fear causing an uncharacteristic loss of control. "Sniff the air and tell me what you smell!"

Puzzled, Jack sniffed. "Wood smoke. Incense. Smells like someone's cooking something."

"Anything else?" The fear had transformed into a dark fury. Bejeezuz felt like grabbing Jack and shaking him. "Don't you smell a slight musty odor?"

"Maybe, Boss. It's kinda hard to say."

Bejeezuz inhaled again, deeply. "It's there," he said, scowling to himself. Jack didn't reply.

The fear that Bejeezuz had felt was totally transformed now into glowering rage. He rocked back on his thick heels, thinking. After such a long time, the peat bog smell was cropping up again, ruining another of his glorious plans. The cords in his neck tightened, and he gritted his teeth as he let rage consume him.

"Incinerate them!" he barked.

Jack regarded his superior oddly, with wonder showing in his simple, squarish face. "Who?" he asked timidly.

"The Freaks, fool! Fry 'em!"

"But, why? I thought we were going on?"

Bejeezuz leaned forward, his black cowl almost touching Jack's face. The underling cringed and stepped backward. "Don't question me, Jack. We're not going on. But I do want to give the locals something to remember me by."

"Whatever you say, Boss," Jack replied, alarmed and confused.

Bejeezuz softened. Sometimes he almost liked his assistant. "Don't worry, Jack," he said quietly. "I think you're going to enjoy what I've got in mind. Tell the boys to meet me at the stable immediately. Make sure the hall is filled to capacity, and then find a way to block the doors and set fire to the place. Make sure no one can escape. Take Vince Venom and Boris with you."

The grin on Jack's face showed his approval. Though only moderately bright, the younger man was loyal and nearly as nasty as his master. "I like this plan, Boss."

"I thought you would, Jack. It does seem a good way to show our Freak friends what a warm guy I can be." As Jack turned to leave, Bejeezuz added, "Don't blow this for me. You know I can put more heat on you than you want to deal with."

"I won't, Boss. You know you can trust me."

When Jack was gone, Sweet Billy Bejeezuz leaped down off the dock, his black cloak flapping around him like the wings of a gigantic bat. Looking down over Covenstead he whispered, "We'll meet someday, Mr. Peat Bog, and when we do, you'll get yours. But for tonight, there's going to be a hot time in this ol' town, and nothing you can do will stop it."

Chapter Six

The lamplit street was nearly empty as he strolled down the boardwalk that ran in front of the closed shops across from People's Turf. Even the usually raucous Bongwater Tavern was closed early in preparation for the concert and the traditional Fire Ceremony that was to follow it. He stopped in front of the Bongwater's large front window and regarded himself in the image afforded by a large campfire in the commons behind him. He adjusted his dusty beret and grinned at the image. He was particularly amused by the reflection of the reflection in his mirrored sunglasses. If he looked closely, he was sure he could see his face repeated on into infinity. "Hey, whoa, daddy-o," he exclaimed. "I do shine on. Like fine wine, I improve with age."

A gentle breeze blew toward him, past the commons and up toward the Concert Hall. Hearing the soft strumming of a guitar, he cocked his head and listened as the music wafted past, accompanied by the subtle scent of mulled cider. There were many good musicians in Street-Corner Earth, but few could play with the expertise and emotion evident in even such mellow music, and only one who would want to hide that talent, reserving it only for campfire gigs. Farther down the street, sitting in the firelight, his back resting against one of the wheels of Ernie Mungweasle's wagon, was the man he sought. He smiled as he approached, knowing what the musician's response to his proposal would be.

"You play a mean riff, man," he said, standing across the fire from his quarry. "I haven't heard strumming like that in ages."

The musician looked up, nodded, and continued playing.

He tried another tack. "You're Tambourine Dill, aren't you?"

"Who wants to know?" the musician replied, seemingly unconcerned.

"Some people call me a prophet. Others call me Beatnik Maynard. It's just Maynard to my friends."

This time the musician looked at him with a faint air of disdain. "You have a very high opinion of yourself, Mr. Prophet."

"Dig it, Tambourine, others lay that handle on me. Still, my opinion of myself doesn't matter. What does is the low opinion you obviously have of yourself."

Annoyed, Tambourine put down his guitar. "What's that supposed to mean?"

"I think you know, but I want us to be friends, so I'll lay it on you straight. You may call yourself Dill, but that handle only goes back maybe three generations."

"You're nuts, man. Leave me alone."

"Hey, like, it strikes a nerve, huh? Doesn't it, Mister Dylan?"

Tambourine acted as if he'd been slapped across the face. "No, it ain't me, babe. My name's Dill."

Maynard grinned and moved closer to the fire. He knew that he held all the cards now. Tambourine would have to listen to his rap. "Hey, I'm hip, daddy-o; your name *really* is Dill. Your granddaddy Woody was the last to wear the Dylan label."

Tambourine's eyes darted back and forth nervously. Tiny beads of sweat appeared on his forehead. "Who are you, really?" he croaked hoarsely.

"Like, a friend of the family, man."

"My father never mentioned anyone like you."

"He wouldn't have remembered me. Little Judas Priest was just a baby the last time I was around. But old Woody Dylan and I were sort of friends at one time."

"My grandfather's name was Woody Dill. And you don't look old enough to have been a friend of his."

"Check it out, man. Looks can be deceiving, particularly when you're as well preserved as I am. Actually, I was older than Woody. I can even remember the day when he changed his name to Dill—he was afraid that he couldn't live up to the Dylan image."

Tambourine's hands strayed back to his guitar. "That was all a long time ago. What does any of this have to do with me?"

"Like, everything, cat. You're the dude I've been looking for. I need your help, same's you need mine." Maynard smiled what he hoped was his most ingratiating smile. "Hey, I'm hip. You find it hard to live up to the old family tradition, as Woody did. But it's there, man, and your time has come."

"And yours, little dude, is gone. Leave me alone."

"No can do, daddy-o. Are you gonna deny that your git-box once belonged to your great-granddaddy, Baby Blue, or that you're descended from the line of Frankie Lee and Bojangles?"

Tambourine fidgeted, running his hands up and down the neck of his guitar. "I don't know what you're getting at," he snapped, "and I don't care. Just go away. Please."

Maynard moved closer, his smile widening into a grin. "No way, man. Like, how would you feel if everyone was to find out who you are?"

"Don't mean shit to me."

"It will. Like, things are getting bad, an' dig it, they'll soon be getting worse. People are going to remember the old legends. They'll be looking for a Dylan to save their butts. That's you, baby, and you ain't gonna be able to do it without my help."

Tambourine hugged his guitar to his chest as if to protect it, and his eyes wore a haunted look. "So what if I am a Dylan? I'm not even that good of a musician."

"You're an excellent musician, man. Probably as good as Ol' Bob himself."

The musician got to his feet and started to move toward the back of the caravan. "I want no part of whatever you've got in mind. In other words, hit the road, Jack."

Maynard moved as quickly as a snake striking at its prey. He grabbed Tambourine by one arm and stood looking up at him. Though the younger man was a foot taller and more muscular, he made no attempt to shrug him off. "Hey, man. You're part of this, whether you want to be or not. I can help you through in many important ways."

"Take your hands off me."

"Not till you listen to me, cat."

"I have a low tolerance for bullshit. You've got two minutes."

Gently, Maynard led Tambourine back to the fire. "There's this book I need. A very special book, you dig? Before long, Fascists and Greasers will invade Street-Corner Earth. There'll be outlanders with them—mean cats who bear an ancient evil. If I have the book, I can, like, stop them."

"So, go get it."

"Again, no can do, daddy-o. There're places you can go that I can't. Who you are will protect you."

Tambourine shook his head. "Why should I believe you, Prophet Beatnik Maynard? How do I know you are who you say you are?"

"The answer to that, my friend, is blowin' in the wind. I'm playing you no false riff. Look around you—all the hard rain fallin', weedwagons getting torched, Fashie troubles. I'm hip to these outlanders. Shit like that's just the tip of their spear. Soon they're gonna push that sharp point right up our asses."

"C'mon. I haven't got time for this crap. I've got a concert to go to.

Talk to me tomorrow."

"Like, maybe you've got a concert to give. Your ancestors wouldn't have shirked their duty; they were no wallflowers."

"Fuck off about my ancestors! You know nothing about my family."

Maynard's hand moved to his spectacles. He lowered them slightly on the bridge of his nose. For a brief instant something like foxfire seemed to flash behind the mirrored lenses. "Dig it when I tell you I know more than you do, daddy-o. I know a lot about you, too."

Tambourine shook his head as if to clear it. "Hey look, something's going on here, an' I don't know what it is."

"History, cat. I'm talking history. Your git-box says THIS MACHINE KILLS FASCISTS. Like it or not, you're the chosen one."

"I don't like it, thank you. Now, leave me alone."

Maynard sighed, a sound like dry leaves skittering over cobbles. Then he did something he rarely ever did; he took off his sunglasses. Tambourine's eyes widened as Maynard stared into them. For a second it seemed as if the musician was about to faint.

"Y-your eyes..." he gibbered.

"Like the eyes of age, man—right? Well, maybe now you can dig it when I say that I knew your granddad, and *his* granddad, and Bojangles and Frankie Lee. Hell, for a while, I knew Ol' Bob himself."

"But, th-that's impossible." The musician's face had gone white and his guitar dropped from nerveless fingers. "Y-you'd be over five hundred years old."

"I told you I was well preserved."

"B-but... That..."

"Can't be? Look into my eyes and tell me you think I'm lying."

"I can't. There's too much there."

Maynard slipped his spectacles back on, extinguishing the foxfire glow. "You're learning, son. I need you to come with me now. Pack your things. We've got a long road to travel and I've got an awful lot to tell you."

"But I can't just abandon my friends."

"Like, you can't abandon your destiny, either. I've come to take you wandering down the foggy ruins of time, just like your name-song says." He touched Tambourine lightly on the arm, and the musician felt all doubt and fear fade away.

Ten minutes later they left. Soon they were gone from the circle of firelight, and not long after, from the city itself. Behind them, unnoticed by either one of them, Covenstead's Halloween celebration began to gear up.

Chapter Seven

Costumed Freaks crowded the streets, many reeling about in drunken glee. The roadways were closed to wagon traffic, and at every corner impromptu dances were going on. As the two Freaks elbowed through one of the many congested alleyways leading to People's Turf, a procession of costumed snake-dancers, all of them bearing lighted jack-o'-lanterns, was working its way up the hill toward the old fortress. For long minutes the procession held up foot traffic, and it was only with the greatest difficulty that the pair managed to cross the street.

Toad grunted. "I wasn't going to say anything but, Dylan's Bones, Ernie, I can't believe you're planning to hand over dangerous weapons like they were candy. You're instigating war, not to mention continually lying to me, your best friend. Ernie, I've had it; I'm going back to Smuttynose in the morning."

"Don't you see what's going on here, Toad? The Freaklands are threatened. Threatened by gun-toting Fascists and possibly Greasers. You're needed in Camp Hoffman, not back on your precious island."

"Ernie, how can I believe you? You haven't told me the truth since this began."

"That's harsh. Sure, I didn't tell you everything I know, but I wasn't lying, exactly."

"I'll bet you didn't tell your friends at that meeting everything you know, either."

"You saw them; they've got major philosophical differences. They can't even agree on what the truth is."

"Truth! You wouldn't know the truth if someone hit you over the head with it."

Ernie shook his head sadly. "The truth is that you are needed in Camp Hoffman. I need your help, more than you know."

"You don't need me; you need my copy of *Cruickshank's*. You're welcome to the damn thing." He thrust the book into Ernie's hand. Without blinking an eye, the tall herbalist took it and slipped it into his frock coat pocket.

"We need more than the book," he said. "We also need your expertise."

Toad snorted. "Sure, I've read *Cruickshank's*. I can tell you the difference between a carbine and a musket, a rifle and a smoothbore. But it ends there. I make pipes, not guns."

Suddenly Ernie loomed over Toad. His eyes roiled with a searing look of pity and anger. "Don't cop out, man."

"I'm not copping out, I'm getting out. There's a difference."

"One of the reasons you came along was because you were interested in history. Imagine seeing history being made, being part of it, making your own place in it. That's the way to write about it. Toad, you could be the historian everybody quotes. You can turn your back and return to Smuttynose, where nothing ever changes, but you'll be turning your back on me, on history, and, most importantly, on yourself."

Ernie had a way of putting things that confused the issues until Toad's mind swam, trying to sort itself out. "I'll think about it during the concert, but that's all I'll promise."

"Fair enough," Ernie replied, a small smile forming in the corner of his lips.

The two Freaks walked along in silence, each wrapped in his own thoughts, worming their way through the crowd in front of The Bongwater Tavern. As they made their way across the street to People's Turf, it occurred to Toad that living on an island all his life had ill-prepared him for the complications of the larger world. On Smuttynose life was simple and decisions were easy to make. Here on the mainland, things were different and the outcomes of one's actions weren't so easy to discern.

When they arrived at the wagon, Tambourine was nowhere to be found.

"Looks like he's gone ahead without us," Ernie remarked.

Toad shrugged. "Maybe he's just catching a nap in back of the wagon."

Ernie went to check and returned a few moments later, holding a scrap of paper. "He's gone, along with his pack and guitar. All he left was this note."

"What does it say?"

"Apparently, he met an old friend of the family, and wants us to go on without him. Weird business, but musicians are always a little off the wall."

Toad frowned. "Still, it seems strange. After all the fuss he made over seeing the concert, he just up and takes off like that."

"I've seen him do stranger things. We can't let that stop us from having fun. By the way, keep your ears and eyes open at the concert. We're not going to the show just to listen to the music."

"Ernie… "

"Stay cool, Toad. I don't mean that you shouldn't have fun. It's just that this isn't Smuttynose and you should always be aware of what's going on around you. Besides, this concert could well figure into your historical accounts; you wouldn't want to miss anything."

Though the larger shops and businesses were closed, the street vendors on the other side of the common were doing a brisk trade. The two Freaks bought hot sausage sandwiches from a cart and picked up a jug of wine from one of the sip-and-toke stalls that were still open. They ate as they walked, and though they didn't talk, they began to feel more relaxed with one another again.

Suddenly, as they entered the broad, crowded street that led directly to the Concert Hall, a bell began to clang furiously in the distance, followed by answering bells nearby.

"Fire alarm," Ernie remarked.

There was a definite smell of smoke in the air, though it was hard to tell which direction it was coming from through the maze of shops and tents. More bells sounded nearby and a disturbance ran through the crowd. Pushing back toward the boardwalk, Toad and Ernie got out of the way just in time to avoid being hit by a horse-drawn pumper fighting its way through the congested street. Behind the pumper, bells clanging and rotating lanterns flashing, an infirmary wagon hurried to keep pace. Suddenly smoke was pouring across the night sky a block away. Even as Toad watched, flames erupted over the skyline of tents and houses. The sounds of screaming filled the air.

"Dylan's Bones!" Ernie gasped, dropping the uneaten portion of his sandwich. "It's the Concert Hall. There must be people trapped in there."

The herbalist took off at a dead run, coat tails flapping. Toad could barely keep him in sight as he tried to follow him through the crowd. Once he tripped and almost fell in front of a second fire wagon, but he regained his footing at the last second and dove into the protection of the crowd. Plowing between protesting bystanders, he dodged from left to right, fighting to keep Ernie's bobbing top hat in sight. As he ran he could see the flames licking up the sides of the fancy, three-storied structure that was the Concert Hall. The fire and the screaming were too much like one of his dreams. He stopped near the mouth of an alley to catch his breath and get himself oriented. Oddly, he suddenly felt responsible for the fire, as if by dreaming about it he'd caused it to happen. As he watched, transfixed by horror, a whole section of the gabled roof collapsed, sending up an eruption of angry red sparks. The screams of the dying reached a crescendo. Hundreds of voices cried out in terror and despair.

From where he stood, Toad could see the pumpers sending up pitiful fingers of water against the blaze. Townsfreaks dressed in bizarre costumes manned the pumper arms or formed bucket brigades, but it was all to no avail. The costumes and the flames made Covenstead look like a painting of Hell. From somewhere a shrill, insane laugh sounded, causing the words of an old folksong, *Merrykin Pyre* to echo in the pipesmith's head. Screams emanating from the burning Concert Hall planted visions in his brain, driven by the song's lyrics. Staccato images of sacrificial rites, and flames dancing high in the night, flashed in his mind ending with the Dark One reveling in delight, the night the music died.

As suddenly as the screaming started, it stopped, as the hall collapsed. A flaming wall fell into the street, sending townsfreaks scurrying for safety. As tears welled in Toad's eyes, he started toward the fire, drawn by the raging terror. A myriad of emotions swarmed at the edge of his consciousness—among them fear, nausea, and anger—but he was only dimly aware of them. Overwhelming horror and disbelief left him almost totally numb.

Suddenly, a cold shock ripped through him as strong hands reached out from the alley, pinning him from behind. Stunned at first, the pipesmith struggled wildly as he was dragged into the alley. Before he could cry out, something heavy crashed down on his head. There was a briefly painful impression of swirling sparks and mirthless laughter; then darkness overwhelmed him.

Chapter Eight

The first sensation was a painful throbbing in his head, followed by the muffled sounds of distant voices. Toad tried to move, but his head hung heavily on his chest and any attempt to move it caused intense pain. As he struggled to consciousness, he became dully aware that his hands and feet were tied and he was propped in a sitting position against a tree. A broken limb jabbed him between his shoulder blades, adding to his misery. Struggling to open his eyes, he saw that it was still night. Then he smelled the smoke. The Concert Hall, he thought. He had to help those people! He tried to get to his feet, but he was bound too tightly. The pain was overpowering.

"Only thing that matters to me is keepin' him alive till we get to Bahston," said a voice from somewhere close by.

"Yeah, but the faggit's so puny ain't nobody gonna wanna buy him," another voice replied. "He ain't fit to be unloadin' no boats."

"Listen up, Cuffer. Them people down there'll buy him just to hold towels and stand by the door. Ain't nothin' to get bent outta shape over."

A hideous laugh followed. "Fuckin'-A, Sonny. Then you and me's gonna buy us some poontang. Ain't that right?"

"Yeah, Cuffer. Sounds like a plan."

Though curious to see his captors, Toad was afraid to raise or even move his head. Their voices carried cruelty the way a breeze carried weedsmoke. Slowly rolling his head to one side, he was just able to make out a campfire with two men sitting in front of it. Firelight glinted off their oiled hair and the shiny blackness of their jackets. Greasers! Toad's heart was ready to burst with fear. Greaser cruelty was legendary, no matter what Wheatstraw had said. The most common story was about the beatings they gave to Freaks after cutting off all their hair. And there were other Greaser stories as well: stories about knives that could flick open as fast as a man could blink, the black, round-toed boots with which they stomped their helpless victims, and the heavy-buckled belts and chains they used to mangle their enemies.

"Hey, Sonny," the one called Cuffer said, the one with the horrible laugh. "Don't you ever get worried that Kham's boys is gonna come lookin' for us? Runnin' out like we done'll get us hung by the balls. That's the law now."

"No shit, that's the law, ever since Kham's been listening to Klaven Thinarm and that weird-ass, Blackcloak."

"I don't like that Blackcloak faggit. Ain't he the one's been sending those—whaddaya call 'em—guns, up from Bahston?"

"That's the bastard, the guy that don't let anyone see his face."

"That bugs me, Sonny. Some of the boys been saying he's really Lord Flatbush, like in the old stories."

The one called Sonny spat into the fire. From where he sat Toad could hear it sizzle. "Sure, Cuff, and others been saying he's The Fonz come back to life. That shit's sacrilege. Blackcloak ain't The Fonz any more than you or I are. He's just some bullshittin' outlander with a good line of crap. That's why I felt I hadda leave, pally. Everything was gettin' way too fucked up."

"Yeah, I know all that. Still, we shouldn'ta cut out like we did."

"Ain't nothin' to get worked up over. I got this escape mapped right-the-fuck-out. Ain't no search party gonna snag us. They ain't gonna send nobody all the way from Lubejob to get us if they don't even know which way we went. Besides, we got a boat and supplies waitin' for us down river."

"You wish."

"It'll be there. My brother Skizzy'll come through. Maybe he don't exactly approve of what I'm doin', but he'll look the other way. There ain't nothin' like blood on blood, you know."

"So you say, Sonny. My brothers wouldn't do jack shit for me. Hey, am I dreamin' or is our faggit waking up? I coulda swore I saw him move."

"Check it out."

Toad groaned inwardly. Though he tried not to move, the sharp-eyed Cuffer had spotted something. He shuddered slightly as the fat Greaser got to his feet and lumbered in his direction.

"Ah, darlin'," Cuffer remarked, as he loomed over Toad. "The pussy's joined the party, Sonny."

"How 'bout that?"

Toad looked up at the dirty, muscular Greaser with his acne-scarred face and rotted teeth. Cuffer's flabby beer gut protruded from beneath his torn T-shirt, a sight that would have made him appear comic except for the cold malice glinting in his eyes.

The pipesmith moaned and wrestled fitfully against his bonds. This seemed to enrage Cuffer. The Greaser cracked him across the mouth with the back of one large-knuckled hand. Toad winced in pain as his head snapped sideways, but he had the presence of mind not to cry out. Cuffer's ugly, pocked face was inches from his own, his breath hot upon Toad's cheek. It smelled of stale beer and decay. Toad found he couldn't meet the Greaser's gaze, so he stared at the black boots planted on the ground before him. They were round-toed and scuffed, with black leather straps running across the top of each one. Tight jeans were tucked into them just above the ankles. One of Cuffer's legs was bouncing defiantly, but his boot never left the ground.

The Greaser backed off a few steps, and with one leg forward and his hands held out at waist level, he made motions for Toad to get up and fight him. "Hey, anytime, faggit," he jeered.

Drained, Toad let his head drop.

Snorting in disgust, Cuffer sat back down by the fire.

The pipesmith seemed to have barely nodded off when he felt himself being shaken awake. Cuffer's face was practically nose-to-nose with his own. The Greaser's eyes were red-rimmed and malevolent.

"Good morning, faggit," Cuffer said, offering a sinister, broken-toothed grin. "Hope you're lookin' forward to a fun-filled day."

As the Greaser untied him, Toad looked around to see that they were in a deep pine forest. It was early; the morning sun was struggling to penetrate the thick overgrowth. Toad spotted the other Greaser leaning against a tree and cleaning his nails with a knife. Sonny was tall and gracefully thin, with a pouty, pretty-boy face and a dark, expertly coifed, duck's ass haircut. From what little Toad knew of Greasers, he judged him to be a Fonzer, a member of the ruling class.

Cuffer tied Toad's hands in front of him and attached a length of chain to the rope. "Start walkin', candy-ass," he snarled. "An' if you don't keep up, I'll drag ya."

Toad took a few experimental steps. The feeling was just returning to his legs, and they felt heavy and wooden. Gasping aloud as needles of pain jabbed at his calves, he staggered and pitched forward.

"Keep walkin'," Cuffer snarled, jerking the chain.

Grimacing with pain, Toad limped along as fast as he could until the circulation returned to his legs. The deep despair that he'd felt last night came back with a vengeance. This had to be a nightmare. He shut his eyes and tried to conjure up a vision of his island home, but the ropes chafing his wrists and the hunger knotting his stomach made that impossible. His former life on Smuttynose was only a vague dream. He wondered about the slave market in Bahston; was it really as horrible as he imagined it to be?

As he stumbled along through the pine woods, snapping twigs beneath his feet and tripping occasionally over dead branches, the pain shot through his legs like hot wires. Several times he almost cried out, but his aching jaw was too clear a reminder of how Greasers dealt with "faggits."

Cuffer obviously enjoyed jerking Toad along by his chain halter. It showed in his small, malevolent eyes and his twisted grin. From time to time, the Fonzer looked back to check out Toad's progress. Somehow his coldly amused smile was far more frightening than Cuffer's stupidly brutal one.

The Greasers moved along at a pace that astounded Toad. Even with no breakfast, they seemed tireless and full of energy. Sonny led the way through the thick forest, carefully moving his lithe body around and under branches without breaking pace. From time to time, he'd pull a long comb out of his hip pocket and repair a dangling lock of his hairdo, but he never stopped moving once. Cuffer, on the other hand, crashed through the bushes like a moose, breaking dead branches with his forearms and sending live ones swinging back at Toad.

In time the three travelers entered an even thicker and darker section of woods that was heavy with brambles and gray, tangled windfalls. Almost overhead, the sun showed intermittently through the tall moss-bearded trees, seeming remote and cold. Toad shivered, wondering if he would ever know its warmth again.

Finally, Sonny called a halt at the edge of an overgrown field and extracted a dog-eared map from the pocket of his leather jacket, pursing his lips thoughtfully as he studied it. Through the trees Toad caught a glimpse of what he thought might be the Covenstead Road.

"So, hippie, how do you like our little trip so far?" Sonny smirked.

"I-it ain't bad," Toad offered, picking up on the Greaser's style of speech.

The Fonzer laughed. "You hear that, Cuffer? He's having a good time."

"Course he is, Sonny. He's with Cuffer Crawley and Sonny Slikback— the two handsomest studs that ever was."

"Ain't no shit, Cuff. When we get to Bahston, we'll pick up some cash, a few women, and then who knows what'll happen."

"Yeah, that'll be somethin'," Cuffer replied. "I don't think them people down there are ready for a coupla bad-asses like us. Ain't no tellin' what we might do."

Avoiding the road, Sonny led them along the edge of the field to another stretch of woods. Toad didn't even have time to reflect on his misery; Cuffer's insistent pulling forced him to concentrate on placing one foot quickly in front of the other. After hours at this grueling pace, they came to a wetland in the woods. The three men fell into a line to stay on the clumps of high ground. Suddenly, after Toad had lagged behind one time too many, Cuffer came back and shoved him toward the muddy turf. "Walk through that shit for a while until you smarten up," he growled.

Toad stumbled to his knees. Cuffer laughed and turned around, tightening up on the chain. Without even thinking about what he was doing, the pipesmith grabbed onto his leash with both hands and pulled back as he began to rise. "Fuck you, scum!" he yelled, jerking the chain with all his might.

Bawling like a calf, Cuffer toppled backwards, twisting around and plunging headfirst into the muck. He jumped to his feet, mud dripping from his contorted face. "You're dead, motherfucker!" he screamed, advancing on Toad. "I'm gonna wrap this chain around your neck until your eyes pop!"

"Cuffer!" Sonny yelled, looking amused.

The fat Greaser stopped dead in his tracks.

Sonny grinned as he looked down from his high hummock. "Hands off the merchandise, Cuff. He ain't gonna be worth nothing if you rough him up."

"Aww, Sonny, I..."

The Fonzer waved him aside. "Come up here, long-hair," he commanded. His eyes were narrow and they twinkled when he smirked at Toad.

The pipesmith obeyed, his heart hammering as he passed the glowering Cuffer.

Sonny's smirk deepened. "What did you just say to Cuffer, faggit?"

"N-nothin'. I didn't say nothin'."

The smirk vanished, but cold amusement still glittered in the Fonzer's eyes. "Did I just hear ya say 'nothin'?"

"Y-yeah. I said nothin'."

"He called me a scum!" Cuffer yelled, wiping mud from his face. "Lemme kill him, Sonny."

"No!"

"By the chrome of the Great Chevy, Sonny! Lookit this black shit all over me. I hafta kill the sonuvabitch!" He began to wade toward Toad, the chain looped between his hands.

Sonny moved between them. "You ain't killin' nobody, Cuffer."

"Fuck you, man! Who says you're the boss?"

"I'm a Fonzer," Sonny replied evenly. "That means I was born to lead."

"Yeah? Well maybe you Fonzers ain't no better than hippies. You think you're special just because you can read them *Shopmanuals*? Readin' don't mean nothin'."

"Not to a dumb bastard like you who can't even read his own tattoos."

Cuffer rattled the chain he held in his meaty hands. "Don't fuck with me, Sonny."

Sonny smiled coldly. "And don't you fuck with me, asshole. We been buddies a long time, but I can still smack you upside the head before you know what's goin' on. When I do, I'll knock you right into the middle of next week."

"You ain't smackin' nobody."

"Keep lippin' off, pally, and you'll be wearing your face inside-out on the back of your head."

Cuffer glared at the Fonzer, but he lowered his chain.

Sonny snickered and went on. "'Course, that won't be no shame. Your face'd scare a freight train down a dirt road."

Cuffer blinked stupidly. "What's a freight train, Sonny?"

"Just an expression, dildo."

"A freight train was a machine made by the ancients," Toad offered without thinking. "They were bigger than houses and could move faster than the fastest racehorses."

Sonny seemed surprised by the reply. "I knew that, but it's nothing Cuffer needs to know. Where'd you get so fuckin' smart, anyway?"

"I read a lot."

"Ain't that somethin'?"

Cuffer scraped the last of the mud from his face and tugged lightly on the chain attached to Toad's wrists. "You know, Sonny, them freight trains sound just like…"

"Quiet, Cuff, no bullshit. Let's get movin' on."

As they worked their way through the mire and out into a series of stubbled cornfields, Toad noticed changes in the Greasers. Their pace was slower and Cuffer didn't yank on the chain anymore. Both men were quiet. Cuffer was sullen and subdued, while Sonny seemed to be brooding.

It was late afternoon when they emerged from the forest onto a small backwater of the Sludge River. The backwater was hidden from the main part of the river by a tangle of weeds and driftwood. In its center a small single-masted fishing boat lay at anchor in the shallow water. When he caught sight of the boat, Sonny's grin nearly split his face. "There ya go, just like I promised," he said. "My brudder Skizzy don't fuck around."

"That's real swell," Cuffer grunted.

"Ain't it though? We better break out some grub. It looks like we ain't goin' nowhere till sunset."

Cuffer tied Toad to a tree by the edge of the backwater while Sonny removed his pointy-toed boots and waded out to the boat. The Fonzer returned a few moments later, bearing a quantity of dried meat and a couple of jugs of beer. He handed Cuffer the meat and one of the jugs. The other he uncorked and began to drain in a series of greedy gulps. When he was done, he wiped his lips on the sleeve of his black leather jacket.

"See what I mean about Skizzy?" he said. "He don't like what I done, but he helped me out anyway. I told him to get me a boat; he got me a boat. I told him to get me food, he got me enough for a coupla weeks. Blood on blood, like I said."

"Food interests me more than family, Sonny. I ain't et since last night."

"I hear that, Cuff. Gimme some of that beef and save some of your beer for the faggit."

"Aww."

"Do it, pally. If we don't feed him, he'll die on us." Reluctantly, Cuffer handed over the meat. Sonny divided it up, even giving some to Toad, along with a couple swallows of beer. The meat was tough and stringy, and the beer warm, but Toad wolfed it all down eagerly.

After the meal Cuffer produced a tattered deck of playing cards and the two Greasers whiled away the time playing cut-throat poker until the sun dipped low on the horizon. At dusk, they trundled their prisoner aboard the boat, tying him to a narrow cot in the vessel's cramped, airless cabin. As darkness built outside the cabin's small dirt-streaked porthole, Toad was dimly aware that the boat was moving. He yawned once, laid back and let sleep claim him.

Chapter Nine

The moon rose three-quarters full, like a silver shield that seemed to float on the scudding clouds. It cast a pale light that Sonny figured was enough to navigate by.

The boat hugged the eastern bank of the Sludge, staying deep within the shadows cast by the forest, and soon passed by the half-rotted wharves of Fat City. Cuffer carefully steered it clear of the rocks and sandbars that made the waters near this deserted town dangerous. The town was dark and lifeless; Freaks hadn't lived there since long before he was a kid. His brother had chosen this place because of its evil reputation; it was the perfect place for an outpost. There was no movement in Fat City's empty streets, but Sonny thought he could see a few lights shining from behind boarded-up windows, and he tipped a salute in passing. Brother Skizzy was in there somewhere.

For now, Cuffer could handle the rudder alone, and with the hippie safely tied up in the cabin, Sonny was free to rig up the craft's single dark gray sail. Good ol' Skizzy, Sonny thought as he worked the sail, he'd taken every precaution. Skiz was an important man now; he was the commander of the small contingent of Greasers that had occupied Fat City in preparation of an attack on Covenstead. Still, he'd found time to help out his brother. Sonny grinned as he hoisted the sail into place. It'd give them plenty of speed if they had to haul ass, and its dark color would make the small craft practically unnoticeable.

Clouds were amassing in the east, building up so thickly that they were beginning to obscure the moon. A wind rose up hard from the northeast, filling the canvas and driving the small craft past dark strands of forest. Once the sail was fully and safely rigged, Sonny stood by the cabin, touching his heirloom talisman, a tiny sliver wrench that hung from a chain around his throat. This world is getting fucked up, he thought. With regret, he remembered his home in Lubejob, now many miles away, and

Temple Sunoc, where he had been one of the youngest Chachis ever to enter the Fonzer priesthood. He had mastered the *Shopmanuals* early and had assisted many times in the yearly Rite of Overhaul, when the sacred '55 Chevy was cleaned and placed before the people of Khamshaft for veneration.

Sonny twirled the silver wrench between his fingers. He recalled being chosen by Overhed Kham himself to learn how to drive the great steam wagons that Blackcloak had sent up from Bahston. Sonny hated Blackcloak and the power he and Klaven Thinarm were exerting on Kham. He refused to go near the ancient machines; he felt that no living man was meant to drive them. It wasn't right for mortals to tamper with the power of The Fonz, who ages ago had breathed life into the great wagons. Kham apparently thought that Blackcloak was The Fonz returned, or at least the legendary Lord Flatbush, but Sonny didn't share these beliefs. There had been arguments, and Kham had threatened to have Sonny stripped of his priestly status, so the Fonzer split. There were no regrets, except maybe for taking Cuffer along. Cuff was all right most of the time, and a Fonzer needed a buddy to do things for him, but the younger Greaser was dull-witted and tended to be a wise ass. Though he liked Cuffer well enough, it had amused him when the hippie had stood up to him. That was something else that was fucked up. As if it wasn't bad enough that a regular Greaser would sass a Fonzer, it was positively weird that a long-haired faggit would know something about ancient machines, and more so that he would show some balls.

Sonny gave up his ponderings and joined Cuffer at the tiller. The lights of Rivertown glowed through the trees. The wind had picked up considerably and the boat was rolling in the swells. A few raindrops fell, and then immediately it started to pour.

"Fucked up weather," Cuffer commented as Sonny grabbed the tiller arm.

"Yeah. I've seen it rain this late in the season, but not like this. The world's fucked up, Cuff. What can I say?"

The wind blew fiercer as they sailed closer to the open sea. Once they reached Rivertown, the storm's full fury let loose. Heavy rain lanced down, reducing visibility to a few yards. Had it not been for the lights of the city off their bow, they'd have had nothing to steer by. Soon they were drenched. Even their heavy leather jackets were soaked through. The little boat pitched back and forth in the choppy water as foam lashed across its deck.

Suddenly a huge shape loomed off the port side—a garbage scow whose bow lanterns glared like eyes as it closed in. Swearing in surprise, Sonny and Cuffer leaned against the tiller, struggling to turn out of the way until it seemed that their arms would tear from their sockets with the effort. Collision seemed unavoidable, but at the last moment they swerved aside and the barge passed by their stern. If anyone on the barge had noticed the near collision, they gave no sign.

Sonny's heart was pounding. The world was getting more fucked up with every passing moment. The relentless rain weighed him down, slowing his movements as he and Cuffer fought to keep the boat on course. It was like trying to walk under water, he thought, as he watched the lights of Rivertown pass off the stern, slowly becoming pinpricks in the distance. He considered shedding his waterlogged jacket, but thought better of it when he felt the cold brine splash in his face. The city lights were gone now and they were heading out into open sea. They'd need all the protection they could get if they were going to survive the night. Pushing aside a wet strand of hair that was hanging in his eyes, the Fonzer leaned hard into the tiller and prayed that the storm would be over soon.

Lightning flashed overhead, revealing a dark line of shoals off the starboard bow. Sonny shoved at the tiller even harder, straining until he was sure his back would break. It did no good. The next flash showed the shoals looming dead ahead and coming up fast. Sonny swore under his breath. He could almost see the little boat shattering on the rocks, splintering into a thousand jagged pieces. He kneaded the heirloom wrench between his fingers and offered up a silent prayer to The Fonz. Above him the sail billowed and flapped; the slender mast creaked threateningly.

"Muckle onto that rudder, Cuffer," he ordered. "I'm gonna haul in this fuckin' sail."

Inching his way across the slippery, swaying deck, Sonny grabbed onto the rigging to steady himself. The shoals were closer now, so close he could hear the waves breaking over them. Working as fast as the wind and the pitching deck would allow, he fumbled with the knots securing the water-slick ropes. He cursed hopelessly as the tangled lines slipped through his cold, numbed hands. The boat pitched wildly as a wave hit it broadside, sending geysers of seawater sluicing over the deck. Sonny yelped as the boat rolled and righted itself. Grabbing the creaking mast between his hands and knees, he held on until the deck leveled off beneath his feet. Ahead of him in the dark, the breakers boomed like funeral drums.

There was no time to haul in the sail. Reaching into the pocket of his tight jeans, the Fonzer pulled out his spring knife. He pressed its release button, popping it open, and began hacking away at the ropes securing the sail. The drumming breakers seemed to be inside his head now.

Holding onto the mast with his left hand, Sonny's right flailed like a pump handle as he slashed at the rigging. The lightning flashed again and the rocks loomed closer. Sea foam ran from them like saliva over a line of jagged teeth. The pounding of the surf filled Sonny's ears. In spite of the cold and wet, he was sweating.

Finally, the first rope frayed and parted. Summoning all of his strength, Sonny started on the others. The wind whipped the severed line out and it coiled around one boot, almost pulling him overboard, but he kept at his wild work, shaking with fear, exertion and cold. Death was near now, and only his puny spring knife stood between him and its clammy embrace.

Suddenly another rope gave way, then another. The sail, freed from its lines, flapped and rippled about the mast like a wounded sea bird. With the forward thrust of the canvas gone, the little craft veered wildly to port, passing by the shoals with only a few feet to spare. As he dropped to the deck, exhausted and trembling, Sonny could hear the rocks grate against the side of the boat. Then, a sudden swell rolled up over the shoals and the little craft rode free.

"It's def'nitely a fucked up world," Sonny said to himself as he cowered on the deck, clutching at his tiny silver wrench. He looked up and watched as the torn remnants of the sail whip-cracked in the wind, twisting back and forth until the overtaxed mast gave way. Sonny ducked out of the way just as it collapsed in a tangle of rigging and shredded canvas on the cabin roof. Shaken and wet, but unhurt, Sonny staggered to his feet and made his way back toward the stern.

It was going to be a long night, a long, fucked up night.

Chapter Ten

Toad awoke with a start, the stifling cabin spinning around him. Something splintered overhead as the cot flew away from beneath him and the floor rose up, smashing him in the face. Dazed, he lay lengthwise across the cabin as the boat rocked from side to side. The grinding of wood against stone was like an earthquake in his ears. We're sinking, he thought. Then, as quickly as it began, the noise stopped and the cabin ceased shaking.

Though bound hand and foot, Toad managed to wiggle to a sitting position, resting his shoulders against the cot as his mind slowly cleared. Outside the cabin he could hear wind and thunder, but the booming of surf against rock was diminishing. He glanced up at the porthole and saw that a sliver of mast had penetrated it. A flash of lightning revealed shattered pieces of glass strewn across the bare mattress. Toad squirmed back onto the cot, moving carefully to avoid the glittering shards. Lying back, he morosely studied the ceiling, trying to come to grips with the fact that he was miles away from land in the midst of a storm that was tearing the boat apart. Maybe, if it survived the gale, the boat might make it to shore. That thought cheered him slightly. Anything, even the slave marts of Bahston, seemed preferable to drowning in an icy sea.

After what felt like an eternity the storm moved on, howling its fury out across the ocean. Dawn was fighting its way into being. Through the ruined porthole Toad could see gray skies and a few shreds of cloud fleeing across the horizon. A breeze blew across his face, bringing a faint scent of pine mixed with the heavier smells of storm and sea. Land was near. Land. If he was lucky enough to escape the insane fury of the sea then maybe, just maybe, he could find a way to escape from his captors as well.

Suddenly, the Greasers' strident voices bellowed outside the cabin.

"Whoo-ee! That was some fuckin' storm," Cuffer hollered. "We're lucky we didn't lose our nuts in that honey."

"F'in A, Cuffer," Sonny replied. "An' it looks like we've come a long way, but I got no clue where we are."

"Me neither, but I got me an idea. See them marshes over there? Back when Blackcloak was sendin' them steam wagons up from Bahston, my cuzzin Cruddy went down there with some of Kham's boys. They got turned around bringin' the barge back and got lost in some marshes south of the city. They called them the Cuttysunk Marshes. Maybe that's the same marshes. If they are, then Bahston's about ten miles north of here."

"I don't know, Cuff. We got knocked around a lot, but south of Bahston, that don't seem likely."

"What, you think I'm stupid? You see that river over there? That's gotta be Squalid Creek. Cruddy said, if you follow that cocksucker north, it goes right into another river that goes up into Bahston. No sweat there. We just gotta paddle upstream."

Sonny laughed. "Sure, why not? Seems I've been paddling up Shit Creek a lot lately. Another pissant creek won't make no difference. Hey, if you're right, we'll be drownin' in beer an' knee deep in poontang by nightfall."

Toad's heart sank. It appeared that he was only a few miles from a life of slavery.

Sonny laughed again. "Sometimes you're almost smart, Cuffer. I don't care what everybody says; you're all right."

"Thanks, Sonny."

"Don't let it go to your head, pally. Now, I'm getting sick of all this salt water. Let's get humping on the rudder and get our asses outta here."

"Should we check on the faggit first?"

"Yeah. We oughta."

Toad lay back on the cot and feigned sleep as the door opened. Sonny stomped into the room and yanked him by the lapels of his coat, lifting him half off the cot. The pipesmith opened his eyes to find himself staring into the Fonzer's. They were filled with a certain cold amusement, but no great malevolence.

"You still alive?" Sonny asked.

Toad nodded weakly.

The Fonzer checked to see if Toad was still tied securely. When he was finished, he let Toad drop back onto the cot. The pipesmith cried out as one of the glass shards dug into his arm.

"What a pussy," Sonny marveled. "You may be smart for a faggit, but you're as wimpy as all the rest. Better get used to the shovin' around. Where you're goin', you're gonna get a lot of it."

As the Greaser exited Toad said under his breath, "Maybe I am a wimp, but I'm smarter than you, wrinkledink." The cut from the glass was painful, but it had given him an idea.

The scent of pine was heavier now, and the cries of sea gulls filled the air. Toad looked out the porthole to see a great marsh fringed by a dark forest. The boat was leaving the open water and entering the mouth of a river. There wasn't much time.

Wriggling into an upright position and twisting halfway around, Toad began working his bound wrists against the sharp glass. It was clumsy work, but after a while the ropes began to fray and separate. With a little more vigorous sawing, they broke apart, freeing his hands. Toad massaged his wrists to restore circulation, then quickly untied the ropes binding his feet. He sat up and looked at the cabin door. It had no lock—only a simple thumb latch. Removing his boots and heavy coat, Toad perched on the edge of the cot and flexed his feet. Once he felt able to move about, he slipped across the cabin to the door and peered out. The boat was about half a mile up a tidal river. Except for a stand of pine that passed off the port bow, the nearest cover was a forest to the north of the expansive marsh.

Opening the door all the way, Toad stood craning his neck from side to side. There was no sign of either Sonny or Cuffer. He crept onto the deck and looked at the river. It was wide, muddy, and fringed with tall reeds that swayed in the early morning breeze. A passable swimmer, Toad felt sure he could make it to the bank and conceal himself among the reeds before his captors even knew that he was gone. Moving quickly to the side of the boat, he worked his way over the edge until his feet dangled mere inches above the water.

"Where you think you're goin', faggit?"

Toad turned to see Cuffer a few feet behind him. The Greaser was holding a spring knife that flashed in the sunlight as it flicked open.

"Well, well, well," Cuffer said, advancing. "What do we have here? I come down to take a piss and I finds me a fairy-boy wettin' his feet. You weren't thinking of going nowhere, were you, fairy-boy?"

Toad slid down the side as fast as he could, but Cuffer moved faster, grabbing Toad's long hair, preventing him from slipping into the river. Crying out in pain, the pipesmith reacted instinctively, punching wildly. The first blow hit its mark and connected solidly with Cuffer's groin. The Greaser screamed as the knife flew from his hand. Red-faced, he toppled into the water beside Toad. The pipesmith started for shore, but Cuffer latched onto him and held him close.

"Help!" he cried, surfacing and blowing like a whale. "I can't swim!"

Toad struggled to get away, but Cuffer held on with an iron grip. Glancing up, he saw Sonny moving down the deck toward them. Toad drove his feet up into Cuffer's face and chest and pushed himself free.

With a couple of strong kicks, he was clear. Taking sharp, even strokes, he stayed under the water as long as he could. When he surfaced he didn't look back until he'd eased out onto the bank of the river. In spite of the intense cold overwhelming him, he concealed himself among the reeds. He watched with grim amusement as Cuffer thrashed about in the water, breaching and sounding while Sonny, white-faced and on the verge of panic, tried to snag him with a gaff hook. Satisfied that the Greasers would be occupied for a while, Toad hurried off through the reeds.

The pipesmith's route took him a long way along the bank of the river. He was tired and shivering, but the daunting fear of the Greasers behind him, Bahston to the north of him, and Dylan-only-knew-what in between, kept him on the move. His feet were freezing but he hurried on, jumping from hummock to hummock as he left the river behind and made for the distant tree line. He knew that to stop for even a moment could prove fatal, and he desperately needed to find shelter.

Toad spied a long, raised area several hundred feet off to his right and slowly made his way toward it. It was part of an ancient roadway that crossed the marsh and led into the forest. Toad clambered up its steep, weed-grown embankment, relieved to find a hard surface to travel on. Shivering uncontrollably and hobbling as fast as his tired legs would allow, he made his way along its broken concrete surface like a crab across a rock, skirting potholes and places where the old stonework had crumbled back into the mire. The ancient roadway dwindled to a narrow woods road that rambled through the high mossy pines; there would be shelter there, he thought.

The woods were dense where the road first entered them. Tangled branches arched over the path and roots snaked through the overgrown ruts, making each step dangerous. Sounds came to him through the trees— bird songs, wind, the scuttling of small animals—and something else.

Toad strained to listen. Something large was moving down the road toward him. There was a steady clopping sound, then a loud snorting whinny. A horse. Quickly, he ran for cover, but his foot snared in a root. He crashed to the ground on one knee. He tried to struggle back to his feet, but his bruised knee buckled and he fell again. Clawing along on all fours, he crawled under the nearest bush just as the horse and its hunched rider came around the bend.

Chapter Eleven

It was nearly midnight when Ernie's wagon rumbled past the series of high, fortified walls that marked the outer perimeters of Camp Hoffman. Torches blazed in sconces every twenty feet along the walls and campfires could be seen at intervals beside the roadway, bathing the grim stonework in an almost festive glow. As Ernie and his escort rolled through the main gate of the city a pair of burly, longhaired soldiers in tight fatigue uniforms stepped out of the shadows of the torchlit gateway. With their heavy crossbows cocked and cradled in their arms, they approached the wagon warily and challenged them.

"Ho there, it's me—Comrade Major Rudy," the Radiclib called down from the seat beside Ernie. "I've returned with Comrade Mungweasle, the traveling herbalist."

"A thousand pardons, Comrade Rudy," said the taller of the two Radiclibs. "We didn't recognize you."

"No need for apologies, Che. A good revolutionary is always vigilant."

"Yes sir," Che replied, lowering his weapon and snapping off a clenched-fist salute. "Raise the gate, Regis."

As Rudy returned the salute, Regis pulled a lever that allowed the iron-barred gate to rumble open. Ernie snapped the reins and his wagon entered the Leftopian capital, its iron-shod wheels throwing sparks as it rolled over the cobbles of Camp Hoffman's main street. They turned left at a row of unpainted barracks, and proceeded to a small park that was dominated by a larger-than-life statue of a muscular Radiclib wearing a long, sleeveless jerkin and wielding a huge war hammer. Behind the statue the Leftopian national flag, a red fist emblazoned on a black background, fluttered in the night breeze, illuminated by red flood lanterns. From the park Ernie could see the lights shining inside the sprawling bulk of Commiemartyr Hall, which for centuries had been the home of the Berkeley clan, Leftopia's traditional rulers.

"Mizjoan's awake," Ernie remarked.

Rudy nodded. "She knows you're coming."

"Waiting for me, or for the Society's proposal?"

"I don't know or care what happened between you and Comrade Leader Mizjoan in the past but I assure you, in these times she only has the welfare of her people in mind."

The herbalist smiled. His affair with Joannie had been brief, and was probably something best left in the past. The Leftopian leader's first love would always be her people and her country. If she ever did take a mate, he supposed it would be one of her own kind.

When Ernie's wagon finally rattled to a stop in front of Commiemartyr Hall, Rudy slipped off the seat and started toward the front door, pausing on the steps a moment.

Turning to face the herbalist he said, "I feel I must thank you for the warning about the concert."

Ernie shrugged. "It was more of a suggestion than a warning. I thought something smelled like ragweed but I sure never expected anything like that. Those poor Freaks."

"A tragedy. Still, I owe you one."

"You can pay me later."

"Mizjoan is waiting for you. You know the way."

Two officers in gray dress uniforms met Rudy at the door. The three of them disappeared inside, closing the door behind them. Ernie sat back and looked up at the high garrets of the imposing four-story Hall. Lazily, he took it all in: the flags and banners waving from the parapets, the red spot lanterns, the uniformed guards patrolling the entryways. Ernie shook his head. He needed a smoke. It was going to be nice to see Joannie again, but it'd be hard to do without a little fortification. He extracted a half-filled pipe from his frock coat pocket and lit it on one of the wagon lamps.

A moment of solitude after the long trip was just what he needed before meeting Mizjoan, and he relished every second. Rudy had been good enough company over the past couple of days, in spite of his gruffness, but like most Radiclibs, Rudy was too serious and political for Ernie's taste. There were also many things on his mind that he could not discuss with the major.

The weed, a pittance of the Thirdworld White that he had left, eased his mind and smoothed his thoughts, but it also reminded him of Toad. He'd panicked at first, when Toad disappeared during the Concert Hall fire. A search of the area failed to locate him. Then Ernie remembered that Toad had threatened to leave after the concert; the fire must have made his decision for him. When the pipesmith didn't show up among the conflagration's injured or dead, Ernie assumed that he was on his way back to Smuttynose. Like Tambourine before him, he'd slipped off onto a trip of his own. Ernie worried about Toad making it safely home and would have gone after him, if matters at Camp Hoffman had not been so pressing.

He sat in his caravan in front of Commiemartyr Hall, trying to sort out all the recent events and work up enough nerve to see Joannie. With a tired sigh he knocked his pipe out, swung his long legs down over the side of the wagon and dropped lightly to the ground. In a way this surprised him, considering how tired he felt.

A young guard challenged him at the door, but after hearing Ernie's explanation, agreed to escort him to Mizjoan's private office. The herbalist followed the guard through a series of cramped, torchlit rooms cluttered with the plunder of two centuries and more. Everywhere he looked, he saw chests of valuables and stacks of weapons. In some rooms political slogans adorned the whitewashed walls. In others, comfortable furniture was arranged around long tables and maps and battle plans were the main decoration.

Little had changed since Ernie's last visit. There was fresh paint in the hall leading to Mizjoan's outer office and a new picture on the wall beside the door. It was a full-length portrait of a stylized figure that Ernie took to represent the Freedom Rider, the legendary leader who would appear to defend liberty when it was most threatened. Quaint old folk tales said he would rise up in the last days to protect Street-Corner Earth. The Freedom Rider was represented as a shadowy figure with a mane of wildly curly hair, holding a guitar over his head. There was a storm going on behind him, and lightning bolts appeared to shoot out of the guitar. Ernie concluded that it was more of a propaganda poster than a serious work of art.

The door to Mizjoan's quarters was open, and mellow candlelight streamed out of it into the hall. Ernie gave a perfunctory tap on the doorjamb and walked in. With Joan he had no need for formalities. The office was empty, but Ernie hadn't expected her to be there. That she would always keep him waiting was a little ritual they had both long recognized and understood.

Like the rest of Commiemartyr Hall, Mizjoan's private suite had changed very little. Her desk was still in one corner, piled high with papers and charts, and the same old overstuffed chairs and couch encircled the plank coffee table in front of the fireplace. Ancestral portraits of famous Radiclib warriors hung on all the walls. Over the mantelpiece was mounted an antique war hammer, its silver head softly reflecting the low candlelight. The hammer was similar to the one on the statue in the park. Originally, so Mizjoan had once told him, it had been carried by Maxwell Eddison Berkeley, "Maxwell the Hammer," who'd been responsible for driving the Fascists out of Covenstead back in the early years of the last century.

Below the hammer hung a new addition, a crudely made black iron sword with a zigzag silver weld mark about halfway down its broad blade. Instinctively, Ernie's hand reached out to touch the ancient weapon.

"Do you always touch things without permission, Ernie?"

Turning to see Mizjoan framed in the doorway, the herbalist grinned. "You of all people should know that," he replied.

Mizjoan grinned back. She was a slender, well-built woman in her early thirties. Standing just over six feet tall, her proud, aristocratic face framed by her waist-length auburn hair, she was, by any man's reckoning, an impressive woman. As she stepped into the light his eyes were drawn, as always, to the black patch covering her right eye—a souvenir of a long-ago battle with a Whiterider raiding party that had taken the lives of both of her parents. As Mizjoan moved toward him, Ernie couldn't help but admire the way her tight gray uniform molded to her lithe body. In spite of, or perhaps because of, the eye patch, black jackboots, and the businesslike silver dagger at her waist, Ernie thought that she was one of the most desirable women he'd ever known.

Mizjoan extended her hand and Ernie took it warmly. "It's been a long time," she said.

"Too long, Joannie. I was just admiring this sword of yours. Something new?"

"Ploughshare? No, it's been in my family for generations, ever since JoJo Lion Berkeley took it off a dead Mansonite priest at the last battle of Darkenwood. Legend has it, it once belonged to the Old Charlie himself."

"I'm impressed."

"You should be. But don't tell me you traveled all this way to talk about my family heirlooms."

Ernie let go of her hand. Though there was no longer anything between them except friendship, he still found it difficult to stand too close to the Radiclib leader. "You know why I'm here. We have some important business to discuss."

"I know," she said, guiding him toward one of the overstuffed chairs. "Rudy's told me a bit about your proposition. Let's work out the rest over a pipe and a drink."

"Consider my arm twisted, Comrade Leader."

Mizjoan laughed, a deep, throaty chuckle that seemed to warm the room. "Same old Ernie," she said, taking a brandy decanter and a couple of goblets from the sideboard. "You could never pass up anything that was free."

"Life's too short. Mind if I help myself to weed?"

She nodded toward a small, carved wood box at the center of the table and uncorked the decanter, filling the two glasses.

Ernie opened the box and took out a short clay pipe and a canister of homegrown. "So what exactly did Rudy tell you?" he asked, filling the pipe.

"Enough for me to suspect it's just another Clear Light gimmick." She sat down in the chair across from him, crossing her long, booted legs at the knee, her drink held lightly in one well-manicured hand.

"You're too skeptical."

"I don't believe one can be too skeptical when it comes to Diggers."

"I'm familiar with your opinion of the Society—snoops and troublemakers."

Mizjoan took a sip of brandy. "Those are your words, not mine. I just prefer to handle my people's affairs without intervention from outsiders. Surely you can understand that."

"Under ordinary circumstances I could. Still, you've yet to see what we have to offer you."

The Radiclib leader took another sip of brandy, bigger this time. "An old weapon, Rudy said."

"It's more than just a simple weapon, Joan. It's a means to destroy your enemies for all time's sake." Putting down the tightly packed pipe, Ernie reached inside his coat and pulled out the old flintlock. With a flourish he passed it to Mizjoan. She took it, gingerly turning it over in her hands as she examined it.

"Interesting artifact. Does it work?"

"It can be made to."

Mizjoan examined the pistol for several more moments before laying it down on the table. "It doesn't look very dangerous to me. I thought these things used thunder and lightning to kill. Yours wouldn't even make a particularly good club."

"As I explained to Rudy, guns take special powders and preparations to do their work. Now, I have this book…"

"Isn't that your friend's book, the one who didn't come with you?"

Ernie was getting irritated. Rudy had no doubt given her a full briefing, and she was playing games with him, as usual.

"That's right," he said smoothly. "His name's Josiah Toad. We became separated during the Concert Hall fire, but he had entrusted the book to me earlier. Now…"

"Horrible business, that fire. The enemy has struck us a deadly blow. But heads will roll for it, particularly Brother John Birch's."

The name was unfamiliar. Mizjoan's traditional enemies were Klaven Thinarm, Furor of the Great Whitelands, and Josuf Manglewurtz, head of the dreaded Brotherhood of Whiteriders. "Brother John Birch?" he asked.

"An outlander. He's also known as Blackcloak. Some say that both Klaven and Overhed Kham work for him now."

Ernie shook his head. He could see now that things were progressing faster than Skulk, or even Maynard, had anticipated. "He's also called The Jiveman, Joannie. If he's involved in all this, you'll need the guns I'm offering, and you'll need them as soon as I can get them to you."

"That's what Rudy seemed to think."

Ernie lit the pipe using the candle on the table. "So now you know what's coming down," he said after a few tokes. "Do you want our help or not?"

"It's under consideration."

For a second he had the urge to toss the pipe at her and leave the room. "Dammit! I didn't leave Covenstead and my two best friends just to hear a lame response like that."

Mizjoan smiled and patted Ernie on the knee. "Keep it cool, comrade dearest. If you hadn't come on your own Rudy had orders to ensure you made it here. Anyway, if you hadn't left Covenstead when you did, you'd probably be dead now."

"What?"

She sat back, regarding him gravely. "As you probably know, I've maintained a spy post near Darkenwood for years. My agents there report that Fascist and Greaser forces have been massing at Ripoff Pass for days. After you left they marched on Covenstead. I believe that the Concert Hall fire was the signal they were waiting for."

Ernie almost dropped the pipe passing it to Mizjoan. "What? Are you saying Covenstead's been taken?"

"No. Didn't you notice that there were an inordinately large number of my people at the Fair this year? That was no accident, Ernie. We suspected something was up, so Kentstate went there with a sizeable contingent of our people; in fact, they are still there. We are prepared to defend Covenstead."

"How long can a handful of your people hold off the Fascist army?"

"Long enough for another battalion of my best to cross the Sludge tonight and catch Brother John and his friends with their britches down."

Ernie took his brandy in one straight gulp. It burned going down, but it gave him strength. "I'm sure Rudy told you that the Fashies have guns now, and great steam-machines. How long can any army, even yours, stand against that?"

"I don't know, but my people are the best."

"That may no longer be good enough. Accept my offer. I wish Toad was here to help, but with his book to go by, and a few guns taken from the Thirdworld, I think we're well on our way to manufacturing all the weapons we need."

"You're no craftsman," Mizjoan said. She handed him the pipe and poured him another brandy. He accepted both eagerly.

"True, I'm not, but you have superior blacksmiths, and…"

"My smiths and armorers can make swords and crossbows. I don't know about these 'guns' of yours."

Ernie disposed of the second drink as quickly as he had the first. A little dribbled down his chin and he wiped it away with his coat sleeve. "Don't you have faith in your own craftsmen?"

"I'm not worried about their abilities. However, these weapons are different and apparently, we only have you to guide us. You've let me down before, Ernie."

"That's low, Joannie! That was an entirely different situation—I was drunk."

"So, you're still sticking to that sorry excuse," Mizjoan laughed.

"Okay, let's drop that and get on with business," Ernie replied. "Look, I've seen this Blackcloak in action. He takes whatever he wants, regardless of price."

There was a knock at the door, faint at first, then repeated more loudly. Annoyance flashed in Mizjoan's eye. She set her glass down hard. "Now what's up? Dammit, I gave orders not to be disturbed."

While Ernie entertained himself with the pipe, Mizjoan rose to greet a young officer at the door. After conferring for a few moments she returned to her seat wearing a deep frown. "You Diggers are an endless source of aggravation tonight," she grumbled.

"What do you mean?"

"Mario just brought me a message. One of your people is downstairs demanding to see me, a skinny young dude in an embroidered yellow coat."

Ernie hopped to his feet. "That's Strutter Lurchkin, Skulk's personal courier. Skulk wouldn't send his courier all the way from Froggy Bottom just for something to do. Let's go see what Strutter's got."

Mizjoan surveyed the half-filled bottle and pipe lying on the table with an obvious air of regret. "It'd better be good, comrade. If this is just another of your Digger ploys I'll have your scrotum for a weed sack."

Chapter Twelve

Toad scrambled out of the road and into the bushes just ahead of the warhorse's thundering hooves. He stumbled through the underbrush, as brambles caught at his clothing and tore into his flesh. Toad shivered uncontrollably; a staccato thumping hammered in his chest. He didn't dare to look back, fearing that the sight of that grim, faceless figure would still his heart forever. He could feel the Dark Man's eyes, flat and pitiless, burning into his back like hot coals. Shark's eyes. Eyes capable of registering only anger and hatred.

As Toad clawed his way through the tangle of brush and half-grown scrub, he looked about hopelessly for a place to hide from those unblinking eyes. A painful stitch burned in his right side and his head was swimming. He needed to stop before he collapsed, but he knew that to stop was to die.

Exhausted, with the horse's hooves echoing in his ears like war drums, he felt his legs give out beneath him and he crashed face-forward on the forest floor. Staggering to his knees, he looked back cautiously, expecting to see the Dark Man riding down upon him. Instead, he saw the silvery shine of a lake through the trees. He dragged himself upright and moved unsteadily toward the water. The pain in his side subsided, but his heart still raced.

As soon as the pipesmith cleared the tree line to the lakeshore he saw it—a high black tower on a promontory above the far shore. Built of a non-reflective stone that seemed more shadow than substance, the tower reared up over the lake, taller than any structure Toad had ever seen before. A constant thrumming seemed to emanate from within the spire. On top of the dark tower a figure appeared who was darker still. The figure turned in Toad's direction and slowly extended a gloved hand, cackling as it gestured directly at him. Toad screamed. Darkness passed over him. Everything faded. The forest and lake swirled away into mists and shadows. And then, the scream ended.

Toad's vision cleared slowly. He was on a lumpy old couch in an unfamiliar room. Though covered by only a light blanket, his body was bathed in sweat. A log shifted in the fireplace and he sat bolt upright, shaking, clutching the blanket.

The figure on the tower had been just another nightmare, more vivid than most perhaps, but still just a dream. As he surveyed his surroundings he began to feel safe. He couldn't imagine such a foul creature as the Dark Man owning a warm, comfortable house like the one he was in. He would have expected a cold crypt or a wet hole in the ground. No, whoever had brought him here was at least human. But although that thought was comforting, it still didn't explain where he was. He vaguely remembered falling down in the road and then being lifted up by a pair of strong arms. Whoever had brought him to this house had taken care of him, removing his wet clothes and making up a comfortable bed for him.

Toad quietly looked about the room, hoping to learn something about his situation and his unseen host. Through the windows he could see trees and a stone water mill, its wheel turning slowly beside a placid river. He heaved a sigh of relief. He was still in the country somewhere and not in Bahston, as he had feared. Judging from the position of the sun, it was late afternoon.

The living room itself, though large and airy, was cluttered and appeared to be used for a variety of purposes. Books and chemical apparatus crowded the mantelpiece while shovels, picks and other digging implements huddled in a corner by the chimney. Several large geared wheels and the decaying remains of a firearm were propped against a large battered desk on the far side of the room. The desktop was a battlefield of books, sheaves of paper, and odd-looking machine parts that were covered with dirt and discolored by age. Between the windows stood a trunk, half open and overflowing with more ancient and indecipherable objects.

The coffee table next to Toad's couch stood in marked contrast to the rest of the room. Neatly arranged on it were a covered food basket, a bottle of some dark beverage, and a pipe and stash jar. Suddenly conscious of his great thirst, Toad uncorked the bottle and put it to his lips. It was cool, honey herbal tea, as fine a brew as he'd ever tasted.

Toad drained off half the bottle in several gulps. He was just getting around to opening the food basket when the door flew open and a burly black-bearded man in a black-and-red checked jacket entered, bearing an armload of kindling.

"Well, well. You're awake," the man said, laying down the firewood. His hair was tied back in a long ponytail that flopped in his face when he bent over. "It's about time you came around. We thought you were gonna sleep your life away."

Toad almost dropped the basket. "You're a Hunter!" he exclaimed.

"Was the last time I checked, lad. Take it you ain't from around these parts." He straightened up and walked over to greet Toad. "The name's Sasquatch. I'm the fella who brought you in. Guess you don't remember that."

The pipesmith shook his head. "Josiah Toad. I don't understand; what's a Freak doing this close to Bahston?"

Sasquatch laughed, throwing back his head so that his long black ponytail danced a jig in the air. "Guess we ain't that close, fella. Bahston's about two or three days south. This is Froggy Bottom you're at—home of my friend and head Digger, Mister Theophilus Skulk."

"B-but, I thought…"

The Hunter dropped heavily into a chair across the table from Toad. "Who told you this was Bahston, lad? Whoever did musta had eel shit for brains."

"Well, there were these two Greasers…"

"You mean the pair that tried to bring that old fishing smack up Whiskey River? What's a nice fella like you doin' hangin' with the likes of that scum? Hell, they had no idea 'bout what to do with a boat. By the time we brought them in, the ugly one had gone and got himself drowned, and the pretty boy was in hysterics. Some friends you got there, son."

"Drowned? H-he said he couldn't swim, but…"

"What's one Greaser, more or less? Obnoxious breed, the whole lot of them."

Toad nodded numbly. The unsavory duo was certainly capable of killing him if the situation was reversed, but Cuffer's death bothered him nevertheless. By not helping the Greaser, Toad had sealed his fate.

"They were no friends of mine. They kidnapped me and were going to sell me into slavery. Still, I didn't want anyone to die."

"Death's never easy, lad. But remember, that boy drowned, so's unless you held his head under…" The Hunter smiled and reached for Toad's bottle. His small, dark eyes shone in his ruddy face. "Anyway, the pretty one's tied up in the root cellar and the other one's only fit for worm food."

"This Mister Skulk you mentioned before, does he know Ernie Mungweasle, the traveling herbalist?"

"I should say so," the Hunter nodded energetically. "You sayin' you know Ernie Mungweasle?"

"I went to Covenstead Fair with him. That's where those Greasers kidnapped me."

Sasquatch took a swig from the bottle and got back onto his feet. "Stay right here, lad. I'll be back in a moment."

"I won't be going too far," Toad replied. "Someone took my clothes."

The Hunter made no reply. He crossed the room and was out the door like a wind, leaving it swinging behind him. Through the opening Toad could see him hurrying along the path to the mill, until he was lost in the glare of the westering sun.

Toad picked up the food basket and drew aside its cloth cover. His stomach rumbled noisily as he extracted a thick slab of yellow cheese, brown bread, and a pair of fist-sized red apples. He finished one of the apples in five well-placed bites, then turned his attention to the cheese and bread. Suddenly, Sasquatch burst back through the door, talking excitedly to a rather short, older Freak in a plug hat and long russet coat that seemed to have endless bulging pockets.

The pipesmith had barely enough time to swallow a morsel of cheese before the older Freak rushed over, grabbed his hand and shook it vigorously. He was an odd-looking little fellow with kinky hair and a square-cut beard going to gray. He moved in quick, jerky motions and his thick spectacles were in constant danger of sliding off his red, potato-like nose.

"Damn glad to meet you, son," he said, finally letting go of Toad's hand. "I'm Theophilus Skulk. Welcome to Froggy Bottom."

"G-glad to meet you, Mr. Skulk. My name's Josiah Toad."

Skulk clapped his hands together gleefully. "Did you hear that, Sas? This is Toad the pipemaker, the fellow Ernie speaks so highly of. That explains everything."

"Except those Greasers, Theo. I don't think they were acting alone."

"Well then, Sas, we'll just have to talk to the surviving one. Maybe he can add a few details. But first, I'd like to hear Toad's story. Why don't you scare up a bottle of wine to sharpen our appetites before dinner, and we'll have a nice little chat."

Toad found that he genuinely liked Skulk and the burly Hunter, but was surprised to hear that Ernie had discussed their relationship with the two Diggers. Sasquatch returned with a pair of bottles and Skulk began filling the pipe on the table. The pipesmith was eager to tell his tale. "Where should I begin?" he asked.

Skulk stoked up the pipe and puffed at it greedily. "From whatever seems like the beginning, son. Chow ain't gonna be for a while yet."

He went all the way back to when he and Ernie first met. The wine helped—it lightened his spirits and loosened his tongue—and Skulk and Sasquatch's interest in his story kept the words flowing. He thought it prudent to downplay what he knew about Ernie's involvement with the Diggers and omitted entirely any references to *Cruickshank's*.

By the time Toad concluded his story with the events at Covenstead, his capture and subsequent escape from the Greasers, the shadows were growing long in the room and the fire was dying on the hearth. Both Sasquatch and Skulk sat on the edge of their seats, looking at him with glowing eyes. Somewhere outside the house a fiddle started up, playing a merry tune, while from the next room came the sound of voices and clattering pots.

"Well, that's sure some story," Skulk said, getting up to throw a log on the fire. "It seems Ernie picked a good traveling companion in you. Your escape from those Greasy-boys showed both courage and cunning."

Toad could feel himself beginning to blush. "I sure didn't feel very courageous; besides, a handful of burnt seeds have more cunning than those Greasers."

Sasquatch chuckled. "You've got a sense of humor, too. That's a handy tool for a man to have in this world."

"Yeah, that's what Ernie always says." Suddenly Toad missed his friend very much, in spite of their recent disagreements.

Once the fire was again roaring on the hearth, Skulk returned to his seat. "If my nose isn't lying to me, it's almost suppertime. Sas, why don't you get one of the girls to bring our guest some clothes, then go see what you can do to help in the kitchen. I'd like to talk to Brother Toad in private for a while."

"Sure thing, Theo. All this tale-telling's made me hungry as a bear anyway." The Hunter heaved himself up out of his chair and walked out of the room. A moment later a pretty, dark-haired teenage girl came through the same door, bearing an armload of folded clothing, which she placed by the couch. Then she too withdrew from the room.

Toad started sorting through the clothing. There was a pair of faded jeans that seemed about his size, thick socks and a baggy woolen sweater with leather patches on the yoke and elbows. Kicking aside the covers he began to put them on.

"So," Skulk said, re-packing his pipe. "What do you think of my little home?"

"What I've seen so far fascinates me, Mr. Skulk. I'd like to see more."

"You will, son. In due time."

The pipesmith buttoned the fly of his jeans and wiggled into the baggy sweater. "This is all very strange to me."

"How so?"

"Well, you and Mr. Sasquatch don't seem like my idea of what a Digger should be. Of course, neither does Ernie."

"What did you think we were supposed to look like?"

"I'm not sure. Duller, I guess, more scholarly."

"A few of us are like that, but not many. A Digger's life is more exciting than you might think. You'll find that out when I show you around the place and you meet some of the others. I hope you'll be staying with us a little while. We're short-handed at present and could use the extra help."

The idea appealed to Toad. It might be interesting to putter around Froggy Bottom for a few days while he was making arrangements to go home.

"Certainly sounds better than what I was headed for. What'll you have me doing?"

"This and that. Doing chores mostly and learning stuff. You won't be bored, I assure you."

"I'm sure of that. Dylan's Bones, I've already got a million questions to ask you."

Skulk lit the pipe with a candle and took a deep toke. It seemed once again that his glasses were going to slide off his rum-blossom nose. He exhaled and pushed the spectacles back into place. "I'll answer all of your questions in time, son. But, right now, I've got a few to ask you."

"Sure. Go ahead."

"You said that there was a musician named Tambourine Dill traveling with you, and that he left right before the Concert Hall fire."

Toad took the pipe from the Digger chief and put it to his lips. "Yeah, he did, but surely you're not suggesting..."

"That there's a connection? Of course not. Ernie's known Tam for years. He says he's a good friend and a fine musician, but somewhat uncommitted. I'm just curious as to why he took off, and with whom. It seems a strange gesture on his part."

"I'm afraid I can't help you there much. I vaguely remember someone asking after him, but that's all. Tam left a note saying he'd met up with an old friend of the family."

"Hmm, most curious. Still, I'm sure he's in good hands at the moment."

Skulk's statement struck Toad as odd. It implied much, but said little. "What do you mean? Do you know something about his whereabouts?"

The Digger shrugged. Behind his thick glasses his dark eyes shifted. "Nothing really. Tambourine is a musician. I'm sure that he most likely wandered off with one of his many adoring female fans. I'm told that stuff like that happens all the time."

"I guess that could be it." Somehow, though, Toad didn't think it was.

"Is there any more you can tell me, Toad, either about Ernie or the fire?"

"Ernie and I were supposed to go to Camp Hoffman. Whether he made it there, I don't know."

"What about the fire? Do you think it was an accident?"

Toad felt uncomfortable. The room suddenly seemed too warm. He nervously stroked his scrubby beard, for the first time disliking it. "I don't know. I didn't get a chance to get very close, but what I did see was horrible. All those poor people."

"A great tragedy—beyond words—beyond understanding. Still, my thoughts are with Ernie now. I hope he makes it to Leftopia. As you've seen, things are moving rather quickly these days."

"I've noticed that, Mr. Skulk. And, I think in a few days I'd like to move on towards home."

"That might be impossible," Skulk said flatly, with a shake of his shaggy head. The kitchen door opened and a thin, blond woman thrust her head out.

"Soup's on, Theo. Bring your guest and let's eat."

"Enough for now. It doesn't pay to ignore Wilma," Skulk observed, smiling at the woman. "It's time you met the family."

Skulk's kitchen was even larger than his living room. It held a long trestle table that must have seated thirty people, though only half the seats were occupied. Several women worked at a preparing table while two of the men rotated a side of venison on a spit in the kitchen's huge walk-in fireplace. Teenaged boys and girls hurried about, setting the table. Sasquatch sat by the sink, patiently whetting a large carving knife. The Digger chief clapped his hands as he and Toad walked in, to get everyone's attention.

"Listen up, children!" he boomed. "I want you to meet Mr. Josiah Toad. He's an old friend of Ernie Mungweasle's, and he's going to be staying with us."

The various Freaks looked up and smiled, then went back to their tasks. Unexplained visitors were apparently common with the Diggers. The group was all fairly young except for Sasquatch, Wilma, and a couple of others who looked to be in their early thirties. But even they were a good two decades younger than Skulk. As the Digger chief had pointed out, with only a few exceptions, none of the Diggers were particularly scholarly looking. In fact many wore loud, outlandish clothing that would have fit right in at Covenstead Fair or Rivertown. Toad observed that there was a seriousness and camaraderie about the group; it was drawing him to them.

Skulk took a seat at the head of the long table and gestured for Toad to sit next to him. They sat and sipped coffee as food was put on platters and last minute meal preparations were taken care of.

"These are less than half of my people," Skulk explained. "Most of our more senior members are out on projects or working on our new dig at Fetid Bog. In a day or so some of us are going to join them at the bog. It's an important site and working it will require all the hands we can muster. If you feel up to it, I'd like you to join us."

An archaeological dig? Toad had to admit that the idea intrigued him.

"Sounds interesting. What's the site? Cellar holes? An old dump?"

"Better than that. Maynard, a friend of mine, told me of the ruins of a manufacturing complex he'd found. With some luck we might be able to learn something about the mass-production techniques of the ancients. It promises to be an interesting dig."

Toad took a sip of coffee. It was hot and revivifying. "Ernie told me about this Maynard fellow, Mr. Skulk. Doesn't he just about run things around here?"

"No, no, no," Skulk frowned. "I'm sure you must have misinterpreted what Ernie said. Maynard *is* an important person locally, a close friend and associate, but he doesn't run the Society. I do. We run an occasional errand for him, and he tips us off about good sites. It's a fair exchange, but nothing more."

"I see. What other sites has he told you of?" Toad didn't want to let on that he knew about the Thirdworld, but it couldn't hurt to pry just a bit.

"Various others, son. Nothing to get into now, with food in front of our noses."

As if on cue, Wilma brought platters filled with venison and boiled vegetables and placed them before Toad and Skulk. The dark-haired girl who had brought Toad his clothing followed behind her, bearing chilled milk in tall glasses. As he worked his way through his meal, Toad kept a sharp ear to the chatter going on around him.

There was a good deal of talk about the new dig, about places Toad had only heard of and about people he knew nothing of, like Strutter Lurchkin and Sam'l Smoot. One of the girls cracked a joke about a professor at Shambullah University that meant nothing to Toad, but got a hearty laugh from everyone else. The conversation shifted to current events, flavored with much speculation and gossip. Toad leaned back in his chair and relaxed, though he had little to contribute. He was beginning to feel like part of the group.

Slowly, the conversation turned to other things: the crops, fruitful past digs, and the daily routine around Froggy Bottom. Some spoke enthusiastically about their personal projects. Though often technical in nature, this talk grabbed Toad's full attention.

A couple in their early twenties spoke at great length about an antique printing press they were trying to rebuild and power using the machinery in the mill. An earnest, freckled youth in a long white coat described the work he was doing on plastic shards uncovered in a cellar hole near Saturday Night. Several times a place named Eppen Dump was mentioned, where a fine trove of ancient machine parts had been unearthed. Wilma was bubbling about her research paper on the site; the paper had just been accepted for inclusion in the library at Shambullah. Sasquatch hugged her, causing much good-natured cheering and clapping. He said that he hoped for the same success from the maps he was working on. The maps showed every important cellar hole and bottle dump in the Zappatown region. By the time dessert was served and the table cleared, Toad was eager to stay at Froggy Bottom. This was the kind of adventure he'd had in mind when he left Smuttynose.

After a post-supper smoke, Skulk gave Toad a guided tour of Froggy Bottom by lantern light. The complex extended far beyond the main house. It included the mill, several barns, and perhaps a dozen smaller homes and workshops. Froggy Bottom was a thriving, self-contained community with its own gardens, blacksmith shop, and horse stables. Skulk explained that what few items couldn't be manufactured locally were imported from places like Saturday Night, Funkyton, and Rivertown.

Over the next couple of days, Toad lost himself in wandering about the village, getting to know the Diggers and helping them on some of their projects. He saw little of Skulk, but went on several long hikes with Sasquatch, once to inspect a deer yard and twice to examine a series of cellar holes that marked the site of an ancient township. While there he uncovered several antique bottles and quite a few plastic shards, which he presented to the freckle-faced boy with the white coat.

On the third morning of his stay at Skulk's, Toad awoke to a bustle of activity in the main house and in the yard outside his window.

Sasquatch burst through his door. "You're not ready yet? If you want to join us, you have to get up earlier than this."

"Huh? Join you?" Toad muttered.

"On an adventure. We're heading out. Get dressed and meet us in the yard," Sasquatch pronounced, exiting as quickly as he'd come in.

Toad hurried into his clothes and rushed his morning toilet, washing sloppily and only desultorily messing with his beard and hair. He was still pushing one arm down the sleeve of his coat as he stumbled outside into the bright morning, where horses were being assembled and young Freaks were busily packing supplies. Skulk thrust a heavy backpack into his chest.

"What's this?" Toad asked.

"Expedition gear. You wanted to go on one, didn't you?" Skulk didn't wait for a reply; he turned and started to give orders to a few Diggers who were tying tools and instruments onto packhorses. He looked over his shoulder and yelled back to Toad.

"There's a plate of breakfast for you in the kitchen. By the time you finish we'll be ready to go."

"Where we going?" Toad yelled back.

"Fetid Bog, my boy."

Toad's heart leapt with excitement. He had heard that Skulk, Sasquatch and some of the other Diggers would soon be leaving for Fetid Bog but he had not expected to be among them.

When Toad came back out to the yard Skulk had a horse ready for him. It was an older mare, but suitable. The expedition left Froggy Bottom, traveling along a narrow road, heading northwest. They passed a root cellar guarded by a young Freak in green and brown motley. He held a cudgel in one hand and wore a skinning knife on his wide belt. Toad thought that must be where they were keeping Sonny.

The Diggers and their horses moved along old forest roads that were overgrown with brush and marshy in spots. They had to ford streams in some places and cut new paths through the undergrowth in others. Skulk and Sasquatch rode at the head of the column, talking and consulting their maps. Between the two Diggers, Toad sat easily on the back of his horse, toking away on his pipe, silent but aware of everything going on around him. The November breezes were chilly, but the heavy wool coat Skulk had given him kept him warm and the smoldering pipe soothed him. Smuttynose Island and the troubles at Covenstead seemed a million miles away.

The line of Diggers and horses moved steadily throughout the day, stopping only for the noon meal and to water the horses. Around dusk they passed over an old stone bridge and through an overgrown area where ruins of broken building stones and piles of rotting bricks pushed up through the underbrush. A few of the company rode off to poke through the ruins momentarily, but the main body of the party kept to the road.

"Tumbledown Acres," Sasquatch said. "If we keep pushing on, we should reach Fetid Bog before morning."

Skulk adjusted his glasses and scratched at his wiry beard. "I'm wondering if we ought to camp down for the night."

"I'd advise against it; I think we'd be safer to keep going. We've got lanterns and the woods roads get better further on. I say we keep on truckin'."

"Well, you know the area better than I do."

"That I do, Theo. A couple of miles from here there's a remarkably well-preserved section of old-time highway that leads right to the bog. We'll make great time then."

By nightfall the forests gave way to scrub-filled fields and swamps that glittered like silver in the light of the nearly full moon. As Sasquatch had promised, the ancient roadway was in good shape and safe to negotiate even by the feeble glow of the party's lanterns.

It was a little past dawn when Toad looked up to catch his first glimpse of Fetid Bog. With all its tents and wagons the excavation site looked like a drabber, scaled-down version of Covenstead Fair. Instead of a maze of roadways and alleys, half-dug trenches ran in all directions. Crews were already at work enlarging the trenches with picks and shovels in spite of the early hour, and other Diggers were cleaning and sorting out what the bog had yielded up. As Skulk's party neared the site, Toad saw several muscular men operating a winch that was bringing up dirt-covered crates from the bottom of one of the trenches. A portly, older Freak in a patched green cloak was moving from crew to crew, yelling instructions and making notes in a logbook he carried in his hands.

"That's Sam'l Smoot," Skulk said, pointing to the cloaked Digger. "He's the man in charge here. Hey-lo there, Sammy! Where's your manners? Can't you see you've got company?"

The portly Freak smiled and hurried toward Skulk and Sasquatch. Several of the other Diggers lay down their tools and rushed to join him. Soon the crew crowded around the new arrivals from Froggy Bottom, talking excitedly as they helped unload the horses and ponies.

"You couldn't have come at a better time, Theo," Sam'l Smoot said, wiping dirt from his hands. "We struck crates an hour ago, and we've found traces of several underground structures. Fetid Bog may yet pay off like Maynard said it would."

"Opened any of the crates yet, Sammy?" asked Skulk.

"No. We've yet to clean them. Most are metal and they're rusted shut. I'd hate swinging a pick at them if I could get them open some gentler way."

"Sound thinking. We can't risk damaging what's inside."

Smoot nodded. "My thinking exactly, Boss. But we've brought up a lot of stuff I can show you. The kids have been doing a helluva job cleaning and cataloguing."

"That's what I want to hear, Sammy," Skulk remarked, sliding down out of his saddle. "Show me what you've got."

Smoot proudly led Skulk, Sasquatch, and Toad to a long table where several women were working, carefully cleaning a collection of rusted iron objects with wire brushes and solvent. He carried a long-stemmed silver weed pipe, which he used as a pointer. "We found these at the lowest level. Worked metal, ingeniously constructed. We think they may be parts of some sort of sophisticated drill system. These larger objects here are gear wheels, though they're so badly corroded that you can't tell at first glance. These," he said, tapping several short, badly rotted metal tubes, "are the first signs of what we're seeking. I believe them to be gun barrels."

So that's it, Toad thought. Fetid Bog had once been a weapons factory. No wonder Skulk treated it with such respect.

"You're certainly getting warmer," Sasquatch remarked, gingerly inspecting one of the metal tubes. "Imagine what those crates'll yield up."

Smoot nodded. "We're holding our breath. It'll be some hours before we dare crack one. As you know, exposure to the air can quickly harm old wood and metal."

"Things'll move faster now," Skulk said. "We've brought you plenty of help and supplies."

As it turned out, one of the crates was opened that evening after supper. The Diggers had made a large campfire in the middle of the site, and the crate was dragged into place as bottles were uncorked and Smoot's silver weedpipe made its way from hand to hand. A guitar and harmonica were produced and several of the younger Diggers did an impromptu clog dance around the rusted old relic as the others joined in joyous song. Toad envied these people their hard work and exciting rewards. Their rapture was contagious. With a bottle in one hand and Smoot's smoldering pipe in the other, he got unsteadily to his feet, watching as Sam'l and Skulk worked on the crate with pry bars. The Diggers held their breath as the ancient metal buckled and gave way with a high-pitched screech. For a moment no one moved, and then Skulk reached with one trembling hand into the crate's interior. A second later he let out a whoop of joy and pulled out a short-barreled flintlock, caked with centuries-old grease. The ossified grease cracked and fell off in chunks as he brandished the weapon over his head. Cavorting about like a man half his age, the Digger chief whooped again, loud enough to sound an echo off the incoming mists of the bog. Beside him, Smoot and Sasquatch pulled out similar weapons. Soon everyone was up and dancing about in frantic excitement.

Toad sat back down, watching the cheering, celebrating crowd. In the mist and flickering firelight, as the Diggers waved the ancient machines of destruction over their heads, all Toad could see was the terror-filled days of Helter-Skelter that he'd read about. He took a deep toke on the pipe and shook his head sadly. As the Greaser, Sonny, would have said, it was a fucked-up world.

Chapter Thirteen

The sides of the trench were soggy and treacherous. Toad moved cautiously as he stepped over the edge and lowered himself onto the floor. He grumbled as his boot went into a mud puddle, splashing muck on his jeans. Twice before today he'd slipped as the crumbly peat gave way under his feet, and once he'd almost fallen on Sasquatch, who had been carefully excavating around an old foundation. With a clumsy leap, Toad reached the lowest level of the trench and started working his way to the half-buried wall that he'd been working on before lunch. The first stirrings of a cold had been nagging him all morning, but he was too excited to give it much thought.

The system of trenches resembled a maze, and Toad had to look around for a moment to make sure he was in the right area. Satisfied that this was the spot, he pulled his heavy work gloves out of his pocket and put them on, flexing his hands gently. Fired up by his first day on the dig, he'd already started to raise a healthy crop of blisters.

Now that eight crates had been opened, five last night and three more that were uncovered this morning, spirits in the camp were at a phenomenal high. As he moved to pick up his tools, Toad could hear the sounds of singing and digging coming from nearby trenches. The pipesmith stopped to examine the exposed section of concrete wall. Humming along with the other Diggers, he took his spade and began to carefully slice away the layers of peat around it.

After about a half-hour, his spade uncovered the jamb of a rotted wooden door. Digging quickly and less carefully than he was shown, Toad exposed it almost fully in another twenty minutes. Though severely decayed, the door was intact and unopened. In fact, the rusted remains of a huge padlock still hung from the jamb. He considered calling over Skulk or Smoot, then quickly decided against it. It was his discovery. If anything lay beyond the door, he wanted to be the one to find it, the one to claim the glory. He struck at the padlock with his shovel and it fell into rusty chunks. He kicked at the door, grinning as it gave way and crashed into the dark interior of the buried chamber. The rotted wood shattered into splinters and dust as it hit the floor inside. Toad stepped backwards, gagging at the musty stench coming through the open portal. He shielded his face with his hands, waiting for the air to clear. Throwing his shovel ahead of him, past the ancient remnants of a stairway that led down three or four feet, he leaped through the opening and landed gently in a thick layer of dust. As it stirred up around him in a boiling cloud, Toad sneezed.

It was as black as midnight in the chamber. Beyond the shaft of light coming through the portal, the darkness seemed almost solid, as thick as time itself. Fumbling in his coat pocket, Toad brought out his tinderbox and a fat candle stub. He held his breath as he lit the candle. It flickered and took. What its pallid light revealed made him gasp: row upon row of crates, packed to the ceiling as far as he could see. Unlike the crates taken from the bog proper, these were unmarred by decay. Even the locks were whole and unspotted by rust. Compared to this find, the eight crates the Diggers had recovered so far were insignificant. Those had yielded up perhaps a hundred guns; these might yield up thousands. Toad sneezed loudly, almost extinguishing his candle. He moved forward like a man in a dream, setting the candle stub on the top of one row of crates. With some effort, he lowered a crate from another row and placed it on the ground. He raised his shovel and, with all his might, brought it down on the lock.

It took several sharp blows to smash the lock and by the time it gave way, he was sweating with excitement. Toad pushed hard at the lid of the crate. It let go and went crashing to the floor in a puff of dust. His hands shaking with anticipation, the pipesmith reached into the crate and pulled out an ancient rifle. Like all the others that had been found, it was covered with dried grease. Cleaning the grease away with his handkerchief, he examined the lettering engraved deeply into the blue metal of the weapon's barrel.

Wahlanger Replica Arms Company
Witchtrot Center, NH, USA

Toad laid the old gun against the crate and stood regarding it in awe for several seconds. Then, in the guttering candlelight, he turned his gaze to the rows of crates. He wondered for a moment if it might be better if his discovery went unmentioned. These thousands of weapons had the potential to change the world forever, to bring back an ancient evil as sinister as anything the Dark Man could devise. On the other hand, if a war was brewing and Street-Corner Earth was in peril, perhaps it was a time for changes, even potentially bad ones. He sneezed again and dabbed at his nose with his grease-stained handkerchief.

A trumpet sounded in the distance. Grabbing the rifle, Toad extinguished his candle and climbed out of the chamber.

Back in the sunlight, Toad started out of the trench. He heard the trumpet again, louder and nearer, followed by the pounding of horses' hooves. Looking eastward he saw a troop of about thirty gray-clad figures riding into view, led by a young man in a long, star-embroidered yellow coat. Beside the young man rode a striking auburn-haired woman in the uniform of a Radiclib officer. When she turned to speak to the young man, Toad was shocked to notice a black patch over her right eye; it seemed to enhance her beauty rather than mar it. His heart skipped a beat when he saw the horse and wagon pulling up behind her. Even at a distance there was no mistaking the lank figure in the black frock coat and top hat sitting in the driver's seat.

"Ernie!" Toad yelled, gesturing with the rifle. "Ernie Mungweasle!"

The herbalist brought his wagon up short, swiveling his head to see where the outcry was coming from. Behind him, a tall officer bearing a bold pennant, red fist upon a black field, stopped and pointed at Toad. Ernie broke formation and drove to meet the pipesmith. The auburn-haired woman with the eye patch followed. Up close, she was even more stunning, easily the most beautiful woman he had ever seen. She smiled when she saw the long flintlock rifle that Toad now cradled in his arms.

"Toad!" Ernie boomed, jumping down from his wagon seat and helping the pipesmith out of the trench. "What in Dylan's name are you doing here?"

"It's a long story, Ernie. Two Greasers kidnapped me at the Concert Hall fire. They wanted to sell me as a slave in Bahston. I escaped. Sasquatch found me and I've been staying at Froggy Bottom since then."

The herbalist shook his head. "A slave? Bummer, man. Dylan, I was worried about you, but I was sure you were headed back to Smuttynose. If I'd known you were in trouble I wouldn't have continued on to Camp Hoffman."

Toad sneezed, almost dropping the rifle. "Well, it all turned out okay, except for this stupid cold. At least I got to meet Skulk and the other Diggers."

"Seems like you've been busy," Ernie stated, pointing at the gun Toad held. "Where'd you get that weapon? It looks brand new."

"In the trench back there. There's a chamber filled to the ceiling with these things. But what are you doing here? Fetid Bog's a long way from Leftopia, isn't it?"

"Skulk sent us word that this site might yield up something interesting," the woman said in a slightly husky voice that Toad found intriguing. She extended a gloved hand for him to shake. "Apparently he was right. I'm Mizjoan Berkeley; I take it you're Comrade Toad. Ernie's told me a lot about you."

Toad took the woman's hand. Her grip was strong and confident. His senses swam. "M-my pleasure," he stammered, unsettled by the gleam in her eye. "Would you allow me to escort you into camp?"

"That won't be necessary, comrade. I see Skulk and Sammy Smoot headed this way now."

Mizjoan rode off to greet the two men while her soldiers dismounted and began tying up their horses. Several of the younger Diggers lay down their tools and clustered around the fellow in the embroidered yellow coat. He seemed to be someone of importance to them; they were hanging on his every word and action. For the moment, Toad and Ernie were ignored in the general hubbub. The herbalist leaned against the side of his wagon and took a pipe out of his coat pocket. Toad rested the flintlock next to the herbalist and offered Ernie a light from his tinderbox.

"I still can't get over seeing you here," Ernie said between tokes. "When I couldn't find you at Covenstead I was sure you'd had enough and headed home."

Between fits of sneezing Toad detailed the story of his abduction, the storm, his escape to Froggy Bottom, and the strange dreams that continued to haunt him even there. During the whole of the narration, Ernie could only shake his head in wonder.

"I'll be damned," the herbalist said when the story was over and he'd passed the pipe to Toad. "I suspected as much, but this proves you've got what it takes. You really were born for the road. Not only did you escape those Greasers, but you made it here to uncover a weapons cache that might turn the tide of history. I'm impressed."

"Don't be, Ernie. I've enjoyed my stay with your friends, but I'll be heading out soon."

"Don't try backing out now," Ernie interjected. "You've started down a new road. There's a long way to go and we're going to need your help more than ever."

Toad sneezed violently and dabbed at his nose with his handkerchief. "Ernie, listen to me. I've had enough of all this."

"Listen to yourself, Toad. When you say that you want out, you lack conviction. I think you're enjoying the adventure and all the attention. It's apparent that the Society thinks highly of you, or you wouldn't have been invited on this dig."

The pipesmith sneezed more violently than before. Ernie always seemed to be able to read him. Toad hated that. For the first time he felt that adventure might be in his blood. The idea of going to Camp Hoffman was appealing; perhaps it was a chance to see more of this Comrade Mizjoan. Still, everything was happening much too quickly, and his island upbringing made him cautious of new acquaintances, even beautiful ones.

"Skulk, Sasquatch, and the others are a great group of people," Toad stated, "but I'm not comfortable with all this. I mean, the Diggers' interests seem about half divided between historical research and political intrigue. Somehow the two things don't seem to go together."

Ernie stroked his long mustaches thoughtfully. "Sometimes they do. The Clear Light Society has been around a long time. We Diggers can be a potent force for good in the world."

Toad shrugged. He looked up to see Sasquatch headed their way. Ernie grinned and waved at the burly Hunter.

"Greetings, Sas," Ernie said. "Come over and join the party."

Sasquatch shook his head. "No can do, Ernie. I'm here to get you two. Theo and Mizjoan want to see you in Theo's tent." He shifted his gaze to the rifle lying by Toad's side. "By the way, Toad—congratulations. Mizjoan told us about your find. You've out-Diggered the Diggers."

Toad's only reply was a chest-wracking sneeze.

The Hunter picked up the gun and laid a friendly arm on Toad's shoulder. "Sound's like a bad cold, lad. Come along to the tent and we'll fix you up."

Toad got to his feet and the three of them walked across the site to Skulk's tent. Although it was bright outside, the light was dim in the tent and on the table between Skulk and Mizjoan a feeble candle flickered, casting foreboding shadows.

"There you are," Skulk said, as Toad and Ernie entered. "Mizjoan and I have just been talking about you two."

"Nothing good, I'll bet," Ernie replied. Mizjoan smiled. Her full lips crinkled at the corners.

Toad sat down beside Mizjoan and suddenly the room felt hot and stuffy. Maybe he was developing a fever, or maybe it was just her effect on him.

"Theo and I were just discussing what a big help you two would be in training my troops at Camp Hoffman," she said.

Toad felt dizzy. Sweat was beginning to bead on his brow. "Wh-what training?" he asked.

"Guns are of no value if my people don't know how to use them. You've found quite a cache already, but Skulk thinks there might be thousands more yet to be uncovered. Isn't that right, Theo?"

"So Maynard seemed to think."

Toad wiped away the sweat from his brow. He envisioned rooms stacked to the ceilings with crates like the ones he'd uncovered.

Beside him, Ernie was shaking his head.

"It must be true, then," the herbalist said. "By his own admission, the great Maynard is rarely wrong."

Skulk glared at Ernie, his eyes flashing from behind his thick spectacles. "This is hardly the time for sarcasm."

Ernie grunted. "If he knew of this site all along, why did he have me tap-dancing all over the Thirdworld? You know how hairy things got there."

"He knew there *might* be a cache here at Fetid Bog," Skulk said, "but he didn't know if it'd still be intact. Bahston was a better shot at the time. Besides, there was more to be studied there than just firearms."

"It spooks me out, Theo. This guy's no Digger, yet lately we always seem to be working on *his* projects."

Skulk adjusted his glasses with his stubby forefinger. "Ernie, we have other business to discuss."

"We can talk business later," Mizjoan interjected. "I would like to know more about this mysterious Comrade Maynard. Hell, for all I know he could be one of Blackcloak's agents."

"That's one thing he's not, Joan," said Skulk. "Though to hear him tell it, he's been just about everything else."

"A real wacka-man? A legend in his own mind?"

"Would you like to hear the story or not?" Skulk asked.

Mizjoan nodded. "Go ahead."

Leaning forward in his chair Skulk rested his chin on his hands: they all but disappeared in his wiry beard. "My association with Maynard goes back several years, when I literally stumbled upon him while digging in some ruins on the edge of Long Swamp.

"It was late afternoon, and I was taking a break from excavating around a large cellar hole. I was leaning against a tree, just about to light up my pipe, when I noticed a hole between the roots of the tree. It was far too large for most animal holes. I bent down to get a closer look at it. There was a definite smell of peat. Peat preserves many things, you know. I was very curious, so, after widening the hole a bit, I lit a candle and lowered myself in. The hole led into a stone shaft with iron rungs set into the stonework at regular intervals. The shaft went down about twenty feet, terminating in a corridor high enough for me to walk through. At the end of the corridor was an iron door, rusty and corroded with years of neglect.

"Trembling with curiosity, I tugged on the door. It opened with a screech of rusted hinges. Beyond the door I was surprised to find a spacious room furnished with antique furniture and several high, glass-front bookcases. The air in the room was fresh, in spite of the ever-present smell of peat. I assumed that the vents I saw running along the ceiling were responsible for this, though I didn't inspect them closely. I was far more interested in the oddly titled books I saw on the shelves. I pored through several of them, mostly histories and works on ritual magick, all quite old. There was a large coffin-sized chest in the far corner of the room. It was near this chest that the smell of peat was strongest.

"Inside the chest, encased in a layer of moldy peat, lay the body of a small man clothed only in a pair of cut-off jeans. At first I was sure that he was dead, that I had uncovered some bizarre ancient tomb. But his skin was warm and dry to the touch, and there was a faint, though irregular pulse."

Ernie shook his head. "Maynard sleeps in peat?"

"A form of sleep, yes."

"And you still take this dude seriously?"

"Sometimes more seriously than I do you, Ernie. He believes the peat prolongs his life. Weird as it may sound, I think it does."

"C'mon."

Skulk gave Ernie a hard stare and continued. "After removing him from the peat I picked him up and placed him on the couch by the door. He was limp and light as a feather, but as I was carrying him he wheezed and moved his lips as if to speak. I took my hip flask out and forced some brandy down his throat, then stepped back to see what would happen. He gasped like an old forge bellows, stiff from disuse, and opened his eyes. Great Dylan, those eyes! They were green and glowed in the dark like foxfire. I couldn't look him in the face again until he found his sunglasses and put them on.

"After draining my flask he told me something of his history. Even now, I wonder if he's given to extraordinary vision or merely mad. He said that he was called Maynard and that I'd awakened him from a state of suspended animation.

"Maynard was neither his given name nor the only one he'd used during his remarkably long life. Then he smiled, saying that I'd probably recognize some of the others from history books."

"Sounds like delusions of grandeur to me," Ernie scoffed.

"Maybe so, but his knowledge of ancient times and his ability to locate sites like this one are phenomenal. I'm convinced he is incredibly old—more than five hundred years by his own reckoning."

Ernie shook his head. "And you believe him? That's impossible, Theo."

Toad thought so too, but a chill raced up his spine. He glanced over at Mizjoan as she leaned forward to listen. He caught her eye for a second and it seemed as though they shared a common thought.

Skulk merely shrugged. "I would have agreed with you before I met the man, Ernie. Those burning eyes; the conviction in that voice. Against my own sense of reality I'm forced to accept him and his remarkable story.

"He claimed that he was born in 1941, in a village not far from the ruins I was excavating. When he was twenty he left his home and journeyed first to Bahston, then to a place called New Yawk. In New Yawk he claims to have met and befriended a struggling young musician named Bob Dylan, who taught him to write poetry and play the guitar."

"Holy Bob," Ernie snickered. "Give me a break."

Skulk ignored him. "After leaving New Yawk, Maynard traveled west and kept traveling for the better part of the next decade. He lived for a while in the fabled land of Haight-Ashbury and came to know many people that we remember now only as characters in our vaguest legends. Those were strange and angry times, he said, and he learned much that was to change him forever. But, he had to return home for the greatest change of all to take place… immortality."

Ernie snorted derisively. "Immortality? Dylan's Bones."

"Maynard doesn't feel that he's really immortal, Ernie, just indefinitely prolonged. He believes he *can* die. He just isn't dead yet."

Mizjoan glanced at Toad, then leaned toward Skulk. "So you say that peat makes him 'indefinitely prolonged'? Not to sound shallow, but as a woman I find the idea intriguing."

"As a Digger, I know that peat does have preservative qualities," Skulk replied.

"What did he do? Smoke it, or use it for a mud pack?"

"Neither. He was buried in it for a long time. Ernie may not think Maynard is a Digger, but he could very well be the original one. It's a point that he's vague on, as he is on many.

"You see, archaeology has always been one of his prime interests. So, after he returned from Haight-Ashbury, he spent much of his time alone, getting stoned and digging in the small bogs in the woods near his parents' home. During the course of one of his excavations a hole he was working in collapsed on him. He was buried alive and soon lost consciousness. When he came to he found himself encased in peat. With almost superhuman effort he clawed his way to the surface, freeing himself from the bog. Shaken and confused, he made his way toward town.

"What he found there was startling. It was as if overnight the village had fallen into ruin. The entire town appeared to be deserted. Half in shock, he staggered into one of the last houses left standing. It had been looted of all useful items. Eventually, in the back of a bedroom closet on the second floor he found some books and journals. From these he learned about Helter-Skelter and the Fashie-Luddite Wars. Though his sleep seemed brief, many decades had passed, and with them the world he'd known. Since then he's roamed the world, making his mark on history, then sleeping for years at a time. He claims that he knows the truth behind the fall of Westcommune and the true nature of the horror our histories call Tommy Two. He also knows the reasons behind the Great Wandering."

"This is heavy," Mizjoan said. "Skulk, is he the Freedom Rider?"

"I asked him that myself, Joan. He just laughed and said he wasn't, but when the Freedom Rider appeared, he'd be his talent agent."

Ernie sighed. "This is all very interesting, but it's been a long hard trip from Camp Hoffman, and there's business to attend to."

At that moment, a Radiclib soldier pushed through the flap of the tent. He looked dusty and worn out. He saluted Mizjoan curtly and handed her a note. She returned the salute and dismissed him. Her eyebrows pinched together. She scowled deeply as she read.

"Mungweasle is right, we have important business," Mizjoan stated upon finishing the note. "He and Toad are urgently needed in Camp Hoffman. My people need guns and training."

Toad sneezed violently, a great, tent-shaking blast that almost put out the candle.

"Toad sounds too sick to go anywhere but to bed," Ernie said.

"We don't have time," Mizjoan replied. "I have grave news. Klaven's army has taken Covenstead."

"What?! I thought you had the situation under control!" Ernie growled.

"They had guns. Greasers were with them. We had to fall back. Now that they've seized the old fortress, they've got their foot in the door on the rest of Street-Corner Earth."

"This news is grave indeed," Skulk pronounced. "I'll give Toad some of my special cold medicine. He'll be ready to travel in no time."

Throughout the entire exchange, Toad's eyes never strayed far from Mizjoan's face. He feared the coming hostilities, but some wild impulse drew him to the gorgeous redhead. His mouth was hanging slack as he regarded her, but with fever eating him up he was past caring.

The Radiclib leader must have been aware of his attention. "You do look ill, comrade, but we sorely need your services. We will rest overnight here. The trip back to Camp Hoffman tomorrow won't be too strenuous. Once we're there, Comrade Mungweasle will see to the arrangements until you're on your feet again." She smiled at Ernie, who avoided her.

Chapter Fourteen

Toad sat under the flap of his small tent, taking a swig from a bottle of Skulk's medicine. It tasted of honey and mint, and possessed a strong alcoholic bite. He'd been up for over an hour, after violent visions had again haunted his dreams. Since then he'd sat restlessly, watching a bank of ground fog slowly advance across the sleeping camp. The only light came from several campfires burning in the Radiclib quarter. He considered lighting a pipe, but thought better of it. It felt good just to be able to suck in the cool night air without sneezing. The medicine had cleared his lungs and nose, but it left him a little groggy. He'd fallen asleep right after the meeting, missed supper, and had awakened long after lights out. Now, even with a few extra sips of the medicine, all he could do was sit and watch the fog tendrils advance like swamp ghosts.

A horse whinnied in the distance. Toad looked up and caught sight of a dim figure moving through the fog. A horseman rode stealthily out of the mist into the circle of firelight. The pipesmith gasped when he saw the rider's long white robes and tall peaked hood. He was carrying a strange flag in one hand, a blue star-spangled swastika on a red field. In the other he held a long bayoneted rifle. The stranger whistled softly and other robed figures melted out of the fog to join him. Somehow, a band of Whiteriders had made its way through miles of heavily guarded Radiclib territory and was now riding into the center of camp.

Toad had never seen Whiteriders before, but he had heard plenty about them, as had every Freakling. They inhabited many of the scariest stories parents told their children on Halloween Eve. A secret within a secret, the Whiteriders were a strange and ancient brotherhood. Some said it was they who really ruled the Great Whitelands. They were above all laws, accountable to no one except the Fascist ruler, Klaven Thinarm. Murder, crucifixion and torture were their main delights. Even other Fascists feared the robed marauders and gave them anything they wanted.

Toad's heart pounded with fear. "We're under attack!" he cried out, without thinking. Several small explosions went off nearby, filling the air with the stench of sulfur as tongues of flame jabbed through the fog. Although the sound hadn't been heard in these woods in half a millennium, he knew instinctively what the explosions were—guns. He slipped out of the tent, dropped into the nearest trench and hurried toward Skulk's tent.

As he made his way along the floor of the dark slippery trench the smell of the fog-dampened peat assailed his senses. It was overpowering, and it reminded him of the eerie story Skulk had told about Maynard being five hundred years old. Toad shivered. The world was most certainly going mad—immortals, Dark Men, and now Whiteriders bearing ancient engines of destruction and searching for more. It felt as if the fever was still upon him, giving his nightmares dimension and shape. Trembling, he ran as though Old Charlie was right on his tail.

Above the trench, a wall of fire rose behind the curtain of fog. Toad heard frightened screams and the desperate sound of swords clashing. Peering over the lip of the trench he caught a fleeting glimpse of a mounted Whiterider bearing down on a fleeing Digger girl. The rider whooped and cheered as he swung a spiked iron ball on the end of a chain, high over his head. A flight of arrows streaked over the trench, followed seconds later by a pair of deadly frisbee discs. The rider fell. Amid the persistent screaming and the clamor of frenzied combat another round of explosions filled the night air.

The sounds of battle were all around. Toad made his way through the maze of trenches. Suddenly, a riderless horse leaped over the trench, nearly decapitating him with its flailing hooves. An instant later, an arrow embedded itself in the peat mere inches above his head. As he rounded a corner in the maze and entered an area where the trenches grew wider and deeper, he looked up to see one of the Whiterider's great crosses stuck in the ground, blazing above him. At the foot of the cross lay the crumpled body of one of the riders, a broken pick protruding from the middle of his back. His robes were soaked with blood, and where their hems lay closest to the cross, they were starting to smolder and burn. A shrill scream sounded behind him, silenced immediately by an explosion. Gasping for breath and feeling pain in his calves, Toad kept running.

Fire erupted off to his left, in the area where he knew the main cluster of tents to be. Suddenly Toad feared for Skulk and Ernie. As he poked his head above the lip of the trench, something whizzed past into the peat sending up a spray of earth that landed on Toad's hair and face. As the flames grew higher he thought he saw something lying huddled near the trench, something covered by a patched, green cloak. Whatever it was, it didn't move.

An explosion, on his right and way too close, showered dirt over him. He whipped around and saw a burly figure in a red and black plaid coat staggering toward him out of the fog. The starred swastika flag of the enemy, erected on a pole above the trench, stood unfurled in the rising breeze. Time seemed to freeze as the stricken man slowly pitched forward into a puddle. The pipesmith groaned aloud when he turned the body over and saw that it was Sasquatch.

The Hunter's face was ashen and his coat was soaked with blood. A half dozen crossbow bolts protruded from his chest and stomach. Sasquatch gurgled unintelligibly and reached out to Toad with one bloodied hand. His small button eyes were glazing over like rime ice on a pond. He tried to sit up and spat out a torrent of blood. The hand clutched at Toad. Shocked, fighting back a well of tears, Toad took it and held on tight.

"I-it's all right." Tears came as Toad heard himself babble, "Y-you're gonna be all right. I'll take care of you, Sas. You're gonna be okay."

Sasquatch smiled faintly and died. The pipesmith shuddered. As his tears waned, he felt cold anger growing inside. He placed his scarf over his friend's face, then slipped Sasquatch's huge hunting knife out of its scabbard and made his way down the trench toward the sound of the heaviest fighting.

Fierce battles raged throughout the bog. Toad saw small parties of Radiclibs and Whiteriders struggling to drive each other off. On his right, he saw a Whiterider shoot a young Radiclib, only to be taken out a moment later by a Digger with a bow and arrow. Flames burned high into the sky on the far side of the camp. He was irresistibly drawn there. Whispering a prayer, Toad slipped up out of the trench and headed through the fog to where the fires burned brightest, the hunting knife clutched tightly in his hand.

Toad saw Mizjoan before she saw him. She was standing on a small rise away from the trenches, clutching a misshapen black sword and watching a row of burning tents as if studying something just out of his range of vision. The pipesmith's heart quickened at the sight of her. Her long, auburn hair hung loose to her waist and her face was flushed with the excitement of battle. As lovely as he'd thought her before, she seemed almost ethereal now. He sneezed and felt his nose filling. He quickly extracted the bottle of cold medicine from his pocket, uncorked it, and drained it in several quick gulps. He tossed the bottle aside and started up the rise. Something moving in the mists behind Mizjoan caught his attention and he shrank back into the shadows.

With a yell that seemed impossible to have come from a human throat, a huge Whiterider leaped out of the fog. Brandishing a long, curved saber, he chuckled evilly as he advanced on Mizjoan. The saber whistled through the air like a scythe through hay, but Mizjoan stood her ground. As the rider swung at her, Mizjoan blocked his stroke with her black sword. Sparks flew as the two weapons met. The Whiterider growled as Mizjoan parried and jabbed, wielding her heavy sword as easily as she might a baton. He retreated several steps, and then charged at her with renewed ferocity.

Toad fought to control his breathing as the two combatants circled one another. The brandy-laden medicine was working on him; he was sweating in spite of the cold and damp. Sasquatch's knife felt light in Toad's hand. The blade seemed to have a life of its own, thrusting and parrying in unison with the two warriors as they resumed their dance of death, slashing at each other in a whirlwind of flashing steel.

The Whiterider had the obvious advantage. Not only was he huge, towering a good six inches over Mizjoan, but his saber was longer and lighter than her clunky iron sword. Still, the Radiclib woman met him blow for blow, spinning out of his way, then driving forward, as the clashing of their swords resonated on the misty bog like the furious ringing of bells. Toad was amazed by Mizjoan's tirelessness and ferocity, and awestruck by the look on her face as she drove at her opponent.

Toad's nose twitched, but the sneeze subsided before betraying him. Gripping the knife tightly, he crouched down and slipped closer to Mizjoan and the huge rider.

Mizjoan fought savagely, her short sword jabbing frenetically at the white-robed giant. Then, the Whiterider made a sudden jab at Mizjoan's stomach; she did a quick half-turn to avoid the oncoming blade and lost her footing on the crumbly peat. She struggled to break her fall, flailing helplessly as she landed on her back in the mire. Her sword flew out of her hand and fell at the Whiterider's feet. He laughed as he kicked it aside and moved in, saber raised over his hooded head.

Toad reacted immediately. Brandishing his knife he ran up the bank and threw himself at the Whiterider.

"Stop!" he yelled as he grabbed the huge rider around the neck with one arm and swung at him with his knife. "Leave her alone!"

The Whiterider grunted in surprise, but shook Toad off as easily as he would a puppy. The pipesmith landed on the ground between the rider and Mizjoan. He scrambled to his feet and stood facing his towering opponent, the knife still locked in his hand.

For a moment, Freak and Fascist stood regarding each other; then the Whiterider laughed, his cold blue eyes glinting behind the eyeholes of his hood.

"Well, well. What's this?" he chuckled evilly. "A little faggit come to save his mommy? Come here, longhair. I'll make short work of you and your slut, too."

"Don't be so sure," Toad heard himself say. His fingers tightened on the grip of his knife as he locked eyes with the Whiterider. He felt hatred welling up inside him like hot bile.

The glare in the Whiterider's eyes hardened. Toad jumped aside just in time to avoid a saber thrust that would have disemboweled him. In the harsh light of the burning tents, with screams and gunshots echoing in the background, the robed giant seemed twelve feet tall.

The Whiterider growled deep in his throat. Courage swelled into the pipesmith's veins with inebriating warmth. Matching the rider's growl, he raised his knife to attack.

Toad's moment of glory never came. The Whiterider suddenly arched backwards with a horrid shriek as an age-blackened sword point burst out of his chest. His robes smeared with blood, the rider lurched forward and toppled to the ground. In his place, Mizjoan stood, clutching her dripping sword.

The fire of victory burning in the Radiclib leader's eye warmed Toad. Overwhelmed by a surge of new and conflicting emotions, he threw down his knife and embraced her. A moment later they were at arm's length, embarrassed and confused.

"I … I'm sorry," Toad stammered.

"Quite all right, Comrade Toad," Mizjoan said matter-of-factly. "You saved my life, you know. Maybe I should have been the one hugging you."

Toad looked down at the sprawled body of the Whiterider. He was shaking slightly. "I think you saved mine as well. I'm new at this fighting business."

"Saving each others' bourgeois butts is something that happens from time to time in this profession. You never take it for granted, though."

"I suppose not." Toad retrieved Sasquatch's knife and stuck it in his belt.

Mizjoan wiped her sword on the fallen rider's robes. "You know, Comrade Toad, I'm really enjoying this conversation, but I don't believe it's wise to continue it at this moment."

Toad agreed. Together, they made their way toward the center of camp. Except for a muffled shriek in the distance, it had become deathly still. There was no more shouting or gunfire.

"It's over," she whispered, touching him lightly on the arm.

As they passed the smoldering ruins of the Digger encampment a sudden, boisterous round of cheering split the silence. Mizjoan clutched Toad's arm impulsively. Her handsome aristocratic face was flushed with excitement. "Those are my people," she breathed. "We've won!"

Mizjoan let go of his arm and raced off toward the sound of cheering. He started to follow her, but turned back. Everything that had happened since he'd stepped out of his tent suddenly pressed in on him. He needed time to clear his head. Like a sleepwalker he stumbled past the remains of an overturned wagon. Beside the wagon a group of Radiclibs were amusing themselves with the starred swastika flag he'd seen earlier. They were tearing the flag into victory headbands, oblivious to the enemy dead scattered about them. Beyond the soldiers Skulk's tent, one of the few to escape the Whiterider raid, had been turned into a provisional hospital. The pipesmith passed a pair of Radiclib medics bearing a stretcher between them. On it lay Sam Smoot, covered with his patched green cloak. Behind them came another pair, their burden covered by a bloodied Hunter's jacket.

"It's too late for them," Toad said, oblivious to the tears starting to form in the corners of his eyes. "Why are you taking them to the infirmary?"

"The dead lie in the next tent over," one of the medics explained. "Five of our people are there, seven of yours."

"Yeah," his partner interrupted. "But the enemy paid for their butchery. Not one of those bed-sheeted bastards made it out of this bog tonight."

Toad looked down, studying the charred refuse scattered on the spongy ground. The breeze brought a stench of burning and death. "Tell me," he said, not daring to meet their eyes. "Is there a Freak in there? Tall, wearing a long coat and... "

The question did not have to be answered. About fifty feet away Ernie and Skulk emerged from the shadows. Skulk was walking with a makeshift crutch and Ernie's left hand was bandaged. Toad nodded to the medics and ran off to intercept the two Diggers. In the east the sky was streaking with the iron gray of dawn.

Chapter Fifteen

The seat of Ernie's wagon was narrow and hard. It moved about under Toad unpredictably as the wagon jounced over the rock-strewn roads of Paranoia Flats. But uncomfortable though it was, it seemed like a haven of safety after the horror of two nights past. The pipesmith craned his neck to look back over the convoy of wagons and horses strung out over the Flats. He was glad to see that Fetid Bog had long since receded from view, leaving only a line of stark trees visible on the western horizon. Soon even the treeline would fade, as they continued on to Camp Hoffman, somewhere miles ahead. Someday his memories of the Whiterider raid would fade too, but he knew that would take a long time.

The difficult work of the past few days, rebuilding the camp and preparing the excavated weapons for transport to Leftopia, had helped to keep his mind off the nightmare he'd been through. Skulk's medicine also played no small role to that end. Now his cold was gone and his mind was beginning to put the carnage in the past.

Suddenly the seat dropped away beneath him as the wagon hit a particularly deep rut. Toad flew forward, and only quick thinking saved him from flying over the front of the wagon.

"Dammit, Ernie!" he sputtered. "Can't you keep this thing on the road instead of in it?"

The herbalist grinned at him. He held the reins with his right hand while his bandaged left rested on his knee. His top hat was cocked low on his head, shading his eyes. "I'm surprised you noticed, Toad. You've been off in a daze for hours."

"I've been thinking, that's all."

"I know what you mean. We've both lost friends. Hell, I've known Sam Smoot and Sasquatch for years. Now they're gone, just like that."

Toad nodded in mute agreement. His eyes drifted toward Mizjoan, riding at the head of the column. He was mesmerized as the sun played through her long auburn hair, turning it to burnished copper. Ernie saw him staring and poked Toad playfully in the ribs.

"Ah-ha. It's Joannie you've got on your mind, isn't it? You'd better forget her, pal. She's a cold one."

"As if you'd know."

Ernie shrugged. "Believe what you want. I've known her for years and I've never known her to keep a man long. Not that there were that many."

"I've never met a woman like her, Ernie. I'd like to get to know her a little better, that's all. Besides, I've caught her looking at me a couple of times and when our eyes meet she starts smiling. "

"She's grateful to you for saving her life. Nothing more."

"I know. I'm sure that's what it is. But she sure has a great smile."

Ernie looked at Toad, sighed, and tipped his hat back out of his eyes.

"Years back I entertained similar thoughts about Joannie. She had just come into power after the death of her father, Righton Berkeley, and I was a friend she needed and couldn't find among her own people. After a while I wanted to be more than friends and she laughed at me. Me—Ernie Mungweasle. So you see, I'm telling you, get those thoughts out of your head right now."

"Maybe you weren't her type."

The herbalist shrugged. "That's probably true, but neither are you. She's a Radiclib, Toad, and a Radiclib would never consider messing with a Freak. We're an inferior people as far as they're concerned."

"Sounds like sour grapes to me."

"Her people are warriors, ours aren't. To them we're weak and unmanly. Check out the way the Leftopians act even to us Diggers. Sure, they're civil enough, but you can sense the underlying contempt."

Toad turned his head, watching the Radiclib horsemen riding past Ernie's wagon. True, there was a certain arrogance in the way they sat astride their great warhorses, but it seemed justified in Toad's eyes. They had comported themselves well in the battle at the bog and they knew it. Mizjoan seemed the proudest of all. She rode with her shoulders arched back, her mane of auburn hair flowing out behind her like a pennant.

"I can't believe they're like that," he insisted.

"Think what you will," Ernie remarked. "I'm too tired to argue."

The pipesmith nodded. There had been little sleep for anybody after the attack; the wounded had to be cared for, the dead buried, the Radiclibs burned on pyres. The excavations then began in earnest and Fetid Bog yielded up a good haul. Fifteen hundred flintlock longarms in usable condition and almost as many pistols had been unearthed, most of these from the cache Toad had discovered. There were other prizes as well: two dozen brass cannon barrels and a wide assortment of bullets, molds and

114

powder flasks. It was a find that would make the Fascists stand up and take notice, and he had been instrumental in both finding and protecting the priceless hoard. He smiled and sat up a little straighter on the seat.

Ernie laughed softly from under his hat. "Feelin' kinda cocky, huh?"

"Well, I think I did rather well—in the battle and before."

"That may be, but war is nothing to feel proud about."

"Look, Ernie, I don't want anyone killed any more than you do, but I got a chance to see how cruel and evil the enemy really is. I've run from things long enough. After seeing Sasquatch die, I realized that some battles have to be fought."

"That's true enough. Dylan only knows, the things I've seen over the years have taught me that. Still, killing's nothing to jack up your ego over."

Toad idly stroked the edge of the wagon seat. "Come on, Ernie. I'm not letting things go to my head, but after all, I was the one who found the major weapons cache and saved Mizjoan's life."

"Yeah."

"Then I don't know why you're ragging on me. Wasn't it you who talked me into this shit to begin with?"

"I asked you to come on a trip with me. I didn't expect you to get into any battles."

"But I did."

Ernie turned his head. The look in his ocean-gray eyes was unreadable. "I wonder if Sasquatch or any of the others would have applauded your attitude, Brother Hero."

"My attitude? What about yours? I'm starting to think you're jealous."

"Holy Bob, do you think you're the only one that's ever done anything brave?" Ernie replied angrily. "I could wack on with stories of my own, and they'd pale into insignificance beside Joan's or any other real warrior's."

"Well, maybe so, but..."

"There are no buts, Toad. I know what I'm talking about, and I can guess what's going through your mind. You've got your first whiff of battle and adventure, and it's gone to your head with its exhilarating scent. Just like when somebody across the room lights up a bowl of fine Gonecian Bluegrass and your nose has to follow the smoke. In this case, though, the rest of the bowl isn't as good as the first toke. Think of the carnage you've seen and multiply it by a hundred. Wait'll you see the real horror: heads lopped off, limbs scattered over a battlefield, entrails oozing out of a dying soldier. Maybe you'll change your tune then."

Toad didn't reply. The conviction in Ernie's voice begged no argument.

"Next time, you could be the one laid out on a slab. Keep that in mind, Toad."

The pipesmith nodded solemnly, watching as a Digger wagon piled high with crates rumbled past them. He suddenly felt cold as he watched the laughing young soldiers aboard the wagon, playfully brandishing their gleaming new weapons. He knew the soldiers would soon be at Camp Hoffman, preparing for coming battles. He wondered how many of them would be alive to see year's end. As he watched the line of horsemen ahead of the wagon ride over the top of the rise, he reflected on what Ernie had said. Next time it *could* be him lying in a trench somewhere with his life's blood running out onto the ground.

Suddenly the soldiers aboard the arms wagon began to shout and wave their weapons over their heads. Ernie's wagon topped the rise and Toad could see the cause of their jubilation. In contrast to the arid wastes of Paranoia Flats, the brown stubbled fields that lay before them seemed lush and inviting. In the distance, barely visible on the eastern horizon, was a great, walled city. Cheering wildly, most of the Radiclib horsemen broke rank and spurred their mounts onward, passing Ernie's lumbering wagon as they made for the city, though it was still many miles away. Toad knew that he was looking at Camp Hoffman, fortress capital of Leftopia. Soon most of the horsemen were gone, leaving only a small contingent to escort the wagons along the wide dirt road.

It was over an hour before Ernie's wagon approached Camp Hoffman's main gate. Toad watched in awe as the towering city walls grew steadily closer and he could make out details, like the banners flying above the battlements and the armed guards patrolling their posts. As Ernie snapped the reins urging his horse forward, the wagons passed the gates and rumbled into the heart of the city. Toad gawked about, spellbound. This was to be his new home for a while, this armed and teeming fortress—and the starting place for whatever fate the future held in store.

Once they came to a stop, Toad took his pack and started to climb off the seat.

"Here, you'd better take this and bone up on it," Ernie said, thrusting the copy of *Cruickshank's* at Toad. "We'll be needing it soon."

"Why don't you read it, Mungweasle?" Toad shot back.

"I have, but there weren't enough pictures for me," Ernie answered. As the herbalist stepped down from the wagon, he added, "You're the real scholar, Toad. You will get more from it than I ever could."

"Thanks," Toad said as he took the book and put it under his arm. "You're a real pal."

Ernie smiled and went about taking care of the horse and the wagon. Toad gazed about in wonder at the vast bulk of Commiemartyr Hall and the long rows of barracks that surrounded it. In spite of how he'd felt before, now he was just worn and hungry. All he could think of was a meal, a hot bath, and a decent night's sleep.

Shortly after Ernie left for a meeting with Mizjoan, some of the young soldiers that Toad had met at Fetid Bog invited him to share a meal with them at the main commissary. He stowed his pack in the room assigned to him, and hurried to meet them.

Chapter Sixteen

Toad lay still under the covers, not wanting to move. Through his bedroom window he could see the sun rising over the row of low barracks on the other side of the courtyard. He had been tossing and turning in his bed for over an hour, suffering from an iron-hard erection that was not responding to his most deliberate ministrations. He cursed it, angered at its unwillingness to either cooperate or go away. Women! They were the last thing he wanted to concern himself with, yet he'd dreamed about Mizjoan last night as he had the night before. He remembered how she'd looked yesterday at the General Muster, in her tight dress uniform and silver eye patch, addressing the people of Camp Hoffman. He remembered the excitement in her face when she'd told her followers about the Fetid Bog gun cache, and the special smile she'd given him when she announced that he and Ernie would head up the arms restoration and training project.

The pipesmith muttered to himself and tried to sit up straight in bed. His head hammered; he'd smoked weed smoked all day yesterday, to try and ease the headache he was suffering after a night of drinking with the young Radiclib soldiers. Moodily, he stared at the clutter on his bedside table. The copy of *Cruickshank's* was there, open face down where he'd left off reading. Next to it was a writing kit and a sheath of note paper. The paper was weighted down with a powdery yellow stone. Toad looked at the stone blearily, trying to recall where he'd acquired it. He dimly remembered it falling off the back of a wagon that had almost run him down in the street two nights ago. The wagon had been packed to overflowing with captured Fascist supplies. The funny thing was, he never remembered picking up the rock. Then again, there wasn't too much he did remember about the last couple of days except smoking his brains out, and reading and re-reading *Cruickshank's*. Shuffling through the papers Toad found his weedpipe, still filled from last night. For a moment he considered lighting it and then, muttering again, kicked aside the blankets and struggled to his feet.

Cold air assaulted his body immediately, bringing him to full wakefulness. He smiled as his erection subsided. Though he was feeling better than he had, Toad still moved carefully as he went about his toilet, cautious of his self-inflicted headache. The night before last, when Ernie and Skulk had gone to their meeting with Mizjoan, he should have gone straight to bed. He hadn't, of course, and now he had more to contend with than just the last vestiges of a cold.

At first he had enjoyed partying with the young Radiclib soldiers. Their weed and wine were good, their stories even better. He felt that after the battle at Fetid Bog, he fit right in with them, a warrior among warriors. But as the evening had worn on and the stories became more horrific, he had paid more attention to his bottle and his pipe than his companions. His one small act of bravery paled beside some of the things the soldiers had experienced in their numerous border clashes with Fascist raiders. After a while he'd excused himself, returned to his quarters and passed into fitful slumber.

As the morning brightened, Toad donned a fresh set of clothes, tucked *Cruickshank's* and a sheaf of notes into his coat pockets, and plodded down the stairs to the street. Skulk and Ernie had been busying themselves setting up a workshop in a barn about a block over, and today was the day Toad would start to help Ernie with their project. Though the way he was feeling, Toad wasn't sure that he was ready to be anything except the town drunk.

Toad's room was located above some stables, so it was no surprise to him that he passed a few young Radiclib horsewomen on his way out the door. Though all quite attractive, none of the lithe young warriors came close to matching Mizjoan's proud good looks. Still, he had to smile when a tall, leggy brunette eyed him flirtatiously as she passed.

It was chilly out on the street, and though it was still early, Camp Hoffman was coming alive. A six-horse armored troop carrier rumbled in front of Toad as he started to cross the main thoroughfare. One street over a group of soldiers marched double-file. Half a block further down he paused for a few moments to watch a half-dozen sweating Radiclibs wheeling a ballista down the street. The huge, wheel-mounted crossbow seemed to have a hard time moving on its axle. The tortured squealing of its bearings testified to its long disuse. Finally, the soldiers gave up and went to work on the axle with a pot of grease. Mindful of his commitment, Toad hurried on his way.

The workshop was easy enough to find. Ernie's horse and wagon were tied up in front of the dilapidated barn and someone, probably Skulk, had painted a Digger shovel emblem on the door. The herbalist opened the door on Toad's first knock. He looked fit and well rested. For some reason, this irritated Toad.

"C'mon in," Ernie said cheerfully. "Looks like you've had a rough night."

"Yeah. Guess I didn't sleep very well."

Ernie showed Toad to a rocking chair by a cluttered worktable and set about pouring him a cup of coffee from a pot heating over the brazier at the center of the room. "Been having dreams about your Dark Man again?"

"No, not last night. There's just a lot on my mind lately."

"Yeah, I've been meaning to talk to you about that. I was acting pretty smug the other day. I apologize."

Toad laughed, though it came out as a dry, wasted chuckle. "Maybe you were, but I think I'm the one who should apologize. Actually, partying with the Radiclib soldiers a couple of nights ago set me straight on a few things. I never want to experience some of the things those guys have. Just listening to them gave me the creeps."

"A soldier's life is hard one, Toad. Still, I'm the one that talked you into this jaunt. I should have known it would affect you."

Toad accepted the cup Ernie offered him and took a tentative sip. The coffee was good, and hot. "Oh, I haven't changed much. It's just that I've never been in battle before and…"

"I know. Well, that's water over the dam."

The herbalist poured himself a cup of coffee and sat down on a barrel. He started playing with the clutter on the worktable, re-arranging the stoppered jars, gun parts and writing materials. Taking a sip of coffee, he toyed with a mortar and pestle. "Toad, now that you're back in the swing, we have to get our collective asses in gear. We're in a hell of a bad situation. If we can't figure out how to make these guns work, we and the Society are going to look awfully stupid."

"What do you mean?"

"Joannie's an old friend and has needed the Society's talents in the past," Ernie said, taking another sip. "But, she still doesn't trust us. Radiclibs have a self-reliant attitude, bordering on paranoia. Secret societies are anathema to them. Except for developing an exploding powder, Leftopia has perfectly good weaponsmiths who could be handling this project, but since we proposed it, she expects us to make it work. The fate of Street-Corner Earth depends on what we do here and yet, everyone's dicking around with politics. That pisses me off."

Toad scratched his beard nervously. "I find it difficult to believe that Mizjoan would play that kind of game."

"Joannie's a great woman; she doesn't see it as a game. She just thinks like a Radiclib," Ernie muttered, turning his attention to a collection of chemicals on a workbench in front of him.

The pipesmith pulled out his copy of *Cruickshank's* and laid it on the table. He picked up one of the flintlock rifles lying on the floor next to his rocker. Taking a screwdriver from the bench, Toad began adjusting the rifle's lock mechanism, playing with the vise-like hammer that held the flint until it produced a satisfactory spark when he dry-fired the piece.

"Everything seems to be in working order," he announced.

Ernie shook his head sadly. "It's not the guns we have to concern ourselves with. For the most part they seem mechanically sound but we can't test them until we've concocted some exploding powder."

Toad felt a moment of slight panic, as if he were being tested. His copy of *Cruickshank's* made mention of gunpowder, of course, but said little of its chemical composition. He looked at the stoppered jars lining the workbench and at the box of mineral samples sitting nearby. He felt sudden irritation at Ernie, who simply remained seated and offered no assistance. "You're the Clear Light Society's representative. You got any ideas?" he asked.

"I only saw it compounded once, and that wasn't under the best of conditions. But I'm sure I got the formula."

Toad watched eagerly as Ernie rummaged through the rock samples. He almost laughed aloud when his friend selected one and sniffed it before tapping away at it with a small hammer. Ernie then broke the stone into small pieces and, selecting a large iron mortar, attempted to grind them into powder. Toad found the sound of iron against rock unnerving, though it didn't seem to bother Ernie in the least. After a few minutes the herbalist looked up.

"What's the next step?" Toad asked.

"We mix up a few things. The proportions should be easy to remember."

"What do you mean 'should be'? I thought you knew the recipe."

Ernie waved one hand lazily and shrugged. He sifted the rock dust into a wooden bowl, then unstoppered two of the bottles and poured their contents in with it. "Charcoal," he explained. "It's kind of a base. This other stuff is niter. When it's all mixed together, just add a flame and poof! Instant explosion."

Toad nodded. Was it really going to be that easy?

When Ernie was done stirring, he transferred a small portion of his mixture to another bowl and set it on the floor, far from the worktable. He took a long splint and touched it to a candle until it glowed and caught fire. "Would you like the honors?" he asked.

The pipesmith shook his head. "No, go ahead. You know what to expect."

Grinning, Ernie moved toward the bowl. "Better block your ears," he advised, touching the splint to the powder.

Toad did as he was told. As seconds ticked by, the splint burned down and dropped into the powder, but nothing happened.

"Oh well," Ernie said and shrugged. "I guess I got the wrong proportions. Back to the mixing table."

"What happened to your formula?"

"I've still got it, but the old black witch doctor, Dreadlock, who gave me the formula, gave it to me in the form of a verse. I watched him work it out only once, and that was in a badly lighted room."

"In other words, you recall everything—but not exactly."

The herbalist tugged at his pendulous black mustache. "Something like that."

"Well, why don't you recite the verse? Maybe we can puzzle it out together."

"Maybe we can. It isn't great poetry, not right up there with Harriman or Kermit Badmoon, but it's easy enough to remember. It went like this:

> There's a funky little recipe that I know.
> It came from way back a long time ago.
> So, if you want to say, 'Burn Baby, Burn',
> Getting Salty Pete should be your first concern.
> The next thing you need is wood from a tree.
> Then burn it up good 'till it's black like me.
> Add another 'gredient and grind it up slow.
> Don't do it right and that baby will blow.
> And, when you're all done, it shake you to the bone,
> As long as you've added that Stinky Stone.
> Now, if you want it wrote down, forget it sucka,
> 'Cause you just one honky, white-ass, motherfucker."

Toad laughed. "I see what you mean about the poetry. I can't make anything out of it, except burned wood must be charcoal."

"It is, and 'Salty Pete' is niter. 'Stinky Stone' has me baffled at the moment, but I'm working on it."

"Correction, Ernie; *we're* working on it. Hand me that mortar and pestle."

Working feverishly, they tried one mixture after another until the shadows grew long outside the barn's dusty windows and the air was thick with the reek of half-burned chemicals. Toad allowed himself a small chuckle several times, as he watched the herbalist fume and swear over defective formulas. Apparently Ernie knew no more about exploding powder than he did.

The next day went no better, nor the day after that. Ernie started coming in hours before Toad and staying long after the pipesmith left. One night he slept on the floor underneath the worktable, using his coat for a blanket and wadded grain bags for a pillow. He grew haggard and muttered to himself constantly. Often he'd sit for hours, staring at the clutter on the table and sighing. For all of this, he accomplished little except for seriously depleting his supplies of niter and charcoal. He became bitter and frequently snapped at Toad.

The morning of the fifth day in Camp Hoffman dawned extraordinarily cold and windy, even for November. On his way to the barn Toad stopped by the fire in the courtyard outside of Commiemartyr Hall and watched the sun rise over the parapets, as he put off going to work as long as possible.

When Toad finally did get to the barn, he found Ernie busy at work as usual, muttering to himself as he played among his chemicals and mineral samples. Unbuttoning his coat, Toad was just about to stoke up the fire when he heard a rap on the door. He opened it to reveal Comrade Rudy and several companions clad in long gray hooded cloaks.

"Good morning, comrade," Rudy said stiffly. "I'm here for a progress report."

Toad fidgeted, not quite sure what to say. "Well ... uh, we're progressing."

"May I step in?" It was more of a demand than a request.

Before the pipesmith could answer, Rudy was inside, leaving his two companions at the door. He strutted past Toad, making no attempt at introductions. "I'd like to see a demonstration of your exploding powder," he said, walking over to where Ernie was working. "Comrade Leader Mizjoan grows impatient. She wonders if you're on schedule."

Toad followed, trying to study the Radiclib's face, half hidden in the shadowed hood. "I wasn't aware there was a schedule," he replied.

"Regardless of what you thought, comrade, we must have the powder now. Fascists are massing at Covenstead. More pour in through Ripoff Pass every day. Refugees are fleeing the area into Sativa Fields. Soon the enemy will attack Rivertown, maybe even Camp Hoffman itself."

Ernie looked up from his work and glowered, but said nothing. It was up to Toad to deal with Rudy.

"We are aware of the situation," the pipesmith offered. "But we won't have anything for you for a couple of days."

Rudy shook his head. "A couple of days! You've had most of a week already. We must be the ones to attack first, at Klaven's Keep. We can't afford any more delays. Some of us on the People's Council think we'd be better off doing this work ourselves."

For the first time, Ernie spoke. "Rudy, we're busting our balls here."

"As I was saying," Rudy continued, "Mizjoan is not pleased with this situation. You have until tomorrow to produce results. If not, this project comes under the control of the People's Council."

"C'mon, Rudy."

"We desperately need results, Comrade Mungweasle."

Ernie smiled, though it was a forced effort. "These things take time, Rudy. As a military man, you should know how much work it takes to develop new weapons."

"I do. Our technicians perfected the M-11 crossbow in three days. If you two had been at it, it would have taken a year."

The herbalist drummed his fingers on the table. His face was flushed with anger. "Don't worry," he said evenly. "You'll have your precious powder."

"See that we do." Rudy exited, slamming the door behind him.

Toad glanced at Ernie, but the herbalist was already back at work grinding charcoal. "You're the man who said we'd have powder by now," Toad blurted out. "Haven't you figured out what that 'Stinky Stone' is yet?"

Ernie looked up. Anger crackled in his gray eyes.

"Robert H. Dylan, Toad!" Ernie raged, slamming his fist down on the table. "I only saw it done once, and that was hurriedly. When I began to recreate it I realized that I didn't know what Stinky Stone looked like."

"Don't you have any idea?"

"No, none. Looking back on it, it was as if old Dreadlock didn't want me to see it. The light was poor in his workshop and he kept his back to me a lot of the time. I actually never saw the stuff."

"That doesn't make any sense."

Ernie shrugged. He looked more relaxed, but weary. "It does if the Blackfolk didn't really want me to know the secret. Maybe to them any White, even a Digger, would constitute a threat."

Toad shook his head and stalked off toward the nearest window. "Great. Where does that leave us?"

Ernie made no reply. Toad stood for some time, gazing out the dusty pane at a group of soldiers standing around a small fire burning in the vacant lot next door. The flames seemed to entice and mock him, and he stared at them entranced, ignoring Ernie. He felt as if everything was sliding away from him—Ernie's friendship, Mizjoan's approval, and his own self-respect. The fire flickered and danced. He stared hard at it, wishing it could yield up solutions to his problems. The door opened and closed behind him as Ernie exited the barn, but Toad's eyes never left the flames.

Chapter Seventeen

Mizjoan fastened the top button of her best dress tunic, regarding her reflection in the bedroom mirror. She straightened the short, stand-up collar and ran her fingers through her thick auburn mane. Dissatisfied, she took a brush from the bureau and stroked her hair until it shimmered in the flickering candlelight.

"Not bad for an old broad," she commented, studying herself from several angles in the mirror. "Not bad at all."

Mizjoan adjusted Ploughshare's scabbard at her waist. She wondered why she was taking so much effort to look good; there would be no man at the meeting who she particularly cared to impress. She shrugged at her reflection, liking the way her broad shoulders rose and fell. Probably just a phase I'm going through, she decided. Satisfied that the ancient sword was secure in its scabbard, she glanced once more at the mirror and walked out of the room.

Mizjoan's top officers were already seated around the great oak table in the council chamber when she strode in. She walked to her customary seat at the head of the table, nodding as three generals and one colonel rose to salute her. One of the generals, a stout middle-aged man with bristling muttonchops, remained standing after the others returned to their seats.

"Yes?" Mizjoan said, eyeing the fat man. "What can I do for you, Comrade Field Marshal Dillon?"

Dillon folded his pudgy arms across his bulging stomach. "I wish for you to know that I don't support your decision to attack Klaven's Keep."

Mizjoan regarded Dillon with a cold eye. The field marshal was a pompous ass who'd wrangled his way onto her staff only through his many connections on the People's Council. He frequently boasted that he was descended from Bob Dylan, but except for the similarity in names, there was no connection, as all but the most naive knew.

"Your opinion wasn't requested yet," she commented. "Please sit down."

With a great huff, Dillon took his seat. Mizjoan smiled at the other generals—young, dashing Starkweather and old, grizzled Prolemkin. Prolemkin's youthful aide, Colonel Kerk, met her glance and looked away.

"You all know what this meeting is about, comrades," she said, gesturing to a map of Great East Lake on the wall behind her.

The officers nodded. The impending attack on Klaven's Keep had been a topic of discussion around Camp Hoffman for several days now. Already war ships were being readied at the Guevarraville shipyards, and long-range ballistas were being moved into the swamps along the lake's western shore.

"The Fascist threat is building daily," Mizjoan continued. "Couriers have already been sent to the Downeast capital at Tinker's Dam to enlist aid in a possible pincer attack against Covenstead, once the Keep has fallen."

Dillon snorted. "Fat chance of any help from them. You can't seriously expect much from a gutless bunch of farmers and fishermen. You might as well try to enlist Oldhips or Freaks."

"I told you to withhold your opinions until they're asked for," Mizjoan flared. Dylan's Bones, was it her imagination or was the fat man being more obnoxious than usual? If it weren't for his support among the more conservative element of Camp Hoffman, she'd have tossed him off the council years ago.

"Comrade Leader's right," sputtered old Prolemkin, as Kerk helped him to his feet. He shook a palsied fist at Dillon. "You're way too negative. All you young people are today."

"Not *all* young people are, General Prolemkin," Starkweather corrected, fingering his elaborate handlebar mustache. "But I do agree with you on this. You are a doomsayer, Dillon. You have no positive input."

The fat general snorted again. "I'm realistic, not negative, comrades. With or without the help of the Downeasters, we're in a tough bind. An unsuccessful assault on the Keep would be our undoing."

Mizjoan glared at Dillon. Some of what he said was true, but she could not afford his negative attitude. "The assault will be successful," she snapped. "At this very moment Comrades Toad and Mungweasle are working on weapons that will make our victory a certainty."

Dillon was unconvinced. "Those outlanders? Of what possible good are the promises of a Freak and a Digger?"

In spite of herself, Mizjoan scowled. He had her there. It had been five days, and though she trusted both Ernie and Toad, there'd been no results. Whatever the reason, she could only hope Rudy had thrown a scare into them. "Their promises are good enough for me," she said evenly. "And they'll have to be good enough for you. Now, kindly be quiet."

"Comrade Leader, I must…"

"QUIET! NOW!"

Grumbling, the fat general slid lower in his seat as Mizjoan turned back to the map. She unsheathed the silver handled dagger she wore next to her sword and used it to point at a patch of green on the eastern shore of Great East Lake. "Our agents near Darkenwood report few enemy craft on the lake, and those are mostly fishing boats and barges. Comrade Field Marshal-Admiral Starkweather, what is the status of our fleet at Guevarraville?"

Starkweather rose, adjusting the linen scarf at his throat. "All is in readiness, Comrade Leader. We need only exploding powder and the great firetubes that our people brought from Fetid Bog to begin our attack."

"The cannons, you mean? We'll have them soon, I assure you. Comrade Field Marshal-Elder Prolemkin, what about the ballista units I ordered?"

Old Prolemkin shuffled to his feet again, steadying himself with his cane. Kerk moved to help him, but this time the aged general shrugged off his assistance. "Things progress well, Comrade Leader," he rasped. "In several days time we will have tripled our strength along the western shore."

"Over half of our ballista are new Steiner MK-3's," Kerk interjected, "capable of delivering a fifty pound load nearly half a mile with unerring accuracy."

"I'm aware of the Steiner's capabilities, Colonel. I assisted in designing it, if you'll recall."

Embarrassed, Kerk sat down, as did Prolemkin.

Mizjoan returned her dagger to its sheath. She nodded to General Dillon. "Now, Comrade Field Marshal-of-the-Armies, you may speak."

"May I be candid?" Dillon sneered, remaining seated.

"Certainly," said Mizjoan.

Dillon cleared his throat. "In hopes that I could dissuade you from your ruinous plans, I have armies patrolling the western bank of the Sludge. All is secure south to Rivertown. We can attack Covenstead soon. I have men and weapons enough to take it in one siege."

"We'll attack Covenstead in time, comrade. First things first."

"Now, Comrade Leader, not later. At this very moment my troops at Eastside-on-the-Westside are building attack rafts."

Mizjoan stiffened. The fat general was pushing his luck. "I don't recall authorizing you to build rafts."

Dillon grunted. "I didn't think I needed your authorization for every miniscule detail."

"Launching an attack without my say-so hardly constitutes a minor detail, comrade."

"I launched no attack, Comrade Leader. I was merely readying for one." Mizjoan tapped her fingers on the polished tabletop. In the quiet room the clicking of her fingernails on the wood was unnerving. "You're drifting very close to insubordination," she stated.

"I was preparing my troops for a *possible* attack, Comrade Leader." Mizjoan's fist came down on the table with a crash that scattered charts and papers. "Comrade Field Marshal!" she thundered. "I will tolerate no more."

Dillon squinted at Mizjoan, meeting her glare. Their eyes remained locked for several seconds; then he slowly waddled to his feet, his mouth pursed in an effeminate pout.

"Your attack on Klaven's Keep depends on some magical powder," he said haughtily. "Where is this marvelous substance?"

"That's already been explained, comrade."

"I know, but I don't share your faith in these outlanders."

Mizjoan felt her patience eroding rapidly. "Comrade Rudy is due to give me a report on the situation this afternoon," she snapped, standing with her hands balled into fists on her hips. "Would the word of a Radiclib officer ease your concerns?"

Dillon shrugged. "Perhaps, Comrade Leader."

"Then, Comrade Kerk, would you please go and find Comrade Rudy? Tell him to report here as soon as possible."

After Kerk left the room, Mizjoan stood silently regarding her generals for a moment. Dillon's pessimism disturbed her. It was like a disease, and she couldn't afford to see it spread to the rest of her war staff. It infuriated her that Dillon didn't share her confidence in Ernie and Toad. In spite of himself, Ernie Mungweasle was intelligent and ingenious. Toad, from what she'd seen, appeared equally capable. Something about him just seemed right. But General Dillon was another matter. In spite of his flabby body and silly pout, a sizable portion of Camp Hoffman admired him and his political posture. It was even rumored that he had some influence among the barbarous Yipps. The fat man was someone who bore watching closely.

Starkweather fidgeted in his seat, toying nervously with his waxed mustache. The silence in the room seemed to disturb him. "Shall we discuss strategy now?" he asked.

"Certainly," Mizjoan replied. "There are still quite a few details to go over."

Once again Mizjoan unsheathed her dagger and thrust it at a star marked on the map.

"Here we are," she stated. "And over here, on a promontory overlooking the eastern shore of the lake is Klaven's Keep. Intelligence reports that the Keep is now being employed as an enemy command center, apparently switched over from Himmlerburg weeks ago. Whiteriders from as far away as Moloch are massing there, not to mention several divisions of Greasers. All of this signifies that Klaven Thinarm is in residence. But, that is not the worst of the news. Intel also reports that black-robed riders have been seen as well. It's believed that Blackcloak is there now too."

"Ahh, Blackcloak," old Prolemkin muttered. "He is said to be sheer evil—the Old Charlie come to walk the earth again."

Dillon uttered a short, hoarse laugh. "Old wives' tales, Comrade Field Marshal-Elder. This Blackcloak is a poseur, a prancing outlander fop— nothing more."

"A very dangerous fop," Mizjoan said. "He is said to have Klaven and Overhed Kham eating out of his hands. I wouldn't discount the man so easily."

"And I wouldn't make such a big deal out of him."

Mizjoan tapped her dagger on the back of her chair. "This talk is leading us nowhere. Now is the time to storm the Keep. Destroy it and we end this war in a matter of days."

"Yeah, and if we lose, we destroy ourselves," Dillon muttered. "It's better to attack Covenstead and work our way north."

Mizjoan was considering using her dagger as something other than a pointer, when the door opened and Kerk and Rudy entered the room.

"Ahh, Comrade Rudy," she said. "I see Kerk found you. How are things going with our Freak friends?"

The major scowled. He looked around the room at the members of the War Council before speaking. "They are—hard at work, Comrade Leader."

"That's good to hear. How much exploding powder do they have ready for us?"

Rudy shuffled his feet uncomfortably. "None as yet, I'm sorry to report. I've given them a twenty-four hour deadline, but they think that's too short."

Dillon chortled loudly, his small eyes gleaming. "Is there *any* chance these Freaks will have the powder by tomorrow?"

Rudy looked away and shrugged. Starkweather and Prolemkin glanced at one another, then at Dillon, who was rising heavily to his feet.

"I told you the outlanders were undependable," Dillon huffed as he headed toward the door. "Just give the order and we'll march on Covenstead. My troops are ready."

Mizjoan shook her head as she sat down heavily in her chair. "You're all dismissed," she said, turning her head as the room cleared.

She sat for quite some time after the others had left, massaging her temples to drive away the pressure building there.

Chapter Eighteen

The carpet outside Mizjoan's office was threadbare, evidence that Toad wasn't the first to pace back and forth on it fearing the Radiclib leader's wrath. He only wished that Ernie was here to share the moment. He hadn't seen the herbalist since yesterday, when Rudy had returned from a meeting with Mizjoan to tell him that his workshop and its contents were being turned over to the People's Council.

Toad glanced up at the sound of boot heels coming down the hallway. The way they reverberated on the wooden floor suggested the tolling of a funeral bell. His heart leaped and then sank as he saw Mizjoan approaching. The grim expression on her face fueled his anxiety and burned away any lust he had felt for her. She'd replaced her normal black eye patch with one of scarlet cloth and she was carrying a riding crop in one gloved hand. He twitched slightly, wondering why she might be carrying it. Behind her, Ernie stepped into view. He was scrubbed and neatly dressed; his hair was combed and his mustache was waxed with a slight curl at each end. He looked like a man going to a party, not the mother of all ass-chewings.

The pipesmith winced when Mizjoan tapped his shoulder with her riding crop. She nodded toward her office door, then kicked it open and stepped inside. Ernie followed. In spite of the Digger's surface bravado, Toad could detect the tension in his face.

Mizjoan sat down at her desk, propping her booted legs on its cluttered top. She gestured with her crop, indicating two high-backed chairs in front of the desk. As Toad slumped into one he noticed a smear of horse dung on the sole of one of her boots. It seemed an appropriate omen. Mizjoan took a small bone weedpipe from her tunic pocket, lit it with a candle and took a couple of quick puffs. She laid the smoldering bowl aside, atop a pile of leather-bound folders, without offering either Toad or Ernie a hit.

"Would you two mind explaining yourselves?" she asked, regarding them coldly.

Ernie stroked his freshly waxed mustache and offered her a toothy grin. "What would you like explained?"

"Can it, Ernie. You know perfectly well what I'm talking about."

Toad sank lower in his seat, wishing he were anywhere but here. Beside him Ernie sat up straighter, adjusting the lapels of his freshly laundered frock coat. The herbalist's grin widened, but the tension was still in his face. "We were doing our best under the circumstances."

"Your 'best' isn't good enough," Mizjoan growled. Her voice seemed distant. "You and your Digger friends promised me you had everything under control."

Toad closed his eyes and tried his best to ignore the exchange. He pretended that he was merely a dispassionate observer. Soon, the conversation became just a meaningless babble in the background as he sank deep inside of himself. He was home, sitting by the fire with a smoldering weedpipe in his hand and a book open on his lap, maybe one of the old histories that he relished so much. Toad could almost feel the pages, soft and dry to the touch as he leafed through the volume, perhaps stopping from time to time to examine some interesting passage or woodcut.

Ernie's voice rose suddenly, dissolving Toad's daydream. "Dammit, Joannie, you've got no right…"

"I've told you before; don't call me Joannie."

"Whatever. Just be reasonable."

"I *was* reasonable."

"Yeah, well it's not my fault that I don't know exactly what 'Stink Stone' is."

"Then whose fault is it?"

The herbalist stiffened in his seat and tipped his hat forward. "Look, you and I go back a long way."

"That has no bearing here."

"It should. Hell, Radiclib leader or not, I've always thought of you as more than just a friend. Honestly."

Mizjoan tapped her boot with her riding crop. The dried piece of horse dung loosened and fell to the floor. "Don't try to charm me, comrade. You know it won't work."

"Joannie… " Ernie pleaded.

"Call me that again, Ernie Mungweasle, and I'll be using your scrotum for a weed pouch."

Toad grimaced, watching the whole scene through squinted eyes. He was glad that, for the moment, it excluded him.

"Dylan's Bones," Ernie continued. "If you had enough weed to fill all the 'pouches' you've threatened to make, Street-Corner-Earth wouldn't have a weed shortage, or for that matter, any children."

The Radiclib leader sat bolt upright. Her boots hit the floor with a crash. "That'll be enough, Comrade Mungweasle!" she snapped. "Quite enough!"

Toad sat up in his chair. He couldn't let Ernie hang by himself. Mizjoan's face was like stone and her eye as cold and empty as glass.

"Comrade Leader," he said, using his best formal tone. "I think all that Ernie is trying to say is that we're getting close to identifying the missing ingredient; it's just a process of elimination."

Mizjoan laughed dryly. "It's too late. The People's Council will be taking over your operation tomorrow morning. I should have known that you two would screw this up. We need competent people, not the Risen Brothers."

Toad winced and shot a glance at Ernie, who seemed absorbed in cleaning his fingernails. The analogy was a harsh one. Like most literate Freaks, Toad knew about the ill-fated Risens, whose very name had become a synonym for bungler or fool.

During the Great Wandering, after Frankie Lee overthrew Tommy Two and Westcommune was abandoned, a company of Freaks headed by Badmoon and Mojo Risen had set out to settle a new community in a place called Teetering Rock. The Risens failed to send out advance scouts, which proved to be their undoing. When they led their people into Teetering Rock, they walked right into a Mansonite ambush. During the battle that followed most of the company, including the Risens themselves, were either killed or taken prisoner, and certain rare books that had been entrusted to their care were carried off by the raiders. All in all, Toad and Ernie had been included in some bad company.

Teetering Rock. Something in the name stirred Toad's memory. As Mizjoan raged on, he turned his ears off and retreated back into his daydreams of cozy chairs and favorite old books. A page formed in his mind, a blurry woodcut in one of Pedanticus's histories depicting savage Mansonites reveling around a campfire. An idea flickered to life in Toad's mind like a candle being lit in a dark room. Survivors' accounts of the massacre mentioned that the Mansonites had planned their ambush well. They lit reeking, smoky fires in the narrow gorge leading to Teetering Rock to confuse and blind their victims. Pedanticus reported that they had used a powdered yellow rock which, when thrown in fires, burned with the stench of rotten eggs. That yellow rock might be the "Stink Stone" that Ernie was seeking. If so, Toad was suddenly sure that he knew where it could be found by the wagonload. What a fool he'd been! The solution to all their problems lay no farther away than his bedroom.

"May I have a word?" he asked, fighting to control his excitement.

"No," Mizjoan sneered. "I think you two have said quite enough. I want your personal gear out of the barn tomorrow morning."

"So that's it, huh?"

"It's quite out of my hands now," Mizjoan replied, her eye flashing like a lighthouse in a stormy sea. "As I said, the Council will be taking over in the morning."

Toad got to his feet. "Then we have time yet."

"What's that supposed to mean?"

"It means," he said, walking toward the door, "that we have till morning to sniff out the answer. I'm not ready to give up yet."

With that, he was gone, leaving Mizjoan and Ernie staring at each other.

Chapter Nineteen

It was just before dawn when Toad slipped out of the dark alley across from Commiemartyr Hall and cautiously made his way toward the low wall that surrounded the statue of Maxwell the Hammer in the middle of Aquarius Square. He glanced quickly from side to side, making sure that no guards were in sight, then ran across the frosty ground toward the statue, his breath pouring out like steam. It was 5:20 by the clock on the tower of the Hall, ten minutes to Reveille. Toad's heart hammered in his chest. He felt incredibly alert, his body pumped to its limits by coffee and adrenaline.

He had worked all night on the exploding powder formula. He'd gone back to his room after the meeting with Mizjoan and retrieved the half-forgotten stone that he'd been using as a paperweight. Later, after Ernie had left the workshop for the night, Toad returned and began his experiments. Just an hour ago he had touched a candle to a batch of powder he'd compounded using the yellow stone. The resulting explosion knocked him happily on his butt.

The pipesmith paused for a moment, hefting the ancient bell-muzzled gun he was carrying. *Cruickshank's* referred to it as a blunderbuss, a lethal short-range weapon of incredible power. It was one of several dozen that the Fetid Bog dig had yielded up. His fingers caressed its frosty brass barrel for a second before he placed it on top of the low wall. He opened his coat to reveal four flintlock pistols thrust through his belt. They were all loaded, primed, and ready to go. Satisfied that everything was in order, he climbed up onto the wall and looked around.

From where he stood, Toad had a clear view of all of Aquarius Square and the four main roads leading into it. There were a few lights on in Commiemartyr Hall and the surrounding barracks, but he was pleased to note that the windows in Mizjoan's chambers were still dark. He grinned, thinking about the loud awakening that she'd soon receive. As he drew two of the pistols out of his belt, he smiled at the small red disk of the sun just cresting above the city walls.

Toad could see all the way past the barracks to the city gates. He swayed slightly on his feet, drunk with success. Soon not just Mizjoan but the whole world would know of his discovery, and hail him as a hero. Or would they? He lowered the pistols slightly, wondering how many might die because of his discovery. Then he shrugged; the enemy already had guns and powder. But perhaps thousands might now live who otherwise would have fallen to the Dark Man's murdering armies. Better ten thousand Fascists die than one Freak, he decided. Grinning wider, he raised his guns over his head and pulled back their hammers.

Suddenly a door flew open down the street and a little man in a badly fitted uniform came running toward the square. It was Cujok, the bugler. Toad snickered to himself at the sight of the scrawny Radiclib with his oversized, peaked cap sliding around on his head and his bugle banging against his side as he ran. You won't be blowing Reveille this morning, Toad thought, not after I've stayed up all night preparing my little surprise for Mizjoan.

Oblivious to Toad, Cujok stopped at the base of the wall and raised his bugle to his lips. Before he could sound a note Toad pulled the triggers of both pistols at once, touching off a blast that rattled windows throughout Camp Hoffman. The bugler yelped and dove into a nearby drainage ditch, cowering as if he'd been struck by lightning. Lights blazed on in windows up and down the street, and confused Radiclibs stuck their heads out of a dozen doorways.

Pistols still smoking in his hands, Toad stared at the lights going on in Mizjoan's apartment. There was movement behind the curtains; then they parted to reveal Mizjoan gawking at the crowd amassing at the base of the wall. Her hair was unbound, cascading softly down over her shoulders, and she was dressed in a light blue nightgown that was surprisingly revealing. Toad thrust the pistols back into his belt and waved jauntily to her. Their gazes touched for a brief moment across the square.

Grabbing a fresh brace of pistols, Toad laughed as he spun them in his hands. "Goooood mornin', Camp Hoffman!" he brayed, waving the guns high over his head. "Let's rock and roll!" He danced a victory jig on the wall, firing twice more at the rising sun as half-dressed townspeople staggered out into the street to investigate the uproar.

Trembling slightly, Toad picked up the blunderbuss and waved it so that the sun flashed off its highly polished barrel. It was his show now. He was determined to make the best of it. The pipesmith held the ancient bell-mouthed weapon over his head for several minutes, while he looked at the crowd with what he hoped was an expression of grim determination and pride.

"Comrade Leader and people of Camp Hoffman," he yelled, pulling back the heavy, viselike hammer, "I give you the New Age. I give you gunpowder!" Slowly, with great deliberation, he brought it to his shoulder, being careful to keep the lethal muzzle up at a forty-five degree angle. He aimed high over the rooftops and pulled the trigger.

The pistols had kicked, but nothing could have prepared Toad for the heavy recoil of the overloaded blunderbuss. No sooner had the flint sparked steel than the gun went off with a roar that reverberated like thunder, blowing the pipesmith clear off the top of the wall. Flipping backward through a pall of sulfurous white smoke, he crashed to the ground at the base of the statue of Maxwell the Hammer. The offending weapon landed in the dirt several feet away, still smoking. Toad's ears rang and his shoulder was bruised. For several moments he lay dazed by shock, his nostrils burning from the acrid smell of gunpowder. From the other side of the wall he heard a babble of excited voices.

"Hey, he disappeared," a gruff voice said. "How'd he do that?"

"It's magick!" another squeaked. "The man's a demon."

"No way!" offered a third. "He just burned up, and there ain't nothin' left. I saw the whole thing."

In spite of pain in his shoulder, Toad felt a warm glow of pride. He rose unsteadily to his feet and tried to climb back over the wall. It was painful, slow work, but he made it. The crowd gasped in surprise as he staggered to his feet at the top of the wall, and then cheered as he collapsed into the arms of Comrade Rudy.

"By Dylan, you really did it!" Rudy grinned, slapping Toad on the back. "I'll be damned if you didn't pull it off!"

Toad winced at the sudden jolt. "Th-thanks, Rudy."

Rudy helped Toad through the crowd while several fatigue-clad officers moved in to keep back the well-wishers. On all sides Radiclibs reached out to touch Toad or to shake his hand. A bugle blatted somewhere beyond the sea of people. Cujok had recovered from his fright and was going about his business.

A murmur passed through the crowd as it parted to admit Mizjoan. Her hair still hung long and loose over a full-length, grey greatcoat she'd hastily thrown on; a sky-blue nightgown peeked out from between the coat's broad lapels. She did not look at all like the stern administrator he'd had to face the day before. For several seconds the two looked at one another, neither one of them speaking.

Finally she spoke. "You'll have to forgive me. I don't usually appear in public without proper dress. But this certainly is not a 'usual' event, is it?"

"No, I g-guess not," Toad stammered, shyly.

"It seems congratulations are in order." She offered Toad her hand, smiling. "I'd given up on you and Ernie."

"I wasn't sure myself."

Mizjoan shook her head in admiration. A tendril of auburn hair brushed against Toad's cheek. "I am amazed and delighted, comrade. How did you do it?"

"It's a rather long story."

She let go of his hand and touched him lightly on his shoulder. "No doubt it is, no doubt it is. Perhaps it would be better if we discussed it in my chambers over breakfast."

The pipesmith blushed. "I'd like that."

Leading Toad by the arm, Mizjoan gently made her way through the crowd. The townspeople stepped back to let them pass, a few reaching out to touch Toad as they went by. He hardly noticed them. A private breakfast with Mizjoan! He walked proudly beside the Radiclib leader, feeling excited and very much alive.

Mizjoan stopped short. The crowd was pushing in again. Several important-looking officers were walking their way. One of them, a fat old fellow with thick muttonchop whiskers, placed himself directly in Mizjoan's path.

"Comrade Leader," he blustered. "I demand to know what's going on."

"Ahh, Comrade Field Marshal Dillon," Mizjoan purred. "It's so nice to see you this fine November morning. Where have you been?"

"Working for the good of the people, Comrade Leader, as always."

"Staying out of everyone's way, you mean. Have you met Comrade Toad yet? Had you been here earlier, you'd have seen a fine demonstration of the power we're going to throw against Klaven's Keep. It's a pity that you missed it." She gave Dillon a sneering look and continued on, raising her voice so that everyone could hear.

"Now that Comrade Toad has demonstrated his achievement to us, let us take heart and redouble our efforts to crush our oppressors. Our struggle, though started, is far from won."

"Sterling words," Dillon snapped as Mizjoan pushed her way past him and started up the stairs of Commiemartyr Hall. "I hope you won't have to eat them some day."

The Radiclib leader made no reply. She looked past Dillon to the people of Camp Hoffman and announced, "We have exploding powder now, and with it deadly weapons. Klaven's Keep and victory are within our grasp. We must strive to strike before the winter ice blocks the lake. Go to your homes now and ponder our coming triumph. Power to the people!"

"POWER TO THE PEOPLE!" the mob responded, whistling and cheering as Toad and Mizjoan hurried up the steps. The doors of

Commiemartyr Hall closed behind them.

As soon as they were inside, Mizjoan turned to Toad and smiled. "I'll send someone to get us breakfast. Double portions. Success always makes me hungry."

Toad returned her smile. He could feel a surge of energy pass between them, as if some karmic connection had been made, linking their two souls together.

The sound of approaching footsteps broke Toad's mood. He glanced past Mizjoan's shoulder to see Ernie and Skulk hurrying down the hallway toward them. The sight of the Digger chief surprised him. He'd heard that Skulk had recently returned to Froggy Bottom.

"What's going on outside?" Skulk asked. "It sounds like a bloody riot."

Toad shrugged, trying to appear modest. "Oh... Well, it seems that I stumbled onto the correct formula for gunpowder. I just gave a little demonstration of what it can do."

"When?" Ernie asked, startled.

"Last night."

"But I was at the workshop after you left us in the office."

"I went back to my room first, to get a couple of things; then I grabbed a bite to eat. When I got back to the shop it was late in the evening. I didn't come up with a workable batch until a little before five this morning."

"But how? We tried everything at least twice."

"Not everything, Ernie. There was this strange yellow stone I had in my room. I'd picked it up off the street after it fell from a wagon. I'd quite forgotten it until last night."

The herbalist shook his head. "Fantastic, man. That gets our asses off the griddle. Only wish I'd been there."

"If you two will excuse us," Mizjoan said. "Comrade Toad and I have much to discuss, privately."

"Oh, I see," Ernie replied with a wry leer.

"I don't think you do, Comrade Mungweasle."

Mizjoan took Toad's hand and led him past the two gawking Diggers. A few steps later, they were going through the door leading to her rooms.

Toad glanced at the painting hanging in the hallway. "The Freedom Rider?" he asked. "I didn't realize that he was revered by Radiclibs as well."

Mizjoan smiled and held the door for Toad. "Very much so, comrade. He is one of our most important legends."

"You don't need to call me 'comrade'. I'm just a common Freak."

"You're hardly common, Toad. Quiet and reserved perhaps, but not common.

"I think we'll be more comfortable in here," the Radiclib leader continued, showing him into her living room, rather than the intimidating office that they had occupied yesterday. She pointed him to the couch by the fire, then left to make breakfast arrangements.

Toad sat back and admired the room, with its overstuffed furniture, family portraits, and the massive warhammer mounted over the fireplace. He watched the door hoping Mizjoan would return quickly. She was the most beautiful, intriguing woman Toad had ever met, and here he was sitting in her private quarters. He couldn't believe his good fortune. Smiling confidently, he settled back into the cushions.

She returned, her greatcoat replaced with a long blue robe. She was carrying a wine jug and two stoneware goblets. For Toad, there was no mistaking the way that she looked at him; her slender hips undulated as she approached the couch.

"Not too early in the day, I trust," she said, looking into his eyes and smiling as she filled the goblets to the rims.

"N-no, not at all," Toad agreed, his head already swimming.

Mizjoan handed him one of the goblets, then sat down next to him on the couch. Toad swallowed uncomfortably. Sparks seemed to snap between the few inches that separated them. He bolted half his wine in one gulp.

"I want to be honest with you," Mizjoan said, leaning toward him slightly. "When we first met I didn't expect a great deal out of you. Hardly any Freak men are worth their salt, and damn few make any great contribution to the world."

Hastily, Toad took another sip of wine. He could feel the warmth radiating from the Radiclib leader. "You think I've made a contribution, then?"

Mizjoan smiled. A faint blush touched her cheeks. "Toad, you are too modest. I'm pleased to admit that I was wrong about you. So much so, that here in my quarters I thought we could dispense with formalities— although in public, I insist that proper decorum must be maintained. I'm sure you understand. For the moment, however, we can relax. You may call me Joan, if you like."

"Or Joannie?"

"For Dylan's sake, no," she said and laughed. "My grandmother used to call me that; I hated it. She used to pinch my cheeks, too."

Toad laughed as well. "I can't imagine anyone pinching your cheeks," he said. Just then she leaned forward and her robe slipped open, revealing her small, firm breasts straining the flimsy fabric of her nightgown. He felt a sudden swelling of admiration for her—and immediately crossed his legs to cover it.

"Are you all right, Toad? You look a little flushed."

"I-I'm fine. Wine's just going to my head, I guess." His pulse was hammering wildly. He glanced back and saw that the top two buttons of Mizjoan's nightgown had come undone. Why was she flaunting herself in front of him like this? He crossed his legs tighter. His throat felt dry in spite of the wine, but fighting back the urge to lick his lips, he took another swallow. This seemed to amuse Mizjoan, and she leaned even closer, smiling.

"If that wine bothers you so much, why are you drinking more?" she asked.

"More? Am I? I-I don't know."

She laughed prettily, like the tinkling of silver bells. "You're funny, Toad. I need that sometimes. Now, are you going to tell me about your discovery, or will I have to drag it out of you? I don't think I can wait until the food gets here."

"Sure. After all, the key to solving the problem came from you."

"It did? How?"

"Yesterday, in your office, you compared me and Ernie to the Risen Brothers."

"An unfair comparison, I'm sorry."

"Maybe unfair, but fortuitous. It made me think of the Teetering Rock Massacre. Did you ever hear the story about how the Mansonites burned a powdered yellow rock in their fires to sicken and confuse their enemies?"

She shook her head.

"Well," he said, spreading his hands, "that reference made me think of Ernie's 'Stink Stone'. Maybe they were one and the same thing."

"Ingenious deduction. And, you said that you had some in your room. Unbelieveable."

"Yeah. As I said, one of the wagons filled with Fashie goods passed us on the street and this yellow stone fell out. I thought it was pretty and put it in my pocket. Later, I used it for a paperweight and had quite forgotten about it. Do you know if your staff has inspected any of the wagons yet?"

"No; but I was told that most of the stuff was junk."

"If you check again I'll bet you find all the Stinky Stone we're going to need."

Mizjoan clapped her hands. "Marvelous, Toad! I love it! Damn, but you're a wonder."

Toad felt the blood rush to his face. The room suddenly seemed to be too warm and the ache in his groin had become a major throb. "It was nothing."

"That's not true. Dylan's Bones, you fascinate me with the way you put information together." She picked up a loose hairpin from the arm of the couch and sat rolling it between her fingers. "You know, Toad, you really saved my hide."

"At Fetid Bog?"

Mizjoan dropped her pin. As she bent over to pick it up her nightgown popped open, offering Toad a quick glimpse of her breast. His throat constricted worse than before and he felt like he was going to faint.

"I wasn't thinking of that," she said, straightening, "though I owe you for that too. I was referring to more recent developments—problems I've been having with Field Marshal Dillon."

"Who?"

"You just met him outside."

"The fat guy?"

Mizjoan leaned back on the couch, playing with her hair. "The 'fat guy' is a dangerous man. He's been dying to see me fail at something. Dillon has opposed me on various occasions, but never so vehemently as he has recently on how the war with the Fascists should be conducted. Coming up with the exploding powder when you did will secure the support of all my people. You'll make me look good."

"Haven't you always? I mean, you look pretty good to me."

She shook her head. "Not with everyone. Dillon may look like a blustering clown, but he's not. He's got his share of followers who believe the House of Berkeley has ruled for too long and would rather see him in power than me."

Toad nodded, but he could hardly hear what Mizjoan was saying over the sound of blood pounding in his head. He was only aware of how beautiful she was, and how she seemed to be opening her soul to him.

Mizjoan noticed his lack of attention. "I have the feeling that you aren't listening to me," she said.

"I-I'm sorry. Please continue."

The Radiclib leader sighed, stroking the fabric of the couch distractedly. "This Dillon thing has been going on for a long time. There's no pleasing or compromising with the man. He wants to be Comrade Leader and he won't be satisfied until he is. The hell of the whole matter is that, in spite of his faults, he's an excellent field commander."

"That must make things doubly hard on you."

Another sigh. "It does. When you're in my position everyone seems to want to get one up on you. After a while it gets so I don't know who to trust."

"I know that feeling."

"Do you?"

"More than you know, trust me. You *can* trust me, you know."

"It's strange, but I almost feel as if I can. I rarely have that feeling about anyone, particularly outlanders."

"We're a little bit alike, I think," Toad said, moving slightly closer to her. "We both know what it's like to be lonely."

"Do you, comrade? Can you even begin to imagine the load I have to carry, being the leader of an entire nation? My decisions affect thousands of lives. When I'm right, my people love me, but when I'm wrong..." Her voice trailed off.

She was looking deep into Toad's eyes, as if she were searching for something there. Instinctively, Toad reached out and slipped a comforting arm around her. She stiffened and her eye went suddenly cold and baleful.

"Who gave you permission to touch me?" she snapped. "I don't let anyone place their hands on me."

Flustered and confused, Toad retreated to the far end of the couch. "B-but, I thought..." he stammered, not really knowing what he thought.

"I can just imagine what you were thinking, comrade," Mizjoan said imperiously. "You men are all alike. I withdraw that comment about trusting you; it seems to have set your juices spurting."

"But, Joan, it's not..."

The Radiclib leader stood up, regarding Toad as she might a cockroach or spider. "If it's a woman you want, comrade, you'll have to look elsewhere. I'm sure there are a few of our local women who would bed you. I don't happen to be one of them. You'd better go now."

Stunned and confused, Toad stumbled past Mizjoan and out the door. His temples were pounding. His erection shriveled away to insignificance and with it his good mood. On his way down the hall he nearly walked into a white-liveried mess sergeant carrying a large serving tray.

"Comrade Toad, sir!" the sergeant exclaimed. "I thought you were having breakfast with Comrade Leader Mizjoan."

"I'm not hungry," the pipesmith muttered, shoving past him. Trembling with rage and humiliation, Toad lurched blindly toward the front door and the fresh air he so desperately needed. Mizjoan's rebuff had been as vicious as it had been uncalled for. She'd used him emotionally, then cast him aside like a used handkerchief. Men were all alike, huh? Well, Dylan dammit, so were women. Kicking the door open with unnecessary violence, he hurried out into the cold November sunlight.

"I told you she was icy," remarked a voice behind him.

Toad turned sharply in his tracks to see Ernie sprawled on a stone bench beside the door. His top hat was tipped low on the bridge of his long nose and he was puffing lazily on a clay weedpipe.

"I don't know what you're talking about," Toad said brusquely.

Ernie tapped out the pipe and slipped it into his coat pocket. Straightening his hat, he got lazily to his feet. "You know damn well what I'm talking about, Toad. There's only one thing that could put that little black cloud over your head today. Joannie shot you down—and probably wasn't too gentle about doing it. I know how you're feeling; I've been there a few times myself."

"Go ahead, Ernie, say 'I told you so'."

The herbalist stretched and started down the stairs. "I probably should do that, but I'll spare you. Joannie's a good woman, but all women are weird—especially these female warrior-types."

"I'll keep that in mind."

Ernie slipped a friendly arm around Toad's shoulders, and guided the younger Freak down the street past Maxwell's monument. There was still a slight smell of powder in the air; that was all that remained of Toad's brief flash of glory.

"Let's get some breakfast, Toad. We can talk about making the world safe for Freakdom."

Chapter Twenty

Thick billows of dank fog hung over Great East Lake like wet burial shrouds. Somewhere above, storm clouds were massing, waiting. The air was heavy with the smell of snow. It was cold—cold enough to dampen the spirits of even the bravest warriors. High in the stern of the *Frankie Lee*, Toad sat huddled in his heavy woolen storm cloak and squinted out through the fog that rolled over and around Mizjoan's flagship. He could see great lumbering shadows that were the twenty-odd other ships of the fleet. On the closest ship, the *Righton*, Toad thought he could make out the shapes of General Starkweather and Skulk. Curiously, the Digger leader had decided to accompany the general rather than join Ernie and Mizjoan on the *Frankie Lee*. Kentstate, newly returned from Covenstead, was reported to be on board the *Righton* as well.

Although the storm cloak offered some protection against the wet cold, Toad still shivered and his teeth chattered. The chilling breeze that tore at the cottony fog and filled the Lee's fist-emblazoned sail was not what made him shake. His coldness came from inside himself, where apprehension and fear formed around his heart like rime ice. Fear of the coming attack was magnified by the return of his nightmares; they had started again several days ago, after the upsetting scene in Mizjoan's chambers.

These nightmares, like others he'd had in the recent past, seemed to presage the future in a vivid and compelling way. Because of their outcome, Toad hadn't shared them with anyone; he just locked them away in the back of his mind. Instead, he'd busied himself overseeing the production of gunpowder and preparing for the trip to Guevarraville, where the Radiclib fleet was readying for the assault on Klaven's Keep. But now that the fleet was actually underway, the dreams were coming back to haunt his waking hours.

The visions had begun much as today was beginning, on a mist-shrouded lake where dim shapes in the fog were the only signs of other ships. The feeling of doom hung over him as heavily as the fog. Somewhere in its depths, choppy guitar chords sounded and a commanding nasal voice arose. The voice was always the same, angry but full of hope. It fired something in his heart. By instinct, he knew who it was; miraculously, after centuries of sleep, old Bob Dylan was on the lake to lead his people to victory.

In the dreams, as the ghostly, stirring music reached a crescendo, the battle was joined. Cries of "Seize The Day" and "We Shall Overcome" rose and mixed with the music. For a while it seemed that the battle was going well, but then the cries died out, followed by a thickening silence that seemed to go on forever. Abruptly, the quiet was shattered by a shrill cackle that even now reverberated in Toad's mind. The scent of gunpowder was replaced by the stench of burning plant matter that was definitely not Honkweed. The Dark Man was somewhere out in the fog. "Pleased to meet you," his voice hissed through the mist. "Hope you've guessed my name."

A hand touched Toad's shoulder, breaking his reverie. He looked up, startled, to see Ernie standing over him. The older Freak was wrapped in a storm cloak like Toad's and his top hat was drenched with mist. Droplets of water dripped from the points of his drooping mustache. He'd just returned from the bow, where he'd been conferring with Mizjoan.

"What's the matter?" Ernie asked. "You look like you're freezing to death. It's pretty cold, but not enough to make an islander such as yourself shiver."

"Not cold. Scared."

"You? The hero of Fetid Bog?"

"Stow it, Ernie."

"I'm sorry," the herbalist said, sitting down next to the swivel-mounted ballista that dominated part of the rear deck. "A lot of people are scared today."

"It's not the same."

"Scared is scared. Whatever it is, try not to think about it too much. If you get shaky now you'll never be able to react properly when the time comes."

"If my dreams are right, it won't matter."

"What dreams? What are you talking about?"

"The ones about the Dark Man."

Ernie tugged at his mustache nervously. "Oh—those."

"Well, I'm having them again. If anything, they're more vivid than before."

The herbalist nodded, but didn't reply. In the thick fog his face looked pale and ghostlike.

"They're getting to me," Toad continued. "I keep thinking of how I saw the Concert Hall fire before it happened. Lately the dreams have been about this lake and Klaven's Keep."

"Strange. That dream you had at Froggy Bottom was about today, wasn't it?"

"Yes."

"Well, it hasn't come true, has it?"

"No, but I'm afraid it's going to, especially after this last nightmare."

Ernie took a packet of crackers out of his cloak pocket, ripped the paper open with his teeth, and offered one to Toad. "Maybe you ought to tell me about it."

The pipesmith related his nightmare between bites of cracker. When he was finished, Ernie got to his feet and walked to the ship's rail. The fog had started to thin, revealing a long dark line of forest along the distant shore. "Sometimes dreams are just dreams, Toad."

Toad joined Ernie at the rail. For several moments they stood side by side without talking, peering off toward the emerging forest.

"I hope you're right," Toad said at last.

The herbalist nodded, but didn't take his eyes from the tree line. "That's Darkenwood," he said, pointing. "That spit of land behind us is Piggie Point, where Jo-Jo Lion Berkeley put down the Mansonites during the Insurrection of 2388."

Toad gazed at the shore through the ragged veil of mist. Shreds of fog hung in the branches of the venerable moss-bearded trees; dark, dense shadows pooled between their roots. Darkenwood looked ancient and mysterious. Perhaps it was like the old stories said—Darkenwood was the first forest, old as time itself, from which all living things came. "Does anyone live there?" he asked.

Ernie shook his head. "Not since the Mansonites were wiped out."

"I've read about Darkenwood in some of Kermit Badmoon's poetic histories. He said human sacrifice used to go on in there, even cannibalism."

"So they say. Because of the legends surrounding the place, even the fiercest Whiteriders won't venture more than a few hundred feet inside it, and then only during daylight hours."

"So it's never been fully explored?"

"I don't believe so. The Fascists occasionally patrol the shoreline as far as the Sludge, but fear keeps them out of the depth of the forest. The Society partially explored the forest some years after the Insurrection, but except for a few bear and lynx, there was nothing there to harm anyone. For a while we maintained a way station in some ruins there and the Radiclibs kept spy posts on the forest's outer borders."

Toad digested this information. "What about Badmoon's accounts? He wouldn't have agreed with you about Darkenwood being harmless."

"Apparently, Kermit Badmoon was your kind of historian," Ernie chuckled. "Before he went mad he spent his whole life at his parents' house in Jukin City, rarely venturing out of his dooryard. His knowledge of the world was severely limited, to say the least. People have disappeared in Darkenwood, to be sure, but that's easily explained. To begin with, most people probably are caught by Fashie patrols at the edge of the forest. Some I'm sure get lost and die of exposure; and then there's the wild animals."

Toad gazed at the eerie twisted trees and couldn't imagine walking in the shadows beneath them without fear. "Are the spy posts still in use?"

"Not so much anymore. Mizjoan found it was easier to pay off, or coerce, wandering Rowdies for information rather than maintain a full-time spy network. Swetshop, the old ruins I mentioned, hasn't been used in years either. A few decades back it was a place to send apprentice Diggers to test their mettle, but that practice has been abandoned now."

"The place still looks evil. I feel like something bad is going to happen here."

"That's just your nightmares talking, Toad."

The pipesmith shrugged. "Maybe it is. But I still can't shake the feeling that I'm going to meet the Dark Man soon. Maybe today."

"Dreams are tricky things, Toad. All they really represent is the fear you feel inside yourself. You've got to learn to face that fear."

"That's bold talk, coming from you, Ernie. You don't feel his shadow looming over you when you sleep. No, we're fated to meet. It's inevitable."

Ernie looked over his shoulder to the stern where the burly, red-bearded tillerman was sweeping the *Frankie Lee's* rudder back and forth as easily as if he were stirring a cup of tea. Looking back at Toad, he leaned against the ballista and started to speak, when a horn sounded somewhere off in the thinning mist. The words died on his lips. Drums pounded, commanding the *Lee's* oarsmen to begin to pick up speed. Over the drums the two Freaks could hear Mizjoan shrilly calling out orders.

"This is it," Ernie whispered.

Toad started down the steps to the lower deck, but Ernie restrained him. Through the ragged fog the pipesmith could make out long, low shapes moving swiftly toward the *Frankie Lee*.

Ernie maintained his grip on Toad's shoulder, guiding him toward the ballista. "Those are Fascist longships, Toad. The fastest things on water. Unpack some of our special bolts while I get this spear-chucker ready. Hurry it up. They're gaining on us."

Unbundling and laying out the six-foot long, iron-tipped bolts, the pipesmith kept a wary eye on the approaching ships. There were perhaps a dozen of the sleek black craft, each equipped with thirty oars and blood red sails bearing either a lightning bolt or starred swastika emblem. Their high bowsprits were carved in the likeness of screaming eagles or wolves. The longships moved in on the *Lee* with a speed that Toad would have thought impossible. In no time they'd have it encircled and cut off from the rest of the Radiclib fleet.

"Quit daydreaming and help me with this winch," Ernie ordered. In spite of the cold, he was sweating as he strained at the ballista's cocking mechanism.

Toad hurried to help. Together they spun the winch wheel until the bow of the unwieldy weapon was cocked and ready. Below, on the main deck, Mizjoan was yelling out orders through a speaking horn while the crew manned the ship's four other ballistas and the pair of small bow-mounted cannon.

"Shall I put on one of those exploding bolts we rigged?" Toad asked.

Ernie looked up from where he was making last minute adjustments on the ballista's sights. "Put in a flamer first and be prepared to torch it when I give the go-ahead."

The tempo of the wardrums increased as the distance closed between the *Lee* and the Fascist wolf pack. Radiclib oarsmen bent to their task, pulling at an arm-wrenching rate. Beside them, archers and riflemen, some whom Toad and Ernie had trained, hastily took their positions and awaited the order to fire.

Toad held his breath. The bulkier Radiclib vessels could not match the speed of the sleek low-slung Fascist craft, but they didn't intend to. He watched as large warships swung into position to block the oncoming enemy pack. Several of the longships swerved and bore down on the *Lee* in a collision course. Toad braced himself and waited for the impact.

The collision never came. The enemy craft, realizing that they'd maneuvered themselves into a dangerous position in the middle of the Radiclib fleet, increased speed and tried to scatter. Two managed to arc around and hurried off toward the northern lakeshore. The other four wheeled about in confusion as the Radiclib fleet circled in around them. As Toad watched, the *Lee's* brother ship, *Field Marshal Cinque*, and four others broke formation and took off after the fleeing enemy craft. Soon all seven ships were lost in the lingering fog.

As soon as the remaining enemy ships were within range, Toad and Ernie swung the ballista around on its swivel and lined up the crosshairs of its sights on the nearest one. Toad had doused the rag-wrapped head of the bolt with flammable oils. He needed only a nod from Ernie to touch a flame to it, turning it into a deadly airborne torch.

Suddenly, the enemy ship increased speed, making for a break in the line of Radiclib craft. It churned by the *Lee* like a frightened waterbug. Archers and riflemen on its deck cut loose on the *Lee*, firing several volleys up at the larger ship before its crew could respond. When they finally did, the hail of arrows and bullets was so thick that half the enemy crew was taken out in one fusillade. The stricken ship listed to one side, but kept on going.

Through everything Ernie had managed to keep a bead on the longship. "Now!" he hissed. "Pop me some smoke!"

Toad fired his tinderbox. Sparks flew from flint and steel onto the oil-soaked rags. They ignited with an audible whoosh, making the pipesmith jump backward. Grinning crazily, Ernie adjusted the ballista's range and pulled the trigger.

The bowstring snapped forward with a jolt that shook the weapon to its mounts. The burning spear arched out over the water like a comet, straight toward the enemy craft's sail. A moment later the longship was engulfed in gouts of flame. Toad could make out a group of figures, some of them on fire themselves, leaping from the blazing decks.

"They didn't know we were coming," Ernie said. "But they sure as hell know we're here."

Toad nodded, but couldn't tear his gaze from the burning ship.

Around the *Lee*, the fleet had made short work of the rest of the longships. Two were ablaze, and the third had been rammed by the *Eldridge Cleaver* and split nearly in two. It lay on its side, rolling drunkenly in the choppy iron-gray water. Wreckage and floating bodies bobbed in its wake. The gunfire died down, and the only sounds on the lake were the muffled screams of the wounded.

Equally sickened and fascinated, Toad watched the final twitches of a Fascist who'd been pinned to the deck of the longship like a bug on a display board, the broken shaft of a ballista bolt protruding from his ruined chest. The dying man's arms flailed and his mouth worked soundlessly as the blood pooled about him and ran in rivulets down the sloping deck. Hot bile rose in Toad's stomach, clawing its way to his throat. Shuddering, he swallowed and forced it back, but the nasty, coppery taste remained in his mouth.

Suddenly, the shooting began again. Radiclib soldiers were taking pot shots at the few living Fascists still struggling in the water, which was already dyed red with enemy blood. As Toad watched, horror stricken, the Fascists tried to swim away. One by one, the gunners and bowmen of the *Lee* took them out.

"What are they doing?" Toad cried. "They're killing helpless men."

"They're doing what soldiers do, Toad. It's none of your affair."

"Yes it is. Those Fashies are unarmed. They know they're defeated."

149

"They do now. They can't be allowed to escape."

"But… "

"Do you really think they'd treat us any differently if the tables were turned?" Ernie shrugged sadly. "Consider it mercy and try to understand. They wouldn't have survived much longer in that icy water anyway."

Toad shook his head sadly. He looked past Ernie, past the carnage, to the far end of the lake where the fog still roiled, thick and deep.

Waiting, somewhere out there, was the Dark Man.

The fog appeared to hang in over the north of the lake forever, but as the fleet approached it began to peel back in ragged streamers. In the east the pallid sun crested the somber tree line of Darkenwood. It looked small and sick, a dingy button sewn onto the billowing black clouds. The air was bursting with the promise of snow. Before long the storm would break.

Toad leaned against the ballista, wrapped in his storm cloak. Absent-mindedly he tapped his foot to the beat of the oarmaster's drum. Ernie had returned to the main deck and now he, Mizjoan and Rudy were engaged in an intense conversation. Toad paid them little heed. Ahead, beyond the mist and fog, lay Klaven's Keep.

As the Radiclib flotilla fanned out across the lake it passed the burning hulks of the two enemy craft that had fled earlier. Of the five fleet ships, four were racing to rejoin the others. Two of these, the *Field Marshal Cinque* and the *Hoachie Min*, were racing in earnest. The *Min* was ahead by several lengths, and its crew was cheering as if they were on holiday instead of at war.

By now the fog had retreated from all but the northernmost rim of the lake. As the last tendrils swirled away Toad could make out the lines of Klaven's Keep. Small and grim in the distance, it stood upon its bleak promontory like a middle finger thrust at the dirty, boiling sky. Breathless, Toad watched it growing closer until it loomed like a rotted black stump. It seemed ageless, and quiet as a grave.

The blast of a horn shattered the silence. Toad turned to see two ships, the *Bojangles* and the *John Lennon*, leave the formation to take after a pair of enemy longships slipping swiftly along the shore near Darkenwood. So far the encounters with enemy craft had been brief and successful. Though nobody knew what might happen once the Keep was engaged, morale on the *Lee* was running high.

Excitement grew as the *Lennon* and *Bojangles* closed on the two enemy craft. Ernie, Mizjoan and Rudy gave up their discussion and went to the rail to watch as the ships engaged.

The *Bojangles* made contact first, bearing down on the lead longship as fast as its oarsmen would take it. When it was within range, its archers rained down fire arrows on its prey until the air between the two craft was alive with sparks. The longship swerved and headed southward, but already its red, swastika-emblazoned sail was afire, spewing smoke and ashes into the gray November sky. Behind it, the *Lennon* had rammed the other longship, splitting it in two and filling the lake with thrashing bodies. History was being made this day. Victory seemed swift and sure.

The *Frankie Lee's* drummer increased tempo. The oarsmen responded vigorously, pulling at their oars until the *Lee* sped across the water. Toad sat down away from the tillerman and the ballista and watched Mizjoan hurrying about on the deck below. Though he'd kept his distance from her since the scene in her office, he loved the way she strode about, her long flag of auburn hair rippling in the wind. Ernie, who had just finished talking with Rudy, was about to take a seat beside Toad when gunshots sounded in the distance.

One of the smaller Radiclib craft, the *Maxwell Berkeley*, had pulled ahead of the fleet and was exchanging shots with a lone longship. Explosions flashed along the decks of both ships as the distance between them closed. For several long, tense moments the enemy outmaneuvered the *Berkeley*. Arrows flew as thick as locusts between the boats. The longship turned and flew toward the Keep; the *Berkeley* slowed, rejoining the fleet, making no effort to pursue.

"Better get a move on," Ernie said, tapping Toad on the shoulder. "Joannie's going to want exploding bolts on all ballista before we run the Keep. She's hoping she can blow it right off the cliff."

Toad moved to the chest containing the special bolts. "Ernie, I hope these work."

"They worked in the tests, didn't they?"

The Keep loomed huge and ominous above them. Within moments it would be in range of Mizjoan's armada. Toad and Ernie wrestled the cumbersome bolts out of their case and began cranking and cocking the ballista. When everything was ready they slipped one of the bolts into the firing groove. The bolt was shorter than usual, just a little over five feet long, but it had an oversized head of thick wadding, wrapped with barbed wire. A coarse fuse extended down the thick shaft to the bolt's hammered copper flights. It looked crude, but the warhead contained about five pounds of exploding powder and metal scraps. In theory it could blow a hole in a stone wall large enough to drive a wagon through. Under Toad's and Ernie's direction about four dozen of these bolts had been prepared and distributed evenly between the *Frankie Lee* and three other ships, the *Eldridge Cleaver*, the *Righton*, and the *Steppenwolf*. Each of these ships sported oversized Ridley ballistas fore and aft. The *Righton*, like the *Frankie Lee*, had cannon as well. A continuous barrage from these four ships would be enough to reduce Klaven's Keep to rubble.

Toad looked up at the Keep in awe. A ghost of his nightmare capered in his mind. Nothing moved on the high headland except for the red and blue swastika flag flying from its high pole on the Keep's roof. He fumbled under his storm cloak, found his tinderbox, and prepared to light the bolt's fuse.

"We're closing," Ernie rasped. He pressed his shoulder against the ballista's aiming stock and swiveled the weapon into position. His eyes narrowed to slits as he lined up the sights on the Keep's summit.

Time ran in spits and spurts as it often does in battle: the flight of one arrow seeming to take hours, a skirmish passing in an instant. The fleet spread out around the point of land that sheltered the Keep. The *Righton* moved past the *Lee*, taking its pre-assigned position. As the *Righton* was Starkweather's ship, Mizjoan had deferred the first strike to him. Cold sunlight glinted dully off the *Righton's* twin cannon. The bow ballista swiveled into position. A moment later the ballista let go and one of the bulky exploding bolts flew to its mark, trailing sparks behind it. It detonated just at the base of the Keep with a roar that rolled back out over the lake. Dirt and chunks of rock showered down like hard rain. Before the dust was even cleared, the *Righton's* twin cannon fired in unison, opening up a hole in one side of the black tower. There was no response from the Keep, no movement except for the flag flapping on its thin black pole.

"Light 'er up," Ernie whispered. "It's our show next."

Toad fumbled with the tinderbox, touching its glowing punk to the bolt's fuse. The fuse sputtered and began to burn, giving off an acrid stench. With a wild grin stretching his features, Ernie shifted the ballista slightly and pulled the trigger. The weapon shuddered, releasing the sputtering bolt. It arched gracefully, meteor-like, for the roof of the Keep. In the next second the whole summit of the tower erupted in a blast of fiery fragments. As Toad watched, the red swastika flag fluttered down to the water like a stricken bird. Victory hung in the air with the smell of gunpowder.

And then, a series of explosions erupted from the tree line to the north and south of the Keep. Toad and Ernie dove for the deck just as something whizzed over the *Lee's* stern before splashing into the water just in front of the *Mad Abbie*. Shaken, Toad tried to get back to the deck as another series of explosions ripped out the *John Lennon's* bow. Listing over on one side, the stricken ship rolled and began to go under. Beside the *Lee*, the *Bojangle's* black, fist-emblazoned sail collapsed over the deck as a cannon ball took out the mast. Toad moaned. The Radiclib fleet was strung in front of the enemy cannon like a line of decoys. Another few barrages at close range could put Mizjoan's ships on the bottom of the lake.

Horns sounded from ship to ship, signaling, relaying orders as the fleet sped apart and moved back out of cannon range. The drummer on the *Lee* picked up a frantic beat. Mizjoan tried to make her voice heard above the turmoil. Toad and Ernie braced themselves as the *Lee* picked up speed, swerving sharply to get out of range. Toad almost jumped when Ernie tapped on his arm.

"Get another bolt ready," the herbalist said. "Maybe we can take out one of those cannons."

The two Freaks moved quickly to ready and load the ballista. Ernie's long arms flailed as he fought with the wheel, tugging on it hard until it rotated smoothly. Wrestling the bolt onto the ballista they looked northward to where the tillerman was pointing. Dozens of gray shapes were emerging from the remaining fog bank. They were ships, smaller and more streamlined than conventional longships, and they were bearing down on the fleet with frightening speed. Toad couldn't take his eyes from the approaching wolf pack, even as all hell broke out on the *Lee*.

Another barrage lit up the tree line. Cannonballs ripped through the fleet, striking the *Mad Abbie*, the *Hoachie Min*, and the *Righton*. The *Righton's* powder chest exploded, taking off the entire bow. The ship was sheathed in flame. Soldiers jumped from its deck as another explosion went off amidships. The *Righton* folded up like a fan and shot straight down into the leaden, icy water of the lake.

Toad and Ernie managed to turn the ballista and sight it in just as another cannonball hit the water not twenty feet from the *Lee's* stern. A geyser of water spewed up over them, drenching them in spite of their storm cloaks.

The pipesmith sputtered as he wiped water from his eyes. Beside him, Ernie was retrieving his top hat from a puddle.

"That was too close," the herbalist said. "Get me some fire. We can't afford to take another one like that."

Though its case was drenched, Toad's tinderbox was still functional. He sparked the fuse a split second before Ernie pulled the trigger. The bolt snaked through the air toward the tree line, riding a trail of smoke. The *Steppenwolf*, though now crippled with a demolished rudder and rear deck, fired as well. The smoke trails crossed in mid-air. The *Steppenwolf's* round hit the beach below the tree line, sending up a harmless spume of sand and water. Ernie's shot hit the trees dead center, taking out a cannon and starting a blaze among the half-dead pines. Enemy powder stores detonated as flames rolled over them.

"Damn, I'm good," Ernie crowed.

"Try for another one," Toad replied. "Maybe we've got the time."

"We haven't. We're losing range. That was a lucky shot and it'll have to stand for now."

But now, the cannon were the least of their problems. To Toad's horror the enemy wolf pack was almost on them.

"Don't let them take us here," Mizjoan bellowed from the main deck. "Head for open water!"

War drums rumbled as the Fashie ships closed in. Mizjoan sounded her horn defiantly, and the call was taken up throughout the fleet. The smaller enemy craft swarmed the lumbering Radiclib ships like fleas on dogs. Barrages of arrows flew between the ships, and at one point the *Lee's* cannons opened fire, sending one of the enemy vessels cartwheeling out over the lake. Above the screaming and gunfire, Toad heard a high-pitched cackle ripple down from the broken crown of the Keep. Looking back, he caught a glimpse of a black-robed figure standing on the ruined summit. Even as the fleets locked in battle, the figure raised one long arm and shrieked louder. It was a sound that seemed impossible to come from a human throat, a sound so evil and old that it turned his marrow to ice.

"D-did you see him?" Toad asked, trembling.

"See who?"

"The D-dark Man."

"I didn't see anything."

Toad looked back at the Keep. The figure in black was nowhere to be seen.

"Load me another bolt, will ya?" Ernie yelled. "These bastards are getting thicker than gnats."

Toad glanced to the south and saw several dozen longships racing to join the smaller craft. As fast as he could he jammed another bolt into the ballista and lit the fuse. Ernie zeroed in on a pair of longships a hundred yards distant. Even as he pulled the trigger, a pack of the little attack boats surrounded the *Lee*, sending up a swarm of fire arrows. Several struck the deck just as the ballista launched its deadly missile. The Freaks dove for cover as another flight of arrows whizzed overhead. An explosion shook the *Lee*, but they didn't have a chance to see if the bolt had hit home. Toad saw Ernie curled up in a ball on the deck.

"Y-you okay?" he asked.

Ernie shook his head. "Yeah, I'm fine. Robert H. Dylan, that was close!"

"I th-think we got one of the longships. Maybe."

"Yeah, but there's too many of the bastards."

From where they crouched, Toad and Ernie could hear screams and gunshots on the lower deck. More fire arrows flew overhead, several embedding themselves in the rigging. The huge canvas sail smoldered and caught fire.

Crawling across the deck, Ernie retrieved a box and pushed it toward Toad. It contained a brass-barreled blunderbuss, several pistols, powder and shot.

"Nice going," Toad remarked.

"I thought we might have need of these, 'ol comrade buddy, so I packed us a lunch. Take the blunderbuss; I want the pistols."

Hastily they loaded the weapons and inched their way to the rail, keeping as low as possible. Below, several of the smaller enemy craft were keeping pace with the *Lee* while a pair of longships moved in on the bow. Above him, the *Lee's* sail was a wall of flame, falling away in burning strips of canvas. Toad popped his head up for a second to get a better look at the longships, then ducked back down just in time to avoid a flight of arrows that embedded themselves in the *Lee's* side, inches from his head. Fragments of burning sail fluttered down as gunshots rang out over the lake.

Mizjoan sounded her horn and Radiclib gunmen and archers opened up on the nearest longship. Toad watched as the marksmen took out most of the enemy crew in the first volley. Fascist soldiers staggered over the sides of their ship in an effort to escape, or fell sprawling across the deck as blood poured out of them. One young soldier was hit in the face with a musket ball, and Toad had to fight back nausea as he watched the man's head explode like an over-ripe melon. He dropped his weapon and inched back from the rail. Ernie's arm snaked out, restraining him.

"Where the hell are you going, Toad?" the older Freak hissed. "Fire, dammit!"

"I-I can't."

"Yes you can. You've got to."

"I can't…"

"Don't cop out on me now, man. Shoot or be shot. It's your life—don't let them take it from you."

Toad nodded weakly. The taste of bile was still strong in his throat. He cocked the blunderbuss and laid it over the rail, taking aim at the longship bearing down on the *Lee's* port side. Toad leveled his weapon at the officer manning the longship's forward ballista and pulled the trigger.

The explosion jarred him, but not as much as the screams that followed. "Ernie," he wheezed. "I don't think I can do this."

The herbalist laid both of his pistols across the rail. "We've got to fight through, dammit. We can't stay boxed in like this for long and survive. The Fashie bastards had this little trap planned all along."

There were more screams nearby. Toad looked up to see the last of the sail fall apart into burning fragments that dropped to the deck like grotesque autumn leaves. The mast was aflame now and all of the rigging was gone. He jumped aside just in time to avoid being hit by a blazing piece of spar. The redbearded tillerman had jumped aside too. He grinned at Toad and went back to manning the tiller arm. A second later two crossbow bolts took him in the chest. The big man clawed at them wildly, then crumpled and fell over the stern before either Toad or Ernie could grab him.

"Ernie…"

"Nothing we can do. Just stay down and follow me."

The two Freaks started down the short ladder leading to the main deck. Though the fire had gone out, the smoldering mast had collapsed across the deck, pinning two soldiers beneath it. Mizjoan and Rudy were struggling to free them, but the charred crumbling wood was still hot to the touch and they had to back off. The screams of the trapped and burned soldiers tore at Toad's ears. Foregoing the ladder, Ernie leaped the distance between decks and ran to help them. Less enthusiastic than his companion, Toad put his heels to the rungs and started down.

Something hit the *Frankie Lee* amidships, making the ladder sway violently under Toad's feet. He reached out to steady himself, but his fingers clutched air. A second shock, more violent than the first, hit the ship and the ladder disappeared beneath him. Toad was thrown through the air. Before he could cry out he hit the frigid water of the lake and went under.

Lights exploded behind Toad's eyes as he surfaced, spewing out a mouthful of lake water. Immediately, he felt himself being pulled back down by the weight of his waterlogged storm cloak and he struggled to free himself. Once rid of the sodden garment, he began swimming back toward the *Lee*. Listing heavily to one side, with flames boiling from its rear deck, the Radiclib flagship was moving quickly, leaving the splintered wrecks of several enemy ships in its wake. The ship retreated too rapidly for him ever to hope to catch it.

Thunder broke over the lake as the *Lee's* cannons flared. Clinging to the nearest piece of debris, the shattered figurehead of one of the wrecked longships, Toad tried to fight back the cold as he watched the *Lee* disappear in the distance, followed by a dozen of the smaller enemy craft. Again, he could hear a shrieking laugh coming from the Keep.

Toad sensed something moving behind him. It was one of the smaller enemy ships, adrift with its oars dragging in the water and its sail ripped and shredded. Scattered across the bloodstained decks of the craft were the motionless bodies of the crew. As the cold began to rob the strength from his arms and legs, Toad let go of the figurehead and swam to the derelict ship. Gasping with exertion, he reached the ship's rail and began to pull himself aboard.

The pipesmith had one leg over the rail when, with a painful grunt, one of the bodies pushed himself to his knees and leveled a large brass-barreled pistol at Toad's face. The Fascist was bleeding heavily from his chest and scalp, but his eyes were alive with rage. Pain and hatred contorted his face as he pulled back the hammer of his gun.

"Kiss yer ass goodbye, faggit," the Fascist wheezed. Blood trickled from the corner of his mouth, but his gun hand was rock steady.

The pistol's muzzle, impossibly huge, was a deep black well of death. But its depth couldn't match what he saw in the Fascist's hate-wracked eyes. They were what he imagined the Dark Man's eyes would be like, twin graves opening onto some fathomless abyss. The Fascist snarled, baring crooked yellow teeth, and slowly began to squeeze the trigger. The muzzle moved only slightly, but it had Toad's fullest attention.

Suddenly, the Fascist froze. The huge pistol shook in his hand and fell out, sliding down the slant of the deck and into the water. It hit with a loud splash and shimmered out of sight. The Fascist spasmed and made strange gurgling sounds deep in his throat. Then, his eyes rolled upward so only the whites showed; he pitched face-forward onto the deck. A knife protruded from between his shoulders, its handle still vibrating.

A blurred shape slipped over the far side of the boat. Toad recognized the top hat and long gray-streaked hair.

"Ernie!" he gasped.

The older Freak quickly cleared the deck, pushing aside the dead Fascist. He reached down, his long arms offering support as he pulled Toad aboard.

"Get out of that water," he said. "You'll catch your death of cold."

"Thanks for taking care of my friend."

"Him? He was on his way out anyway. I just helped him along."

The battle was moving away from them. The *Frankie Lee* lay on its side, burning, valiantly firing back at the smaller ships swarming in around it. Ernie reached down and pulled his knife from the Fascist's corpse. He wiped it on the dead man's coat before sticking it in his boot. Suddenly, he grabbed Toad and forced him to lie on the deck. The pipesmith almost cried out in surprise, but Ernie's hand was clamped over his mouth. Long dark forms moved through the water on either side of the derelict craft. Once, signal lanterns flashed between the ships, but no one seemed interested in the wreck. Another longship passed by a moment later, oars blurring as it took off after a Radiclib ship cut off from the fleet. Silence set in and the derelict ship drifted slowly southward toward the dim tree line of Darkenwood.

"What'll we do?" Toad whispered. "We're sure to be discovered."

"Not necessarily. I've got a plan that just might get us out of this alive."

"I'm all ears."

Still crouching, Ernie began to peel off his storm cloak and frock coat. He rolled one of the corpses over and removed the long blue greatcoat and uniform. He tossed the bloodstained garments to Toad.

"Here, try this on. We'll disguise ourselves as Fashies and hide under the bodies. If nothing else it'll keep us warm."

"I-I don't think I can do it," he said, and pushed the coat away. It stank of death.

"Look there, Toad," Ernie said pointing across the lake.

A disabled Radiclib ship was under attack by four longships. Toad could see Fascist archers shooting at Radiclibs thrashing about in the water. One soldier even went so far as to hack at floating bodies with his sword, laughing gleefully. Toad's stomach churned. The coppery taste returned to his throat, and before he could control himself, he puked on the deck.

"I-I'm sorry," he sputtered, wiping vomit from his beard.

"It's okay, Toad. I understand. Put that coat on and do what I do. It's our only chance."

Ernie stripped the uniform from another of the dead Fascists and put it on, and then he lay down among the bodies. Toad gagged as he buttoned the greatcoat all the way up and slipped under the still warm body of a corporal. The corpse's flaccid face rested only inches from Toad's; its lolling tongue and cracked-glass eyes mocked him. He closed his eyes tight and waited, trembling. It seemed like hours before the sounds of battle died away and he felt Ernie stirring beside him.

"Wh-what's going on?" Toad asked.

The older Freak sighed. "See for yourself."

Toad slid out from under the dead Fascist. The corpse settled back on the deck with horrible, gelatinous ease. Toad peered out over the lake. Radiclib ships were burning everywhere.

"We're losing," he moaned.

"Correction: we've lost. We've only got ourselves to worry about now."

"What'll we do?"

"At present, nothing. The way this boat is drifting, we'll hit land near Piggie Point. We can seek shelter in Darkenwood." The thought brought Toad little joy, but after the horrors he'd seen, Darkenwood could be no worse.

Chapter Twenty-One

A few fat snowflakes were drifting down by the time the boat nudged the shore just below the tip of Piggie Point. Moving quickly and efficiently, Toad and Ernie gathered up some weapons and slipped over the bow onto the sand. It was a short run up the beach to the shrub-covered slope, and no more than twenty yards to the forest beyond that.

Even though he was wearing dry Fashie clothes, Toad shivered violently. Fighting for breath as branches snapped under his booted feet, he stumbled over a root and fell, almost dropping the musket he was carrying. By the time he was back on his feet Ernie was nowhere to be seen. Soon the herbalist reappeared from behind a bush at the forest's edge, looking slightly ridiculous in his top hat and long, gold-braided Fascist overcoat.

Toad started to call out, but Ernie motioned him to silence. Sounds of battle could be still heard, but they were muffled and distant, like a passing thunderstorm. An occasional explosion in the distance indicated that the ships were moving southward.

"This is too much like the dream I had," Toad said, catching up with Ernie. "The Dark Man's watching us, I'm sure."

"Dreams are only dreams, Toad. But if your dreams are correct, your boy will find us. It's best that it happens under our conditions on our own turf."

Toad looked about the silent, forbidding forest. Nothing stirred; no sounds came from within its vast darkness. The shadows beneath the ancient trees seemed to pool and thicken. The snow sifted down quietly, but none of it quite reached the forest floor.

Our?" he asked.

"Our. Darkenwood belongs to no one except itself, but the Clear Light Society once had a stronghold here. If we can get to it we'll probably be safe."

"Probably?"

Ernie grinned. "It's best we head deep into the forest. Enemy patrols will be combing the shore looking for survivors and you've seen what they do to them."

Toad drew back as Ernie plunged into the darkness beneath the venerable moss covered pines. Snow was settling onto their thickly twined upper branches; the deep carpet of spills beneath them was dry and smelled of resins and must. Here, under the dense canopy, the shadows seemed almost solid.

"Hurry up," Ernie called. "Get moving, before somebody sees us."

Nervously, Toad followed the herbalist. It was nearly as dark as night in the forest. Neither wind nor light penetrated the thick vegetation. The two Freaks moved on, enveloped in the cold silence of Darkenwood; the only sound was the soft rustle of their footsteps. The air was oppressive, heavy with the scent of moss and decay.

With little to distract him, other than the sight of Ernie's back in the gloom, Toad's mind began to dwell on the day's events. He began to shudder uncontrollably and he stopped to lean against a mossy trunk for support. The battle replayed in his mind and he realized that, except for Ernie, everyone was probably dead or captured. Skulk and Kentstate had been on the *Righton*, which had sunk, and when Toad last saw Mizjoan's ship it was under attack and burning. He feared he'd lost her without really ever having her—without at least becoming her friend. Toad's life, like the forest surrounding him, suddenly seemed dark, without center. He hung his head. Shocked, he noticed that one boot was almost resting on a large, well-chewed bone. Something about its size and shape made him gag with terror. He turned and rushed after Ernie.

The pipesmith fought against a growing irrational fear that caused him to sweat under his heavy clothes; he drew what comfort he could from Ernie's self-assurance. Hardly speaking, they pushed their way through the undergrowth for what seemed like hours, moving deeper into the forest, picking their way around vast deadfalls and through gloomy avenues of giant pines. The snow was beginning to filter through the branches in places, lightly dusting the thick moss underfoot.

Suddenly Ernie stopped at the edge of a small clearing. He cocked his head attentively, as if listening for something. Faint, yet distinct in the distance, were the sounds of human voices. The herbalist crouched behind a stump and signaled for Toad to do the same.

As the two Freaks watched, blue-clad figures emerged from the trees directly across from them, into the snowy clearing. There were seven of them in all—Fascist soldiers carrying swords and crossbows. At the head of the column walked a burly, scowling brute distinguished from the others by the chevrons on his coat and the heavy wheel lock pistol he carried in his meaty hands.

One of the soldiers, a skinny, jug-eared specimen whose uniform seemed much too large for him, hesitated at the edge of the clearing. He stopped, looked up at the snow drifting down, and sniffed the air timidly. "Hammers and thunderbolts," he whined. "It ain't right you make us go through this, Krakker. We wanna turn back."

Krakker spun around, leveling his gun at the complainer. "That's Sergeant Krakker, Likspittle, and I'm tired of your whimpering. Quit sniveling, or I'll grease your faggity ass on the spot."

"B-but, Sarge. Ain't nobody ever came this far into Darkenwood that's come out alive or sane."

Krakker grinned knowingly. His finger strayed to the wheel lock's trigger. The glint in his eyes was unmistakable.

"You've got only one shot, Sarge," a hulking blond soldier remarked, moving toward him. "That ain't gonna take out six."

The pistol shifted slightly. "You got a complaint, Kokbrett?"

"Yeah, I do. We're supposed to be patrolling the shore, not dick-dancing around in these woods. You're making us disobey orders."

"Orders change, boy. I don't need shit from you."

Likspittle moved closer to Kokbrett, as if for protection. "How come you didn't tell us?" he squeaked.

"Cause it ain't none of your business," Krakker shot back. "We're moving to meet with the other patrols at Indian Stream HQ."

Kokbrett relaxed slightly. Standing behind him, Likspittle inquired, "Ain't that where the Seventh Thundertroop is located?"

"Smart boy. Maybe we won't have to recycle you through Basic after all."

"We gonna attack something?" another soldier asked hopefully.

Krakker offered a lopsided, sneering grin. "Another smart one. I got me a buncha fuckin' geniuses here. What in the hell do you think we're doin' here, boy? Them Raddyclibs got their butts whipped today. An' what's the first thing you learn in boot camp? Kick 'em when they're down, co-rect? Word is, people, we're gonna blitz Guevaraville."

The soldiers brightened at this. Even Kokbrett seemed to have forgotten his anger.

"Holy Himmler, ain't that somethin'?" he said. "But we still got plenty of time, Sarge. We can't do nothin' at Indian Stream until them Greasy Boys are there to help."

Krakker chuckled. He lowered his pistol, but the look of cold amusement never left his eyes. "That was before. Now we won't need no help takin' Guevaraville. Hell, we just might waltz over an' kick the shit outta Camp Hoffman, since we're in the neighborhood. It's gonna be a great day for the White and Right."

None of this seemed to have affected Likspittle. He still hung close to Kokbrett, whining. "I still don't see why we gotta go through these woods."

In the shadow of the stump that concealed them, Toad moved closer to Ernie. His heart hammered as he mulled over what he'd just heard. It was beginning to seem that he and Ernie were condemned to hide in the gloomy forest forever while the world outside fell apart.

"Those is my orders," Krakker was saying to his troops. "Like it or not, you're gonna obey them. Let's move it out, boys."

He turned and strutted through the clearing, but no one followed. Kokbrett seemed to have regained some of his former arrogance.

"It's always what you want, ain't it, Sarge?"

Krakker stopped. His eyes flashed as he raised his weapon again. "Yeah, it is, shitheels, and you'd be wise not to forget it."

"Well, we ain't going any further, Sarge. There's haunts and boogies in this damn forest. It ain't right for us to be here."

Krakker's face twisted in an evil grin. The wheel lock swung up, pointing directly at Kokbrett. "Don't push me, boy. We gotta make time."

"Ya shit!" Likspittle bawled. "You just wanna look good to the brass."

"Tell someone who cares, wimp. Break's over, you slugs. Let's move it on out."

Grumbling, the soldiers shifted their packs on their shoulders and headed off toward the trees. Krakker, his pistol still trained on Kokbrett and Likspittle, took up the rear, forcing the others to march in front of him. Toad and Ernie held their breaths, waiting until the sound of the Fascists' voices faded into the distance. Ernie nudged Toad and pointed to the other side of the clearing. It was time that they too moved out.

As he slipped through the trees behind Ernie, Toad mulled over all that he'd heard.

"We've got to warn Leftopia," he whispered to Ernie. "If the Fascists take Camp Hoffman, we might as well pack it up for the rest of Street-Corner Earth."

Ernie shook his head. "We'd have to go through the entire Fascist army to do that. By the time we got to Camp Hoffman, if we even made it that far, it'd be too late. Besides, who would there be left to warn?"

"Well, we've got to do something."

"That's right, and at the moment that means surviving. If I can get us to Swetshop, we might have half a chance. After that, who can say?"

"But... "

"But nothing. C'mon, it's only a couple more miles."

The undergrowth grew thicker as they traveled deeper into Darkenwood. Great twisted branches intertwined over their heads, and creepers with large, menacing thorns tore at their clothing. The air was oppressive. It stank of half-rotted vegetation. From time to time Toad thought he heard something moving through the underbrush behind him. He paused and cocked his head, but the sounds ceased. Bear, he thought, and picked up speed. Soon he was following Ernie into a vast snow-covered clearing that had magically appeared out of the storm.

It was snowing harder in the clearing. The wind gusted, picking up the snow and swirling it around so they could see no more than ten or twenty feet ahead. Toad grabbed the shoulder of Ernie's coat and allowed the herbalist to guide him until the wind shifted and he could look about without shielding his eyes. Through the churning snowflakes he could make out the outlines of a massive ruin. The snow and wind momentarily subsided, allowing Toad to see that the edifice was breathtakingly huge. Made of age-blackened brick it stood, even in its roofless state, six stories high. As they passed through the iron portal on the ruin's outer perimeter, hundreds of shattered windows gazed down on the two Freaks like dead eyes.

Toad gawked as they crossed the rubble-strewn yard leading to one of the building's side doors. He looked up at the sheer walls, and at the gigantic chimney that towered above them. The ancient stone pile seemed alive—and watching.

"This is Swetshop," Ernie announced. "Shelter from the storm." Toad nodded. Somehow the thought brought him little comfort.

As Ernie tried to force open the scarred and sagging door, Toad gazed up at the ruins with a mixture of awe and dread, letting the large, wet snowflakes splash against his cheeks. As far as he could see, there were endless lines of walls. It seemed to him that nothing less than a race of giants could have constructed Swetshop. He took a deep breath, and followed Ernie through the battered door into the ruin's black interior.

To Toad, entering Swetshop was like entering a void where time had no meaning; it was as if they were stepping backward into a darker age, where eldritch forces still held sway. Holding his breath, he waited for his eyes to adjust to the gloom.

Ernie fumbled with the large belt pouch that he wore under his Fascist coat. He produced a candle and his tinderbox, and after a few tries succeeded in getting the candle lit. Toad squinted as the sudden glare revealed rusting piles of ancient machinery crouched in the corners resembling shadowy, nightmarish beasts.

"Some shelter!" Toad griped, releasing a plume of breath into the frigid air. "It's colder here than it is outside."

Ernie nodded. "Swetshop is cold even in summer."

Toad shivered again, drawing his bloodstained coat closer about him. The decaying walls were covered with a whitish-gray mold. In the flickering candlelight, the mold appeared to grow and spread. He took another deep breath and dutifully followed Ernie deeper into the ruin.

Swetshop did not appear to faze the herbalist. He walked ahead of Toad, keeping up a steady line of chatter about its history.

"There's an old Digger outpost at the far end of the building," he said. "The Radiclibs used to use it once in a while, too."

Toad looked around the gloomy chamber they were in with growing suspicion. Shadows shifted and changed shape, reaching out toward him.

"What did this place used to be?" he asked nervously.

"For centuries it was a Mansonite stronghold; they used to keep a temple around here somewhere. Before that, the Society isn't quite sure. The remains of what looked like a huge loom were once unearthed here, so it's possible that Swetshop was once a vast weavery."

Toad exhaled. The cloud of breath swirled about him and dissipated in the dark. "A place this size? You could fit a whole town in here."

"The Mansonites did, while they occupied it. Our research indicates that the Old-Timers built many such places. There were very few artisans back then. Most people worked for the handful that owned places like this, the majority of them for pitiful wages. In Bahston the Massas still maintain pale imitations of these workhouses manned by Prole slaves."

"Strange concept."

"Strange times. Let's hope we never see their like come around again."

Toad fell into step beside his friend. Ernie seemed to be finding his way by instinct, as if something was drawing him onward. They passed through a seemingly endless series of dark rooms that got mustier and more debris-strewn as they penetrated deeper into the heart of Swetshop. In one room they found rusty chains hanging from the walls and a pile of human bones. In another the walls were covered with illiterate graffiti, like "Die Littul Piggies" and "Heltah Skeltah," written with what looked like blood. The air seemed to grow heavier, almost solid, as if it contained the ghosts of all who had lived and died at Swetshop. He caught his breath as he almost tripped over a large, broken toothed gear lying in his path. Up ahead Ernie was testing a door that, judging from its covering of cobwebs, hadn't been opened in years.

"This way," the herbalist said, shoving the door open with a screech of complaining hinges. "The floor's fallen into the cellar beyond here. Be careful where you step."

As they entered, Ernie held the candle high over his head. A smell emerged from the cellar, an overpowering stench of some ancient rottenness that made Toad gag. The candle threw long flickering shadows about the two Freaks as they crept along an exposed floor beam spanning the open cellar. Though the stench rising up seared at Toad's nose, he dared not look down. Far below something squeaked and chittered in the darkness. He stumbled once and felt like he was going to faint before reaching the safety of the next room.

"The Mansonites used to throw the bodies of their victims in that pit back there," Ernie remarked.

Toad clenched his teeth and made no reply.

"You know, Toad, I'll bet it's been twenty years since I was here last. But, I can still find my way, even in the dark."

"Why were you here?"

"Digger initiation. Mine."

"None since?"

"There weren't many. The initiations held here were only for the best and brightest. It's probably been over ten years since the last."

The Freaks passed through a rubble-strewn corridor into a large room where more chains hung from the walls, and the remains of a pillory lay rotting in one corner.

"Charming place," Toad remarked.

"Isn't it, though?" Ernie stopped short. "Hey, look at this!"

The pipesmith looked where Ernie was pointing. There, in the thick dust, were the unmistakable prints of boots. The prints led from a side door into a dark corridor longer and more ominous than the first.

"These are heading in the direction of the old outpost," Ernie said, stooping to look at them like a Hunter examining spoor. "They're recent—too recent."

"Wh-who do you think made them?"

"Hard to say, but these prints didn't come from a military boot. That rules out both Radiclibs and Fashies."

"Who then?"

Ernie scratched his chin as he studied the prints more closely. "These were made with square-toed boots like you or I would wear. That rules out Greasers, who wear round-toed boots, and Fonzers who wear those pointy-toed Freak-stabbers."

"Then a Freak made these—maybe a Digger?"

"Not likely a Digger. No member of the Society has been near here in ages. It could be just a regular Freak, but most likely, it's a Rowdie."

Toad hadn't considered that possibility. His hand strayed to the Fascist musket he wore strapped across his back. "You really know how to cheer me up, Ernie."

"Just stating facts, Toad; it's more likely for a Rowdie to be in

Darkenwood than a Freak. From now on, we'll have to be more cautious." He slipped his knife out of his boot and checked the double-barreled pistol that he'd brought from the Fascist ship. "I don't want to use these things if I don't have to, but I don't want any nasty surprises either."

Toad nodded as he unslung his musket.

The footprints led down the corridor and through a fenced-in area that had been used for storage. Rats squeaked and scurried away as the two Freaks approached, disappearing amidst piles of rotting crates and barrels. The prints were placed erratically; as if whoever made them was having a hard time walking. In several places dust was disturbed where he had fallen and gotten back to his feet.

"Looks like our man's in a bad way," Toad remarked.

"Maybe so, but we'd still better be careful. He might be dangerous."

Swetshop was getting to Toad; he cursed himself for being timorous. After all he'd been through already, the old ruin should seem like the haven of safety Ernie said it was. Even the presence of a Rowdie shouldn't make Toad feel like he did, but Swetshop's history still crouched in the shadows, and much of that history was evil. If Old Charlie existed anyplace it was here. As he trudged along behind Ernie, Toad thought that soon his world would be as desolate as this old ruin, centuries of its culture ground to dust under the Dark Man's heel, entire nations and peoples brushed away as if they never existed. It seemed as if they were gone already. Only he and Ernie existed now—and one more.

Huddling deeper in his coat, Toad gripped the musket until he could feel his knuckles go white. His thumb stayed firmly on the hammer as he followed Ernie through the maze of litter-strewn aisles, past seemingly endless rows of deteriorating crates and barrels. When the herbalist stopped suddenly, Toad almost collided with him. Ernie signaled the younger Freak to be silent, flattened himself behind a huge crate, and slipped into the shadows as comfortably as he might a smoking jacket. His every nerve ending charged with electricity, Toad followed cautiously. Together they crept toward a hallway just ahead. Gray light filtered down through the broken upper stories illuminating the entryway; a body lay on the floor in front of it.

Toad approached the still, cloak-draped form from one direction, while Ernie circled in from another. The pipesmith didn't lower his musket until Ernie was bent over the body, cautiously examining it.

"I-is he dead?"

"I don't know, Toad. Help me roll him over."

Though the body under the fire-charred brown cloak looked bony and frail, it turned out to be surprisingly heavy.

"Dead weight," Ernie grumbled. "It ain't just a cliché."

The two Freaks strained to get the body on its back. It rolled and sprawled. The cloak rode up, revealing faded jeans tucked into a pair of scorched, down-at-the-heel square-toed boots. The hood obscured the figure's features. Slowly, gently, Ernie peeled it back to reveal an angular, sallow face framed by curly brown hair. Even in the dim light, the face was immediately recognizable.

"Dylan's Bones!" Toad gasped. "It's Tambourine."

Ernie nodded. His face lined with worry; he reached down and took Tambourine's wrist in his hand.

"He's got a pulse, but it's weak. We've gotta move fast, or he won't make it."

"Wh-what can we do?"

"The old Digger outpost isn't far from here. There might be things there we can use. We'll have to get him there."

"Isn't that dangerous? If he's in such bad shape, wouldn't it be a risk moving him?"

"He'll die for sure if we leave him here. This building is loaded with rats. They have a most peculiar talent for knowing when animal or man is helpless, and they're always hungry. There's also a fireplace at the outpost. Warmth is what he needs most right now."

"We'll need a litter."

The herbalist pointed to one of a half-dozen doors opening into the hallway they were in. It hung askew, clinging to the jamb by one rusty hinge.

"That'll do," he said.

Toad had no trouble tearing the door from its jamb. Though warped and discolored with age, the paneled pine slab was solid, certainly strong enough to carry a man.

Carefully, they slid Tambourine onto the improvised litter. The Freaks each took an end of the door and started out down the corridor. They passed through several more rooms before coming to a pair of grimy glass doors marked OFFICE.

"The outpost is right through here," Ernie said. "If we're lucky we might find some supplies and medicine."

"I though you said the place was abandoned years ago."

"It was, but we always leave emergency supplies, just in case."

"In case of what?"

"In case of something like this. If you knew how Diggers thought, you wouldn't ask that question. We often leave caches about, known only to us. They're always left at some place where one of our order might find himself in need, and always near important archaeological sites."

"Interesting concept."

"It's called planning ahead."

Toad accepted this with a faint shrug. He shifted the makeshift litter slowly and followed as Ernie kicked open the cobweb-covered doors. Making their way carefully, the two friends entered the old outpost.

Light filtering in through holes in the ceiling revealed the outpost to be a series of several interconnected rooms cluttered with a few dust-mantled chests and the remains of desks and other bulky furniture. At the far end of the second room, a crude stone fireplace took up most of one wall. Flanking it were a tall wooden cabinet and a rusty metal trunk.

"Supplies used to be kept in that cabinet," Ernie said as they set the litter on the floor. "Chances are there's still something in there we can use."

The latch on the cabinet was corroded with rust. It disintegrated when Ernie tried to work the mechanism. He tossed the remains on the floor and tugged on the cabinet door. It swung open to reveal shelves of jars and stoppered bottles, blankets, cooking utensils, and a box of medical supplies, all covered with a thick coat of dust. Ernie started grabbing things and handing them to Toad, oblivious to the clouds he was stirring up.

"Clean this stuff up while I check Tam out," Ernie said. "Get a fire going too."

Toad took the articles and began cleaning them with his coat sleeve. "What'll I use?"

"Bust up the furniture. There are candles and a tinderbox in the cabinet too. I'm going to need all the light I can get."

The pipesmith did as he was told, breaking up several small chairs and a coffee table and depositing their remains in the fireplace. With the aid of a few rags and the tinderbox, he soon had a warm blaze started. In the meantime Ernie had partially undressed Tambourine, examining him for wounds. In the flickering firelight the musician looked horribly pale and emaciated. His chest and arms were discolored with purplish bruises and long scratches. A horrible cut zigzagged across his chest. Dried blood stained his ragged underclothes.

"Open those bottles and pass them this way," Ernie ordered. "Some of that stuff might be useful."

"Would any of it be good after all these years?"

"It's possible. Some compounds only last a few months, but under the right conditions others are good for decades."

While Ernie shook out the blankets and used them to cover Tambourine, Toad wrestled with the stopper of a large brown bottle. He was still fighting with it when Ernie took one of the other bottles, opened it and poured its contents out into his hand. The small pile was brown and crumbly—plant material of some sort. Frowning, the herbalist touched his tongue to the dried leaves.

"Hawthorn," he announced. "If fresh, it would make an excellent sedative."

"Just what Tam needs now, right?"

"Unfunny. Need help with that bottle?"

"No, I've got it." Toad lifted the stopper and sniffed at the bottle. The smell that reached his nostrils was unmistakable. "Hey, this is like the cold medicine Skulk gave me. It's probably no good now though."

Ernie reached for the bottle. "Are you kidding me? Properly sealed, this shit would keep its potency for a century."

"We should all be so lucky. Still, it looks like Tam's got more than a cold."

The herbalist took the bottle and poured some of the thick liquid into a cup. "This isn't just cold medicine, Toad, it's a general restorative. If this stuff doesn't help him, nothing will."

Once Tambourine was bundled in more blankets and moved to a sagging, overstuffed couch, Ernie forced several sips of the medicine down his throat. Though he shook slightly and moaned, the musician didn't waken.

Ernie hurried to the cabinet and began reading the faded labels on the jars and bottles. He selected a cobalt blue bottle and took it nearer to the fireplace. Quietly, he began to read off its contents.

"Plantain, mullein flowers, lungwort. I could use this to ease any fevers or colds. There's willow bark here, too, good for pain. That is, if this stuff is still usable."

"I thought what you gave him was supposed to be enough."

"It's a big help, but it won't cure all his ills. He's emaciated and suffering from exposure. Whatever he's been through, it's left him pretty banged up. That wound on his chest will need dressings and something to fight infection. There isn't much we can do except keep him warm until morning. Most of these herbs are no longer much good. At first light, one of us will have to go in search of fresh ones and some food. It's late in the year but there's still things out there we can use. For now, I'm going to gather up some snow to boil down for water."

Ernie picked up a couple of pans and headed out. While he was gone, Toad added a few more scraps of wood to the fire and set about organizing the contents of the cabinet. When the herbalist returned fifteen minutes later, he had it almost finished.

Ernie set the pans on the fire. As the snow melted to water and began to boil, he extracted a packet of dressings from the box of medical supplies they'd found, and began to unwind them. Toad had just taken a jug out of the cabinet and was dusting it off when Ernie looked up.

"What you got there, kid?" he asked.

"I've no idea. There's no label."

"Pass it here, then."

Ernie took the jug and uncorked it. He sniffed it, then took a sip from it and smiled. "Aaah! The best kind of medicine, Toad. Apple brandy. Untouched and quite tasty. A vintage '37 if nose and palate serve me right. Fetch some cups and we'll have a nip."

Toad produced a pair of earthenware mugs from the cabinet and wiped them free of dust. Ernie filled them to the brim with the dark, sweet-smelling liquor. The herbalist took one and passed the other to the younger Freak.

"Drink up," he advised. "It's gonna be a long night, and we'll need something to take the chill out of our bones."

The two Freaks huddled by the hearth, sipping on their drinks. Ernie tipped a little of the brandy into the boiling water, then threw in one of the bandages.

"Don't swill up all this toddy," he said. "I want to use some of it to clean Tambourine's wounds. Tomorrow, one of us will have to scare up some yarrow so I can make a proper poultice. We'll need other herbs as well. I'll do up a list later."

When the bandage had boiled sufficiently, Toad and Ernie drained their mugs and went to where the helpless musician lay. The large gash on Tambourine's chest looked particularly troublesome. With Ernie's guidance, the pipesmith helped wash and bind Tam's wounds. When they finished, the herbalist administered another sip of restorative and they returned to the fire. From time to time they looked over to see how Tambourine was doing. Color was slowly returning to his cheeks and he was breathing more easily, but he showed no signs of regaining consciousness.

"I wish there was more we could do," Toad said sadly.

Ernie poured another half cup of brandy and moved closer to the fire. "There's nothing more we can do tonight, Toad, except make sure that he's warm and comfortable. Once that restorative takes effect, and we get him the herbs he'll need, he should pull through all right."

"How can you be so sure? Are you a doctor on top of everything else?"

"No, but an herbalist learns more than a little about healery in his line of work, especially if he's also a Digger."

"Is Tam a Digger, too?"

"No."

"Then why's he here in Swetshop?"

"That's a very interesting question. We'll have to ask him."

"I hope we can." He reached over and touched the musician's brow. It

was hot with fever. "Do you really think he'll live? He looks terrible."
"Infection is his worst enemy right now. If we can stop it he should be
okay. At least he's got a better chance now than he did." Ernie took a big
sip of his brandy and swallowed hard. "We'll have to watch him in shifts
tonight," he declared. "You might as well turn in. I'll take first watch."

That was agreeable to Toad. It had been a harrowing day, one that had
thoroughly sapped him of energy. He drained off the last of his brandy and
rolled out one of the blankets to sleep on. Using his coat for a pillow, he
curled up by the fire and closed his eyes.

Toad fell into the dream almost immediately. He was someplace cold.
Snow danced all about him, driven by a howling wind that gnawed at him
with frozen fangs. He was not alone. Indistinct figures moved through the
snow on all sides of him, shapes that seemed to shift and alter with the
wind. Though he squinted and shielded his eyes, he couldn't determine
whether they were friends or enemies. At times they seemed to be both.
They were moving toward some high cliffs. He could see the hulking
blackness of the mountains through the snow. Behind him the horizon
glowed orange, flickering eerily through the gusting snow. Screams came
from that direction, riding on the wind, and a shrill bitter laugh—the Dark
Man's laugh. The sound ripped at Toad's nerves. When the unseen hand
clamped down on his shoulder, Toad almost screamed himself.

"One of these days I'm going to learn to wake you without scaring you
half to death," said Ernie, holding a cup of hot brandy in front of Toad's
sleep-dimmed eyes. "C'mon, get up. You've been out for hours, and from
the looks of it, you've been having some wild dreams."

Toad accepted the cup eagerly, taking a large swallow. It was warm and
soothing. It washed away the last vestiges of his nightmare.

"Is it morning already?" he asked, wiping his mouth with his sleeve.

"That and then some. Sun's been up for over an hour."

"I thought you were gonna wake me to stand guard."

"What can I say? You looked so cute, just like a baby. I didn't have the
heart."

"How's Tam?"

"Actually, he seems a little worse. You should go ahead and find the
herbs we need while I stay and tend to him."

"Why me? You're the herbalist. I wouldn't know what to look for."

"Tam needs me here."

"But I don't know a lot about herbs."

Ernie grinned and produced a scrap of heavy paper covered with closely
crowded script. "No offense, but you don't know much about healing
either. I made a list for you. You're familiar with everything—bloodroot,
ginseng, sweet flag—the usual stuff. I also need staghorn sumac, grape

171

burdock, juniper berries…"

"Enough with the juniper berries," Toad said. "I'll go."

Toad took the list from Ernie. He shrugged into his coat, and taking his musket and a blanket to carry his finds in, headed out of Swetshop following Ernie's directions.

The sun was just lifting above the treetops as Toad stepped out into the snowy field behind Swetshop. He squinted, temporarily blinded by the light reflecting off the huge expanse of snow ahead of him. Slowly, his eyes adjusted and he could make out details: the snakelike mound of a half-buried stone wall, the runic shapes of leafless bushes, and the numerous tracks of small animals that transformed the snowy field into a magical scroll, recording furtive comings and goings.

Frozen stalks of grass crunched underfoot as Toad made his way toward the area where the tracks seemed thickest—a small swampy area near the edge of the clearing. Sometime during the night, after the storm had passed, the field must have hosted a flurry of activity. Near the forest, Toad observed the delicate spade-shaped tracks of deer, along with the spoor of squirrels, rabbits, field mice and birds.

The deer tracks led past a stand of twisted old apple trees that stood sooty black against the clear blue of the sky. Beyond the trees, the field was overrun with juniper. Toad squatted among the bushes and started to strip them of their berries, taking only the firmest and darkest ones.

Beyond the junipers lay the swampy meadow, where willow and birch grew in ragged groves. After Toad had stuffed enough of the berries into his blanket bag, he headed toward the nearest stand, breathing in the cold, crisp air. When he reached the grove, he pushed his way into it, oblivious to the scratchy branches and the spongy frozen swamp beneath his boots.

Picking up a sharp stone, he began stripping bark from the largest willow. As he spread out the blanket and placed the berries and strips of bark on it, he took time to scan the list Ernie had given him. Most of the items could be found in the clearing, but he knew that he'd have to venture into the forest to find the all-important ginseng. The thought didn't please him. The woods were dark and forbidding, even in daylight. He winced as his stomach rumbled, reminding him that he hadn't eaten since the previous morning.

Once Toad had completed a circuit of the field, stuffing everything he could find from the list into his makeshift bag, he unslung his musket and headed into the forest. As he made his way through the undergrowth he used the sharp stone to make blaze marks on the trees. The bag on his shoulder was beginning to feel heavy, but it could still hold a few more items.

At the base of an old oak Toad found what he was seeking. The brown leaves of several ginseng plants poked up through the thin snow cover. Making sure not to injure the delicate man-shaped roots, Toad carefully dug up the plants with his stone. He shook the dirt from his prizes and placed them carefully in his sack. When he looked up, he was surprised to see a fat rabbit, its fur already half gone to white, regarding him with curious eyes.

Toad smiled. "Hello, little bunny," he said, pulling back the hammer of his musket.

The rabbit clearly understood Toad's intentions. As the Freak drew a bead on him, the little animal jumped and scampered off into the bushes. Cursing under his breath, Toad shouldered his bag and followed. The rabbit's tracks led straight to a wind-fallen maple. It had taken refuge among the exposed roots.

Toad kicked at the roots until they caught and tore at his pantleg. In disgust he threw down his bag and poked at the tangled roots with his gun. The muzzle nudged something soft. With a shrill squeal the rabbit emerged from its hiding place in a brown and white blur. Grinning triumphantly, Toad aimed at the disappearing shape and pulled the trigger.

The gun went off with a roar, kicking Toad so hard in the shoulder that he almost lost his footing. When the smoke cleared, he was amazed to see the shot had taken the animal off its feet, blowing it halfway down an incline that led to a small gully. Shouldering his bag and weapon, Toad raced toward his prey.

Toad found the rabbit lying on its side in a patch of bloody snow. He washed off the small corpse as best he could and placed it in his bag. There'd be rabbit stew tonight.

As he started back up the incline, Toad noticed some large tracks off to his left. They too were headed uphill, but veering off towards the deep woods. The small hairs on the back of his neck prickled. Something had been moving out there, perhaps observing him—something much larger than a rabbit. Bear, he thought, maybe a moose. Gripping his musket like a club, Toad went to check out the tracks.

He froze when he saw them. Though blurred and partially filled with snow, they were unmistakably made by human feet, apparently by a man of fairly good size. His scalp tingling, Toad stooped to examine them. They weren't made by any kind of boot or shoe he was familiar with. A shred of coarse gray material sat in the middle of one of the tracks. He picked it up and examined it. It was half rotted and smelled bad. Whoever had made the tracks had bound his feet in rags for lack of proper shoes.

Toad threw away the shred of smelly cloth like he might the remains of a dead rat. Wiping his hands on his trouser leg, he stood and looked both ways, half expecting to see a pallid face staring at him from the shadows. Moving quickly, he retraced his steps out of the forest and crossed the field

PIPEDREAMS

toward the crouching dark ruins of Swetshop without looking back.

Chapter Twenty-Two

As the days passed, Toad and Ernie maintained their habit of sleeping and standing guard in shifts. The two Freaks discussed the mysterious footprints often, pondering their meaning until more important things took precedence. At one point, Ernie took a stroll outside to examine the tracks and returned shaking his head—a hermit or some poor refugee, he theorized, fleeing from earlier border troubles.

The snow returned, burying the tracks under five inches of fine white powder. When no new ones appeared, the topic dropped from their conversations and they turned their attention to surviving and taking care of Tambourine.

Under Ernie's knowledgeable care, the musician was making good progress. Color had returned to his face and his fever had abated. Aided by poultices made from the herbs Toad had gathered, Tambourine's wounds were healing without infection. Though lucid from time to time, and able to eat with a little help, the musician hardly spoke and only vaguely acknowledged his surroundings. The restorative, plus Ernie's various broths and herbal teas, kept him groggy. When not eating or having his dressings changed, Tambourine slept, waiting for his body to finish repairing itself.

On the fourth night of their stay at Swetshop, Toad was keeping the midnight-to-dawn vigil while his friends slept soundly not ten feet away. Though it seemed odd to admit it, Toad was beginning to feel comfortable at Swetshop, or at least in the corner of it where he and Ernie had settled. The room exhibited the small, comfortable signs of occupation, and was no longer a barren, dust-filled box like the others surrounding it. The pipesmith brewed some herb tea and surveyed the now-familiar objects crowding every surface. Bundles of herbs dried on the mantle, surrounding the rack of antlers from the deer Toad had shot the morning before. A haunch from the same deer roasted slowly over the fire.

Taking his mug from a table littered with Ernie's doctoring paraphernalia, Toad sat by the hearth and poured himself a cup of herb tea. As it cooled, he reached into the pocket of his dirty Fascist overcoat and extracted a pipe and a sack filled with some wild Honkweed that he'd found, nicely dried on the stem, in a cluster near the far end of the swamp. Toad hummed as he cleaned the weed, separating sticks and seeds from powder. From time to time he'd toss a handful of seeds into the fire, smiling as they popped.

When the weed was clean, and his pipe well packed, Toad lit it with a splint from the fire. Taking a couple of deep hits, he leaned against the wall and blew the sweet-smelling smoke out over the sleeping forms of his friends. He closed his eyes for a moment, letting the weed warm his body as it loosened his mind. For some reason it felt more powerful and relaxing than before. When he opened his eyes he saw Tambourine sitting bolt upright and staring at him. The musician's lips were moving, weakly forming words.

"Are you going to share that bowl," he wheezed, "or am I going to have to beg?"

The pipe dropped from Toad's fingers, showering sparks on the hearthstones. Tambourine spread his arms. The blanket slid from his shoulders, revealing the bandaged cut on his chest.

"You're awake," Toad said, feeling foolish as soon as the words had passed his lips.

"Of course. I try not to make a habit of talking in my sleep."

Tambourine still looked flushed and sickly, but his eyes were clear and they shone with high spirits. He tried to get to his feet, but the effort seemed too much. Groaning, he sat back down, still gazing questioningly at Toad.

"Are you going to fill that pipe up and pass it this way, or not?"

Toad picked up the pipe and sat at Tambourine's side. Whatever the fever had done to Tam's body, his mind was still clear.

"I'm not sure you should be having any of this," he said, repacking the pipe.

"Why not?"

"You're still pretty sick."

The musician smiled, though it was more of a grimace. "I look a lot worse than I feel. It's been a while since I've smoked; I deserve it."

Toad lit the pipe from the candle on the nearby table, took a quick toke and passed it to Tambourine. "Just take it easy. And, when you're ready, you can tell me how you got here."

"Fair enough. I was wondering the same about you."

The musician smoked most of the pipe by himself, sharing the last of

176

the bowl with Toad. When they were finished, Toad began relating the events that had transpired since they parted ways in Covenstead.

Slowly at first, then with greater speed as the events of his travels replayed in his mind, Toad told of the Concert Hall fire and his capture by Sonny and Cuffer. He noticed a look of concern darken the musician's features as he related how he'd been tied up and dragged through the woods. The look deepened as the pipesmith talked about his boat ride and subsequent escape to Froggy Bottom. By the time he was relating the battles of Fetid Bog and Great East Lake, Tambourine was leaning far forward.

"Quite a story, Brother Toad, and not good news. Apparently, you've been through as much as I have."

"Meaning…?"

"A lot I'd care never to go through again."

There was silence between them for a moment; then Tambourine began to tell his story. "I should begin at Covenstead Fair," he said. "That was where I met the person whose quest sent me here."

"A quest?"

"Yeah. But maybe we should wait until Ernie wakes up."

"Ah, let him sleep. I'm dying to hear your story, and it will give me a one-up on Ernie for a change."

"Fair enough, but if I get too tired I'll have to stop." He paused for a moment, then settled in and continued.

"I was at the Fair, playing my guitar by the fire, when this stranger stepped out of the shadows and started talking to me. He was a short little dude, dressed oddly, even for Halloween in Covenstead. His clothes were so old that they smelled like mold and, although it was dark out, he was wearing sunglasses—a strange pair, with mirror lenses. He called himself Maynard."

"I-I saw him, too. He was asking a lot of questions about you and Ernie. He acted like he knew you both pretty well."

"Well, he knew a lot about me, but I'd never met him before."

"You said in your note that he was an old friend of the family."

"He claimed that he knew many of 'em, back a ways."

Toad shrugged. "I've heard about Maynard. Some things I believe, some things I don't. What did he want from you?"

"He wanted me to find an old book for him here in Swetshop."

"A book? Here? Why didn't he come himself?"

"I'm still not quite sure. I got the feeling, though, that something awful must have happened to him in a similar place, in his youth, when places like this were common."

"Then, he's as old as they say?"

Tambourine nodded. "Probably older. I've seen his eyes, man. Like the old song says, 'he had the eyes of age.' Everything's written in them. See them and you see the history of our kind."

"And the book…?"

"He wants some old thing on ritual magick." The musician rubbed his hands and moved closer to the fire. "Once Maynard got me convinced of the urgency of his mission we left Covenstead right away. Traveling most of the night on foot, we reached the area of Indian Stream and Ripoff Pass just after daybreak. The place was a madhouse. We passed mobs of Freaks heading south, fleeing from the Fascists who were setting up a base camp in Indian Stream. Taking to the fields and woods, we got into some secret mountain passes that Maynard seemed to know well. In that way we skirted Ripoff Pass and came within sight of Darkenwood late the next day.

"At first I hadn't trusted Maynard very much, but as we traveled together I became fascinated with him and his endless knowledge of old lore. Beside him, the elders of the Clear Light Society, or even the nameless writers of the *Book of Love* seem to know practically nothing. He told me of the days before Helter-Skelter in a way that only one who had actually been there could. When we parted, I headed to Darkenwood, and he continued on to Hillcommune. I gave him Fashie Killer, my guitar, for safekeeping. Once I had the book, I was supposed to meet him there."

Toad's eyes widened. "Really. Ernie said that the three of us would head for the Oldhip stronghold once you're well enough to travel."

"That's not surprising," Tambourine replied. "We both have been there a few times, and it's probably the safest place in Street-Corner Earth."

For a moment, with a slight smile tugging at the corner of his mouth, the musician's thoughts drifted. Then, regaining his train of thought, he continued.

"As I was saying, I needed to get the book so I waited until dusk before heading into Darkenwood. I had to cross over a mile of open fields, and I knew that enemy patrols were thick as fleas in the area. As it turned out, I should have waited longer than I did.

"I was more than half way to the edge of the forest when I spied a troop of Fascist cavalry passing in the distance. I took to the high grass, keeping low as I edged toward the tree line. Every time I looked back they seemed to be getting closer. It was a stupid move, but I panicked and broke for the woods. I ran until I thought my heart and lungs would burst. The trees seemed to rush toward me; before long I could almost reach out and touch them. I was aware of the dread most people had for Darkenwood and I hoped that my pursuers would turn back at forest's edge. I thought I would be safe, but then the clamor of hoofbeats shook the ground around me.

"I was almost into the first row of stunted pines when something hit me over the head. I collapsed face-first into the brush. When I rolled over, I was surrounded by Fascists, their spears and swords pointed at my throat."

Tambourine signaled for another pipe, which Toad quickly packed and lit. The musician took a toke and held it until his eyes watered.

"That's better," he wheezed. "Where was I? Oh yeah... At first the Fashies wanted to kill me, but the officer in charge wouldn't let them. After he checked me out, he decided to have me tied up and taken to the regional commander, a fat-ass Whiterider named Krotchlow. The guy looked me up and down with those cold, piggy eyes of his, then kind of nodded his approval.

"'You did real well not to kill this faggit,' he said to the Fashies that had brought me in. 'Fact is he could be the one Overcommander Klaven told us to be on the lookout for. We're gonna take him back to the Keep with us and let Brother John decide what to do with him.'

"By now you probably know that Brother John, or Blackcloak, or whatever you call him, is the outlander that started all the trouble between the Fashies and our people to begin with. Though it seemed impossible, I was beginning to fear that he'd found out about my mission.

"Next thing I know I was on my way to Klaven's Keep. Once there, they turned me over to the Whiterider guards. I hadn't eaten for several days and I was so battered from being tied up and moved around like a sack of potatoes that I could hardly stand upright. Still, the Sheets had to get their licks in. I was bounced through torchlit corridors and dragged up seemingly endless flights of stairs until we reached a small waiting room outside of Klaven's quarters. I was thrown on a cold stone bench outside of the huge oaken doors. Behind the doors I could hear cursing and harsh laughter.

"One of the Riders opened the doors and went inside while his buddy stood guard over me. I slumped onto the bench, exhausted, but my ass hardly hit the seat when he grabbed me by the hair and forced me to sit upright. I cried out and he poked me with his spiked truncheon.

"After what seemed hours, the other rider returned. 'Overcommander Klaven will see you now, scum,' he said. 'It's best that you kneel on the floor before him and don't speak until spoken to.'

"He jerked me off the bench. Then, he half dragged, half threw me across the floor and forced me to my knees beneath a high stone throne.

"On the throne was a short, dumpy man dressed in the elaborate blue and gold uniform of a high-ranking Fascist officer. The wide-brimmed white hat he wore shadowed his face, but I could still make out the jowls and the beady eyes, set close to either side of his long thumb-shaped nose. I was in the presence of Klaven Thinarm.

"Around Klaven's throne stood various officers, Whiteriders, Greasers, and slutty-looking women. Everyone was holding a jug or drinking horn, and several had already drawn weapons. One of the Greasers wore several lengths of chain hanging from the shoulder of his leather jacket and a crown of crudely worked iron on his head. I guessed he was Overhed Kham. None of the company spoke, but they all fixed on me with mocking, hate-filled stares. At last, Klaven nudged me with his heavy boot. The hobnails dug into my head.

"'Is this the faggit we were told of?' he asked, his reedy voice out of place with his heavy-set body.

"'It is,' one of the Whiteriders told him. 'He was caught right outside of Darkenwood. We think he's the one Brother John is looking for.'

'Lord Flatbush,' Overhed Kham corrected.

"Klaven gave Overhead Kham a look that could melt stone. Then he turned and glared down at me, long and hard. 'Darkenwood, eh?' he grunted, scratching his chin. 'What was your business there, faggit?'

"I sputtered out some bullshit story but Klaven cut it short with a shove that sent me sprawling on my back to gales of laughter. I tried to get up but he tromped down on my chest, pinning me to the floor. He pressed down hard, until I thought my ribs would crack. Then one of the sluts leaned over me and hit me in the face with her huge boobs and everybody laughed even louder.

"'I think this faggit's lying,' Kham said, stepping up to kick me. 'Send for Lord Flatbush.'

"Suddenly the laughter stopped..."

"Did you see him?" Toad asked with some apprehension.

"I did," Tambourine said, hunching closer to the fire. "And I hope I never see his likes again—death-black robes and burning eyes. I swear the temperature dropped when he entered the room. The only sound was his thick-soled boots knocking on the cold stone floor. Everyone's eyes were alive with fear, even Klaven's and Kham's."

"What'd he look like?"

"Tall. Real tall, and all black. He even had black gloves and shiny black boots, with soles that must have been six inches thick. A long black stick protruded from his cowl; its smoldering tip was no match for his unblinking blue eyes. His face was hidden deep in the shadows of his hood, but those eyes burned a hole clear through me. He leaned over, putting his cowled head close to mine. I felt a horrid chill, as if the heat was being sucked from my body. Then, I swear, he sniffed me like a dog would a bone. Suddenly, he stood up and ground out the stub of his stinkstick on the arm of Klaven's throne.

"'You waste my time,' he hissed. 'This isn't the one.' Then he wheeled and left the room."

"Holy shit. Close call," Toad said. The hairs were standing up on the back of his neck.

Tambourine picked up a stick and poked at the fire with it. "Yeah, it was close. After that, Klaven and his cronies lost interest in me. They took me to the dungeon below the Keep until they could think of an entertaining way of killing me.

"My cell was a horror, small and dank, with only a hard slat to sleep on. I was lucky in one aspect, though; the guards' main interests seemed to be drinking and playing cards in the station next to the cells. So, for the most part I was ignored.

"Then one night, Klaven's birthday, or so I'd guessed from listening to the guards talk, the drinking and carousing were going on much heavier than usual. The turnkey brought me my food, but he was so loaded that he spilled most of it. When he left he fumbled at the lock for a while and then lurched off. The asshole never locked the door."

Tambourine stopped poking at the fire and accepted the pipe that Toad passed him. "You can't imagine how I felt. I wanted to shove the door open and make a blind dash for freedom, but I had to be sure everyone was asleep. I don't want to think of what they would have done if they'd caught me. The waiting was agony. Hours later, I pushed the door open gently and crept out of my cell. Several rats chittered and ran past my feet. I stole an old cloak and got the keys from one of the guards, as he lay sprawled across an empty keg. Using the keys to get through the doors in the upper passageways, I made my way toward the main gate. Several times I had to slip past guards who were on patrol and on the way out I almost walked into a pair sharing a bottle by the gate. I just barely got by them."

Toad accepted the pipe back from Tambourine. "Dylan's Bones, that's quite a story..."

"That's not all of it, Toad. Not by a long shot."

"There's more?"

"Unfortunately, yes. I had to hurry. It was already getting light in the east, so I took a more open route, following the lakeshore south to Darkenwood. I glanced over my shoulder and almost shit myself. Eight Whiteriders on horses were bearing down on me."

Toad nearly dropped the pipe. "Oh no."

"Oh yeah. The Riders cornered me on the edge of a steep hill overlooking the water. They encircled me and dismounted. I wanted to run, but every avenue of escape was cut off. At first I thought the riders were the ones from the Keep, but they wore an unfamiliar skull emblem on their sleeves and none of them had firearms.

"The Whiterider nearest me produced a short knobbed club, which he lay right across my shins. I fell in a ball of agony. As the pain subsided they were clustered around me, uncoiling long, scary-looking bullwhips.

"Their leader, a tall thin Sheet with a red lightning bolt stitched on his hood, was the last to dismount. He strode through the line and stood towering over me, carrying a wide-bladed dagger that seemed neither too clean nor too sharp.

"'Looks like we caught us a faggit,' he said, toying with that frog-stabber of his. He snickered in a way that made the sweat pump out of me like sap out of a maple.

"'What we gonna do with him, Kleegle?' one of the other riders asked.

"Kleegle began whipping his knife from side to side. 'Kill 'im, I imagine. You boys can pick how.'

"'How about the cross?' one piped up. 'We ain't done one of those in a while.'

"Kleegle seemed to like that idea. I'm sure that under his hood he was grinning to himself. He made a gesture and half of the Riders rode out to the nearest grove. I'd heard of people dying that way, lashed to a cross and set aflame. It was no way I wanted to depart the world, writhing to death on a Whiterider fire tree.

"When the Riders returned, maybe twenty minutes later, they were carrying two huge tree limbs, and armloads of brush and kindling. The branches were fitted together into a cross and set into the ground at the crest of the hill. Then they tied me to it.

"One of the Riders produced a soiled handkerchief to gag me, but Kleegle made him put it away. He wanted to hear my screams when I started cooking. I decided not to give him the satisfaction. Even when the kindling was placed about my feet and torched, I held my tongue. As soon as they lit it, the heat was intense, and I could smell my clothes beginning to smolder."

His face drawn, Tambourine took a few quick tokes from the pipe and went back to poking at the fire.

"In spite of the unbearable heat on my feet, I was aware enough to notice that the bindings around them had charred and fallen away. When Kleegle began poking at me with his knife I let out a blood-curdling yell and flailed at him with my feet. My thrashing loosened the cross, causing it to lurch backward at a crazy angle, slowly tipping over the hill. Suddenly, the cross broke free and slid down the muddy embankment toward the lake.

"I used my feet to propel the cross faster down the hill. When it went into the lake I used them like paddles to put some distance between the Riders and me. The last I saw of them, the whole hilltop was on fire and they were flapping around like fools trying to put it out.

"As it turned out, I hit the current where the lake empties into the river. The cross crashed against some rocks and broke apart, freeing me, but I got this big gash in my chest. I crawled out of the water and made my way into Darkenwood."

Toad fished out the carefully rationed jug of apple brandy and offered it to Tambourine. The musician lay down the pipe and accepted it eagerly.

"It seems like you've been through enough to kill two men," the pipesmith said.

Tambourine finished off the jug and wiped his mouth with a corner of his soiled cloak. "I would be dead if it weren't for you and Ernie. I owe you guys. And with your help, maybe now I can finish what I set out to do. The *Necronomicon* may yet be found and delivered to Maynard at Hillcommune."

The hairs on the back of Toad's neck stiffened again. "*Necronomicon?*"

"Yeah, that's the name of the old magick book Maynard wants. According to him it should be here in Swetshop somewhere."

The pipesmith's mind raced. He knew of the *Necronomicon*, and of some of the legends surrounding it. A partial copy had been in his family for generations, though it was written in a language that nobody could understand, and was defaced with footnotes scrawled in it long ago by someone named Lovecraft. In spite of this, the sheath of crumbling pages had given off an aura of power. He hardly ever picked the book up; something about it felt wrong, almost evil. He wanted to mention that to Tambourine, but something told him to keep it to himself, for now.

"I've heard of it before," he said blandly.

Tambourine nodded, stifling a yawn. "It's kind of famous I guess, though I don't take much stock in that stuff, legends and such. People trust too much in legends and they're always disappointed when they learn the truth. Anyway, Maynard says it's really old, so it must be worth a lot. It was ancient even in the days of Westcommune, when Frankie Lee liberated it from the library of Parakwat, Tommy Two's chief poisoner. If Maynard's got his story straight, this copy he's got me looking for was one of the priceless volumes that the Risen Brothers were taking to Teetering Rock. When the Mansonites killed the Risens, they kept the book, supposedly bringing it east with them."

"Here?"

"For centuries Swetshop was a Mansonite stronghold. When Jo-Jo Lion Berkeley put them down the book was not found, but was thought to be hidden here somewhere."

"But…"

The musician yawned and shook his head. "I've talked enough for one night. I'm worn out."

Toad nodded.

Tambourine turned away from Toad and before long was snoring softly.

Toad sat watching him for a long time. In his head he replayed the story, going over parts of it time and time again. He sat by the fire and stared off into the shadows. Somehow they seemed blacker and deeper than before.

Chapter Twenty-Three

Toad eyed the broken shovel lying in the rubble at his feet with disgust. It was the fifth one he'd ruined, the third since yesterday morning. Muttering, he sat down on a pile of rusty machine parts. Ernie and Tambourine were busy with wrecking bars, tearing out a wall on the other side of the cavernous storeroom. They seemed to be enjoying themselves, laughing and joking as they scattered plaster and lathwork on the already cluttered floor. To look at Tam, Toad found it hard to believe that just a few days before he'd been knocking at death's door.

Swetshop was working on the pipesmith's nerves. He was growing tired of its gloom, its smell of rot and decay mired in a darker time and place. Also, he was bored with Tambourine's endless search for the *Necronomicon*. Regardless of what the musician said, Toad doubted that it had ever been in Swetshop. Even on the slight chance it was, the ruin was so huge that years could be spent hunting for the old book. At the rate the half-rotted tools they'd discovered were falling apart, they'd soon be digging with their bare hands.

The herbalist lay down his wrecking bar and glanced in Toad's direction. "Hey, wrinkledink," he yelled. "You gonna screw off, or you gonna work?"

"Screw off, if it's all the same to you."

Ernie and Tam started walking toward Toad. "It'll be dark soon. 'Bout time to call it a day, anyway," Ernie commented.

"Toad, we've got to be more careful with these," Tambourine said, looking down at the broken shovel. "We have to make them last."

"Is all of this worth the effort?" Toad asked.

The musician wiped the plaster dust from his clothes. "What do you mean? We have to find the *Necronomicon*."

"If it's here to find."

"It's here. I'm sure of it."

Toad shrugged, watching Ernie light the pair of lanterns they'd brought with them. "Even if we do find it, what then?"

"Then, we'll take it to Maynard in Hillcommune."

"What's he going to do with it?"

"He didn't give me the details, but he has a plan to use the book's power to defeat our enemies."

"You trust him?"

"You forget, Toad, I've seen his eyes. He's no ordinary man. Yes, I trust him."

Toad shook his head. "I'm not sure I do."

Ernie finished fiddling with the lanterns. The storeroom was bathed in mellow light. "Do I detect an argument brewing, you two?"

"Not really, Ernie. I'm just getting tired of this place."

"We all are," Ernie replied. "I may have made my comments about Maynard in the past, but Skulk trusted him and said that he had great wisdom and a rare kind of strength. If Maynard says he can use this old book to save Street-Corner Earth, then I say we should continue looking for it."

"Even if we have to spend the rest of our lives in this hole doing it?"

"Until we've found it, we've got nowhere to go."

Toad looked at the shovel blade at his feet. Angrily, he kicked at it. It skittered several yards across the dust-covered floor and hit something with a ring of metal on metal.

"There's no need for that," Ernie said. "C'mon. We'll knock off for the day and have something to eat. You'll feel better about everything in the morning."

"What's the point?" Toad continued. "Leftopia's probably charred ruins by now. Covenstead's gone. Even if the book could have helped, it's too late."

"Giving up already? We survived the lake battle and made it here. For what?! I can't believe this was all for nothing."

During their discussion Tambourine had moved away from his friends. He stood idly examining the broken shovel blade, nudging it with the toe of his boot. "Hey, you guys," he said. "Come over here. I've found something. There's a ring set in the floor. The shovel hit it just now."

The musician got down on his knees and began to clean away the dirt and debris around the large iron ring. By the time Toad and Ernie joined him he'd cleared out an area that revealed a door set into the floor.

"A trap door," Ernie marveled. "There must be a cellar underneath."

"It's worth a look. Help me clear out some of this trash. Toad, would you bring one of those lanterns closer?"

Curious in spite of himself, Toad brought over a lantern and the three

Freaks set about brushing aside the accumulated dust and rubble. Grabbing the ring with both hands, Tambourine gave a hard tug and the trap door opened with a groan of long-rusted hinges. A dank, nasty odor, that suggested slimy creatures crawling under rocks and debris, issued from the darkness below. Holding the lantern over the pit, the Freaks could see a series of iron rungs leading down into a stone shaft.

"This could be what we're looking for," Tambourine said excitedly.

"So's every other place we've looked in," Toad replied. "Why would this one be any different?"

"Because it looks dangerous," Tambourine answered with a slight smile.

Toad shook his head. "Yeah, well screw that; I've had my fill of danger."

Ignoring Toad's protests, Tambourine and Ernie started to climb down into the moldy, dark shaft, taking the lanterns with them. As the light disappeared below him, Toad looked about the storeroom, grimly aware of the gaping mouth of a hole in the ceiling above, the decayed and broken beams jutting from the old plaster like teeth. Long shadows stretched up the walls, gobbled up by the hungry maw of darkness above.

"Hey, wait for me," Toad called out. "If you insist on looking for the book down there you're going to need my help."

The pipesmith started down after his friends, nearly slipping on the wet rungs. The air grew rank as he descended, but the light below him beckoned. Paying as little attention as possible to the dripping stone walls of the shaft and the cold slimy feel of the rungs on his hands, the pipesmith stepped on Ernie's hand in his eagerness to reach the bottom. The shaft ended about twenty feet down, terminating in a tall, wide tunnel. Sagging beams and the corroded remains of intricate copper pipe work crisscrossed its ceiling.

The lanterns revealed that at some time in the past sections of the masonry walls had given way and been repaired with concrete. It must have been done long ago, Toad thought; the concrete was crumbling and cracking apart. Water had collected on the earthen floor of the tunnel, and in several places the Freaks found themselves sloshing through puddles several inches deep.

At the end of the tunnel was a door made of riveted iron. It was caked with the rust and discoloration of centuries. Toad held his breath as his two friends worked the heavy door open, revealing the yawning blackness beyond. The door led into a large chamber. Inside the air was heavy and thick; the shadows cast by the lanterns seemed almost solid.

At one time the chamber must have been a meeting hall of some sort. Rows of crude wooden benches were lined up across the middle of the room, facing a stone altar. The altar was littered with a jumble of ceremonial objects, including a skull, several rusty daggers and a pair of large black candles. It was what the lantern light revealed behind the altar that grabbed Toad's attention, though. There, over six feet wide and reaching to the ceiling, a bearded mosaic face glowered down at them. Its mad, stone eyes seemed to follow the Freaks as they approached the altar. Smeared on the icon's forehead, in what looked like dried blood, was a jagged scar-like cross.

"I'll be damned," Ernie whispered. "It's the Old Charlie. We've found the lost temple of the Mansonites."

Toad felt a chill pass through him as he looked up at the huge portrait of Manson. The face seemed to mock them, sneering down at those who dared disturb its sanctuary.

"The *Necronomicon* is here somewhere," Tambourine said. "I can just feel it."

"We might as well start around the altar area," Ernie stated. "If it's here that is where it will be."

Toad didn't move. He kept staring up at the great mosaic face as if hypnotized. "I hate this place," he muttered.

"As a Digger you get used to this sort of environment, but in truth I'm not too fond of it myself," Ernie replied. "If the book *is* here, the sooner we find it the better."

The herbalist placed his lantern on top of the altar. He and Tambourine began rummaging through the litter.

Beneath the portrait, Toad felt the ancient cult leader watching him. "I think I'll look around," he said.

"Suit yourself," Ernie replied.

Toad made his way through the aisles between the benches. He could see his friends' shadows looming huge against the portrait as they chattered back and forth. As he approached the far wall he noticed a curious iron grating next to a rotting bundle of dark red rags. Bending down to investigate the grating Toad nudged the rags with his knee. He stifled a cry as a gray, misshapen human skull fell from the pile and clattered around his feet. It stared at him with its empty sockets and eternal, knowing grin. He wondered if the Dark Man grinned like that.

"Toad, come here, we've found it!" Ernie yelled.

"Take a look, Toad," Tambourine said, stretching out his hand as the pipesmith reached the altar. "You know, it's not as big as I expected."

Tam held a small packet wrapped in coarse red cloth, but Toad knew what it was before his fingers touched it. There were markings on the cloth, laboriously stitched in what looked like human hair. At first they were indecipherable, but as Toad studied them he could see they were ordinary letters, though some were reversed and all were misshapen, as if copied down by someone who didn't know their meaning. Once his mind had deciphered them, they read CHRLI:BK—Charlie's Book. Trembling with such excitement that he almost dropped the little packet, Toad quickly unwound the cloth. Inside the wrappings he found a small worm-eaten volume bound in black leather and stamped with intricate silver filigree that spelled out NECRONOMICON.

Tam was right; it seemed small. His own partial copy at home was a lot larger than this obviously newer edition. Excitedly, the three Freaks passed the book from hand to hand, marveling at the eldritch phrases and disturbing diagrams that filled its pages.

"We can leave for Hillcommune tomorrow; our search is over," Tambourine said, slipping the slim volume under his cloak.

"The sooner we're out of here, the better," Toad agreed.

Ernie picked up his lantern and started toward the door. "I'm afraid we'll all have to put up with Swetshop a bit longer. It'll take a while to get supplies together for the journey to Hillcommune. Even under the best of conditions, that'd be a three-day trek. These days it'll probably take even longer."

"You're right," Tambourine replied, "but right now all I can think of is the pot of venison stew that's waiting for us."

Toad's stomach growled happily at the mention of food.

After they ate, Toad borrowed the *Necronomicon* from Tam and sat down by the fire to read, while Ernie and the musician cleaned up and began planning their journey to Hillcommune. Toad studied each page of the old book carefully, trying to absorb what it said. Fortunately, most of it was in the Common Tongue, but many of the chants it quoted were in a language Toad found difficult to pronounce—a language almost totally devoid of vowels. The references to beings like Nyarlathotep, Cthulhu, and Yog-Sothoth confused him more, as did the odd and disturbing diagrams. Some of the diagrams were similar to the ones in his copy at home, but others were unfamiliar and done in a cruder style. This *Necronomicon* had a different feel as well. His copy, in spite of its unreadable text, had an evil aura about it; this one just felt like an old book.

Toad thumbed backward to the front of the book. There were several pages missing, but in what was left of the prologue he caught references to "Lovecraft". Could it be the same Lovecraft that had scribbled marginalia on his copy? This *Necronomicon* had notes in it as well, but they didn't match the spidery script that he remembered.

Ernie brought Toad a cup of tea and placed it on the hearth. "Really getting into that book, huh?"

"It's confusing, but interesting."

"It's a hell of a lucky find."

Toad nodded. "It sure is. You know, the way we found it seems unnatural—not right, somehow."

"Don't know how you can say that, pal. It was right where it should have been."

"That's not what I mean, Ernie. I just don't see how it survived so long. It was damp in that temple. A book should have rotted to pieces in that kind of environment."

"You'd be surprised. Back in '62 Skulk and I excavated an old library a couple of miles from Summerluv. It was in a bad spot, just where a swamp empties into Summerluv Pond. By rights, we shouldn't have come up with anything of value, but in fact we got almost eighty volumes out of that dig. Over half of them were in good condition and dated back to Helter-Skelter and before. In the Society we call that 'Digger's Luck'."

"Still, I've got a funny feeling about it."

"You're just letting this place get to you. Why don't you wolf down this tea and do a bowl with Tam and me? You'll need it since it's your turn to pull guard tonight."

Toad picked up the mug and drained half of the boiling liquid. The herbal brew revitalized him. When he'd drunk it all, he set the *Necronomicon* to one side and helped Ernie clean their remaining supply of weed.

Much later, after Ernie and Tam had turned in for the night, Toad returned to the book, but found the passages of the small, close-set type to be overly grand, too pompous to read in long stretches. The margin notes were fascinating, though. They gave references to other magick books and expanded on various underlined passages. Again Toad wondered who'd made them. From what he'd read about Mansonites, it seemed unlikely that one of them would be capable of such knowledgeable commentary. But if the notes hadn't been done by Mansonites, then who?

A noise in the hallway made Toad forget the book. An old building like Swetshop creaked and settled with age and winter weather, but what he'd heard, or imagined he'd heard, sounded like footsteps. It had to be rats, he thought. The ruin was filthy with the little beasts.

There was another sound—a creak, as if a loose board had been stepped on. Toad stuffed the *Necronomicon* into the backpack he'd fashioned out of a blanket and started for the corner where his musket sat propped against the wall. He halted, thinking better of it, and sat back down. He considered waking Ernie, but talked himself out of that too. The older Freak wouldn't appreciate being awakened in the middle of the night just because Toad was letting his nerves get the better of him.

Toad reached for the kettle bubbling on the hearth and poured himself another cup of tea. He thought about Hillcommune and everything Tambourine and Ernie had told him about it. Tambourine had visited there in his younger years and Ernie was still a frequent visitor. Both said there was no place like it in all of Street-Corner Earth. It was a paradise, where the sun almost always shone and flowers bloomed even when it was winter beyond the mountains, where the days passed slowly and the heart was never troubled. It was an island of peace and plenty in a world going dark, where the women were beautiful beyond description, the wine flowed like water, and Honkweed plants grew twenty feet tall. He sipped his tea and sighed.

Again he heard noises—stealthy footsteps and the quiet murmuring of voices in the hallway. Dropping his teacup, he dove for his musket just as the door flew open. A knife whistled through the air and stuck, vibrating, in the baseboard inches from his hand.

Suddenly, the room was filled with a howling mob of skinny, ragged figures brandishing spears and clubs. Several of the invaders moved toward Toad, their spears leveled. Others fell on Ernie and Tam, kicking them and hitting them with large sticks.

The room swarmed with mad-eyed barbarians, and more stood watching from the doorway. Male and female alike were a singularly disturbing sight. They were gaunt to the point of emaciation, with glazed rolling eyes and fish-belly white skin. Some had running sores on their faces and all displayed teeth that were in varying states of decay. Their clothing was mostly tattered rags—weird combinations of Freak, Fascist and Greaser garb that was filthy and crudely patched. When they spoke it was predominantly in grunts, with an occasional recognizable Freak or Fascist phrase. They all had long hair and most of the males were bearded; the creatures looked like no Freak, or even Rowdie, that the pipesmith had ever seen.

When the mob had finished beating Tambourine and Ernie senseless, several of the creatures dragged the Freaks from the room. The leader, a male taller and gaunter than the rest, turned his attention to Toad. He was a frightening sight in his graying Whiterider robe, cut short and worn over an almost new pair of black leather pants. He had a Radiclib campaign cap pushed back on his greasy hair, and instead of shoes, his feet were wrapped in rotting gray rags. He grinned as he approached Toad, revealing teeth long gone to green and black. In his hand he carried a long wavy-bladed knife that looked badly rusted.

"No move, little piggy," the creature hissed. "You move, me cut balls."

Numbly, Toad nodded. He was sure the gaunt man would enjoy doing what he threatened to do.

The creature gave him a cold grin and moved closer. His breath smelled like an open sewer. Hate blasted from his tiny, close-set eyes as he held his knife against Toad's crotch. The knife moved up, pricking Toad's stomach.

191

"No talk, till Geekus say talk."

The pipesmith stood like a stone, hardly daring to breathe. The knife drew back an inch, two inches. For the first time he noticed the livid, cross-shaped scar between his tormentor's eyes.

"Good, little pig. Charlie like us be good children."

Toad felt close to fainting. Mansonites! But they were supposed to be extinct. Somehow a whole tribe of Charlie-worshipers had not only survived in Darkenwood, but had returned to their old temple. Now he and his friends were their prisoners.

The Mansonite who called himself Geekus turned to his companions and barked, "All gots?"

"All gots, Godspawn," they grunted in unison.

"Good. Can go. Make boogie now."

A short, grinning Mansonite wearing jeans and a Greaser jacket approached Geekus. He scratched his crotch and giggled. "Don't kill? Not good, Geekus Godspawn."

"Not kill here, Squeakyson," Geekus replied. "Charlieday soon. Kill then."

"Not now?"

"No, Squeakyson. What me say, you do."

Squeakyson shook his misshapen head. With disgust, Toad noticed that the little Mansonite's chin was slicked with drool. He eyed the pipesmith up and down and turned back to Geekus. "Me be hungry," he whined.

"Eat shit then," Geekus growled. "We go now."

The little Mansonite shrugged stupidly, but there was a dangerous glitter in his eyes. "Me do what you say. You Chosen, not me." He sneered as he tromped off.

When he was gone, Geekus gestured at Toad with the knife. "Okay, move now, piggy. Beat feet."

Toad needed no further prompting. He reached for his pack, but Geekus grabbed it from him. Ever mindful of the knife at his back, he allowed himself to be herded into line behind the two Mansonites carrying the bundled forms of Ernie and Tambourine. One of the Mansonites had retrieved Ernie's top hat and wore it perched ridiculously on his large, knobby head. Though frail looking, the Mansonites proved surprisingly strong. They carried the two unconscious Freaks with no apparent effort.

Other Mansonites joined the procession, carrying food and other items that they'd pillaged from the room. A stringy-haired girl with a cataract on one eye had taken Toad's musket and was employing it as a staff. Mindful that he'd left it loaded, Toad wished that it would go off and scatter the Mansonites.

Outside of Swetshop the wind pulled a caul of ragged clouds over the moon. Yet, in the darkness, the Mansonites had no problem navigating. It appeared that despite their obvious inbreeding and degeneracy, they possessed good night vision as well as strength.

Toad looked about, thinking of escape even though he knew it was futile. As if reading the pipesmith's thoughts, Geekus uttered a grunt and two Mansonites, burlier than the rest and dressed in matching red-and-black checked Hunter's coats, moved up to flank Toad. They said nothing, but grinned in a way that made the pipesmith's skin crawl. The smaller of the two giggled and drooled slightly. Avoiding their hungry glances, Toad put his head down and concentrated on placing one foot in front of the other.

As he plodded along, oblivious to the dark forest around him, Toad mentally catalogued everything that he'd ever read about Mansonites. It wasn't much—just a few references in one of Kermit Badmoon's works to a scholar named Evan Copralallius who'd made several expeditions into Darkenwood before disappearing there early in the last century. According to Copralallius, the Mansonites were murderers and expert torturers who delighted in killing slowly and inflicting great pain. Worse yet, Copralallius maintained that sometimes they cooked and ate their victims, having developed a taste for human flesh during their long wanderings. Toad closed his eyes and tried to fight back the fear that was consuming him. Like most Freaks, he wasn't particularly religious, but he considered praying to the Freedom Rider to deliver him. Even death, that old grinner, seemed better company than the shambling subhuman forms that muttered and moved about him.

The Mansonites walked quickly but stealthily, moving through the moss-covered pines and down the rocky banks of gullies. Toad had to scramble to keep from tripping several times as the Mansonites hurried along the floor of one particularly long gully to a low, scrub-covered hill crowned with a high standing stone.

"Family near," Geekus grunted, pointing to the stone.

Squeakyson wandered over to the two Hunter-coated Mansonites flanking Toad. They stepped aside, allowing him to prod the pipesmith with one bony finger. Toad flinched, sickened by the hungry look in the little Mansonite's cloudy eyes.

Geekus shoved the smaller man aside. "Watch step, Squeakyson. Leave piggy to me."

"Hungry, Geekus."

"Not be hungry long, be dead. Move ass."

Squeakyson shrugged and walked on, but not without giving Toad another appraising glance. "Party soon," he mumbled.

Under his dirty overcoat Toad was sweating. Something in the way

Squeakyson had said "party soon" froze Toad to the marrow. He could smell his own fear rising like mist from a swamp. His guards must have sensed it too, because they laughed and elbowed each other in the ribs. The pallid moon broke out from behind the clouds, bathing the hilltop in light. He looked up at its gloating face and shuddered.

The Mansonite village lay in a wide gully surrounded on all sides by high, wooded cliffs. The buildings were rude, tumbledown huts made of wattle or rough-sawn planks, though one appeared to be constructed mostly of the bones of large animals. Some of the buildings nestled under overhangs while others appeared to be little more than false fronts propped in front of natural caves. Toad was taken to one of these caves and shoved roughly inside. The still forms of Ernie and Tambourine were dumped in beside him. The Mansonite who had taken Ernie's top hat must have become bored with it. He tossed it in after the herbalist where it landed in a half-frozen puddle at Toad's feet. As the pipesmith stooped to retrieve it, he heard a heavy iron grating swing shut, closing off the entrance to the cave.

Two torches guttered in their wall sconces, throwing lurid shadows. It was damp in the cave and the air was heavy with the smell of excrement. Slime grew on the walls and water dripped constantly from the low ceiling. Looking around, Toad saw that the cave wasn't natural at all. It was a man-made tunnel lined with fieldstone and brick with the same type of beams he'd seen in the tunnel under Swetshop. The tunnel ran back about thirty feet and came to a dead end, where bricks, newer and more crudely made than those in the walls, sealed it off.

Toad moved to where his friends lay, placing Ernie's hat on a rock to dry. Ernie and Tam's labored breathing told him that they were alive, although they were still unconscious. He made them as comfortable as possible, then sat down on a rock away from the dripping walls and watched the flickering camp fires of the village. In the distance he could hear drumbeats and muffled chanting. The thought of what the Mansonites had planned for him and his friends horrified him.

The drumming increased tempo and the chanting grew more frantic and strident. Toad looked up to see a tall figure approaching the guards who stood watch outside the cave. The Mansonite wore a studded Rowdie vest over a Radiclib tunic that was falling apart at the seams. A cat skull dangled around his neck on a string of beads. His jeans were filthy and crudely patched, but the hob-nailed Fascist boots they were tucked into were shiny and almost new. Toad caught his breath when he saw the man's face. Ugly even by Mansonite standards, it was crisscrossed with burn scars that gave it a melted, puckered look. One eye was almost closed shut by knotted scar tissue. Mercifully, a black cloth that moved with his breathing covered the lower part of the Mansonite's face.

The guards snapped to attention as the tall man drew closer. Hideous though he might be, he was obviously someone of importance.

"Hail Charlie, Dhambum," the guard in the sleeveless red shirt said. Beside him his companion averted his head, seeming to study his rag-clad feet.

"Hail Charlie, Atkins Steeltooth," the tall man replied. "I come for the hippie-pig."

Steeltooth grinned, revealing long yellow incisors. "Which piggy?"

"That one," Dhambum said, pointing at Toad, who tried in vain to melt into the shadows.

"Ahh, he make good munchies."

"You bad as Squeakyson. Get him now."

Atkins Steeltooth pulled a key from the ring at his belt and opened the grating. Grabbing Toad by the arms he shoved him toward Dhambum and kicked the grating shut behind him. Dhambum produced a slender dagger, which he held to the pipesmith's throat while the guard bound Toad's hands with rope.

"He yours," Steeltooth announced when he was done.

Dhambum nodded and withdrew the dagger. Grabbing Toad roughly by the back of the neck, he shoved him toward the clearing where the campfires were burning.

One of the houses they passed was larger and better built that the others. It had a real wooden door instead of a skin flap, and it was painted all over with mystical symbols. It was from this house that the chanting and drumming came. In the long shadows beside the house, robed and shaven-headed women sat rocking and howling in the dirt. Dhambum tightened his grip on Toad's neck, pushing him toward the clearing, but as he passed the house Toad looked back to see one of the women stand and point to the sky.

"Charlie die, Charlie live!" she cried. "All hail Charlie's love!"

In the middle of the clearing a fire blazed between two high-standing stones. Atop a granite altar, in front of the fire, stood Geekus Godspawn. He was now wearing a robe of coarse red material, an empty sword scabbard hanging from his belt. In his hands he held the *Necronomicon*. Toad's pack lay on the altar by his feet. Dhambum's fingers dug into Toad's neck and he was forced to kneel before the altar.

"I bring the hippie-pig, Chosen," Dhambum announced.

Godspawn grinned. "Good, Dhambum. You leave now."

"But, Chosen…"

"Go, Dhambum."

After Dhambum had moved back off into the darkness, Godspawn tapped Toad's shoulder with one rag-covered foot. "Can stand now," he said.

Was it Toad's imagination, or was there a trace of friendliness in the Mansonite's voice? Slowly, the pipesmith got to his feet.

"Dhambum is High Charliepriest," Godspawn explained.

Toad nodded, though he wasn't sure that he understood.

The Mansonite held out the *Necronomicon*, waving it tantalizingly close to Toad's face. "This in your bag. You steal Charliebook?"

There was no sense in lying. "Y-yes, I took it."

"Can read?"

"I can read."

A look of interest crossed Godspawn's slack face. His eyes glittered. "Long time go some Charliepeople read, write too. No more. Now be stupid. Not even Dhambum know what book say."

"You want me to read this book?"

"Just so. You read at ceremony, you live. This holy book. Maybe if you read, Charlie come—real Charlie, Old Charlie."

Something like hope flickered to life inside of Toad. "Let's get this straight," he said. "If I read for you, you'll let me live?"

"That so."

"And my friends?"

"Other piggies must die."

Toad squared his shoulders, standing firm as he met Godspawn's cracked gaze. His heart hammered against his rib cage as he spoke. "No. If my friends die, I wish to die with them. Spare them and I'll do as you say."

The Mansonite laughed a dry, cunning chuckle. "Worse things than death, hippie. Pain make you read."

"I'm sure that it would. However, since you can't read, I could say that your book says anything that I want it to. Spare my friends and I'll read true."

Godspawn considered this for a moment, idly picking at a sore on his chin. "Some of Family not like that."

"And you?"

"I Chosen. Soon I be next Charlie."

"And… "

The Mansonite grinned. "I say there be other piggies to kill. You read true, you be Family. Friends live too. You not read true, all die."

"I'll read true."

Godspawn snapped his fingers and two Mansonites stepped out of the shadows behind the nearest standing stone. One was Squeakyson, the other a thin redhead lacking front teeth. "You take hippie back now. Give food. He help at ceremony. Bring back then."

"No eat?" Squeakyson said, licking his lips.

"No. Go now."

Squeakyson and the skinny redhead led Toad back the way he'd come with Dhambum. They stopped at one of the huts and Squeakyson went inside. He returned moments later with a loaf of black bread and a crockery jug stoppered with a corncob. He undid Toad's bindings and handed him the food.

"You eat," he said, giggling. "Me hungry too. Maybe eat later."

Toad scowled. "Yeah. Maybe someday you'll eat somebody's fist."

The little Mansonite found this amusing. "Too bony. Like tripes best."

Another fifty feet and Squeakyson turned Toad over to Atkins Steeltooth and the other guard, who were sitting beside a fire they had started in Toad's absence. They pulled Toad roughly to the cave and locked him inside. Back by the fire, Squeakyson and the redhead sat down with the two Mansonite guards. They talked softly, but from time to time they laughed and glanced in Toad's direction.

Stupid animals, Toad thought. He ripped off a piece of bread from the loaf and began to eat it. It was dry and tasted like it was made out of acorns, but he ate a third of the loaf anyway before setting the rest aside for Ernie and Tambourine.

Toad followed the bread with a pull from the jug. It was wine of a sort, but heavy and slightly bitter tasting. He took a second pull to pass clearer judgment. It tasted no better, but it warmed his stomach. Taking a third swallow Toad re-corked the jug, placing it on the ground beside his sitting rock.

Geekus Godspawn and the priest, Dhambum, seemed to be the top men in the village. Maybe, if he played it right, he could use one of them to get his hands on the *Necronomicon* again. Then, if he and his friends could somehow find a way to escape, they could still deliver the book to Hillcommune. He looked over at Ernie and Tambourine. They were no help, just now. His friends were still out of it, but they were breathing easier.

Toad stared at the jug, letting his thoughts wander. How they might get out of the Mansonite village wasn't clear, but then neither was anything else at this point. His vision blurred momentarily, doubling, then tripling, then doing interesting kaleidoscope effects. Whatever this wine was made of, it was damn potent stuff.

He reached for the jug, but the shadows circled in and he was asleep even before his chin hit his chest.

Chapter Twenty-Four

The shadows had substance, thickening about Toad like gelatin as he moved down the long tunnel toward the distant light. It was difficult to move forward, impossible to move back. Nameless fear churned his guts as he was inexorably pulled toward the distant pale flickering light, like iron drawn to lodestone.

After what seemed like hours, the shadows finally gave way to the radiance of many candles and he found himself in the underground temple standing before a high dark altar. In the dancing candlelight he saw the twisted face of Manson leering down at him. The portrait's eyes fascinated him. A timeless evil seemed to brood in their stony depths, and he found that he couldn't look at them for very long. They were eddying pools of black hatred that threatened to suck him in.

Toad was not alone in the chamber. He sensed something was moving in the shadows, something ancient and malignant. A sudden snicker startled the pipesmith and he looked up to see a black-robed figure standing in front of the portrait of Manson. The figure laughed again, long teeth flashing briefly within the deep shadows of its cowl. From the folds of its robes it produced a twisted black stick, which it lit on one of the candles. Toad whimpered softly as acrid smoke filled the chamber. This was it, the final confrontation.

The air grew heavy and oppressive. The walls of the chamber began to change and move inward. The altar wavered and melted into a new shape. Within moments it was gone, and in its place stood a strange metal coach, all glittering glass and brightly painted steel. Despite his fear, Toad couldn't help but be fascinated by the great metal wagon. It was like nothing he'd ever seen before, yet there was an eerie familiarity to it as well.

The Dark Man found it fascinating too. Ignoring Toad, he inspected it closely, running a black-gloved hand over its top, and cackling appreciatively as he stooped to examine some minute detail of its design.

Toad moved back into the shadows, feeling immense relief when the Dark Man opened one of the coach's doors and, laughing gleefully, swirled inside. Suddenly, he felt himself falling. Invisible hands reached out to grab him.

Toad awoke with a start to find Ernie and Tambourine lifting him up from the floor of the cave. "Wh-where am I?" he said thickly, not quite comprehending that he'd been dreaming.

"We might ask you the same," Ernie replied, helping him to his feet. "The last thing I can remember is somebody beating the crap out of me in Swetshop. I came to about an hour ago. Dylan, I feel like one big bruise. Tambourine was already awake, in pretty much the same condition as me. You were sleeping like a baby on this rock, but just now you were twitching so much that you almost fell off. Tam and I stopped you."

Tambourine stood peering out of the iron grill at the Mansonite guards sitting by the fire. The moon was hanging low over the rim of the gully beyond and it was starting to get light out.

"Where are we?" the musician asked quietly. "Who are these people? Are they some kind of Rowdies, or something?"

"Worse," Toad replied, dusting the mud from his clothes. "They're Mansonites."

Ernie shook his head in disbelief. "How could that be? The last Mansonites were destroyed ages ago."

"Apparently some survived. Judging from what I've seen of their settlement, I'd say there must be about a hundred of them."

Tambourine let out a low moan. Though he was standing at the front of the cave with his back to them, they could see how tightly he was gripping the iron crossbars. He was shaking his head slowly and kicking at the grating.

"I can't believe it," he raged. "After all I've been through, to end up as supper for some slimy Charlie-sucker."

"We're not going to die," Toad said.

"I wish I shared your belief, Brother Toad."

"We're safe for the time being, Tam."

"But the legends say…"

"I know what the legends say, but I've got this little deal with their chief." Quickly, he related his conversation with Geekus Godspawn. When he was done, Tambourine left the front of the cave and came to sit beside him.

"Then there's a chance of getting out of here?" the musician asked, the tension in his face lessening.

"Almost none," Toad nodded solemnly. "Still, as their Bookreader, I may be allowed some freedom."

The conversation was curtailed by the appearance of Squeakyson and his redheaded companion. Squeakyson was carrying a basket filled with food and the redhead staggered under an armload of firewood. One of the guards let the pair into the cave, where they deposited their burdens on the floor.

"Godspawn give these," Squeakyson said. "Eat lots, get fat."

"Squeakyson, you've got a one-track mind," Toad remarked. The Mansonite gave a slack-jawed grin and rubbed his belly; then he and the redhead departed, slamming the grill behind them.

"I guess my little talk with their leader has reaped a few benefits," the pipesmith said to his friends as he opened the basket. Besides food, it contained torches for the wall sconces, a flint-and-steel, and several coarse blankets.

The three Freaks assessed the food. There was black bread and dried meat that looked like it might be venison. There were also several jugs of heavy dark beer.

Tambourine grabbed a hunk of meat and sat by the fire while he nibbled on it. "At least the food's better here than at Klaven's Keep," he said glumly.

"Yep, literacy's a powerful thing," Toad replied, munching thoughtfully on a chunk of black bread.

The next few days passed without event. Every morning Squeakyson and his companion brought supplies, but other than that, and one brief visit from Godspawn and Dhambum, the Freaks were left to their own devices. Late at night when they couldn't be observed by the guards, they chipped away at the brickwork at the back of the cave, more from boredom than from any real hope that some way to escape might lie beyond. On the evening of the fourth day of captivity, Squeakyson and the redhead came for Toad.

"Make quick," Squeakyson said as the grillwork was opened and the guards brought the pipesmith out. "Ceremony soon."

The two Mansonites led Toad through the village, taking him to the clearing where he'd first met with Godspawn. A huge bonfire burned between the standing stones where Godspawn and Dhambum stood. Most of the villagers were lighting torches by dipping them into the fire, while a handful readied a canopied litter that lay on the ground by Godspawn's feet. As Toad was forced to kneel in front of the Mansonite chief he noticed an old man in ragged red robes and several figures in Fascist uniforms being led into the crowd. The uniformed figures wore bags over their heads and were tied together in a human chain. Before Toad could get a closer look at any of them, Godspawn tapped him on the shoulder, indicating that he could rise.

The chief wore the same red robe that he'd had on the night he and

Toad had talked. His feet were encased in heavy black boots and a sickle-shaped knife was thrust under his belt, next to the empty scabbard. In his hands he held the *Necronomicon*. He grinned slightly and passed the book to Toad.

"Ceremony soon," he said. "You walk with me and Dhambum."

Taking the book, Toad looked around at the crowd. They eyed him suspiciously. "Isn't the ceremony going to be held here?"

"No. Tonight special, go special place."

Toad nodded. Was this place the one he'd dreamed of, the old temple under Swetshop? His stomach clenched at the thought of that musty chamber with its glowering portrait of Manson and its ancient, dark secrets. Drums sounded in the village, as they had for the past several nights. They were followed by a series of high, keening wails. As Toad watched, a half-dozen shaven-headed women in identical red robes placed the old man on the litter. He sat regarding the crowd with rheumy, bloodshot eyes as the women lifted him and the litter over their heads.

The drums increased their tempo as the litter bearers started through the village with Godspawn, Dhambum, Toad and the rest of the Mansonites following behind. As he walked along, Toad kept glancing at Dhambum, but the priest's masked and scarred face was unreadable.

The procession left the village, taking a path that led them deep beneath the moss-bearded trees. The torches cast long, flickering shadows that danced between the venerable pines like wood sprites. Except for the drumming, the procession was silent. Feet shuffled noiselessly over ground too deep in the forest to be covered by snow. To Toad the silence between the drumbeats was frightening. It seemed that something evil was near, something that might reach out of the darkness and seize him in its black-gloved hands.

After a while the forest gave way to a moonlit clearing, snow-covered and dotted with clumps of brush and juniper. In its center, Swetshop loomed black and ominous against the star-flecked sky. The sight gave Toad no comfort.

"Temple near," Dhambum croaked. "Where you steal Charliebook." The ruined face above the mask hardened and became even more hideous.

Toad sensed the priest's barely contained hatred. "We thought you were all gone. The temple looked like it wasn't used in years."

"It only be used when new Charlie named," Godspawn intervened, picking at his teeth with a dirty fingernail. "Last be True-Knife, long year past. Tonight be me ... have Bookreader. Last Bookreader many Charlies ago."

Toad tried to hold back as the procession neared Swetshop, but Dhambum pushed him forward. He had no desire to see the stygian temple again, where his nightmares might become realities. Still, he knew that he had to face what was ahead, for his friends' sake and for his own. Ernie and Tam's lives were in his hands now, so he tried to shrug off his fears and followed Godspawn through the ruined entryway that led into Swetshop.

Drums now sounded within the ruin itself. Once the trap door was opened, Toad could hear them pounding far beneath the floor. Apparently some Mansonites had been sent ahead to prepare the temple, for as the women lifted the old man from his litter and eased him down the shaft, light poured up to greet them.

After the old man and the women were safely through the opening, Dhambum followed. Toad froze up in spite of himself, unable to place his feet on the iron rungs leading downward. He nearly cried out as Godspawn's fingers dug into his shoulder.

"Move," the Mansonite hissed, "or throw you down."

The pipesmith responded quickly, scurrying down the shaft, fighting back fear and nausea.

At the bottom of the shaft, Mansonites lined the tunnel leading to the glowing temple. Godspawn forced Toad past the host of inbred miscreants and into the chamber, which was as brightly lit as it had been in his dream. Sitting on a bench near the altar, Toad watched Dhambum prepare the ceremonial objects as several acolytes in sleeveless black shirts lit the last of the candles in the wall sconces.

Unnoticed by either Dhambum or the acolytes, Toad got out of his seat and wandered toward the back of the chamber. Except for himself, Dhambum, the acolytes, and Godspawn, the temple was still empty. The rest of the Mansonites were waiting outside in the tunnel until the start of the ceremony. As he moved along the far wall, he stooped to examine the iron grill he'd noticed on his previous visit to the temple. A smell of wet earth and decay came from beyond the grill. The light from the candles revealed a tunnel, walled in crumbling concrete with the now familiar pattern of beams and pipe work along its ceiling. Toad put his hands on the rusty grillwork and began to pull.

"Bookreader!" Dhambum boomed. "Get away. Come here."

Reluctantly, Toad let go of the grill and walked back toward the altar.

The priest seized Toad as soon as he was within range. Shocked, the pipesmith offered no resistance, though he tensed up when one of the acolytes, a pimply youth with a leather cap worn backward over his greasy, plaited hair, grabbed his other arm and dug in with his long dirty fingernails.

"You listen," Dhambum said, his fetid breath blasting in Toad's face. "This be my son, Beatleskin. You do what him say. Gots book?"

"Y-yeah, I got it."

"Read true. No fuck up."

Toad watched numbly as Dhambum pushed aside a rag curtain behind the altar, revealing a low passageway about the height of a man's waist. Gesturing hurriedly, the priest indicated that Toad was to enter it. Already Beatleskin was on his hands and knees, crawling into the passageway. Toad hesitated, but a shove from Dhambum sent him on his way just as the rest of the Mansonites began filing into the chamber.

The narrow crawl space was dark and confining, but it soon widened into a small, candlelit cell that was large enough for him and Beatleskin to stand in. Toad was all too aware of the Mansonite's closeness and his overpowering body odor. Directly in front of the pipesmith was a small aperture that revealed the altar and the chamber beyond it. Below the opening the end of a wooden tube protruded from the wall.

"This special place," Beatleskin said, with an air of adolescent importance. "Old times, Charliebookreader talk here."

"I see," Toad said, realizing that speaking into this tube would make the Mansonites think that Old Charlie himself was talking to them. "When was that?"

"Long time before Graycoat pig-soldiers came."

Toad nodded. The *Necronomicon* hadn't been read since before the Mansonite Insurrection late in the last century, so these people had been illiterate way before then. It would be easy to say that the book said anything that he wanted it to. Still, he reasoned, though crude and violent, the Mansonites seemed to possess high animal cunning. They might be able to detect a fabrication, so like it or not, he'd "read true."

"So, Beatleskin, when I read, your people will think the picture of Charlie is talking to them?"

"That be so."

"What do you want me to read?"

Beatleskin seemed confused. He scratched one acne-scarred cheek as he pondered the question. "When I say, just read."

"Okay." As he watched Dhambum and the others through the aperture, Toad slipped a finger into the book. When it came time to speak he'd read more or less at random.

Outside of the hidden cell Dhambum strutted in front of his audience like a carnival mummer. The chamber was filled with Mansonites now, and more were standing in the doorway. They were a wild looking mob, with their mismatched ragged clothing and gaunt faces that had been painted with crosses and swastikas. As Dhambum worked on them, they became openly agitated. Some squirmed in their seats while others leered and played with their knives. When Godspawn joined Dhambum at the altar, several got to their feet and began grunting loud cheers, but when the priest raised his gloved hands they dutifully took their seats again.

"Tonight we make new Charlie," Dhambum boomed, his voice echoing throughout the chamber. "Charlie die. Charlie live. All hail Charlie's love."

"ALL HAIL CHARLIE'S LOVE!" the crowd responded, eyes glowing in slack, gray faces. Some giggled insanely, and the fidgeting and knife-play became more noticeable. Several of the more ecstatic twitched and drooled.

Dhambum's face crinkled, and it occurred to Toad that under his mask he was probably smiling, or making what would pass for a smile on that ruined visage. The pipesmith saw Godspawn's green teeth flash as the priest reached out to touch his shoulder.

"We all be Charlie's children," Dhambum intoned. "All be Family."

The crowd murmured, agreeing.

"Many be Family. Only one be Chosen."

The Mansonites became more agitated, louder and more enthusiastic. The shaven-headed women cried out ecstatically. "CHARLIE! CHARLIE! CHARLIE!"

"Geekus Godspawn Chosen—he that be son of True-Knife."

"CHARLIE DIE! CHARLIE LIVE! ALL HAIL CHARLIE'S LOVE!"

Dhambum wiped his forehead with one gray sleeve. The elation burning in the eyes above his black mask filled Toad with dread.

"Tonight we have piggies to eat," the priest continued, gesturing languidly with one gloved hand. A commotion erupted in the doorway and a pair of tall Mansonites in denims and leathers shoved several cowering figures into the room. The prisoners were all dressed in the remains of blue uniforms. With a start, Toad recognized Krakker, Kokbrett, and the other Fascists he and Ernie had observed in Darkenwood. They were gaunt now, and looked like they'd been badly beaten. Even as Toad watched, the one called Likspittle began to cry uncontrollably as he was forced toward the altar.

Dhambum gestured again. He was agitated, excited.

"Long time Family live Dark Woods; long time our enemies keep us from sun. Soon that change. Soon Family be strong again. Old Charlie weak, we make new Charlie."

"CHARLIE DIE! CHARLIE LIVE! ALL HAIL CHARLIE'S LOVE!"

He waited until the crowd settled down again. Then, Dhambum leaned forward as if to impart some great secret. "Soon Karma Circle close. We make new Charlie, yes, but First Charlie come too—Old Charlie. He be with Family again, make them strong."

Toad felt the sweat beading on his forehead. His time to read was drawing close. When he read, the simple Mansonites would believe that the picture of Manson was speaking to them, confirming Dhambum's prophecy. The wily priest needed Toad as much as Godspawn did, and the pipesmith was determined to turn that to his advantage. Somehow he'd find a way to gain full possession of the *Necronomicon* and plot a way to set himself and his friends free.

Dhambum threw his arms up, giving the ready signal. "Tonight Charlie speak to Family," he boomed. "He speak to us like he did before piggies drive us into Dark Woods. He speak and we be mighty people again! All hail Charlie's love!"

"ALL HAIL! ALL HAIL CHARLIE'S LOVE!"

The priest pointed at the captured Fascists cowering before him. He reached under his mask to wipe his mouth, then took the long sickle-knife one of the acolytes offered him. He ran his fingers over it lovingly and held it above his head so the candlelight flashed from its shiny blade. Toad wasn't listening to his words anymore; they were just more rantings about Charlie and how he loved his children. He searched the *Necronomicon* for something to read. In it lay his destiny and that of Street-Corner Earth. He hated wasting even a morsel of its wisdom on the shambling, half-human Mansonites, yet they too were now part of the cosmic plan.

Toad noticed again how the book felt lifeless in his hands. The old family copy felt far different; it gave off waves of dark energy. He looked down at the yellowed, fly-specked pages he'd randomly selected. The type was faded and hard to read in the dim light. Somehow, he had to convince the Mansonites to let him have the book for a while.

Beatleskin leaned close to Toad. He smelled like rotting fish. "Get ready. Read soon," he advised.

Toad flipped quickly past the seemingly endless perfunctory notes and appendices. The text he had chosen seemed to have no bearing on the ceremony that was taking place in the temple. Turning page after page, he could not find any text that fit. He settled on a passage that made little sense, but seemed impressive, filled with bombastic phrases.

In front of the altar Dhambum strode back and forth, ranting and waving his hands in the air. Reflecting the candlelight, the sickle-knife in his hand scribed stroboscopic tracks in the air. The effect was hypnotic. Toad turned his attention to the mob and the knot of Fascists cowering in front of them.

Dhambum's followers had been whipped into a fine froth. They were banging on the benches and shaking as if they were having fits. Several of the women had fallen to the floor and were rocking back and forth, moaning. The Fascists were huddled together, trembling like cornered rabbits, their faces a ghastly fish-belly white.

Toad felt a momentary pang of compassion for the enemy soldiers. They were broken men. Their fierce pride was gone. The pipesmith hugged the book in his hands. Were it not for his ability to read, he and his friends might be the ones cowering before Dhambum, not the Fashies. He took a deep breath, and when Beatleskin tapped his shoulder, he started to read.

"Long have I dwelt among the shadows, holding converse with the Old Ones..." Toad intoned in his best oratorical style.

The effect of his words was instantaneous. The Mansonites grew suddenly silent and stared gape-mouthed in Toad's direction. Even the Fascists had looked up, their eyes widening in terror. Dhambum and Godspawn had turned to face the portrait of Manson as well, so only Toad could see the gloating look in their eyes.

Reading into the speaking tube, Toad continued, *"Yog-Sothoth is the Keeper, Yog-Sothoth is the Gate. Cthulhu, long have the Old Ones waited. Ia! Ia! Shub-Niggurath..."*

A murmuring rolled through the crowd and a scowl like a nest of squirming snakes erupted on Dhambum's forehead, but Toad hardly noticed it. Though lacking the evil emanations of his copy at home, much of the *Necronomicon* was powerfully written. The passage he was reading, had force; the words flowed off his tongue. *"...They walk unseen and foul in lonely places where the Words have been spoken and the Rites howled through in their Seasons. Nyarlahotep, the Crawling Chaos, the wind gibbers with your voice."*

Toad paused in his reading, to turn a page.

"Charlie speak too much!" Dhambum yelled from the altar, making Toad jump. "Talk of things Family not understand. Maybe he speak to himself only. Maybe better if he speak to Dhambum."

Suddenly, Toad realized that what he was reading was far from what the Mansonites expected. They didn't have an inkling of what was being said. The reading had apparently driven the dull-witted Mansonites to distraction. Dhambum was having trouble getting them back under control. He closed the *Necronomicon* and waited to see what the mad-eyed priest was up to.

"You fuck up bad," Beatleskin remarked.

"I was just reading what was there."

"Sound stupid. Just answer Dhambum's questions now."

Toad shrugged. The Mansonites were supremely screwed-up, particularly their ugly priest. But, this was Dhambum's show.

When the mob had settled down a bit, the priest turned his back to them and faced the portrait of Manson. Through the aperture Toad could see Dhambum's eyes boring into his. The pipesmith blinked and licked his lips nervously. Suddenly, Dhambum threw his hands over his head and spun about to face his congregation again. "Charlie speak big words Family not understand. Charlie be very wise. All hail Charlie's love!"

"ALL HAIL!" the crowd responded, happy to be back in the familiar pattern again.

Dhambum spread his arms as if to embrace the whole room. "Yes, Charlie be god, speak great mysteries. But me think he come, tell he love us. That be right, Charlie?"

Summoning his most spectral voice, Toad replied, "That be right." It seemed a good idea to slip into Mansonite argot. If words bothered them so much, he'd use as few as possible.

"Charlie say he be tired of words. Charlie say he bless new Charlie. It not so?"

You must be reading my mind, Toad thought. "It be so."

Dhambum arched his back. It was a surprisingly graceful movement for one so deformed. He clapped his hands like the crack of musket fire. Almost at once the drums sounded in the back of the room and a procession began to form. As he watched the rites unfolding, Toad slipped the *Necronomicon* into his overcoat pocket. Beatleskin squeezed in next to him, fighting for his share of the aperture.

The drumming became louder and more rhythmic. Chanting began guttural and low, then swelled to a rolling, thunderous mumble as more Mansonites joined in. From time to time, the women screamed out in ecstasy—the long yipping cries of hungry dogs. Then they got to their feet and began clapping, all the while doing a shaking, hip-rolling dance that soon had the rest of the congregation up and dancing in the aisles.

A gong sounded and the dancing stopped. The crowd parted, revealing the old man in the tattered red robe. Slowly, he made his way to the altar. Two of the shaven-headed women rushed to help him, but he brushed off their assistance. His steps were uncertain and his rheumy eyes showed that he was heavily drugged. Somehow he made it to the altar. He wavered feebly as he took his place in front of Dhambum and Godspawn.

"Hail, True-Knife Godspawn," Dhambum said. He reached out and laid his hand on the old man's scarred forehead. True-Knife grinned up at him toothlessly.

Dhambum withdrew his hand. "True-Knife, son of Greentooth, long time you be Charlie on earth. Tonight you join Old Charlie."

The old man licked his cracked lips and looked up at the portrait of Manson. For a moment the cloudiness left his eyes as his face burned with religious fervor. The light faded from his face. Waving the women away one last time, he lowered his head and stood stooped but proud in front of Dhambum and his successor. Then True-Knife Godspawn uttered his final words. "Show Charlie's love."

As Toad looked on, horrified, Dhambum pushed back the old man's head and made one quick slash with the sickle-knife, ripping open his throat. Blood flew in all directions as the body quivered and fell across the cowering Fascists. The pipesmith looked away. What kind of monsters were these that would slaughter one of their own as casually as they would butcher a hog?

Repulsed, he turned back to watch the ritual with morbid fascination. A swarm of Mansonites was hunching forward to dip their hands in their dead chief's blood. Then they reached up to wipe the gore on Geekus Godspawn's robe, as if to transfer its magick from the old Charlie to the new.

"Make fun soon," Beatleskin giggled breathlessly. "Spread old Charlie's strength to Family. Take Bluecoats' strength, too."

Toad felt nauseous. Beatleskin's body odor permeated the air in the cubicle. He closed his eyes and breathed slowly and methodically until the queasiness passed.

When he reopened them, Toad could see Dhambum as he moved about, while blood-smeared and half-naked Mansonites danced around the huddled knot of Fascists. Entranced, they shuffled slowly from foot to foot as Dhambum clapped. When he threw his hands into the air they leaped and capered. Drawn knives flashed in the light as they shambled closer to their intended victims. Their eyes were blank, devoid of humanity.

Toad kept looking, knowing as he did so that forever after he'd wish he hadn't. Squeakyson, shirtless and growling, rushed out of the mob. He grabbed Likspittle, the youngest Fascist, and dragged him, crying and pleading, to the altar. Likspittle tried to fight him, but the Mansonite was too quick and strong for him. Laughing hysterically, Squeakyson drew a long, wavy-bladed knife and plunged it into the soldier's chest. The young Fascist convulsed and lay still. Gouts of blood poured from his nose and mouth. Giggling, Squeakyson leaned over and began to lick it up.

While Squeakyson was occupied with Likspittle's corpse, some of the other Mansonites dragged the body of the old Charlie off to the back of the room, where they squatted around it. Toad couldn't see what they were doing exactly, and something in their movements suggested that he didn't want to.

"Me hungry," Beatleskin complained. His fetid breath was hot on the back of Toad's neck. The pipesmith gasped for air. The walls of the cubicle seemed to be pressing in on him, driving the breath from his lungs.

His face smeared with blood, Squeakyson started to drag his victim's body to one side. Others tried to join him, but he brandished his knife at them and snarled. When they retreated he used the knife to slowly cut open Likspittle's chest.

The remaining Fascists huddled closer together, their eyes huge with terror in their pallid faces. They were no longer the swaggering warriors Toad and Ernie had seen in the forest. Now they were just frightened men facing a gruesome death. Toad felt pity for them and lightheaded relief that their fate wasn't his—at least not yet. He swore that he'd hold onto the *Necronomicon* and turn its magick against the Mansonites. For the meantime though, he was doing well just to keep from fainting. He felt himself slipping off into darkness, draining away into some cold abyss far from the present horror.

A sudden scream brought him back. Dhambum had hacked off Krakker's head and was dancing about, holding the grisly trophy in the air. The other Mansonites were dancing along with him, shuffling clumsily from foot to foot as they closed in on the Fascists again. A fang-toothed Mansonite was brandishing something that looked like a large fork. He and three companions grabbed Korkbrett and hoisted him to their shoulders as he struggled to get away. Laughing, the Mansonites threw him to the floor. Fangtooth took his fork and drove it into Korkbrett's stomach until the Fascist stopped screaming and lay still, bleeding.

Beatleskin was getting more excited by the second. His breath came in great, ragged bursts as he leaned over Toad's shoulder for a glimpse of the blood ceremony. The pipesmith tried to move away, but the lank young Mansonite was in his way. He tried closing his eyes, but that didn't filter out the sounds and only increased his feelings of dizziness. Trapped with his face pressed to the aperture he could only watch the slaughter and pray that the madness would soon end.

The Mansonites fell upon the remaining Fascists and slaughtered them one by one. The red-stained uniforms were stripped from the bodies and distributed among the worshipers. Blood covered the altar and was splattered on the walls. The pack of Mansonites around the dead Fascists was so thick that Toad was spared from witnessing what they were doing. From time to time, a Mansonite or two would run off to some dark corner clutching a bloody lump, but Toad's eyes refused to follow them. Beside him, Beatleskin was slobbering and moaning in ecstasy.

Godspawn walked among his followers, smiling at their unholy feast. When he reached the Mansonites who were cutting up the old Charlie, his father, he stopped and watched for a long time. With great ceremony they presented him with a wooden bowl piled high with bloody fragments. He received the bowl with equal ceremony and returned with it to the altar. Making a stiff bow, he handed the bowl to Dhambum.

"Make good," Beatleskin twittered, nudging Toad. "Eat soon."

Dhambum held the bowl close to the portrait of Manson, affording Toad a close hand view of its sickening contents. The pipesmith gagged. With all his strength he fought back the urge to puke.

"Hear me, First Charlie," Dhambum boomed. "This is True-Knife Godspawn. We give him. Eat and make us strong."

With that, he took globs of the bloody flesh and began stuffing them into the speaking tube right under Toad's nose.

Shoving past Beatleskin, Toad staggered blindly to the back of the cubicle. The sight and smells were more than he could take. Dropping to his knees, he gagged and started to vomit. He pressed his forehead against the rough stonework and shook. Darkness was closing in fast. The last sounds he remembered before it overtook him were those of Beatleskin giggling and slobbering over his grisly meal.

Chapter Twenty-Five

Though wet and slimy to the touch, the wall in the cave was cooler than the one in the cubicle. Toad laid his head against it and sighed, letting the coldness seep into his skin. His head throbbed with the onset of a piss-ripper headache. His body felt soggy and dead, as if it refused any connection with his wildly racing mind. This is what insanity feels like, he thought.

Toad hugged the wall closer. The caress of the cold stone helped soothe him. It reconnected him with his body and took away some of the pain and fear. He stank, and he knew it. The front of his coat was crusted with dried vomit. His throat was raw from retching. Groaning, he turned his head and looked over to where Ernie and Tambourine were sleeping beside the fire at the mouth of the cave.

He envied them. After what he'd been through, he doubted if he'd ever be able to rest that peacefully again. In spite of his discomfort, Toad had to smile at the sight of Ernie's battered top hat sitting on a rock next to the herbalist's head like a watchful spirit. He'd wished he had such a guardian when Godspawn and Dhambum confronted him after the ceremony. As it was, he'd had only his scrambled wits to save him from possible death.

Toad remembered little of the end of the ceremony and even less of the return to the village. When they brought him back, however, instead of being taken directly to the cave, Dhambum and Godspawn had escorted him to a house set aside from the others, the one constructed of animal bones.

There, he was taken inside and forced to kneel in front of a fireplace made entirely of human skulls. For some time Dhambum and Godspawn had stood over him not speaking, their faces cold and impassive in the light of the fire. The *Necronomicon* had been taken from him and placed on the mantelpiece. Dhambum had circled him twice, glaring angrily. Then the interrogation began.

"You no read true," the priest growled, his flimsy mask moving with the effort. "Talk bullshit at ceremony."

The pipesmith had fought to find his voice. "I-I only read what the book said."

"It be crap. No make sense."

"I read what the book said," Toad repeated.

Dhambum growled and, with a sweep of his gloved hand, indicated the room they were in and the collection of chains, flails, and thin sharp knives hanging on the far wall. "This place Fun House. Many die here; few die fast. You be useless hippie-pig, maybe you die here too."

In spite of his fear, Toad knew that this might be his only opportunity. If they had even an ounce of reasoning power, possibly he could work out a deal with them. Ignoring the priest, he spoke directly to Godspawn. "If you want to kill me, go ahead, but you wanted me to read, so I read. Charlie's words were strange and powerful. I could barely understand them."

Toad paused momentarily, for effect, and then continued, "I suppose that I could translate it … but not if I'm dead."

A dim understanding showing in his eyes, Godspawn spoke. "What you be saying, hippie?"

"Your Charliebook was written a long time ago, when people talked differently than they do now. I could make it so that you can understand it."

"You could do this?"

"Yes, I could," Toad nodded eagerly.

Godspawn smiled, but Dhambum had hung back, glowering at the two of them. "This be more bullshit, Geekus. You be Charlie now. Kill him."

"That right. Be Charlie now; want book. Be like Old Charlie."

Dhambum had growled deep in his throat. Before Godspawn could stop him he'd lashed out, cracking Toad across the face. The blow had sent the pipesmith sprawling onto the packed dirt floor. He'd tried to get up, but Dhambum kicked his ribs and stomach.

Asserting his new position as Mansonite leader, Godspawn turned on the priest like a whirlwind, pinning Dhambum to the wall with one hand while the other held a dagger to his throat. "Leave him be, priest. He speak Charlie's words."

Dhambum's eyes had blazed. "No. He speak lies. Make Dhambum look stupid."

The knife had drawn closer. "Look more stupid with tongue for necktie."

"I Charliepriest. Can't kill priest."

"I Charlie now, maybe don't need priest. Give book to hippie-pig."

Toad scrambled to his feet, amazed at the viciousness with which these two had gone at one another. Dhambum had snarled some more, but faced with Godspawn's knife, he'd relented and handed over the *Necronomicon*.

"Little-piggy, listen," Godspawn said, his eyes burning into Toad. "Take book. Learn. Then read for Charlie. Read good, be Bookreader. Read bad, give you to Dhambum."

An hour later Toad was back in the cave, with the book safe in his greatcoat pocket. He took a splint from the fire at the mouth of the cave and lit torches in the sconces near him. It had been that simple: Godspawn had wanted the power contained in the *Necronomicon* for himself, and nobody, not even the high priest, was going to stand in his way.

The pipesmith reached into his coat pocket and extracted the ancient book. The scene in the Fun House still fresh in his mind, he turned to the first page and began reading. After several pages he noticed that the style varied greatly from the selection that he'd read at the ceremony. Thumbing forward in the book he found the passage, which he re-read. It seemed to be a quotation of some sort, hardly in keeping with the blander text surrounding it. Confused, he abandoned the text altogether and tried to decipher the crabbed footnotes. They were faded and virtually indecipherable; even those that were legible gave references to beings and books unknown to Toad. But on one of the pages he found something he recognized. Unmistakably, near the very top edge was the name Evan Copralallius.

"I'll be damned!" he muttered to himself. At last he knew the identity of the original Bookreader.

A sound near the mouth of the cave diverted his attention and Toad lay the book down. He could see Ernie stirring in the firelight. Yawning, the herbalist stretched and started to get up. Beside him, Tambourine mumbled and rolled over in his sleep.

"Hey, Toad, man," Ernie said, patting his sleep-rumpled hair into place. "When the hell did you get back?"

"About an hour ago."

"So, did you have fun with your Mansonite buddies?"

"Hardly."

As Ernie rummaged about for something to eat, Toad related to him some of the night's events. Just as he was getting to the part about the murders in the temple, Tambourine awoke and wordlessly joined them by the fire. He seemed abnormally quiet and distant, staring into the flames as Ernie fixed a chunk of grayish meat on a stick and began to cook it.

"Toad was just telling me about his adventures at the temple," Ernie said, trying to draw the musician into the conversation.

"That so?"

"Tam, you're too quiet. What's with you?"

"I can't take this dump too much longer. We've got to get out of here." Toad nodded. "I know."

"They like you, Toad. What don't you just ask them to let us go?"

"Yeah, right. Mostly they would like me for lunch. Thank Dylan, Godspawn thinks he needs me."

"We've got to do something soon," Ernie remarked.

"Maybe I could use Godspawn's interest in the book somehow—but Dhambum is going to be watching me like a hawk." Toad stopped and studied the iron bars of their jail, and then looked to the back wall. "When the Mansonites took me to the temple I noticed iron grills set into the rear wall—iron grills very similar to the ones keeping us here. I snuck a peek into one, and the construction is similar to the tunnel that's the main entryway to the temple. My guess is that they're all part of the same network, which was sealed up ages ago. The more I think about it, the more I'm convinced that beyond that brick wall there's a tunnel that leads to Swetshop. We should keep working at it."

"If there is a tunnel, there's a good chance that it may be caved in all the way back," Ernie answered. "Though, the thought of doing something to get out of here will help keep our minds off our current situation."

"It's a long shot, but we don't have many alternatives. I've got some pull with Godspawn, but it won't last."

The other Freaks considered this. "Let's get back to it," Ernie said.

Tambourine agreed. "If we work when the Mansonites are resting and cover up what we're doing, we could have a long head start on them, before they even know we're gone."

Ernie took the piece of meat from the stick and began to nibble at it. "I've got some food set aside that we can ration, and we've got torches. For weapons, we've only got my boot knife."

"Well, let's work in shifts. One of us can watch the entrance while the other two dig. If we get back to work on it quickly, maybe we can get out of here in a few days. We've got a pretty good start already."

Leaving Tambourine to watch the front, Toad and Ernie took a torch and moved to the back of the cave. The ground was wet back there and Toad swore softly to himself when he nearly slipped and fell in the mud. He picked up one of the flat rocks he and the others had been employing as digging instruments and began to chip away at the crumbly mortar where they had already worked a few bricks loose. The water seeping into their prison must have been doing its work; they hadn't been at it long when several bricks and large chunks of earth fell out of the wall and splashed at their feet. They continued digging until a soft whistle from Tambourine signaled that someone was coming.

The two Freaks returned to the front of the cave just as the guards opened the door for Squeakyson and his redheaded buddy. The Mansonites were bearing the usual basket of food and supplies. Toad accepted the basket, but he couldn't look Squeakyson in the face. All he could think of was the scene, hours earlier in the temple, of the little Mansonite licking blood from the corpse of the young Fascist he'd just killed.

Over the course of the next few days, things returned to normal in the Mansonite village. The three Freaks were left to themselves, and except for the morning food delivery and the occasional jeering remark from the guards, they were largely ignored by their captors. Working in shifts, they patiently chipped away at the back wall, removing mortar and loosening brick. On the third day they finally broke through. Toad and Ernie had been working on the wall for little over an hour when a small section, already weakened by their previous efforts, suddenly collapsed. The pipesmith stuck his arm in the resulting hole, inhaling sharply when he felt nothing but air beyond.

"I think we've got something here," he whispered to Ernie.

The older Freak stopped working and bent low to examine the hole. He held his torch up to it; a current of cold stale air made it flicker.

"See anything?" Toad asked.

"Not yet, the hole's too small. "

Fervently, the two scraped and pounded at the brickwork, until finally they worked a few bricks loose, and then a few more, opening a hole big enough for Toad to stick his head and arm through. Without thinking he let out a yelp as the torchlight revealed a wide tunnel leading off into the darkness. The cry echoed throughout the cave, and by the time Ernie had clapped a grimy hand over the pipesmith's mouth, the damage had been done.

The Mansonite guards were standing at the grating, yelling hoarsely at Tambourine. Leaving Ernie at the back of the cave to cover the hole with his body, Toad ran to intercept them before they unlocked the door and came in. One of the guards had reached through the grating and had grabbed Tambourine by the front of his cloak.

"No gimme bullshit, piggy!" the guard bellowed. "What noise about?"

The musician struggled to get free of the Mansonite's grasp. "Uh, it's nothing. I think my friend burned his finger. Isn't that right, Toad?"

"Yeah, that's right," the pipesmith said sucking on his finger. "I burned myself moving a torch."

The guard let go of Tambourine and glowered at Toad. "That so, huh? No more noise, or Atkins Steeltooth eat piggy's tongue."

"R-right, Mr. Steeltooth," Toad nodded. "I'll be quiet, I promise."

He glowered at the Freaks a second longer, then he and his partner turned and went back to their campfire.

"We're almost through," Toad whispered to Tambourine. "Get your stuff together and let's boogie."

The musician pulled the hood of his cloak up over his matted curly hair. "You don't have to tell me twice," he said.

By the time Toad and Tambourine had gathered up their few possessions Ernie had widened the hole to where a man could easily squeeze through. Dawn was still an hour or so away as the trio started into the tunnel.

Atkins Steeltooth shuffled uneasily at his place by the fire. He drew his dagger from the belt of his sleeveless red shirt and ran his fingers along its blade. Beside him, his partner Slash dozed, leaning on his spear. Atkins spat into the fire, grinning as the embers sizzled. It had been a quiet night, except for when he'd had to go quiet down the noisy hippie-pigs.

Slipping his dagger back into its sheath, Atkins shifted his weight onto his left buttock and yawned. He gazed disinterestedly at the mouth of the cave where the prisoners were kept, watching for any signs of movement. He growled deep in his throat. Atkins hated guard duty, but he hated the hippie-pig faggits more. They were weak, and always huddled together, whispering.

The prisoners' fire had burned down to a few embers and he was waiting for them to add wood to it. Time passed and there was still no sign of movement. The cave was quiet—too quiet. Something wasn't right. With a grunt of disgust Atkins got to his feet, picked up his heavy knobbed cudgel and approached the grating. He took a key from the ring at his belt and turned it in the lock. Slowly he pushed the door open with his left hand as he gripped his cudgel in his right. The silence in the cave disturbed him. The piggies were in there somewhere and he was convinced they were waiting to jump him.

Atkins was quick and well muscled. He knew that no matter what they tried, he could handle the three with no problem. Closing the grating behind him, the Mansonite crouched in the darkness, his predatory instincts in total control. There were no sounds in the cave except for his light footsteps and the steady trickle of water down the walls.

Atkins grumbled, swiveling his shaggy head from side to side. There was nothing to be seen in the cave except for three sets of blurry footprints leading toward the back wall. If that was where they were planning to jump him, they had a surprise coming. He shifted his cudgel to his left hand and drew his dagger again. He licked his lips in anticipation, his nerve endings alive with the thrill of the hunt. Atkins craved blood, and he was going to have it—and maybe a hunk or two of fresh hippie meat to go with it. He and Slash had been denied the right to attend the ceremony. Their energies, which could have been better spent celebrating the making of a new Charlie, had been wasted guarding these piggy-faggit prisoners. Well, he was hungry now and he was going to do something about it.

The Mansonite howled with pain as he tripped over the small mound of rubble at his feet, and he fell to his knees on the broken bricks and mortar. When he looked up, he was facing a gaping hole in the back wall. For a moment he goggled at it, not fully comprehending what he was seeing. Then he let out a bellow of rage that reverberated down the tunnel and echoed back into the village.

Chapter Twenty-Six

Toad ran, his heart hammering against the ancient book he'd stuffed under his shirt. Panting heavily, he sucked in the miasmic air, fighting to keep pace with his companions. The flickering light of their torches threw crazy shadows on the dripping walls and made the lumpy fungus growths underfoot seem to glisten and move. As he ran, Toad avoided the slimy mounds. Ernie had stepped on one earlier, and the stench had been unbearable.

The tunnel seemed endless and the walls felt closer at every turn. Toad felt claustrophobia crushing in. For one crazy moment he considered running back toward the cave. Suddenly he felt lightheaded; he couldn't keep going. Calling out to the others, he slumped down on a rock, fighting to catch his breath. Tambourine and Ernie stopped and ran back to him. The tunnel was filled with the sounds of their heartbeats and labored breathing. Gasping for air, Toad became acutely aware of the smell of his filthy clothing and unwashed body, and he wrinkled his nose in disgust.

"Dylan's Bones," he wheezed. "We stink."

Ernie shrugged. "Worry about that when we get to Hillcommune. We can find a nice tub and soak for two days."

"We haven't gotten out of this mess yet," Tambourine remarked. "But, if it's three days to Hillcommune, we'll be pretty ripe by the time we get there."

Toad smiled at his friends' banter, but the smile froze on his face. Far back in the tunnel a faint light flickered and distant voices could be heard. "We're being followed!" he wheezed, struggling to stand.

His friends pulled Toad to his feet and they hurried down the tunnel. Toad stumbled several times, but managed to keep pace with the others as they trotted past piles of rubble and skirted pools of stagnant water. Farther along the tunnel, the debris piled higher; sections of the walls and ceiling lay collapsed, nearly choking the tunnel with broken masonry. They scrambled up one of the ancient cave-ins and found it entirely sealed off. The three Freaks dug and scratched and pushed their way through the crumbly dirt and broken stone with their bare hands. By the time they'd opened a hole large enough to crawl through, they saw torch lights closing in and heard the strident voices of Mansonites echoing in the tunnel.

The Freaks squeezed through the small opening and scurried down the pile of rubble. The tunnel beyond led up a steep incline. The air was cleaner and they could feel a draft moving against their faces. They followed the draft forward to the top of the incline. The tunnel terminated in a rusty iron grating. Beyond it their flickering torches revealed long rows of wooden benches.

"It's the temple!" Toad gasped. "I was right."

"And here we are," Tambourine replied. "We've still got to get through that grating."

Ernie squared his shoulders and stepped toward the opening. "Stand back," he commanded. "I'm gonna try to force it." Running as fast as he could, the herbalist slammed against the grating, first with his shoulder, then with his feet. The grating shuddered and showered down a few flakes of rust, but it didn't give. Behind the Freaks the babble of approaching voices grew louder.

Toad felt the color drain from his face. Peering into the darkened temple, he remembered only too well the carnage that had taken place there. He did not want it to happen again. "We're trapped," he moaned.

"Not necessarily," Tambourine said, working his way back down the incline. "I saw some iron beams and pipes back here. We could use them as battering rams and pry bars."

Nervously, Toad followed his friends back down the incline. A rusted steel beam about seven feet long lay at the bottom of the rubble pile. Though not very thick, it was half-covered with mud and debris and difficult to move. Kicking away chunks of masonry with their feet, the three Freaks grabbed the beam as best they could and with a mighty effort ripped it from the muck that held it.

"Damn," Toad whispered softly, as they hoisted the beam onto their shoulders. The old girder was heavy, even for the three of them.

The voices on the other side of the rubble pile were louder and more intense. Pebbles trickled down the side as if someone was trying to climb over.

The Freaks hefted the beam and loped back up the long incline. They hit the grating going at full speed. There was a terrible screech of tortured metal and a shoulder-wrenching impact as the beam connected. The grating showered down more rust and bowed slightly, but held in its casement.

An inhuman scream sounded behind them as the first Mansonite wriggled over the rubble pile. It was the red-shirted guard, Steeltooth. He held a dagger in one hand and his eyes burned with murderous hatred. The Freaks slammed the beam against the grating again. It bowed some more; then several bars snapped and it parted from its frame and fell crashing to the temple floor. Toad glanced back to see Steeltooth starting up the slope with several other Mansonites right behind him.

Grabbing their torches, they squeezed through the opening and ran across the temple, leaping over benches as they went. A stone-tipped spear whizzed past Toad's head just as he collided with a bench; searing pain shot through his leg. A rock flew past him, followed by another spear. Hopping in several exaggerated leaps, he managed to cross the temple and through the door into the corridor beyond. Forcing himself to run, he dashed along the tunnel with the Mansonites close behind. Without warning, the *Necronomicon* popped out of his shirt. Dropping his torch, he bobbled the book three or four times before regaining control of it.

Ernie and Tam were already scrambling up the ladder's treacherous rungs as he reached the end of the corridor. By the time the pipesmith's hand fell on the ladder, Steeltooth was close behind. Toad's foot slipped on a slime-covered rung. He started again, expecting the Mansonite to fall upon him. Halfway up he felt a hand close around his ankle. He looked down; Steeltooth had Toad's ankle in one hand and a knife in the other. Wobbling, the Mansonite drew his knife back to strike.

Without thinking Toad struck at him with the *Necronomicon*. Steeltooth grunted with surprise as the old book hit him in the face. Already off balance, the guard started to fall backwards. His fingers clamped on the front cover of the book like a vise, as he fought to right himself. Freak and Mansonite looked at each other in shock as the *Necronomicon* tore along its spine. Bellowing, Steeltooth fell to the floor in a flurry of worm-eaten pages. Clutching the back cover and the remaining handful of pages, Toad scrambled up the shaft.

The pipesmith exploded out of the shaft's entrance, rolling over and over on the dusty floor of Swetshop. By the time he'd stumbled to his feet, Tam and Ernie had slammed the trapdoor shut and were piling machine parts and other heavy debris on top of it. Angry, muffled voices came from beneath the pile; fists pounded on unyielding wood.

"That'll hold the bastards," Ernie said. "But not forever. Let's split."

The trio ran through Swetshop and out into the early morning sunshine. Without looking back, they plunged across the snowy field, with Ernie leading them into the secretive darkness of the great forest. Toad did his best to keep up, feinting and dodging between the tall conifers until Swetshop was lost from sight.

They ran until Toad thought his lungs would burst. His leg ached. He stumbled along until they broke into a small clearing, then dropped to the ground retching and gasping, the remaining pages of the *Necronomicon* still held tightly in his hand.

"You've got to get up, Toad," Tambourine urged, pulling the pipesmith to his feet.

"I can't. Give me a couple of seconds to rest. My leg hurts; I banged it in the temple."

"We have to keep going," Ernie advised. "It isn't that much farther to the edge of Darkenwood. I don't think the Mansonites will follow us beyond its borders, particularly in daylight."

"Look at this," Toad wheezed as his friends steadied him. He held out the remnants of the book. "I've lost most of the *Necronomicon*. All we've got left is just a few torn pages."

Tambourine patted him on the back. "Nothing we can do about it now. Maybe what's left will prove useful when we reach Hillcommune."

"We've got to get there first," Ernie commented. "We have to get going. Now!"

Toad tested his leg. It hurt, but he could go on.

Tambourine stiffened. "Do you hear that?" he whispered.

Ernie nodded. "Something in the bushes..."

Suddenly, the air was rent with a blood-curdling shriek as a Mansonite jumped out of the bushes in front of them. His black mask flapping around his face, Dhambum charged at the Freaks wielding a huge battle-ax. He swung, just missing Ernie.

Pushing Toad out of the way, Ernie and Tambourine spun around; the herbalist kicked the priest sharply in the balls as the musician simultaneously punched him in the face. Howling in pain, Dhambum dropped to the ground and doubled over. The ax fell out of his hand and landed in the snow. Ernie reached down and threw the ax into the woods. As an afterthought, he kicked the priest again for good measure.

"Glad to see our old bar brawl routine still works," Tambourine said.

Ernie grinned. "Once you got it you never lose it."

As the Freaks started back into the woods, Dhambum made an unearthly noise, halfway between a growl and a dog yelping. Cupping his injured crotch with one hand and drawing a long knife with the other, he staggered to his feet, bellowing, and charged at the Freaks like a bull. Ernie sighed and pulled out his boot knife. With a flick of the wrist, he sent the little knife whipping end-over-end through the air. It embedded itself in the priest's chest with an audible 'thunk'. Dhambum clawed at the crimson stain spreading across his chest and fell backward. He twitched once and lay still. Ernie retrieved his knife, calmly wiping it off on the Mansonite's

221

tunic.

"Let's get truckin'," he said, returning the knife to his boot.

The trio re-entered the deep forest, trotting through the shadows, their breath coming out in silvery blasts. Though it was hard going, they pressed on until the thick woods gave way to scrub pine and juniper-choked clearings brilliant with undisturbed snow.

They emerged at last from a stand of stunted pine. As far as they could see, great expanses of snow-dusted grassland spread out to the east until they merged with the foothills of the Purple Mountains. A frozen wind rolled down out of the north, bending the icy spikes of grass before it until the stubble-covered fields rippled like an undulating crystal sea. Toad breathed deeply of the frosty air. It seemed to clear his head and ease his tired body. His leg was feeling better. The sun was riding high over the two tallest mountains, like a small gold coin set in the sky. Raising his hand to shield his eyes, he gazed intently at the distant twin peaks.

"Those mountains are called Mount Lennon and Mount Leary," Ernie said. "Hillcommune lies in the valley beyond them. But we've got to cross the southern fields of the Great Whitelands and the Dragstrip Plains of Khamshaft to get there."

Toad considered this. "Have we got the supplies to make it?"

"Don't know. You want to wait around and ask the Mansonites to help us out?" Tambourine remarked.

"Stop bumming me out," said Ernie. "This whole expedition doesn't have to be any more hazardous than sneaking through someone's back yard, if we're careful."

"Dylan's Bones," Toad cried. "We almost were lunch for a tribe of degenerate inbreds and now we have to cross miles of open enemy territory with almost no food. How can you be so cavalier about it?"

"What's your point, Toad?"

"Don't you get tired of the endless adventuring, constantly risking your life?"

"Actually—no. It's exciting. Look at the sorry condition we're in, and yet I, for one, couldn't feel better. Ha! Think about it, Toad; we've escaped death. There is no better high."

Tambourine's eyes seemed fixed on the distant line of mountains. "We aren't out of the woods yet, so to speak. We don't have much food, and what we've got for clothing may not be adequate out there. We could die trying this jaunt."

"But, we'll definitely die here. Hillcommune's a two-day journey, three at the most. Before you know it, we'll be swapping stories about this over a pipe or two of Red."

After a moment Tambourine asked, "Do you know the way in?"

"Don't you? Didn't you say that you were going to meet Maynard there?"

"Wait a minute!" Toad interjected. "I thought you'd both been there before. You don't know how to get in?"

"I don't remember; I was just a kid then," Tam replied. "But Maynard said there would be a watcher posted to lead me in."

"That'd be Moonshadow," Ernie declared. "To answer your question, Toad, no one ever finds their own way in. That's Moonshadow's job. He knows when there are visitors. He leads them in. Believe me, he'll find us. We'll make it okay."

"I certainly hope so."

"We can avoid Ripoff Pass. So, once we cross the main routes, we shouldn't run across any enemy patrols."

Tambourine shuddered slightly and gazed once again at the distant mountains. "Then let's get a move on. I don't want to stand around waiting for the worst to happen."

Cautiously the three friends started across the plain, keeping to the high grass and dropping low where the cover was scanty. Within an hour they came to the edge of the wide, well-beaten track that Ernie explained was the main road leading to Ripoff Pass. They started to cross just as horns sounded in the distance.

"We've got visitors," Ernie said. "Get down in the grass and don't make a sound."

Toad did as he was told. As the three Freaks lay shivering among the tufts of high grass, they saw a long column of horse soldiers approaching from the north. Toad watched in wonder as the advance guard rode into view not twenty yards from where he and the others lay.

The standard-bearers came first—young soldiers in brilliant gold-trimmed blue uniforms. The sunlight reflected off the shiny buttons of their tunics and their highly polished jackboots and cap visors. They sat up arrow-straight in their saddles, holding aloft long spears from which fluttered the lightning bolt insignia of the House of Klaven, the flaming cross of the Brotherhood of Whiteriders, and starred swastikas. Behind the standard-bearers rode a group of high-ranking Fascist officers, distinguishable by their wide-brimmed white hats and the elaborate gold-fringed epaulets on their shoulders, followed by a dozen Whiteriders in their snowy robes and tall hoods.

Once the advance guard passed by, the main body of the column rode into view: mounted cavalry armed with pikes, sabers, and in some cases, flintlock rifles. Behind them straggled foot soldiers with spears, longbows and crossbows, followed by lumbering supply wagons and troop transports. At the rear of the procession, huge draft horses dragged the artillery pieces:

massive catapults, siege ballista and, Toad was disturbed to note, four-wheeled brass cannon.

It seemed to take an hour for the enemy ranks to pass by, as the three Freaks lay on the cold ground, not daring to move or make a sound. Once the column had disappeared in the distance they leaped to their feet and ran for the high grass on the other side of the road. Moving as fast as they could, they traveled eastward, stopping briefly to rest and consume some of their tiny store of food, which they supplemented with tasteless roots and dried berries that Ernie gathered. After eating handfuls of snow in an effort to quench their thirst, they set off once again for the mountains.

It was late afternoon and growing bitterly cold when they finally decided to stop and set up camp. In the west the sun was dipping low over the black tree line of Darkenwood, and a wind came howling down from the north that made them huddle deep into their ragged coats. The land was low and flat, offering little protection from the elements, but brush was plentiful and they gathered it up to build a makeshift shelter.

"A fire would be nice right about now," Tambourine remarked as they piled the brush into a crude windbreak.

Ernie shook his head. "We can't risk it, Tam. The smoke would be visible for miles."

"Like that over there?" Toad asked, pointing to a thin tendril of smoke that rose against the eastern horizon.

"Exactly."

Tambourine studied the line of smoke thoughtfully. "I thought these plains were uninhabited, Ernie."

"They are. That smoke's probably coming from a campfire where some patrol's bunking down for the night."

"Kind of out of the way for a Fashie patrol, ain't it?"

"I suppose it is, now that you mention it."

"Maybe it isn't a campfire. Maybe there's a settlement over there."

"No, we're miles and miles from the closest town. It could be a solitary, I suppose. Strange wanderers can sometimes be found in regions like this—odd folk of no particular race or occupation, who live far from the main centers of civilization. Whoever it is, you can bet your last guitar pick they won't be hospitable to Freaks."

"Maybe we should check it out," Tambourine said, scratching his chin.

"I suppose you're right. Whoever our neighbor is, he's got a fire and, I'm sure, a supply of food as well. If he's alone, maybe we can convince him to share it."

Picking up their meager gear, the Freaks headed off in the direction of the plume of smoke, slipping quietly across the landscape as twilight thickened and the first stars twinkled on overhead. Half an hour later they crested a small rise and, hiding in the grass, looked down on a house in a small valley.

The house was run-down, a sorry-looking hovel—a dismal dwelling that might take pride in being called a large shack. The building appeared to have been thrown together out of raw logs and scrap timber. For all of its shabbiness, lights shone in its windows and a thick stream of smoke rolled out of its chimney, laying a pall across the newly risen moon. A sway-backed mare of indeterminate age stood in the corral next to the house, grazing among the decaying remains of at least a dozen wagons of different sorts and sizes.

Toad peered out from behind a clump of grass, taking in the house, the corral, and the littered yard. "Is this how your average Fashie lives?" he asked.

Ernie shook his head. "No Fascist would live in a dump like this. I don't think it belongs to a Greaser, either."

"Then, who? One of those solitaries you were talking about?"

"Must be. Looks like it might be a hermit's digs."

Tambourine leaned forward, grinning. "Well, oddball or not, this guy's got a fire and a roof over his head."

Ernie picked up a rock, hefting it in one hand. "Perhaps he'll be a hospitable sort, with a little persuasion."

"What's the plan?"

"I'll go to the door and talk to the man while you two hide beside the house. I'll draw him out and you guys can jump him."

The trio slipped out of the high grass and moved quietly to the cabin door. They were in position and Ernie was just about to knock when the breeze brought the slight smell of burning rope to their nostrils. Something moved behind them, and an ominous click disturbed the evening silence.

"Move and you're dead men," a low voice said from the shadows.

Toad turned his head ever so slightly. A massive figure with long plaited hair and a full bushy beard hulked out of the gloom of the dooryard. Though his face wasn't visible in the dark, the huge matchlock arquebus in his hands was. Its glowing match cast a feeble glow that did little to reveal the black bulk behind, but Toad saw enough to know their captor was a Rowdie—a creature as totally out of place in the Great Whitelands as themselves. The Rowdie gestured with his weapon and the three Freaks filed into the cabin with their hands held high over their heads.

Chapter Twenty-Seven

Toad had never seen the interior of a Rowdie's house before, but he imagined this one to be typical. It was spacious enough for one person, but it also was severely cluttered and dirty. Wagon parts were stacked in a far corner, along with several heavy chests and a pile of moldy clothes. A crude wooden table dominated the area in front of the fireplace, surrounded by crates that served as chairs. Pieces of shattered beer crocks lay everywhere, particularly in front of the scarred door that seemed to lead to a side room. The wall near the fireplace held the room's only decoration, a sloppily daubed bull's eye from which several rusty knives protruded.

As the Rowdie motioned for them to sit by the table, Toad noticed that he was no tidier than his surroundings. He wore filthy pegged jeans that did little to conceal his swollen beer gut and a denim vest over a leather Greaser jacket that had seen better days. The vest was embroidered with strange symbols: coiled snakes, lightning bolts, and skulls whose broken-toothed grins and fiery eyes matched the Rowdie's own. Chains and various odd implements hung from his belt, and a swastika-shaped earring dangled from his left lobe. Without changing his expression, the Rowdie brought up his heavy arquebus and leveled it at Tambourine's head.

"Ahhrr, what's this I got here?" he rumbled. "Fuckin' hippies dressed in Fashie rags. What you little hairballs doin' sneaking around Scuddy Lout's? You weren't thinking of trying to rob me, were you?"

Tambourine's face had turned a strange shade of gray. He moved his lips like a beached fish, but no sound came out. Toad cleared his throat, but all he could manage was an anguished peep. Beside him Ernie, his right eyebrow jittering wildly, sat quietly.

Scuddy Lout pressed the muzzle of his weapon closer to Tambourine's face. The musician trembled violently and looked like he was about to pass out. "You better talk," the Rowdie advised, "or you'll be wearing your hat on your shoulders."

"It's freezing outside. We w-were just looking for shelter for the night," Ernie blurted out.

"Ahhrr, were you now? That still don't explain what you're doing in Fashie lands, dressed in Fashie clothes."

Lout fixed Toad with a piercing, homicidal stare. Something in his crazed eyes looked familiar to Toad. In fact, the Rowdie's whole face looked like one he'd seen before. Then it struck him; the similarity of face and surname had to be more than a coincidence. In spite of his fear, an idea began to form in his mind, based on his knowledge of Smuttynose Rowdies and their ways.

"We're traveling merchants who were captured by the Fascists," the pipesmith said, trying to act casual. "We escaped and stole these uniforms as disguises."

Lout grunted in disbelief. "Maybe that's true, and maybe it ain't, but it don't mean shit to me. My problem is, am I gonna kill you fast or am I gonna kill you slow? I haven't had any fun in a long time, so I guess I'll kill you slow."

Toad forced himself to smile. "Kill us, Mr. Lout? Surely, we are no threat to you. Where we come from, your people and ours get along. In fact, we live side by side."

"Ahhrr? Where's that?"

"Smuttynose Island—many miles from here."

"I know that island, hippie. My cousin, Gumma, lives there with some of his bros."

"Hey, I should have guessed. I know Gumma; he's a good man."

Scuddy Lout relaxed slightly. He took his finger from the arquebus's trigger, and some of the hostility left his eyes, but they lost none of their shiftiness. "Rowdies and hippies never like one another," he said flatly.

"Maybe in other places, but on the Island we've learned to get past our differences. We come from common stock, you know. Under the skin we're more alike than different."

"Ahhrr, maybe so. Still, I never heard of such a thing." The Rowdie's manner was becoming friendlier. He took his gun away from Tambourine's face, leaving a white circle on the musician's cheek where the muzzle had been pressed against it.

Toad smiled to himself. Experience had taught him that Rowdies were a stupid and unpredictable lot, capable of great deceit, but also capable of being deceived. They either wanted to kill you on sight or, if they were drunk, attach themselves to you like leeches. In the past, Toad had often been hard pressed to decide which fate was worse.

"Well, maybe I won't kill you then," Scuddy declared with an evil, unsettling grin. "I can't see why, but Gumma might get pissed if I wasted you. We'll have some grub and talk. Then I'll decide what to do with you. Why don't you take your coats off and I'll see what I got for food."

The Freaks removed their coats and sat back as Scuddy moved to the fireplace, taking his arquebus with him. Once the Rowdie turned away to fiddle with a rank-smelling concoction bubbling in the kettle over the fire, Toad glanced at his friends and wiped his brow. They nodded at him gratefully.

"Ahhrr, we eat soon," Scuddy announced. "Hope you like groundhog stew. Plenty of groundhog around here."

After the mystery substance that the Mansonites passed off as meat, groundhog sounded promising. Toad glanced at his companions again. They looked hungry enough to accept their gastronomic fate.

When the wooden bowls were placed in front of them, the pipesmith looked down at the fatty lumps of meat and smelled the gamy steam rising from the bowl. It made him think that the woodchuck might have done something in the stew before it was fully dead. Fishing out a chunk of meat with his wooden spoon, he popped it in his mouth. At least it was better than Mansonite chow. He swallowed the morsel, but it wanted to fight its way back up.

Scuddy Lout watched Toad's discomfort with obvious relish. "Ahhrr, you're not eating," he growled, as stew dripped from his matted beard. "Don't you like my cookin'?"

"We've been out in the cold so long, I just felt a little ill. I think I'm coming down with something."

"That's too bad," Scuddy grunted, draining his bowl and ambling over to the kettle for a refill. "Means all the more for me."

Toad looked up from his bowl and contemplated the winged wheel emblem on the back of Scuddy's vest. He and his friends could easily jump the Rowdie, but Toad sensed that Scuddy would like that. Though fat and slovenly, he had wide shoulders and powerful arms. In their weakened condition, the three Freaks would be no match for the Rowdie. He knew that, and he flaunted it.

Scuddy came back to the table, bearing not only a second helping of stew, but also a wooden box which he set next to the candle guttering in the middle of the table. He patted the arquebus, which lay across the table in front of him, its match now extinguished. "We'll smoke and you can tell me your story. After that, I'll decide what to do with you."

Toad cleared his throat as the Rowdie opened the box and produced a skull-shaped iron pipe and a handful of weed. "Why do you live here in the Great Whitelands?" he asked. "I thought your people mostly lived in Sativa Fields, and along the coast."

"Ahhrr, I like it here better. Everybody leaves me alone: Greasy Boys,

Bluebellies, everybody."

"But, how do you make a living? "

Scuddy lit the pipe from the candle and took a toke. "I live free, Hippie, like a man should oughta. Sometimes I do some trading to get the things I need."

"Is that how you got your gun?"

"Ahhrr, not exactly. Sometimes I find things. The Greasy Boys lost it; I found it. I found this here 'Commune Red the same way," he said, poking the heavy iron pipe at Toad. "C'mon, smoke."

Toad took the pipe and lifted it to his lips. Like its owner it was crude, ugly, aboriginal. He accepted his host's weed, but he did not accept his story. The gun and the weed, like everything else in the cabin, hadn't been "found"—they'd been stolen. Toad had no doubt that Scuddy Lout was one of the brigands who'd been robbing weedwagons and killing their drivers. The weed was red, all right—red with blood. "Interesting pipe," he said between hits. "Did you 'find' this as well?"

"No. It belonged to my grandfather, little bro."

The pipesmith smiled momentarily. A bro was a Rowdie's social peer—his equal. The endearment was a red herring; Scuddy's eyes held no warmth. Still, he tried to hold the grin as he passed the pipe on to Ernie.

"Okay," Scuddy growled. "You can start by telling me why you're dressed in Fashie colors."

Toad held his breath for a moment. The house was silent, except for the wind rising outside.

"My friends and I had a traveling herbal show, which did the Rivertown, to Smoky Waters, to Little Woodstock circuit," Ernie offered, taking Toad off the hook. "Maybe you've heard of *Mungweasle's Magical Mystery Tour*?"

The Rowdie merely grunted.

"Right. Well, because of the situation in Covenstead we decided to hit Leftopia for what was left of the season. We left Camp Hoffman and had just arrived at Guevarraville when the Fascists attacked. Before we could get turned around and out of town we found ourselves surrounded by Fashies."

"Ahhrr, too bad," Scuddy said, feigning sympathy.

"To make a long story short, that night the Fashies were sending us to the slave pits at Moloch, when the wagon we were in hit a rock and overturned right outside of Krakkerton. We escaped, and later that night snuck into their camp and stole these uniforms."

"You didn't steal them," Scuddy corrected. "You *found* those uniforms, same way I find things."

"Okay. Anyway, we've been on the run ever since, hiding out by day and foraging for food."

The Rowdie looked Toad right in the eyes. "So, that's the straight poop, is it, little bro?"

"Leaving out a lot of boring details, yes," Toad answered.

Scuddy nodded and looked out the window's cracked panes. He gave an exaggerated yawn. "Ahhrr, it's cold tonight. Hear that wind ripping down? A man'd freeze to death in that shit, and it'll get worse before it gets better. Sometimes the wind blows across the plains faster than a Greaser's chariot. I swear, if I needed to pluck a chicken, alls I'd have to do is hold it out the window when the wind blows like it can some nights." He paused, then added, "You stay here tonight and then leave in the morning."

The glint in the Rowdie's eyes was unmistakable; he was planning something. "Th-that's really kind of you. I don't know how we'll ever pay you back."

"Ahhrr, don't worry, little bro. Finish your story and in the morning I'll rustle up some grub for you to take with you."

"There's not much more to tell," Toad replied, glancing at Ernie and Tambourine.

The Rowdie produced another yawn, as phony as the last. Outside the wind howled around the eaves and tore at the windowpanes. "Okay, we'll have a little more to smoke and then I'll make a place for you to sleep. I need some sack time myself."

He reached for the pipe, and was in the process of filling the bowl when the wind set on the house in full fury. The door blew open, slamming against the wall. With a grunt of disgust, the Rowdie lurched to his feet and moved toward the door to close it.

Toad saw his chance and seized it. Leaping across the table he grabbed the heavy arquebus and pointed it at Scuddy. With his free hand he got hold of the candle and held it over the weapon's flash pan. Ernie moved just as quickly. As he and Tambourine got out of Toad's line of fire, he whipped out his boot knife.

"Ahhrr, damn you!" Scuddy roared. "I knew you was lyin'. I shoulda killed you when I had the chance."

"Too late for that, friend," Toad said. "Ernie, cover this guy. Tam, find something to tie him up with."

The Rowdie took a small step forward, but the determination he saw in Toad's face stopped him. His eyes shifted momentarily as Ernie moved in on him, but he remained as still as stone. "What are you going to do with me?" he asked.

"Nothing, if you behave yourself. You'll find us a lot more merciful to you than you would have been to us."

Tambourine dug through the clutter in the corner and returned with a coil of stout hemp rope. While Ernie held his knife to his throat and Toad covered him with the arquebus, Scuddy lay down on the floor and allowed Tambourine to truss him up in a cocoon of intricate knots. When the Freaks had finished, Ernie bolted the door while Tambourine, wielding a heavy wagon spoke, stood guard over the inanimate Rowdie.

Scuddy's face was crimson with rage. He tried to thrash about, but he was bound too tightly. "Ahhrr, you fuckin' bastards! I coulda sold you to the Fashies for thirty gold Nixons each!"

"Life's tough all around," Tambourine reminded him.

"I got friends, hippie."

Ernie toyed with his knife, flipping it in the air and catching it expertly by the handle. "Not here you don't. Now be a good boy and shut up."

"Kill me if you're gonna, then," Scuddy raged.

"That's one possible solution, but, as long as you don't piss us off, you'll live."

As the Rowdie lay mumbling to himself, Toad took the candle away from the arquebus and lit the pipe with it. He took a few hits, then passed the pipe to Tambourine, and fished in the pocket of his greatcoat for the remaining pages of the *Necronomicon*. When the pipe came his way again, he brought it over to the fire and sat down to read.

"Hey!" Scuddy bellowed. "Who are you guys, really?"

Toad just smiled and went back to his reading.

In all, about twenty pages of the *Necronomicon* had survived the escape from Swetshop. Of these, perhaps fifteen were actual text. The remaining pages comprised a diary kept by Copralallius, the original Bookreader, and were heavily crowded with his distinctive broad scrawl, though in some places the ink was badly faded.

Toad yawned as he stared into the fire. In his mind he tried to reconstruct all he knew about Copralallius. His memory yielded little of much use, just bits from the *Wackaveda* and some of Kermit Badmoon's other writings. Apparently, the mystic poet of Jukin City and Copralallius had been good friends, delving together into the lore of the Old-Timers. Badmoon had hinted that of the two, Copralallius was the more adept. Not only had Copralallius held the post of Dean of Eldritch Studies at Shambullah University before his disappearance, but he had also been considered an authority on Ritual Magick. He must have had some power about him, because he'd traveled into Darkenwood on several occasions before the last. Badmoon claimed that these expeditions had been made to search for certain relics of "most ancient evil." For over a century there had been much speculation among historians and folklorists as to what happened to Copralallius but no one, not even his friend Badmoon, could come up with a satisfactory answer. Toad held the answer to that riddle in his hands now, but even the thrill of such knowledge wasn't enough to keep him awake. Yawning, he tucked the pages into the front of his shirt and closed his eyes.

The wind slamming against the sides of the cabin awoke him some time later. He stirred and saw Tambourine standing beside him, attending to the kettle over the fire.

"What are you doing?" Toad asked, stretching.

"Boiling up some water for tea. Want some?"

"Sounds like a hell of an idea. Maybe it'll give me some energy."

Leaving Tambourine to brew the tea, Toad got up and joined Ernie at the table.

"That book we got from the Mansonites must be pretty boring," the herbalist said. "One minute you were reading, the next you were keeled over sawing lumber."

"I really needed it."

"We all did. Tam and I swapped off naps while you were out."

"Actually, the book is fascinating for several reasons. Parts of it, like the one I read at the Mansonite ritual, are powerfully written. Other parts are poor at best. It's like the whole thing was just a bad rewrite of an older text."

Ernie shrugged. His battered top hat slipped down on his forehead. "So what if it is? As I understand it, the thing is supposed to be incredibly ancient."

"Something doesn't feel right somehow. The first Bookreader, Copralallius, kept a diary in part of it. It's interesting, though cryptic."

"What's he say?"

"I haven't read it all, but I get the feeling that Copralallius thought the *Necronomicon* was a fake."

"Mind if I look it over?"

"Go ahead." He handed Ernie the sheath of pages while stealing a glance at the still form of Scuddy Lout tied up in the corner.

"Don't worry about him," Ernie said, taking the pages. "He started getting mouthy again, so I slipped him some of my special sedative. He'll be out for hours."

Tambourine had just finished with the tea and was ladling it into some mugs when Toad stepped over to the fire and accepted a cup.

"I think some of the clothes I found here might fit you," the musician said.

"Oh?"

"Yeah, there's a pile on that crate over there that you might want to look at. Our host has been a busy lad. He's 'found' all kinds of good things, and most of it looks brand new. My guess is that he's one of the brigands who have been robbing the weedwagons. At any rate, a lot of this stuff is of

Oldhip manufacture."

"I was thinking that too," Toad stated as checked out the clothing pile. It contained some articles of Greaser and Rowdie attire, but it was mostly Freak garb of the highest quality. He selected some new underwear and a sweater and jeans. "I'm going to need a coat," he said.

Grinning, Tambourine produced a heavy sheepskin coat with wooden buttons. "This ought to do the trick. I also found a leather coat for me and a cloak for Ernie. This place is a regular treasure trove."

When he had donned his new clothes, Toad rejoined Ernie at the table. The herbalist was toking vigorously on Lout's pipe as he studied the pages spread out before him.

"Find anything interesting?" Toad asked.

"Maybe. I don't understand a lot of these references to old books and fancy-ass gods, but there's a little poem here that you should find interesting."

"A poem? Let's see it."

Ernie pointed to a short set of verses scrawled on the margin of one page. Squinting as he leaned forward, Toad could just make them out:

> *I searched for the book from dusk to dawn*
> *By the "X" on Charlie, dead and gone.*
> *"X" marked the spot, they hadn't lied,*
> *There on the altar I espied,*
> *The evil tome of Charlie's brood.*
> *They caught me then and now I'm screwed.*
> *I read to live, so that's the deal,*
> *The worst part is the book's not real.*

"Well, that's that," Toad said. "The book's a fake. I wonder where the real *Necronomicon* is."

Ernie flipped through several pages, stopping to point out another fragment of verse:

> *Charliespawn revere this book,*
> *A thing worth only scoffing.*
> *The true Black Text lies to the East,*
> *Secure in its swift, iron coffin.*

Toad grunted in disgust. "What's that supposed to mean, 'swift iron coffin'?"

"You've got me. Maybe you can find some clues in here somewhere."

Ernie got up and ambled over to Tambourine, who was still digging through the pile of clothes. Toad sipped his tea and settled back to read. Twenty minutes later, he put the book down, dismayed.

Copralallius's diary hadn't revealed the location of the real *Necronomicon*, but it had hinted strongly that it was somewhere in the Greaser nation of Khamshaft. During Copralallius's internment in the Mansonite village he had often struck up conversations with other prisoners. One of these, a Greaser Aayfonzer, or chief priest, had informed him that a book of real power had been captured by his people years before and was kept somewhere known only to a few of the elect. The Aayfonzer might have revealed more, but he was killed soon afterward and the secret of the 'swift iron coffin' died with him. Khamshaft is a big place, Toad mused. The book could be anywhere there, if it still existed.

Ernie and Tambourine returned to the table. Toad listened as his friends discussed their plans to reach Hillcommune within the next couple of days.

"Food'll be no problem now," Tambourine was saying. "Ol' Scuddy has this place pretty well stocked. But I wouldn't want to be out in this weather long. That wind sounds like it could cut right through you."

"It won't last forever," Ernie replied. "But while it does, we're safe enough here. Lout may claim to have friends, but they're not likely to drop by on a night like this. If we start out around dawn tomorrow, we should reach the mountains in two days' travel, but we'll have to cross the Plains of Dragstrip to do it. Fortunately, they're deserted this time of year."

"Let's hope."

Ernie grinned and clapped the musician on the back. "Hey, no problem. You forget that I know something about Greaser culture. Their chariot-racing season runs from April until October. Nobody lives on the Plains year round, not with these winter winds. They can rip across unprotected flatland."

"Well, at least the Greasers have some sense." Tam paused, and then continued. "You make it sound like it'll be clear sailing from here on in."

"Sure thing. If we don't take any foolish risks, it'll be as simple as…"

"…sneaking across someone's back yard," Tam retorted. "We know; we've heard that before."

Ernie smiled as he reached over and took the smoldering pipe from Toad's mouth. "Things'll go better this time."

"Leapin' Lennon, I can't wait to get to Hillcommune," Tam offered. "I haven't been up to the mountains in years, though I used to go there a lot with my old man. Hillcommune weed's the best in the world and Oldhip girls are the prettiest."

"Is that what old Judas used to go there for—the women?"

234

Tambourine laughed. "No way. He loved Mom too much, but he did like to jam with some of the old git-box pickers he knew there—guys like Lemon Verbena and Smokin' Joe Wildthistle."

"I've heard of Wildthistle. Wasn't he the guy that composed the *1968 Overture*?"

"He's the one, but his real forte was the old songs. My pop always said he and Verbena played like Lennon and Old Bob must have played." Tam grinned in remembrance. "Hell, I can remember sitting on the dock in front of Lemon's shack when I was no more than six years old, listening to my pop and his friends jamming. Joe and Lemon were old men even then, but they played with a fire that would put a guy like me to shame. When they played the old songs I'd just sit back and listen, look up at the stars and dream. I can even remember how the breeze off the river smelled, all sweet and perfumey from the wildflowers that grew along the riverbanks."

As Tambourine got up from the table, Ernie began languidly refilling the skull pipe. His sea-gray eyes took on a distant look, as if his thoughts were miles away. "You've got a real treat in store for you, Toad," he said so quietly that the pipesmith almost couldn't hear him. "Yeah, there's no place like it in the whole of Street-Corner Earth."

"It sounds like it."

"Uh-huh. I envy anyone who sees Hillcommune for the first time. Words can't convey what the place is like."

"I don't know about that. Tam was doing a pretty good job."

The herbalist chuckled. "Well, you'll see what I mean soon enough."

A low moan came from the corner. Scuddy Lout stirred and tried to sit up, but he was too securely bound and gagged. Handing Toad the pipe to light, Ernie wandered over to where the Rowdie lay. He picked up a heavy wagon spoke from the corner and whacked him over the head with it. Lout groaned and slumped back, unconscious.

"So, that's your 'special sedative'?" Toad asked laughing.

"Seems to work as good as anything."

"What are you going to do with him when we leave?"

Ernie grabbed the pipe and took a quick hit. "I'm still working on that. It probably wouldn't be polite to kill the sorry bastard."

Just then Tambourine joined them, bearing a wheel of yellow cheese and three crocks of beer. With a mock bow, he placed them on the table in front of his friends.

Ernie examined one of the crocks closely. "Aah, Black Thirtyweight, good Greaser stout. Our host shows impeccable taste."

The beer was heavy and dark, more powerful than Toad was used to, but it went down smoothly. He drained the crock in a couple of gulps and reached out for a hunk of the cheese Tambourine was slicing up. "This is pretty good suds. There wouldn't be any more around, would there?"

"Cases. Friend Lout is apparently quite the juicer."

Later, after most of the cheese was consumed and another bowl smoked, Tambourine brought out a case of the Greaser beer. Between the talking and the smoking, several crocks were emptied and hit the floor. Soon after, the three Freaks did the same.

The wind howled through most of the night, clawing at the cabin until it wore itself out. Tam shook Toad awake about an hour before dawn. "Wake up and eat," the musician said softly. "There's tea and dried meat on the table. The wind's died down and it's time to go."

Apparently Tambourine had been up for some time. Packs of food and supplies for the journey ahead were lined up by the door. Ernie was nowhere to be seen. Toad started to ask about him when the door opened and the herbalist appeared, swaddled in the long gray cloak from Scuddy's stores.

"So, where've you been?" Toad asked through a mouthful of food, finishing the question by washing it out with the last of his tea.

"Outside checking on Lout's horse. I thought she might be of some use to us, but she's too old to be much good. So, I kicked down the corral gate and let her wander off to forage."

"We don't need a horse anyway," Tambourine remarked. "I've rigged up some packs to carry food in. They're pretty light."

"That gun isn't," Toad said, indicating the arquebus propped against the fireplace. "The sucker must weigh over thirty pounds."

Ernie raised one eyebrow. "Carry it if you want, but don't let it slow us down."

Toad took the ancient matchlock from its place by the hearth and examined it closely. It was covered with rust and its thick heavy stock was pitted with wormholes, but it seemed serviceable enough. He hefted it, grunting with the effort. "The least you can do is rig up some kind of carrying strap for me."

Tambourine grinned. "There's plenty of old harness around. I guess we can manage something. But you'll have to wait until I make sure we've packed all the food and clothing we'll need."

"Don't forget the weed," Ernie remarked, taking the skull pipe from the table and slipping it under his cloak.

Lout awoke and watched them with hate-filled eyes. Beneath the bandanna covering his mouth he gurgled something unintelligible.

"Ah, Friend Lout," Ernie said as he shouldered a backpack. "How are you? We seem to have overlooked you in our preparations."

The Rowdie growled, his eyes narrowing to pencil points.

"What are we to do with you? Well, you've been such a generous host that killing you wouldn't be at all polite." He pulled one of the knives out of the bull's eye on the wall and whipped it through the air. It landed, quivering, a foot from the Rowdie's head. "You might try cutting yourself free with that, or, if you don't mind getting singed a bit, you could burn off your ropes in the fire. The choice is yours."

Scuddy Lout thrashed about on the floor, his face flushed with effort and rage. Ernie grinned at him as he opened the door, ushering Tambourine and Toad outside. "Oh, don't carry on so. We'd like to stay, but there's places to go, people to see ... I'm sure you understand."

The herbalist slammed the door behind him, and the three Freaks headed east, leaving the shack and its occupant to their solitude.

Chapter Twenty-Eight

The ground was frozen hard underfoot. Blown free of snow by the frigid night winds, the long grass wafted gently in the mild morning breezes. Having left the Rowdie's shack as soon as the wind showed signs of abating, the three travelers managed to cover a few miles in the hour or so before sunrise. Now, with dawn breaking, they stood on the edge of the great barren expanse of the Plains of Dragstrip. Beyond the Plains the Purple Mountains stood high and dark against the horizon.

Toad yawned and leaned heavily on the arquebus. He rubbed his eyes and looked at the long, straight tracks slashing across the Plains and at the skeletal rows of bleachers and high observation towers that ran alongside each track. Nothing moved on the Plains except the wind, muttering and hooting among the vacant structures.

"Eerie sight, isn't it?" Ernie remarked, as he set down his backpack and stretched. "In the summer this place will be packed with Greasers racing their chariots and partying it up. Now it's deserted."

"Actually, I was more interested in the mountains. They look so close."

"If we make good time, they're only one more day's journey, Toad. We should be there by late tomorrow afternoon."

"I hope that Moonshadow fellow is there to meet us."

"Don't worry about Moonshadow. He's the Keeper of the Gate. The dude's got powers that help him spot travelers over a long distance. It's just a matter of whether we find him or he finds us."

Shouldering his pack again, Ernie led the way across the Plains, skirting the track area and giving the deserted observation towers a wide berth. Soon the grassland gave way to bare dirt, and after a few miles turned into rocky, low-rolling hills.

The morning passed uneventfully. As the day wore on, the travelers came to an area where boulders the size of houses loomed large all about them. Here and there, a lightning bolt or swastika was carved into the rock.

Fascists had once passed through the area and defaced the boulders, as though by doing so they could lay claim to them.

Finally, as the sun rode high over the tops of the distant mountains, they stopped to eat in a narrow, rock-strewn gully. Ernie opened his pack and extracted a loaf of black bread, a small wheel of cheese, and some chunks of dried beef. "Thank you, Mr. Lout," he said.

Tambourine undid the wineskin he wore about his shoulder and took a long pull from it. "Yes, here's to our benefactor, Scuddy Lout," he said, offering the skin to Toad.

Toad smiled, laying his gun against a boulder. He accepted the skin and drank eagerly. The dark Thirtyweight beer tasted full and rich. He belched happily and passed the skin to Ernie. "A most generous fellow, Brother Lout. May he find happiness."

"Or at least a way out of those ropes I bound him in," Ernie added. "Help yourself to food, guys."

Toad laughed as Ernie sliced the bread with his knife. "I'm so hungry I could eat a horse."

"I could have brought Lout's old mare." The friends laughed heartily and dug into their meal.

When they'd eaten their fill and packed away the leftovers, Ernie produced the skull pipe and a flint and steel. The trio sprawled among the rocks, passing the pipe between them.

"I can't wait to get to Hillcommune," Tambourine said. "The first thing I'm going to do when I get there is get my guitar back from Maynard and find someone to jam with. I wonder if Smokin' Joe and Lemon Verbena are still around."

Ernie shrugged. "I heard Wildthistle died a few years ago. I never even heard of the other guy, so he's probably gone too."

"That's too bad. Still, my fingers are itching to hold a guitar pick again."

"Pick what you want. Me, I'd like to find a woman to snuggle up to. For the moment, though, I need to wander off among those rocks and leave a marker—you know, a colon cairn."

Toad reached into the pocket of his sheepskin coat and removed the remaining pages of the *Necronomicon*. "Here, take these to wipe with. That's all they're really good for."

"I'll take them, but only for safekeeping."

After Ernie walked away, Toad turned his attention back to the pipe in his hand. It had gone out. He was just about to ask the whereabouts of the weedsack when Tambourine motioned him to silence. In the distance a horse whinnied.

Tambourine put his finger to his lips. "Get your gun, Toad. I think we've got visitors."

Pocketing the pipe, Toad grabbed the arquebus. Fumbling with the flint and steel, he fought to light its match, but the charred cord wouldn't take. In desperation he pulled up a clump of grass, and after several clumsy attempts, got it to smolder. He blew on the tinder with all his might. Finally, it smoked heavily and burst into flame.

"Quickly!" Tambourine whispered. "Someone's coming this way."

Toad plunged the match into the flame, trembling as it caught fire. Then, balancing the heavy weapon in his hands, he aimed toward where Tambourine was pointing.

Several figures were moving through the rocks toward the Freaks. Though they were still distant, Toad saw that one of them had a long musket and the others held small, one-handed crossbows. They all wore leather jackets. The sun reflected off the chains that the musket-bearer wore looped around his shoulders.

"Greasers," Tambourine moaned. "We're screwed."

The Greasers sauntered toward the Freaks as casually as if they were attending a party. Toad opened the flashpan of his matchlock and drew a bead on the lead Greaser. More Greasers appeared among the rocks, until their numbers swelled to over twenty. Beside Toad, Tambourine was moaning and shaking his head.

"Why me?" the musician wailed. "Why does this always happen to me?"

"I've come to believe it's because we've had the misfortune of being Ernie Mungweasle's friends," Toad growled.

Without warning, one of the Greasers fired his crossbow. The bolt dug into the arquebus's stock an inch from Toad's fingers. With a yelp, the pipesmith dropped the weapon as if it were glowing hot.

"Well, well, well," the Greaser with the musket chortled as he approached the Freaks. "Faggits—playing with firesticks. Ain't that somethin', boys?" He was close enough now that Toad could see the scars crisscrossing his face and the gold-capped tooth winking in his mouth. He swung the musket up so that Toad could get a clear look at its yawning muzzle.

"Yeah, that's somethin', Pozzi," the Greaser who had fired the crossbow said. "These must be the faggits that Rowdie told us about."

"You think so, Bondo? I only see two faggits. Lout said there was three."

"Ain't that strange? Where's your buddy, faggit?"

"Uh, h-he split. He headed south hours ago," Toad answered.

The Greaser with the crossbow nudged his companion. "The pussy can talk, Pozzi. What ya think? Ya think he's tellin' the truth?"

"It's the truth," Tambourine stated.

Pozzi grinned and fondled his musket. "Now this is really somethin'. Both of the pussies can talk. You faggits better not be lyin'. Nobody lies to Pozzi Pozzburn and lives to tell about it."

Bondo stepped closer, cocking his crossbow and slipping in a fresh bolt. "I think they're lying through their teeth, Boss. What say I take some of the boys and check in the rocks?"

"Sure, suit yourself. Make it snappy, though. I wanna be in Lubejob before nightfall."

About half of the Greasers went with Bondo, fanning out through the gully with their crossbows cocked and ready. The rest remained behind, forming a circle around the Freaks and eyeing them with silent hostility. Several produced spiked brass knuckles or short iron truncheons, which they fingered eagerly. Pozzi seemed to take delight in the Freaks' discomfort. He aimed his musket at Toad's midsection and grinned. In the bright sunlight his gold-capped tooth flashed like a warning beacon.

"If my boys find your buddy, you'll be hurtin' units," he said. "I'll put you pussies through a world of hurt like you won't believe. Maybe it won't be here and now, but I'll do it sure'n shit."

Toad nodded numbly and glanced at Tambourine. Though still pale, the musician's face was set and grim, his robin's-egg blue eyes expressionless. He seemed reconciled to his fate, a feeling Toad found hard to share. The Greasers were dangerous, that much was clear, but they weren't subhuman like the Mansonites, or stupid like Scuddy Lout. The pipesmith looked down, studying the ground, while he tried to come to grips with his fear.

"What we gonna do with these pussies?" one of the Greasers asked. "We gonna stomp 'em?"

Pozzi shook his head. "That ain't for me to decide, Spudder. You know Overhaul's coming up, and I got my orders."

"Shitfire, Boss. We ain't had no action in weeks."

"I know, but Kham wants us taking prisoners these days. 'Sides, there's people that might wanna talk to these faggits."

"That ain't no fun. Taking prisoners sucks. Lookit that pussy we caught last week; you didn't let us stomp him either."

"Orders is orders, Spud. I do what Kham and Kwikshift tell me to do, and I suggest you do the same. There'll be stompin' enough at Overhaul."

Spudder looked like he wanted to argue the point more, but just then Bondo and the others appeared from the rocks at the far end of the gully. To Toad's relief, Ernie wasn't with them.

"No luck?" Pozzi asked.

"Not so much as a footprint. These fuckers might just be telling the truth."

"Ain't that somethin'? Still, he ain't gonna get too far if he headed south. Fashie soljers or Bed-Sheet Boys'll make fast work of him."

"We woulda too, if we caught him."

Pozzi grinned. "You boys are just pissin' for a fight, ain't you? That time's coming soon enough. Then, you'll have all the scrappin' you can handle."

"Yeah, but how much action we really gonna see?" Bondo asked. "Sure'n shit Klaven's boys and Ol' Creepy Crawler are gonna hog most of the glory."

"Maybe that's so, and maybe it ain't. All's I know is I wanna bomb out of here and get back to Lubejob. I got me some fancy stickin' set up for tonight, and damned if I'm gonna miss out."

The other Greasers laughed and made crude comments, but they rushed to comply with Pozzi's wishes.

Toad tensed as a pair of smirking Greasers grabbed him and bound his wrists with chains. Beside him another pair was doing the same to Tambourine. The musician didn't resist, but anger sparked briefly in his eyes when he was shoved toward the trail leading back through the rocks. One of the Greasers had picked up the arquebus and prodded Tambourine along with it. Toad fell into step beside Tambourine and his captors. He tried to remain calm even though a pair of crossbows was aimed at his back.

Within a few minutes the Greasers were through the gully and back to where they'd left their chariots. Eight of the sleek, brightly painted vehicles were lined up next to the gully entrance, their teams patiently grazing on the dead grass. To Toad, the Greaser chariots were odd-looking to say the least; they looked ominous. They had high, narrow wheels and their sides sloped back into tall tail fins decorated with shiny metal and glass. The front of each vehicle was equally as ornate; grinning shark jaws were painted on one, surreal flames on another. The one Toad was being shoved toward was decorated with a grotesque cartoon rat wearing a tall shapeless red hat. Beneath the misshapen rodent ran the legend "Mother's Worry." Tambourine was seated behind the driver of a sleek, black chariot emblazoned with the words "High Roller" and a pair of oversized dice.

Toad made no resistance as he was chained to the bar directly behind Pozzi's head. The Greaser grinned and took up the reins. "You're going for a ride, boy," he informed Toad. "One you ain't never gonna forget."

The pipesmith made no answer. As the chariots rolled out onto the level grassland he concentrated on the squeak of the wheels and the clopping of the horses' hooves, listening to their rhythms. He let his head drop and closed his eyes.

In less than an hour the rutted road through the grasslands gave way to a section of ancient throughway that, though crumbling and riven with cracks, led as straight as an arrow across the barren expanse of Dragstrip Plain. Toad was only dimly aware of the roadway. As the chariots rolled over the expanse of rotting concrete, he sought solace in daydreams of home. Closing his eyes, he fell into a half-doze. Pictures of his book-lined study on Smuttynose turned round in his head.

He was in his overstuffed leather chair, a mulled cider in his hand and a well-worn book on his knee. A short clay pipe protruded from his mouth and fragrant weedsmoke drifted lazily as he gazed into the fireplace. The flames on the hearth leaped up and fell back, dancing as if some invisible presence had passed by them. The flickering shadows against the far wall solidified and pooled in on one another, taking on the form of a stooped, black-robed figure with glowing eyes. Straightening, the figure moved toward Toad—a puddle of darkness with outstretched talons and a smoking grin.

Toad jerked awake. Looking around, he saw that the highway was giving way to packed dirt. Along the road tumbledown houses with wagon-littered yards were becoming a frequent sight. Traffic was heavier, too. Several times other chariots sped past, and once a huge armored troop carrier rumbled by, drawn by eight straining workhorses. Sullen Fascists peered out of its bow slits, needling Toad with their eyes. They passed through several villages—tiny hovels clustered around a wagon shop or livery where the locals seemed to spend most of their time. More than once these idlers yelled out comments as Pozzi's troop rolled by, but often they just waved.

The packed dirt road finally led to cobbles and brick at the outskirts of Lubejob. Rows of grim, multistoried tenements and long barn-like structures became common. Toad looked about Lubejob with interest. The wide cobbled streets bustled with activity. Another troop carrier rolled by, followed by a team dragging a wheeled siege ballista. A pair of tall Whiteriders clattered past on their matched white stallions, seemingly oblivious to the pedestrians and gaudily painted chariots moving all about them.

Suddenly, Pozzi gave a hard tug on the reins. The chariot whipped around a corner, almost running over a knot of teenaged Greaslets converged in front of a pool hall. Several of the larger kids yelled obscenities and shot the finger at Pozzi, but most just goggled at Toad. Pozzi swore back at them and reined his team harder. The kids scattered in the dust. The chariot rolled up over the curb before proceeding down a narrow side street, then joined the others as they clattered by a row of the huge barns. The door of one barn was open. Through it Toad saw Greasers in gray overalls working on a metal vehicle that stood as tall as a small house. From its cylinder-shaped front end with its pair of chimney-like stacks, Toad guessed that it must be one of the steamwagons Ernie had told him about. He whistled involuntarily, impressed by its glittering bulk. "You like that firewagon, eh?" Pozzi said. "We got more of 'em— shitloads more. Maybe you'll get to see 'em in action real soon."

Toad didn't reply. He imagined a fleet of the metal monsters—dozens, maybe hundreds—rolling over Street-Corner Earth, smoke blasting from their stacks, darkening the sky, as people and houses were crushed to mash under their relentless spiked wheels.

Pozzi's chariot wheeled to a stop in front of one of the barns. The other Greasers pulled in right behind it. Rough hands seized Toad, and he was half-shoved, half-dragged to the side door of the cavernous structure. Pozzi kicked open the door and Toad and Tambourine were hurried down a long corridor cluttered with crates and barrels, apparent overflow from the storage rooms on either side. At the end of the corridor was a narrow door with a small barred window. The Freaks were pushed through it into a gloomy cell that smelled of urine. There was another smell as well—a faint odor of peat. Before the Freaks could turn around, the door was slammed shut behind them and the lock bolted.

"Welcome to your new home, faggits," Pozzi jeered from the other side. "Sleep tight and don't let the bed bugs bite."

Toad slumped onto a pile of moldy hay. Except for the cone of light coming through the small window in the door, the room was in total darkness. After a moment Tambourine sat down next to the pipesmith. "I can't believe this shit," he said. "I'm getting awful sick of getting captured by one inbred bunch of rat-bastards after another."

"Yeah, it sucks. I knew I should have stayed on Smuttynose. I should have never let Ernie talk me into this escapade."

Something rustled among the thick shadows at the far end of the cell. The air grew dense with the increasing odor of peat.

"Hey, like, quit your bitching," a gritty, familiar voice instructed. "There's time enough for grief in the grave."

In the dim light Toad could see Tambourine's jaw drop. It was several seconds before the musician could utter a sound.

"Maynard! What are you doing here?" he exclaimed.

A shadow detached itself from the others and moved toward the two Freaks. Maynard stepped into the light, still shadowy except for the glint coming from his reflecting sunglasses. Dust motes swirled about him like a protective fog, drifting down to settle on his moth-eaten beret and powder the shoulders of his threadbare turtleneck sweater. With the exception of the long gray scarf that he wore casually looped about his neck, Maynard looked much as Toad had seen him at Covenstead Fair.

"Hey, like, when you didn't show up in Hillcommune I got worried and

244

decided to come looking for you," he said. "I made the mistake of holing up in one of the towers at Dragstrip and got my ass captured."

Tambourine shook his head. "That sounds like something I'd do. Still, it looks like you managed to find me."

"It does indeed, daddy-o. And Brother Toad, too. I'd heard that you were traveling with my man Tambourine again."

Toad was startled. "Wh-who told you that?"

"Moonshadow, the Gatekeeper at Hillcommune. He's got a gift for far-seeing. He said Tambourine had fallen on hard luck and was gigging with you and Brother Mungweasle. Like, where is that tall cat?"

"He managed to escape."

"Hey, dig it, then there's still hope."

"Dylan's bones, how can you say that? We're stuck in the middle of Lubejob with a thousand Greaseballs around us."

"Man, I've been in worse places than this and managed to escape. Given time, I'll blow this scene too. I'm sure our friend Mr. Mungweasle will have a plan."

Getting to his feet, Tambourine peered through the grating at the top of the door. "We won't be leaving soon. There are guards with crossbows posted at the far end of the corridor. Somebody wants us to stay put."

"That'd be Hurst Kwikshift's doing," Maynard grunted. "He's the Aayfonzer, and he likes to interrogate all prisoners personally. The cat's worked on me a couple of times, but I jived him."

Toad got up off the hay and began examining the cell. Though the light was poor, he tapped the walls and ran his hands along the floorboards. "This place doesn't look all that sturdy. I'll bet we could dig our way out like we did the last place we were held."

"Like, I've contemplated that, man. This pad's a warehouse, not a real prison. Thing is, security here is tight. Besides the local fuzz, Lubejob's crawling with Whiteriders and Fashie soldiers. Nothing'll get past those cats."

"I thought you said there was hope," Tambourine said.

"Never say die, man. If you brought the *Necronomicon* along, I could use it to blow this burg to kindling."

"You're going to have to ask Toad about that one. It's kind of a long story."

"Lay it on me, pipesmith. We've got nothing but time."

Leaning against the nearest wall, Toad took a deep breath and slowly related everything that had happened since he and Ernie had found Tambourine and nursed him back to health. When he got to the part about their discovery of the *Necronomicon* in the underground temple and their subsequent capture by the Mansonites, Maynard could hardly restrain his excitement.

"Real gone, man," he said, rubbing his hands together. "So, like, the Charlie-cats are still around. I thought they couldn't *all* have been killed off."

Tambourine made an odd noise low in his throat. "Is that why you sent me to Swetshop instead of going yourself—because you thought they might still be haunting the place?"

"You read me all wrong, daddy-o. Sure, I was kept prisoner by those cats centuries ago, just after they stole the book, but that wasn't the reason I won't step foot in Swetshop."

"What is, then?"

"Man, I used to work in a place like that and I hated it so bad that I, like, vowed I'd never go in another."

"That's it!?"

"Hey, you ever heard of mandatory overtime? Never mind—forget that. Let's just say I've got a strong aversion to that place. But, like, this is getting us nowhere. What I want to know is, do you have the book now?"

Toad shook his head. "Ernie's got it, or what's left of it. We lost most of it fighting our way out of Swetshop."

"Shit. Still, a part's better than nothing. At least it's safe with Ernie."

"It doesn't matter if it's safe or not. The book's bogus."

Maynard's jaw dropped. "What? Like, how do you know that?"

"Because of the diary in the back."

"Diary?"

"Yeah, a journal kept by the first Bookreader, Evan Copralallius."

"Unreal, man! I knew Copralallius; he was a heavy cat."

Toad's jaw tightened. Sure, you know everything, he thought. But he said, "Quite an accomplished scholar. According to him, the real *Necronomicon* is somewhere in Khamshaft—maybe here in Lubejob, for all we know."

Maynard tugged at his goatee thoughtfully. "Like, it's possible that there might be multiple copies, some phony, some not. Back before my time there was a cat named Lovecraft who mentioned the *Necronomicon* in some of the stories he wrote. According to him, there were several editions floating around in this part of the world, both in the Common Tongue and in an ancient language we called Latin."

"That might be so," Toad replied, not mentioning the copy he had at home. "But this copy Copralallius mentions is concealed in a 'swift iron coffin'—whatever that means."

Maynard shrugged. He started to speak, but was cut short by the sound of footsteps outside the door. A key rattled in the lock and the door swung open to reveal a fat, toothless Greaser carrying a club. Beside him stood a

246

pair of leather-jacketed guards wielding Fascist-style crossbows.

"Hope you boys been enjoyin' your stay," the fat Greaser sneered. "Now, the Aayfonzer would like a little talk with one of you new guys."

Maynard chuckled. "Waste of time, daddy-o. Like, he ain't going to get any more out of them than he did out of me."

"Stow it, faggit. You," he said, pointing to Toad. "You're the lucky one."

Toad shuffled out into the corridor with the three Greasers right behind him. Without the presence of his friends, he felt his confidence waning. Still, if anyone knew where the *Necronomicon* might be, it was be the man he was about to meet. Perhaps, if he played it right, he might get the Aayfonzer to let out more information than he intended. It was a slim hope, but it lent Toad courage. Straightening his shoulders, he stepped through the side door that the fat turnkey indicated.

The room that they entered was huge—a storeroom, judging from the crates and barrels lining the walls. Several windows provided enough light for him to make out the bales that were stacked ceiling high at the far end. He glimpsed them for only a moment before being prodded through a door leading into an adjoining chamber, but the sweet musty odor told him all that he needed to know. The Greasers were hoarding stolen Honkweed— thousands of kilos, probably fine Hillcommune Red.

Beyond the chamber, which was filled to bursting with chariot and wagon parts, the Greasers moved Toad quickly through a great open room where swarms of overalled Greasers were putting the finishing touches on a huge steamwagon. Even as he watched, they crawled over the machine like ants, polishing metal and painting stylized flames that swirled over the front of the engine's mammoth boiler. Beyond the steamwagon lay a short corridor, at the end of which stood a scarred wooden door bearing a sign that said: "HURST KWIKSHIFT-AAYFONZER. Knock Before Entering."

The fat turnkey rapped twice on the door, giving Toad a toothless smirk as he did so. "Here's where the fun begins," he said.

The door swung open on the second rap. Inside, behind a crude wooden desk, stood a hard-faced Greaser in his late forties, dressed in spotless white overalls. A large silver wrench hung from a chain around his neck, dangling just above his small potbelly. When he walked out from behind the desk, Toad saw that he was wearing a fearsome set of spiked brass knuckles on his right hand. He looked like he knew how to use them.

The Aayfonzer regarded Toad like he might a new species of insect. A sneer twisted one corner of his thin mouth. "This is the new prisoner?"

"Sure is, Boss," the turnkey replied. "One of the scumbags Pozzi brought in."

"Don't look like much to me, Turbo."

"Hah, you oughta see the other pussy."

"Yeah? Well, that's gonna make my job real easy. What ya wanna bet I can make this here he-man talk really pretty?"

"Ain't bettin', Boss. I seen your work before."

Kwikshift nonchalantly polished his brass knuckles on his left sleeve. "An' you'll see it again, Turbo. Why don't you leave now, so the faggit and I can get better acquainted."

The turnkey and the two guards gave a thumbs-up salute and closed the door behind them. Kwikshift glared, his close-set dark eyes boring into Toad's. There was craziness in their black depths, but there was intelligence too. The pipesmith decided that the Aayfonzer wasn't one to be easily deceived.

Kwikshift made a step forward. His eyes sparked cold malice. "We're gonna talk, faggit. You give me any shit, you get hurt. Understand?"

Toad nodded.

"That's real good. Maybe I won't have to rearrange your face after all. Now, I wanna know what you and your buddies were doin' on my turf. The truth, not what you told that weaslin' Rowdie."

Toad nodded again. He doubted he could lie extensively and get away with it, but he could omit details. "Wh-what do you want to know?"

"Everything. Every fuckin' thing."

The pipesmith looked past Kwikshift, focusing on the painting behind the desk. It was a crude rendition of a nude woman sprawled across the front of a strange horseless wagon, like the one he'd dreamed about at the Mansonite village. Acting as contrite and timid as possible, he began his story at the Battle of Great East Lake, without mentioning his or Ernie's role in it. When he got to the part about his adventures with the Mansonites, the Aayfonzer grew excited.

"Back up right there, boy," Hurst Kwikshift said. "I wanna ask you a few questions."

"S-sure."

Kwikshift began pacing the room, nervously playing with his brass knuckles. He stopped suddenly and fixed Toad with a cold stare. "Did you hear the name Isky Kwikshift mentioned while you were there?"

"No."

"Think real hard, faggit. He was my great-great grandfather—an Aayfonzer like me."

A light went on in Toad's brain. "Well, I heard that one of your people had been a prisoner there long ago. There was no name given, but he was supposed to be someone important. Could be the same guy."

"Maybe we're getting somewhere. Tell me more."

"I really don't know much more."

"Strain your brain. Back in the old days an Aayfonzer passed certain—uh—relics, from father to son, things that maybe other people didn't have a need to know about. When Isky disappeared he never had a chance to pass these things on. I want what's mine."

"I'm not sure I understand."

Kwikshift leaned forward, his eyes glittering. "I'll spell it out for you: things could go easy for you here, or things could go rough. What the old Aayfonzer's secrets were, I don't really know. If you know anything at all, it could work to *our* benefit."

Toad had to fight to maintain his composure. The hell of it was that he was beginning to suspect that he did know something. If he weren't careful, Kwikshift would know too. Old Isky's secret had been the *Necronomicon*, and where it could be found.

"*Our* benefit? Now I'm really sure that I don't understand."

"It's real simple, pally. Before Isky's time, Fonzers ruled Khamshaft, and the Aayfonzer ruled the Fonzers. The Kham clan was nothing more than what you might call figurehead rulers. They didn't dare take a shit without asking the Aayfonzer what color and how much. That meant that Isky and all my ancestors before him were the real honchos around here.

"Once Isky disappeared into Darkenwood, that all changed. Over the years the Khams got more power and now it's the Fonzers that's gotta dance to their tune."

Toad nodded. "And you want things the way they were."

"Damn straight. It ain't entirely for me, you unnerstand; it's for all Khamshaft. Bad enough the Khams have been screwing things up for generations; now they're playing footsies with Klaven Thinarm and his Bed-Sheet Boys."

"And, you don't like Fascists very much."

"You got that right, son. But it don't stop there. Lately, in the last few months, we've had that Ol' Creepy Crawler, Lord Flatbush, to contend with. He just rode in here with his pack of black-cloaked outlanders and started taking over the joint. Now it's getting so Klaven and Kham are taking orders from him."

Toad suppressed a shudder. The Dark Man was close, too close. "What's all this got to do with me?"

"Smarten up, pally. There's some of us want things back the way they oughta be. You been to Darkenwood and you say there's still Charlie-scum there. You heard about Isky, and maybe you heard about more. I think you know about his secrets and just ain't tellin'."

"Mansonites are inbred troglodytes!" Toad blurted out. "They were only concerned about getting us into their stomachs. I'm sorry, but I can't help you."

Kwikshift moved quickly, slamming his brass-knuckled fist down on the desktop so hard that it split the wood. "Can't or won't?!" he roared. "Them that ain't with us is against us! Now, answer my questions!"

"I-I'll try." Dylan's Bones, the Aayfonzer knew. Toad didn't know how, but he really knew.

"Good. Now, I wanna know about your buddy, the tall skinny pussy the Rowdie told Pozzi about."

"Him? Oh, he left hours before your men caught us. He headed south to The Freaklands."

The Aayfonzer laughed. "Shit lot of good that'll do him. He won't get far. Ripoff Pass is crawling with Fashies and Bed-Sheeters. He woulda done better to stay with the Charlies."

"He'll get through."

"Maybe he will, 'n maybe he won't. That don't explain you, though. Where were you headed?"

There was no sense in lying. "We were on our way to Hillcommune."

"Now, ain't that somethin'? Hippies hanging around with Flower Faggits. You're full of surprises, ain't you, boy?"

"It's a safe haven, that's all."

Kwikshift's eyes narrowed. They bored deeper into Toad. "Well, I'll tell you what: I don't give a jack-shit about you and your fancy buddies. I just want what's mine, and I intend to get it, even if I have to cut you apart inch by inch to get the info I need. You believe that, faggit?"

Toad nodded.

The Aayfonzer's eyes narrowed further, until they were like dagger points. "Why is it I don't believe you? Way I see it, you got a choice: either your memory improves, or you and your buddies got ringside seats at Overhaul."

"I've t-told you all I know. Honest."

Kwikshift smiled humorlessly. He removed his brass knuckles and flipped them into the air, catching them deftly with one finger. "I could make you talk, boy, but now ain't the time. You oughta think on it awhile. Get goin'. You're free."

"Free?"

"Free to go back to your cell, hippie. You ain't got much time, so use it wisely. Try and improve your memory before Overhaul."

Slowly, Toad got up and moved toward the door, not quite daring to turn his back on Kwikshift. His feet and legs felt like they were made out of lead. "Wh-what's Overhaul?" he asked.

"You'll find out soon enough, boy, if you don't level with me."

Back at the cell, as soon as the guards slammed the door shut behind him, Tam and Maynard bombarded him with questions.

"Like, what did he do to you?" Maynard asked.

Toad stretched out on the moldy hay. He was weary and his head felt too heavy for his shoulders. "Threatened me, mostly. He seems to think that I'm onto something, but I wouldn't tell him anything."

"The cat's not stupid, I'll give him that. He's been playing the same riff on me. I wouldn't worry, though. I don't think he's going to be around much longer."

"What makes you say that?"

"Like, he's stepping on too many toes, dig? The Dark Man's running this gig now, and he won't stand for anyone who doesn't go along with his way of thinking."

A chill went through Toad. "The Dark Man's here in Lubejob?"

"Hey, I haven't seen him personally, but a cat hears things, even in the slammer."

"What does he want?"

The Beatnik sat down on the hay next to Toad. "He wants what every other megalomaniac wants—power, the ability to make everyone his slave, to rule the world. The usual stuff."

"So why is he here in Lubejob?"

"Who knows? But, he's here just in time for Overhaul. Seems like more than a coincidence to me."

"What is Overhaul, anyway? The Greasers that captured us said something about it; even the Aayfonzer mentioned it, but nobody said what it was, really."

"It's, like, the main Greaser holiday, when they venerate their holy '55 Chevy. A ritual gang beating highlights it. A stupid concept at best, but it just goes to show that Greasers haven't changed much in five hundred years."

"I'd just like to beat feet out of here," Toad sighed, "and forget that stupid book."

"We need the book. You said that Copralallius thought it was here in Lubejob. If we get out of this hole, I'd like one quick look around."

"I said, he thought it was somewhere in Khamshaft. I was the one who mentioned Lubejob."

"We won't have a chance anyway," Tambourine interjected. "Especially during Overhaul. You can bet your ass that porky jailer's gonna be keeping a close eye on us until everything's over."

"He'll be more interested in what's going on with the holiday than in us," the Beatnik offered.

"Yeah. Well, my guess is that we'll be part of the celebration," Tambourine stated. "At least one of us will be attending Overhaul—as the victim."

"One of *us*?" Toad asked, fearing the musician's suggestion.

"You see any one else in this rat hole? It might be all three of us—who knows. But unless they have other cells with more promising candidates, I'd say we're all they've got."

Toad glanced from Tambourine to Maynard. "You guys really know how to brighten my day."

Maynard adjusted his sunglasses on his nose. "Hey, dig it; the situation isn't *entirely* hopeless."

The pipesmith took little comfort from Maynard's words. He was formulating a reply when he heard the jailer's key in the lock.

Turbo came in bearing a trencher filled with watery soup and a loaf of moldy-looking black bread. "Eat 'em up, faggits," he said, placing the trencher on the floor. "We want you fat 'n healthy for Overhaul."

When Turbo had closed the door behind him, Maynard broke the loaf into three pieces and shared them with Toad and Tambourine.

Toad took his bread and dipped it in the soup until it became saturated. Then, sitting off to one side by himself, he began to chew on it methodically. The bread was tough and grainy, and the soup he'd sopped it in had an unpleasant undertaste, but he hadn't eaten since noon, so anything was welcome. When he'd choked down his last morsel he stretched out on the hay and closed his eyes.

Toad found himself in a warm and beautiful place. Stretching, he opened his eyes to the westering sun as it cast long shadows across the flowered meadows below the mountains. Birds wheeled in the sky above him, their faint cries musical and enchanting. A narrow band of clouds hung over the distant peaks, flushed crimson and violet with the setting sun.

In the distance, beyond the meadows, a peaceful village lay along a river. Though he could see no people in the streets, Toad heard singing and merry laughter coming from one of the larger buildings. He hurried toward the sound, with a lightness of step that he found surprising. Somehow, he knew that beyond the mountains the world was gripped by winter, but here in this land with no name, summer reigned forever.

The music grew louder, more compelling the closer he got to the village. Insects buzzed in the tall grass, joining in with the guitars and flutes. In the marshes beyond the river frogs added a cheery bass. Huge, multicolored butterflies capered in the air, dancing fancy arabesques in time to the music.

There was movement in the village—a flash of turquoise that shimmered brightly in the darkening twilight. A figure started across the field toward Toad, a woman whose flowing red hair was set off by the rich blue of her dress. Toad's heart gave a leap, his feet picking up speed as he ran toward her, toward Mizjoan.

Chapter Twenty-Nine

Toad's eyes jerked open. There was no sunlit meadow, only the dank cell. No Mizjoan. No music. Just the soft breathing of his friends huddled on the hay beside him, and the harsher sound of Turbo arguing with the two guards at the other end of the corridor.

"Lug! Tach!" Toad heard the jailer yell. "What've I told you losers about drinking on duty? Lookit this place: beer crocks all over the floor an' you bastards are hardly able to stand up. Why, for two hubcaps I'd…"

"Aww, Turbo," one of the guards whined. "Have a heart. It's Overhaul Day. We was just celebratin' a little early."

"I'll give you something' to celebrate, dickface. I'll bet you assholes ain't checked on them prisoners once all night. Probably been too busy butt-blasting each other to take care of business."

"That ain't so. I looked in on them 'bout an hour ago. They was all sleepin' like babies."

"Awright, get your wimpy asses in gear. I want this pigsty cleaned up by the time I get back, an' I want that one prisoner readied up for Overhaul. Think you jerkoffs can remember that, or do you want me to send you a letter?"

"No, we'll get right to it. You can depend on us."

"I'm sure I can, or it ain't gonna be some pussy-boy longhair that gets his brains kicked out tonight."

The door slammed, and Toad could hear the two Greasers muttering to themselves as they went about cleaning up the guard station. "Boy, was he pissed at you, Tach," one said.

"Me? Do your ears lap over? He was yelling at both of us."

"Mostly you, though."

"That's only 'cause you were actin' like a scared rabbit."

"Aww. Did ya check on the faggits like you said?"

"Yeah. Where were you, sleepin'?"

"Maybe. I don't remember. Whatcha wanna do with the one that's getting stomped tonight?"

"Holding cell. 'Fact, let's get him right now."

Toad could hear their footsteps coming down the corridor. Before he could get to his feet, the key rattled in the lock and the cell door opened. The two guards stood in the doorway, smirking stupidly. One held a club, the other an open spring-knife. They both smelled of beer.

"Get up, get up," the one with the club said, hovering over Toad. "Nappy time's over."

"Wh-what do you want with me?"

"We gonna take you for a walk. Get you ready for a party."

The Greaser with the spring-knife grabbed Toad's collar and jerked him to his feet. His eyes were glazed and red, and he literally stank of brew.

"Wh-where are you taking me?" Toad demanded.

"You'll see. Now, you come along nice-like, or am I gonna have to drag you?"

Grabbing Toad's arm and twisting it around behind him, the Greaser yanked the pipesmith out into the corridor. His partner fell into step beside him, prodding Toad along with his club. Toad looked back at the cell before the door swung shut. From inside, he could hear his friends' protestations.

Halfway down the corridor the Greasers paused. The one with the club fumbled with his keys. He selected one and opened a narrow door opening off to the left.

"Wh-what's this?" Toad asked. The room was tiny, hardly bigger than a broom closet.

"Your new home—least until tonight. You're gonna be the star of the party."

"Wait! Kwikshift told me if I cooperated and told him what he wanted to know, he'd spare me."

"That so? Well, it don't matter what he says. Kham calls the shots around here, not him."

In spite of the Greaser's grip on his arm, Toad struggled to free himself. "No! I want to see Kwikshift, right now!"

"All's you're gonna see is stars," the Greaser replied, raising his club and slamming it down on Toad's head.

The pipesmith had no idea what time it was when he finally came to. Groaning, he worked himself up into a sitting position and leaned against the wall. It was stifling in the tiny cell. There was no ventilation, save for the crack under the door, and barely enough room to lie down in. Gingerly massaging his throbbing head, which now had a considerable lump, he put his ear to the door. Beyond it he could hear movement in the corridor and the muffled sounds of the Greasers talking among themselves.

"So, you checked on the faggit lately?" he heard Turbo ask.

"Yeah, I looked in about two hours back," the Greaser that had held the club replied. "He was startin' to come to, so I sapped him again."

"You better not've killed him, Tach. That's for others better than you to do."

"Nah, he'll live. Look, Turbo, can me an' Lug go home now? We been up over twenny-four hours, an'..."

"An' you'll be up twenny-four hours more. It's gonna be a busy night tonight, an' I ain't got no replacements for you."

"Hey, that ain't fuckin' fair."

"So, when you known me to be fair? You assholes wanted to be party boys last night, an' I'm punishing you for it. Now, get his ass out here. I gotta get our boy over to Temple Sunoc, an' I'm runnin' late as it is."

The guard grumbled and Toad heard the squeak of a chair being pushed aside. A moment later the door to his cell was pulled open and Turbo and Tach were jerking him to his feet. Turbo's vapid, toothless grin looked like a half-healed wound.

Without saying a word, the fat turnkey pressed a knife into the small of Toad's back and led him out of the building and down a litter-filled alley between two of the large barns. Turbo seemed to take great delight in prodding the pipesmith with his knife.

Soon, the alleyway turned into a narrow street leading past rows of seedy tenements. Greasers of all ages sat on the door stoops, eyeing them as they passed. Turbo shoved Toad through a vacant lot that was filled with rubbish and overgrown with tangled weeds. The evening was cold, and a few lazy snowflakes drifted down out of the leaden sky. Once the lot was behind them, Turbo maneuvered Toad onto a street illuminated by the harsh light spilling from the game rooms and sleazy bars that lined the way. Though it was barely dusk, most of the inhabitants of Lubejob were out carousing in the streets, drunk.

Greasers, both male and female, catcalled from windows and doorways as Toad went by. Several threw garbage, one even chucking a full crock of beer at Toad's head, barely missing him. A slutty-looking girl with teased red hair giggled and threw Toad a kiss.

"That'll be enough of that shit," Turbo snapped at the onlookers.

"Can't wait for Overhaul," yelled a young Greaser from the shadowy doorway of a pool hall.

"Gonna hafta, kid. C'mon, move aside here. Let us through."

Grudgingly, the crowd parted. Turbo and Toad proceeded across another empty lot toward a strange, sprawling building set apart from the tottering houses and shops that encircled it. In spite of his fear, Toad forced himself to be stoic.

As they approached the building from the street side, Toad saw it was actually a series of additions built upon and around a central structure of whitewashed concrete. Though the concrete was flaking in places and the unpainted wooden additions showed signs of dry rot, the building looked better maintained than anything else he'd seen in Lubejob. The torchlit lot was freshly swept, and only a few weeds poked up from the cracks in the concrete. Directly in front of the building stood three wooden monoliths, painted red and yellow and emblazoned with the words REGLAR, REGLAR UNLEAD, and ULTRA UNLEAD. Toad gaped at them, wondering what dark Greaser gods they represented. Above the monoliths a sign was suspended from a high pole. It was in the shape of a yellow diamond with one end broken off, pierced by a red arrow. In large, faded letters it bore the legend: SUNOC.

Turbo shoved Toad toward the huge double doors that took up most of the front of the concrete structure. Large blocks of rusted iron and piles of sinister objects that resembled huge black doughnuts flanked the doors. Still holding the knife to Toad's back, Turbo reached out and rapped loudly on one of the doors. After a moment the door rolled upward noisily and Toad was propelled into the torchlit interior of Temple Sunoc.

Toad blinked until his eyes became accustomed to the light. He fought to catch his breath. The floor of the temple was swarming with Fonzers dressed in gleaming leather or overalls of various drab colors. Scores more sat on long rows of wooden benches along the back wall, where it appeared that part of the original structure had been knocked out crudely for a wooden addition. As the door rolled back down behind him, the Fonzers turned and fixed on Toad with hostile stares. Several nudged friends sitting next to them and made comments that evoked harsh laughter from the crowd.

Hurst Kwikshift stood behind a low podium at the far end of the room. Torches burned on either side, illuminating the rows of antique tools mounted on the wall. He held a heavy, cheaply bound book in his left hand and a massive black wrench in his right. In front of the podium, a line of Chachis stood at rigid attention, neophyte Fonzers in blue overalls wielding short iron bars in their gloved hands. When he saw Toad a scowl rippled across the Aayfonzer's features, and he looked up toward the high vaulted ceiling of the temple.

Toad looked up too. There, among the webbing of scaffoldings and catwalks, a light shone in a makeshift balcony. A dark figure gazed back down at Kwikshift, a man wearing a shiny leather jacket with a crudely wrought, iron crown cocked rakishly to one side of his head. With a quick jerking motion, the man gave a thumbs-up salute. Even at a distance, it was apparent that the gesture was an act of defiance and not a greeting. Kwikshift's scowl deepened, and when he looked back at Toad his face had hardened into an unreadable mask.

Toad started toward the Aayfonzer, but Turbo's knife bit into his back, even through the pipesmith's thick jacket. "You bastard, Kwikshift," Toad snapped. "I was going to tell you what you wanted to know."

If the Aayfonzer had heard Toad he gave no reaction. Ignoring the pipesmith, he addressed the crowd instead. Gesturing with his wrench he said, "The Fonz smiles on us tonight, boys. He's sent us a faggit to stomp."

The crowd murmured its approval. To Toad, the sound was like angry storm waves breaking on the shore back on Smuttynose. He was scared and angry, but he was determined to act as impassively as Kwikshift. He tried to look the Aayfonzer straight in the eyes, but Kwikshift ignored him, giving his full attention to his audience.

"Yeah," he boomed, clutching the book and waving his wrench like a sword. "Tonight faggit blood will grease the wheels of the holy '55."

The Fonzers cheered and whistled. The young ones who stood in front of Kwikshift slapped their iron bars on the palms of their hands, grinning wolfishly.

Kwikshift's eyes glittered as he motioned the mob to silence. "Tonight our young Chachis become full Fonzers. They've worked long and hard for this moment, studying the *Shopmanuals* and learning the mysteries of the '55 Chevy. Before the night is over, their tools will have tasted faggit blood and they'll take their rightful place in Temple Sunoc."

The crowd grew wilder, more excited. Most of the Fonzers were out of their seats by now, stomping on the grimy concrete floor with their heavy boots. Their eyes burned with a feral light.

"Let it begin," Kwikshift said, glancing up to where the light burned in the single balcony box.

With a thundering chant of, "OVERHAUL! OVERHAUL! OVERHAUL!" the crowd of young Fonzers swarmed around Toad, tearing him away from Turbo. Strong hands grabbed him and hoisted him high over the heads of the cheering celebrants.

Quivering with fear, Toad suddenly remembered the night at the Mansonite temple. He turned his face from the coarse, sneering Fonzers. In the balcony far above the scaffolding there were now three figures, shadowy and indistinguishable from one another in the faint light, except for the jagged crown worn by the figure on the far left.

The Chachis danced in a clumsy circle, passing Toad from hand to hand like a sack of meal. Hard fingers dug into his flesh; harder faces leered at him. Their stale beery breath rose about him like fog, driving him to the brink of nausea. Suddenly, without warning, they released their hold and

Toad fell to the oil-stained concrete floor in a bone-rattling heap. Before he realized what was happening, a heavy hobnailed boot pressed down on his neck, forcing him to eye level with the yawning rectangular pit that opened up in the floor.

The boot crushed down harder, causing sparks of pain to flash in front of the pipesmith's eyes. Toward the back of the room a drum sounded a long, slow beat and a noise came out of the pit like that of squeaking winches. Slowly, ominously, something began to rise out of the depths. Whatever it was, it was huge—a great shiny expanse of red that seemed to grow as it rose into the torchlight. At first the object seemed to be made mostly of glass, but it soon widened into a crouching form made of brightly painted and polished metal. Toad forgot his fear for a moment, and gaped in awe as its great metallic face loomed over him with two huge, expressionless glass eyes and a steely grin that was wide and menacing. The thing from the pit was a vehicle of some sort, not massive like the steamwagons, but more like the one he'd dreamed of in the Mansonite prison—the one the Dark Man had seemed so interested in.

The drumming slowed. Kwikshift flexed and opened the timeworn book he'd been holding. He smiled and leaned forward, speaking so softly that he was barely audible: "Hey, lookit my car... "

"IT'S ONE HOT RIG!" the frenzied Fonzers barked in unison, stamping their feet.

The Aayfonzer's smile widened. "I got me... "

"A '55 CHEVY TWO-DOOR HARDTOP WITH A 427 AND DUAL QUADS ON A HIGH-RISE MANIFOLD."

"I'm runnin'... "

"HOOKER HEADERS AND A 411 POSI."

Toad squirmed as the meaningless invocation thundered about him. Short iron bars and wrenches slapped against open hands, keeping time to the drumming. The boot lifted from his neck and he was jerked to his feet. Hands were all over him again, forcing him to circle the ancient vehicle. He caught a glance at the interior.

Unlike the Chevy's outside, which was cleaned and polished to a mirror finish, the inside was a mess. The seats and banks of strange instruments were covered with dust. Spider webs hung from the pair of oversized dice dangling below the mirror and crisscrossed the windows like old lace curtains. More webs draped over the odd wheel on the left side of the compartment. As Toad was forced to pass around the vehicle's front right side, he wondered about this wheel and the various dials and meters beside it. To the right of the dials, he made out the faint cracks marking a built-in compartment. To it was affixed a small blue cross, wider than it was tall.

Suddenly, he was hit with an inspiration that almost took his breath away. Maybe this ancient vehicle, this '55 Chevy, was the 'swift iron coffin' Copralallius had alluded to. Maybe the odd little cross marked the true repository of the *Necronomicon.*

The drumming in the background rose to a frantic beat. The crowd moved in on Toad, eyes glittering, short iron bars and wrenches beating time in eager hands. The Chachis were grinning broadly, but their grins held no warmth.

Kwikshift's voice rose, booming out over the rising drumbeat. "I GOT ME A..."

"HURST CLOSE-RATIO FOUR WITH A REAL SHORT THROW," the Fonzers responded, nearly deafening Toad. "A STRAIGHT-X FRONT END AND AIR SHOCKS ON THE REAR."

"I DON'T SCREW AROUND. I GOT ME..."

The Chachis pushed in closer. Iron bars whirred in their hands as they muscled their way toward him. He closed his eyes and tried to steel himself. "G-FIFTIES WITH CHROME REVERSE MAGS," they howled. "BUCKET SEATS WITH A TACH ON THE DASH."

The response pleased Kwikshift. He leaned over his podium, his cold voice boring into Toad's ears. "MISTER MAN, I TELL YOU. I GOT..."

Chapter Thirty

There were three kinds of people Billy hated—women, children, and everyone else. There were, however, a few he could tolerate: ones he could use, ones he could abuse, and one or two like Jack Rabid, who were more like pet dogs—which, come to think of it, wasn't necessarily to their credit, because his heart held no warm spot for dogs either. Still, the latter type shared with dogs two qualities that he found endearing. One was blind loyalty; the other was their willingness to nuzzle his genitals. In Lubejob, however, it was the abusable type that had led him to Bardahl Street.

Simply known as The Strip, Bardahl Street was the heart of the Fonzer section of the city. With its many bars and game rooms, it was Lubejob's cultural center, and perhaps the epitome of culture in all Khamshaft. It was on The Strip that the young Chachis usually congregated, with their swaggering little asses molded into tight blue jeans. The sight of their succulent buns was what lured Billy to include Bardahl Street in his route, regardless of where his business took him.

Tonight though, there were no Chachis to ogle. Only a few common Greasers strolled the streets, watching in awe as he and Jack Rabid marched past toward Temple Sunoc, their thick boots clomping on the cobbled streets. Most of the Fonzers were at Sunoc already, awaiting the Rite of Overhaul, when the young neophytes would finally be inducted into the priesthood. No outsiders were allowed entry to the secret ceremony but every common traveler, from Moloch in the Great Whitelands to the border town of Saturday Night in the south of Street-Corner Earth, knew what went on inside. Given enough to drink a Greaser, even a Fonzer, would tell you anything.

Tonight tradition would be broken. Much to the Aayfonzer's chagrin, Billy and Jack had received Overhed Kham's personal invitation to attend the ceremony, which Kwikshift officiated. Kham ruled the country, but Hurst Kwikshift was the Fonzer high priest, and was a man not to be regarded lightly. The Aayfonzer led the annual Rite of Overhaul and was steadfastly against outsiders attending. Even though Greaser rituals held no value for the Dark Man, he was fully aware of the role he was playing. His attendance was a show of strength for Kham.

The majority of the Radiclib forces had been wiped out on Great East Lake and the mop-up operations in Leftopia were progressing nicely, but there were still many things that could go wrong. He needed allies, no matter how stupid or weak. Without The Book, he had to count on all of the Greasers; he could not afford to let the pitiful Overhed Kham lose control to the smarter, more devious, more difficult to handle Aayfonzer.

Billy also knew that he would not need his allies much longer. Once The Freaklands were wiped out he could easily set the Greasers and Fascists against one another and then he would pick up the pieces. He was even beginning to think that he could do without the elusive book, though it still frequently occupied his thoughts. However, to achieve his larger goals, possession of the *Necronomicon* was necessary. It contained certain chants, certain combinations of arcane words that could bring his magic spear to its fullest potential. Finding it was the problem. There were reports that The Book was somewhere in Darkenwood, where the Mansonites had secreted it long ago, but it was well known that the scabby cult of Charlie worshipers was extinct, and since then The Book could have been moved or destroyed. Other, more speculative reports had The Book lost in the Great Whitelands, guarded to the death by the fierce Yipp tribesmen of Leftopia, or hidden magically by the mystic Oldhips in Hillcommune. Wherever it was, sooner or later he'd find it.

The Dark Man puffed meditatively on his cigar. There was snow in the air, a high clean smell signaling a storm. As he sniffed a light snowflake fell on his nose; his nostrils quivered. The flake seemed to bring another scent with it—the hated aroma of peat. It was barely perceptible but it concerned him. He was also bothered by reports of roving bands of Radiclib soldiers apparently headed for a rendezvous at Ripoff Pass. One of the larger groups had even had the nerve to attack his supply caravans as they headed for the Sludge. The wagons were burned and the weapons carried off by the marauders. Billy spat and took another drag off his cigar. He couldn't afford any more setbacks like that. He wanted to get as many supplies as possible to his forces in Covenstead before the first big blizzard closed Ripoff Pass, and the bitter cold that usually insinuated itself on the region choked the Sludge with ice.

Billy felt confident that his latest ploy would take care of both of those problems. A number of steamwagons dispatched with a contingent of well-armed Greasers was accompanying a large caravan, scheduled to be the last through the Pass. By holding the steamwagons and the accompanying troops back from the convoy, he was certain that the Radiclibs would be unable to resist attacking it. While they were striking their "significant blow" to the supply route, his forces would roll in and crush their puny effort.

"We're here," Jack announced as they approached Temple Sunoc's main entrance.

"Astute observation, Jack," Billy replied, smiling in the shadows of his cowl. He looked at the painted SUNOC sign and at the leonine engine blocks and pile of rotting tires that guarded the entrance and laughed aloud. "You know, if these pathetic Greasers fully understood what they were worshipping here, they'd probably throw a fit."

"Why's that, Boss?"

"You wouldn't understand either, I'm afraid. Come, let's go inside."

They skirted the front of the temple and entered by a side door. A pair of Greaser guards gave them the thumbs-up salute and allowed them to pass into a small lobby, where they mounted the stairs that led to the catwalks overhead. Off the catwalks was a long corridor that led to Overhed Kham's private box. The sound of their boots echoed like thunder in the hall. Billy saw the guards at Kham's door cringe as he and Jack approached. Without a word the two guards moved aside and let them enter. To Billy's silent satisfaction, neither of the young Fonzers seemed able to meet his gaze.

Inside the box Overhed Kham turned and regarded them. His ridiculous iron crown was askew on his head, and he held a crock of Black Thirtyweight in one hand. "You're late," he whispered. "Overhaul has begun."

"You don't have to remind me of the time, dearie," Billy replied, as he and Jack took seats back from the railing. "Overhaul, my ass," he whispered to Jack. "Gang beating is more like it."

Jack grinned. "Too many cooks—right, Boss? Takes the fun out of it."

Billy nodded and blew a couple of large smoke rings. Sometimes he wondered how Greasers even managed to take a piss alone. They were always in gangs. They worked in gangs, partied in gangs, fought in gangs, had ritual gang beatings, and even ceremonial gangbangs. It was his personal opinion that a quirk of nature was responsible. It seemed that for the last three hundred years the Greasers had been producing a vast majority of male offspring, and just enough females to keep the race from dying out altogether. This situation provided them with an army larger than one would expect for the size of their population, and tended to leave them with quite irritable dispositions. As a young Greaser entered puberty, the lack of female companionship drove him to stronger bonds with his buddies. This often led to homosexual encounters, which were outwardly frowned upon but commonly practiced. Billy particularly relished this aspect of Greaser society.

Such women as existed in Khamshaft were second-class citizens. They were looked down upon for the friction they caused in society and were, for the most part, considered whores and breeders. Occasionally, a couple would fall in love and want to get married. When that happened, it was the duty of the groom's buddies to try and talk him out of it, and if a little "cuffing up-side the head" was considered in order, that was okay too. Should the swain still be insistent, and a marriage actually took place, then another ceremony followed wherein the groom allowed all his buddies to "have a go" at his wife, to prove where his loyalties lay.

Billy fiddled with the spearhead hanging around his neck. He could feel its power, now mostly dormant, waiting for The Book to unleash its potential. He puffed on his cigar and sneered. Ceremonies were for the feeble minded, he thought. Indeed, they were useful for just that reason; they kept the rabble in line. He was sure that Kham was dimly aware of that fact, but as he watched the proceedings, he knew that Hurst Kwikshift grasped it totally. Greasers were like sheep—stupid and easily led.

Hurst was a master showman. From the way he manipulated his audience, alternately keeping them spellbound and whipping them into a chanting frenzy, Billy could see that he was better equipped to handle power than Kham. The relationship between Overhed and the Aayfonzer was strained at best and always had been, because of their different heritages. The Fonzer gene pool that produced Kwikshift and all the Aayfonzers before him was innately more intelligent than the common Greaser stock from which Khams had risen. It seemed logical that the Aayfonzers should be the rulers of Khamshaft and not the Kham clan. Indeed, he'd heard that once this had been the case, back when Khamshaft had been called Pitstop, and the ancestors of the present inhabitants were little more than nomadic bands of cutthroats. Over the years something had changed that and the Khams had become the seat of power.

Hurst would have made a more cunning ally than Overhed Kham, but he was *too* smart—another reason Billy was glad things were the way they were. Sweet, stupid Kham let Billy tell him how to use his power, and was dull enough that he wouldn't be able to conceal any subversive plots. Kwikshift, with his superior intelligence and popular power base in the Fonzer priesthood, would not be so easy to handle. Taking another drag off his long black cigar, he exhaled it in a fog that obscured his view of the ceremony going on below him. Billy dreamed of the pageantry and brutal splendor of the ceremonies that he'd orchestrated in his dark tabernacle near the Great Brine Lake back in Yewtah. Kwikshift knew how to run a sideshow like this mindless machine cult, but it was nothing compared to those spectacles.

"I'm runnin'…" the Aayfonzer shouted.

"HOOKER HEADERS AND A 411 POSSI," the Fonzers chimed in as they closed in on their victim.

Billy stubbed out his cigar on the railing. The gyrating, chanting Fonzers below were starting to amuse him. The Dark Man hadn't paid much attention to the hapless soul who was chosen for the ritual, but now that the Fonzers were about to get down to the serious work of pounding him to a helpless pulp, he had to watch.

Kwikshift's reaction to this sacrificial Freak was surprising. Billy noted that the Aayfonzer scowled deeply and kept looking up at Kham. Each time, Kham smirked and gestured for Kwikshift to go about his business. The exchange intrigued Billy. He scrutinized the victim closely, realizing with a jolt of surprise that he recognized him from somewhere. This was unusual; to the Dark Man all Freaks looked pretty much alike.

Hurst and the Fonzers continued their litany. Billy fingered his spear again, detecting a slight variation in its power. Then it came to him; he'd sensed this Freak's presence before. In the shadow of his cowl he licked his incisors. This was not the Peat-Bog Stinker. This was the cowering, yet defiant, Freak Billy sometimes detected when he withdrew into the dark wreckage of his soul to rest. This Freak's destiny and his own were somehow linked. The Dark Man's highly tuned psychic sense told him that this one knew something about The Book.

Bejeezuz could hardly contain himself as the Fonzers dragged the squirming Freak to the edge of the pit that held their object of worship, the ridiculous old Chevrolet. He leaned far over the rail, his unblinking eyes taking in everything. The blood pounded in his temples as the Chachis cavorted around the Freak, mindlessly chanting off a list of auto parts as a sacred mantra. Every time Kwikshift gave them an "I got me," their response became louder and more excited. Finally, as their bloodlust grew so heavy that he could almost smell it and they moved in on their cowering victim, Billy could restrain himself no longer. He rose out of his chair, his gloved hands clutching the railing. Beside him, Jack and Overhed Kham shifted uneasily in their seats.

"MISTER MAN, I TELL YOU. I GOT…" boomed the high priest.

"YOU HAVE NOTHING, KWIKSHIFT," Billy bellowed. The ceremony stopped abruptly and everybody turned toward the Dark Man. "Bring that poor lad to me and find yourself a new victim. I have need of him. Do you understand?"

Hurst Kwikshift's face darkened with rage, but there was nothing he could do. He gestured for his acolytes to step back and let Toad go.

Billy turned to Jack. "Bring that one to my rooms," he said. "I wish to

265

interrogate him there."

"I understand, Boss," Rabid replied, though his face showed that he did not.

Ignoring the shocked look of the crowd below him, as well as Kwikshift's surly pout, Bejeezuz swirled out of the box and within minutes was hurrying down Bardahl Street toward his headquarters. It was snowing lightly but steadily. The Dark Man was so caught up in his own thoughts that he didn't notice the tall Whiterider approaching him until they nearly collided. He glowered at the Rider as if he'd stepped in a fresh dog turd. Bed-Sheeters were very high on his list of people that he didn't like. These vermin haven't changed in half a millennium, he thought. They've always been the stupidest and most violent of their lot. His scowl deepened as the figure in white stood directly in front of him.

"What do you want, scumbag?" he growled as the Rider deliberately got in his path. "Move aside or I'll cut a door through you."

Billy pulled out a long, wavy-bladed dagger, and the Whiterider backed off.

"Pardon me, sir," the Rider said contritely. "My name's Geist, and I've been sent to find you. It's most important."

"Then speak quickly. I have business of my own."

The Whiterider bowed. "A fire has broken out in number four warehouse, and it's getting out of control. Commander Manglewurtz says that your steamwagons are in danger."

The Dark Man stood stock still. His nostrils quivered, again picking up a faint scent. It could have been the smell of something burning, but it had a faint underscent of peat. "That's what Manglewurtz says, huh? I'll have his balls if he loses those wagons. How bad is it?"

"Not sure, sir. The flames started in the prison section. They spread quickly to the entire warehouse. The Commander sent me to find you."

Rage filled Billy like a black flood. He returned his dagger to its sheath and clutched nervously at the spearhead hanging from his neck. The smell of burning was stronger now, and he could see smoke rising through the softly filtering snow. "Get my man, Jack Rabid, and tell him to meet me at number four."

Without waiting for a reply, Billy stormed away. Above him, iron clouds heavy with the promise of more snow boiled out of the north; they seemed to follow him down Bardahl Street.

Toad felt a chill race through him as a black-cloaked figure moved through the crowd in his direction. The Chachis released their hold on him and backed out of the way. Toad lay unmoving as the dark figure loomed over him. A face stared down from out of the cowl, ruddy and square jawed, with pale blue, unintelligent eyes.

"You oughta be more careful with the merchandise, Kwikshift," the figure said, scowling at the Aayfonzer "The Boss wants this boy in good shape; he's got plans for him."

"I'm sure he does, Rabid. Just like he has plans for Kham."

Toad scrutinized the man in black closely. This wasn't the one that he feared, the one that crawled through his dreams. This one called Rabid, frightening as he was, was just one of the Dark Man's servants.

"Hand over the hippie, NOW!" Rabid commanded.

"Don't tell me what to do, outlander. This is still my temple. I will not kiss your ass— or Lord Flatbush's, either."

Sneering at the Aayfonzer, Rabid grabbed Toad by the scruff of his neck and effortlessly hauled him to his feet. "You'll kiss ass in time, greaseball, and beg for the privilege. Out of my way, the Boss is waiting." He pushed his way past Kwikshift and propelled Toad out through the door into the lighted parking lot. Snow was coming down more steadily, settling on Rabid's black robe.

"Wh-where are we going?" Toad managed to blurt as he was hurried toward Bardahl Street.

"To see the Boss. He wants to talk to you."

"The D-Dark Man?"

"Yeah, that's one of his names. Around here he's called Lord Flatbush, or Blackcloak, or Brother John Birch—though he calls himself Sweet Billy Bejeezuz. But no matter what you call him, he's a real powerful man, and he don't like to be kept waiting." Rabid grinned. He obviously took pleasure in bragging about his master.

The chill Toad felt earlier intensified. "B-but, what does he want with me?"

"That's the Boss's business, hippie, not mine. Still, if I was to have my guess, I'd say he's taken a liking to you."

"I don't understand."

Rabid winked knowingly, his vapid face twisting into a leer. "You'll find that out soon enough. What the hell...?"

A Whiterider was approaching them from the direction of the darkened tenements on the other side of Bardahl Street. He was apparently in a great hurry, for he almost ran into them.

"Hey, watch it, spook," Jack growled.

The Whiterider came to an abrupt halt and stood regarding the pair. He was quite tall, and with his high, conical hood, seemed to tower over Rabid. He was breathing heavily, as if from great exertion, but when he saw Jack he bowed with sufficient respect. Toad marveled at how the proud Whiterider seemed to grovel in the presence of the Dark Man's servant.

For a moment the two figures stood silently, regarding each other.

"I beg your pardon," the Whiterider said, once he'd caught his breath. "But there's a fire at number four warehouse. Your master sent me to seek out one of your number—Jack Rabid."

Toad's ears tingled. The Rider's voice was familiar, but he couldn't quite place where he'd heard it before.

"That's me, spook," Jack replied.

"Brother John wants you to meet him at the warehouse. He's gone there to oversee the rescue of the steamwagons, but it looks hopeless. The flames are already spreading to number five and some of the nearby tenements."

Jack grabbed Toad's arm with a ferocity that made the pipesmith wince and started running down Bardahl Street. To the west flames licked up over the tenements and black smoke boiled up to meet the storm clouds. The air was thick with the smell of burning Honkweed, a surprisingly sweet odor like that of a thousand pipes all going at once.

The Whiterider ran beside them, clutching at Toad's sleeve. "Wait," he said.

Jack growled low in his throat. "There's no waiting, spook."

"You don't understand, sir. Your prisoner is to come with me—orders of Brother John."

Jack stopped in mid-stride. "That don't seem right. What's your name, anyhow?"

"Geist, Kaspar Geist. Your boss has no time to interrogate him now. The faggit will be safe with me until the fire's under control."

The flames and smoke were climbing higher now, adding chunks of soot to the snow that was falling on Lubejob. Jack still looked doubtful.

"Brother John needs you. He was afraid the prisoner might escape in the confusion."

"Okay, Geist. Watch that faggit close, or you'll have Jack Rabid to answer to." Jack paused, then released his grip on Toad and hurried away. In the distance horns sounded and scurrying Greasers filled the streets.

"Dickhead!" the Whiterider snorted, shoving Toad toward a nearby alley. His obsequiousness was gone, and his voice sounded different. "You can thank me for this later, Toad."

"Ernie!"

The robed figure nodded, pushing Toad into the darkened alley. "The same."

"But, how? I-I mean…"

"It was simple, really. I followed the gang that captured you and Tam. When it got dark I slipped into town, stole this robe, and did a little snooping around."

They were far down the alley now, but the glow from a tenement window lit their way. Two Whiteriders stood in the alley, guarding four white warhorses. Toad caught the glint of something reflective behind the eyeholes of the nearest rider's hood.

"Maynard?" he whispered. "Tambourine?"

One of the counterfeit Whiteriders laughed. "You can dig it, daddy-o. My main cat, Mungweasle here, sprung us from the slammer and torched the place. Like, you shoulda seen those hoods wig out when the place went up, man. Endless good karma."

"I kind of envy them, though," Tambourine chuckled, stepping forward to shake Toad's hand. "There must be a ton of weed in that storeroom Ernie set on fire. Before long, this whole town will be stoned."

"Not us, though," Ernie added. "We've got to get going."

Maynard laughed again. "Hey, not to worry, cats. While Ernie was doing his thing I filled up my pockets with primo boo. We can, like, light up after we split this nowhere scene."

Ernie went to the nearest warhorse and pulled a set of robes from its saddlebag. He thrust them into Toad's hands.

"Here, put these on. It won't be too long before your buddy, Jack Rabid, comes back looking for us."

Toad slipped into the robe. It was intended for a taller man, and he had to roll up the sleeves to keep his hands free. The tall pointed hood fit as poorly. Try as he might, he couldn't seem to get the eyeholes to line up properly. "We can't go just yet," he said.

"Why not?" Ernie asked. "The sooner we get out of town, the better."

Tambourine nodded his approval. "My sentiments exactly. I have no wish to get caught again."

"You guys don't seem to understand. I think I know where the *Necronomicon* is hidden."

Ernie paused. "Are you positive?"

"I think so, yes. I believe it's in that metal wagon the Greasers worship. At least that's the closest thing to Copralallius's 'swift iron coffin' that I've seen."

"I don't know, Toad. Wouldn't someone have discovered it by now? Hell, it's been right under their noses for centuries."

Toad shook his head. "I don't think the wagon's been opened in that long. Its interior is filthy with dust and cobwebs."

"Hey, like, maybe someone lost the keys," Maynard interjected, hopping about excitedly. "Greasers have always worshipped their rods. They'd never think of breaking into it."

"Maynard's got a point, Ernie. That steel wagon's like a god to them. They'd rather die than hurt it. Besides, I've got the impression that few knew about the existence of the *Necronomicon* to begin with. Of those, Kwikshift's great-great grandfather was probably the last."

The herbalist tugged at his hood, adjusting it. "That settles it. Toad, you and I are going back to the Temple. Maynard, you and Tambourine bring the horses and meet us in front of Sunoc in about ten minutes."

"That's cool. On the go, daddy-o."

Taking Toad's arm, Ernie led them back toward the mouth of the alley. Behind them, Maynard and Tambourine vaulted onto their horses, and taking the reins of the other two steeds, rode out of the alley in the opposite direction.

Bardahl Street was remarkably empty of people, though a few could be seen in the distance, moving in the direction of the fire. Alarm horns sounded several blocks over, and the smell of burning Honkweed lay heavy in the air. Just as the two Freaks emerged from the alley, a trio of black-cloaked figures rode by, spurring their horses toward the flames that licked over the tenements and warehouses on the West Side. A moment later a huge water tanker drawn by eight frothing horses rumbled past, and then Bardahl Street was deserted again, except for the two white-clad Freaks hurrying toward Temple Sunoc.

A handful of Fonzers were clustered around the main door of the temple goggling at the flames in the distance. As he and Ernie approached, Toad saw them and started to move away, but Ernie tugged at his sleeve, urging him forward. Smoke drifted toward the temple, mixing with the snow that was now coming down heavily. For one crazy second, Toad wanted to lift his hood and suck in the cool, smoky air, but the urge passed as soon as it came and he hung back, letting Ernie lead.

"FIRE!" Ernie barked, approaching the knot of Fonzers. "What are you screwing off for? Can't you see what's going on? The warehouses are burning and we need every hand to save the steamwagons."

The Fonzers regarded him with blank, red-veined eyes. The rolling clouds of weed smoke had obviously already gotten to them. Several giggled foolishly, and one particularly stoned Fonzer sat down in the snow and laughed until he was red in the face. Muttering under his breath, Ernie grabbed him by the lapel of his overalls and pulled him to his feet. "Hurry!" he urged, shoving the Fonzer toward Bardahl Street. "There's no time to lose."

Hurst Kwikshift staggered out of the temple. Glaring at Toad and Ernie, he shoved his way through the group clustered at the door. "What's going on?" he demanded. "What are you spooks doing here?"

"What you should be doing, apparently," Ernie replied imperiously, as he aimed a fat, giggling Fonzer toward the road with a few well-placed kicks. "This town's burning down, and your people are sitting around with their thumbs up their asses."

Kwikshift goggled at the boiling clouds of smoke. "Hubcaps and lug wrenches, lookit that!" he exclaimed. "How'd it start?"

"That doesn't matter, you fool. Get your people motivated, or I will."

"Izzat so? Well, emergency or no emergency, I give the orders around here, not you."

Ernie drew himself up to his full height. In his long, white robes and tall peaked hood, he appeared twice the Aayfonzer's size. "Then give a few. Order your people to the warehouses. Otherwise Kham and Klaven Thinarm will be interested to learn that you sat by and watched Lubejob burn."

Kwikshift stepped back, obviously angry at being ordered around. He glanced past Ernie to where the flames were licking at the sky. "We're going, spook," he said flatly. "But I'm taking this up with Kham in the morning."

"Do that."

The Aayfonzer snapped his fingers, urging the Fonzers into action, and started off down the street. As he was leaving he turned and glowered at Ernie skeptically.

Once the stragglers were out of sight down Bardahl Street, Ernie and Toad hurried inside Temple Sunoc. A few Fonzers milled around the podium. Ernie sent them packing after Kwikshift and the others. When the building was deserted, Toad removed his hood and stuck it in the cord belt of his robe. "Dylan's Bones, it smells of weed in here," he commented. "Couldn't really notice, with that pillow case over my head."

Ernie nodded. "But this is no time to be thinking about catching a buzz."

"I know, I know. But that hood was driving me crazy. You could have scarfed one that fit better."

"I'm an herbalist, not a tailor. Now, where do you think that book is?"

"In the steel wagon. I'll get something to bust the windows with."

Moving to the podium at the other side of the room, Toad pulled a wrench and a pry bar from the display board on the wall. Pushing Ernie gently aside on his return, Toad took a vicious swipe at the Chevy's side window with the wrench. The glass spider-webbed on the first blow and flew apart into crystal popcorn on the second. Laughing excitedly, he reached into the vehicle's dusty interior, oblivious of the shattered glass all over the seat. He fumbled with the lock on the compartment built into the dashboard. It was sealed tight.

"Dammit!" he yelled.

"Calm down," Ernie advised, pointing to the pry bar. "Where there's a will, there's a way."

Hands trembling, Toad fitted the end of the bar into the crack between the compartment door and the surrounding padding. He jammed down hard and the door bulged outward, but didn't give anything except a cloud of dust. Sweat beaded his forehead as he hammered at the lock, soon reducing it to a flattened mass. One more swipe and the door popped open releasing a faded and much-folded map, a greasy comb, and a cylindrical metal container with the word "BUDWEISER" painted on it.

Toad reached deep into the confines of the compartment, pushing aside clutter as he went. He nearly cried out loud when his fingers closed on the ribbed spine of a small leather-bound book. It was thick, heavy, and exuded a force that tingled up his arm like lightning. In his excitement he almost dropped it as he pulled it out of the compartment that had held it for centuries.

Ernie leaned close as Toad brought the book out into the light. It was bound in cracked black leather that felt vaguely repellent to the touch, and its cover bore no title. Still shaking, Toad undid the rusty iron clasps that held it shut and flipped through the worm-eaten pages until he found the title page. The print was old and faded, and the letters ill-formed, but he could read it plain enough:

Ye NEKRONOMIKON
of Ye Arabb, Abdul Alhazred,
Called by himm Al Azif.
Tranſlated by Dr. John Dee,
Alchemiſt of Ye Queeneſ Court
Paternoſter Row, London, Anno 1598

"Dylan's Bones," Toad muttered. "I've found it. I've really found it!" He held the millennium-old volume gently, marveling at the power emanating from its dusty pages.

Ernie grabbed him gently by the shoulder. "Hurry it up. I just heard someone outside."

Clutching the book to his chest, Toad followed Ernie toward the temple entrance. But it was too late. They'd hardly gone three steps before Hurst Kwikshift stepped through the door into the torchlight. His face was contorted with anger. He looked at the shattered window of the '55 Chevy and snarled. Brass knuckles glinted on his right hand. "You!" he bellowed. "You're gonna die." With a howl of rage, he ran at Toad, driving at the pipesmith's face.

Toad jumped aside just in time. The Aayfonzer's fist hit a wooden sign advertising Black Thirtyweight, toppling it to the floor. Shoving the precious book under his robe, Toad backed away, his eyes locked on

Kwikshift's.

Suddenly, Ernie rushed at the Aayfonzer. He stumbled as Kwikshift lunged out with one heavy-booted foot and knocked him sprawling over a row of benches. Kwikshift pounced on the herbalist. Torchlight tracked off from his brass knuckles as he drew back his fist to punch. Ernie feinted at Hurst's wrist with his forearm. With his free hand he clutched unsuccessfully for his assailant's throat.

Toad dove at the struggling pair. While Ernie had one hand on Kwikshift's face, his other was trying desperately to free his boot knife. For his part Kwikshift was swinging violently at Ernie with his brass-knuckled fist, but the herbalist's longer reach was keeping him at bay. Toad took the only weapon at hand, the pry bar he'd just used to free the *Necronomicon*, and brought it down on the Aayfonzer's head. Steel met greased pompadour with a sound like a melon would make being dropped from a second-story window. Kwikshift uttered a single strangled moan and slumped across Ernie's chest. The herbalist rolled the unconscious Aayfonzer onto the floor, where he lay staring blankly upward with glazed, slightly crossed, eyes. Blood oozed from a long laceration on Kwikshift's scalp. Only the slight rising and falling of his chest indicated that he was still alive.

"Are you all right?" Toad asked, helping Ernie to his feet.

"Yeah. Thanks."

"You're lucky, Ernie. He could've done a number on you with those knucks of his."

The herbalist dusted off his robes and retrieved his hood, which he'd lost in the scuffle. He placed the cowl squarely on his head and adjusted it slightly. "I don't think he'll be doing much for a while, Toad. Get your hood on, and let's get out of here."

Together, the two Freaks left Temple Sunoc. Smoke and snow swirled about them, reducing visibility. Even through the folds of his confining hood Toad could smell burning weed.

Soon, white shapes loomed out of the smoke and snow. For a second Toad was startled; then he recognized the white warhorses and the robed figures standing patiently by them.

"What took you so long?" Tambourine asked, handing Toad a set of reins.

"We ran into a little trouble with the Aayfonzer," Ernie replied. "But Toad ironed it out, so to speak."

"Did you find the book?"

Ernie smiled broadly. "Yeah."

Maynard joined them, slapping Toad and Ernie each on the back. "This is like the height of coolness, kitty cats. We're free, we've got the book and there's enough boo in the air to have one groovy party. But I guess it's too dangerous to stand around rapping. Let's split."

The four Freaks clambered up onto their mounts and galloped down Bardahl Street and out of the city. They did not slow down until Lubejob was a glowing point of orange light lost in the swirling snow.

Chapter Thirty-One

Ashen clouds boiled overhead, reducing the late afternoon sun to a dull silver spot in the sky. Bitter winds blew through the pass. Leaning into the frigid gusts, a shadowy shape slowly made its way up the narrow footpath, pausing from time to time to lean on a long wheel lock musket. After an arduous climb the gray-cloaked figure stopped before a large clump of brush clinging to life under a rocky overhang. Nodding to almost invisible sentries that were camouflaged to blend in with the rocky terrain, the figure pushed through the bushes and stepped into a large cave. A small, warm fire burning in the center of the cavern was a welcome respite from the knifing winds outside. The hood of the cloak fell back revealing a tall, red-headed woman in her early thirties, her proud good looks only slightly marred by the black patch she wore over her right eye. Leaning the captured enemy wheel lock beside the cave entrance, she undid the clasp at the throat of her heavy woolen cloak and laid the garment carefully over the small cannon beside her. Frowning slightly, she wiped some dust from its ornate barrel with the sleeve of her tunic. It was a good, sturdy weapon, one of the pair that had once graced her flagship. It hadn't been easy salvaging it and transporting it here to the cliffs overlooking Ripoff Pass, but it had been necessary.

Removing her gloves and slipping them under one of the epaulets of her tunic, Mizjoan strode to the fire at the center of the high-roofed cavern that she shared with over a hundred of her compatriots. They were a ragged, motley group, battered veterans of Great East Lake and numerous guerrilla raids—good warriors, but all that remained of the proud Leftopian army. They were tired and hungry. Their uniforms were ragged and inadequate for winter weather. Counting the twenty-odd fugitive Freaks that had joined their camp, the Radiclibs were still few in number. Many of them were sick with flu or malnutrition. A handful of moderately successful raids on enemy supply routes were all that kept morale from disappearing completely. However, the raids had not yielded anywhere near enough provisions to safeguard her troops from continuous hunger and cold. Mizjoan managed a smile as she sat down on a rock across from Rudy and Kentstate.

"Enjoy your walk?" Kentstate asked, her dark eyes bright with reflected firelight.

"As much as I could, 'State. There's a storm on the way, but along with it, if I'm not mistaken, there's an enemy supply train."

Rudy scratched his dark beard and grunted. "Maybe we should forget about more raids. The sooner we're in Hillcommune, the better for all of us."

The smile left Mizjoan's face. She seemed to grow tense. "I know how you feel, Rudy, but this raid is necessary." She pointed to a corner of the cave where a woman wearing the red mortar-and-pestle armband of the People's Medical Corps was tending a pair of flu victims swaddled in blankets. "Our people are sick and hungry. This last supply train will be carrying medicines and food for the garrison at Covenstead. Once the storm strikes, Ripoff Pass may be closed off until spring."

"If Comrade Mungweasle was here, we'd have all the medicinal herbs we could use," Kentstate said.

Mizjoan turned her face toward the cave entrance. She shrugged sadly. "Well, we all know what happened there."

"There's still hope."

Picking up a stick from the floor, the Radiclib leader poked at the fire. There was no use trying to hide her feelings from Rudy and Kentstate. "I suppose there is, slim though that might be. I miss Ernie, and Comrade Toad as well. For Freaks, they were brave men."

A horn sounded in the distance, followed by another just outside of the cave. All discussion ceased as the Radiclibs scrambled for their coats and weapons. Below, in the floor of the pass, shots rang out.

Mizjoan jumped to her feet, gathering up her cloak and gun on the way out of the cave. "This is it, comrades! Seize the day!"

Outside the wind had died down, as if nature was holding its breath. The gunfire in the pass rose from a sporadic rattle to a full fusillade as the Radiclibs who were stationed along its length caught sight of their quarry. Though they did not have much in the way of food or medical supplies, Mizjoan's troops were well armed and had acquired a good supply of powder and shot in their previous raids.

Followed by Rudy, Kentstate, and a score of her best marksmen, Mizjoan ran to the edge of the rock face and began to scramble down. On the other side of the pass similar groups moved, keeping to the cover of boulders along their way and emerging only to fire at the caravan of twenty

Fascist wagons stranded on the floor of the pass. As one wagon tipped over, its drivers hurried to untangle their terrified team from the twisted harness. Another wagon was burning, a victim of Radiclib fire arrows. A Fascist was slumped over the seat with a crossbow bolt buried in his spine. Even as Mizjoan watched, gunfire cut into the wagon's screaming, plunging team. She winced. It pained her to order her men to shoot defenseless animals, but it was the least hazardous way for her soldiers to stop the caravan. A musket sounded nearby and a Fascist warhorse rolled over, pinning its blue-uniformed rider underneath it. Another shot ended his agonies before he could even cry out.

Taking a small spanner from her trousers pocket, Mizjoan wound her gun's firing mechanism and positioned the hammer over the wheel. She had one shot before she had to resort to using her sword, Ploughshare, and the steel frisbee throwing disks that she carried in a pouch on her belt. She was so intent on watching the battle in the pass that she flinched when Rudy approached and touched her arm.

"This should be quick," she said, pointing to her soldiers as they fired on the caravan from the cliffs above the pass.

Rudy nodded. "I hope so. From the looks of that sky, the storm isn't going to hold off forever."

"We'll wrap this up before the first flake falls." Above them the clouds were growing darker. Snow would be coming any time now.

Once the initial shock of the attack was over, about fifty mounted and armed cavalrymen who accompanied the caravan tried to mount a counteroffensive, shooting at the Radiclibs while attempting to form the wagons into a circle. One more of their teams went down in a flurry of gunshots and arrows. The horses neighed shrilly and rolled over, taking the wagon with them.

As Mizjoan started cautiously down the slope, gripping her heavy wheel lock in both hands, she saw other Radiclibs filtering down from the cliffs on the opposite side of the pass. The gray-clad figures moved like shadows, slipping from rock to rock behind the smoke boiling up from the burning wagons. Above them, comrades still stationed in the cliffs opened up on the encircled caravan, matching the Fascist gunmen and archers shot for shot.

Along the far wall, three Radiclibs made it to the floor of the pass. They moved quietly behind the smoke, edging toward a pile of crates that had spilled from the shattered side of an overturned wagon. As Mizjoan moved further down the slope she could make out the markings on the crates, even at a distance. The white stenciled letters and bold red RX symbols told her all that she needed to know. She smiled. Just as she'd suspected, the caravan was hauling foodstuffs and medicines. She hurried her pace. Over her shoulder she saw Rudy and Kentstate following at a distance.

Mizjoan crouched lower, until she was almost crawling, and waited for the smoke to drift her way and cover her movements. When it did, she gripped her cumbersome wheel lock as tightly as she could and ran for cover behind a fallen horse. She moved from there to a boulder on the other side of the pass. Behind her, riflemen opened up on the Fascist riders. One of the enemy went down, sprawling across a broken wheel. He was dead even before being impaled on the shattered spokes.

The three Radiclibs Mizjoan had spotted earlier were almost to the crates of food and medicine. One of the three, a lanky blond barely out of his teens, made a mad dash for the nearest box. Snatching at it eagerly, he began to pull it back toward the rocks. Mizjoan took several steps toward him when she saw something moving in the wreckage of the overturned wagon.

A Fascist soldier, bleeding from a slashed cheek, staggered to his feet and fired a blunderbuss. The young Radiclib didn't even have time to register surprise before the grapeshot tore away half of his upper torso. The Fascist's moment of glory was brief; Mizjoan touched off her wheel lock and he crumpled to the ground.

Another Fascist popped out from behind the wagon and fired his crossbow at the Radiclib leader. The bolt went wild, bouncing off the boulder near her head. Before he could get back to cover and reload, two of Mizjoan's frisbees sliced through the air toward him. The first took off his right hand; the second took the top of his skull. He crashed to the ground beside his companion.

Suddenly a piercing scream reverberated down the pass and the ground shook as if some primordial beast had risen from a timeless sleep. Startled, Mizjoan crept from her hiding place and pulled an unfired pistol from the belt of one of the downed Fascists. She cocked the weapon and poked her head from behind the wrecked wagon. The scream sounded again as the first of the steamwagons rumbled into the pass. It was huge, as large as a house, and the grinning jaws and bloodshot eyes painted across the front of its boiler made it seem almost alive. Smoke blasted from the behemoth's twin stacks, blackening the sky. The great engine's giant spiked wheels tore furrows in the ground as it rumbled toward Mizjoan. Behind the steamwagon two more of the massive machines lurched into view, followed by twenty or more Greaser chariots.

About half of the Radiclib forces were in the floor of the pass now. The combined Fascist and Greaser cavalry troops and chariots fanned out, trying to encircle them. Mizjoan ran for the rocks, arrows and bullets whistling around her like hornets.

Once she was safe among the boulders, Mizjoan uncocked her pistol and feverishly reloaded her wheel lock. From a crack between the rocks she watched the lead steamwagon roll to a stop. Its enclosed cab was high and protected by iron plates. A small swivel cannon was mounted on top. A Greaser popped out of a trap door and began to move the cannon, training it on a spot halfway up the cliff face where Radiclib soldiers were firing down on the chariots. The Greaser was only exposed for a moment, but that was enough. As he readied the cannon fuse, Mizjoan lined him in her sights. A second later he lay sprawled over the cannon, the fuse sputtering harmlessly in one dead hand.

With an ear-piercing shriek, the steamwagon lurched forward, bearing down on an abandoned wagon that some Radiclibs were using for cover. Gunshots erupted from the mouth of the cavern she and her troops were using as a headquarters. Bullets ricocheted harmlessly off the great machine as it picked up speed.

"The cannon," Mizjoan thought, glancing up toward the cavern. "Why don't they use the cannon?"

Another volley of gunshots erupted from the cliffs, answered by sporadic fire from the wagon circle. Four Fascist horsemen and a pair of Greasers went down during the exchange. After that, the enemy abandoned horses and chariots and fled for the safety of the huddled supply wagons. The second team of steamwagons rolled into formation behind the first. The cannons on top of their cabs swiveled back and forth as the Greasers sought out targets on the cliffs.

A thunderous explosion erupted near the front of the cavern. The flame that issued from the lone Radiclib cannon lit up the pass like midday. A nine-pound ball whistled through the billowing smoke, taking aim on the closest steamwagon. A geyser of dirt and pebbles spewed into the air as it slammed into the ground just in front of the lead wagon. Mizjoan saw the gunner on the second steamwagon swivel his weapon toward the cave mouth. Laying aside her wheel lock, she tried to draw a bead on him with her pistol. Her target jounced around quite a bit as the steamwagon reduced speed, but he held his cannon as steady as an accusing finger. Gently, she squeezed back on the trigger.

Nothing happened. Flint struck steel, and the pinch of powder in the weapon's flash pan went off with a smelly whoosh, but the gun didn't discharge. A heartbeat later the Greaser cannoneer fired. The rock face above the cavern blew to pieces, showering granite fragments down over the floor of the pass.

Mizjoan pulled a powder flask and shot pouch from her tunic pocket and hurriedly reloaded her wheel lock. Rudy and Kentstate, carrying crossbows, were moving toward her through the boulders; a short-barreled pistol protruded from Rudy's tunic belt. They reached her just as Fascist soldiers left the shelter of the caravan and fanned out into the rocks, shooting at anything that moved. Cannons fired from the cabs of the steamwagons, blasting out more holes in the cliffs. As Mizjoan and her friends crouched among the rocks, more Greaser chariots poured into the pass, the wind at their backs.

"This is slaughter," Kentstate said bitterly. "We're being massacred."

Mizjoan nodded as she unsheathed Ploughshare. In the dying light the zigzag weld on the age-blackened blade seemed to writhe and twist. "It's bad, 'State, but we can still go back into the hills faster than they can come after us. There's no way their steam-buggies and chariots are going to climb cliffs."

The lone Radiclib cannon opened up again, sending down a shower of pebbles and shale. The shot hit right in the middle of the caravan, blasting one of the wagons to splinters. Pieces of wagon, driver and horses scattered up and down the pass.

"That's one for our side," Rudy murmured.

Kentstate shook her head. "Joan, you've got to sound retreat before they roll all over us."

The Radiclib leader nodded again. She scrabbled in her pocket for her small signal whistle. Her fingers closed on it just as the cannons on top of the steamwagons homed in on the single Radiclib gun emplacement. Before she could get the whistle to her lips, they opened fire and the front of the cave exploded in a starburst of rock. Blown free of its carriage, the cannon barrel rolled down the wall of the pass. Mizjoan looked up at the smoking, rubble-choked hole that had been her headquarters and almost cried out in rage. Below the ruined emplacement the steamwagons were rolling again. Mizjoan put her lips to the whistle and blew.

Up and down the pass horns and whistles answered her. In small, furtive groups, Radiclibs abandoned the cover of boulders and overturned wagons and zigzagged back up the slopes. Silent as mist, Mizjoan and her companions slipped out of their hiding place and, using the growing darkness and wind-whipped smoke for cover, made their way toward the rock fall halfway up the canyon wall. Suddenly, Rudy let out a gasp and ran back down the slope.

Below, on the floor of the pass, several Radiclibs were barricaded behind an overturned wagon. Nearby, one of their comrades was pinned under a broken wheel. Seeing his plight, two of his friends rushed to free him. As they struggled to move the wheel, a steamwagon bore down on them. Frightened by the spectre, the trapped Radiclib's companions panicked and abandoned their attempt to rescue him.

Dodging enemy fire, Rudy ran across the floor of the pass to the stricken Radiclib. He pulled at the wreckage covering the young soldier and tossed it aside. Just as he pulled the wounded man to his feet, a huge shadow loomed over them. Rudy and the Radiclib screamed together as the steamwagon's huge, spiked wheels ground their bodies into the dirt.

Kentstate let out an anguished shriek and started toward her mate's crushed body. Mizjoan stopped her. Grabbing the younger woman, the Radiclib leader held her tightly in her arms. Kentstate struggled, alternately screaming and crying. Blindly, crazily, she pounded her fists on Mizjoan's arms and back. Supporting her grief-stricken friend, Mizjoan stumbled toward the cover of the cliffs. All around her, her people were pushing back, stopping only momentarily to fire at the advancing enemy before scrambling to the upper slopes. The wind was stirring now, ruffling Mizjoan's cloak as she stumbled up the rubble-strewn path.

"It all happened so fast," Mizjoan murmured. "There was nothing I could do for him. Nothing."

As if giving solace, the first snowflakes drifted down from the sky, caressing her tear-streaked face.

Chapter Thirty-Two

Bone-chilling winds racing down from the Plains of Dragstrip drove snow deep within the confines of Toad's thick traveler's cloak. Pulling back his hood and wiping snow from his face and beard, Toad glanced toward Lubejob, many hours and many miles back. The thin Whiteriders' robes that had provided their disguise during their escape from Lubejob had been replaced by heavy winter cloaks, which Ernie had commandeered from one of the warehouses before setting it on fire. Grinning in spite of the cold, he raised a clenched-fist salute. Hillcommune was close at hand—shelter from the storm.

To the east the cloud-smeared, morning sky was growing lighter. As the wind and snow tapered off and the curtain of gray pulled back, Toad could see the sheer cliffs of the Purple Mountains looming dead ahead. In front of Toad, Maynard rode hunched over in his saddle. Snow powdered his beret and hung over his shoulders like a mantle. He was lost deep in thought. Ahead of the little Beatnik, Ernie and Tambourine rode side by side, talking quietly and gesturing occasionally toward the towering cliffs before them. If Maynard and Ernie had their directions straight, it wouldn't be long before they'd all be journeying through the hidden passes under the escarpment into Hillcommune.

By the time the Freaks reached the foot of the rocky heights, the storm had died out entirely and the iron gray of dawn had crept into the eastern sky. Tambourine dismounted and gazed up at the sheer rock face. He shook his head. "So, what do we do now?"

Maynard brushed the snow from his sweater as he and the others slipped off their horses to join the musician.

"I'm sure Moonshadow will be waiting for us," the Beatnik offered. "Like, we must be close to the entrance; let's keep going east and see if he'll find us."

With the Beatnik taking the lead, the Freaks followed along the base of the precipice. The path took them around various rock falls and into an area where the walls towered straight up for a thousand feet. Here their four-legged transportation was of no value. Taking what they needed from their saddlebags, they sent the horses on their way. The sun was just cresting the horizon when they stopped at the base of a boulder that was shaped like a huge loaf of bread.

Toad looked up and recoiled in surprise. Standing on top of the boulder was a tall black-bearded Oldhip, swaddled in a colorful patchwork cloak. He pointed at the Freaks with a long staff topped with a multicolored god's eye. The pipesmith swore that the man hadn't been there a second before; it was like he had materialized out of thin air.

"Welcome, my brothers," the Oldhip said. "We have awaited your arrival." A breeze shifted the man's coal black, shoulder length hair, revealing a tiny gold hoop dangling from his right earlobe. His eyes were blank and colorless. He seemed to stare through and past the Freaks.

"This is Moonshadow?" Toad whispered.

"Yes," Ernie replied. "He guards the entrances to Hillcommune."

"He's weird. Those eyes…"

Ernie motioned him to silence. Then, raising his voice, he said, "Peace, Brother Moonshadow. It's been a long time since I met the Seer of the Gates."

Moonshadow nodded solemnly, though his eyes remained unreadable. "Ahh, Brother Mungweasle, so it has been, though I knew you were coming."

"Then you must also know that we're cold and tired."

"I do. You have brought with you others: Beatnik Maynard, Tambourine Dill, and one who is unknown to me. You come here under a cloud. Your souls are like swirling dust devils and you bear with you a great power. You seek sanctuary to use this power against your enemies."

"Right now, sanctuary is what we need most. Beyond that we will need time, and counsel."

The Seer smiled and gestured with his staff. "All is as I thought. I would not deny you passage, but I warn you to be cautious with what you bring into our home. Ours is a land of light, and peace, and love—abandon hate all you who enter here." He hit the boulder with his staff. It rumbled to one side, revealing a dark opening about eight feet high. Bowing, he gestured toward the hole. "Follow me from darkness into the light."

With surprising agility, the tall Oldhip leaped down from his perch and entered the cave, gesturing for the others to follow. He was soon lost in the darkness.

Toad shook his head. "Is he for real?"

"You mean the way he speaks?" Ernie replied. "Don't let that put you off. All Oldhips are a bit spacey and mystical, though I'll admit Moonshadow's more so than most. He has powers that others don't; he can see and understand things others can't."

Still bemused by Moonshadow's strange appearance, Toad followed the others into the cavern. They did not venture far inside before Ernie produced a candle from his pocket and lit it with his tinderbox. The feeble glare revealed seemingly endless stone stairs leading up a steep shaft into which Moonshadow had already disappeared. Toad flinched as the boulder behind them rolled back into place with an eerie grating sound. Beyond the pale circle of Ernie's light the darkness was absolute.

"Where is he?" the pipesmith wondered out loud. "How can he see in this?"

Ernie chuckled. "Moonshadow's blind, Toad; at least in the ordinary sense. Yet, like the true visionary that he is, he has an inner light that shows him things lesser men miss."

"Oh."

"As to where he is, he's gone ahead to disarm traps that protect Hillcommune from invaders. There's great magick in the land of the Oldhips, particularly in some of its people, like Moonshadow and Foreseein' Franklin, but magick isn't always enough to keep away evil."

Toad digested this information. "But why would the Oldhips have a blind man guarding their tunnels?"

"Because it's what he wishes to do. His powers enable him to know when visitors are coming long before they arrive. Others, like Franklin, possess some of this unworldly talent, but they have to work hard at it. Indeed, Franklin's powers come from the fact that he's a scholar and the keeper of the *Book of Love*; Moonshadow was born with his. In Hillcommune, many look up to him more than they do Franklin and Wheatstraw."

"Why isn't he Tribechief, then?"

Ernie smiled and adjusted his top hat, which had slid down on his forehead. "The Seer has little interest in community politics and surface doings. His heart beats with the inner pulse of the rocks and trees. Nature is his weird, not the affairs of men."

A light appeared in the stairwell above them and Moonshadow materialized, his sightless eyes unblinking in the glare of the torch he held. "I know that others need burning sticks to guide them," he explained, handing the torch to Ernie. "Follow me, but do not walk ahead. There are still traps that I must disarm to make the way safe. Careful, the path is long and steep."

In silence, Toad and his companions followed the bobbing torch. The stairs seemed to go on for miles, and frequent stops to rest their weary legs became necessary. Finally, the stairs gave way to another long tunnel. In the distance a small light appeared.

Sunlight showered down over the mountains as the company emerged from the cave like groundhogs coming out of a burrow. For a moment they stood transfixed, smelling the sweet warm air blowing in their faces. They were in a grove of huge pines, and the ground around their feet was radiant with scores of trilliums and lady slippers. Beyond, verdant fields and meadows spread off in all directions. Sunlit swards of grass and wildflowers were dotted with copses of hardwood and rambling orchards of flowering fruit trees. Dozens of tiny silver streamlets wound their way through the gently sloping meadows. Berries of all types grew in abundance. Off to the right, in the distance, a pond shimmered beside an apple grove. Around its banks cattle and sheep grazed lazily. The air was sweet and heavy with the spice-like aroma of growing things.

Toad blinked and looked out over the valley of Hillcommune with awe. Was that a river and village he saw in the far distance? Was this the country of his dreams?

"Where's the snow?" he asked. "It's like summer."

Moonshadow chuckled, a sound like water running over timeworn stones.

"It *is* summer. It's always summer here. We call it the *'Summer of Love'*, for like love it is eternal."

It was said that in the valley of the Oldhips was centered the undying spirit of its people—The All, the culmination of the original Dream, untouched by the cares of the outside world. Such a mystical explanation could account for the balmy weather in the valley, but Toad thought that the hot springs he saw bubbling up along the way probably played a part as well.

The company had not gone far before Toad found it necessary to remove his cloak and coat. Before long, Ernie, Maynard and Tam did the same. In the perfumed air Toad felt slightly lightheaded, but he had no trouble keeping up with the others as they passed through a field of chest-high grass. Everywhere he looked there were flowers, bigger and brighter than any he had ever seen. Insects droned around every bloom while huge butterflies danced to the songs of bobolinks and meadowlarks. Overhead in the clear blue sky a pair of doves wheeled and pirouetted. It was very much like his last dream, except that Mizjoan was not there to greet him.

In spite of himself, Toad started to sing an old tune that his mother had sung to him when he was small. It hadn't meant much then, but these days the words seemed to fit his mood.

"Oh, I'm Barney McDougal, The Third.
I'm a magical merchant of dreams.
An' I'm here to tell you nothin' is real -
Nothin' is quite what it seems.
I've been a lonesome traveler,
A sometimes-soldier, it seems.
There's music in my heart all day;
Rockets and fire in my dreams…"

The others smiled and looked his way, gladly accepting Toad's off-key voice. They soon reached a gentle flowered slope and patches of carefully tended gardens, laid out in a roughly circular pattern. In the center of the gardens, a huge dead oak dominated a small open park. The enormous tree was decorated like a Yule fir. Garlands of flowers encircled its trunk and streamers, wind chimes, God's eyes, and ornaments of every type hung from its branches. Beyond the gardens and the park, the village of the Oldhips spread out along the near bank of a winding river. Bathed in the early morning sunlight, the brightly painted houses of Hillcommune looked like a scattering of children's blocks. The houses, some of them several stories high, stretched for nearly a mile along the river, interconnected by porches and common rooms so that the entire village seemed like one continuous, eccentric structure.

Smaller houses nestled behind the ones along the bank. Some were clustered together; others were separated by large flower beds. In the places where small creeks and brooks fed into the river some of the house lots and gardens were like islands, linked to the rest of the village by footbridges. Longer bridges snaked out over the river to connect the wharves of the village to the rolling fields of vegetables, flowers, and Honkweed on the far bank. Toad smiled as he looked about him, thinking that this was a place completely at peace. Maybe in a place such as this, he could be free from dreams of the Dark Man.

The path down through the field was long and narrow, and for a while the village was lost from sight. Widening to where the travelers could walk three abreast, the path leveled off until it was almost flat. The Freaks stopped to drink from a spring that bubbled up from the rocks amid a riot of wild speckled lilies and sweet flag. The water was cold and seemed to tingle with an unseen energy. Moonshadow shrugged out of his patchwork cloak, revealing a shirt and trousers made entirely of fringed leather that was beaded and quilled in strange designs. Even Maynard took off his moth-eaten beret, running his fingers through his short blue-black hair.

Moonshadow suddenly cocked his head and smiled. From the direction

286

of the village came the faint sounds of music and singing.

"Hasten," the Seer said. "Your arrival is expected. There are those who are eager to greet you." He paused and sniffed the air. "Aah, and unless I'm much mistaken, breakfast awaits."

Perhaps it was the bubbly spring water, or perhaps the promise of a hearty meal, but they found themselves running. The sightless Seer led the way as they raced through the last few acres of field, laughing as they went. His destination was a whitewashed longhouse beyond a small creek. The Freaks slowed to cross the stream over a narrow footbridge, only wide enough to accommodate them one at a time. On the other side, Moonshadow was far up the path, past an elegant garden, knocking on the longhouse's back door with his staff. Puffing and panting, the Freaks reached him just as the door opened on the third rap.

Tendrils of smoke curled out to greet the travelers. The air was thick with the smell of incense and weed. Toad took a deep breath of it as he followed Moonshadow and the others into the house.

The room they entered was large and airy, and cluttered with bright throw pillows and low tables and filled with the sweet, lighthearted notes of a panpipe. Wind chimes and mobiles hung from the open rafters. The walls were covered with colorful tapestries. Some depicted images from nature—sunsets, woodlands and oceanscapes. To Toad, the most interesting hangings were scenes from Freak history. One in particular showed a city of ancient times, gray and grim except for the area immediately surrounding a group of brightly garbed Freaks. Standing on a street corner, the Freaks were in the act of scaling a street sign and placing a placard on it. The sign said HAIGHT-ASHBURY, but a slim youth, shirtless and bathed in golden light, was replacing the HAIGHT with a sign that read simply LOVE.

Another wall was covered with a single huge depiction of the near-mythical Festival of Woodstock. Thousands of Freaks filled the tapestry, all of them gazing intently toward a distant stage. There, dwarfed by the huge skeletal towers and banks of equipment, a solitary male figure stood hunched over a guitar. The silhoulette had his face turned from the audience. Something in the man's stance made Toad think "Dylan," though Freak tradition held that Old Bob had never played at the great festival.

Wheatstraw, the Oldhip Tribechief, and a slim, dark-haired woman in a white dress, sat on cushions in front of the huge tapestry; a guitar rested between them. The woman, who was playing a panpipe, put it down to accept the hose of a waterbong that Wheatstraw offered. Both of the Oldhips wore strands of beads and silver bells around their necks and garlands of flowers crowned their heads. A button, painted in the likeness of a peace symbol surrounded by the rays of a sunflower, adorned the breast pocket of Wheatstraw's chambray shirt. Below it, a smaller button spelled out LOVE in flowing letters. Without missing a hit on the hose, Wheatstraw smiled and gestured for the travelers to sit down.

"An interesting company!" he laughed, exhaling. "Moonshadow told me to expect you. Welcome to Hillcommune."

Maynard grinned as he took a seat beside the Tribechief. "Thanks, Brother Oldhip. But, like, I haven't been gone that long."

"True, Brother Beatnik, but I haven't seen Ernie since the Fair, and Brother Dill perhaps not for a decade."

"Your loss on both counts," Ernie remarked, good-naturedly.

"It is a pleasure to have Brother Toad as well."

Toad smiled, warming to Wheatstraw and the quiet woman at his side. "The pleasure is all mine, Brother Wheatstraw," he said, glancing at the Oldhip woman. "I've heard much about your land, but nothing prepared me for its great beauty."

The woman blushed slightly. Wheatstraw noticed this, and patted her on the hand. "Pardon my rudeness, friends. This is Hashberry, my mate and one of my best advisors."

"Your best," Hashberry corrected, reaching out to shake Toad's hand. "You people have traveled far, and from the looks of it, you haven't eaten well."

"The places we've been recently aren't noted for their fine cuisine," Ernie said.

"I can well imagine, Brother Mungweasle. If you'll excuse me, the Eatery has a glorious breakfast prepared this morning. I'll see about having some brought over."

Once Hashberry had left the room, Ernie reached over and took the waterpipe hose without being asked. "You're looking well," he said to Wheatstraw.

"I wish I could say the same of you, Friend Mungweasle. You look like you've been down to sticks and seeds for a while. Even the Beatnik looks like he's aged a decade in a month."

"Dig it," Maynard remarked. "Bad Karma, man. This cat's usually, like, vice-versa."

"Things aren't going well in Street-Corner Earth," Ernie added between tokes.

"Even worse than when last we spoke?"

The herbalist nodded. "Much."

"Moonshadow has told me something of these things. Day and night Foreseein' Franklin has been poring over the old books, trying to decipher the meaning of these events."

"What's to decipher? The Dark Man's kicking up a storm out there."

"We Oldhips are aware of the Evil Weed's doings, Ernie. We see and hear more than you might think. Already, we've given shelter to various refugees."

"Lowland Freaks?"

"A few, some of them members of your own Clear Light Society. Strutter Lurchkin brought in about a dozen Diggers bearing books and records from Froggy Bottom. It's been turned into a Radiclib garrison and as such, is more open to attack from the enemy. Before too long we expect to have Skulk with us as well."

Ernie shook his head sadly. "That's impossible; Theo's dead."

"Not according to Moonshadow. Skulk will be heading here soon, along with others."

"What others?"

"The Radiclib, Mizjoan, and some of her people," Moonshadow offered.

Toad felt his heart leap. He couldn't be hearing right. The possibility that she was alive stunned him. He wanted to yell for joy, but somehow he restrained himself.

Ernie seemed equally as moved. "That's fantastic news. Mizjoan is an old friend, as dear to me as family. Do you know who the others are?"

"I don't know their names," the Seer stated quietly. "But there was a girl with long, dark hair, like Hashberry's, and a burly man with a black beard."

"Kentstate and Rudy. This is too much to be hoped for. How'd they all manage to survive?"

"There was a great lake battle. Many ships sank or were burned."

"Yes, at Great East. Toad and I were there."

"Indeed. One of the Leftopian ships, though severely damaged, escaped the enemy pack. It sank in shallow water at the narrows below Piggy Point."

Ernie shook his head again. "Outrageous! Then, Mizjoan was no more than a few miles from us the whole time."

"The All works in mysterious ways, Brother Mungweasle."

"Are there any more headed here? Lowland Freaks? More Diggers?"

"My powers aren't infallible. Sometimes I don't sense visitors until just a few hours before they arrive. My powers seem to wax and wane according to the dictates of The All. I see what I see. In that, I'm like other men."

Hashberry returned from the Eatery carrying a heavy wooden tray laden with covered dishes, goblets, and a stoneware jug. She placed the tray in front of Wheatstraw and began to uncover the dishes. Soon the Freaks found themselves feasting on thick slices of oatmeal bread smeared with apple butter and washing down the tasty mouthfuls with goblets of sparkling, cold cider. Before them, a dazzling display of fresh fruits, berries, and cheeses was laid out. Toad grinned when Hashberry ladled him out a dish of yogurt, honey and finely ground nuts. His smile broadened when she added a topping of sliced strawberries.

"You see much, Moonshadow," the little Beatnik said. "Like, tell me this then—does The All tell you why we've come here?"

"It shows me enough. I sense you bear with you an object of great power, a book of dark knowledge."

"Dig it, we do. But it can only bring peace."

The blind man shook his head. "We have peace here already. What need would we have of your talisman?"

"You may have peace, but others don't."

"This is known. Still, what you bear disturbs the fabric of The All. I sense strong vibrations from it; they speak of great evil."

"Dig it again. These are heavy times, Moonshadow, and heavy times call for heavy solutions. Still, it is only a book—a simple weapon to use against our enemies."

The Seer rubbed his temples with his long, white fingers. A few minutes passed while he seemed to be in deep concentration; then he continued. "Now I understand more fully. How can you call this a simple weapon, this Black Book?"

"In the proper hands that's all it will be."

"This thing is darker than you know, Brother Beatnik. Who has these 'proper hands'?"

"Me. And Skulk, if he's headed this way."

Moonshadow grunted and shook his head. "I fear neither of you may be up to the task."

"Like, that's for me to decide."

Wheatstraw reached out a hand and rested it on Maynard's shoulder. "Now is not the time to discuss such matters."

"As you wish, man."

"Good. Enough of this for now. You've all traveled a great way. You must rest while I meditate. Someone will show you to your quarters." He jingled the strand of bells around his neck and a moment later a slim blond girl in a flower-print dress entered the room.

"This is Northstar," he said, indicating the girl. "For as long as you stay among us, she'll be in charge of your quarters. If you have need of anything, just ask her. For the rest, we'll meet here tomorrow night."

Maynard looked like he was about to speak, but Northstar opened the side door and smiled, indicating that their audience was at an end. As he followed his friends out onto the porch Toad looked back at Wheatstraw.

The Tribechief had already engaged in a hushed but earnest conversation with Moonshadow and Hashberry.

Chapter Thirty-Three

Barely two hours past dawn the day was already warm. Toad undid the last few buttons on his shirt and leaned back in the rocking chair. A slight breeze blew off the Peace River. He put his bare feet up on the deck railing, wiggled his toes experimentally, and smiled as the moving air tickled them like the lightest touch of a feather. With his head thrown back and his eyes closed, Toad let the warm sun play across his face and chest.

Rising just before sunup, he had been surprised to notice that the coverlet of Ernie's bed had been turned down neatly, but the herbalist was nowhere to be found. After bathing, Toad had picked out a pair of jeans and an embroidered blue shirt from a pile of clean clothes that lay on the table. He made a quick survey of his new lodgings as he buttoned the cuffs and tucked the tails into his pants. Though small, the cabin was well stocked with food, clothing and other supplies. To his delight, he even found a bulging leather sack of weed lying on the kitchen table. The Oldhips were remarkable hosts.

The one thing the Greasers hadn't taken from Toad was Scuddy Lout's his iron pipe; it lay on the railing next to his rocker. Toad picked it up and lit it with a few deft flicks of his tinderbox. He smiled as the first toke hit him. As he'd discovered before, this Oldhip weed was primo, far better than the Hillcommune Red that they peddled to lowland Freaks.

To Toad's left a long bridge set on high pilings arched out over the Peace to the fields on the far bank. As he was taking his second toke, a group of laughing children passed over the bridge, followed by a pair of barking, cavorting dogs. A few boats moved on the river—elegant canoes and small sailboats with colorful patchwork sails fluttering in the warm morning breeze. Haze still hung over the distant fields and meadows, but it was rapidly burning off as the sun rose higher over the mountains. The bright blue sky was flawless, except for a spot in the west where a long tentacle of black clouds unfolded between the peaks of Mount Lennon and

Mount Leary. Toad's grin left him. He knew that beyond the valley of the Oldhips it was cold and snow was falling. A chill passed over him, and he thought of Mizjoan.

Toad laid his pipe to one side. The sound of footsteps behind him tore his gaze from the distant clouds. A pair of odd-looking Oldhips approached from the direction of Wheatstraw's house. The two Oldhips were young, probably no more than twenty, but there the resemblance between them stopped. The taller of the two had curly carrot-red hair that bounced when he walked. He was lanky, and so skinny that his clothes barely fit. His jeans bagged sadly and his billowing white T-shirt ended inches above his navel. Though he looked frail, the redhead carried a bulging backpack seemingly without effort, as he concentrated all of his energy on chewing on the Honkweed stem that protruded from his vapid, good-natured face.

The redhead's companion was shorter than him by a good six inches and had straight black hair that hung limply down over his bare chest, barely moving as the little man jittered and bounced along. As the pair neared, Toad noticed that the smaller Oldhip possessed a small pencil-line mustache and had crude tattoos, the type of primitive artwork usually seen only on Greasers, decorating both arms. FLO wavered across his right bicep, while MOMMA'S BOY graced his left forearm. In spite of himself, Toad gawked at the pair.

"Peace, Brother Toad, and good mornin'," the short Oldhip said, waving familiarly. He extended his hand to be shaken while his companion just grinned foolishly and moved the Honkweed twig to the other side of his mouth.

"Peace yourselves," Toad replied, hoping that the pair would exchange pleasantries and be on their way. He shook the Oldhip's hand politely, but with no great enthusiasm.

The short Oldhip smoothed his absurd mustache, but made no sign of leaving. He said nothing for a moment, as if mulling something over in his mind. "Call me Flo," he said at last. "This here's my brother, Eddie."

"I see." Better to keep it curt, Toad decided.

"We heard that you'd arrived with Brother Ernie and The Beatnik, so we rushed right over to meet you."

"You wanted to meet me? Why?"

"Well, because you're somewhat famous around here."

Toad thought this over. Since leaving Smuttynose he'd been involved in quite a few adventures, but he really didn't feel famous at all. "Thank you, but you flatter me."

"Not at all. You are *the* Josiah Toad, right? Of Smuttynose Island?"

"I confess that's me, but what of it?"

"What of it? Such modesty! Hell, it isn't every day that a craftsman with your reputation visits Hillcommune. Eddie and I are great fans of yours; we've been collecting your pipes for years. Some of them cost us a pretty Abbie, I don't mind telling you."

Toad smiled. In a company that included mystics, adventurers, and an immortal, Flo and Eddie had singled him out for attention because of his trade. "I-I'm pleased that you like what I do," he said, somewhat lamely.

"Did you hear that, Eddie?" Flo said, jabbing his companion in the ribs. "'I'm pleased that you like what I do.' Now that's modesty—and this from a man whose work surpasses that of the great Wheelen himself."

Toad felt himself blushing furiously. Cernunnos Wheelen of Summerluv was considered the greatest pipesmith who ever lived. Even before his death in 2278 his pipes commanded prices of several hundred Rubins each. "You exaggerate," he mumbled.

"Not in the least, Brother Toad. I've got several Wheelen clays in my collection, plus a couple of pre-Helter-Skelter bongs, but mostly I collect Toad pipes. I've got eight of your works in all: three briar churchwardens, four deer antler shortpipes, and a half-lid, dual-chamber party pipe that Brother Mungweasle charged me an ounce of Mt. Leary Black hash for."

The pipesmith shook his head. "I'm afraid Ernie robbed you on that one. Those dual-chambers were my least favorite design. The draw on them was too hard for most people."

"That may be so, but they're great collector's items. I got mine hanging over the fireplace at me and Eddie's pad. I've even got some far-out weed that we could smoke out of it, if you want."

"I thank you for the invitation, but as you can see, I've got a pipe going right now."

Flo nodded, studying Scuddy Lout's pipe with some interest. "Fascinating bowl. Rowdie design if I'm not mistaken. Made of cast iron. As effective as a club as it is a smoking instrument. Where'd you get it?"

"I found it. That is, it's rather a long story."

"Then, why don't you tell us the story while we give you a tour of Hillcommune?" Eddie asked, speaking for the first time. This shocked Toad momentarily. The lanky redhead hadn't looked bright enough to remember his own name, much less construct a sentence, yet his speech was that of a cultivated man.

"Well, I w-was thinking of touring the place with my friends."

"They've all been here before. Besides, they're all over to Wheatstraw's at the moment. We just came from there."

Toad felt a momentary stab of jealousy. Were they holding a meeting without him? "Uhh, it's nice of you to consider me, but I was thinking of spending some time alone right now."

"What for?" Flo asked. "So you can pout and be miserable? The look on your face when we approached you wasn't entirely that of a happy man."

"I have to admit, I've got a few things on my mind."

"I'm sure we've got a cure for whatever troubles you. The weed at our place is far better than that stuff you're smoking."

"I don't know; this stuff's pretty good."

Flo grinned devilishly. Toad's resolve started to crumble. Maybe the two brothers were just what he needed to cheer up.

"What's in your pipe might be better than what you're used to," the little Oldhip persisted. "But it can't match our private stash of Green Ruin."

"Well, you know, I…"

"You better listen to what my brother says," Eddie interjected. "You might not know it, but he's an important dude hereabouts."

"Hush up, Eddie. I'm only an assistant Horticulturist."

"You're Head Assistant Horticulturist, Flo, and I'm your helper. That makes me Assistant Head Assistant Horticulturist."

"Oh, then in that case I take back what I said. We're both important dudes, Eddie. Maybe we ought to run for Tribechief next."

"Maybe."

Toad grinned. "Hillcommune weed's well thought of in the lowlands. If you two had anything to do with it, then your skills *must* be greater than mine."

Flo blushed. "Well, except for some of the later strains like Green Ruin, weed is only a hobby for us. Mostly, we work with magick mushrooms, wheat molds, and stuff like that. Still, we've managed to come up with a few minor improvements on the local crop."

Eddie laughed and slapped his brother on the back. "Haw! Haw! Minor improvements, the man says! Wait'll you try some of our Green Ruin, Brother Toad; the improvement is more than minor."

"I don't believe Brother Toad is interested, Eddie."

"Of course he is. Aren't you, Brother Toad? We can smoke it out of your dual-chamber pipe. I've modified it so it works real well now. Maybe you could even give me some pointers on pipe design."

Toad cocked an eyebrow. "Pointers?"

"Eddie has ambitions of being a pipesmith himself someday," Flo explained. "But his real talent is in scheming up things."

"Brother Toad doesn't want to hear about that, Flo. You're the only one I show my inventions to. Everyone else laughs."

"You're exaggerating, Eddie. Nobody laughs."

"No, I'm not. You're the one people listen to, not me."

Toad had to smile at the obvious love between the two brothers, which seemed to drape around them like a well-worn cloak. "What sort of things do you scheme up?" he asked.

"Promise you won't laugh?"

"I promise."

Eddie fumbled with his knapsack and produced several parchment scrolls, which he handed to Toad. The pipesmith took them and unrolled them, squinting as he attempted to make out the delicate diagrams and curlicued notations. One was of a windwagon, one of a pair of huge parabolic mirrors, another was of a complicated hydraulic system, apparently for pumping water uphill, but the one that caught his attention depicted a man strapped into a kite-like device that swept back into an exaggerated triangle. He studied it closely, shaking his head in confusion.

"It's a sky-glider," Eddie explained. "A device that'll make it possible for men to fly, just like the *Book of Love* says the Old-Timers could."

Toad studied the drawing closely, frowning as he tried to read the scrawled notations. "Have you made one of these?" he asked.

"No. Right now my plans are to construct the wings out of thin leather, but leather is heavy and a rare item in Hillcommune. We don't slaughter animals like you do in the lowlands, though we do use the hides of creatures that die naturally."

"I've noticed that Moonshadow dresses exclusively in leathers."

"Moonshadow is Moonshadow; he gets first pick of many things. Me, I show these plans to people and they just mumble until I go away."

"Why? I'd think something like that would interest them."

"New ideas aren't always welcomed here," Flo interjected, "especially ones that smack of the ways of the Ancients. Some think that such things disturb The All. Besides that, Eddie's thought to be slower than most."

"Why's that? Obviously he's not."

"Superstition. We're twins, though we don't look much alike. We were born two minutes apart—me at one minute to midnight, the seventh of December. Eddie was born the second minute of December Eighth."

Toad nodded, "John's Day."

"Need I say more?"

Toad shook his head. Like any Freak he was aware of the superstitions surrounding the anniversary of Lennon's death. To be born on that darkest of all days was to be considered unsound of spirit and mind. Known also as "The Day the Music Died," December Eighth was a day of sadness and reflection, not of jubilation like Yule, Dylan's Day or Halloween. The stigma attached to it unfortunately often stuck to those born then. This often led to people lying about their birth dates and brooding over astrological charts, moaning, "Why me?"

"You look sane enough to me," Toad informed Eddie.

The lanky Oldhip chomped thoughtfully on his weedstick. "Maybe so, but you can't prove that by a lot of people. I've been assigned to help Flo, because they don't think I'm suited for anything else. I'll show 'em someday, though."

"Eddie's got guts," Flo beamed. "I think that's why I love him so much."

Eddie blushed. "Aww, that's okay, Flo. You've had to take your share of grief for your nickname."

"Flo isn't your real name?" Toad asked.

"Nope, name's Harvey, but I've been called Flo for so long that it might as well be my name. I copped that moniker because of these," Flo said, displaying his tattoos as a man might an old scar.

Toad scratched his beard. It was way overdue for a trim. "How'd you come by those? I thought only Greasers and Rowdies wore such things."

"Usually that's so. It's rather a long story."

"Good tales usually are. Go ahead."

Flo folded his arms behind his back and rocked to and fro on his heels. "Well, about thirty years ago, Eddie and I went to Covenstead Fair with our folks..."

"How can that be? You barely look twenty."

"Huh? Oh, we Oldhips live longer than you lowlanders. As a matter of fact, Eddie and I just celebrated our forty-eighth birthday last week."

"It's clean living and good weed that does it," Eddie explained. "With any luck we'll see another hundred years. Hell, look at Foreseein' Franklin; he's all of 136, and still going strong."

Flo chuckled. "And I'll be that age before I finish this story. Now, hush up and let me go on."

"Just trying to help."

"Right ... anyway, we were just kids at the time and it was only our second trip out of Hillcommune, so I guess we were pretty unhip in the ways of the world. Our folks told us to beware of outlanders and all that. But who listens? Well, one evening I left our wagon alone and wandered around the Fair, past the bright tents and down lantern-lit streets. After a while, I found myself by the horse barns.

"I heard some raucous laughter coming from a camp at the end of the stalls. A group of Greasers was drinking and playing dice. I'd never seen such folk before so I stopped to watch them."

"That was a big mistake," Eddie remarked.

"Maybe so, brother mine, but in those days Slickhairs weren't considered life-threatening, and I really didn't know what to make of them. After a while they noticed me watching them and invited me over to have a beer with them. In spite of their rough language and strange ways they seemed to be having so much fun that I joined them.

"I liked their strong beer and their bragging talk about fights and wagon racing, but after a while they started to get real drunk—uglier—and some of them started to look at me with dangerous smiles. I made my excuses and tried to leave. When I tried to get up a thin, blond Greaser with no front teeth grabbed me by the arm. 'Where do you think you're goin?' he asked. 'You can't be leavin' your new friends already.'

"Before I realized what was going on, they were on me, holding me down. The blond reached inside his jacket and produced a huge pair of metal shears. I just about fainted when I saw them."

Toad felt his stomach clench. He was all too familiar with Greaser violence.

"The rest was kind of a blur. They cut off huge hunks of my hair and I started crying, so one of them hit me in the face, hard, calling me a 'momma's boy.' The others found that funny, and soon they all took up the chant.

"'That's a real good name,' a fat Greaser said. 'Let's write the little fairy up.' He produced needles and ink, the type they use for tattooing.

"While four or five of them held me down, the fat one started stitching on my arm. It hurt bad, but I didn't dare let out a peep. When he was done with that arm, he announced that he wanted to 'write up' the other one."

By this time Toad was fascinated. "How'd he come up with Flo?" he asked.

"I was getting to that. One of the Greasers had a girlfriend named Florence. He wanted to immortalize her on my arm. The Greasers were so stupid, that once they started, they couldn't decide how to spell her name. An argument broke out and soon escalated into a brawl. While they were busy swinging fists and busting jaws, I walked off with the first three letters of the girlfriend's name stitched on my arm. Flo I became, and Flo I am to this day."

"I tell him Flo is the first three letters in flower," Eddie remarked. "That cheers him up sometimes."

Toad wanted to hear what, if anything, happened to the Greasers after Flo's assault, but his questions were cut short. Ernie, wearing patched up jeans and a red and yellow flower-print shirt that was too small for him, was coming his way, waving his hands excitedly. Toad's heart leapt when he saw the others, following in Ernie's wake. There was a short bespectacled Freak with a plug hat, and a rangy youth wearing a star-printed yellow frock coat.

"Skulk! Strutter Lurchkin!" the pipesmith yelled, running to greet them.

There were others with Ernie—Maynard, Tambourine, Wheatstraw and his advisor Foreseein' Franklin, whom Toad had met in Covenstead—but it was the two Diggers that Toad grabbed, hugging them both.

"Brother Toad!" Skulk boomed. "I thought you were dead. Seeing you and Ernie again makes me think there might be something right with the world after all."

"Brother Skulk, Lurchkin. Dylan's Bones, but it's good to see you. I must admit, I thought you were goners."

"Nearly were, nearly were," Skulk continued in a softer, more serious tone. "If Mizjoan hadn't plucked me out of the water after the *Righton* sank, I'd have been a goner for sure. But Ernie's been telling us about the adventures you've been having. Makes that little muss-up at Great East seem like a tea party in comparison."

"I wouldn't go that far," Ernie interrupted, clapping them both on the back. "Let's just say we've had more than our share of fun, travel, and adventure." He patted Toad on the back again. "You were still asleep when Moonshadow came and told me that he sensed Skulk was near. We wanted to get to them quickly so I didn't bother to wake you."

Toad shrugged. "It's okay. I had Flo and Eddie here to keep me company. What happened at Froggy Bottom?"

"General Dillon's turned it into a military outpost," Skulk replied. "We moved out all our books and valuable artifacts and brought them here."

"Things have really gone that far?"

"They have, but let's not speak of that right now. I'm interested in hearing more of your adventures. There hasn't been an initiation like this since Ernie joined us."

Ernie grinned nervously. "It wasn't all that much, Theo."

"That isn't the way you made it sound before. I say we should attend to Brother Toad's swearing in very soon. We need people like him."

Toad didn't like the direction the conversation was taking. Something was going on that he couldn't quite fathom; he felt like he was being set up. He glanced at Flo and Eddie, then back at Skulk. "Initiation? Swearing in? What in Bob's name are you talking about?"

Skulk cleared his throat importantly. "Son, you found the *Necronomicon*! That accomplishment deserves a reward."

Toad glanced at his friends. There was a look of grim expectancy on Wheatstraw's face, and on Franklin's. Flo and Eddie drifted off toward the fringe of the group where they watched the proceedings warily. "Look," he said. "If you really insist on doing something nice for me, get me back to Smuttynose."

"That would be impossible," Skulk said.

"I was afraid of that. Listen, everything that I've done was more by accident than anything."

"The All permits no accidents," Foreseein' Franklin rasped. "To all things there are seasons and reasons. In the *Book of Love* it is written that when the Age of Peril falls upon our lands there will come a host of outlanders bearing secrets both wonderful and terrible. Armand Barwackadae, the famous scrollist, said that this knowledge would be a two-edged dagger, as capable of cutting its bearer as his enemies. Yet, close upon the heels of these strangers would come the Freedom Rider, the promised savior of our peoples."

A sticky fearfulness enveloped Toad. "Surely that's just an old folk tale."

"It's one of our most revered legends, Brother Toad. The Rider will come, though it is said we will not know him at first. He could be walking among us right now, unseen as anything but a mortal man."

"Let's not get into this lame old story," Tambourine scoffed. He was trying to look bored, but Toad sensed unease in the musician's manner.

"You might think these are only stories," Franklin countered. "But they were written down long ago by those who had the gift of prophecy. Many people believe that these events are soon to come to pass—that the end of an Age is upon us."

Toad cleared his throat. He looked around for Flo and Eddie, but they had disappeared. "This is getting heavy," he said. "Can we talk about something else?"

Franklin nodded. "Perhaps that would be best—for now."

Suddenly a mountain horn sounded in the distance—three loud blats followed by a long, wavering note that seemed to go on forever. "Moonshadow is sounding the distress call," Wheatstraw announced. "Someone's coming through the West Gate. They must be in trouble."

Before Wheatstraw could explain more, Toad was caught up in the mob of Oldhips that had boiled out of the houses along the wharf in response to the signal. Shoving and jostling, they made their way through town toward the West Gate. The horn blew again, closer now, repeating its signal. He looked around for his companions, but they'd been swallowed up in the mob. He caught a brief flash of something yellow, possibly Lurchkin's coat, but it was far ahead of him in the swarm of running bodies. Another time he saw Ernie's top hat bobbing over the heads of the crowd, but soon that too was lost to sight.

Toad was caught in a knot of people who surged over one of the bridges leading to the far bank of the Peace. Cautiously making his way through the packed bodies he glanced toward the west. There in the distance he could see a line of gray-clad figures approaching through the fields. At the head of the column he could see Moonshadow with his staff in one hand and a huge carved horn strapped over his shoulder. Beside the Seer strode Mizjoan, urging her troops along.

Toad tried to elbow his way through the mob, but too many people stood in his way. By the time the advancing line was almost to the bridge he could see that most of the Radiclibs were wounded and limping. Those who weren't, were bearing the most seriously hurt on stretchers. He pushed harder through the crowd, but the huddled Oldhips hardly budged. Mizjoan passed within hailing distance, but his heart was hammering so fast that he found he couldn't cry out. She looked drawn and weary, defeated. When he finally did call to her, she was out of earshot, swallowed up by the churning mob.

Chapter Thirty-four

The westerning sun streamed through the stained glass windows of the gathering room, hitting Toad full in the face. Moving through the crowd of Freaks, Oldhips and Radiclibs, he nearly collided with a low-hanging mobile as he situated himself, using Ernie to block the harsh glare. The pipesmith rubbed his temples and closed his eyes, trying to get comfortable on the pillow-strewn floor.

"Will you stop fidgeting?" Ernie complained, taking a toke from Toad's iron skull pipe. "What's wrong with you, anyway?"

"I guess I'm just a little edgy," Toad offered. "Since I left Smuttynose I feel like I've lost control of my life, like getting caught up and pushed along by a crowd. Some of the older Islanders have a saying for it, 'like rowing a dory in a hurricane'."

Ernie exhaled a blast of smoke that wreathed about him in a cloud. "You call how you were existing on Smuttynose, being in control? To extend your maritime analogy: some people ride with the rough seas and maintain their bearings and some flounder in a tide pool. You, Toad, were floundering.

"Look, these are heavy times, and getting heavier. We all feel tossed around by fate. Did you know that there was a light snow in the pastures north of town last night?"

"Really?"

"That's almost unheard of in these parts."

"It seems like an insignificant event after seeing Mizjoan limp in with her people."

"Is it?" Ernie gusted out rings of smoke that wobbled as they rose toward the raftered ceiling. He handed the pipe to Toad. "But hey, I know where you're coming from. Her people aren't used to losing. Rudy was like family to Joannie; it's going to take a long time for her to get over his death.

It must have reminded her of when her parents died. She witnessed that too."

Toad took a deep toke and held it until his eyes watered. "By the time we reached Hillcommune I thought I'd been through it all, but looking at Mizjoan—I can't begin to imagine what she's feeling."

"Grief, like anybody else. But how she handles it is a different story. Radiclibs are hard to figure out, and women are almost impossible. So therefore, a Radiclib woman is beyond human male comprehension. I do know this: Joannie can get over losing a comrade, even a dear one. But losing Leftopia..."

"I wish I could do something," Toad sighed. He took another toke and let out a silvery stream of smoke just as the door whispered open and Wheatstraw, Foreseein' Franklin, and Moonshadow entered the room. A moment later Skulk, Tambourine, and Maynard followed.

"That's odd," Ernie remarked. "I thought Moonshadow never attended these things."

Toad said nothing. As the Freaks and Oldhips took their seats the crowd parted, admitting Mizjoan and Kentstate. Though they had changed out of their uniforms and into fresh jeans and blouses, both women looked tired and beaten.

Wheatstraw raised his hands, signaling for silence. The crowd gathering in the room sat down on the pillows scattered about the floor while he remained standing. When the room was silent, he began to speak.

"In the *Book of Love*, it is written, we are the dust of stars, and we are golden. But it is not the gold of commerce or idolatry, but the gold of the earth, of the harvest. And so, we must each, in our own way, tend our gardens.

"Brothers and sisters," he said, "friends from home and friends from afar: this is *our* garden. The All has brought us together, Oldhips and Freaks, Diggers and Radiclibs, young and old—even the very old," he added, nodding at Maynard. "We have gathered here for a common purpose: to attempt to resolve our current struggle between Good and Evil.

"I don't have to tell you what's going on beyond the safety of our mountains. Something stalks the outside world, raising up our enemies against us—a Dark Man with a hundred names but no face. To some he is known as Blackcloak, Brother John Birch, The Jiveman, Bejeezuz. In our legends he is called the Evil Weed, the weed with its roots in hell. But whoever he is and wherever he comes from, his intentions are clear: he means to destroy Street-Corner Earth and everything in it."

"Amen," Toad heard Maynard mutter.

"Another thing is clear as well, brothers and sisters," Wheatstraw continued. "It is our part, as the children of Hillcommune, to offer you a safe haven and such aid as we can give. Most of you have followed dark and perilous paths to be here. The cost has been great. All of you have lost friends; all of you have lost parts of your souls. Though we can't arm you, or help you in any violent acts, we can shelter and feed you until you can fight again. This help, in love, we give freely.

"Perhaps if each of you, in turn, could unfold your stories before us we might divine the patterns in The All, that they may give us guidance for what must be done. Brother Beatnik, would you be first?"

Beginning with Maynard, each of the travelers rose to tell their stories. The Beatnik's was quite brief. To Toad it seemed he was being particularly evasive, acting more as a master of ceremonies than a direct participant in the tale telling. In the end, Maynard managed to go into some detail about the background of the *Necronomicon* and how he had sent Tambourine in search of it. No more enlightening, Skulk's speech dealt mainly with the events at Fetid Bog and Great East. To Toad, it was Ernie's tale that was the most wanting. The herbalist went into great detail about everything that had transpired from the Island to Hillcommune, but carefully worded his story so that it appeared he was as surprised as Toad about the turns of events from Covenstead on. Ernie never mentioned the incident with *Cruikshank's* or any other of his half-truths and obfuscations, which he'd liberally dispensed since leaving Smuttynose.

Though Toad listened to all the stories, only Tambourine's tale captured his full attention. Perhaps it was the sincerity in the musician's voice or the pain in his eyes that elevated his narration beyond that of his fellows.

Tambourine sat down and Mizjoan walked to the front of the room. She brushed a strand of auburn hair out of her face and looked out over the gathering without seeming to see anyone. In the light that streamed through the west windows she looked tired and thin. She sighed deeply and began speaking. Her voice was flat and weary. Saddened by her worn appearance, Toad leaned forward and listened intently.

"Comrades, brothers and sisters, old friends and new," Mizjoan intoned. "The People's Republic of Leftopia, or what remains of it, extends greetings and thanks. We thank you for safe refuge in a world gone mad, we thank you for whatever aid you can tender, and we thank you for your love and caring.

"By now you have heard of my defeats at Great East and Ripott Pass. I say 'my defeats' because I gave the orders; I made the decisions that sent many brave warriors to their deaths. I should never have tried to storm Klaven's Keep. I should have ordered my troops into the mountains rather than keep up sustained guerrilla raids against enemy supply trains long after the need for such raids was past. I have lost friends, comrades, and kinsmen in the defense of our peoples. I have lost one who was more of a brother to me than a comrade in arms.

"After much brave resistance, the People's Army is broken and scattered. Except for Field Marshall Dillon's forces at Froggy Bottom, the few of us who made it here are all that are left. Already, the Dark Man's armies have rolled over Leftopia and the rest of Street-Corner Earth. We who remain are weary and filled with despair."

She pushed aside another strand of hair. Toad noticed that her hand trembled slightly. "Yet for all this, Comrade Skulk and Beatnik Maynard tell me that there's still a glimmer of hope—this mystical book. However slight the chance might be, I would embrace it rather than think of our freedom as gone forever, crushed beneath the Dark Man's iron heel."

As Mizjoan returned to her seat, Skulk stood up. "There is indeed hope," he said, adjusting his spectacles. "But the story is not mine to tell. We Diggers have suffered greatly on our journey here, but our trials are nothing compared to those undergone by Brothers Mungweasle, Toad and Tambourine. Even my own escape from Starkweather's burning ship at Great East and the long trip back to Froggy Bottom pale in comparison to what they have endured. These men are heroes, as brave as any Radiclib warrior. They have traveled far and fought hard to bring us a weapon of great power—an ancient book that will prove the undoing of the Dark Man and his minions."

"I would ask to hear how this book was obtained," Wheatstraw stated. "The manner of its recovery may provide important insight to our future actions. Since Brother Toad found the book and was the first to hold it in his hands, I would like his story, starting from the very beginning."

Toad stood up, feeling a little nervous about being asked to speak, but also quite pleased.

"Some of you already know my story. A few probably know it better than I do myself," he said, nodding towards Skulk and Maynard. "What began as a simple excursion has become much, much more. A wise man once said, 'I don't like adventures; they make me late for dinner.' I couldn't agree more; I've missed many since I left the safety of my home. I've been kidnapped by Greasers, shot at by Fashies, threatened by a Rowdie, and nearly been lunch for Mansonites. I've been almost drowned, frozen to death, insulted and cuffed around more than I care to remember, imprisoned on numerous occasions, scared senseless on more, and nearly sacrificed to an antique metal chariot. Front to back, it's been a cosmic bummer.

"It began for me when I came to the mainland from Smuttynose Island with my friend, Ernie Mungweasle, to visit Covenstead Fair..."

For the next hour, everybody listened intently to the pipesmith's tale. Then, after relating how he found the book, escaped from Lubejob and safely arrived in Hillcommune, he offered a comment.

"There's not a great deal that I can tell you about the *Necronomicon*, except that when I hold it in my hands I can feel it pulsing with vast power. The other day, Moonshadow said that the book possessed great evil. I can't say that it feels *evil* exactly, but it does feel menacing. One thing is certain: the Dark Man is out there, and he *is* evil—evil beyond words. I've seen him in my dreams and we've all experienced his intentions first hand. If the book can be used to destroy him, then I say use it."

A worried look flickered across Wheatstraw's face before disappearing behind a forced smile. "Thank you, Brother Toad. What do you say, Brother Franklin?"

The elderly Oldhip nodded sagely, his bony fingers kneading at his sparse gray beard. "What Brother Toad says is reckless and contrary to our basic values." Franklin paused before continuing. "I have searched The All and it is intensely disturbed around the book, but that doesn't prove that the book is evil. However, even as we are gathered here, the light of freedom pales. I do not see another option."

"I've heard enough of this madness," Moonshadow snapped, rapping his staff against the floor. A cold fire flashed in his sightless eyes. "You people speak of things beyond your ken as if they were child's toys to be used at will. That book is the very Avatar of Doom."

The Seer threw his head back so that his hair and beard waved like battle standards. "My All-sense tells me it is anathema. Already there is snow in the high pastures."

"Cool it, man," Maynard cautioned. "Like, it's true that the *Necronomicon* is heavy stuff, but I can handle it."

"Hah! Have a care, Brother Beatnik, that it doesn't handle you."

"I'm hip."

"Your vanity blinds you, Maynard. This Black Book of yours is no mere artifact; it has a mind and a will of its own. It disturbs the fabric of The All, and of our society. I sense its evil even if others do not. It is subtle and pernicious—deadly."

Maynard sighed in exasperation. "Cat, I'm not saying this book is *A Child's Garden of Grass*, but desperate times demand desperate measures."

"It will bring down ruin upon us all. The *Necronomicon* will turn upon he who holds it, destroy him with madness, infect those around him, and set brother against brother, father against son."

"Hey, better it's in our hands than the Dark Man's."

"Is it? I say let him have it; let it destroy him instead of us."

"If you're right, and he gets the book, he will surely destroy us before it destroys him."

"Already the disruption I've spoken of has started, right here in this very room. Rid Hillcommune of this book, now!"

"No! If there's disruption here it's not from the *Necronomicon.*"

The Seer jumped to his feet and strode towards the door. He stopped abruptly and turned to address Wheatstraw. "In the end you will do as you wish," he cursed, "but I'll have nothing to do with that foul book." Ernie got to his feet to stop him, but Moonshadow was gone in several swift strides.

"Let him be," Wheatstraw said. "He has spoken his peace. Now he goes back to the fields to commune with his friends, the plants and stones. He'll return when he feels the need."

"Touchy cat," Maynard commented.

Wheatstraw shook his head. "If he's touched, Brother Beatnik, it is by The All. You would do well to consider his words. But for now, we need to know more about the intentions of our Digger and Radiclib friends."

Toad listened half-heartedly. He looked toward the door where the Seer had recently exited. Moonshadow's words haunted him. The pipesmith shifted his attention to Mizjoan, who also seemed distant and preoccupied.

Just then Kentstate got to her feet. Hope, mixed with trepidation, shone in her dark eyes.

"We know little of this book you speak of, comrades," she said diplomatically. "It seems a matter of confusion even to you. Comrade Maynard sees it as a blessing, Comrade Moonshadow as a bane. Yet both say it is dark, powerful, not easily controlled.

"It is not for a mere soldier like myself to contemplate the good or evil of such a talisman. But, whatever its properties, it can be no more evil than that which already stalks us. A wolf is loose among the sheep, comrades. A shadow covers the land.

"Our people are battered and weary, but we'll fight to the last drop of blood to defeat the Dark Man. If this book can give us a chance, no matter how small, then I say it's worth any risk to use it."

Mumbles of approval filled the room.

Skulk stood up. He had loosened the buttons on his vest and now had his thumbs hooked around his suspenders. Rocking slightly backwards on his heels he nodded thoughtfully. "Brave words for a grim time, Sister Kentstate. Still, you speak of fighting as if that is all that must be done. The *Necronomicon* will be a great weapon in our hands, and its use will require cooperation among all of our peoples.

"But, because its power is so arcane and capricious, it should be entrusted to those who have the best chance to master it—the intellectuals. We, therefore, suggest that Maynard and I..."

"Stop right there," Kentstate asserted. "A power for the good of the masses should never be retained for the usage of the few. Holy Mao taught us that from bourgeois elitism stems all…"

"This really isn't the time for Radiclib philosophy, Sister Kentstate."

"We Radiclibs are warriors. We are trained in the use of weapons, and you have said that this book shall be our weapon."

Skulk snapped his suspenders loudly. "This is not a matter for soldiers."

"It isn't, comrade? How do you expect to defeat the enemy, give him a daffodil and a pat on the ass?"

"That isn't what I mean. The book is a weapon, to be sure, but scholars must unlock its powers and learn how to direct them."

Kentstate crossed her arms and scowled. "You've been a friend of ours for years, Theo, but you can try our patience. If everything were left up to you, your tight-lipped Society would rule the world." From her pillow nearby, Mizjoan looked up at her friend with approval.

"There's, like, not gonna be any discussion over who wields the book," Maynard interrupted, slapping one of his sandals on the low table in front of him.

"But, comrade…"

Maynard waved her to silence, then reached inside his sweater and fished out a dented and very rusty harmonica. "And there's not going to be any discussion over who wields this, either."

The Oldhips in the room gazed at the old instrument with awe. Wheatstraw looked shocked, then angry. "You took that from the Love Archives. Why?"

"Dig it, I placed it there years ago for safekeeping."

"But, you have no need of it. Please put it back. It's a priceless relic of our people's history."

Something flashed behind Maynard's mirrored spectacles. "You've hit the bongo dead-center, man. It's a part of history, our living history. What it represents and who it rightfully belongs to is here, in this very room."

Smiling knowingly, Maynard walked over and placed the ancient instrument in the hands of the startled Tambourine. The room grew so quiet that Toad could hear his heart beat. It was a moment frozen in time, like the tapestries on the walls.

"Damn you," Tambourine hissed, dropping the harmonica as if it was red hot. Quietly, Maynard retrieved it and placed it back in his hands. This time Tambourine held it as if it were offal. He looked pale and upset.

Maynard raised his arms as shards of sunlight reflected from his glasses. "Some of you can dig what I'm doing here. This harp is the same one that Bob Dylan himself laid on me back in the old days. Today, at last, it goes to its rightful owner. This is Tambourine Dill, born of the house of Dylan. He's the one you've been waiting for—the Freedom Rider. With the magick contained in the *Necronomicon*, and the music of this man, victory will be ours."

For a long moment nobody said anything. In fact, Mizjoan seemed to be sinking ever further into her despondent mood. Finally, Kentstate spoke. "Oh, come on!" she said. "Tambourine is a fine musician, but the Freedom Rider? Guitars and magick books, wielded by musicians and scholars, aren't going to win this war. We still need warriors and weapons."

Maynard shrugged. "You'll soon see the truth in what I'm saying."

Toad watched the proceedings with a growing sense of unreality. The distance between Tambourine and himself became an expanse. The musician's face was a pallid oval in the sunlit room; his eyes were misty and vacant. He seemed frightened, as he clutched the battered harmonica tightly in his hands. Toad felt a pang of sympathy for his friend. Tam was a good man and they'd been through a lot together, but it was hard to believe that the scruffy, leather-jacketed wanderer could be the Freedom Rider of legend.

Kentstate was still standing and staring at Maynard. Her hands were on her hips and she tapped one booted foot impatiently. Suddenly she pointed at the musician as if she were thrusting a sword. "This is absurd," she said. "He can't be the Freedom Rider. Where's his horse? Where's his sword? He doesn't look like a great hero."

"Like, 'Freedom Rider' is just a title, you dig?" Maynard replied. "He doesn't need a horse when he rides the winds of freedom. His music will prove stronger than any sword."

"He's no warrior."

"Neither was Frankie Lee, neither was Old Bob. Yet, warriors will follow him."

A murmur rippled across the room. All eyes were fixed on Tambourine. He could not meet their stares and stuffed his hands deep into the pockets of his frayed leather jacket. In truth, he looked like a very unlikely savior.

"You all doubt my words," Maynard said. "That's cool. But when the time comes you'll know the truth."

"The truth as you see it, Beatnik," Mizjoan said quietly from her place on the floor.

"Hey, chick, the truth shall set you free."

The Radiclib leader scrambled to her feet, glowering. "Chick! Nobody calls me 'chick'."

Wheatstraw stepped between them, taking them both gently by the arms. "Peace, Sister Mizjoan," he soothed. "Please remember that this is The Beatnik, who was old when our people were young. He's used to different ways."

Mizjoan shook him off. "It's great to talk of folk tales and magick books; our comrades died from guns and steel. If this book is to be our weapon, then we who have given the most lives toward liberty should wield it, not a Beatnik and a Digger."

"Sister, we are here to explore the options."

"Then, it seems to me that if anyone deserves the right to hold the book, it should be Josiah Toad. After all, he found it."

The idea took Toad by surprise, for two reasons: one, he had never even thought of it, and two, it came from Mizjoan. Her proposal stirred passionate feelings within him.

"It's true, Toad has done us all a great service," Maynard stated grandiloquently, "and I'm sure history will honor him. But there's a play being written here and we'll all have our parts in it, like those roles or not." Stroking his small goatee dramatically, he walked around the room. "My role is like, clear. I am the one who tuned everybody on to this *Necronomicon* gig. I sent Tambourine to locate the book. If The All saw fit to have Brother Toad and Brother Mungweasle share in the same scene, then so be it. But the fact remains that without me, no one would have even known about the book. It was at my request that this search began. Tambourine's journey was part of his karma, and it helped mold him for his new role. Now, the book and the Freedom Rider are both here."

Toad glanced at Mizjoan, then back to Tambourine. The Musician seemed a reluctant participant. He looked nothing like the grim icons Toad had seen of the original Dylan; he was more like a man caught in the pincers of fate. Dimly, Toad felt those same pincers tightening about himself as well. He thought of the remarks Skulk had made earlier in the day about an "initiation"—an initiation into what? The Clear Light Society? Had anybody ever thought to ask him if he even wanted to join?

Suddenly Maynard stopped his pacing and snapped his fingers loudly. A side door opened, and Strutter Lurchkin entered, cradling a battered guitar in his arms. The young Digger walked straight and tall, carrying the instrument as if it were beyond value. For the first time since Maynard had exposed him, Tambourine smiled.

Maynard took the guitar from Strutter, offering it to Tambourine. "Maybe these cats will dig the truth if you play."

"They've heard me before. They know…"

"They think they do, man," the Beatnik said. His demeanor had changed; it was almost fatherly. "You'll play differently this time, I guarantee."

Tambourine took the guitar, holding it gently. A wire harmonica holder had been affixed to it. Carefully, he fitted the rusty old harp into it and blew a few experimental notes. Satisfied with the sound, he took a thin wooden pick from his pocket and began to tune his guitar.

"Listen, and dig it," Maynard said. "Like, there's no escape from the

Dark Man—not even here. If he is Tommy Two, like I'm certain he is, he'll hate Oldhips most of all. Given time, he'll find a way into Hillcommune. The only thing that will lay him low permanently is the Freedom Rider's music. Listen to him, then tell me what you're going to do."

As Maynard's voice trailed off, Tambourine's playing took over. Notes strung themselves together easily, forming the refrains of beloved old songs. The audience leaned forward, mesmerized as Tambourine's fingers breezed over the strings. The musician's breath howled and wheezed into the harmonica, bringing the old instrument to life. His back straightened and a wild look came into his eyes, the look of a man raging at the inequities of life.

Toad felt a tingling sensation at the base of his spine. He'd heard Tam play before, but nothing like this. The musician's normal style was low key, mellow, devoid of any heavy emotion, save joy. What Toad was hearing now was angry—raw, primal rage that grabbed the listener by the throat. Though the songs were familiar, Toad felt as if he were hearing them for the first time. As Tambourine wailed, his fingers chopping out the chords, the tingling sensation spread, fighting its way toward Toad's chest and head. The pipesmith felt his muscles twitch involuntarily. The hairs on his arms and the base of his neck stiffened. The air in the room grew thick and charged, like a thunderstorm about to break.

Tearing his eyes from the figure playing his guitar beneath the Woodstock tapestry, Toad glanced about at the others in the room, trying to read their reactions. In their eyes he caught the unnerving glint of rapture. As his emotions took over, the tingling in Toad's body grew into a fire that raged along his nerve fibers, spreading its message faster than logic could drive it back ... He's the One ... He's the Freedom Rider. Hot tears welled up in the pipesmith's eyes. When he looked at Mizjoan, he saw that she was fighting back tears too. He wanted to cross the room and embrace her, but the music's magick spell held him in check.

After Tambourine stopped playing the music hung in the air, fading slowly like a chime in a quiet room. Stunned by what they'd witnessed, no one spoke. Nor did they have to; their faces told the story, a silent patchwork of varying emotions. Though he was fighting to conceal his feelings, Tambourine's face glowed like that of a man who, searching in darkness for far too long, finally discovers the light. Wheatstraw and the other Oldhips were enraptured. They too had found the same glow. Skulk looked both humbled and proud. Ernie's face struggled to hold back emotion. The Radiclibs, for all their studied stoicism, were affected too. Mizjoan surreptitiously dabbed away a tear as a look of quiet resignation stole across her features. Kentstate, obviously moved, also looked oddly disappointed.

At last Maynard stood and surveyed the group. "Like, I think the Tambourine Man has said it all. I intend to continue with my plans, unless anyone has any objections."

Kentstate made a motion as if to speak, but Mizjoan laid a hand on her arm and whispered something in her ear. She relaxed and sat back.

Wheatstraw stood. "We Oldhips are all too aware of the terrible evil outside our valley." He turned toward Tambourine. "But we also see the magick in this room. As I said before, our beliefs do not allow us to be a party to violence. Nor, would we attempt to control the book that you now possess. We can offer you assistance, comfort, and the natural protection of our valley. But, there is one condition we request. Since we all agree that this Black Book contains powers that we do not understand, and in deference to Brother Moonshadow, who has warned us against it, I request that one of our tribe be included in whatever group you choose to use the book. To help insure the safety of Hillcommune, I would like that person to be Foreseein' Franklin."

"I'm cool with that," Maynard said. "Franklin is a genuine scholar, and he's got the crazy All gig going for him too."

Later, after the meeting had broken up, Toad walked back to his quarters, alone with his churning thoughts. He paid little attention to people he passed as he tried to sort out his confused emotions. Faces flashed behind his eyelids: Mizjoan, Ernie, but most of all Tambourine. Toad marveled at how quickly a simple musician had been transformed into a legend.

The music had opened up too much inside of him—intense feelings of both hope and doubt. Aided by a pipeful of weed and the night air, he allowed the feeling part of himself to run free, something he rarely did these days. Emotions rose up, welling to the surface. He was aflame with desire for Mizjoan. At the same time he felt a growing distrust of Ernie and Skulk. Ernie was a lovable character, but the Clear Light Society ruled his life. It appeared that the Society had plans for Toad. Toad was sure that Ernie would play his part to bring him into the fold.

The pipesmith trudged along the nearly deserted wharf. Lanterns hanging from poles cast oblongs of light across his path. As he passed the mouth of an alley not far from his quarters he heard the low excited voices of a man and woman talking. Something in the voices seemed familiar; Toad slipped into the shadows behind a pair of rain barrels. Crouching low, he peered out at the pair. They were half in shadow, but he could see that they were both tall. The taller of the two wore a battered top hat. The other figure, the woman, toyed with her hair as she spoke. Even in the feeble light thrown by a porch lantern halfway down the alley, Toad could see that it was a vibrant auburn.

Suddenly, Ernie wrapped his arms around Mizjoan and she embraced him back, reaching to his ear to whisper something. Toad almost jumped out of the shadows; his stomach felt like it was packed with ice. I've been betrayed, he thought. First, Ernie conspired with the Clear Light Society to Dylan-only-knows-what end and now he's moving in on Mizjoan. Toad crept closer, almost crawling to get within earshot. The voices were too muffled for him to make out much that was said. After a few minutes the pair unlocked from their embrace, and with a few more murmured words, parted company. Mizjoan walked quickly down the alley and was soon lost in the darkness. Ernie stood by himself for a moment, then turned on his heel, walking past Toad's hiding place. A black cloud engulfed the pipesmith; he clenched his fists.

"It's clear to me now, Ernie Mungweasle!" he bellowed, jumping out from behind the rain barrels. "'Weasel' being the operative phrase. I should have known not to trust you when I caught you stealing *Cruickshank's*."

Ernie leaped into the air, spinning around and instinctively placing his back against the wall of the alley. His hands were up; he was ready to defend himself. His hat slid down on his forehead.

"Toad! What are you doing here?"

"Finding the truth. "

Ernie put down his hands. "The truth?! I'm afraid I don't know what you're talking about."

"You know, you snake. I can't believe you're putting the moves on Mizjoan. You know how I feel about her."

"If you still refer to her as 'Mizjoan', I guess not," Ernie answered. "I was just comforting her; she's been through a lot. But understand this: Joannie decides who she wants and when. You've already seen that it isn't me."

Toad shook his head. Blackness was swimming in front of his eyes.

"Oh, hell. It's bad enough that you're trying to trick me into the Clear Light Society. Do you have to lie about this too?"

"Have you gone mad? What are you gibbering about?"

"I'm not mad, I've just finally realized what's going on."

Ernie moved to the center of the alley, straightening his hat. "Nothing is going on, Toad."

"Well, I'm not becoming a Digger to please you or anybody else," Toad scowled, "and if you have one ounce of decency you'll leave Mizjoan—Joannie—alone."

"You're not making sense." Ernie's tone was soothing, even patronizing. "If you want Mizjoan that bad, you're certainly free to try. But, why complicate your life?"

"My life got complicated the day you talked me into going to Covenstead with you. The only way I can simplify it is to stay away from you and your Digger buddies."

Turning his back on the herbalist, Toad strode out of the alley and down the lonely, lantern-lit wharf.

Chapter Thirty-five

The night air was alive with the scent of growing things. As Toad strolled along the moonlit path above the village, he paused from time to time to savor the calming effect of the sweet fragrance. Since moving out of the cabin he shared with Ernie, Toad's long solitary walks had become nightly meditations. Drawing on his pipe, he buttoned up his hemp-cloth jacket against the slight night chill and looked back at the town in the distance. A few lights burned along the streets and in houses, but mostly Hillcommune was a dark jumble in the pale moonlight. The village, and everyone in it, seemed far away—inconsequential.

Frogs thrummed and sang in the distant river marshes. In the high grass beyond the apple orchard night insects took up the counterpoint, overlaying the night with sound. Toad tapped out the cherry wood pipe he was carrying and slipped it into his pocket. The pipe, a gift from his new roommates, Flo and Eddie, was plain and lightweight. After the first of these long nocturnal jaunts, Toad had left his heavy iron skull pipe at the brothers' place and relied on the cherry wood to accompany him on his wanderings.

Each night Toad took a different path, roaming the far fields, often until dawn, his pipe and his thoughts his only companions. Tonight, drawn by the sweet smell of apple blossoms, the orchards to the north of Hillcommune were his destination. Climbing a small knoll that led to the nearest orchard, he remembered one of the many facts about Hillcommune that Flo and Eddie had inundated him with: apple trees here produce two crops a year.

Reaching the top of the knoll, Toad settled himself between the roots of one of the gnarly trees and sat looking out over the pond at the foot of the orchard. The moon hung between the peaks of Mount Lennon and Mount Leary, like a pearl set in the sky. The pond mirrored its milky beauty, occasionally distorting it when a breeze passed, rippling the waters.

Much had happened in Hillcommune in the days since the meeting. And since he now slept days and roamed the Oldhip land at night, avoiding involvement with Ernie and his Digger friends, Toad relied on Flo and Eddie to keep him informed of current events. The pipesmith suddenly missed the brothers, and took out his pipe again. As he packed it, he played recent developments over in his mind, reflecting on the changing climate of Hillcommune—not just the chill air at night, or the light snows in the high pastures, but the way people were changing, too.

The night after the meeting, Tambourine had played another concert for all the people of Hillcommune. Flo and Eddie had come back from it all bright-eyed and excited. "He's the One," they said. "He's the Freedom Rider."

Though Wheatstraw had agreed to Maynard's plan at the meeting just a few days ago, Flo and Eddie reported that rumors abounded in Hillcommune that experiments were already being conducted atop Mount Lennon. The mountain was chosen for its karmic significance and inaccessibility. Even though every Oldhip made at least one pilgrimage to its lofty summit in their lifetime, the pathway up to it was kept secret. Blindfolded, the pilgrims were led there only by those said to be touched by The All: the Gatekeeper, the custodian of the *Book of Love* and the Tribechief.

Toad fiddled with his tinderbox, stoking up the cherrywood until it glowed like a red eye in the darkness. He inhaled deeply, taking in equal parts of weedsmoke and night air, and leaned back to watch the setting moon make its slow descent between the mountains. He knew from former night jaunts that it would become darker, almost rust colored, as it slid over the horizon. It pleased him to think that only he and the night creatures shared its eerie glow.

The moon dropped comfortably lower between the twin mounds of Lennon and Leary, darkening to a deep orange as it went. Bright stars flared up around it. One that shone with an odd, pale blue light seemed to dance on the summit of Mount Lennon itself. Toad smiled. It reminded him of the stars that he'd wished upon when he was a child. As he gazed at the little star, wondering what to wish for, he noticed shadows creeping across the moon. The shadows seemed to form faces. At first he thought he recognized Ernie, and then Maynard. But as the blue star flared and dimmed, it was her face that he saw on the dying moon.

The thought irritated him. "Mungweasle!" he grumbled to himself. "He got me into this mess and if Mizjoan wants him, then to hell with them both."

As if in reply to Toad's outburst, a sliver of dark cloud bisected the face of the moon, spreading like a knife slash. The temperature seemed to drop a few degrees, making it necessary for Toad to turn up his coat collar. As he watched the cloud thicken across the moon, Toad noticed the blue star flare up again and then go out.

Toad huddled deeper into his coat, feeling agitated and confused. Some of the elder Oldhips maintained that the weather had been growing progressively worse since Maynard and his party had arrived. A few, encouraged by Moonshadow, went even further, saying that the Clear Light Society and the *Necronomicon* were to blame. Toad was ambivalent about the Society's doings as long as they didn't try to involve him any more than they already had.

According to Flo and Eddie, not everyone agreed with Toad. Though Tambourine was held in high esteem in Hillcommune, some of his companions were not. If it weren't for Wheatstraw and Franklin, many more of the Oldhips would be siding against Maynard and the Diggers. Clearly something was in the wind, something that could strain the closely woven fabric of Oldhip society. Toad tried to shrug off these thoughts but they persisted, adding to his restlessness. With a sigh, he pushed himself to his feet and walked down the knoll toward the pond.

Walton Pond was several hundred feet across and man-made, as evidenced by the low earthen dam at its southern end. Walking carefully past the clumps of tangled weeds that marked the swampy areas, Toad stopped at the edge of the pond. Perhaps all of his troubles weren't Ernie's and the Diggers' fault; much of it was just fate. It was he who dreamed of the Dark Man while others only knew of his presence secondhand. Although Toad's dreams had rarely been invaded by the Evil One since he'd been in Hillcommune, the Dark Man was still out there, beyond the mountains, watching and waiting.

With the cloud now gone from the moon, fish jumped in the moonlight, making silver splashes that broke the surface of the pond into a delicate web of ripples. In spite of the chill, it seemed to Toad a perfect night. The frogs and night insects chirruped their chorus, and fireflies winked on and off among the trees, adding their magick to the scene. As he walked along the bank of the pond toward the dam, Toad pondered the Oldhip belief that everything in nature was connected—part of a great eternal All, without end or beginning. In Hillcommune some now believed that The All moved among them in the guise of a young man with a guitar.

Toad had never been one to take religion of any sort very seriously, but he'd always been fascinated by the legends surrounding Dylan and some of the other musicians of old. Part of him found it hard to accept that Tambourine was really Old Bob's flesh reborn, but on the night of the meeting at Wheatstraw's he'd been astounded by the musician's performance. He shook his head. It really didn't matter what he thought;

plenty of others were willing to believe, and that belief was already changing his world. Whether Tambourine truly was the Freedom Rider or just a pawn of Maynard and the Diggers was of no consequence; the end result would be the same.

A movement in the moonlight caught Toad's eye. A cloaked shape emerged from the brush and began walking along the bank of the pond away from him. Suddenly the figure stopped and took a seat on the trunk of a fallen tree by the water's edge. Curious as to the stranger's identity, Toad crept closer, keeping to the shadows among the bushes. The figure reached up and lowered the hood of its garment, releasing a spill of long, thick hair. Something in the gesture seemed very familiar. As he stealthily approached, Toad was surprised to hear the soft sounds of a woman crying. He was almost up to her when the woman turned her head and he saw the patch covering one eye. His first impulse was to slip back into the shadows and disappear, but Mizjoan's obvious sorrow moved him and he took a step closer, snapping a twig under his boot heel.

Mizjoan spun around. "Who's there?" she demanded.

"It's just me—Toad."

At first she didn't seem to comprehend. "Toad?"

"Yeah. Look, maybe I better go."

"No. Please stay. Sit with me. We haven't talked in a long time; I could use the company."

Toad hesitated. "You sure?"

"Yes. I need someone to talk to—someone who doesn't wait on my every word, expecting me to have a solution for every problem. I'm afraid that I'm all out of answers."

"I'll stay with you for a few minutes, but I can't promise that I'll be any help."

"A minute or an hour, I'll be grateful for the company, and that will be help enough." She smiled wanly and patted the log beside her. "Please. Sit."

Toad nodded. He eased nonchalantly onto the log beside her, but when he tried to speak, his throat constricted. For several long seconds all he could do was toy nervously with the lapels of his jacket. He hadn't been this close to Mizjoan since Camp Hoffman. The urge to touch her was unbearable, but he remembered what had happened the last time. Mizjoan seemed to sense his turmoil, for she laid her hand gently on his.

"So, how are you doing?" the pipesmith asked lamely.

"Not so well, as you probably can guess."

"I don't know why I asked such a stupid question. I'm sorry. The day you came in to Hillcommune—I wanted to say something then, but I couldn't find the words. I still can't."

Shrugging, Mizjoan dabbed at her eye with the hem of her cloak. "I should be the one who's sorry. I'm not used to people seeing me like this."

"We don't have to talk," Toad said, brushing imaginary dust from the knees of his jeans.

"I want to." Mizjoan leaned close. "We should have talked before, but…"

"I thought…" he started, but could not find the right words.

"The day I arrived here," Mizjoan continued, "I saw you, and I was glad to see that you were alive. But my people had just taken many casualties at Ripoff Pass. I thought we could keep attacking the enemy in small raids, much like a dog nipping at a wagon wheel. I forgot that sometimes the dog gets crushed under the wheel."

"I know. I heard about Rudy. I'm sorry, Joan; I liked him."

A tear slid down Mizjoan's cheek. In spite of her drawn appearance, Toad thought that he'd never seen her look so lovely, or so vulnerable. He squeezed her hand. Gently, she squeezed back.

"It was all my fault," she said. "Kentstate and Rudy have always been like family to me, and I failed them. It happened because of a stupid decision … my decision."

"Don't be so hard on yourself. You couldn't have foreseen what would happen."

She shook her head. "I should have seen that I was pushing my luck. I took chances with my people's lives. Rudy and others paid the price."

Mizjoan began to cry again, shaking as tears coursed down her cheek. Toad slid his arm around her shoulders and held her until the sobbing subsided.

Perhaps it was the full moon and the sweet night air; perhaps it was the beautiful, troubled woman beside him. Whatever it was, Toad felt strong and protective.

Time passed. Fireflies flickered over the still pond. Except for some crickets chirping in the high grass, the night had gone quiet. The entire world seemed to be holding its breath.

"I have a confession, Toad," Mizjoan whispered, edging out the silence. "I'm—lost. It seems like every decision I make is the wrong one. I don't know if I can lead my people any more. I can't even trust my own judgment. Why, I even think I'm seeing things. On the way up here I thought I saw a strange light in the sky. It was shaped like a giant frisbee. It hovered over the eastern mountains for a few seconds and then flew away at great speed. I must be losing my mind; such things don't exist."

"Maybe it was a big firefly, or swamp gas—who knows? Whatever it was it doesn't matter. What matters is that you don't drive yourself crazy. I know it's gone badly for your people, but it's not your fault. You need time to rest and, Dylan knows, there's no better place for it than Hillcommune."

"Hillcommune's magick may not be enough, Toad."

"Once the power of the book is harnessed and the restorative powers of this valley have done their work, you'll be back leading your troops to victory." But seeing Mizjoan in her present state, however, Toad was not convinced of the truth of his words.

"I'm not sure that I want to. I'm tired—tired of being responsible for everyone and everything. I'd like to be a normal woman with someone to take care of me for a change."

"That's not you. You're too strong a person for that kind of life."

"I may have been once, but not any more. I'd always thought of myself as a warrior, a leader of warriors—the oak that stands against the storm. Back in Ripoff Pass that oak snapped. You may not realize it, Toad, but you have real strength."

"Me?" Toad blushed. "No, I'm just a simple pipesmith."

"You are like the reeds at the edge of the pond. Storms can blow you about and push you down, but you stand back up after the storm passes."

Suddenly, she leaned forward and kissed him. He backed away, as if burned. His mind was going in a dozen directions at once. He wanted her more than ever, but he wasn't sure that he wanted it to happen this way.

"What's wrong?" Mizjoan asked, releasing her embrace.

"I'm not sure." Toad's heart was racing like a trip hammer. "It's just … I'm me, and you … you're…"

"A woman. A human being, with feelings just like yours."

"But, what about Ernie?"

"What about him?"

"I saw you two together—in the alley."

"The alley?" Mizjoan thought, then smiled. "Oh, yeah, that night. That was just one old friend trying to comfort another."

Toad did not respond immediately but mulled it over for a minute. "And tonight?" he asked.

"Tonight?" Mizjoan spoke, appearing for the first time soft and vulnerable, with a slight smile creasing her lips. "Tonight, I believe I need a different kind of comfort, with someone who doesn't view me as a leader of a great nation—someone who sees me as a woman, flesh and blood."

Resistance was futile; Toad helped Mizjoan to her feet and together they strolled toward the orchard. He stole a backward glance. The blue star on top of Mount Lennon was shining again, and it seemed to be winking at him.

On the other side of the dam, a hundred yards or so around the pond from where Toad and Mizjoan had been sitting, Flo and Eddie were crouched close to a very small campfire hidden by reeds near the water's edge. A small grove of pear trees just behind them formed a protective canopy. It was the brothers' favorite spot. Eddie tended to the fire while Flo spread out a cloth on the grass and laid out a series of small containers from his pouch. Carefully extracting their contents, he weighed each in his hand, ceremoniously placing them apart from each other on the cloth in front of him: a pile of leaves here, some dried mushrooms there and, near the edge, a sticky ball of black hash. Lastly, he produced a small wooden mortar and pestle, which he set down carefully in the center of the other objects. Scratching his chin nervously, he studied the arrangement with an artist's practiced eye.

"Ahh," he murmured. "Where to begin? Where to begin?"

"Hey!" Eddie called from his place by the fire. "You gonna take all night to do this?"

"Patience, brother mine. We can smoke no bowl before its time. This is Flo's Purple Haze, a select blend of herbs and condiments. Candy for the brain."

Flo chuckled as he placed a pinch of dried mushrooms, aged ergot, and several varieties of weed in the mortar, including a bud of Thirdworld White. Paring off several slivers of hash with his penknife and dusting in a touch of datura for body, he stirred the mixture together with his bony forefinger. When that was done, he began to pulverize the mixture with his pestle.

After several minutes, Flo finished grinding and peered into the mortar, examining its contents closely by the firelight. Satisfied that the concoction was properly mixed, he picked up his antique Wheelen clay from the cloth and began to pack the bowl. "Prepare to get high, Brother Edward," he said. "Higher than you've ever gotten before."

Eddie's eyes shone. He scuttled over closer to Flo. "We'll see about that, brother mine. Boy, I'll bet Brother Toad will be disappointed that we didn't let him in on this one."

"Believe me, Eddie, I thought long and hard about inviting him along."

"Why isn't he here then?"

"Well—uh—it's his condition. I don't wanna imperil the man's health."

"Aww, he's plenty healthy."

Flo grinned. "For a lowlander, maybe. This stuff could completely fry the man's brain. I wouldn't want to subject Brother Toad to that kind of risk."

"That's just a polite way to say that you just want to bogart the first batch, huh?"

Flo tamped the bowl tighter and reached for a splint from the fire. "Not exactly, Eddie. Toad's carrying something around in his head that he don't wanna talk about. In that condition, it's better that he don't smoke any of this Purple Haze. Brother, we have his best interests at heart."

Flo touched the burning splint to his pipe. He took a hit and held the smoke until his eyes began to water. Eddie's eyes glistened as he watched his brother exhale.

"Get off yore ass, there's a pipe to pass," Flo jibed.

The redhead chuckled as he placed the pipe to his lips. He liked it when Flo made up silly poems. For years, rhyming banter had been their signal that the weed they were sharing was exceptional. "Ain't no joke, this is righteous smoke," he replied.

A second later, Eddie inhaled like the next breath would be his last. It was another two minutes before he exhaled, coughing until it seemed he'd turn his lungs inside out.

Flo patted Eddie on his back until the coughing fit passed. "Brother mine," he said. "Flo's Purple Haze puts you in a daze."

Eddie leaned back against the nearest pear tree, gazed out at the fireflies over the pond, and listened to the cries of the night birds. To his left he could see the moon nestled in between the two mountains, and over Mount Lennon a small blue star winked on. At least, he thought he saw it wink on; in his condition it was hard to tell.

"Outasite smoke," he commented.

"And worth another toke," Flo agreed.

Moonshadow strode quickly through the high grass rimming the western edge of the pond, his staff tapping on the soft ground. From time to time he sniffed the air, his nostrils quivering as he filtered through the myriad night smells for the one he was seeking. Suddenly it came to him: a sweet flash of wildflowers signaling that he was close to his private little garden, nestled at the end of a small cove. Moving onto the dirt path, he headed unerringly toward the scent.

When his nose told him that he was in the middle of his garden at last, the Seer lay down his staff and seated himself among the flowers. He sat there for a long time without moving, listening to the frogs and the gentle flow of the water among the reeds. Here, at last, he could be at peace as the world around him went mad.

There was tranquility in the garden, a sense of well-being and order that Moonshadow could no longer find in town. The outlanders with their strange ways, their weapons, and their Black Book had changed all that. At times he cursed himself for letting any of them pass the gates, but he couldn't have refused them. In this crazy world, Hillcommune was their last refuge.

The Seer plucked a lily from the bank and buried his face in it. Its sweet fragrance soothed him, helping relieve the tensions of the last week. Still, it wasn't quite enough. Even here, in his private garden on the banks of Walton Pond, he could feel the disruption in The All. The delicate webbing of life force that held all things together was straining and bucking as if attacked by a dark, invisible hand. The center of this disruption seemed to come from the mountains in the west, where Maynard, Skulk, and Franklin had gone to work with the *Necronomicon*. Something sinister was stirring in those hills, but he seemed to be the only one who sensed it.

The book was the wellspring. Its corrupting force lay behind much that was going wrong in Hillcommune: the changes in the weather, the attitudes of his fellow Oldhips, and Franklin's growing flirtation with the occult. Moonshadow had felt the *Necronomicon*'s foulness from the first moment he'd been exposed to it; he knew it was a dark thing from another age, with great potential for destruction. Using it to combat the enemy would be like trying to douse a fire with seed oil. And who could say who might be consumed in the ensuing conflagration?

Placing the lily on the ground beside him, the Seer turned his face to the west. Even as he sat by the still, peaceful waters, disruptive forces were building there. They were like a hot breath upon his skin. The time for words was over, he thought, and the time for action near. Gone were the days when he could be content to let the rivers run and never run against them. The thought distressed him, because he really had no idea what form this action should take. Like all Oldhips, he was not a violent man. Shaking his head wearily, Moonshadow reached into the pocket of his fringed leather jacket and extracted a granola cake, which he slowly began to eat.

Suddenly, Moonshadow stopped chewing. He sensed something moving toward him—a mass of raw energy rolling down from the mountains at ferocious speed. Dropping the cake, he hobbled to his feet, clutching his staff. Before he had gone two steps it struck, slamming him to the ground. The force enveloped him, tearing at his body with a cold fire. The Seer tried to cry out as it rolled over him, but all he could manage was an agonized wheeze that sent half-eaten globs of granola spewing out of his mouth. The air sizzled around him and he felt as if his body was being pierced with a million frozen needles.

Flo had just finished a second bowl when he caught sight of the flashes of blue light rolling down the slopes of Mount Lennon. "Wow! Look at that!" he gasped.

Beside him, Eddie sat upright, rubbing his eyes. "Outtasight light show, Flo. Is this smoke doing that?"

"Must be, brother mine. Hell, this shit's better than I thought it'd be."

323

PIPEDREAMS

As the brothers watched, one of the blue bolts rolled across the fields, heading toward the pond. It struck about two hundred feet from where the brothers sat, sending up a geyser of purple sparks as it exploded on the western shore. The sparks whirled together, taking on the form of a man, then winked out, leaving behind the faint odor of crushed violets.

"Eddie, old son," Flo drawled, "I do believe we've outdone ourselves with this batch. Wait'll we spring this shit on the masses. They'll flip."

"I don't know, Flo. This stuff's intense. The world might not be as ready for it as we are."

"Hell, we'll be heroes, Eddie. When Purple Haze hits the market, our fame will be assured."

"Don't let it go to your head," Eddie laughed. "Still, I ain't never seen anything like those blue flashes before. They're kind of scary."

"I'm sure we'll have to tame her down a bit for the public, little brother. But, there's nothing to fear here, just a few hallucinations."

"Even that one headed this way?"

Flo got to his feet, weaving unsteadily, as a ball of the blue fire skipped across the field toward him, throwing off sparks in its wake. The air was thick with the smells of violets and ozone. "S-sure," he said. "It's nothing to worry about; it's just a psychotropic manifestation brought on by blending 'shrooms, datura root, and ergot. The effect will—oh, shit!"

The ball crashed between the two brothers, scattering their small fire. The blue orb exploded silently in a brilliant flash of light. Flo was knocked off his feet by the concussion. He rolled around on the ground; his skin felt like it was being attacked by thousands of stinging insects. When the sensation passed and he finally managed to crawl back to his feet, he could hear Eddie calling his name.

"I'm okay," Flo wheezed as he braced himself against the nearest tree.

"Flo! Flo! Over here," Eddie called out.

The moon was mostly down over the horizon and dawn was growing in the east. Flo shook his head; his vision cleared slowly. The explosion had left a constellation of spots swimming in front of his eyes. Just part of the hallucination, he supposed. Staggering toward the sound of his brother's voice, Flo almost fell into the pond. His legs, somehow his entire body, suddenly felt wrong. As the spots cleared, he could make out Eddie in silhouette, apparently standing on one leg in the water.

"What's the matter?" Eddie asked, in a voice that was more like a harsh croak. "Come closer, Flo. I can't see you too well."

Flo shook his head again. The last of the spots were gone and he could see clearly, but now he wasn't sure he wanted to. The voice was Eddie's all right, but the figure standing in the pond was that of a six-foot tall whooping crane with a mop-like tuft of red feathers crowning its head. As

324

it stood regarding Flo it shifted a soggy weedstalk back and forth in its bill. In spite of himself, Flo burst into hysterical giggling. As he laughed the absurd crane appeared to laugh with him

"Dylan's Bones, Eddie," Flo cackled, fighting to regain composure. "You ought to see yourself; you look like some kind of screwed up bird."

The Eddie-crane nodded thoughtfully, still chewing on its weedstalk. "You don't look so great yourself," it replied. "I can't imagine anything stupider looking than an overgrown muskrat with tattoos and a pencil-line mustache."

Flo made his way to the edge of the water, but didn't dare to check out his reflection. Instead, he just gazed up at the blue star twinkling on the summit of Mount Lennon. "Next time," he said, moving closer to his brother, "I think I won't use quite so much datura."

With dawn ready to rise over the eastern mountains, Toad smiled dreamily as he helped Mizjoan to the edge of the pond. He cleared a place on a fallen log for her to sit, then took a seat next to her. His hand trembled when it accidentally brushed against her leg. He wanted to say something, but was afraid to, worried that it would break the spell. The moment had come on with the sudden fury of a summer thunderstorm and had spent itself as violently. Neither said a word as they sat side by side, gazing up at Mount Lennon.

Sighing happily, Toad groped in his pocket for his pipe and tinderbox. As he lit and drew on his pipe, he watched Mizjoan out of the corner of his eye. Even now, with her tousled hair and the color high in her face, she was beautiful. He leaned back, resting his shoulders against the trunk of a half-grown apple tree, and passed her the pipe. She took it, her fingers brushing gently against his, but her gaze remained fixed on the mountain.

Mizjoan passed the pipe back and their eyes met. Toad realized that he was now deeply in love with this strange, proud woman. It saddened him to think that she probably didn't feel the same about him. When she passed the pipe back to him he smiled at her hopefully. She smiled back.

"What are you grinning about?" she asked.

"Just feeling good, I guess," Toad replied, slipping his arm around her. She lay her head on his chest and he buried his face in her hair, savoring its rich, clean smell. He ached to tell her how much he loved her, but he fought the temptation. He didn't know a lot about women, but he knew better than to utter *those* words too soon.

Mizjoan stiffened as Toad began nuzzling her ear. Gently, she pushed him away.

"What's wrong?" he asked.

"Look. Something's happening on the mountain."

He glanced to where she was pointing. Blue lights were flashing at the top of Mount Lennon again, but with more energy this time. As he watched, two lights rolled rapidly down the mountainside, gaining momentum as they went. One skimmed over the fields until it struck the opposite side of the pond in a tremendous flash. The air seemed to crackle as the blue light exploded soundlessly. The second light continued on and exploded just on the other side of the dam. Wriggling free of the pipesmith's grasp, Mizjoan got to her feet. "That first flash looked like it hit someone," she yelled, starting to run. Toad ran after her.

Mizjoan ran with long, sure strides. Blundering through the reeds at the pond's edge, Toad found it hard to keep up with her. As he ran he noticed that the frogs and crickets had ceased their night songs, and the air tingled with a strange energy that stiffened the hairs on the back of his neck.

Mizjoan was already across the dam ahead of him, moving quickly. As Toad crossed the dam he called out to her, but she continued on. In his haste, he stumbled on an exposed root and fell face down in the mud, stunned. As he pushed himself to his hands and knees, he glanced toward the pond. For a brief confused second he thought he saw a huge red-tufted crane and a large, mustached muskrat regarding him from the shadows of the reeds. He closed his eyes, rubbing them with his hand. Before he could look again, Mizjoan had returned to his side, helping him to his feet.

"Hurry up—I think there's someone in trouble in the little garden over there."

Toad wanted to tell her what he'd seen, but Mizjoan grabbed him by the arm and pulled him along behind her, causing him to stumble several times before they reached the garden. The area still glowed with a faint bluish light and the smell of crushed violets hung heavily in the air. A body lay sprawled among the flowers at the center of the garden, face down, clutching a staff in one hand. The fringed leathers and the staff could only belong to one person.

"Moonshadow!" Mizjoan gasped.

Toad knelt by the unconscious Seer and felt his face and wrists. "He's still alive."

The last of the bluish light evaporated with the dawn. Moonshadow moaned and shuddered slightly. His face was beaded with clammy sweat and his breath came in shallow gasps. Quickly, Mizjoan removed her cloak and handed it to Toad, who placed it over the struggling Oldhip. The Seer moaned again and tried to speak.

"Be still," Toad said gently. "Try to stay calm."

Moonshadow's breath rattled in his throat. His chest rose and fell feebly, and he seemed on the verge of shock. "Help me," he rasped. "My head feels strange. There are lights.... forms.... "

"Sssh. Everything's gonna be cool."

Moonshadow shook uncontrollably. His eyes opened for a moment, radiating a strange light, but closed again as he slumped back, unconscious.

"I'll stay with him while you go for help," Mizjoan said.

Toad nodded and hurried toward town while Mizjoan tended the fallen Seer.

Chapter Thirty-Six

Flashes of sunlight sparkled off the clear water of the Peace. On the bow of a bulky, slow moving barge, Toad lay sprawled across a large heap of bright orange pumpkins, as the houses of Hillcommune slowly slipped past. For a tranquil man this would have been the ideal form of transportation, but Toad was far from calm. He was reviewing the events of the previous night.

His perfect moment with Mizjoan was overshadowed by what followed. Of those nearly catastrophic events, he now recalled only a series of blurred images. Most distinctly, he remembered the agonizing run into Hillcommune. Sprinting through the dawn-splashed fields, his heart hammering in his chest, he'd reached Wheatstraw's door just as the sun was climbing over the mountains. A frantic dash to the town's Healery followed, where they rousted Doc Aloevera and a pair of stretcher-bearers.

By the time Moonshadow was brought to the Healery, it was nearly nine o'clock in the morning. Exhausted, Toad had dragged his weary body back to Flo and Eddie's and collapsed on the couch; his new roommates were nowhere to be found. Strangely, as he drifted off to asleep, the image that seemed planted in his brain was that of the huge crane and muskrat he thought he'd seen by the pond. When he awoke a half hour ago, trying to piece together the jumbled fragments of a bad dream, they still had not returned, though the clock on the mantel showed that it was past one in the afternoon.

The barge stopped and its crew scrambled about to tie it up to the wharf just below Doc Aloevera's. Toad was reluctant to move. Getting slowly to his feet, he stood on the deck for a moment, regarding the rope ladder that hung down from the wharf.

"They say the Seer is feeling much better," one of the crew remarked pleasantly.

"News seems to travel fast here," Toad replied, hoping that the news was accurate.

"It does when it concerns Moonshadow, Brother Toad. Careful on that ladder now."

Toad made his way up the swaying ladder. He crossed the wharf to a low white building with a green mortar and pestle painted above its door. As he walked into the clean airy interior of the Healery he saw gray-haired old Doc Aloevera, still in the wrinkled green tunic he'd had on earlier, deep in conversation with Wheatstraw, Skulk and Ernie Mungweasle. They were gathered around the cot upon which lay a pale and silent Moonshadow. The Seer was dressed in white robes and a cloth was bound across his eyes.

Ernie's presence bothered Toad. Had the tall herbalist not looked up and given him a tight smile he might have backed out of the room and left. Instead, he returned the smile, but kept his distance. Maybe he had misinterpreted the herbalist's involvement with Mizjoan, but Ernie's apparent scheming with the Clear Light Society did little to lessen Toad's mistrust. Skulk and Wheatstraw noticed him and gestured for him to join them.

Ernie nodded at him as he approached the group. "How's Moonshadow doing?" Toad asked.

"Quite amazing, really," Aloevera announced.

"That's putting it mildly," Skulk interrupted. "This man is nothing less than a genius at holistic medicine."

The elderly healer laughed, shaking his head. "You flatter me, Theo. If I could get around like Brother Mungweasle does, then I'd consider myself a great healer. Unfortunately, not all medicinal plants grow in our valley. More than once I've had to rely on cuttings and sets that Ernie's brought from the lowlands for me. It's partly due to his efforts that we've got such a well-stocked medicine chest."

Toad glanced at Ernie, who was obviously enjoying the praise. "Is there anything I can do to help, Doc?"

"Only if you can tell me exactly what it was that hit him. I've never heard of anything like that rolling blue fire you described to me. Does any of this make any sense to you, Theo?"

The Digger chief shook his head, but Toad noticed that he avoided looking the healer in the eyes.

"Perhaps it was ball lightning," Ernie suggested. "It's rare, but I have seen it once or twice."

Aloevera shrugged. "Lightning? Out of a clear sky? No, I think it was something else."

"Like what?"

"I have no idea, but I've never seen anything quite so miraculous, or as troubling. When we brought him in I thought he was past hope, but now ... amazing ... he's not only recovering, but he's gained his sight."

"You mean he can see?" Toad asked, startled.

"Yes. When he regained consciousness he was greatly disturbed by this new sense, so I gave him a mild sedative and bandaged his eyes. He should be all right now, if you'd like to talk with him."

Toad stood beside Doc Aloevera as he leaned down and gently touched the Seer's shoulder.

"There's someone to see you," Doc said gently. "Do you feel up to having visitors?"

The pale figure on the cot stirred and tried to sit up. "I am better, medicine man. When will you take this cloth from my eyes?"

"Very soon, but you must be careful. It'll take time for them to adjust to the light. Remember how you were complaining about that earlier?"

Moonshadow reached for the bandages, but Aloevera gently brushed his hands away. "You must be patient, Moonshadow. What has happened to you is a miracle; I've never seen anything like it in my life."

"I'll go you one better, medicine man—I've never seen *anything* in my life. Who's this I hear beside you?"

"Brother Toad. He found you last night."

"Of course. I remember a woman as well. And these others?"

"Old friends, Seer: Wheatstraw, Brother Skulk, and Ernie Mungweasle."

Moonshadow clutched at the bandage again. "Take this rag away, so I can see them."

"This is not the proper time."

"I think it is." There was steeliness in Moonshadow's voice that Toad had never heard before. Somehow it chilled him. He looked at the others, registering the concern in their faces, then watched Doc work on the bandages. With slightly trembling hands, the healer began unwinding the cloth from around Moonshadow's head.

"You must be careful," Doc admonished. "The light in here is strong."

"It can be no stronger than the darkness that I've known all my life. Get these rags off, and be quick about it."

Once the bandages were removed, Moonshadow sat up and silently regarded his visitors. Amazingly, he didn't blink, and though his smile was friendly, his eyes glittered with cool amusement.

"How do you feel?" Aloevera asked, winding the bandage and slipping it into his tunic pocket.

"I feel fine, medicine man. Introduce me to our friends."

Doc did the introductions, and Moonshadow solemnly shook hands with everybody in turn. When it was Toad's turn, he noticed that the Seer's hand felt cold and dry, not warm as he had anticipated.

"You're all very much as I expected," the Seer said, "but with greater detail and individuality. Sight cures the partial ignorance that I've suffered with all my life."

Wheatstraw sat down on the corner of the cot and regarded his old friend closely. "Tell us what happened. Toad said you were struck with blue fire from the mountain. What can this mean?"

The Seer smiled, ignoring the question, his long teeth flashing behind his beard. "Who knows? I miss Brother Tambourine from this company. Where is he?"

"He's been keeping to himself lately."

"Ahh. So he has time to meditate, I suppose."

"Yes. Moonshadow, we're interested in what happened to you."

"Does it matter? It is past."

"Of course it matters. You've undergone a change."

Moonshadow laughed, a very unpleasant laugh. "As you surmised, Wheatstraw, I was struck by lightning. It was just no lightning of this world."

"Then what was this blue fire?"

"A force from beyond, perhaps some of that raw energy from which everything is derived. A pure jolt of The All, if you will."

"Magick?"

"I think so, Tribechief. I don't know what summoned it, but it's a good thing. It has given me sight."

Wheatstraw nodded slightly. His eyes never left Moonshadow's. If he had an opinion, he was keeping it to himself.

Toad, however, was forming some very strong opinions of his own. He didn't like this new Moonshadow very much. The steely voice and sardonic eyes seemed to belong to another person. He saw the same doubts reflected in Wheatstraw's face.

Finally the Tribechief spoke. "So you have no idea at all where this force came from?"

"I believe the Black Book somehow summoned the power that healed me."

"Considering your prior opinion of the book, Seer, doesn't it concern you that the *Necronomicon* may be responsible for this change in you?"

"With my new sight I see many things differently. Maybe I was too hasty condemning the book. How can something that does good be considered evil?"

"How, indeed?"

Moonshadow sat up straight on the cot, though it seemed that the effort cost him. Blotches of color flared on his waxy cheeks. "Brother Wheatstraw, I'm now able to see things that I've only known by touch.

Other things, like the night sky or the view of the mountains surrounding our home, are now open to me. I've been reborn, Wheatstraw, son of Bambu."

To Toad the conversation was eerie. Moonshadow had changed dramatically, but nobody seemed to notice it except himself and Wheatstraw. At least, if they did, they were giving no indication. Something had crept into the Seer's personality, something Toad didn't like.

"Your eyes may not have served you before, but your sight was better than ours," Wheatstraw said.

"Not everyone shared that opinion."

"True, but what of your All-sense now?"

"It is still there."

"What do your spiritual eyes see now that your physical eyes are open?"

"Why consult The All now, Wheatstraw? You didn't heed its advice before, and you were correct; it's not infallible."

"Can you at least tell us what's ahead?"

"Nothing has changed. The sun still rises and sets for us all."

"Can you be more specific, Moonshadow?"

"Later. I will be better able to answer all your questions after I have rested and become more comfortable with my sight. Its effect is overwhelming." Suddenly he seemed distraught. He glanced at Aloevera, then at the door.

Doc took the hint. Gently he led Wheatstraw away from the cot and motioned for the others to follow. "The Seer is very tired now. You may come back and see him tomorrow."

As they were all ushered from the room, Toad glanced back at Moonshadow. The Seer closed his eyes and lay back on the pillow. A thin smile crossed his face.

Outside of the Healery, the friends stood around in thoughtful silence. At last, Wheatstraw spoke. "Did Moonshadow seem strange to you?"

Skulk shrugged. "After all he's been through, it would be more strange if he didn't act differently."

"Then you don't agree with him, that the book caused this?"

"The *Necronomicon*? Ridiculous. We haven't come that far with it, yet. I'm sure it was lightning."

"Brother Skulk, I think we should discuss this further, over some herbal tea."

"Thank you, Wheatstraw, but another time."

"Time is something neither of us can afford to waste."

To Toad it seemed as though the Digger chief was reluctant—concealing something.

"Walk with me, Theo," Wheatstraw stated flatly.

Skulk looked like he was about to object, but Wheatstraw was quite insistent. He tugged on the Digger's sleeve and led him away. With a polite nod to Toad and Ernie, they were soon walking briskly down the boardwalk.

"Odder and odder," Ernie remarked when they were out of sight. "Curiouser and curiouser."

Toad didn't respond at first. He felt uncomfortable around Ernie. "Strange indeed," he finally remarked.

"Then again, I guess everyone's been acting a bit strange lately."

"You mean me?"

Ernie toyed with his mustache. "For one."

"Look, Ernie, I realize that I was way out of line with the remarks I made about Mizjoan. I'm sorry."

"It's okay, Toad. You've been through a lot. We all have. And, well— you know what my thoughts on the issue are."

"Is this going to turn into one of your lectures?"

"Do you want one?"

"No, I'd rather hear your thoughts on Moonshadow."

"What's to think? He's alive. He can see."

"I think Wheatstraw is right; he's changed."

"Of course he's changed. He can see now."

"That's not what I mean. He seems to be a different person now, and I'm not sure that I like the change."

Ernie clapped the pipesmith on the shoulder. "Give him time to adjust. After what he's been through, he needs it. You know, Yule is only a couple of weeks away. It's a great celebration here in Hillcommune and Moonshadow plays an important role in the festivities. Let's see how he's doing then."

"That's only fair, I guess," Toad relented, although he doubted that the time before the Yule holiday would bring any changes for the better.

Chapter Thirty-Seven

A circle of standing stones crowned Mount Lennon, great henges twice the height of a man. Toad stood in the middle of the ring—the fool on the hill. He touched the mossy sides of the stones and felt dark energy thrumming in their cores. It was as if the megaliths spoke to him. Somehow he knew that the circle was no natural formation, but had been created long ago in the distant morning of the world. No Freak planned their symmetry; they were far older, more ancient than even the Old-Timers. These henges had stood sentinel even before the legendary Red Men—the people who once ruled this land, gliding silently through the forests when the world was young.

Beyond the circle Toad saw the whole of Street-Corner Earth spread out before him. Its forests and fields straddled the Sludge and stretched out toward the White Mountains in the hazy distance. In the dying sunlight the lands looked gray and desolate. Here and there, he spotted huge fires burning out of control. Was this the future, or the present; a vision of what was to be, or a remembrance of Helter-Skelter with its Night of a Thousand Fires?

The stones thrummed louder as Toad approached the huge rock altar they encircled. On the altar the *Necronomicon* lay open, its pages riffling in the night breezes. He was drawn to the crumbling volume; his hands twitched as he reached out to touch it. Suddenly, he wanted to clutch it to his chest and run away with it over the mountains, far away from the valley of the Oldhips. As his fingers brushed the decaying vellum pages, he sensed something stealing up behind him. A twisted imitation of a man cast a long shadow over the altar.

"I need you," a spectral voice intoned.

Toad jumped at the sound of that hollow voice. It did not relieve him when he spun around and saw the shadow shrink, drawing itself into the shape of the wizened old Beatnik, the dying sunlight flashing from his mirrored spectacles. There was no comfort in Maynard's presence. He smiled at Toad, but it was a cold, hungry smile.

"Wh-what do want from me?" Toad asked.

"Your help."

"My help? Why?"

"Because, daddy-o," Maynard said, advancing, "we all need a little help from our friends."

Gripped by inexplicable fear, Toad shuddered. Then, in an instant, the mountain was gone. Maynard and the stone circle were swept away like mist in the wind. Confused, he found himself sprawled in the grass at the forest's edge. Beside him lay his pack and tools. His cherry wood pipe, half-filled with weed, lay in his hand. For a long, frightening moment Toad had no idea where he was or how he got there.

Far below him lay Hillcommune Village, a garland of multicolored houses set along the Peace. Beyond the village the river wound its way through a patchwork of fields and orchards, glistening in the late afternoon sun. In the west loomed the peaks of Mounts Lennon and Leary, brooding and silent like the gods they were named after. A chill seized Toad as he gazed at Mount Lennon. He half expected to see blue fire dancing on its summit, the same blue fire that had changed Moonshadow.

"Just a normal dream," he reassured himself as he clutched his pipe. "I've only been asleep a few minutes, not enough time to have another one of *those* dreams."

He reached for his tinderbox to light the pipe, but thought better of it. The powerful weed in it, from Flo and Eddie's personal stash, had no doubt been what zonked him out and precipitated his nightmare.

Earlier, as he and Ernie had left the Healery, the herbalist made mention that the holiday was fast approaching. Yule was only two weeks away and Toad found it necessary to continue his solitary jaunts. Here, in the high pastures and orchards above the village, he could find the materials he needed to make pipes for Yule gifts. Several old cherry trees grew near the spot where he was now sitting; he knew from previous examination that their twisted roots would yield fine materials for his pipes. Toad picked up his shovel and hatchet, along with the knives he'd need for shaping the tough cherry roots.

Wandering over to the most promising of the old trees, he kicked at a few of the exposed roots with the toe of his boot. It was one of his rituals as a pipesmith. It really didn't tell him anything about the quality of the wood, but he'd done it since he was an apprentice. Satisfied, he jammed the shovel into the dirt and began digging. As he worked, he thought about Mizjoan, knowing that his finest pipe would be for her. There would be many more pipes as well, one for each of his friends in Hillcommune.

Having succumbed to the holiday spirit, Toad decided to put aside any animosity he might have, at least until after Yule.

The holiday was taken much more seriously in Hillcommune than it was in the lowlands, where it was primarily a children's festival. Here, adults as well as the young gathered around the Importance Tree on that day to await the coming of Daddy Lay-On, usually portrayed by Moonshadow, with his bell-bedecked scarlet suit and bulging sack of gifts. Once the gifts were handed out, the feasting and merrymaking began. The festivities could go on for days.

As Toad cut the wood for his pipes he thought about his dream. In it, he had expected to see the Dark Man moving in on him. He'd never been to the mountain, of course, or heard of the standing stones before, yet the dream was so real that he knew they existed. Even now, Toad wasn't sure what it all meant, but it was as disturbing as any dream he'd had of the Dark Man. He unstoppered his canteen and took a pull of clean spring water. Even though it had only been a dream, it caused him to wonder what role Maynard really played in the scheme of things, and what the Beatnik had in mind for him. No matter what it might be, Toad was sure he wanted no part of it.

Gathering up pieces of root that he'd cut, he glanced towards the tree line. There, to his surprise, was Tambourine, hurrying along at an agitated pace through the lengthening afternoon shadows. The musician appeared to be deeply engaged in a conversation with himself, his arms flailing wildly. The wilder the gestures, the more distraught he seemed. Fearing that his friend was becoming unhinged, Toad dropped his tools and hurried towards him. Suddenly, Tambourine flailed his arms one last time and plunged into the forest. Toad ran after him.

The forest was old and heavily overgrown and the musician was soon lost in the thick undergrowth. Toad attempted to follow, slowed, and then stopped. As he turned to go back to his cutting, a shadow detached itself from the darkness beneath the great pines and moved into his path. Instinctively, Toad backed up, right into the trunk of a dead spruce. The shadow nodded its head, smiling, and light flashed from the odd spectacles that it wore. Maynard's sudden appearance was too much like Toad's dream. For a moment the pipesmith felt panic.

"Like, leave Tambourine alone, man," the Beatnik said, raising his hand. "He's packing trouble enough."

"It looks like you've been adding to it," Toad replied.

"Not so, daddy-o. I'm just keeping an eye on him."

Except for flashing points of light reflecting off his sunglasses, the little man faded deeper into the shadows, blending with and becoming one of them.

"What makes you think Tambourine needs watching, Maynard?"

"He's no longer Tambourine, man; he's the Freedom Rider. It's a heavy role to play and it's freaking him out a bit. But, heroes drop out of the most unexpected places—you know what I mean? Sometimes they don't even know they're heroes until, like, somebody makes them hip to it."

"Or forces them into it."

The shadow pointed behind Toad. "Look at Mount Lennon, man. All Freaks should stand at the summit at least once in their lives. I'd like to show it to you sometime."

Toad turned and glanced up at the peak, just barely visible over the trees. "It's only a mountain," he lied.

"Hey, it's more than a mountain, daddy-o. It's, like, your karma, your fate."

Toad shuddered slightly. "I take it you know all about fate?" he asked, becoming irritated with Maynard's performance.

"Like, I know yours."

"You mean, in the Clear Light Society?"

"You're on the beam, man. You might groove on what we're trying to do."

"I don't think so."

"Hey, consider it carefully, man. You want to write history; we help make it. If you're into ultimate truth, you could learn a lot from us."

"I'm not *that* curious."

"Give us a chance. What have you got to lose?"

My sanity, Toad thought. A breeze stirred between the trees and he knew that he was now alone. He called out to Maynard, only to be answered by a cryptic "Koo-koo ka-choo," and distant loon-like laughter.

The pipesmith's head spun as he made his way out of the forest and back into the clearing. The little Beatnik was a hard one to get a handle on. Like the *Necronomicon*, he was enigmatic, and not entirely to be trusted. Life was becoming stranger than Toad wanted it to be.

After he'd collected the sections of cherry root that he wanted for bowls, Toad repacked his bag and started west across the fields to the wetlands that lay beneath the orchards. There he would find apple wood and the reeds from which he would fashion stems and one-hitters. Whistling as he walked, he tried pushing uncomfortable feelings from his mind by turning his attention to thoughts of Mizjoan. Yet, try as he might, no amount of daydreaming would keep them at bay, and grim forebodings kept slipping back in.

West of the woodlands, the countryside opened up into sprawling hillside pastures thick with high grass and wildflowers. In the growing twilight, he passed grazing flocks of sheep and herds of cattle lowing softly, as they wandered near the many brooks that meandered southward toward the Peace. As he crossed a log bridge spanning one of the streams he replayed the incident with Tambourine and Maynard over and over in his mind. He had thought that he knew both of them fairly well, but … maybe not. Maynard, in particular, seemed to be growing less predictable, more sinister, but both were becoming elusive and strange.

Nearing the spot where he and Mizjoan had sat before the blue fire sped down the mountain, more questions surfaced to haunt him. With the moon rising behind him, he stood looking at the pond, reliving the incident. The *Necronomicon* must have been involved, and by association so was Maynard. Perhaps the little Beatnik was involved in other things even more dark and mysterious, things that Toad didn't want to know about.

The pipesmith followed a path along the edge of the pond, eventually leading him across the dam. As he set down his pack he realized that he was in the same spot where, last night, he'd imagined that he'd seen the crane and muskrat. Toad began to examine the tall, straight reeds growing by the bank; with proper drying and painting they'd make excellent pipe stems. Selecting several dozen, he pulled them up and laid them beside his pack. Just as he drew his knife to cut the reeds to the proper length, a movement in the bushes caught his attention.

"Yo!" called a hearty male voice. "Hey, Brother Toad!"

Peering through the reeds, Toad saw Flo and Eddie standing by the water's edge. Flo was barely in the water. It just touched the tops of his bare feet as he stood waving and toking on a short clay pipe. Further from the shore, Eddie stood on one leg, his head resting on his shoulder. He was either sleeping or very stoned, probably both. Something in the redhead's birdlike stance bothered Toad, and he looked away quickly.

"Yo, yourself," he said to Flo. "Where have you been keeping yourselves?"

"Mostly, right here."

"Last night, too? It was … I mean, it must have been chilly up here."

"It wasn't too bad. Eddie and I managed to stay amused."

"Eddie looks like he still is."

"Yeah, we were trying out some new smoke. It's got a few disturbing side effects."

Toad looked at the pipe in Flo's hand, then back at Flo. The little Oldhip caught the glance and laughed.

"Don't look so worried," he said. "This here's Peace River Green. It's very mild stuff."

"I'm glad to hear that. I don't need any more intensity in my life. But, what kind of side effects did you get with the other stuff? Looking at Eddie, it seems like they must have been heavy indeed."

"You don't know the half of it. Look, don't go telling this to anyone else, okay?"

"No problem there."

"Good. This new stuff—I don't think the world's ready for it yet."

Toad took a toke from Flo's pipe and handed it back. It was all he wanted. "What do you mean? Is it too good?"

"Way too good. It makes you see things."

"A couple of six-crocks of Stumpwater Ale will do the same thing."

Flo shook his head. "Not the same, Brother Toad. It's not like smoking, or even tripping on shrooms or ergot. I've had hallucinations before but never like the ones last night. I saw Eddie change, and I saw myself change too."

"What do you mean, 'change'?" Toad asked nervously.

"I mean that after we smoked, it seemed like this blue fireball rolled down out of the mountains and smacked right into us. It turned Eddie into a crane, and made me a muskrat. We only just came down off that high a few hours ago."

Toad shivered. He sat down and began cutting at the reeds with studied casualness. "That is strange, Flo. I think you're right—it's best you don't tell anyone what happened."

Flo crouched down beside Toad, still toking from his pipe. He took a clasp knife out of his pocket and began to help Toad trim reeds. "Yeah, it was too weird for me. Even if I was to leave the datura out of the next batch and cut back on the rest of the ingredients, I'm still not sure that I'd want to touch it again."

"Like you said, maybe the world's not ready for it. There's a lot of things in nature that shouldn't be tampered with," Toad remarked, his apprehension growing faster than Honkweed in June.

Chapter Thirty-Eight

Toad was so intent on carving his pipes that he didn't notice the storm brewing outside his window until the wind ruffled his hair and the first drops of rain spattered heavily on the sill beside him. Vivid blue lightning lanced the night sky, silhouetting the ragged mountains. He gently placed the churchwarden he was carving for Mizjoan on the table and glanced out at the approaching storm.

Nearly a week had passed since he left the apartment he shared with Flo and Eddie and secured himself this flat over a warehouse near the edge of town. Though crowded and dingy, his new flat provided him with an excellent work area and the seclusion he needed. Keeping his hands busy with the task of carving and polishing the numerous pipes required for Yule, his mind had the freedom to examine the strange events taking place in Hillcommune. There was more brewing than just this storm. Maynard, The Clear Light Society and everyone connected with the book troubled him. Also, there was the news of Moonshadow's disturbing transformation. The Seer, to all reports, was not returning to his former self but was continuing to exhibit strange behavior; even his manner of dress showed radical change. And then there was Mizjoan...

Another, closer, flash of lightning and its accompanying roar of thunder prompted him to close and latch the window. He usually paid little attention to thunderstorms, but something about the way the blue bolts jabbed down from the clouds like accusing fingers made him nervous. It was disconcerting that in an idyllic place like Hillcommune he found so much that worried him, even his newfound relationship with the Radiclib leader. Awash in the ever-changing sea of illusion and machination that was now Hillcommune, the pipesmith, more than ever, needed solitude to find his bearings.

On Smuttynose life was simple and the people were genuine and forthright. In this respect Hillcommune and Smuttynose were alike; life didn't change, people didn't change. But now, Hillcommune *was* changing and the people he knew were changing—including Flo and Eddie, literally.

Last week Mizjoan had come to see him twice, both times rapping softly on his door and sweeping in, dressed in a dark cowled cloak. They sat and drank large mugs of honeyed wine, smoked, and chitchatted, always skirting important issues. They never talked about military misfortunes, and never, ever, about real feelings. By the end of the night, Mizjoan would initiate sex. In bed, or on any other item of furniture in the flat, she was energetic, almost animalistic. Therein also lay the rub; her passion did not seem to be driven by love for him, but by a deep desire to escape herself. Toad hoped that in time she could learn to love him, but for now he would have to be satisfied with what she could give him.

Lightning sizzled, and the immediate, resounding explosion sent showers of dust sifting down from the rafters. The night was alive with flashing light and booming thunder. One bolt of lightning hit a tree on the opposite bank of the river, momentarily transforming it into a blazing blue beacon. Toad curled up nervously in his chair and sat for what seemed like hours watching the display before it slowly rumbled into the distance and finally passed.

Sleep came slowly. When Toad awoke dawn was fighting its way through the ragged scud of clouds. Slipping into his coat, the pipesmith scrambled down the narrow staircase to inspect the damage the storm had left. It was cool outside. Mist was rising from the river and the huge puddles along the wharf. In places the fog was thinning out. Through it, Toad could make out the stark outline of the tree that he'd seen struck the night before. Other than that, and a few shingles torn from the roofs of the buildings, there seemed to be very little damage. Looking up the wharf, Toad could see a lanky top-hatted form approaching from the direction of Wheatstraw's place.

"Hey! The elusive Toad," Ernie boomed. "I haven't seen you in so long, I thought you were lost in the woods somewhere."

Toad smiled. In spite of himself he was somewhat glad to see his friend. "Nothing that dramatic, Ernie. I've just been real busy working on Yule presents."

"Ahh. Working with your hands again, eh? That's good."

Toad nodded.

"Well, what brings you out of hibernation, then?" Ernie continued.

"That was a piss-ripper of a storm last night. I wanted to check out the damage."

"Me too. I don't think I've ever seen a thunderstorm so late in the year or one that came up so suddenly and behaved so strangely."

Toad scratched his beard and nodded. "I'm no expert on Hillcommune's weather but I've never seen anything like it either, even on Smuttynose. Maybe we should talk to Moonshadow about it."

"Moonshadow? Why?"

"I thought he could explain it. After all, he's in contact with The All— or was before he started acting so weird."

"You can stop right there. I admit it, you were right." Ernie shrugged. "I thought that gaining use of his sight wouldn't change Moonshadow all that much, but it has. He hasn't snapped back to his old self at all."

"You've seen him, then?"

"Oh yeah, several times."

"I heard that he's acting stranger."

"It's true," the herbalist said, scratching at the back of his neck. "All of a sudden, material things seem very important to him. It's almost impossible to engage him in a philosophical discussion. He refuses to talk about anything mystical, though I think he still retains some of his old powers. What makes it even more odd is the fact that, while he won't talk of mystical matters, he's most adamant on seeing the *Necronomicon*. Really strange. What do you make of it, Toad?"

Toad felt a slight chill that had nothing to do with the morning mists. He knew what Ernie was getting at. Hillcommune these days seemed to be teeming with plots and conspiracies and at the bottom of all of them lurked the Clear Light Society and the *Necronomicon*. What Toad really wanted to know was why the herbalist was asking him. Ernie was a Digger, and should have firsthand knowledge of what was going on. "Your guess is as good as mine," he remarked noncommittally.

"I don't like to guess. Look, I'm on my way to visit Skulk. Care to join me?"

Toad shook his head. "Not today, thanks. I've got too much to do for Yule and too little time to do it in."

Ernie tipped his hat and started down the wharf. Toad watched him as he sauntered toward the west end of town. As Ernie disappeared from sight, Toad resolved to find out what was really going on with the herbalist and his friends in the Clear Light Society.

Chapter Thirty-Nine

Yule in Hillcommune traditionally began right after sunrise with a communal breakfast under the Importance Tree. Unlike lowland Freaks, who decorated their trees only at Yule, the Hillcommuners kept the Importance Tree decorated all year as a symbol of eternal peace. The Yule breakfast was very special indeed, and the gift giving and entertainment that followed were better still. Unfortunately, the feast in the park surrounding the Tree was all but over by the time Toad arrived on the scene; he'd been up all night putting the finishing touches on his pipes and hadn't risen from bed until late morning.

As much as he regretted missing the ceremony at the Tree, it was the party at Wheatstraw's that Toad was really looking forward to. Soft sounds of laughter and the sweet scent of weedsmoke told Toad that the party was already well under way as he nervously clutched his bag of gifts and hurried up the path to the Tribechief's house.

Though it was a warm sunny day, candles blazed in all of the windows and a ceremonial brazier burned on either side of the door. Entering, the air was heavy with the scents of food, incense and weedsmoke, and the sounds of music and laughter were all around him. Somebody uncorked a bottle of bubbly wine just as Toad stooped to lay down his sack. The cork whizzed over his head and disappeared out the door.

As his eyes adjusted to the interior light, the pipesmith surveyed the room. Evergreen boughs and garlands of bright flowers were strung everywhere; bells, streamers, and multi-colored glass balls hung from every beam and casement. Only the clothing and beads worn by the partiers were more brilliant. That is, except for Moonshadow, who wore only a plain white shirt unbuttoned halfway down and tight, dark trousers. The Seer stood off by himself, eyeing everyone disdainfully. His beard had been trimmed relatively short and his hair was tied back in a severe ponytail.

As Toad walked by him, Moonshadow reached out and grasped his hand, shaking it forcefully. "Damn glad you came, Toad. Damn glad," he said, patting the pipesmith on the back with his other hand.

A small fire burned on a dais that had been built in the center of the room. As Toad watched, Wheatstraw and Foreseein' Franklin threw handfuls of Honkweed into the flames, filling the room with pungent smoke. A cheer went up from the crowd when Ernie Mungweasle walked importantly up to the fire, stuck his head into the billowing smoke, and held it there as the others clapped and called out his name. As the cheering reached a crescendo he reeled back, coughing. Toad was just about to walk to the fire himself when Maynard approached, holding out a foaming bottle. The little Beatnik looked quite cheery, not at all like the menacing figure Toad had encountered in the woods two weeks ago.

"A cool Yule to you, daddy-o," Maynard said, pushing the bottle toward Toad. "It's time for celebration; finish it."

The pipesmith accepted graciously, taking the bottle and hoisting it to his lips. "Thanks. We haven't had much to celebrate for a while."

"Hey, man, don't sip that stuff—chug it. Like, this ain't no pink tea party, dig?"

Toad took several deep gulps. It was excellent, dry and lightly spiced—a tribute to the grapes that had spawned it. When he finished the bottle he noticed that his friends had congregated around a table where Hashberry was laying out more food and drink. He dragged his sack over and placed it on one of the nearby chairs. As he started to unpack the gifts, his friends gathered around. Ernie rubbed his hands and looked over Toad's shoulder eagerly.

"What's the matter?" Toad asked, grinning. "Can't wait?"

"You're the one that's opening the bag, man. I'm just observing."

"Typical lowlanders," Wheatstraw said, coming over to stand beside Hashberry. "They possess no patience. They can't wait even a minute."

Toad chuckled as he emptied the bag into a heap on the chair. "I'm an Islander," he said. "We're even less patient; we can't wait a second."

Maybe it was the wine, maybe the holiday revelry; but Toad hadn't felt this good in a long time. The Yule spirit was in him, making his recent worries float away like weedsmoke.

Walking unsteadily, Skulk ambled up to join the others. His red potato-like nose glowed like a beacon. "Who says anyone here has any kind of patience?" he rumbled. "We've all brought gifts, and we've been waiting on you to share them."

"Well, there's no time like the present, if you'll excuse a small pun," Toad replied.

Ernie and Wheatstraw booed good-naturedly, and Skulk pulled a flask from his pocket, gesturing to Toad with it. "I'll drink to that," he said, upending the flask.

Mizjoan appeared from one of the side rooms, carrying an armload of gifts wrapped in colorful paper. Toad almost sighed aloud at the sight of her. She was dressed in her best uniform, which had been carefully cleaned and patched for the occasion, and her billowing auburn hair was tied back with a scarlet ribbon. She smiled as she handed Toad a narrow box done up in silver paper.

"I've been waiting to give you this," she said.

Toad unwrapped the box carefully. Inside was a short sword in a leather sheath. Set into its staghorn handle was a small silver medallion, depicting a clenched fist superimposed over a peace symbol. Toad unsheathed the weapon, admiring the way the light rivered off its polished blade.

"It's beautiful," he said simply. "Thank you."

"You're welcome. It was my father's, and his father's before him. Now it's yours. May it serve you well."

Mizjoan smiled, and Toad felt a tingle run up his spine. Laying the sword carefully on the arm of the chair, he reached into the gift pile and presented her with the churchwarden that he'd worked on for so long.

The Radiclib leader smiled as she unwrapped her gift; she held up the pipe so everybody could see it. "It's marvelous, Toad. What exquisite workmanship!"

When she kissed him lightly on the cheek, Toad felt the color rise in his face. To hide his embarrassment he dug back into the pile and quickly began to distribute its contents around the room.

Toad sat back in the chair, basking in the admiration of his friends as wrappings were torn from boxes and colorful wads of paper and ribbon flew in all directions, revealing the pipes he'd made for them. When it was his turn to receive his gifts, he did it with a dignity and grace that he didn't know he possessed.

He slipped into the vest Ernie had given him. It was of fine embroidered hemp cloth and had many pockets and pouches for storing things. Around his neck he placed the strand of silver and quartz lovebeads that had been Wheatstraw and Hashberry's offering, and the stained oak peace medallion Franklin had given him. There was a fine embossed belt from Tambourine. On it he placed Mizjoan's sword and the beaded stash pouch he'd gotten from Skulk. Inside the pouch was a fist-sized chunk of black hash from Flo and Eddie's personal larder. By his feet sat a jug of Old Southslopes '42 that he'd received from Moonshadow. He was packing his presents away and just reaching for the jug when Maynard motioned him to one side.

"This is for you, daddy-o," the Beatnik said, patting a bag that hung from a strap around his shoulder. It was of finely woven hemp fiber, embroidered with beads that spelled out the word PEACE in flowery curlicues. Instinctively, Toad reached for it.

"Hey, like, not so fast," Maynard laughed. "This here ditty-bag's my present from Wheatstraw. Your gift's inside." He reached into his bag and palmed a small object, which he pressed into Toad's hand. "They may not appear very useful now, but someday…"

Toad studied the gift. It was a pair of round gold-framed spectacles, slightly bent up and obviously quite old. A tiny crack ran along the edge of one smoked-glass lens. He unfolded them and placed them on his nose. The lenses were smudged and almost impossible to see through.

Toad thought the glasses an odd gift and wondered at the Beatnik's motive but said, "Uh-h, thank you. They're very nice. Really." He removed the glasses and placed them into one of his vest pockets.

"Treat 'em well, man. Like I said, someday they'll be of use."

"I'll take good care of them."

But Toad was talking to air. Maynard had wandered off into the crowd around the weed fire and was lost to sight. Shaking his head, Toad wondered what use he'd ever find for the glasses. Like many things about Maynard, the gift didn't seem to make much sense.

In the center of the room, Wheatstraw had thrown another handful of weed on the fire and smoke swirled through the crowd like a playful mist. While the others breathed in the smoke or made their way to the buffet table, Toad uncorked his jug of Old Southslopes and stood sipping it by the window as he watched the main celebration going on in the park behind the house. Old Southslopes was Oldhip honey wine at its best. It went down smooth and tasted of flowers and soft spring nights.

As Toad nipped at the jug, wagons began pulling up to the Importance Tree and crews of Oldhips started unloading gifts, produce, and kegs of wine and beer. One wagon, swaying under a load of weed bales, almost overturned as it made its way through the packed crowd.

Suddenly, a figure dressed in scarlet and bells jumped out from behind the Tree. In his hands he held a long list, which trailed to the ground and dragged along between his booted feet. From the wild cheering of the crowd, Toad surmised that this must be Daddy Lay-On, the capering Yule spirit usually played by Moonshadow. This blond and beardless Daddy Lay-On was obviously a last minute replacement for the former Seer. The pipesmith felt his apprehensions starting to creep back, but was determined not to let them in, at least not until the day was over.

Toad's determination toppled when he spied Moonshadow sitting on the other side of the room, beside a mistletoed arch, anxiously conferring with Maynard and Franklin. Their manner had an intensity that disturbed Toad. He had to find some way to eavesdrop on their conversation.

Just then, Mizjoan brushed by him.

"Ahh, Joan," he breathed as he touched her on the arm. "I need to talk to you. Please, come where it's quieter."

Mizjoan, mildly puzzled, allowed herself to be led to the arch.

Toad and Mizjoan approached the archway; the three conspirators never looked up. Toad strained his ears to hear what they were saying as he positioned Mizjoan under the mistletoe.

"Well," Mizjoan whispered. "What do you want to say?"

"This isn't easy," Toad replied softly. "Please, just one second."

"Dylan's Bones, don't take too long. As I told you before, I can come to your flat but I cannot be seen alone with you in public."

Toad concentrated on the conspirators behind the archway. They appeared to be arguing. Their voices were rising to the point where he could easily make out what was being said.

"So, I say again," Moonshadow demanded. "You must let me work with you on the book. It's something I have a right to be part of."

Maynard shook his head. "And I tell you again, no. Franklin, Skulk and I have this gig under control. You have no need to be involved."

"No need!" The Seer's voice raised an octave and his face became quite red. Moonshadow balled his hand into a fist. "You don't know what you are dealing with. You are like ants trying to move an oak tree. I must have a say in this. Do you hear me?"

Moonshadow was on his feet now, looming over Franklin and Maynard. The muscles in his jaws twitched violently, and it was obvious that he was just barely keeping himself under control. Mizjoan stared at the Seer, and if Toad hadn't held her back she would have intervened in the argument.

Tambourine also noticed the exchange. The musician stood up and walked to the front of the room, adjusting his battered harmonica in its makeshift holder.

"My friends," he began quietly. "Brothers and sisters, may I have your attention?"

Moonshadow and Maynard ceased their arguing. Something in Tambourine's manner suggested that he had an important announcement. The Seer shot Maynard a venomous stare, then resumed his seat and turned to watch Tambourine. Throughout the room conversations halted as the frail musician shifted his guitar in his hands and began to run his fingers lightly over the strings.

"That's better," he said, smiling. "Most of you know me. I am a Dylan, the last of my proud line. For most of my life I've denied that fact, and have lived quietly under an assumed name. I can't do that any longer."

There was a hushed expectancy in the room. All were holding their breath as they hung on Tambourine's every word.

Absent-mindedly caressing his guitar, Tambourine continued. "There may be some among you who doubt that I can do what destiny decrees I must. I confess that I've often doubted it myself. Recently a friend helped me realize that I can deny my destiny no longer."

Maynard, Toad thought. That day in the woods, the little immortal had been working on Tambourine, preparing him. No wonder the musician had seemed distant and strange; he was being transformed from man to legend, from Tambourine Dill to Freedom Rider.

The musician bowed his head for a second and then began to play. His fingers flew along the guitar strings, picking out the chords of a familiar melody. Without looking up, he said softly, "My feelings are best expressed by something Old Bob, himself, wrote centuries ago."

As the crowd remained hushed, he touched his lips to his antique harmonica and blew out a few sad notes. They hung in the air for what seemed minutes; then the guitar strumming grew more frantic and Tambourine began to sing. Toad recognized the opening lines of *Chimes of Freedom*. From the moment Tam began, the musician's audience was completely silent, spellbound. His voice was the voice of the people, a resolute proclamation of hope. The performance went beyond mere singing. Toad's eyes closed. It was sunset and he could hear the tolling of distant bells. Then, suddenly, he was huddled in a doorway, shivering as thunder rolled overhead and lightning flashed in the darkening sky. Overwhelmed by the imagery, Toad opened his eyes and surveyed the room. Eyes closed, slowly swaying to the music, the others were obviously experiencing profound visions of their own.

Gradually, the musician's voice took on an eerie, hard, nasal quality. The effect was chilling. Toad was compelled to sing along as the words took hold. Around him, faces flushed with rapture opened their mouths in song. Never were the ancient words so alive, so full of meaning.

Tambourine's eyes were closed; his face was strained and intense as his fingers snaked along the neck of his guitar. He sang of soldiers, warriors brave enough to lay down their arms. He sang of refugees, the poor, the abandoned and the forsaken. He sang of all the luckless, outcast and misunderstood people of the world.

Tambourine's face aged, growing haggard, suffused with ancient sorrow. His voice became even more cracked and nasal until it was not a singular voice at all, but a pleading howl of the downtrodden and dispossessed. It was the aggregate crying of the people, the trumpet of The All.

When the playing was over, and the last few notes hung in the air, the people in the room jumped to their feet and cheered the musician. There was rapture in their faces, fire in their eyes. Toad knew what they felt in their hearts: here, without a doubt, was the true descendant of Dylan, the promised Freedom Rider.

As people got up and crowded around Tambourine, Toad felt strangely sorry for his friend. Freedom Rider or not, the musician was a pawn. Without knowing why, Toad wondered if his own fate would be the same. Mizjoan, who was still standing next to the pipesmith, looked as if she was waking from a trance. She turned to Toad and asked, "I'm sorry, you wanted to say something to me before?"

The Radiclib leader's eye followed Toad's as he glanced up at the mistletoe. Before she could protest, Toad put an arm around her and kissed her forcefully.

"Don't you ever do that again!" Mizjoan sputtered, pushing him away.

"It's just a tradition, Joan."

Before Mizjoan could chastise Toad, Skulk approached and put a fatherly hand on his shoulder.

"I'd like a few words with you," the Digger chief said quietly.

"Can't it wait?"

"No."

Toad smiled to Mizjoan as he sauntered off with Skulk. "A very cool Yule to you, Comrade Mizjoan."

Mizjoan scowled.

Skulk led the pipesmith to a deserted corner along the back wall. "Have you thought anymore about joining the Society?"

"No," Toad lied.

"I wish you would."

"Why?"

Skulk smiled, his eyes twinkling behind his thick glasses. "We like you, son. And, you never know ... it could come in handy someday."

"I can't see how."

The Digger leaned forward and whispered, "I understand your reluctance. But, maybe we can compromise. The Society considers you terrific Clear Light material; we'd hate to lose you, son. So, for your efforts and achievements this far, we are going to make you an honorary Digger. If, at a later date, you wish to be a full member, just say the word."

"Is there nothing I can do to stop you?"

Skulk laughed. "C'mon, Toad. It's a great honor. You've shown enormous bravery and self-sacrifice. You obviously care about what happens to our people."

"Of course I care, but that's hardly qualification to be a Digger."

"Maybe so, but it counts for a lot. There are many benefits to being a Digger, even an honorary one. But none if you decide to exclude yourself.

At least agree to the honorarium."

Was Skulk merely suggesting that, as a member, much of the Society's arcane knowledge would be available to him, or was it a veiled threat?

"Sure," Toad replied with as big a smile as he could muster, deciding that, for now, it would be best to play along.

"Good, good. You've made the right choice," Skulk said as he patted the pipesmith on the shoulder.

The party was now in full swing. Toad stood with his hands jammed deep in his pockets and watched as the dumpy little figure in the plug hat threw a small sack of gifts over his shoulder and left the room. For a moment, it seemed as if Skulk was carrying away the remainder of Toad's holiday spirit in that sack.

Chapter Forty

It was the last night of 2468. Toad hurried along the empty wharf. Lights shone in nearly every window. Music and laughter issued from open doorways, evidence of the New Year's Eve parties that began at sunset, as was the Oldhip custom. The revelry would continue well into the next morning; for the most determined celebrants, parties would go on for days. Toad looked over the town as if seeing it for the first time, admiring the way the houses, with their varying paint schemes and styles of architecture, seemed to blend into one another. Here, a simple white A-frame was connected to a blue three-story house that in turn was connected to a low shed of unpainted logs. Different, yet all part of a greater whole, like the people who built them. Breathing heavily of the night air, he smiled as singing wafted down from a high balcony.

The waning moon cast a silvery sheen on the waters of the Peace as it flowed beneath the wharf supporting the single-story house that Mizjoan occupied with Kentstate. Usually, the two were inseparable, but tonight Mizjoan would be alone. Earlier, he was surprised to find a note slipped under his door. The message, in the Radiclib leader's bold script, was concise: "Must see you. 'State will be gone all night."

Since Yule, Joan had visited his garret flat only once, and that was the night after the holiday. Their conversation was brief; Joan cut short any attempt by Toad to communicate. Their lovemaking was only slightly more successful than their dialogue. From the start Mizjoan seemed preoccupied, and then suddenly asked if Toad would mind finishing quickly. Immediately after, she dressed and almost ran out the door. Given the stresses she was under, her reaction was to be expected. At least that is what he told himself. But, after a few days with no word from her, doubt about their future crept in. Her note did nothing to lessen it.

Flickering firelight danced in the window of Mizjoan's front door. He hesitated. Was this the end of 2468 and the end of their relationship, or was he going to see in the New Year with the Comrade Leader? Either way, he needed to know. Glancing quickly up and down the wharf to be sure that he wasn't being observed, he pushed the door open and stepped inside. Rufus, the scroungy alley cat that shared the apartment with the two Radiclib women, was sprawled by the fire. He glared at Toad and growled. Toad growled back.

Toad thought of calling out to Joan, but decided instead to surprise her. Quietly, he crossed to the sofa. The pipe that he'd made for Mizjoan lay on the coffee table. He took a chunk of hash out of his pocket and, breaking off a piece, began to fill the pipe.

"Making yourself at home, Comrade Pipesmith?"

Toad looked up. Mizjoan stood in the doorway to the bedroom, dressed in a long, blue chambray dress. Her auburn hair cascaded down over her bare shoulders in soft, curly tendrils. He felt his heart jump a beat, like it always did when he saw her.

"I got your note," he said.

"I'm glad you came."

Mizjoan sat next to him on the sofa. The light perfume she wore had both a calming and arousing effect on him.

"I wasn't sure you'd want to see me again ... after the other night."

"That was my fault, I'm sorry. I'd just left an argument with Kentstate. I should have postponed my visit until I cooled down."

"We could have just talked; it might have helped."

"There was nothing I wanted to talk about," Mizjoan said sharply, "then or now."

"Sorry."

Tension eased from Mizjoan's face. "No, I'm the one who should apologize. That's why I invited you here. I wanted to make it up to you."

"What about Kentstate?"

"She's partying with Wheatstraw and the others. She won't be back till morning."

Toad arched one eyebrow and Mizjoan smiled seductively. "Are you going to light that pipe this year?" she laughed.

Hours later, as the town horn sounded and bells and whistles welcomed in 2469, Toad slipped back through Joan's door. Once again he and Mizjoan hadn't really talked, but somehow that didn't bother him. Raucous celebrants began spilling onto the wharf, cheering in the New Year with loud hoots and noisemakers. Bumping from shoulder to shoulder in the reeling crowd, Toad dodged and pushed his way along the wharf until he escaped the crowd by slipping into one of Hillcommune's few alleyways.

The alley was dark except for a light shining in a window at the far end.

As he approached, Toad spied a tall, furtive figure lurking in the shadows nearby. Something in its movements suggested Moonshadow. Whoever it was, he was interested in what was going on behind the window. As stealthily as Toad approached, the spy must have heard him; the dark figure scurried away.

Curious as to what interested the shadowy interloper, Toad eased up to the window and peeked inside. A single candle illuminated the small, shabbily furnished room. In the center, Maynard and Skulk sat at a table cluttered with papers and writing instruments. Between them lay the open *Necronomicon*; the pair seemed to be discussing one of its passages.

Toad crouched beneath the casement and pressed his ear against the wall. The voices were low and somewhat muddled, but he could hear enough to piece together the conversation.

"It doesn't seem fair," the voice that Toad recognized as Skulk's was saying.

"Hey, dig it, man; life isn't fair."

"That's philosophical bullshit, Maynard. We're talking about a life here."

"I'm hep, but what other choice is there? At least the cat doesn't have a family."

A shudder shot up Toad's spine. Dylan's Bones, he thought, they must be talking about me. He pressed his ear closer to the wall and held his breath.

"That's pretty cold-blooded."

"Dig it, Theo, it is. I don't want to lose the cat any more than you do, but he's, like, in a position that could cost him his life. You know he could prove to be a problem later on."

The shudder intensified. Toad fought back the urge to run.

Inside the room, Skulk's voice grew louder. "Maynard! You're not suggesting...?"

"No way, man. It's just that if he lives through this—if any of us do—well, he'll have to go along with the rest of the plan. He's been pretty reluctant so far."

Slowly Toad got to his feet, his mind whirling with what he'd just heard. That was all he needed to hear; he was going to leave Hillcommune tonight! He was going back to his rooms, and...

Suddenly, someone grabbed him from behind, cupping a hand over his mouth before he could cry out. Toad struggled, but he was pinned fast. He tried to bite the hand covering his mouth, but his assailant was too quick. Raising his leg to kick back, he stopped abruptly as a familiar voice whispered in his ear.

"What's this, the ever elusive Peeping Toad or a common snoop?"

"Damn you, Ernie," Toad muttered as the hand was removed from his mouth. "What are you trying to do, scare me to death?"

"No, but I'm curious as to why you're spying on our friends in the middle of the night."

"Friends? Yours, maybe. Do you know what they're planning? What am I talking about—of course you do. You're all in it together, aren't you?"

"All in what together?

"Don't give me that. You know perfectly well what I'm talking about."

The herbalist looked puzzled, then suddenly brightened. "Oh, you mean about trying to recruit you for the Society? It's hardly something to get all bent out of shape over."

"Isn't it? It could mean my death."

Ernie shook his head. "Honestly, Toad. Where in hell are you getting such ideas?"

"Ideas? You people are planning to kill me!" Toad's voice grew shrill as he jabbed an accusatory finger in Ernie's face.

The herbalist scowled and took a step backwards. "Pipe down. You're getting hysterical."

"Hysterical, bullshit! You know damn well what they're planning in there. Don't you?"

"I might, if I was in the habit of eavesdropping, but I'm not."

Ernie stepped forward quickly, grabbing Toad by the arm. Behind them, the window flew open and Maynard and Skulk peered out.

"What's the row out here?" Skulk exclaimed.

Maynard adjusted his sunglasses and squinted at the Freaks. "Hey, like what are you cats doing?"

Toad clenched his teeth and said nothing.

"Everything's under control," Ernie said. "Toad here has been celebrating the New Year a little too zealously. I'm trying to escort him home, away from the wharf and all that madness. He's decided to take exception to it."

Skulk frowned.

Quickly appraising the situation, Toad followed Ernie's lead. He lolled his head and blinked his eyes woozily. "I think I'm going to be sick," he slurred, then puffed his cheeks in just the right way.

"Maybe you'd better let Ernie take you home," Skulk remarked. "That way we can all get a good night's sleep."

Thrusting two fingers aloft, Toad displayed an exaggerated peace sign and staggered slightly. Ernie grabbed his arm and began to guide him down the alley. Toad resisted and made sure to stumble convincingly.

"I guess this Islander is not used to Hillcommune's New Year's partying," Ernie said.

"Apparently. Happy New Year, gentlemen," Skulk replied, closing the window. In the light of the room, Toad could see him lapse back into conversation with Maynard.

"That was close," Ernie remarked.

"Yeah, it was. Thank you for covering for me."

"Sure, but it'll cost you an explanation of your behavior. For now, be quiet until we get to your place."

When they arrived at Toad's garret, Ernie flopped into an overstuffed chair by the foot of the bed. Toad busied himself stoking up the fire under the teapot and breaking up some of his remaining hash.

"Nothing like your place at Smuttynose," Ernie commented, examining the clutter on Toad's small worktable.

Toad shrugged. "I sure hope Gary's keeping the old place up—wonder if I'll ever get to see it again."

"Oh, you'll return once this war thing is over."

"I wish I had your confidence. It seems my days are numbered." Toad set a mug of fragrant tea in front of Ernie and began to crumble hash into his cherry wood.

Ernie took a sip of tea and sat with the mug cupped in his hands. "After all we've been through, what would make you say something like that?"

"Knowing what your friends have planned for me, how can I think any other way?"

"This has something to do with what you heard at the window, doesn't it?"

Toad finished packing the pipe and lit it with the candle on the workbench. Puffing furiously, he said, "Of course it does and I'd be shocked if you didn't know already."

"Let's assume that I don't. Now, pass that pipe."

The pipesmith accommodated him, and as Ernie toked away, Toad related everything that he'd heard pass between Maynard and Skulk. The herbalist listened thoughtfully, and when Toad was finished, he passed the pipe back to him.

"Why are you so sure they were talking about you?" Ernie asked.

"What do you mean?"

"Tambourine would be my first guess, or it could be someone you haven't even thought of. The Society may be small, but it's got its fingers in a lot of pies. It seems to me that you're inferring quite a bit from just a few lines of conversation."

Toad puffed on his cherry wood meditatively. "Maybe so, but it's all your Society's secretive ways that set the stage, so to speak. Why can't you guys just be more open, less mysterious? You really put people off."

"Think of it as a game."

"Game? Horseshit. I want no part of any game. Now, what does the Clear Light Society want from me?"

Ernie took another sip of tea. "I really can't get into this now."

"If my life is in peril you should. I mean, what kind of friend are you anyway?"

"A good one. Better than you know. Still, there's things I can't tell you."

"Which is more important to you, the Society or the life of a friend?"

A worried look crossed the herbalist's features. He pointed to the mug, indicating that he'd like more tea. Toad complied, filling it to the brim.

"Maybe I do owe you an explanation after all," Ernie said. "We've been through a lot together since Smuttynose, and it's likely we'll go through more before this play is finished."

He pushed his hat back on his head and took a sip of tea before continuing. "Toad, it's no chance of fate that we met. I also want to say that our friendship was never planned or arranged."

"I don't understand."

"It's simple really. The Clear Light Society knew about you long before you'd ever heard about us. In fact, I was sent to Smuttynose that first time specifically to check up on you. If you hadn't made the first contact I would have."

Toad shook his head as if to clear it. "That doesn't make any sense. How could the Society have known about me? Why would they care?"

"You have a solid reputation as a master craftsman, and somewhere along the line they learned you were a scholar of sorts, interested in history. How they found that out I'm not sure. Skulk has his ways, many of which are a mystery even to me."

"So you were sent to spy on me?"

"Make contact."

"And now you expect me to believe that our friendship was not planned in the same way—that it was a random event?"

"I'm not sure that 'random' is the right word, but I certainly never planned it. As a matter of fact, I initially couldn't see the value of keeping an eye on a Freak as sheltered and housebound as you. Don't take this wrong, but at first I thought you were—well—too much like ragweed for us to ever have much in common."

Toad leaned forward. "You've been manipulating me from the beginning, haven't you?"

Ernie sighed. For a moment he seemed older, sadder. "I wish you wouldn't put it that way. I was assigned to observe you, nothing more. Still, be that as it may, our friendship is real enough. If you weren't a true friend I wouldn't be telling you the things I'm telling you now."

"Then why do you let the Society conceal things from me and the world?"

"Because there are certain things, particularly things about the Old Order, that are best left unknown."

"You would have made a good Luddite."

Ernie stroked his mustache and took another sip of tea. Outside of Toad's window the sounds of celebration had died down. All that could be heard was the wind soughing through the deserted streets.

"That's an unfortunate comparison," Ernie said, "and inaccurate. The Neo-Luddites were madmen who destroyed the Old Order and its technology. The Society merely tries to preserve what's left and regulate how much of the old knowledge enters our culture. The old technology was dangerous, often evil, and best kept from the unwary."

"So I've always heard."

Ernie caught the sarcasm in Toad's voice. "You may think the machines of the Old-Timers were wonders, and some were, but they were destructive as well. Their horseless wagons and flying machines gave off poisons that destroyed the air. In those days the skies drizzled corrosive acids; the rivers and lakes were clogged with sewage. Even the earth itself became barren, unable to sustain life."

"That sounds like cant. Surely..."

"Toad, you're arguing just for the sake of argument. You've seen some of their inventions, their steamwagons and firearms, and you've been dazzled by their destructive ability. What about the weapons and machines you haven't been told about?"

"Such as?"

"Well, have you ever heard of *The Bomb*?"

"Some sort of exploding device, wasn't it? Like the ones we used at Great East Lake."

The herbalist laughed coldly. "Somewhat, only a trillion times more powerful. The device I'm talking about could devastate a whole city. Not just a city like Rivertown, either, but one of the mega-urban areas like Bahston or New Yawk used to be. One of those Adam Bombs could kill millions of people and poison the land for generations to come. How would you like to see something like that preserved and re-introduced to the world?"

"I wouldn't. But, you Diggers were pretty eager to bring back firearms."

"Yes, but let's not forget your role in that escapade."

Toad winced.

"You've seen what the Dark Man is capable of," Ernie continued. "Introducing guns was our only chance."

"I suppose. Still, I'm not too clear where I fit into this great scheme of things."

"I can only relate what Skulk told me, Toad. By rights I shouldn't even tell you that."

"But you will."

Ernie put down his mug. "Skulk once said that the Society wanted you to write a history of Street-Corner Earth. They knew that you'd been toying with the idea, though I don't think I'd said that much about it in my reports."

"And that's what got me into all this?"

"Yes. Skulk would really like to recruit you into the Society."

"There's got to be more to it than that, Ernie. After all, from what I've seen you people have plenty of your own historians and scholars."

"Maybe there is more to it, but I don't know what. Theo keeps me in the dark about a lot of things."

Toad shook his head. "I like the idea of doing my own history, but being a Digger...?"

"You won't be able to do one thing without doing the other."

"Why not?"

"Because, one way or the other, whatever history you wrote would be the Society's. It would have to be what they wanted or nothing at all."

The pipesmith's eyes flashed angrily. "They can't do that! I can write what I damn well please!"

"You'd be surprised what the Society can do. Sure, you can write what you damn well please, but who has the great research facilities that you'll need and the printing presses to get it into circulation? Believe me when I say that any unauthorized edition can be stopped by fair means or foul."

"What the hell ever happened to free will?"

"Nothing. If you believe it ever really existed."

Toad started to repack his pipe. "I can't believe that. Not in Freak society."

"Believe it; Freak society and every other one that I've ever heard of. Look: the Old-Timers believed they had free will too, but they didn't. Our culture has as much freedom, more probably, than any ancient one, but we still have our taboos, our unwritten laws. The Clear Light Society is only guarding us against what has already been proven to be evil."

"So you say. But, who runs the Society ... I mean really?"

"Right now, Skulk does. You know that."

"Does he?"

"I know what you're implying, Toad. Maynard has a lot of influence— but why not? We may not see eye-to-eye on everything, but the dude *is* over five hundred years old, after all. He knows what's going on. And he knows how to deal with Bejeezuz."

Toad stared moodily at the pipe in his hand. "Do you trust him, Ernie?"

"I don't know if there's any choice in the matter."

"I can't trust anyone without knowing the whole story. And I'm sure I won't get it."

"I'm telling you what I know, pal. I'll admit that I've lost some faith in the Society lately, but it's been my life, my family, for as long as I can remember. If I can't trust them, then who can I trust?"

Toad lit his pipe and inhaled vigorously. "I wish I could share your faith, Ernie. But, I can't now that the *Necronomicon* is involved in this. I'm afraid of it."

"I have to abide by Skulk's decisions."

The pipesmith snickered. "Ernie Mungweasle listening to someone besides himself? I never thought that I'd live to see the day."

Ernie tugged at a strand of his hair nervously. "Okay, that damn book worries me too. Just about everything worries me these days. Still, the fact is that people like you and me don't have all the answers. Sometimes we have to let others, wiser than ourselves, make our decisions for us and hope their decisions are the right ones."

Toad didn't answer. He looked out the window at the fine dusting of stars spread across the night sky. Were they really wiser, the Digger chief and the little self-proclaimed immortal? Perhaps someone should find out.

Chapter Forty-One

His conversation with Ernie did nothing to ease Toad's worries. Indeed, it had magnified them so much he had to spend the next two days trying to calm down, doing little more than reading through a stack of dusty comic almanacks that he'd found in the storeroom behind his flat. He brooded over them as if he could truly discern the nature of reality from thirty-year-old copies of *Tokin' Tales*, *Zowie* and *The Hellacious Hirsute Hippie Brothers*. Whether he found anything of value in the almanacks or not, he was never quite sure. But at noon on the third day, when he put the last volume to rest, he resolved to get to the bottom of everything that was coming down in Hillcommune. Dragging himself out of hibernation, he set off to a nearby eatery for lunch.

Rumor had it that since Yule Tambourine was spending most of his time wandering the fields and forests high on the mountain slopes. So it was with some surprise that Toad almost collided with the musician on the wharf. Tam seemed distracted and registered the pipesmith's presence with some difficulty.

"Hey, Tam," Toad greeted him cheerfully, "I've been looking all over for you."

Tambourine blinked like a startled owl. "You have?"

"I thought we should talk."

The musician blinked again, like he was having trouble bringing the world into focus. "About what?"

"The Clear Light Society."

"Very heavy subject, man. Very heavy."

"True. Skulk's been pushin' the Society's offer for me to join. I wanted your opinion."

Tambourine ran his hand across his chin, where the traces of a curly brown beard were beginning to show. "The Diggers have taught me a lot lately."

"Like?"

"Well for one thing, they taught me that a man can't escape his fate."

"Certainly, not if the Society won't let him."

Tambourine favored him with an enigmatic smile. "You think I'm being used? Maybe I am, but we're all used one way or another; we all have to serve somebody. Fate toys with us, man. My destiny is written in the stars and in my bloodline."

"C'mon, where's the old Tam? What are they doing to you?"

"My birth was not their doing, Toad."

"I know, but…"

Tambourine's smile softened. "Brother Toad, you have to understand. How would I feel if the Dark Man gained complete control of Street-Corner Earth and I did nothing to prevent it? To think the Diggers might be using me is naive. History is using me. Surely, fate is using me."

Toad shook his head. All that Tam said was true, but the pipesmith still felt something was wrong.

"Times are changing, Toad, as surely as they were in Ol' Bob's day. If you're looking for answers, remember the song. As it says, when the water starts rising, you'd better recognize it and start swimming, or you'll sink for sure."

"If the Clear Light Society is involved," Toad asserted, "answers are blowing in the wind."

"Toad, all that Maynard and the Diggers have done is to help me learn how to swim. What road you're meant to walk, I can't say."

Toad searched for a reply but Tambourine was already making his way down the wharf.

The next day, the fourth day of January, Toad was crossing the field behind Wheatstraw's, embarking on an afternoon jaunt in the hills. The Tribechief emerged from his garden on a small rise, his arms loaded with large multicolored sunflowers. Oldhips were, by nature, suspicious of outsiders, but it occurred to Toad that if he chose his words carefully the Oldhip might be able to help him find answers to his questions.

"Peace, Brother Toad," Wheatstraw called, smiling. "Righteous day, isn't it?"

Toad held up his hand and climbed the knoll to meet him. They stood silently for a moment looking out over the valley. With the sun hanging almost directly overhead, the long stretch of Hillcommune Village resembled an eccentric mountain range. When Toad commented on this effect Wheatstraw nodded solemnly.

"That is no accident, Brother Toad. We Oldhips are children of the river and the mountains. We feel that everything about our lives should

361

reflect that fact."

Toad nodded back, solemnly. "The mountains are beautiful. I hope to climb one of them someday."

"Have you given any thought to which one?"

"Either Lennon or Leary, I guess."

"Excellent choices, though given the times, Leary would be preferable. Mount Lennon is rather a busy place these days."

"So I've heard. When are Skulk and Maynard going back up there?"

"They should be there already. With Brother Franklin, as well."

"Oh? Yes, of course, I knew he'd be joining them."

Wheatstraw fixed Toad with a penetrating look. "It's hard not to be interested in their doings."

"Like most people, I'm curious. The Beatnik and Skulk are a fascinating pair, difficult to read sometimes."

"Those concerned primarily with matters of the spirit and the mind often are hard to fathom. They dig deeper, and see more, than other folk."

"And change things?"

Wheatstraw shook his head a little sadly, "Yes. Yes, they do. Change sweeps through this valley like a wind."

"Does it bother you?"

"Change is often unsettling."

"Unsettling?" There's something happening here that goes far beyond just the peculiar weather and the odd way Moonshadow's been acting."

Wheatstraw nodded. "It's interesting that you should mention the Seer. He was by the other day and inquired after our three pilgrims, much as you are now."

"He did?"

"Yes, and he wanted to know more about the *Necronomicon* too. He was very insistent—acting stranger than usual."

"What do you mean?"

The Oldhip shrugged. "He has altered his appearance so much that I almost didn't recognize him. He looked like no Oldhip. At the Yule celebration you may have noticed that he'd given up his leather attire; now he's changed his manner of dress again. He wore plain white trousers and a matching jacket over a black shirt. His hair was cut short, like a Greaser's, and his beard was trimmed down to almost nothing. He was most adamant on seeing the book. He claimed that it was his right, since he was the most affected by it. I explained that it was not my privilege to grant; it was Maynard's and Skulk's. I'm ashamed to say, I wasn't sorry when he left."

"Wow."

"In spades, Brother Toad."

Wheatstraw gazed off past the pipesmith. "In a few months it'll be spring. Perhaps things will return to normal then."

"You mean we will be out of here and you'll have your valley back to yourselves?"

"It sounds cruel, but ... yes, something like that. I wish that cursed book had never come here."

"I'm surprised that you allowed it to."

"Whatever my personal feelings, Brother Toad, I still listen to what others like Franklin and the old Moonshadow, think are best. Besides, with his violent aggression, the Evil Weed has offered us little choice. It's a dangerous thing, this book, and I'll breathe easier once it's far from here."

"It'd be even more dangerous if it were in the Dark Man's hands."

"I fear it could still end up there. Evil draws to evil, you know. I'm sure the Dark One will let nothing stand in his way to possess it. It may even find its own way to him."

Toad scratched his chin. "You seem to know a lot about this, Wheatstraw."

"I do."

"And the Clear Light Society? What do you know about them?"

"More than they might suspect."

"What can you tell me?"

"Nothing. Yet, I imagine you will find out for yourself soon enough." Wheatstraw sighed. "Things will never be the same for their being here. Times change as they must, and it is written that there is a time for every purpose under heaven."

Toad was disturbed by the haunted look on Wheatstraw's face. "Please..."

"Brother Toad, the *Book of Love* contains great knowledge. You know, it is not one volume but many."

"Sure, Pedanticus wrote that..."

"I wouldn't credit too much to what that one said. He was a known liar. Few outlanders have glimpsed our sacred volumes, and he was not among them. Nor, do I think, would he have wanted to be. Our books differ, sometimes greatly, from what is written in your lowland histories."

This intrigued Toad. A tingle of excitement rippled up his spine. "Please, isn't there information you would share?"

"It would do you no good." Wheatstraw's eyes clouded, as if he were gazing off towards a different time and place. "Long ago, when I was young and bursting with curiosity like yourself, I spent all of my free days poring through the *Book*. Over the course of five years I read through the entire collection of volumes several times over, dissecting every phrase for its inner truth. What futility!"

"What do you mean, futility?"

"Just that. It was foolish, immersing myself in the past of our peoples only to come back to what I knew all along."

"Which was?"

Wheatstraw's gaze met Toad's and held it. "That I am a child of the sun and rain, a brother to the rivers and the mountain mists. I am an Oldhip, and we are as we are. Life holds great meaning for us, its cycles and eternal patterns."

"But surely things change all around you."

"That too is as it must be. We are all as individual as the flowers of the fields, but all part of the same cosmic plan. Each of us must find our own way through life, never forgetting that each individual is part of The All. Sometimes great changes come, thrust upon us unbidden. Choices made in a situation like that are particularly difficult, for they can affect others, perhaps thousands of others, and forever alter the flow of history. But, The All remains."

Toad nodded. He was becoming irritated with the Oldhip's obfuscations, but tried hard not to let it show. "Why all this talk of choices?"

"I can tell you what you wish to know, but I choose not to. Wisdom comes from living what is to be and uncovering life's secrets. No man can do this for you. However, Toad, I will tell you this: the song of your life is always in your ears, but you refuse to hear it. The composer is before your eyes, but you refuse to see him.

"You're on your own path to enlightenment. I can't help you there. We both must do what we must; you go to seek your truth, and I remain to tend my garden and help my people."

After a few more minutes of Oldhip wisdom and platitudes, Toad realized that he would get no useful information from the Tribechief. Leaving Wheatstraw, he continued west, crossing the footbridge that led to the meadows north of town. He pulled his cherry wood out of his pocket and lit it with his tinderbox. Toking deliberately on his pipe, he walked through the high rolling pastures towards the scattered patches of forest that lay beyond them. Tendrils of smoke swirled about his head and danced away as elusively as his own thoughts. The midday sun beat down on his shoulders, but he was only dimly aware of it as a dozen hopeless plans flitted through his mind. He had to know what was happening on Mount Lennon. Wheatstraw had spoken of Toad taking his own road to enlightenment. As far as the pipesmith could see, that road led in only one direction. Somehow, he had to get to the summit, just as he'd dreamed. It was his appointed path and his boot heels itched to be wandering it.

Toad kicked aside a stone that lay in his way and entered a tall stand of pine trees that stood as a wall separating this field from the next. A few minutes later, he emerged from the trees and stood overlooking rolling pastureland that spread before the feet of Mounts Lennon and Leary. Smiling, he took a breath. The air was sweet with the scents of wildflowers and ripening Honkweed. Birds chirped and fluttered among the trees. As he started out across the pastures, multicolored butterflies flew out of the grass beneath his feet. In the distance beyond the next rise he could hear excited laughter, like children at play. The sound drew him like a lodestone, and he hurried toward it. After the gloomy thoughts that had been plaguing him the innocent laughter was medicine to his soul.

As Toad reached the crest of the rise a huge, brightly-colored bird swooped up over it, nearly hitting him. He barely had time to duck as the monster bird whooshed over his head. It wheeled and flew off into the sun, but not before he saw that it grasped a man in its talons. Banking sharply, it headed back.

Scrambling to his feet, Toad took off after it. As he stumbled over the rise he saw Flo at the edge of a Honkweed patch, laughing and dancing about. Even though the bird was now little more than a grotesque shadow flying at him out of the sun, Toad knew that it was Eddie that he had seen clutched in its claws.

"Brother Flo! Brother Flo!" Toad cried. "Run away! It's coming back!"

Flo stopped and gawked at the pipesmith barreling down the hill towards him. "Heeey, Brother Toad," he said, grinning. "What's up?"

"Run! You'll be killed! Run!"

"Killed? Whoa, what are you talking about?"

A shadow swept down over them. Instinctively, Toad threw himself between it and Flo. Reaching up to fend off the bird, his hand closed on what felt like a man's foot. Before he could let go, the pipesmith was jerked off his feet and sent careening into Flo. Together, they and the monstrous bird crashed into the towering sticky-leafed plants. Toad saw the bird falling towards him, a wide-eyed Eddie still clutched in its claws.

The bird landed on Toad amid a rustle of dry wings, with Eddie sprawling across him. He thrashed about to extricate himself from his predicament. When he finally managed to stagger to his feet he saw that the bird was no bird at all, but a kite-like artificial wing resembling the one in Eddie's drawing.

"D-Dylan's Bones!" Toad sputtered, spitting out bits of leaf and topsoil. "You really made this thing? It actually flies?"

Clumsily, Eddie got to his feet, freeing himself from the harness that had held him beneath the wings. "Yeah, it works, or it did until you made me crash."

"I'm s-sorry, Eddie. I thought it was a giant eagle or something."

"Thought it was a big bird, huh? See, Flo, I told you this paint job was convincing."

"A little too convincing, brother mine. Brother Toad was freakin' out on us."

"No fooling? Any damage that you can see?"

"Freebird's a little bent up, but it's nothing I can't straighten out in a few moments."

While Flo set about repairing the glider, Eddie stripped a few dry leaves from one of the trampled Honkweed plants and stuffed them into a corncob pipe. Toad offered him a light from his tinderbox, and soon the three friends sat basking in the afternoon sun, passing the pipe between them.

"What's it like?" Toad asked. "Flying, I mean."

Eddie grinned. "It's the ultimate trip, man."

"I wouldn't go that far," Flo remarked.

"You haven't been up as many times as I have. Hell, the feeling of freedom up there is un-freakin'-believable."

"So's the feeling of fear, which is what I get every time I get into that kite."

Toad puffed on the pipe briskly, exhaling a roiling cloud of sweet-smelling smoke. "You guys are really lucky. You're probably the first people who have flown since Helter-Skelter."

"We are," Eddie stated proudly. "How about you? Would you like to give it a try?"

"Me? Isn't it dangerous?"

"Not really. Just takes some getting used to. C'mon, I'll teach you how."

"This thing's really light," Toad remarked, as Eddie strapped him into the contraption and showed him how to work the moveable harness and steering bar. "What is this fabric? It can't be leather."

"It ain't. Me and Flo eighty-sixed that idea long ago. Instead, we devised this special paper out of 'weed fiber. It's light and strong, really tough and weather-resistant. The struts and supports are treated with shellac. As you've seen, Freebird can take some rough use without a lot of serious damage."

"What about the pilot?"

Eddie laughed. "This bird's pretty stable once she's in the air. The challenge is to not crack up when you're landing her."

"I'll keep that in mind."

"It's simple enough, really. Keep the wings level on the down-swoop, bring her in slow and easy and hit the ground running."

Toad nodded and made some final adjustments on the harness. "I guess I'm ready."

"Fine and dandy. We'll launch from that hill over there. Don't try to take her too high on your first flight."

"You don't have to worry about that."

Toad hardly breathed as Flo and Eddie helped him to the top of the low hill. Below him the fields rolled off towards the horizon like the waves of the sea. Beyond them Mounts Lennon and Leary reared dark and ominous even in the afternoon sun. A breeze swept down from the mountains, stirring the grass and caressing Toad's face.

"Wind's coming up," Eddie commented. "Tilt the wings up into it and run."

Toad gave the glider one final adjustment and charged down the hill as fast as he could go. The wings billowed slightly as they filled with air. Suddenly, his feet left the ground. He pulled his legs back so that his body lay parallel to the earth. Slowly, gracefully, the delicate craft rose into the air until he was flying about fifteen feet above the grass. Behind him, Toad could hear Flo and Eddie's excited whistles and cheers.

Then, as suddenly as it had risen, the wind dropped. Toad and the glider plummeted into a juniper bush. Sputtering through a mouthful of spills and berries, the pipesmith staggered to his feet. Flo and Eddie tried to look concerned as they untangled Toad from the bush, but he noticed them both suppressing laughter as they lifted the kite out of the bushes.

The next attempt was conducted from higher up, about a hundred yards from the weed patch. A strong, steady wind was coming down from the mountains. This time when Toad lifted off he rose gracefully into the air and banked to the right, swooping low over the fields, which were now crossed with the lengthening shadows of late afternoon. The breeze ruffled his hair and swept over him in a gentle stream. He laughed aloud, exulting in the total freedom of flight. As he banked to the left and headed to the hill where Flo and Eddie waited, he turned to watch the sun settle in between the peaks of Mounts Lennon and Leary.

Toad grinned. He knew how he was going to get to the mountain.

Chapter Forty-Two

Silently, Toad glided over the moonlit fields, the roots of the mountain rising up before him. Shifting his weight to catch the mountain thermals, Freebird rose into the land of his nightmares. As dark stands of twisted pines flashed beneath him, something flew by, chittering and flapping. A leathery wing brushed his face. The near collision caused him, for one scary instant, to lose control of the craft. A bat, nothing more, he convinced himself. Thankfully, additional flights under Flo's and Eddie's tutelage had given him enough experience to steady Freebird quickly. For an instant, he felt guilty for commandeering their contraption without their permission, but he couldn't risk the possibility of anyone preventing his flight.

Earlier, when he had stepped out onto the wharf, the first evening stars were shining through the last rays of sunlight. The dark sweater and black wool cap he was wearing would offer protection from prying eyes and would insulate him against the cooler air of the high mountains. He'd found the clothes, a week ago, in the bottom of a battered trunk in the garret's storeroom. Curiously, when he'd gone to retrieve them earlier in the day, an old guitar lay on top of the trunk. He was sure that it hadn't been there earlier.

By the time he reached the shed where Flo and Eddie kept Freebird, the dark of night blanketed Hillcommune. He'd eased the spidery contraption through the door, and setting the bundle over his shoulder, had stolen out of town on one of the less-frequented trails.

Below him now, pines were giving way to barren outcroppings of jagged rock. The night breezes soughed by him, answered by the mournful hoot of an owl. Higher up the air was cooler. Above him the crescent moon, as cold as a polished scythe blade, beckoned him onward.

Nearing the summit he heard the faint but frantic beating of drums. He banked Freebird to the left and landed in an open area beyond a pile of boulders. Curiously, the drums stopped. After stashing the glider, he crept cautiously along a narrow path leading to the mountaintop.

Startled, Toad almost cried out when the drumming started up again, louder and closer. The urge to find its source was overpowering, as if the mountain itself was calling him. Slipping from boulder to boulder, he stopped short of the stone circle that crowned the mountain's summit.

The stones were huge, blackened with age. Some stood by themselves, others side by side, crowned by massive lintels. Most were straight, but a few listed sideways, bent under the weight of countless centuries. To Toad the circle was a vortex, drawing him into its center, while his heart beat in time to the drums pounding in the darkness beneath the megaliths.

Something moved among the ruins. Toad crept closer, rolling behind a fallen menhir for cover. Crouching as low as possible, he stared out from beneath the brim of his woolen cap. There were two figures moving in the darkness, faint black blotches on the fringes of the fire that burned in the center of the ruins. Toad saw a brief flash of light reflecting off a pair of spectacles and breathed a sigh of relief. These were no demons, only Maynard and Skulk. Nothing supernatural, no bogeymen with slack, grinning faces. Curiously, Franklin was not in sight.

The drumming intensified. Toad could see now that Maynard was pounding away on a small pair on bongos that he held between his knees. From time to time he'd lean his head back and bellow out words or phrases in a harsh-sounding tongue that was like no language Toad had ever heard before. Skulk responded in the same language, holding a book over his head. Even at a distance Toad knew it was the *Necronomicon.*

As the pipesmith watched, spellbound, the drumming and chanting became wilder and more frantic. The air on the mountaintop seemed to thicken and grow heavier. The shadows between the stones swayed in time to the music. They lengthened and started to swirl together, bobbing and billowing upward until they spread out over the circle of stones, obliterating the stars. Before the shadows crowded out the light entirely, Toad saw a figure move on the far side of the circle. Was it Moonshadow, Ernie or someone else? All he could be sure of was that he wasn't the only person curious about what was happening here. In an instant the figure was gone and only the drumming and dancing shadows remained. Suddenly the wind came up with such ferocity that it almost snatched away Toad's cap. The inky pulsing mass above the stone pillars was unaffected; the mountain rumbled and twitched as if it was stirring in its sleep.

Inside the stone circle lights moved; blue flashes flickered and danced like manic fireflies. They pulsed in time to the drumming, capering to and fro. When Skulk held the book up again, the lights flew up and swarmed around him. Skulk placed the *Necronomicon* on the high stone altar before the fire. Blinking on and off in random patterns, the lights followed the book, clustering around it in a protective aurora. The effect was hypnotic, like the northern lights Toad had seen as a child. He held his breath, and time itself seemed to stand still. The lights formed into pulsing, erratic groups only to swirl apart and form new combinations. In the misty light caused by their gyrations, Toad again saw the figure lurking behind the lightning-blasted remains of a tree that lay just outside of the stone circle.

Toad watched the furtive form closely. Apparently unseen by the others, the interloper huddled closer to the ruined tree trunk. Something in his shadowy movement suggested that it might be Moonshadow, but he couldn't be sure. The pipesmith tried to get a better look, but the haze from the lights around the altar obscured his vision. As Toad crept closer, Skulk turned and glanced in his direction. The pipesmith froze, crouching low behind a boulder just as the bongos increased their tempo. He watched the lights slowly rise from the altar and form a throbbing halo over the ruins. He held his breath as the light ring began to spin.

At first the circle of light spun slowly, wobbling slightly on its axis. It seemed alive, tensing, waiting for something. Suddenly it began to pick up speed, spinning faster and faster. Occasionally it threw out sparks that showered down over the ancient megaliths. It seemed to Toad that he'd never seen anything so beautiful, or so dangerous.

Maynard's drumming became more frantic as Skulk resumed chanting in a high cracked voice, "PH'NGLUI MGLW'NAFH CTHULHU R'LYEH WGAH'NAGL FTHAGN! IA! IA!"

As the eldritch words rang out, reverberating off the stones, a most remarkable thing happened. The lights stopped circling and formed into several spheres of blue fire that hung, quivering, in the air. Suddenly, one of the fireballs separated from the others and flashed towards Toad's hiding place. Maynard ceased drumming. He and Skulk stood silently, watching its flight.

Toad didn't dare move. He pressed himself close to the ground as the fireball arched overhead, a sizzling blue comet that smelled of lightning and violets. It quickly changed course and veered into a long sparking curve towards the shattered tree where Moonshadow was hiding. Toad trembled as he watched it rip through the night sky, awed by its fiery grace and beauty.

The fireball seemed to move with growing intelligence. It hovered over Moonshadow's hiding place for a moment, and then slowly made its way back toward Toad, sputtering and sparking furiously. The hair on the back of his neck stood on end.

Again the fireball veered off uncertainly towards Moonshadow's tree. Not wanting to be another victim of the blue light, Toad slipped from his hiding place and quickly crawled back towards the trail leading down the mountain, not daring to get to his feet until the stone circle was well out of sight behind the boulders. Swiftly and silently he made his way down the trail.

There was a tree in the bend of the path, an old stunted fir, naked except for a few clusters of needles on a couple of its twisted branches. As Toad ran past it the tree seemed to lunge out at him, trying to trip him with its knotted roots. He dodged it and hurried on his way, zigzagging over and around brush and boulders.

Someone moved out of the shadows beside the trail. In the pale moonlight Toad caught a glimpse of a white-haired figure—Franklin. The elderly Oldhip moved towards him slowly, hands outstretched.

"Brother Toad," he croaked. "Wait! We must..."

Turning sideways to avoid the Oldhip, Toad noticed a blue ball streaking down the trail towards them. Unaware, Franklin clutched at Toad's sweater, holding him back. Toad broke away too late.

Suddenly, he was slammed to his knees. He felt like he was burning and freezing at the same time, jabbed through with a million sharp needles, his nose seared with ozone and the surreal scent of crushed violets. He fell to the ground, writhing as the flames licked over him without scorching. Beside him Franklin lay unconscious, enveloped in an aura of flickering blue light. Toad tried to cry out as he slowly spun off into darkness.

The pain and darkness passed. Toad, still numbed, found himself lying on the ground. With a groan he staggered to his feet and looked about for Franklin, but the old man was nowhere to be seen. Above him great black ruins loomed toward a star-flecked sky. Slime dripped down the sides of the huge towers and spires as if they'd just emerged from the ocean floor. They were covered with strange symbols that might have been the writing and hideous carvings of beings that seemed to be part lizard, part man. More disconcerting was the distortion of angles and arcs of the buildings; and, as he became more aware of his surroundings, the place itself. Something about its geometry was wrong, horribly wrong.

The sky, too, was strange. It was filled with constellations that Toad had never seen before. The stars were close and unblinking, staring down like a million multi-lobed eyes.

With dread and awe, Toad made his way towards the closest ruin. He looked about desperately for any sign of Franklin. A feeling of formless terror seized him as he looked up at the great windowless structures towering above. They seemed to rise up, spire upon spire, for miles. Though silent and brooding, this was not a dead place. Something lived and moved here, something monstrous. There were signs of its passing on the wet cobbles beneath his feet—wide, slick trails of slime that looked like a snail the size of a house had recently lumbered by. A stench of corruption and decay tore at the pipesmith's nostrils, making breathing difficult.

Stopping at the base of a set of stairs, too steep and tall for any human to ascend, he looked up at the ruin. It was flat black, devoid of ornamentation, taller than those nearby. A movement at the top of the stairs caught his eye. A pair of figures stood in the shadows there. For a moment, before the figures became shimmering and indistinct, Toad thought he saw a muskrat and tall red-tufted crane looking down at him. As they winked out of existence he heard something moving behind him.

It was like nothing he'd ever heard before—a wet, slithery sound announcing the appearance of something mammoth and formless. Toad froze in his tracks, shuddering but not daring to turn around as the presence lurched closer. Growing sounds of sucking and smacking told him that the thing stalking him was hungry. Out of the corner of his eye, he caught sight of a tentacle the size of a large tree trunk uncoiling towards him. He screamed as something clamped down on his shoulder and gripped him hard.

He did not scream again. A hand was covering his mouth and the voice of Ernie Mungweasle was whispering harshly in his ear, "Toad! For Dylan's sake calm down!"

The pipesmith opened his eyes. There were no searching tentacles, no towering dark ruins, only the lonely mountainside and his friend kneeling over him. Close by a white-haired form lay motionless under Ernie's cast-off longcoat.

"E-Ernie!" Toad wheezed. "Franklin, is he d-d...?"

"No, but he's in rough shape."

"We've got to do something, Ernie. We can't leave him here."

"We? You don't look in much better shape than Franklin."

"I-I'm fine. Really I am."

Ernie seemed doubtful. He reached into his shirt pocket and took out a small leather bag, which he opened and held under Toad's nose. The pipesmith sniffed at the bag and almost sneezed. It smelled of wildflowers and acrid leaves, but almost immediately he felt his head clearing and warmth returning to his limbs. Slowly he sat up as Ernie returned the bag to his pocket.

"What in hell is that?" Toad muttered.

"One of my inventions—a simple, but effective, restorative. I only wish that it had worked on Franklin."

Toad tried getting to his feet. He still felt lightheaded. Shifting about slightly, he sat back down. "We can't leave him here, Ernie. Somehow we have to get him to Doc Aloevera."

"In a moment. You're looking better than you did, but you still have to take it easy. Holy Bob, for a moment there I thought you'd lost your mind. You were babbling some strange stuff."

"It seemed so real…"

"I'm sure it did. What in hell were you doing up here anyway?"

Toad flashed on the figure he'd seen sneaking about on the far side of the ruins. He'd thought it was Moonshadow, but obviously it had been Ernie. "I might ask you the same question. Are you in on all this with Maynard now?"

"No. I was just curious."

"How'd you get up here?"

Ernie chuckled softly. "You know me. I gotta be where the action is."

"Right."

"Look, if you feel up to it, I'd like you to help me rig up a litter for Franklin."

"I've got just the thing stashed in those boulders over there."

Ernie helped Toad to his feet. Within minutes they'd retrieved Freebird from its hiding place, and using the wing sections as a makeshift litter, gently placed Franklin on it. Starting down the mountain, Toad looked over his shoulder; there was nothing there but the stars and the night wind.

Chapter Forty-Three

A pitcher of cold herbal tea sat on the workbench, a plate of cheese and fruit beside it. Toad crawled out of his sweat-soaked bed and drank the tea greedily as he watched the early evening sunlight play over the wharf below his window. Grabbing a couple of apples and a hefty chunk of yellow cheese, Toad moved slowly to his overstuffed chair. He felt weak; whether it was exhaustion from carrying Franklin down the mountain or some effect of the strange blue fire, he wasn't sure.

Ernie hadn't left Toad's flat until well after dawn, most of the time coaxing the pipesmith to talk about the incident on Mount Lennon's summit. It wasn't until Ernie stomped down the stairs, that Toad realized the herbalist had done it to him again. While his friend had managed to get Toad to unwittingly reveal more information than he wanted, the older Freak had offered almost no explanation of his own presence on the mountain.

As much as that omission troubled Toad, other concerns weighed more heavily on his mind. Chief among them was Franklin. When they finally got him to Aloevera's, Doc couldn't find much wrong with him physically, but his mind seemed to be gone.

Toad put a thumbnail-sized portion of hash in his pipe and sank back in his chair. Through light puffs of smoke, he looked at his workbench. It was littered with sheaths of notes and drawings held down with half-finished pipes that he employed as paperweights. None of this interested him. He tried to concentrate on his unfinished work, but the one image that kept filling his mind was the dusty old guitar that he'd found in the back storeroom. Toad had never been interested in playing an instrument, but inexplicably he now possessed a strong urge to dig out the battered guitar. He shook his head; the urge made no sense. Still, every time he closed his eyes the image of the guitar welled up before him. Finally he gave in. Setting his smoldering pipe on the table, he traversed the hall to the storeroom.

Returning to his chair, Toad set about cleaning and tuning the guitar. He waxed it with a compound that he often used to put a soft finish on pipe bowls, then buffed all the woodwork with an old sock. When it shone to his satisfaction he started tightening the strings and plucking out experimental chords. Tuning came easier than he'd thought. He'd watched Tambourine do it on several occasions, and though he'd always thought he had a tin ear he seemed to know instinctively what he was doing.

Satisfied with the sound of the guitar, Toad played a few more chords. They were perfect. The tips of his fingers tingled when he touched the strings. He launched into a rather sloppy rendition of *Sludge River Boatman*—not the best he'd ever heard, but it sounded a lot better than it should have, almost as if some strange energy was flowing from the guitar into his hands. The tingling in his fingers remained even after he placed the old instrument on the bench.

"I'll be damned," he muttered to himself. Entranced, Toad stared at the guitar. There was definitely something strange going on here—eerie, in fact.

As if emanating from the door itself, a soft persistent knocking roused the pipesmith from his spell. Slowly, Toad got to his feet and opened it. He was taken aback when he found Maynard standing just outside.

The little Beatnik grinned. "Hi-ho, daddy-o. Is it cool if I come in?"

"S-sure," Toad mumbled, backing up a step.

Maynard walked past him and took a seat by the window. He seemed absorbed in studying the guitar lying on the bench. A sly smile spread across his face. "Hey, man, nice ax. I didn't know you played."

"I... I don't... didn't," Toad replied. He found the Beatnik's presence disconcerting, but was curious as to why Maynard had come. "That is, not really. I'm just learning."

The Beatnik's smile broadened. His small perfectly formed teeth seemed out of place with his leathery skin and strange blue-black hair. "So, like, tell me," he asked. "How do you feel?"

"How should I feel?"

Something seemed to flash behind Maynard's mirrored spectacles. He snorted, almost gleefully, regarding Toad closely as he stroked his small pointed goatee. The silence hung heavily in the musty air of the small room. "I thought you could tell me, man. Like, you saw the light, so to speak. I just came by to make sure you're feeling okay."

"I feel fine, thank you."

"We tried to keep things under control, but—well—your presence upset the balance."

"Control? Balance? Franklin's an empty shell and you're talking about control and balance."

Maynard leaned forward. His face was a mask of squirming tension. "Hey, man, don't lay that at my door. He should have stayed in the circle. But, don't sweat it, daddy-o. Franklin will be all right. He's a real gone cat."

"Yeah, he's gone all right. But where?"

"He'll be okay; it'll just take some time. But hey, I didn't come here to discuss what was going down on Mount Lennon. I only came here to make sure you were all right. Dig it?"

"I dig," Toad replied, still wondering what the Beatnik was up to.

Maynard picked up the guitar and examined it with interest. "This is a righteous instrument, Toad. It'd be nice if you got into playing it."

"It's just something I found. A decoration for the room really."

"Oh no, this box is begging to be used."

"As do many things, I suppose, but it doesn't mean they should be."

The Beatnik ignored Toad's thinly veiled insinuation. Putting the guitar back on the bench, he got to his feet. "I gotta split this scene, man. Places to go and people to see, ya know."

Adjusting his beret with an odd little gesture that looked like a salute, Maynard started for the door. Toad opened it for him.

"Just one thing," Maynard said before vanishing down the stairwell.

"Yes?"

"By tomorrow everyone will know what happened to Franklin. Let's just say, people could get hysterical if there were too much talk."

"The truth shall set you free," Toad stated.

"Ah, but whose truth?" the old Beatnik smiled slyly back.

Toad attempted to reply, but he was speaking to the shadows clustered at the bottom of the stairs. The Beatnik was gone.

Staring into the growing darkness for a few moments, the pipesmith turned and closed the door behind him. He returned to his guitar, playing it far into the night. Eventually, he nodded off in his chair, cradling the ancient instrument in his arms.

Violent gusts tore up the hill behind him, rippling his long cloak and shredding the dense fog that had hidden the fortress from view. Far above him a tiny sun struggled against leaden clouds. Toad laughed triumphantly and held the book and guitar over his head. He felt strange—powerful, confident, and wonderfully aware of himself and the world around him. Behind him, legions of his followers held their breath, waiting for his command.

Continuing to hold the guitar over his head, he slipped the book inside his shirt, placing it over his heart. It felt warm against his skin, faintly humming with power. With a toss of his head he lowered the guitar and held it with both hands. As his followers watched reverently, he flexed his fingers and began to play. Sliding sensually along the instrument's silver strings, his fingertips tingled with power as they caressed each chord. Soon they began to race up and down the neck, fretting out one angry note after another. A nasal, raging voice erupted from his throat, declaiming truths in convoluted magical images.

The music seemed to pour out of some place deep in the pipesmith's soul, gushing up from the dark well of racial memory. It flowed from some great gulf of time and space, channeling itself through his heart and hands. At his feet wraiths curled out of the ground, the long-dead ghosts of his people's ancestors summoned from Strawberry Fields to stand beside their living brothers and sisters. Faces loomed in front of Toad, appearing and disappearing like will-o'-the-wisps. The faces had strange half-forgotten names like Che, Janis, Jerry, Jimi, Abbie and John. Beside the phantoms Toad saw both his friends and enemies. Maynard, Ernie and Mizjoan were there, but so was the Dark Man. The face he saw most clearly, however, was Tambourine's. Even as he watched, the young musician's visage aged and darkened into one familiar from a thousand icons, the face of Dylan himself. Toad shook from the energy pouring through him, but his fingers never wavered on the strings. Tambourine, Dylan—was that what Toad was becoming, part of their mythic heritage?

The wind slackened. The words, howled and chanted from the Black Book, had done their work. Toad's song had dispersed the mists, reducing them to scattered tatters that cowered at the feet of his followers. As the last note faded away and the angry voice stilled, a cheer rose from the crowd, a single roar from thousands of throats assailed the heavens like waves pounding upon the shore. As Toad moved toward the fortress, an earthquake of two hundred thousand marching feet followed him. Covenstead lay ahead and nothing could stand in their way. Seize the day; the time was now.

The war drums began their low, measured beat. As Toad strode forward the scene began to change. The landscape altered and shrank until it fit into the confines of his room. His armies and the foggy hillside faded slowly away. Only the beat of the war drum remained, and that soon became the insistent sound of someone knocking on his chamber door.

He laid his guitar aside and shuffled, half awake, to the door. The first rays of dawn filtered through his window as he fumbled with the latch. The door creaked open to reveal a young dark-haired woman dressed in the uniform of a Radiclib officer. "Kentstate," he said foggily.

Without a word Kentstate entered and sat down in the chair by the window. She crossed her long jackbooted legs and stared at Toad for a moment, appraising him closely. "I need to talk to you," she said at last.

"Well, you've made a good start," Toad said as he closed and latched the door. "But, this isn't exactly a social call, is it?"

Kentstate shifted in her seat, but her eyes never left Toad's face. "No. I think you know why I've come. Lately you and Mizjoan have been, shall we say, close."

The pipesmith stiffened. He didn't like the course the conversation was taking, nor did he like the tone of Kentstate's voice. "We're friends. That's never been any great secret."

"You've been a lot more than that, Toad. Comrade Leader told me everything."

"Did she?"

"Your relationship concerns me—and quite a few others. It could even affect the entire course of history."

"Then, I trust, she described our relationship as 'earth shattering'?"

"This is no joking matter," she snapped.

Toad returned Kentstate's cool stare. He was beginning to get irritated. "What are you getting at? If Joan and I love each other that's our business."

"Who says she loves you, comrade? She may have some tender feelings, but love is out of the question."

"That is not for you to judge, in my reckoning."

The Radiclib leaned forward until her face was no more than a foot from Toad's. "Can't you see?" she asked. "Is it male vanity? You're her poultice, not her paramour. A leader like Mizjoan can never allow a mere man to come between her and her duties to her people. The wounds she's suffered in battle run deeper than simple cuts and bruises. The loss of my dear Rudy and all the others has wounded her spirit. You've been the salve that has allowed her wounds to heal."

"Toad, the human bandage, is that it? You think she's using me?"

Kentstate smiled weakly. "Not consciously, I'm sure, but she's better now and it's time for her to resume her duties."

"Without me."

"Certainly. Further romantic interludes would be counterproductive. It would only hamper her ability to rule."

Toad scowled at the pretty, dark-haired officer. "Mizjoan wouldn't have sent you here to tell me this," he said flatly. "Furthermore, if what you say has any truth to it then she will have to tell me herself."

"Comrade, the needs of the people come first."

"We have needs, too."

She shook her head. "The feelings of two people don't amount to a pile of potseeds next to the future of Street-Corner Earth."

378

Toad shrugged and began to fill his pipe. He lit it from the candle on the workbench and took a deep toke, not offering any to Kentstate. "You should go now," he said, exhaling

Kentstate got to her feet. "End it!" she demanded.

Toad looked out his window and watched Kentstate march down the wharf. He blinked; dawn was fully upon the world, pouring sunlight through the dirty garret window. He casually picked up the glasses that Maynard had given him for Yule from the clutter on the bench next to him and slipped them on. It was strange, but they fit him like they'd been made for him. Their slightly smoked lenses reduced the glare, and oddly enough they also seemed to improve his vision slightly, though he never needed spectacles before.

Kentstate's visit upset him. He knew that much of what 'State said was true. He had to talk to Mizjoan. And now that Kentstate knew of their relationship, he saw no reason not to go to the Comrade Leader's apartment. As Toad folded his spectacles and placed them next to the guitar, he remembered his dream and shivered. Like most dreams he'd had over the last few months, this one was disturbing and prophetic.

"Nobody told me there'd be days like these," he mumbled as he closed the door and started down the stairs.

It was already quite warm as Toad walked along the wharf. As he passed an alley between a warehouse and a residential building he was certain he saw Maynard and a taller companion walking away from him. Morning shadows still lurked in the alley, but even in a quick glance, there was no mistaking Kentstate's gray uniform and long, dark hair. The two of them together explained a lot, a hell of a lot. Toad slipped into the alley, trying to keep them in sight, but they soon exited the opposite end and disappeared around the corner.

Emerging from the alley, he looked quickly to the left and right, but there was no sign of the pair anywhere. Mumbling to himself, he hurried along the pebbled path and through the flower gardens clumped behind the various homes and business establishments of Hillcommune. Ahead, Skulk was lounging by the back door of the town bakery. The Digger chief was breaking up a loaf of bread and sharing it with a companion sitting on a bench by the door. As Toad drew closer he saw that it was Maynard. Straightening his shoulders, he hurried towards them.

"Hey-ho, daddy-o," Maynard said as Toad approached. "I'm, like, surprised to see you up and about so early. Feeling better?"

Toad shrugged. "I'm fine."

"That's cool."

"I was feeling a little cooped up in my room so I decided to catch some air."

"Must get lonely, staying to yourself as you do," Skulk commented, dusting some breadcrumbs from the front of his russet coat.

"Oh, I get plenty of visitors. Ask Maynard; he popped in for a chat last night and this morning Kentstate was by for a while."

Maynard grinned. "A classy chick, that one. Did you, like, have a nice rap with her?"

"Don't *you* know?"

"I'm not hip to what you're saying, man."

"I saw you talking to her just a few minutes ago?"

"Wasn't me."

"It's true," Skulk interjected, "Brother Maynard and I have been together all morning."

Toad wondered why Skulk would lie for the Beatnik. Suddenly, he felt dizzy, as if he'd stood up too quickly. For a second everything seemed blurry and distant.

"Most peculiar, Mama," he said in a voice that didn't seem to be his own.

Maynard leaned forward. Though Toad couldn't see them, he could feel the Beatnik's eyes on him. They were like pinpricks of sheer energy sweeping over his face. Maynard stroked his goatee thoughtfully and nodded, regarding Toad as a healer might his patient. "Yes, like, most peculiar. You seemed a little woozy, cat. Are you sure you're completely recovered from your trip to Weirdsville, up on the mountain."

"I'm fine," Toad replied; the dizziness passed as quickly as it came on.

"You sure?"

"I'm feeling fine, okay? But, I've really got to get going."

"Keep on truckin', man."

Toad started to leave, but stopped short at the sight of the bizarre creature emerging from a nearby doorway. It was Moonshadow, or at least what might once have been Moonshadow. This new Moonshadow wore a tight white jacket and trousers outfit over a black shirt that was unbuttoned almost to the waist. A gold-colored chain hung around his neck, beneath a sallow face on which the once luxuriant beard had been cut to less than an inch in length. Even the Seer's hair had been severely barbered, trimmed short like a Greaser's and combed and pomaded until scarcely a strand was out of place. On his feet, pointed-toed shoes had replaced beaded moccasins.

To Toad's relief the new Moonshadow ignored him and set upon Skulk and Maynard in a fast-talking frenzy. "Hey, hey, dudes, what's shakin'?" he asked, performing a bopping dance step as he spoke. "I been up n' down this little ol' town looking for my two main men. I got shit I wanna rap with you about."

"These things have already been discussed," Maynard said quietly.

"Hey, I can't seem to get no satisfaction, big guy."

"Sorry, cat."

Moonshadow stopped his dance and glowered down at Maynard. "I want in on that book, dude. There's no one around this dirty old town that's better qualified than me…"

"No! Case closed." Maynard snapped.

Moonshadow clenched and unclenched his fists. His face flushed scarlet, and the cords in his neck tightened until it seemed that they'd snap the fragile gold neck chain. He spoke clearly and evenly, but his words hissed out like steam from a teakettle. "You'll regret this decision."

When Maynard made no reply, Moonshadow turned and stormed off. The Beatnik watched him until he was out of sight. "Strange days," he said, glancing at Toad.

The pipesmith nodded. "Strange days indeed." Again, the words didn't seem entirely his own.

Maynard only smiled in reply. That smile was destined to hang in Toad's mind for days afterwards.

Chapter Forty-Four

Toad knocked three times. Mizjoan answered, opening the door slowly. The new uniform she was wearing was crisp and clean. It seemed to be trying its very best to brighten her weary face. At her feet, Rufus eyed the pipesmith suspiciously while weaving around Mizjoan's boots, as if polishing them.

"Toad, what are you doing here?" Mizjoan asked, drawing out the words as she crossed her arms over her chest.

"I had a visitor," Toad replied.

"She shouldn't have…"

"Then you told her?"

"Everything, yes. I had to."

"So, what now?"

Mizjoan's eye was red and watery, her face pale. She looked like she was in imminent danger of vomiting.

"Are you okay?" Toad asked.

"I'll be all right," she replied, gathering herself. "Lately, I wake up and my stomach starts doing rolls and flips. I try to eat, but it continues performing acrobatics the rest of the day. 'State says it's nerves from shirking my responsibilities. I suppose she's right."

"I should go," Toad pronounced, suddenly unsure, doubting his own wisdom in coming.

"No, we need to talk. I'm sure I'll feel better once we do."

Mizjoan motioned for Toad to enter. Rufus, who had taken up position behind her, hissed as the pipesmith stepped through the door.

"Don't worry," the Radiclib leader said. "He just doesn't seem to like men."

"What about Kentstate?"

"Oh, she likes men just fine."

"No. I mean, will she welcome me?"

"Don't worry about her. She wanted to blame you for distracting me, but now she knows it wasn't your fault."

"Right."

Mizjoan led Toad into the simply furnished living room and sat next to him on a threadbare sofa facing the fireplace. She sat close, but purposely left some distance between them.

"New uniform?" he asked awkwardly.

"Yes. 'State had it made for me; it's of the finest Oldhip hemp. Should last a century or one good hand-to-hand battle, whichever comes first."

Toad's heart began a long descent; she was thinking about combat.

As often happened when they were alone, he watched Mizjoan's every movement. Her hands fluttered like birds as she retrieved her churchwarden from an oak coffee table that stood between them and the fireplace. As she packed the pipe with a dark, resinous weed, Rufus jumped on the table and eyed her closely. The old cat seemed to be expecting a toke.

"I've never seen weed like that before," the pipesmith commented.

"It's unique, blended exclusively by and for the women of Hillcommune. Hashberry tells me that few men have ever experienced it. I don't believe that even Flo and Eddie have ever had any."

"What's it called?" Toad asked as he accepted the pipe and toked deeply on the pungent smoke.

"Black Widow."

He exhaled methodically. "They kill their mates, don't they?"

"Not in this case," she answered, smiling sadly.

The pipesmith was now aware of the weed's effect, rising warmly around him. Its name belied the calming, introspective mood it produced.

"I know where you're coming from," Toad said. He felt only sad resignation. Perhaps the weed had served its purpose.

"Look," Mizjoan explained, "I don't want to put you down, and I certainly don't want to simplify you, or crucify you. All I really want to do is be friends with you."

Friends. Toad felt a twinge of pain, as even the weed could not safeguard him from *that* dreaded pronouncement. He reached for the pipe.

"I guess, in my heart, I always knew it wouldn't work," he offered, "but it really gets under my skin that Maynard and Kentstate conspired to hurry it along."

"What are you talking about?"

"You knew that Kentstate came to see me, but what you didn't know was that right after she left I saw her talking to Maynard."

"For Dylan's sake, don't succumb to paranoia. Hillcommune is a small place. They are bound to bump into each other."

The pipesmith shrugged. Rufus, still waiting impatiently, growled as Toad re-lit the pipe, watching the contents of the bowl begin to glow. Suddenly a stray seed exploded, showering the cat with hot ash. Rufus retaliated, launching a vicious attack. Toad shielded himself with his hands. The collision spilled the cat, pipe and smoldering ash into Mizjoan's lap. The pipesmith fell across her as he tried to remove the alley cat and the churchwarden.

"Get off me!" Mizjoan cried.

Suddenly, a sarcastic female voice called out. "Hey, hey, party time."

The Radiclib leader pushed Toad away forcefully and jumped up, depositing him on the floor. Over the sofa, Toad saw Kentstate at the door, smirking.

"Don't you know how to knock?" Mizjoan barked, slapping ash from her uniform.

"I'm sorry for the intrusion," Kentstate said, trying to appear properly contrite, "but, I *do* live here and I didn't expect you'd be entertaining."

Mizjoan's cheeks glowed as red as the embers in the pipe.

"Comrade Major Kentstate! Remember whom you are talking to. What I was doing with Comrade Toad is none of your business."

Kentstate came immediately to attention but seemed almost glad to be reprimanded. "Yes, Comrade Leader," she replied, "It's just that ... the War Council."

"I'm fully aware of the War Council, major, but my business with Comrade Toad couldn't wait. Now that it is concluded, we may have our Council." Mizjoan was looking her major square in the face, her back turned to Toad. He could tell from the set of her shoulders that she would not turn around until he was gone.

Chapter Forty-five

Toad listened to the night winds. His heartbeat quickened as his ears caught the sound of drums; the beating was deeper and more resonant than the bongos that he'd expected to hear. The mountain seemed higher than he'd remembered it, and younger somehow. The alignment of the stars overhead was horribly wrong—incomplete—alien. Instead of the rude stone circle ruins on Lennon's summit, he found himself wandering among odd-angled cyclopean towers. Nearby a bonfire burned next to a huge stone altar. Sporadically, flames exploded upward, rolling to the tops of the towers and blotting out the alien stars. A faint sound behind him made Toad turn. He caught a brief glimpse of a fleeting figure swaddled in a tattered robe—Franklin was here.

Suddenly, Toad was aware of another sound behind him, as if something huge was approaching out of the dark, something too massive to be truly stealthy. Toad ran. The altar fire erupted again, sending gigantic bursts of flame toward the sky. Hot winds tore down the mountainside leveling everything that wouldn't burn and igniting everything that would. Trees snapped in half like twigs, bursting into flames in mid-air. He wanted to call out but the heat sucked the wind from his lungs. Jabbering with fear, he fell. Clutching at some tufts of grass to stop from being blown off the mountain, he screamed as the grass beneath his fingers caught fire. Toad screamed louder as his hair and clothing smoldered and began to burn. Above his screams he could hear hellish panting, coming nearer ... nearer.

The pipesmith awoke with a convulsion that sat him half on his feet. His breathing returned to normal as he realized there were no monsters, no fires or howling winds. There were only warm breezes coming off the river and wafting through his open window.

Slowly his mind turned to thoughts of Mizjoan. Something's happening here, he thought, but, what it is ain't exactly obvious. Or was he just being paranoid? Regardless of the Comrade Leader's comment about not giving in to paranoia, he knew that these days he couldn't be paranoid enough. Thoughts of plots and conspiracies bubbled in his brain like water boiling: Maynard, Kentstate, Skulk, Moonshadow and even Ernie were all involved somehow. The *Necronomicon* seemed to be responsible for much of what was wrong in Hillcommune; of this he was certain. Moonshadow and Franklin were obvious victims, as was Maynard, whose desire to possess and wield the book's dark power seemed almost maniacal. Its influence could also be seen in the unusual weather and in the growing rift among Oldhips over their part in the struggle against the Dark Man. There had to be a way to counteract the book's malignant presence, but he had no concrete plan. If he could get the book ... no, he wouldn't know what to do with it. If he could somehow release Moonshadow or Franklin from its grasp, maybe one of them could help him control the book. But, where to start? Moonshadow was skating on the edge of insanity, and in his current state Franklin was totally unresponsive. Some choice.

An hour later Toad ambled through the front door of the Healery. Inside, Doc Aloevera was just finishing up with a patient, a boy in his early teens with a nasty looking cut on his forearm.

"There you go, Brett Nettle," Aloevera said as he cleaned and bandaged the wound. "Now stay out of trees for a while, and if the urge to climb another one becomes too strong just remember to hold onto the branches."

"Sure, Doc," the kid said, scampering past Toad on his way out. "Thanks."

Aloevera smiled as the boy disappeared up the wharf. The smile broadened as he noticed Toad standing in the entryway.

"Hello, Brother Toad," the physician boomed. "What can I do for you today?"

"I just dropped by to see how Franklin's doing."

"I wish I could say he's doing well, Brother Toad, but I can't. His body seems to be recovering; with help he can be fed and walked. Still, he doesn't speak and seems unaware of his surroundings. Foreseein' is an old man and I fear the worst."

"He says nothing? Nothing at all?"

Aloevera shook his head.

"I'd still like to see him, Doc."

"Certainly, but don't expect him to recognize you, or even be aware that you're there."

Toad nodded and Aloevera led him into the same room that Moonshadow had occupied. Dressed in his brown robe and sandals, Franklin sat in a chair by the window. He looked waxy and cold. If it hadn't been for the rising and falling of his thin chest Toad would have taken him for a corpse.

"You have a visitor," Doc announced softly.

The pale figure in the chair did not respond.

"I believe," Aloevera continued, "that he has the ability to see, but it's as if his mind is elsewhere, concentrating on something inside."

"Or outside," Toad murmured. "Do you think he'll ever recover? I mean, Moonshadow did, after a fashion."

"And you as well, Brother Toad. You know, if you could tell me what this blue fire is, it might give me a clue how to treat Franklin."

The pipesmith shook his head. "I don't know what I can tell you. It's not like anything I've ever known. Some kind of energy, I guess. It seems to affect everyone differently."

"What was it like for you?"

"Weird dreams, mostly."

Aloevera looked at Toad, then at his patient. "I don't see how that will help, but, if you would like to help Franklin in another way…"

"Of course. What can I do?"

"Well, other than young Master Nettle, it's been a slow morning. I was thinking about taking Franklin for a walk, but since you're here and you've both had experience with that blue light … walk with him, talk with him. Maybe a walk would do both of you some good. And don't worry too much about his step; he seems quite sure on his feet."

"I'll walk with him, but I have no idea what to say."

"Anything. Everything. Chat about whatever you like, but take care to watch his face for any reaction to your words. Somewhere, something in what you say might give us a clue on how to get through to him."

"Is it possible?"

"I don't know, but it may be our only chance."

After leaving the Healery, Toad led Franklin out of the village. As they climbed the meadows above town together, Toad barraged Franklin with a steady stream of chatter, peppered with sour commentaries on Maynard, Skulk, Mizjoan, and just about everyone else who'd irked him lately. Franklin gave no response. Still, Toad talked about the *Necronomicon* and the copy he had on Smuttynose, half expecting a surprise reaction. He also spoke of the changes the book had brought to Hillcommune, the disruption of the weather patterns and the growing schism in the community between those who held fast to the Oldhip ways and those who favored the *Necronomicon's* use as a karmic weapon against the Dark Man. He spoke of the Other Place that he'd seen in his dreams, of the strange, eldritch structures that he'd visited there and the nameless horrors that inhabited them. He spoke until his voice was as rusty as a gate hinge, but it was to no avail. Franklin remained still and impassive, his eyes as murky as those of a man lost in a dream from which there is no waking.

Leading Franklin by the arm, he crossed the fields to the low hills that supported groves of cherry, and apple, and pear. Without really thinking about it, Toad led him to the banks of the pond where he had spent his first night with Mizjoan, now seemingly so long ago. Gazing across the pond he saw the spot where he and Joan had found Moonshadow. It occurred to him to show Franklin the place. It might still contain some magick, some faint stirring of The All that could provoke a reaction in the old man.

As Toad led Franklin along the edge of the pond he saw Flo and Eddie sitting on a log by the shore. They were engaged in passing the iron skull pipe he'd given them and didn't notice his presence for several seconds. When he cleared his throat they looked up, startled, and almost dropped the pipe into the pond.

"Hey, check it out!" Flo exclaimed. "It's Brother Toad and he's got Foreseein' Franklin with him."

"All right," Eddie called, smiling. "He's okay then?"

"Well, no," Toad explained. "His body is functioning but his mind seems to be gone."

"Not to worry," Flo joked. "Eddie and I frequently suffer from the same condition, but we always manage to pull through."

"But that condition is self-induced."

"True, and coincidentally, we were just starting to induce ourselves when you came along. Would you like to join us?"

"If it's the same stuff you were smoking before Yule I'm not sure I want any."

"We took your suggestion, Brother Toad, and toned down the formula. No more animal hallucinations, I promise you."

"Then torch it up, boys." Toad smiled as he rubbed his hands together eagerly.

"Eddie's got the tinderbox. Little brother, spark up the boo; we got some serious toking to do."

Soon the smoldering skull pipe was passing Toad's way; tendrils of smoke curled up from the bowl as the pipe passed under Franklin's nose. To Toad's astonishment, he thought he saw the Oldhip's nose twitch and his eyes clear; but the dreadful murkiness returned almost instantaneously. Toad choked in surprise, nearly dropping the pipe.

"Whoa there," Flo said, reaching for the grinning bowl. "It's rough stuff, but not that rough."

"Sorry. It's just that I thought I saw Franklin move."

"I didn't notice anything. Did you, Eddie?" Flo asked his brother, who, because he was struggling to hold in his last hit, just shook his head and shrugged. "Brother Toad," Flo continued, "I said we toned this stuff down; I didn't say we tamed it."

"It's just that…" Toad started, then stopped. "May I have the pipe?" Eddie passed it to him, the heavy iron bowl almost too hot in his hands. Before involving the brothers, he wanted to test Franklin's response to a more intense stream of smoke. The pipesmith filled his lungs and exhaled directly into Foreseein' Franklin's face. He waited, but whatever reaction he expected failed to occur. Toad shook his head.

"What are you doin', Brother Toad?" Eddie asked.

Toad surveyed the pair and decided that he trusted them more than anybody in Hillcommune.

"The same thing that hit Moonshadow also hit Franklin and me on Mount Lennon. I believe it hit you as well, the same time Moonshadow was struck, though in your case the effects were quite different."

Toad continued, describing what had happened to him after being hit by the blue light—his vivid visions and experiences in the dream world. He stopped short, however, of sharing his suspicions that Franklin's mind was trapped in the Other Place.

"That's a pretty heavy tale," Flo commented, "but we never had any dreams like that, did we, Eddie?"

The lanky brother shook his head. "No way, dude. Nothing like that."

"It was just a thought," Toad said.

The brothers shrugged in unison and the subject was dropped.

Much later, after Toad returned Franklin to Aloevera's, he acquired a jug of apple brandy at an eatery near his garret flat and sat late into the night gazing out his window toward the distant, dark shadow of Mount Lennon. He couldn't stop thinking about the brief look on Franklin's face when the burning weed had passed under the Oldhip's nose. Was it a clue to something important or just another trick of the blue light? Maybe there was no Other Place, no eldritch ruins or unspeakable monsters. Worse yet, maybe it was only his imagination.

Imagination or not, when Toad dreamed that night he was again in the Other Place among the ancient ruins. Franklin was there. too—a dim presence that cried out for help.

Chapter Forty-Six

Beyond the fertile, well-tended fields fringing the Oldhip village lay the steeper, less-traveled pastures north and east of Hillcommune. A few footpaths, narrow and overgrown with weeds, led through the pastures to scrub-covered foothills where they nearly disappeared. As he left behind the last few tufts of timothy the pasture had to offer he hesitated, plucked a thin stalk and slipped one end into his mouth. The bristly end of the grass bobbed up and down slowly as he mulled over his activities of the last few days—walking Franklin and searching for a way to get through to him with no success. It was desperation that led Toad to these high pastures to search for Moonshadow.

Toad was beginning to think that the *Necronomicon* might be his only chance to save Franklin from the Other Place. But before he traveled that treacherous road, he wanted to find out if Moonshadow knew of a safer way to bring Franklin back ... though dealing with the new Moonshadow might prove to be perilous as well.

The pipesmith had to admit, though, that the idea of getting the book away from Maynard was becoming increasingly appealing. The little Beatnik had shown his inability to direct the text's power. In fact, it was obvious to everyone that the book was now controlling him. It was no accident either, Toad decided, that *he* was the one who found the book, not Maynard, nor was it merely coincidence that *his* dreams of the Dark Man seemed to predict a confrontation. Perhaps it was ordained that he should wield the *Necronomicon* against Street-Corner Earth's ancient foe. Perhaps.

Logic and emotion collided in Toad's head with equal force, as the pipesmith struggled to keep on a trail that appeared to be little more than a chipmunk byway. Finding his way through the nearly pathless foothills was proving to be almost as challenging as plotting what course he should take with Moonshadow and the book. Even now, as he climbed to seek out the ex-Seer, he knew bone-deep that the man could not be trusted. Still, hope that the Oldhip might be of some help urged him on.

The sun was straight overhead by the time Toad scrambled up the last slope and found Moonshadow's old log shack, nestled in the overhang of a shallow mountain cave. Except for the plume of smoke curling up from the chimney, the shack appeared little used, as if its owner only occupied it on the rare occasions when his business didn't take him elsewhere. Its plank door stood open, listing slightly on worn leather hinges. Feeling a flash of apprehension and doubt, he rapped timidly on the doorjamb. He heard someone shuffling around inside and soon Moonshadow appeared at the door. He was shirtless and white foam dripped from his short beard. In his hand he carried a long shiny straight razor.

Moonshadow grinned mockingly at Toad. The grin faded into a smile that never quite touched his flat, sardonic eyes. "Say-hey, Brother Toad," he said, lowering the razor. "Come on in. I've been expecting you."

"Have you? I wasn't really sure myself that I was coming, until I left the village. And with all you've been through—gaining sight, resigning the Gatekeeper gig—I thought… "

Moonshadow's smile deepened, appearing almost genuine. "Just because I'm no longer the Gatekeeper, it doesn't mean that I don't know when a visitor is coming."

"I'm curious. If you no longer watch the Gates, who does?"

"It *should* be Foreseein' Franklin, but once he started dick-dancin' with the Beatnik and the Digger, Wheatstraw's cousin Thaddeus Shroom had to take over, at least until another Gatekeeper is chosen. But, you didn't come all the way up here to talk about that."

"N-no. I didn't."

"You know," Moonshadow continued, eyeing the razor closely, "Maynard, Skulk and company are nothing but fakers and con artists. You're different from those dudes; there's more to you than just a ripple in The All. I sensed it the moment you entered Hillcommune. It's no fluke that you've come by today. It was woven in the fabric of The All long ago."

"It was?" Somehow, Toad had expected Moonshadow to be more reticent, maybe even openly hostile to visitors. His willingness to talk came as a welcome surprise.

"Believe it, guy. We've got loads of things to rap about. Come on in and make yourself at home while I scrape off the last of this chin-fuzz."

Toad entered the dim, low-ceilinged shack and took a seat at the rickety table in front of the fireplace. On the other side of the room Moonshadow stood in front of a grimy mirror, keeping up a steady stream of conversation as he razored off his beard.

"I prefer to keep to myself these days," he said, "even more than I used to. It is true that I've experienced many changes. And, I need a little time to adjust. Still, I enjoy a bit of company from time to time, and I keep my ear to the ground. You can learn a lot by listening to the world around you.

"I heard about the night you and Brother Franklin got zapped on Mount Lennon. I knew then it would only be a matter of time before you'd want to talk about it. That blue light opened my eyes in more ways than one, dude."

Moonshadow finished with his shaving, set his razor down by the washbasin and began to towel off his face. Without his beard, and with only a well-pruned mustache adorning his upper lip, his jaw line was long and angular, almost wolf-like. The effect startled Toad.

"I-I'm not sure I know what you mean," the pipesmith muttered.

Moonshadow stared hard at Toad. His eyes seemed to glow with a feral light. "You know exactly what I mean, man, or you wouldn't be here. It's that place you came to rap about, isn't it?"

"What place?"

"Don't dance with me, dude. The place you saw after the blue light hit you. The one you dream about."

Toad found that he couldn't meet Moonshadow's fierce gaze. "T-then you've seen it too?"

"Of course, just like you and Franklin. Only you and I came back while he's still there."

"If he is there, can you help me bring him back? "

"Oh, he's there all right, and you need me to get him. That's why I was sure you would come."

"Then you can do it?"

"It all depends on you, little bro."

"What do you mean?"

Moonshadow's eyes glittered. "To bring him back I need the Black Book. Bring it to me. You had it before; you can get it again."

"I was hoping we wouldn't need it. You and I have both been to the Other Place and come back. Hell, Flo and Eddie were struck by the same blue light and they didn't even go; at least, they have no memory of it."

"Interesting, but irrelevant. If you want the old man back, get me the Book."

"But what about Flo and Eddie?"

"Obviously, the Place is accessible only to those who have some spiritual quality that the brothers lack; you know, people who are tuned to The All in some way."

"That might explain you and Franklin, but it doesn't cover me."

Moonshadow smiled coldly. "Oh? You have your strange dreams, do you not? Dreams that seem to foretell the future?"

"I've had dreams about the Dark Man, if that's what you mean." Dylan's Bones, Toad thought, just how much does this man know about me?

"Toad, the aura about you is strong. You are no ordinary Freak."

"But what about Franklin? Why is he still there and you and I are not?"

The ex-Seer laughed—a strange bitter laugh that seemed to fill the tiny room. "You were not struck with as much force as Franklin and I were. As for me, I was a Gatekeeper; I already knew the way." In the dim light his lean, clean-shaven face seemed even more wolfish than before.

"Then can you go through and bring Franklin back with you?"

"Impossible, Toad! I've lost some powers, gained others, but I've changed too much. I can do nothing without the *Necronomicon*."

Toad shrugged. "Maynard never lets the book out of his sight."

"Or, it never lets him out of its sight. The Beatnik is mad. He doesn't own that book, guy; it owns him. How you get it from him is your problem."

Toad nodded as if he agreed. In truth he suspected that Moonshadow was as mad as Maynard.

The ex-Seer put a finger to his lips and thought for a moment. Suddenly, his eyes widened and a sly smile crept over his face. "Little brother, I do believe there is a way," he said. "Is it true that the Clear Light Society is busting their buns to get you into the fold?"

"Yeah, but how would that help me to get the book?"

"Hey, you're a smart guy. Do I need to spell it out? Walk their walk, talk their talk," Moonshadow rubbed his hands together evilly. Toad thought he looked like a praying mantis. "Tell them you want in. Dance with them awhile, and before long an opportunity will present itself."

Toad thought about this. Inside he felt cold. The hungry look in Moonshadow's face told him that the book was no safer in his hands than Maynard's. "What will you do with it after I get it for you?"

"We'll return poor ol' Foreseein' to Hillcommune, of course."

"And after that?"

Moonshadow's eyes blazed like torches. "That's a good question. What do you think we should do with it?"

"I haven't given it a thought," Toad lied. "Maybe we should destroy it, burn it, and scatter the ashes to the wind."

"Potentially dangerous, Brother Toad. Destroying the *Necronomicon* inside Hillcommune may be more harmful to this valley than Maynard could ever be."

"You think so?"

"It is a powerful book, dude, and it will protect itself. But hey, bring me The Book and we'll dance that dance when the song plays."

Moonshadow's mouth turned up at the corners. There was something Toad feared in that back-slapping, damn-glad-to-meet-you, wouldn't-trust-you-with-a-sheep kind of smile; he'd seen it on many a traveling herb salesman. It was usually accompanied by the lying phrase, "Trust me."

Toad rose slowly, coldness growing inside him. "Well, I guess I have to be going if I want to get back before dark."

Moonshadow nodded as Toad moved to the door. The ex-Seer's eyes followed his every movement.

"I'll be back," Toad said and eased out the door.

From behind the door he heard, "I know. Franklin and I will be waiting," followed by a long low laugh. A chill shot down Toad's spine.

Chapter Forty-Seven

The strings flashed in the bright sunlight as the battered guitar sang mournfully under his adept fingers.

"*Ranger's Lament*," a voice behind him commented.

Startled, Toad spun around. As he played the old sad folk song of his youth, he hadn't noticed Mizjoan approach. Franklin, sitting beside him on the wharf outside the Healery, hadn't noticed her either; his mind was still far away.

"I haven't heard anyone play that in years," she continued. "You do it justice."

"Thanks." Thank Dylan, he thought. His newfound talent was one of the few good things that had happened to him since arriving in Hillcommune. Without it, he would have snapped like an ill-seasoned twig.

"You never told me you could play."

Toad shrugged uneasily. "Do you always sneak up on people?"

"That depends on the situation." She smiled as she adjusted the bow that held her hair straight back in a severe ponytail.

Toad pulled a red bandanna from his hip pocket and wiped his sweaty forehead. Hillcommune slowed down in the heat; even the river barges seemed to creep along. The weather in the valley was unseasonably hot—one might say, preternaturally hot.

"After that day at your place I wasn't sure we'd be talking again," he said, letting his fingers fall slowly across the guitar strings.

"I said we'd still be friends. We are friends, aren't we?"

Toad rolled his eyes up at her. "Yeah, I guess, but let's not go on about it, okay?"

"Okay," Mizjoan laughed.

Scarce breezes off the river did little to dispel the heat, but Toad was relatively comfortable in the brightly colored tie-dyed T-shirt he had chosen to wear, expecting the day to be warm. Mizjoan, however, tugged constantly at the collar of her well-patched fatigues, while Franklin, still staring into empty space, remained unaffected.

"Toad, I was on my way to a staff meeting, but since we've run into each other, I'd like to talk with you. I'm a little pressed for time. If you wouldn't mind walking with me, we could talk on the way."

Before long, many more people would be out on the wharf, bound for their favorite eatery. Right now, hardly anyone was about. In fact, the only person he could see was an elderly Oldhip woman approaching from the opposite direction.

"Why not? Franklin needs the exercise," the pipesmith replied as he put a hand under Franklin's arm and gently lifted the Oldhip out of his chair. "Let's boogie," he added, shouldering his guitar. Mizjoan hooked Franklin's other arm with her own. For a moment the trio strolled along the wharf in silence.

"Josiah Toad—Digger," Mizjoan said finally, seemingly amused.

"Where did you hear that?" Toad snipped. "I didn't expect it to be advertised all over Hillcommune."

"It's no secret. I heard it at the meeting I just had with Wheatstraw and Maynard. Maynard told me you were being sworn in tomorrow night…"

The ancient Oldhip woman stopped directly in front of Mizjoan, interrupting her. The old woman struck her cane loudly on the wharf, looked at the Radiclib leader and said, "Hrumpf," with as much elegance as a Downeast sailor hawking up a huge wad of phlegm. As she moved aside her cane kept tapping, less stridently, like the sound of a distant woodpecker. All the while, muttering to herself, her eyes remained fixed on Mizjoan.

"What was that all about?" Toad asked as they continued walking.

"Hillcommune is a small community, Toad. Small enough to keep up with the latest news, but also small enough to know when your welcome is wearing thin."

"Is it that thin?"

"You've seen the changes since we came here. The Oldhips are hospitable beyond any expectation, but after all, we are outlanders with different ideals and different problems. Our presence disturbs their way of life. Many think our ideas are infecting their youth. The awful truth is that they are right. Recently, a dozen or so young men of the village approached me about going to Covenstead with us. That's unheard of here. I agree with Wheatstraw and Maynard; we shouldn't need to corrupt Oldhip values to defeat our enemies. So far I've put those young men off, but I'm not sure I'll feel the same way in two weeks or a month. Fortunately, the weather in the lowlands is reported to be improving rapidly and the time to leave is close at hand."

Toad's pulse quickened at the unexpected news. "What do you mean?" he asked nervously.

"As I said, I had a meeting with Wheatstraw, and Maynard and company. With the improving weather outside and the growing pressures inside, we decided that as soon as the necessary preparations are complete, we will be on our way to Covenstead."

"So soon? I thought your troops weren't ready yet. I mean, don't we need more? And ... and, what about the book?"

"Toad, my troops are as ready as they will ever be. We could always use more warriors, but we do have General Dillon's forces to count on. Messengers have been sent throughout Street-Corner Earth asking for help and volunteers. I even sent someone to the Downeasters, though I suspect they are too isolationist to care about getting involved unless they are directly threatened. The messengers should return within the week. As for the book, Maynard feels he has enough control over it to give our forces the edge in battle. Barring any unforeseen complications, we will be marching out of the gates of Hillcommune in two or three weeks."

"No ... no, that's too quick. It won't give me, I mean you, enough time."

"It will have to be enough," Mizjoan answered.

Toad stood in the heat of the day, at a loss for words. He glanced up and down the wharf, avoiding her.

"I have to go," she said hurriedly.

"I know. I should be going too. I promised Franklin a well-packed bowl of Red before I brought him back to the Healery."

Mizjoan looked at Franklin's empty face and smiled. "Don't let him bogart the whole thing," she said.

"Might do him some good," Toad replied.

"I have to go—really."

Toad saw something in her face, as if she wanted to say more but couldn't.

When Toad returned to his apartment, with Franklin still in tow, he found a note tacked to his door, carelessly folded and attached to a small leather weedsack. Once inside, he helped Franklin to a comfortable sitting position on the corner of the bed and sprawled out in his chair by the window. He unfolded the note attached to the weedsack.

Yo, Brother Toad, (it read)

Thought you looked pretty bummed out the other day. Eddie and I've been workin' out a new variation of our famous Purple and decided to send you a sample. Tell us if you like it. Enjoy!

Your Buddy, Flo.

P.S. We replaced some of the more dangerous ingredients with a higher content of the Third World White. Knock your socks off.

Toad crumpled up the note and tossed it aside. Smiling, he emptied out the contents of the sack onto the table and drew the candle closer so he could better examine the weed. Like before it was dark maroon in color, but in the flickering light it sparkled silver like the Milky Way. Toad licked his lips as he ran a pinch of it between his fingers. It was moist and had a rich earthy aroma. Casting a glance at the impassive Oldhip on the bed, Toad packed his cherrywood and fired it up.

Toad's mind began to melt as soon as he inhaled it. After that, it took all he could do to exhale, blasting out a cloud of pungent smoke in Franklin's direction. The smoke swirled around the old man's head like a nimbus, but his stolid expression never changed.

Toad took another toke and set the smoldering pipe down on the table. His brain felt as if it had come unglued in his skull. Objects in the room seemed to swim in and out of focus. He took several deep breaths and melted back into the chair. Once his vision cleared he found that in spite of the buzz he felt more rested than he had in days. He was amazingly clear-headed as well, and felt preternaturally aware of everything around him. Sitting with his fingers steepled in his lap, he stared directly into Franklin's blank eyes and began to formulate a plan for the future.

"Mizjoan's right, we have overstayed our welcome," he said more to himself than to Franklin. "I think if it weren't for you, I'd just grab the book and go far away, home maybe."

The elderly Oldhip continued to stare through Toad.

"I have somewhat of a plan, you know," he confided to his silent companion. "I suspect that Maynard is arrogant enough to leave the *Necronomicon* hidden in his room when he attends the induction ceremony tomorrow night. If he does, the book will have a new owner.

"What did you say?" he asked the inanimate Oldhip. "I know I'll be late for the ceremony, but I can make excuses. I'm just not sure what to say when Maynard notices that the book is missing. I certainly can't tell him the truth, that it belongs to me more than it does to him or Moonshadow. Ah, Moonshadow—if I didn't think that he was the only person who could bring you back, I would never trust him with it."

Toad began to massage his temples. On the table beside him the pipe fumed away, its pleasant odor beckoning. He picked it up and cradled it in his hands. Its warmth was reassuring and soothing. Toad took another hit from the pipe, holding in the smoke until his eyes watered. When he exhaled, the sweet-smelling smoke blasted from his mouth, settling around Franklin more like a fog bank this time. The Oldhip remained immobile but his glazed, washed-out eyes blinked twice rapidly.

"After Moonshadow brings you back…"

Across from him, Franklin began to twitch and stir. Suddenly, the Oldhip's arm jerked up, one long gnarled finger pointed right at Toad. The eyes were as dead as ever, but the old man's wrinkled face convulsed with effort.

"No!" his harsh voice commanded. "Beware the book! Do not trust Moonshadow!"

Toad sat speechless as Franklin crumpled on the bed. He jumped to Franklin's side and tried to rouse him but the Oldhip's slow, soft breathing signaled that he had slipped back to his Other Place.

"I'll be damned," he whispered, covering Franklin with a blanket.

Returning to his chair by the window, Toad took one last small toke from the cherrywood and set it aside. Had he really just seen what he thought, or was it just the product of wishful thinking and mind-twisting weed? If the old man's warning was real, then giving the book to Moonshadow could be disastrous. Thoughts tumbled through the pipesmith's head like stones falling down a mountain. He exhaled slowly. Maybe something in the weed was acting as a catalyst, establishing a contact with Franklin. If a small amount of Flo and Eddie's weed had some effect, could a larger dose bring him all the way back? Or perhaps, only one ingredient of Flo and Eddie's mixture was essential and the brothers could help him isolate it; then he wouldn't need Moonshadow's help. On the other hand, if the weed didn't work he'd be right back at square one. Groaning, he reached for the weedpipe. He still had to have the book. But that really was never in question.

Chapter Forty-Eight

Water thundered down in cataracts from the eaves on both sides of the alley, spawning a stream several inches deep that cut down its center. Under an overhang, protected from the torrents of water by a small dormer on the roof above, Toad drew his cap brim low over his eyes and huddled out of the weather. Rain was coming down in sheets so heavy that he could barely see across the alley to the dark, dirty windows of Maynard's flat. For a second, he fancied he saw a flicker of light within. He faded back into the drizzling shadows. You're paranoid, he thought; it's just a trick of the lightning.

Earlier in the day, he'd had high hopes that he would not need to set upon this path. Following breakfast he'd gone by Flo and Eddie's to pick up samples of their Purple Haze and its individual ingredients. Then, he practically ran to the Healery to get Franklin and towed him, as fast as the Oldhip's condition would allow, back to his garret apartment. Pulling the rocking chair over to the table, he sat Franklin in it, making him as comfortable as possible. Once the Oldhip was settled, he carefully laid out a variety of small leather sacks. First, he chose the one containing the Purple, packed a bowl, lit it from a candle burning in the center of the table and blew the smoke directly into Franklin's face. He waited. The first bowl produced no effect. Neither did the second, or third.

Smoke was starting to hang around the rafters, reaching down in long wispy tendrils. Mildly disheartened, Toad stared at the other sacks: Hillcommune Red, ergot, powdered mushrooms. Bemused, he gently knocked around the sacks with the back of his fingers. None of them felt right. Suddenly, one caught his eye. Specks of white dust sparkled around its pursed opening, as if The All was blowing him a kiss flecked with twinkling stars. In that instant the pipesmith believed in The All more than ever before. The Thirdworld White in the small pouch was a sign, a portent. It seemed more than coincidence that the magical weed, which was the catalyst in starting him on this journey, would now present itself in Hillcommune at the very moment his future course stood at a momentous crossroads. He shook his head. Thirdworld White's roots must grow deep into The All, indeed.

Reverently, he picked up the weedsack and filled the bowl of his pipe. With great expectation, he leaned close to Franklin and puffed furiously, cloaking the Oldhip's head in a dense cloud. After a few moments, Franklin twitched. Then, he twitched again, blinked his eyes, coughed slightly and went silent. Toad nearly jumped out of his chair; it was working. Emptying one bowl he lit another, and another, but the Oldhip remained silent. The pipesmith called to him hoarsely. He nudged Franklin's shoulder and patted his face. Nothing. Smoke swirled around the duo like the mists of time. But time, and his supply of Thirdworld White, were running out.

Desultorily, he tried bowls of the other ingredients, but to no avail. Admitting defeat, he leaned back in his chair and rubbed his puffy, red-veined eyes. The All mocked him. Reluctantly, he returned Franklin to the Healery.

After leaving the Oldhip at Aloevera's Toad paused, glancing up and down the wharf. His stomach growled angrily, reminding him that he'd missed lunch and was suffering from a near-terminal case of the munchies. An eatery was conveniently located just up the wharf from Aloevera's. Hurrying to it, Toad went in and picked up bread, honeyed wine and cheese to bring back to his flat. A few young Radiclibs, along with a scattering of townsfolk, were seated for an early meal. Vibes between the two groups were not mellow. An Oldhip, probably a field worker, about Franklin's age but broader and more muscular, seemed to delight in wry comments aimed at the soldiers. Several of the locals laughed encouragingly. Though the Radiclibs paid him no mind, the place possessed a disturbing atmosphere. Toad was relieved when the waiter handed him a crock and a package wrapped in heavily waxed paper. He slid out with both tucked safely under one arm.

Now here he was, a few hours later, a stout walking staff in one hand and his short sword snugly belted to his waist under his cloak, trying to muster enough courage to cross the alley. He hunched his shoulders as water trickled down his back. Lightning struck close by. The resulting thunder shook away any lingering apprehension. He scanned up and down, a futile effort considering the torrential rain and the staccato bolts of lightning that provided the only illumination. He scurried across the alley to Maynard's flat. As his hand fell on the pitted iron doorknob a sudden thought chilled him—what if the *Necronomicon* wasn't inside? What if Maynard had taken it with him after all? Taking a deep breath, he turned the knob and slowly inched the door open. It squeaked slightly. He ducked inside the doorway as thunder crashed overhead.

Lightning strobed through the rain-streaked window beside the door. It provided enough light to show that the room was furnished with a table, two chairs, and some empty shelves. On the table lay a clay pipe, a scattering of papers, and a candle jammed into the neck of a wine bottle. A particularly bright flash revealed doors leading off to the side—bedrooms perhaps, or storage areas.

Even with the din of the storm outside, Toad was aware of his rapid heartbeat and quick, shallow breathing. With unsure hands he fished his tinderbox out of his coat pocket and lit the candle. Shielding the flickering light with his left hand, he quickly explored the room. Except for the clutter on the table, a pair of soiled tea mugs and a single, holey sock on one of the chairs, the room was bare. Creeping towards the nearest door, he nudged it open with the toe of his boot.

The room beyond the door was a shambles. Clothes were everywhere, either hanging out of the open drawers of the dresser or scattered across the unmade bed. In the corner, a beaded satchel hung from beneath a shirt draped over a coat rack. At first it seemed that someone had ransacked the room before him, but as he poked around it became apparent that the mess was just extreme sloppiness. The room had no window. The air was close and heavy with the unmistakable odor of peat.

Toad rifled through the dresser drawers, knowing somehow that he would not find the book there. As he glanced around the room again his eyes fell on the beaded bag. Something was drawing him to it. As he approached he could see the word PEACE embroidered on its side in brightly colored beads. Toad recognized it as the ditty bag Wheatstraw had given Maynard for Yule. The *Necronomicon* was inside; he could feel it. He could almost smell its ancient pages slowly crumbling into dust.

Resting the candle on the windowsill, he tucked his walking staff into the belt of his jeans, reached inside his cloak and produced the used waxpaper he'd saved from his evening repast; the paper would protect the fragile tome from the rain. He opened the bag and gently lifted out the ancient book. As soon as he touched it he felt giddy. Though slightly warm to the touch, the vellum pages brushing against his fingers sent a chill up his spine. Suddenly the room was all dancing shadows and impossible angles. In the shadows he saw the tumbled cyclopean ruins of the Other Place. Fires burned here and there in the twisted streets. A shape, huge and dark, bulked up against the starlit sky, patiently waiting.

Another flash of lightning brightened the room and the vision disappeared. Toad wrapped the book securely in the paper and slid the bundle under one arm. Tiny particles of rotting vellum, like scales from a moth's wings, clung to his fingers. They tingled with unnatural warmth. Blowing out the candle, he quickly left the room.

Toad stopped halfway across the front room, pausing to stand by the paper-strewn table. The warmth emanating from the book felt soothing now. It was coursing through his entire body. He could hear sweet distant voices, clear as wind chimes, chanting foul words. In the shadows of the room he saw another vision: he was standing on a high cliff overlooking a long low valley. As in the dream he'd had the previous week, he was holding his guitar and the *Necronomicon* over his head, while below him in the valley thousands stood gazing up in silent awe. He liked what he saw in the enraptured faces. Smiling to himself, he stepped out into the alley.

As soon as Toad cleared the door, lightning flashed overhead outlining a tall, cloaked figure standing in his path. Before he could even cry out in surprise the figure jabbed at him with the long staff it held in its bony hands.

"Give it to me!" a rough voice commanded.

Toad stepped backwards, feeling his way along the wall of the alley. Rain sluiced down from the eaves, pounding on his head and shoulders. "Moonshadow!" he squeaked.

The figure moved closer, holding the staff with one hand while grasping for the book with the other. "Give me The Book!"

"No ... I ... I mean I was just on my way to bring it to you," Toad rasped, edging slowly along under the dripping eaves. He clutched the book tightly to his chest. The warmth from the book slipping away— retreating before shivering-cold fear. With his free hand he felt first for the pommel of his sword, then for the handle of his walking-staff.

In the shadows of his cowl Moonshadow flashed a twisted grin, but his eyes were deadly cold. "Were you now?" he chuckled.

Toad stopped moving. He held the book tighter.

"Just as I thought," Moonshadow sneered. "You meant to keep it for yourself, didn't you?"

Toad shook his head. His right hand closed on the head of his staff and slowly began to draw it from his belt.

Suddenly, Moonshadow uttered a low growl that was more animal than human and swung at Toad. Toad ducked the blow, breaking past his attacker as the staff rebounded off the wall. It descended again, cracking across his forearm with a force that made him drop the book.

Toad grabbed for the *Necronomicon* just as Moonshadow's hand closed over it. He fought to tear it from the larger man's grasp, but a vicious kick sent him sprawling. He landed face down in a puddle. Sputtering, he staggered to his feet as lightning stitched the narrow band of sky above the alley. Moonshadow was gone. In the lurid glare of the lightning Toad could see his hunched form running in the direction of the river with the *Necronomicon* bundled under his arm.

Moonshadow was getting away with *his* book. Wielding his staff, he ran off after the loping black-robed figure. In the dark and driving rain, with only the flashing heavens to help him, Toad was barely able to keep the Oldhip in sight. It appeared that Moonshadow intended to cross the Peace and lose Toad somewhere south of the village where the fields met the base of the mountains. The tunnel through which Mizjoan and her troops had entered was there. As the former Gatekeeper, Moonshadow would know how to navigate it quickly and safely.

The pipesmith gained ground as thunder shook the valley and a spectacular lightning bolt arched over the bridge leading to the southern fields. Halfway across the span Moonshadow's silhouette appeared in the flickering light. The ex-Seer was bent over, running slower than before, as if carrying a great weight. Wind and rain whipped around Toad as he ran toward the retreating shadow. Needles of pain shot up his legs and his chest heaved with exhaustion, each breath more ragged and burning than the last. In the next brief flash of lightning he saw Moonshadow, closer now, moving through a field of wind-whipped rye toward a mass of black boulders. It's there, Toad thought, the tunnel to the outside world. If Moonshadow reached the boulders he'd be gone, worming his way through the dark passages that he knew so well, out of Toad's reach forever. Summoning the last of his rapidly failing strength, Toad hurried on.

"HALT!" the pipesmith roared in a voice that competed with the thunder. About ten yards from the boulders, Moonshadow stopped and turned to face him. He was hunched over nearly double and his eyes shone with unnatural brightness in the rain and dark. In his right hand his staff twitched menacingly.

"The Book is mine!" he hissed.

"No! It's mine," Toad insisted as he slowly advanced. His grip tightened on his knobbed walking-staff. For a moment they stood facing each other as the thunder and lightning boomed around them.

"Leave now or die," Moonshadow sneered, baring his teeth.

"One of us may die," Toad replied firmly, "but it won't be me."

The former Seer growled deep in his throat. Blue fire flashed in his eyes as he hurled himself at Toad. Toad quickly sidestepped and lunged with his staff. Moonshadow missed his mark, but Toad didn't. With the first blow he knocked the paper-wrapped bundle from Moonshadow's hand; on the second its knobbed handle connected with the side of the ex-Seer's head. The larger man stood dazed for a second, then toppled to the ground where he lay unmoving among the rocks.

Ignoring the book for a second, Toad approached the still form.

Moonshadow lay in a widening puddle of rainwater. The lightning revealed a bright welt on the side of his head where Toad's staff had hit home. A string of saliva drooled from the corner of his mouth. Toad laid his staff aside for a second and wiped Moonshadow's face. His hand trembled slightly; he feared the blow might have been a killing one.

Suddenly Moonshadow's eyes fluttered open. Though dazed they looked clear, free of the insanity that had previously animated them. "It has you," he rasped.

Toad's hand strayed towards his walking-staff. "What do you mean? What has me?"

"The Book, Brother Toad; it's starting to own you. Its grip is not yet as tight as it is on Maynard and me, but it will be. Do not let it consume you."

Moonshadow's face contorted violently. The blue fire flared in his eyes again, brighter than before. With incredible speed he leapt to his feet, shoving Toad to one side. With a low throaty growl he snatched up his staff from the ground and stalked towards Toad. "Give it to me!" he grunted in a thick slurry voice. "The Book is mine!"

Scrambling for his own staff, his hand barely closed on it as Moonshadow's crashed down on the back of his neck. Dazed, Toad took a clumsy swipe at his adversary. Parrying the pipesmith's blow, the Oldhip knocked the stick from Toad's hand. A second blow caught the pipesmith just above the ear.

Blinded by thousands of fragments of light that danced before his eyes, Toad fell backwards, banging against a rain-slicked boulder. Instinctively he reached inside his cloak for his sword. His fingertips just brushed the timeworn pommel as Moonshadow's staff connected with his shoulder, driving him to the ground. With a victorious howl, the ex-Seer came at him again.

"Stop!" ordered a soft but stern voice from the shadows among the boulders.

Moonshadow growled and turned, his black cloak swirling about him like smoke. A brown-robed figure stood among the boulders confronting him. In one hand it held the *Necronomicon*.

"You!" Moonshadow spat. "Foreseein' Franklin!"

The old man bowed mockingly. "That's right, Brother Moonshadow. And not a moment too soon, it would appear."

"Franklin!?" Toad murmured, still dazed from the blows he'd received.

The blue fire flared brightly in Moonshadow's eyes. "Give me The Book, old man."

Franklin stepped toward him, his face impassive but his movements quick and sure. In the harsh glare of the lightning it seemed that some arcane force glowed and crackled about him. "You do not really want it,

Moonshadow. More importantly, it does not want you."

"We'll see, maggot."

Brandishing his staff, Moonshadow advanced. Franklin stood his ground, holding up the *Necronomicon* like a shield as Moonshadow's staff descended. On impact the cane shattered into a dozen pieces, consumed by a bolt of blue fire. In that moment the ex-Seer seemed to diminish in size, as if some great power had been sucked out of him. Then, with a howl of insane rage, he shoved his way past Franklin and ran into the tunnel, hidden in the darkness of the boulders. Toad struggled to his feet and stumbled after him. Franklin's hand fell gently on his shoulder.

"Are you all right?" the old man asked softly.

"I'm okay, I guess. But, Moonshadow…"

"He's gone."

"We have to go after him. We can't let him escape."

Franklin shook his head. "What good would it do? He's probably halfway through the tunnel by now. It would be folly to pursue him in those dark passageways."

"But … he … you … the book … wha…?"

"Try to be calm, Brother Toad. Moonshadow is no longer a threat to anyone but himself. Come, let us get out of this storm."

Toad allowed Franklin to help him to a protected spot under a rock overhang. When they were settled on a bed of dry moss Franklin reached into his belt pouch and produced a small silver flask, which he offered to the pipesmith. Toad accepted it gratefully, taking a generous swig of what proved to be excellent blackberry brandy. It warmed his throat and stomach. He leaned his aching head back against the rock.

"If I'm not mistaken, you are late for an appointment," Franklin said.

"I know, but how can I go now? Wait a minute; how'd you know about that? I mean … you were …?"

"I know, I know, Brother Toad. And all will be revealed, in time. But suffice it to say, I seem to have acquired much knowledge since returning."

"I don't understand. How did…?"

"How did I get here? Quite simple, really. Though the outcome was delayed, your infusions of the white weed worked. Fortunately I returned just in time; I was almost too late to help you."

"But how did you know what was happening?"

"My time in the Other Place seems to have changed me. When I awoke in Aloevera's Healery, I found that my perceptions of things were stronger than before. In fact, I may have absorbed Moonshadow's lost abilities. I felt a great distortion in The All and knew that Moonshadow meant to steal the *Necronomicon* and leave Hillcommune. I also knew that you were planning a similar move. You two were bound to clash. Although I couldn't prevent the initial theft, I knew that I needed to prevent either of you from escaping with the book."

Toad bowed his head, feeling suddenly ashamed. "I suppose you're going to tell everyone about this."

"Not at all, Brother Toad. When I said that I needed to stop either of you from leaving our valley, I wasn't quite accurate. I mean to see this evil book out of Hillcommune, but on our terms. The book has caused nothing but trouble and has ruined one of our most notable brothers in the process."

"Let's light a fire. We can destroy it now."

The old man shook his head. "Not in Hillcommune. This land is connected to The All, as no other. Destroying the book might shatter that connection. If that happened, Hillcommune would surely perish."

"Then, what can we do?"

"You must take the book away from here and destroy it utterly, before it falls into someone else's hands … if you can."

"I'll do it! I know I can do it," Toad replied.

"Can you? That's really the question, isn't it? I can see many things in The All and I know that the book has infected you. Its hold is weak, but grows daily. My biggest concern is that when the time comes you will not be able to do what you must."

Toad knew in his heart that Franklin's concern was well founded.

"But, you will leave well prepared, and not without company," the Oldhip continued. "Alone, the book would consume you in no time. However, it would not be wise for those who go with you to know your design. With the best of intentions they might persuade you to use the book against the Dark Man. That would start you on the same path as Moonshadow and Maynard. Trust that, even without knowing, your friends will protect you and make your task easier."

"I can't ask anyone to go with me, Franklin."

"Are you sure that you will have to?"

"What do you mean?"

Franklin took a sip off his flask and then offered it to Toad. "Tell everyone that you saw Moonshadow running from Maynard's. They will think that Moonshadow took the book and fled. I'm sure Maynard will insist that someone follow him and retrieve the book. You will offer, as will others. Once you and your companions are clear of Hillcommune, and the opportunity presents itself, you must destroy the book."

"I will do what I can."

"No! It is not a matter of what you *can* do; it is what you *must* do."

Maynard paced nervously back and forth in front of the podium. Every now and then he glanced at the others, sitting on pillows around the room, smoking and talking sporadically amongst themselves. In the vastness of Wheatstraw's meeting room the handful of Diggers and two Oldhips seemed like small children camping out in a barn.

"Man, the cat is late," Maynard fumed. "Like, what is keeping him?"

Ernie shrugged. "I checked his rooms about half an hour ago; he wasn't there. He's got to be on his way."

Strutter Lurchkin, newly arrived from Froggy Bottom, reached into the pocket of his star-bedecked, yellow frock coat and produced a watch the size of a small apple. Squinting nervously, he consulted it. "It's twenty of nine," he reported. "He could have crawled in here on his hands and knees by now."

The Beatnik nodded, candlelight flashing from his reflective glasses. "I don't dig this!"

"I'll go check on him again," Skulk offered, getting up from the pillow next to Wheatstraw and Hashberry.

Suddenly, the door to the outside flew open admitting a gust of rainy wind. Two figures stood outlined against the flashing lightning, one in a cap and cloak, the other in tattered brown robes. Everyone fell silent as the pair entered, closing the door behind them.

Ernie was the first to speak. "It's Toad and ... Franklin!"

"You're way late, man," Maynard snapped. "This is no time to be playing nursemaid to Franklin."

"Friend Beatnik, perhaps you underestimate Brother Toad's healing abilities," Franklin said, smiling.

Maynard reeled back. Around him, the others goggled in amazed silence.

"Franklin!" everyone echoed.

"Brother Franklin, it's you! I mean, you're all right. You are, aren't you?" Wheatstraw cried, hurrying to the Oldhip, with Maynard right beside him. "This is heavy, very heavy. Aloevera has worked a wonder, indeed."

"Wonders have happened, Brother Wheatstraw, but Toad and I have been through quite an ordeal. Right now we need a place by the fire and something to warm us."

"Certainly. Come rest yourselves." Wheatstraw signaled to his mate for some tea.

Maynard led the pair to a place by the hearth while Hashberry hurried off. She returned moments later bearing two quilts and steaming cups of herbal tea. Franklin and Toad wrapped themselves in the warm covers and sipped the some of the strong brew. Everybody gathered about, barely able to contain their curiosity. A pipe started around and the questions began.

"This is truly miraculous, Brother Franklin," Wheatstraw declared. "We must summon Aloevera and see what brought about this recovery." However, after eyeing the Oldhip and Toad closely, he added, "or maybe one of you can offer an explanation."

Franklin wiped his mouth on the sleeve of his robe and took a hit from the pipe as it passed his way. "I will say only this," the elderly Oldhip began, choosing his words carefully. "I do not remember much of my experience, except that it was dark and cold and frightening. I awoke, not long ago, in a bed at Aloevera's Healery. However ... I am not here to rejoice in my re-awakening, but to bring ominous tidings. When I opened my eyes, I immediately sensed danger, a powerful disruption of The All, emanating from near the Gate west of town. I was drawn there with a feeling of overwhelming dread. At the Gate I found Brother Toad engaged in a mighty struggle with Moonshadow."

Maynard's brow furrowed. He glanced around the room at the other Diggers and Oldhips, but their eyes were riveted on Franklin and Toad. "Moonshadow? What's he got to do with this?"

Now it was Toad's turn to speak. "He's the reason I was late. He's left Hillcommune."

Wheatstraw shook his head sadly. "This is terrible news."

"I don't get it. Why'd he leave, man?" Maynard asked. An urgent edge hardened his tone.

Toad rubbed his hands together nervously, then related as much of the tale as he and Franklin had deemed prudent. "I was on my way here, taking a shortcut through the alley where you and Skulk are rooming. Just as I was passing your door, it flew open. Someone clutching a bundle under one arm burst out and slammed right into me, knocking me to the ground."

"And this was Moonshadow?"

Toad nodded. "Before I could get up, he attacked me with his staff and ran off. He seemed like he was out of his head, crazy. I ran after him and finally caught up just before he reached the West Gate tunnel, the one the Radiclibs came through. He turned on me and was about to bust my head open when Franklin showed up. I guess seeing Franklin scared him, because he ran into the tunnel."

"You said he had a bundle under one arm; do you know what it was?"

"No. It was dark and I was trying to cover up so he wouldn't kill me."

Maynard's look of concern deepened. "Franklin, did you see what was in the bundle?"

"No ... but it was the book. I could feel it."

"Why didn't you try to stop him?"

"Moonshadow was like a crazed animal. Once he was in the tunnel there was no point; no human could catch him in there. Besides, Brother Toad was injured and needed immediate attention."

Outside the thunder boomed louder than before and rain pelted against the windows. No one spoke as Maynard stared into the fire, rubbing his hands together frantically. "This is horrible. Moonshadow has really wigged out. He's taken my ... *the* ... book outside the valley. It could fall into the Dark Man's hands. Doesn't he realize that? We have to get the *Necronomicon* back."

Franklin nodded. "The book's power is strong. Moonshadow will not give it up willingly."

"Dig it, man. Sooner or later he'll be captured and Bejeezuz will learn of the book. Whatever the risk, we have to get it back."

Wheatstraw had been silent until now. "And what of Moonshadow?" he interjected. "After all we've seen, is the book more important than his soul?"

Maynard glared at the Oldhip leader. "We need that book! We can't win against the Dark Man without it."

"And with it, what would you win? Do you wish to save Street-Corner Earth, or rule it?"

"Whoa, man! Totally uncool," Maynard exclaimed, glaring at the Oldhip.

Franklin interrupted, "I'm sure we all agree that the book cannot fall into the Evil Weed's hands—what we do with the book is another matter. And, I am also sure that we are all concerned for Brother Moonshadow's safety. We need not argue while we share a common purpose. We need to act."

The Oldhip shrugged off his quilt, slowly stood up and paused for a moment to survey the bewildered faces in front of him. "What if there was a way we could rescue Moonshadow and secure the book?"

"How can we do that?" Skulk asked. "There's not a thing we can do that won't jeopardize our plans. We're not ready to send out an armed force of any size."

"I'm not suggesting a large force; two or three would do," Franklin offered, "a band small enough to go unnoticed while they track down Moonshadow, before he gets too far. I'm sure Aloevera can concoct some potion to help Moonshadow become ... cooperative."

Toad shuffled uneasily by the fire. "I'll go," he said. "I found the thing in the first place, so I should be the one to bring it back."

"You can't go alone," Tambourine remarked, rising from the corner where he'd been sitting. "I'll go with you. After all, Maynard first assigned me to look for it, long before Swetshop and Lubejob."

Maynard shook his head. "You can't go. It's way too soon, man. You're needed here."

"For what? As a figurehead? Some bloody icon? Haven't we already decided that I've got to go to Covenstead anyway, to pave the way for Mizjoan's army? What difference will a few days make? After we find the book, Toad can return here to Hillcommune, and I can continue on to Covenstead."

"That's *not* the plan."

"One way or another I have to go to Covenstead; Moonshadow has just altered the timing."

Toad looked up from his place by the fire. "What's this plan you're talking about?"

"A simple one," Tambourine replied. "Before Mizjoan's army attacks Covenstead on All Loveday I will leave Hillcommune and allow myself to be captured by the enemy. Once I'm taken to Bejeezuz I'm going to present him with a challenge."

"What sort of challenge?"

"To play against me in concert, on All Loveday. As a fellow musician he can't refuse me."

"What good would that do?"

"At the very worst, it will buy us time. But if I can defeat him, it will rally our forces and confuse his."

"What if he refuses?"

"He won't."

Maynard coughed loudly. "We can't be sure, daddy-o. This is not some wiggy old-timey 'battle of the bands.' The Dark Cat, like, has no honor."

"But you yourself said that he has a huge ego. He couldn't refuse to play against a descendant of Ol' Bob."

The little Beatnik shook his head. "That is our hope—but what if you both get caught before you find Moonshadow? We can't ask Toad to risk his life."

"I found the book," Toad stated. "I'm going. Besides, I'm the one who has dreams of the Dark Man. I'm in this up to my ears, like it or not."

Outside, the thunder had moved on; it boomed hollowly beyond the western horizon. The rain had fallen off to a light drizzle. Before Maynard could frame a rebuttal, Franklin joined in. "Toad is right," the Oldhip interjected. "The Dark Man, the *Necronomicon* and Josiah Toad are somehow all bound together in The All. I believe that he must go."

"I can tell you one thing," Ernie added, "You guys aren't going anywhere without me. We've all been in this from the beginning, and that's not going to change now."

"There's a good chance you won't make it back," Maynard said.

"How bad could it get? The Dark Man's biding his time in Covenstead while Greasers and Fascists roam the countryside stomping every Freak they find. We've been in worse fixes. Right, guys? Anyway, somebody's got to keep these two from screwing up."

Maynard looked agitated. He tugged furiously at his goatee. "I don't dig this at all, man. What if you cats are jumping the crossbow here?"

"The All tells me that they must go," Franklin said.

"I don't know, daddy-o."

"There's no alternative," Ernie declared. "If we want to catch Moonshadow, we must leave as soon as possible."

Maynard shrugged. "I suppose you're right. Go then. May Dylan speed your journey."

Beyond the window the clouds were breaking up and the stars were coming out one by one.

Chapter Forty-Nine

Toad slipped from sleep like a moth emerging from its cocoon. His first sensation was warmth, his second almost supernatural stillness. Opening his eyes, he saw that the fire had died down. Beside it Ernie and Tambourine were softly snoring.

The pipesmith yawned and sat up. Without giving a thought to what he was doing, he checked his gear, reshuffling the contents of his pack and tightening the straps of the oilskin that covered his guitar. Then he unsheathed his short sword and ran his fingers along its blade to check the edge. He did these things to keep his body occupied, while his mind tried to recall the dream that had caused him to wake in a cold sweat. But, try as he might to retrieve the dream, it existed only in cloudy fragments. Scary at the beginning, the dream ended with him on a high place, holding The Book aloft, surrounded on all sides by many followers. He remembered feeling powerful, omnipotent. Scattered throughout his dream were bits about the Dark Man too; it was odd that he'd had so few dreams about him in Hillcommune.

Toad reached for a stoppered jug that sat beside the fire. The cork came out with a slight pop, and he took a tentative sip. To his delight it was a cold, flowery herbal tea, sweetened with hint of honey. After taking a larger swig, a surge of energy shot through his body. Yes, there were many things he would miss about Hillcommune.

The pipesmith grinned as he thought about the swaying fields of corn and grain, mountain breezes, comfortable mornings by the Peace and evenings in the moonlit orchards. His smile broadened as he thought of his last glance back at the village—a last glance that found a solitary figure, with hair the color of flame and dressed in Radiclib gray, standing on the wharf watching Franklin lead them into the tunnels beyond the West Gate.

They had traveled through dark passages lit only by the torches they carried. From time to time the flickering light danced on faint hieroglyphs painted on the walls. There were various symbols: peace emblems, flowers, Honkweed leaves, graffiti scrawled in long flowing script and others too dim to make out. Some seemed to be crude murals depicting events from history or folklore, though in the dim light it was hard to tell. Whatever they were, there hung about them a sense of great age. There was little discussion as the four passed through the twilight world under the mountains. The deeper they went the more Toad became cognizant of the oppressive mass of rock above him. In every flickering shadow he expected to see Moonshadow's capering form leering out at him, mad-eyed and hating. But for now, nothing disturbed the eternal stillness of the caverns.

Overhead, unseen, the sun was completing its diurnal march across the heavens as the group stopped at a long footbridge that stretched across a wide chasm into the darkness beyond the candlelight. Water roared as it rushed under the bridge and tumbled over a precipice.

"What you are hearing," Franklin shouted, "is an underground branch of the Peace. It can only be crossed by this footbridge. The bridge feels rickety, but it is strong enough. Cross it one at a time." He motioned Ernie and Tambourine over as Toad stood listening to the waters boil over into the void below.

As Tam was making his crossing, Franklin turned to the pipesmith. "Not far from here, you will stop in a large cavern to spend the night before leaving the tunnels and Hillcommune. At the first opportunity, once you are outside and away from our world, destroy the book. To do so, you must burn it until it is nothing but ash."

"I know."

"It will fight you. You cannot let it win."

"I understand."

The Oldhip patted Toad softly on the back and helped him onto the bridge. "Know this, Brother Toad; you have no need of the book's magick. There will be magick enough to aid you when the time comes."

Toad blinked. "What are you talking about?"

"We Oldhips have our own earth-magick. There is a little of it in each of us, and slightly more in a few like Moonshadow and me. We will be praying for you. The All will see you through in ways that the Black Book never could. Remember, your friends must not suspect that you have the *Necronomicon*."

Now, after spending the night in a large, high-ceilinged chamber at the end of one of the tunnels, Toad sipped again from the jug of tea and offered silent thanks to the departed Franklin. He and his friends were going to need its restorative powers in the days ahead. He tapped his pack, feeling for the book though he knew it was there. Here, alone in the dark, it seemed a shame that he had to burn it. If only there was a way he could keep it—preserve it for history.

Toad re-stoppered the jug as the first faint stirrings of life came from the bedrolls on the other side of the fire. First there was a snort from Ernie's roll, then a stifled yawn from Tambourine's. The two sat up almost at the same time.

"You guys ready for the real world?" Ernie inquired sleepily.

Tambourine rubbed his eyes and gave the herbalist a playful kick with his foot. "Question is, is it ready for us?"

"I don't know about you and me, Tam, but it was never ready for Ernie Mungweasle," Toad remarked, smiling.

"Let's eat and get to it," Ernie exclaimed, jumping to his feet. "The world may not be ready for me, but I'm raring to get back to it."

After a light breakfast of bread and cheese they packed their weapons and gear, slipped into winter clothes, and rolled aside the stone separating them from the outside. A patch of scrub pine stood in front of the doorway, and once Ernie and Tam slid the stone back in place no cracks showed in the cliff face behind them.

The three companions scrambled down over the scree to the bottom of the slope. Tambourine tightened the straps on his guitar case and checked the short-barreled pistol that protruded from his belt. "Okay," he said. "What now?"

"Well," Ernie replied, taking out his own pistol and giving it a quick once-over, "to the best of our knowledge Moonshadow left Hillcommune unprepared. Crazy or not, he's going to need supplies. Covenstead's about two days journey from here and he won't get far without food or drink. The nearest town is Ozone, so he'd probably head there first."

Though the weather was much cooler here than it had been in Hillcommune, it was still unseasonably mild. Spring had come unnaturally early to Street-Corner Earth. The morning was sunny, and the sky was a high, bright blue with just a few rags of clouds near the horizon. South of the mountains the rocky foothills gave way to bands of dense forest, where remnants of the winter snows huddled in the shadows beneath the towering pines, and the dried-out spikes of last year's weeds rimmed the unused logging roads. Save for the occasional scurryings of small creatures through the underbrush, the three Freaks encountered no signs of life. They passed an abandoned squatter's shack, its door off its hinges and the roof collapsed into the interior. Beside the shack the gray mossy bones of some large animal lay rotting among the weeds and litter. After hours of walking, they encountered recent footprints in the snow. Though blurry and indistinct, the prints revealed pointy-toed boots, the same type Moonshadow had recently taken to wearing.

415

By the time the sun was directly overhead the thickest part of the forest was behind them. Ahead lay a region of overgrown fields dotted with charred remains of farms, a harsh reminder of the Fascists' slash and burn tactics. The roads, wide and muddy from a recent thaw, were deeply rutted in places where many heavily-laden wagons had passed through. Judging from the hoof prints they were all headed south. Several times Toad thought he saw ragged, emaciated figures hiding among the ruins, figures that looked more like scarecrows than human beings. These poor souls must have suffered unspeakably as the Dark Man's minions drove them to the brink of extinction. Anger welled from the pit of Toad's stomach. With the book he could teach the enemy a few things about annihilation. But of course, the book must be destroyed. Toad studied his friends for a moment as they continued along the road, unaware of his burden. His backpack felt perceptibly heavier as he hurried to join them.

As the long shadows of early evening overtook the trio, the fields and decimated houses retreated behind them and they were again trekking forested roads. The Freaks made camp in a clearing well back from the nearest road. They started a small, smokeless fire and cooked some of their meager supplies. After eating they passed a pipe around, and Toad volunteered to sit the first watch. Ernie and Tambourine rolled into their sleeping bags and settled in for the night. Their snores were soon competing with the soft cries of the night birds.

Toad busied himself by adding enough wood to the fire to keep it going, without it becoming a beacon for the enemy. Even though the weather was incredibly mild for February there were still sizable patches of snow under most trees and a lingering chill in the air. When the fire was burning to his satisfaction Toad sat down on his bedroll and repacked Tambourine's briar.

Puffing on the pipe, Toad began to feel pangs of uneasiness. He found himself doubting the wisdom of his quest. He thought about the miles behind them since leaving Hillcommune. Except for the indistinct footprints, there'd been no sign of Moonshadow. And, confronting the ex-Seer was not the only problem. The further they traveled from the Oldhip village the more Tambourine talked of a confrontation with Bejeezuz. In the safety of Wheatstraw's meeting room Tam's quest had sounded very daring, even romantic. But out here on the Dark Man's turf the idea was positively scary, unless ... unless he could find a way to control the book and use it to against the Dark Man. It could be the great equalizer. And, once Street Corner Earth was safe from that evil, destroying the book would be a cinch. What could possibly be wrong with that? But then, from the depths of his thoughts, Forseein' Franklin's words reverberated through his mind. As the echoes of the Oldhip's words faded, Toad reluctantly conceded that Franklin was right.

When the pipe was spent, Toad tapped it out on his bootheel and placed it next to Tambourine's pack. Then, checking to make sure that his companions were soundly asleep, he reached inside his pack and pulled out the *Necronomicon,* which seemed to fall open of its own accord. At Hillcommune he'd only skimmed through the old book, but curiously, now that he was on the verge of actually destroying it, he felt compelled to read it. It didn't seem right somehow, that he should burn it without knowing what secrets lay hidden in its musty pages.

He stared down at a page entitled, "Ye Curiou*f* and Arcane Rite*f* of Ri*f*ing and Opening." Toad ran his finger over the musty vellum and looked across the fire to the dead apple tree that stood on the other side of the clearing. In the flickering firelight it seemed to move slightly. Hardly realizing it, he began to read, his lips silently mouthing the words. Though they were seeming nonsense, he could feel their power. As he recited the words, he found that he could not tear his eyes from the page:

"Krogg-gogalog Megagog.
Ia! Cthulhu-Krogalog,
Mekatoom!
Yog-Sothoth Dragnagog,
Azathogg-Nogagog,
Mekatoom!"

Suddenly, the pipesmith was aware that the slight breeze playing around the clearing had dropped away and the night birds had ceased their plaintive cries. In spite of the fire, the night was growing perceptively colder. Moving to add more wood to the fire, Toad stopped abruptly when he saw something approaching from across the clearing. A tall figure, swaddled in black robes smeared with mud, neared the fire, its face completely concealed by a deep shadowy hood. The stranger walked with a slow unnatural gait. Trembling, not daring to take his eyes from the apparition, Toad edged towards the place where Ernie's pistol lay across his pack. How could the Dark Man have found him so soon?

The grim visitor uttered an eerie rasping laugh and reached up to lower his cowl. Ernie's pistol was too far away, so Toad fumbled to draw his shortsword instead. The spectre laughed again, louder this time. "Put away your weapon," he said in a voice like wind stirring autumn leaves, "I mean you no harm, and they will do you no good anyway."

Toad's right hand slid away from the sword, but his left still firmly clutched the *Necronomicon.* "W-who are you? What do you wan...?"

The words died in the pipesmith's throat as the stranger threw back his cowl, laughing. It was Moonshadow, not Bejeezuz, who stood before him—or what had once been Moonshadow. The jawline and thin mustache were unmistakable, but the rest of the face, from the bridge of the nose up, was a shattered, gouted horror. One side of the ex-Seer's head was gone, as if from a close-range blunderbuss blast. The remaining eye was a milky, unblinking orb that stared out from the flayed remains of the face. The thing that had been Moonshadow shambled closer, almost walking into the fire.

"Y-you're dead!"

"That I am."

"Dylan's Bones, h-how can this be?" Toad backed away, clutching the *Necronomicon* to his chest.

"A Greaser patrol caught me. I should not have tried to escape."

"I-I'm so sorry. I..."

"Save your pity. I am with The All now."

"W-what do you want from me?"

Moonshadow smiled. On that ruined face the expression was an obscenity. "You know already. Why do you ask?"

The pipesmith shuddered. "It's the book, isn't it? You can't have it; i-it's mine!"

"Your desire for the book blinds you, Toad. Its hold over me is gone, but its power over you grows with each passing minute. Soon it will consume you completely."

"That's not true. Nothing has control over me. I left Hillcommune to destroy it ... to keep it from you ... from Maynard."

The spectre chuckled, an unpleasant sound like fingernails scraping over a slate. "That is the lie you tell yourself. But, in your heart you know the truth. Maynard should not have the *Necronomicon*, but neither should you. You tell yourself that you can destroy it whenever you want, that it cannot affect you, but already you dream of the power it can bring you, as did I before I passed into Strawberry Fields."

"That's not true!"

"No? Did not you dream last night that the entire world worshipped at your feet? And did not you enjoy that feeling? Destroy the book, Toad, before it destroys you—and the world."

Toad suddenly remembered the dream vividly. "No! Tam plans to challenge the Dark Man. I ... we will need to use it against him."

"Another lie! You must destroy it tonight, now, as planned, before it is too late. Others want it; they are coming."

The pipesmith shook his head. He could feel the warmth of the book. As he clutched it against his chest, memories of his dream returned: great power and all people of Street-Corner Earth chanting his name. It could all come true if he just had time. "I'll hide it," he said. "Bejeezuz will never find it."

"*If* you make it through this night. There are things out there, far worse than the Evil Weed. Truly evil things, whose thirsts are far greater and far more malevolent than his."

"What do you mean? What could be worse than the Dark Man?"

"Emissaries of the Old Ones; they who were ancient before this planet was ever formed. The Black Book was once theirs. They mean to have it again. It unlocks the portals between their world and ours. They need it to take form and reality in our world, to unleash their terrible powers. Without it, they are but menacing shadows."

Dread consumed Toad. In spite of the fire he felt cold. He shuddered uncontrollably. "N-no. I don't believe you. You're lying; you're trying to frighten me. You still want the book!"

Moonshadow replaced his cowl. "Before this night is out you will come to believe me. Destroy it, before it is too late. Send the Old Ones back to the darkness that spawned them. Nyarlathotep, who is called the Crawling Chaos, and Yog-Sothoth, who is the Keeper of the Gate, they are near. You have been warned. Do what you must."

"But…"

"Do it quickly."

The thing that had been Moonshadow turned and, like smoke dispersed by a gentle breeze, disappeared into the darkness beyond the fire. Immediately, the blackness beyond the clearing seemed to deepen. Suddenly Toad was afraid of the dark; he didn't want Moonshadow to go. Instinctively he reached out.

"Stay," he begged. "Help me."

A faint voice drifted back from the darkness. "I cannot. Their presence smothers The All."

Toad looked anxiously to his companions. Remarkably, they continued their peaceful sleep.

The pipesmith hurriedly piled wood on the fire. The dry branches were quick to burst into flame, but the light was too weak, losing the battle against the inky darkness building beyond its feeble circle. He threw on more wood. Still the blackness moved in. More horrible yet, it seemed to be breathing.

Toad clutched the *Necronomicon* to his chest, tighter, until he could feel his heart beating against its timeworn covers.

The shadows billowed and swelled, swirling in closer. The silence of the night was disturbed only by the crackling of the fire and the wild beating of Toad's heart. In the darkness something moved, something immense. It stayed just out of the light, but he sensed it shift to one side, then another, then behind him as it ponderously circled the camp, slithering and hissing.

Toad pulled the book out and held it towards the fire. He wanted to toss it in, but couldn't. This had to be a dream, a weed fantasy. No sane human mind could make up what was happening now. Through the growing haze of fear Moonshadow's ominous words echoed back to Toad. The book opened a pathway to another world, a world where the affairs of Freaks and Fascists were no more than the fornications of fleas.

The blackness surrounding the camp gained strength, suddenly crackling with obscene life, a cacophony of insane raw power. In the clearing something stirred, something evil. To Toad's horror, the tree on the far side of the clearing began to sway, even though there was no breeze. Its trunk began to writhe and twist violently, and its limbs shook and waved wildly. It began to change shape, much like the tree on Mount Lennon weeks before. Toad watched, transfixed. The tree trunk was transforming itself into a scaly body, while the broken limbs twisted themselves into arms and tentacles.

"Ernie! Tam!" Toad shouted frantically. "Wake up! For Dylan's sake, wake up." All attempts to wake them were futile. Near complete panic he realized that some evil enchantment must be keeping his friends shrouded in deep slumber, oblivious to his plight.

The tree thing cackled insanely. Toad jerked back, cowering but unable to look away, as it assumed its final form, looming at least ten feet above him. Its face, hideously disfigured, was a chinless, goatish travesty with eyes that burned phosphorescent blue. It had hands as well, but with far too many fingers to be human. Its chest was manlike, but covered with heavily ridged scales of piebald brown and green. Below the waist it bore thick, moss-like black hair, and from its abdomen sprouted long gray-green tentacles terminating in red sucking mouths. Wheezing and grunting, it pulled itself out of the ground, revealing long spindly legs, backward-jointed like those of an insect. Its tail was like a writhing length of knobbed root ending in a long, scythe-like stinger. The creature drooled as it reached out with one misshapen arm, its long polydactylous hand clutching. "The Book," it demanded, in a voice that sounded like a man talking through a mouthful of seaweed.

Toad felt himself drawn to it. He lifted the *Necronomicon* in his numbed hands, holding it like an offering. The darkness sighed and hunched closer. Terrified, Toad tried to break its spell, tried to cry out to his friends, tried to wake himself from this grandfather of all bad dreams, but the only sound to escape his throat was a tiny peep like the cry of a tree frog.

Blue light flared deep in the thing's eyes. Its many-jointed fingers twitched and its tentacles thrashed angrily. Panting and drooling, it lurched closer. "THE BOOK!"

Pulling the book back to his chest, Toad recoiled as the cold terror of the creature confronted him. If this horror was only an emissary of the Old Ones, then the Old Ones themselves must be horrible beyond human understanding. His heart slammed against his ribcage. Fighting to keep the book tight against his chest, his arms slowly extended. He was powerless to prevent them from offering it to the hideous creature. Suddenly, the flame of desire for the *Necronomicon* flared within him, and he pulled the book back slightly, grinning strangely as he held it just out of the monstrosity's clutching fingers.

The thing's eyes blazed. Yellowish drool slathered from the corners of its lipless mouth. Its breathing became hoarse, erratic. Long, many-fingered tentacles swirled in front of him, snapping, grasping air, moving closer. With the cold terror of the beast inches away, Toad's mind raced. The *Necronomicon* is mine! Can I keep it and control the creature? Will it kill me and take the book? Keep it or let it go? Suddenly Franklin's voice was in his head. "Either way you would be lost, Brother Toad," the Oldhip's voice intoned. "You have the strength. Do what you must."

"THE BOOK! GIVE ME THE BOOK!" thundered around him, as one monstrous hand, with fingers as jagged as lightning bolts, poised overhead ready to squash him like a bug.

"Never," Toad screamed. Suddenly, without thinking, he ripped the *Necronomicon* in two along its rotted spine and tossed the unequal halves into the fire.

The ancient volume exploded as soon as the flames touched it, sending a flurry of sparks swirling upward. The tree-thing bellowed in pain, thrashing its arms and tentacles. In its madness and rage it tried to grab the burning pages. Flames jumped from the book, igniting the very tips of its fingers. Fire raced up its tentacles, causing it to scream louder. Tambourine and Ernie remained sound asleep.

Raging clouds boiled overhead, moving at unnatural speed; the skies rumbled. As Toad watched, a bolt of lightning slammed straight down, piercing the monster through its scaly chest. It screamed again, clawing at the smoking hole in its breast, and then exploded in a blue flash that knocked the pipesmith over. When he looked up, the monster was gone; only a shattered, blackened tree trunk remained. Suddenly awake, Tambourine and Ernie leaped out of their bedrolls and ran to where Toad lay sprawled on the grass.

"Toad! Are you okay?" Ernie asked breathlessly. "What happened?"

Toad stared numbly at the smoking ruins of the tree scattered about the clearing. "Yeah. J-just a little shook up. I think lightning hit that tree."

"Well, you look like you've seen a ghost ... but I guess lightning will do that to you."

"I'll be okay in a bit."

Toad trembled violently. After a few minutes, he ventured to his feet. Unsteadily he wandered over to examine the smoldering wreckage of the tree. Maybe he'd imagined the whole frightening episode—just another crazy dream. He was tempted to kick at the tree trunk for reassurance, but he felt a sudden wave of revulsion sweep over him, and he turned to stare at the fire instead. As his companions busied themselves preparing a pot of herb tea, Toad noticed a few pages lying on the ground. Somehow they had escaped the fire, and his friends' scrutiny. As he picked up the pages, they tingled warmly in his hands. Only a few pages ... nothing ... a mere souvenir, what difference could they make? Why should he destroy them now—now that the rest of the book was gone? He folded the pages neatly and started to slide them into his pocket. His friend's backs were to him; they were conversing in whispers as they worked. A faint rustling in the grass distracted him. One of the fragments of the demolished tree, a claw-like branch with a few brown leaves still hanging from it, was inching its way towards him. Stifling a scream, he jerked his hand away from his pocket and quickly tossed the remaining pages into the fire. They flashed as they hit the flames and were instantly consumed; the branch shuddered and lay still. Toad drew his sword and poked at it, but it didn't move. With a grunt of disgust he flipped the limb into the fire and watched intently as it started to burn. He didn't notice Ernie approaching, and jumped back a step when the herbalist held out one of the two cups he was carrying.

"Drink this," Ernie said handing him a cup of tea. "You sure you're all right? You're shaking."

"No! I mean, yes. I mean ... thanks for the tea, okay?"

"Don't mention it. Hopefully it'll calm you." Ernie looked up to a clear, star-filled sky. "Lightning, huh?" he asked, glancing at Toad.

Toad nodded.

"Strange," Ernie added, lifting his cup to his lips.

"Yes, very."

Toad's hands were shaking so badly that half of his tea ended up on the ground. As he sipped on what was left, he considered telling his friends what had happened. With Moonshadow and the book gone there was no reason to continue on their quest. But, even as he considered it he knew, book or not, it was already too late to turn back. There was no real safety in Hillcommune. His destiny, and undoubtedly Tambourine's, lay in Covenstead, and if they were going, Toad knew that Ernie would go too.

Draining off the last of his tea, he set his cup on the ground.

"How about a little weed?" he asked.

Grinng, Tambourine walked over to Toad and handed him a newly loaded pipe. "Way ahead of you, friend."

"I don't want to get too sentimental," Toad said, accepting the pipe, "but if I'm forever destined to go on adventures, there's no two Freaks I'd rather be with. You two are great friends."

The pipesmith thought he saw Ernie blush. "Don't think twice," the herbalist said. "It's all right."

The pipesmith smiled briefly. But looking out into the darkness, he sensed that somewhere out there the Dark Man waited.

Chapter Fifty

Sweet pine-scented breezes washed over the three Freaks as they made their way along the road to Ozone; the warm weather was a signal that spring had indeed come early to Street-Corner Earth. Breathing the cool, fragrant air the pipesmith allowed himself a momentary smile, noting that the remainder of the previous night had passed uneventfully—proof that the book and its evil influences were banished from the Freaklands for good. The warm morning sunshine resting on his shoulder like a friend's comforting hand would usually have been enough to lift Toad's spirits, but visions of Moonshadow's horrible fate kept his mood subdued. Ernie and Tambourine's sporadic grousing over their inability to find any signs of Moonshadow weighed heavily on him as well. Only Tambourine's conviction that his fate lay in Covenstead with the Dark Man kept Toad from telling his friends the truth.

Several hours later, after following the higher, drier center between the wagon tracks they took to the woods, keeping the road on their right, just barely in sight. By midday they reached the Freak town of Ozone. Peering through the thick underbrush, they were dismayed to observe the silent, smoldering ruins of the once prosperous hamlet. The devastation was complete; hardly a beam was left standing. Nothing moved. There was nothing left. It was as if there was a giant hole where Ozone had once been.

Ernie pushed back into the small clearing behind the bushes. He tore off his top hat and threw it on the ground. "What in the hell are we going to do now?" he growled.

Tambourine snapped back. "What'd you think? We'd stroll into town and find Moonshadow in the local tavern with his feet on a table, holding a mug of Stumpwater in one hand and a bowl of Red in the other?"

"Very funny," Ernie replied. "You know what I mean. Other than the first footprints which, by the way, may or may not have been

Moonshadow's, we don't have a clue where he is. Now that Ozone is burned to the freakin' ground our best shot at getting any information at all is, shall we say, up in smoke."

"He may not have even come to Ozone," Tam offered.

"That's true; he may not have been here. However, if there were anyone left to ask, we might know one way or the other if we were on the right track. Instead, we're just dancing in the dark."

While the two argued, Toad came very close to telling them both about Moonshadow's fate. Instead, he backed away and leaned against a gnarly oak that harbored a patch of icy snow around its base, and kicked at the snow determinedly with the heel of his boot.

"So, what are you saying, Ernie?" Tam continued. "You want to turn back?"

"No. But, I don't know where we should go either. What about you, Toad? You haven't said anything."

Toad did not reply immediately.

A stiff breeze picked up. Tendrils of smoke from the smoldering remains of Ozone carried to where they stood. There was something familiar in the burnt wood smell. Seeing his friends shrouded in the wispy, gray veil, he remembered: dreams of thousands massing with burning expectancy in their eyes, the scent of a coming storm ready to sweep away the old ways and usher in the new, and he was there to lead them. He shook his head. He could not allow that to happen. "I have a strong sense that Moonshadow was never here," he stated.

"A sense? What does that mean?" Ernie asked, cocking his head slightly to the left and eyeing the pipesmith intently, as if trying to read his inner thoughts.

"All I'm saying is that I have a feeling. Call it intuition. Call it a premonition. But somehow I know that Moonshadow never reached Ozone."

"But how do you know?"

"I don't. It's only a feeling, but I'd bet my life on it."

"Even if you're right, how does it help? Where do we go from here?"

Smoke sifted through the bushes around the clearing and permeated the silence surrounding the three Freaks. For a long time no one said anything. They avoided eye contact, generally finding the mud on their boots more interesting. Finally Tambourine spoke.

"It seems to me," he said, "that we assumed that snow would be blanketing the ground outside Hillcommune, and tracking Moonshadow would be a cinch. At least I thought so. We just didn't know how little snow there actually was. There's still time, but I can't look for him forever. Ultimately, my fate is in Covenstead. It's reasonable to think that the book is headed there as well, that it's somehow drawn to the Dark Man. So, why not head in that direction? If we find the Seer, then you two can decide what you want to do."

Ernie looked at the pipesmith and shrugged. Toad knew that there was no other course. Regardless of Moonshadow's fate, the three friends would all be going to Covenstead.

They continued on, skirting the remains of Ozone. Staying deep in the shadows among the trees, they slipped through the bushes, making as little noise as possible, as if the least sound would bring down upon them the same fate the village had suffered.

Once they were well past Ozone they took to the road again. Before long, they arrived at a place where the road forked in two directions. The right fork, wider and better maintained than the road from Ozone, ran in a more or less southerly direction and looked more promising. Taking this route allowed them to continue at a quicker pace, but by mid-afternoon they slowed. Since they had barely stopped since early morning, Ernie suggested that they get out of sight of the road and rest. Leading them deep into the bushes, he found a small clearing where they could slip out of their packs. Relieved of their load, Tam and Ernie sprawled on the ground. Toad dropped his pack beside theirs and started back toward the road.

"Where are you going?" Tam asked.

"Got the urge to write my name on something—rock, snow, whatever," he replied. "I'll be back in a minute."

Toad walked almost all the way back to the road before he found a boulder worthy of autographing; satisfied, he re-buttoned his fly. Suddenly, something crashed through the woods near by. His heart skipped a beat as a young doe ran into view and then bounded back into the underbrush. Laughing to himself, he started back toward the clearing with the kind of contentment that could only come from being at one with nature, and of course an empty bladder. Suddenly shots rang out. As they echoed through the forest, his hand instinctively reached for the Radiclib short sword at his side. Another shot sounded and he drew the sword from its scabbard. Without thinking, he ran headlong toward Ernie and Tam. Dashing past two large trees, he tripped and sprawled into a patch of half-melted snow. Barely hitting the ground, he rolled over and tried to get to his feet. The cavernous muzzle of a blunderbuss stared him in the face. A Greaser with the heavy features and slack-jawed expression of a congenital idiot wielded the ancient weapon. As he pulled back the gun's hammer, he smiled evilly, revealing a mouthful of rotting broken teeth.

"Aay, Skummer," a growly voice intervened, "don't splat him here."

Toad opened his eyes to see a larger Greaser dressed in the garb of a Fonzer.

Reluctantly, Skummer lowered his weapon.

The big Fonzer laughed. "Let's get motorvated. Bring the faggit with you."

Skummer jerked Toad to his feet, and placing the blunderbuss squarely against his back, pushed him along until they reached the clearing where Tambourine and Ernie crouched with twenty muskets and crossbows leveled at their heads. One of the tormentors, a short wiry fellow whose leather jacket looked way too large for him, noticed the Greasers approaching and hailed them. "Aay, Skummer, Reemer, another faggit, huh?"

"Fuckin' A, Skragg," Skummer replied.

"We gonna waste them right here?"

"Fuckin' A, that's what I say. We ain't had us a good killing in a while."

"What about that one you wasted a few days back? Nailed him pretty good, didn't you, Skum?"

"You mean that weird-lookin' hippie? No shit," Skummer answered. "I ventilated him right between the headlights. Wasn't enough of that pussy's face left to stuff up his asshole. You jerk-offs had your chance at glory, but you was too scairt. His black robe and short hair threw you off, but I knew he was a flower-faggit, all right. He died whimpering, like they all do."

"You took a helluva chance," Reemer stated. "If he was one of Lord Flatbush's men our lives won't be worth shit."

"They ain't worth much anyhow."

"Ain't dat da truth?" Skragg added. "But, what I wanna know is, how could ya tell he was a hippie?"

"Shit, it was easy. The way he was stumblin' around, he had to be blind, or doin' some of them hippie drugs. Besides, only a fairy would own some of the stuff we took off him."

Ernie and Tambourine shot quick, puzzled glances at each other, and then at Toad. The pipesmith gave a slight shrug.

"Now, ya see," Skummer continued, knowledgeably, "when he heard us shout, he went and tried to fly the coop. If he was one of Lord Flatbush's men he woulda waited for us."

"Yeah. Well, I still think you was lucky," Skragg stated.

"Lucky, shit. Plus, we found them fancy hippie drugs on him, didn't we? Sure sign he was one of those mountain faggits."

"Maybe… "

"Har, har, har," Skummer guffawed explosively. "You know what I was thinking? It just come to me; that pussy didn't need them drugs, I blew his fuckin' mind for him. Har, har, har."

All the Greasers burst out laughing. Spittle flew from Skragg's mouth as he roared, "Fuckin' A right!"

"Maybe we oughta do the same for these boys," yelled one of the Greasers.

"Maybe we should," Skummer agreed. "We wouldn't want anybody callin' us impolite, 'cause we didn't offer all our guests the same hospitality."

"That would be a mistake," Tambourine remarked quietly.

"Hey, pussy-boy, you talkin' to ME?" Skummer swiveled his blunderbuss at the musician, but Reemer gestured for him to stop. Walking up to Tambourine he looked him over appraisingly, as if shocked by the act of defiance. "Since when has it been a mistake to kill a longhair faggit?" the Fonzer inquired reasonably.

"Your Lord Flatbush would be more interested in us being alive."

"You are def'nately a fucking funny-man, now ain't you? Why do you suppose he'd be interested in you, one way or the other?"

"Because we bear news from Hillcommune, and a proposal."

"As if he fuckin' cares." Skummer growled and raised his gun again. "Screw this shit, Reemer; say the word and I'll waste the fairy."

Tambourine laughed, though it was a weak effort. "Go ahead, and then see what your friend Lord Flatbush has in store for you."

"I ain't afraid of him, or you. Kiss your ass goodbye, faggit."

Reemer grabbed Skummer by the arm. "Cool off, pally. "

"What? You believe that bullshit story? They're faggits; we kill faggits."

"Not this time. If what they say is true, the Dark Man might reward us for bringing 'em in."

"Why do we have to bring them all back? One oughta be enough."

Reemer nodded. "You got a point there, Skum."

Ernie spoke up for the first time. "You could do that, but how would you know which one of us to keep alive and which ones to kill? You take all of us, or none. If you kill two of us, the other will tell the Dark Man that you killed his spy. You see, that is one of the reasons we are here. That Oldhip you killed back there *was* one of the Dark Man's spies," he lied. "We were trying to catch him before he got back to Covenstead."

"See," Skragg said, "I told you…"

"Shut up, asshole!" Skummer growled.

"Kill 'em and be done with it!" snapped an authoritative voice that Toad recognized immediately. "Can't you limpdicks see that they're lying?"

The crowd parted to reveal a darkly handsome Fonzer in faded jeans and gleaming leather. Toad blinked, but it was no hallucination; the pouting, arrogant face was all too familiar. It had been months since the two Greasers had abducted him, but there was no forgetting Sonny Slikback. But, except for a brief flash in Fonzer's eyes telling Toad that Sonny hadn't forgotten him either, the Fonzer glowered and looked past him as if he didn't exist.

"So what's the hold up here?" Sonny demanded. "Why ain't these faggits dead yet?"

Reemer tensed and scowled. "Because I'm the Fonzer in charge here, Mister Man, not you—a point you seem to be constantly forgetting. We're taking these boys to Lord Flatbush, an' that's that."

Sonny sneered and toyed with the small silver wrench hanging at his throat. He opened his mouth as if to speak, then closed it again.

"Got a problem?" Reemer asked. "'Cause if you do you better tell me about it."

Sonny glowered at Reemer, then at Toad, then back at Reemer again. "Naah, there ain't no problem, 'cept maybe your face."

Toad laughed to himself. Sonny was in a hard situation and he knew it. If he tried to harm the Freaks, Toad could reveal him for the turncoat that he really was. The Fonzer scowled darkly when Toad grinned at him, but he said nothing.

"I don't care what you think of my face, Slikback," Reemer snarled, "as long as you know who's boss."

Sonny offered no reply.

"Okay, then. Let's get goin'." Reemer ordered his troops to mount up. A pair of swarthy Greasers grabbed Toad and tied him up with rope. When they were done they picked him up and none too gently put him over the saddle of one of their horses. They did the same with Tam and Ernie. Toad looked around, trying to keep his eyes on Sonny, but the young Fonzer was nowhere to be seen. Sighing, he settled on the saddle and tried to make himself as comfortable as possible. It was then that he noticed that his guitar and pack, along with his sword, had been tied to one of the other horses with Tam and Ernie's gear; the thieving bastards would likely be selling it all in Covenstead for a few Abbies.

The Greasers rode in slow, solemn silence on the journey south, as if they dreaded their homecoming. From time to time Sonny rode past Toad and glowered at him. Whenever this happened, despite his discomfort, Toad would give him a wink and a nod. The Fonzer offered a menacing sneer, but it was a false gesture. Sonny looked worried. There was only one penalty for a deserter in wartime. Toad wondered if there would be a way to use that to his advantage.

The patrol rode on until well after sunset, when Reemer called for everyone to halt and set up camp by the side of the road. The same pair who had handled Toad before removed him from the horse and tied him to a tree. Tam and Ernie were also bound to trees, well away from each other. The Greasers loosened Toad's bonds slightly and forced a little hot broth down his throat. The hate in their eyes was all too evident, but he was confident that they would not harm him—at least, not yet.

Before the Greasers left him they tightened his ropes. As they returned to their camp, Toad settled back against the tree and tried to get comfortable. It was easier to do in theory than practice, but he finally managed to wiggle around until the ropes didn't bite into him quite so cruelly. When he looked up he saw Sonny leaning against a nearby boulder, eyeing him sullenly. Toad nodded to the Fonzer. "Why don't you come over and chat, Brother Sonny?" he offered. "After all, we're practically old pals."

Surprisingly, Sonny complied. With false nonchalance he swaggered over to the tree and stood glaring at Toad quietly, his thumbs jammed into the belt loops of his tight jeans. Sonny's expression was one of cool, studied disdain, but a hint of fear showed in his narrowed eyes. "Whaddaya want?" he demanded.

"I was just curious what you were doing here."

"Where I been and what I been doin' ain't none of your business," Sonny smirked, picking at his teeth with his fingernail. "But I could ask the same of you."

"It seems, Brother Fonzer, that we both would prefer to keep our reasons for being here somewhat confidential," Toad replied, glancing back at the Greasers milling around their campsite.

A muscle twitched in Sonny's jaw. "Don't go planning on spilling your guts about it. You think Reemer'd take the word of some hippie prisoner over that of a fellow Fonzer?"

"What I think is, that Reemer doesn't like you very much. And, who knows what he might believe—if it came to that."

Sonny continued to pick his teeth as his eyes narrowed into suspicious slits. "What's that 'sposed to mean?"

"It means, Brother Sonny, that if you feel the need to make it difficult for me and my friends, well... Let's just say that I'm willing to bet that any account you've made of the time you were 'missing in action', so to speak, would not hold up to close scrutiny."

"Screw what?"

"Scrutiny. It means, scoping something out, real close."

Sonny shifted uneasily. Pulling his finger away from his mouth, he inspected it closely as if he had found something of great interest.

"So, what do you want?" he asked, looking up at Toad. "What's the catch?"

"No catch."

"There's always a catch."

"Well, perhaps a small one."

"I knew it," he whispered disgustedly.

"Cheer up. I'm not asking for much. See, me and my friends are dead men, anyway. I just don't want you pushing to get us killed before we reach Covenstead, that's all."

Sonny kneeled down, balancing on the heels of his boots as he stared Toad straight in the eyes. "Why you so het up on goin' there? Death'd probably be better than what the Dark Man will do to you."

"I can't tell you."

There was still hate and fear in the Fonzer's eyes, but there was also something else—hope, maybe.

"That's it? That's all you want?"

"That's all I want."

"I'll never understand you longhairs. Me, I've always believed in paybacks."

"The time for payback is long past, Sonny. Besides, when I was your prisoner you kept your buddy Cuffer from beating me to a pulp."

"That was business, man. You were valuable property. I couldn't have Cuff damaging the merchandise."

"Whatever your reasons, you kept Cuffer off me. You know … it's strange, but I was sorry to see him die."

"Cuffer? That fucker was never too bright."

"That may be so, but you liked him enough not to desert him. You could have recaptured me if you hadn't taken the time to try to save his life."

Sonny ran his hand through his brilliantly oiled hair. "Aah, he was okay I guess."

"So, what happened? After he died, I mean."

"What's it to you?"

"I just want to put the pieces of the story together while I can."

Sonny looked over at his companions, sullenly. For a while he seemed lost in thought. Finally, looking as though he had come to some inner decision, he said, "What the fuck. Why not?"

He took a seat beside Toad and before too long his manner became conversational, even friendly. "I thought for sure I was going to rot in that root cellar your buddies put me in," he said. "I musta been locked in there for weeks, but I guess it wasn't so bad; they fed me well, and didn't beat me up or nothin'.

"Anyway, one day some Lefties came and pulled me out. Judging from their uniforms, they were officers. They hustled me into a prison wagon and we headed north—for Leftopia, probably. I wasn't sure what they had in mind, but I was sure it weren't nothing I wanted any part of. I was on the verge of kissing my young ass goodbye when, what do you know, the Leftie patrol was attacked by some Whiteriders just south of Eastside.

"The Bed-Sheet Boys were some surprised to see a Fonzer prisoner of

PIPEDREAMS

the Raddyclibs. I told them that I'd been caught and put in the slammer because they thought that I was the one that set the Concert Hall fire at Covenstead. It was a lame story and I knew it, but it was the best I could come up with on the spur of the moment. Well, the dumb bastards believed me. They treated me like some kind of hero.

"After awhile I got back to my own people. I kept to the same dumbass story I told the Whiteriders and everybody was happy. Then, a few weeks ago I was assigned to Covenstead Garrison as Reemer's second in command. Now it looks like I'll be stuck in that Fashie dump for the rest of the war with that butt munch."

"You could always boogie again."

"I tell you, Mister Man, it's crossed my mind. The Dark Man and his blackrobe boys give me the willies."

"Well?"

Sonny snickered bitterly. "No fuckin' way. He's got eyes everywhere. There ain't no chance in hell, the way he keeps us so closely checked. Besides, cuttin' out ain't something you do on your own. Ya gotta have someone watching your back, ya know? An' Cuffer was a good man to have along. Ya also gotta have a little nest egg to pay for the things you can't steal ... I mean, the things you can't find in the woods." Sonny smiled. "It sucks, but my last meal ticket is all tied up, waitin' to go to Covenstead."

"Very funny," Toad commented. "I have to go to back there ... but I have the same feeling about going to Covenstead that I had about leaving there with you and Cuffer, if you know what I mean."

"Me an' Cuff persuaded you pretty good, didn't we?"

"Quite vigorously, as I remember."

Sonny looked back at the Greasers settling in around their campfire. "Look, I probably don't have much time. They may get to wonderin' what I'm doing over here. But I got to know, what's got you firing on all cylinders to get back to Covenstead? After all, Cuff and I did our best to get you out."

"Don't get upset if I don't thank you," Toad replied. "But all things considered, my ... adventure with you and Cuffer was a joy ride compared what I've been through since."

"Hey, Cuff was no pussy. Me neither."

"I know. And without meaning to, you and Cuffer started me on a path that would, to borrow a phrase, scare a freight train down a dirt road."

"Tell your tale, pussy, and let me decide," Sonny laughed softly. "Or are you all bullshit?"

Settling back against the tree as comfortably as he could, Toad began. He left out things that the Fonzer had no need to know. He skipped over

432

the particulars of his stay at Camp Hoffman and made no mention of the *Necronomicon*, but went into great detail about his capture by the Mansonites.

Sonny hunched forward and listened intently as Toad related all that had gone down in Darkenwood. He rubbed his hands frequently as Toad told about the bloody ceremony that took place deep under Swetshop. Though the Fonzer tried to hide it, a growing respect showed in his eyes.

"Charlies," he marvelled. "Ain't that somethin'? And I thought those crazy fuckers had all taken the long dirt nap years ago."

Toad laughed. "You and everyone else, Sonny. The only problem is nobody told the Mansonites they were supposed to be extinct."

"X-stinked?"

"Extinct. You know, dead."

Toad continued, relating more about being held captive by the Mansonites, and how he and his friends had escaped, only to be recaptured by Greasers. Sonny stopped him when he mentioned the Rite of Overhaul.

"Overhaul, huh? It can get a little messy, but it's considered an honor to participate."

"For you, maybe."

Sonny leaned closer. "How in the hell'd you get out of that one?"

"Fate. I was only seconds from being beaten to death, when a fire broke out in one of the warehouses and everyone rushed out to fight it. In the confusion, my friends and I escaped and made our way to Hillcommune, where we stayed until a couple of days ago. Now we're on our way to Covenstead, and you catch me again. I'd say everything has come full circle."

"You definitely got balls, hippie, but your luck's run out. The Dark Man will take care of that. That guy don't dance around."

"I know."

The Fonzer shook his head and got to his feet. He started to walk off towards the shadows under the trees when he turned around and said, "You know, for a longhair you ain't so bad."

Chapter Fifty-One

Covenstead Hill loomed in the distance, silhouetted by the dying sun. The ancient fortress crowning its summit had been rebuilt with towers and battlements, so that it stood much as it had centuries before. The road to the crest of the hill was lined with squalid huts made from scraps of lumber and rotted canvas. As the company approached the base of the fortress Toad noticed that some of the huts were made of charred timbers. From the size of the beams he guessed they were sad remains from the Concert Hall fire. Faded tarps used here and there as rooftops, curtains, and doors were the only evidence of the colorful tents that were once Covenstead's hallmark. Smoky cooking fires sputtered in vacant spaces between the hovels. Yet, no matter how wretched the remains of the Fair City looked, its inhabitants looked worse.

Though it had only been a few months since Covenstead had fallen, the Freaks that remained were pitifully emaciated. Their eyes were glazed and lifeless in the harsh glare of the fires, as if the minds behind, seeing the futility of conducting business in their current location, had closed up shop and skipped town. Some Freaks cluttered the doorways of their poor dwellings; others stood about in the street leading to the main gate of the fortress, silently shambling out of the way as the patrol approached. Several moved too slowly for the liking of the Greaser guards and were set upon with clubs and gun butts.

Beyond the cluster of huts, barred barricades guarded by glowering Fascists blocked the huge oak doors of the fortress. Reemer spoke a few words to the guards and they opened the gates, admitting the patrol into the garrison courtyard.

Inside, they passed a long line of ragged Freaks working by torchlight, repairing the walls of the inner courtyard. The Freaks were chained together and overseen by a handful of whip-wielding Fascist soldiers. As Toad watched, the half-dressed Freak men and women dragged heavy stones on rollers and laboriously set them into place on the nearly completed wall.

Headquarters was housed in the building where the old Fair Commission once had its offices. The Greasers dismounted and led their horses away, leaving Reemer and Sonny to usher the Freaks into the building.

In the main office two Fascist officers were playing cards at a table in the corner, while a corpulent Whiterider sat at his desk under a red, white and blue lightning-bolt banner. Setting aside the sheath of papers he was studying, he took a pull from the crockery jug sitting on the edge of the desk, lifted a cheek and noisily broke wind.

"Hey, what's this? Fresh meat?" he asked, noticing Reemer and the others as they entered the room. "Big Brother John'll be proud of us for this one. Most of our indigenous faggits are just about wore out."

Reemer snorted loudly. "He ain't gonna be proud of you for nothin', Krill. You scumbags ain't grabbin' credit for something my boys did."

"Show some manners, greaseball," one of the card players growled without looking up.

"Manner this," Reemer snarled, grabbing his crotch as he thrust it in their direction.

"It's bad enough we gotta look at your type, without havin' to listen to your lip too," the Whiterider snapped.

"These faggits are special," Reemer replied, cracking his knuckles, "and we're gonna take them to The Man ourselves. They got a message for him."

"If you know what's good for you, you'll just leave these boys with us. We'll take real good care of 'em for you."

Sonny pulled out his spring-knife and clicked it open. Sneering, he made a great show of cleaning his nails with it. "Maybe we'll just decide to take care of you instead."

Across the room the two card players rose from their seats. They started towards Sonny with their hands resting on the pommels of their swords. The Whiterider rose to his feet as well. From under his robe appeared a long-barreled flintlock pistol, which he leveled at Reemer. "You assholes need a severe lesson in the chain of command," he stated, "and the boys and I are gonna give it to you."

Reemer reached down and quickly pulled a heavy hunting knife from his boot just as the Whiterider cocked his pistol and swiveled it towards his face. The two Fascist officers drew their swords. So intent was everyone on the confrontation that nobody except Toad noticed the stocky, black-robed figure standing in the doorway.

"Put down your weapons and stand clear!" commanded a gruff voice.

The black-robed figure moved between Reemer and the Whiterider. Instinctively both men lowered their weapons and stepped back. "That's better," said the newcomer. With a sweep of his gloved hand he pushed back his cowl to reveal a heavy square face and close-cropped blond hair. Toad groaned to himself as he recognized Jack Rabid, Bejeezuz's lieutenant. "What's going on here?"

Reemer was the first to reply. "We were delivering these prisoners to Lord Flatbush and these ass ... uh, these officers..."

"Silence!" Jack Rabid sneered. He obviously enjoyed the fear that he instilled in these underlings. "HE will hear about this. For now, go about your business and leave these vermin to me."

"B-but... " Reemer began. "These faggits are special. They... uh, that is... "

"Billy Bejeezuz will judge how 'special' they are." Jack glowered at the Fonzer. His eyes were flat, lusterless blue, as devoid of expression as a shark's and just as menacing. "He may even reward you, if you don't cause any further delays."

Reemer sputtered and backed off; he and Sonny left the room quickly while the Fascists quietly returned to their duties. Jack Rabid smiled at their discomfort. Then, when his eyes rested on Toad the smile fell from his face. "You!" he thundered. "You're the one from Lubejob!"

Toad nodded weakly.

"Well, well. 'Special' indeed. You caused me a great deal of discomfort. I'm sure *he'll* be very interested to see you again, my friend. Come with me now."

The pipesmith could feel the sweat trickling down the back of his neck as Jack Rabid ushered them through corridors and up long stairways leading into the oldest part of the fortress. It was cool in the high chambers, but that did nothing to alleviate the sweating. As much as he tried to remain calm, Toad was rapidly losing his courage. He would soon face his worst nightmare, literally.

Jack knocked on a heavy oak door at the end of the last corridor and a thin, reedy voice bade them enter. The door swung open to reveal a dark candle-lit chamber. Heavy black chests were scattered about the floor and gloomy tapestries hung from the walls. A particularly bizarre one showed a band performing on a dimly lit stage. The musicians were frightening, barely human forms with leering painted faces and outfits of black leather studded with spikes. Their eyes were glowing beacons of hate.

A cowled figure sat at a desk across the room from the tapestry. A shaft of bloody red light from the setting sun knifed through the room's single slit window, illuminating the charts and battle plans scattered on the desk. As Jack approached, the figure looked up and waved them in—far too affably—but did not rise from its seat.

There was no face visible in the deep shadows of the hood, but a pair of pale unblinking eyes peered out, scrutinizing the Freaks closely. This was Sweet Billy Bejeezuz.

The Dark Man took a long joint-like object from a container on his desk and lit it from a nearby candle. He puffed on it greedily until its tip glowed a bright red. Acrid smoke blasted out of his cowl. He leaned back in his chair and propped his boots up on the desk; the soles were as thick as the span of a man's hand. The smoke was coming out of his cowl in a series of rings that circled over his head like vultures. "Introduce me to our friends, Jack," he requested pleasantly, in a voice filled with good humor.

"These hippies say they're from Hillcommune, but this one here is the one we lost at Lubejob."

Bejeezuz toyed with the rusty spearhead hanging from a chain around his neck. "Oh, yes. Yes, I think you may be right. Well, at least we are not complete strangers. And, you know, it's always nice to have visitors, isn't it, Jack? Especially when they hail from a place I have such an interest in. I'd ask you gentlemen to have a seat, but as you can see I have no chairs, nor any of the other customary comforts. Dear me, wartime, you know. It can be such a bother."

The Dark Man's voice was soothing—a voice you could trust, a far cry from the reedy croak that had answered Jack's knock. He took a pull from his smokestick and held it in his hand like a burning scepter.

"Why don't we have a chat," he continued. "I'm sure it was a long trip from Hillcommune. You must have many stories. Don't be shy. I would like for you to think of me as an old friend." He chuckled and put the smoldering stick back in his mouth. "I understand your reticence. It's the cowl, isn't it? Don't think me an ungracious host, please, but it's become a strict rule with me never to show my face, comely though it might be." He paused and blew out another series of smoke rings. "Though, when the time is right, I will reveal myself."

Toad trembled. Although he tried to control it, Bejeezuz seemed to detect his fear. "Are you cold, dear?" the Dark Man asked.

The pipesmith shook his head.

"Please, introduce yourself and your friends."

"Toad—Josiah Toad. These are my friends, Tambourine Dill and Ernie Mungweasle. We come from Hillcommune with a proposal."

"Toad—that's what I shall call you, as I'm sure all of your closest friends do. I congratulate you on your ingenious escape from Lubejob, dear Toad. It was most resourceful."

"I can't take credit for that."

"Still, it was very clever, though vexing to me personally." Deep in his cowl Bejeezuz's eyes glittered. He steepled his gloved hands and exhaled a blast of bluish smoke. "A most remarkable group, you three. But what matter is so important that you'd come to see me, putting yourselves in such peril along the way? With all the goings-on, the roads are just not safe."

"A matter of cosmic importance," Tambourine stated. "I'm a musician, as are you."

"As is our little friend here. Leastwise, he is in my dreams."

"But it's me you have to contend with."

"Contend?" Bejeezuz said, stroking his spearhead pendant. His voice was as smooth as honey being poured on toast. "Oh my, that sounds very confrontational."

Tambourine, confused by Bejeezuz's response, looked blankly at the Dark Man, and then turned hopelessly to Toad and Ernie.

Without warning, Bejeezuz became enraged. "Come on man, spit it out. You wasted my time at the Keep; you're wasting my time now," he snarled.

"You remember that?" Tam asked stoically.

"An insignificant moment to be sure, but yes," Bejeezuz growled. "The important question is, why are you here now? Are you auditioning for a gig?" he demanded. "I have no need of minstrels here. The cries of my victims are music enough for me."

"That is not why we are here," Tam countered sternly.

Bejeezuz paused for a moment, and angrily took a long hit off his smokestick. The end burned menacingly, like a glowing branding iron, but it trembled slightly. The Dark Man turned his back to the trio and gazed out the window. He stood still for a moment, and then took another, slower hit off his smokestick. His hand steadied. As he turned back he exhaled a blast of smoke. "You'll have to forgive me," he offered coolly. "As you know, we live in very stressful times. When you put yourself forward in such an adversarial way, it disturbed me. But, I'm a reasonable individual. Perhaps we can work together. I've been thinking of forming a combo. What do you say about you and Toad and I going on the road? We could play a few taverns, have a few laughs?"

Angered by the Dark Man's taunting, Tambourine drew himself up to his full height. "No! I am here to challenge you!"

"Challenge me?"

"I am a Dylan, sir, and the son of a Dylan. I am the Freedom Rider."

"Sorry, I left my autograph book in my other robe."

"You must play against me. It is our destiny."

Bejeezuz yawned audibly. "Is it? Your Dylan was a vastly overrated performer, you know. Never in a class with AC/DC, Twisted Sister, Kiss, Ozzy Osbourne, Metallica or a hundred other metal bands. In short ... I'm not interested."

"I don't know who they were, nor do I care. I am challenging *you*, Bejeezuz. You must accept."

The Dark Man laughed. A horrible, raspy cackle filled the room. Jack Rabid joined in, harrumphing like a dog with dry heaves. "You are really quite amusing. Are you forgetting who I am?"

"No, but my request can't be denied," Tambourine insisted. "It's the Musician's Code."

Bejeezuz was no longer laughing, nor was Jack Rabid. The room seemed to be growing colder by degrees. "I'm older than your foolish code, boy, and far stronger than either you or your pathetic ancestors. You fools have such delightfully simple minds. Don't you think that I've anticipated your silly little plans all along? I predate your Oldhips; I'm more ancient than Street-Corner Earth itself. I was old even on the Night of a Thousand Fires. Indeed, I participated in it. I know better than you where this puny little tradition of yours comes from, and it makes me laugh."

Tambourine was becoming flustered. His face grew red and he trembled with sudden rage. But he restrained himself, not speaking again until he was calm. Then he looked Bejeezuz straight in the eyes.

"The challenge is you against me, for all the world to see."

"And what would that gain me, Friend Dylan?"

"If you win you will have defeated the Freedom Rider and destroyed the rising spirit of my people. You will have proven your superiority."

"It seems I've proven that already."

"You fear me and my music. You don't dare play against me!"

Bejeezuz laughed again, smoke boiling out of his cowl. "You are even more vapid than I thought, because you also think me a fool. Do you seriously believe that I would ever let my ego overrule my common sense? I made that mistake once and I intend to never make it again. There is nothing for me to gain from your proposition. If you were to win, which is clearly impossible, the consequences for me would be obvious. But my victory could be worse. I don't want to create a martyr, especially a Dylan. Besides, we all really know what's going on here. This charade is pointless. I can see this is just a feeble attempt to buy time so that Hillcommune can fortify against attack."

"The fact remains that I am here and thousands know of my existence," Tambourine countered. "If you kill me, or if I simply disappear into your dungeons, I'll still be considered as much a martyr as if you defeated me in honest competition. By not daring to face me you will be considered a coward and your rule of fear will be weakened."

"Then you, Master Dylan, underestimate my ability to instill fear. You waste my time. Hillcommune can fortify all it wants; I'll conquer it easily when the time comes."

Toad found Bejeezuz's sneering disheartening. But the Dark Man was wrong; his ego *was* getting in the way. He seemed incapable of imagining that Freaks and Radiclibs might attack first.

Bejeezuz stubbed out his smokestick, lit a fresh one immediately, and got up out of his chair. He stalked around the room like a carrion crow sidling up to a rotten carcass. Hovering around one Freak, then another, not uttering a sound, he scrutinized them carefully, his cold eyes attempting to penetrate theirs. As the Dark Man stared down at Toad, it was all the pipesmith could do to keep from trembling. It took every ounce of his effort to stay put; he could not show Bejeezuz any signs of fear. Finally, the Dark Man settled on Tambourine.

"I have no inclination to indulge your ego or your curiosity, Mr. Dylan. Freedom Rider indeed," he spat. "I'll not allow one of your odious tribe that privilege. But I will extract my amusement from you. And, when I'm done with you, I'll give you to Jack to play with. You'd like that, wouldn't you, Jack?"

Jack grinned in a way that made Toad's skin crawl.

"You may have seen through our plot," Ernie interjected, "but it might be to your advantage to let us live awhile."

"Rest assured, I *will* keep you around for a while. It will be entertaining to see how long each of you can survive my games."

"Tambourine is a useful political prisoner and I am a member of the Clear Light Society."

The Dark Man exhaled a long tendril of smoke that wreathed about Ernie's neck before dissipating. "I have little interest in you Diggers and your childish projects, and even less in this Freedom Rider. In fact, the only one of you that holds any interests at all for me is Mr. Toad here. He and I have important matters to discuss."

Toad turned his head, no longer able to meet Bejeezuz's mocking stare. The Dark Man's proclamation didn't surprise him. His nightmares had long foretold this meeting.

"Why Toad?" Ernie asked.

"The Book, among other things."

"What book?"

"Don't try to be coy, Digger. Such attempts at slyness ill-becomes you. You know that I speak of the *Necronomicon*, the same *Necronomicon* that you maggots stole from the glovebox of a 1955 Chevrolet Bel-Air in Lubejob. Perceptive of you to find it before I did; but I must have it."

"W-we don't have it," Toad blurted.

Bejeezuz hissed. One gloved hand flew up like a snake poised to strike. "You lie! You have it and you will give it to me now!"

"What makes you think we've got the book?" asked Ernie. "Even if we did, we wouldn't be stupid enough to bring it along with us."

"I know that Toad has had his hands on it recently; I can smell it on him."

"That's not true. The *Necronomicon* was stolen."

"I believe my dreams, and they tell me otherwise."

The herbalist shrugged. "Believe what you will."

Toad nodded slightly. He knew what the Dark Man meant.

"Dreams?" Tambourine asked. "Dreams are fragments of undigested thought, brain droppings. What have they got to do with anything?"

Bejeezuz snickered and flicked an ash onto the musician's shirt. "Dreams are everything, especially *my* dreams. I have dreams, waking dreams. I had them even before I left my home to visit your tiny corner of the world. There's a link between Toad and me, a strong link even I don't fully understand. My dreams tell me the truth. They've led me to you, and they'll lead me to The Book. We are not strangers … are we, Toad?"

The pipesmith shook his head slowly. It felt heavy, leaden. A bitter coldness was stealing up from the pit of his stomach.

Bejeezuz flicked another ash and continued to prowl the room. "And you wouldn't lie to an old friend, would you?"

"No."

"Excellent. Now, give me The Book."

"I don't have it."

"Liar! Would you like to see how I deal with liars? It's not pretty, I assure you."

Toad cringed as the chill worked up his spine. But suddenly he realized that, perceptive as he was, Bejeezuz wasn't all-knowing. If he knew the book was destroyed, Toad and his friends would surely be dead. In spite of his fear, a plan swiftly formed in the pipesmith's mind. Though the copy of the *Necronomicon* that Bejeezuz wanted was safely destroyed, there was another copy that Toad could use as a bargaining chip, a partial copy that was miles away, unheeded and safe from prying eyes, and in an unreadable language.

The Dark Man ceased prowling the room. He stood beside Toad, looming over him as his eyes bored deep into the pipesmith's. It was as if he'd guessed part of Toad's secret. Then he laid his hand on Toad's shoulder, his fingers digging into the soft flesh beneath the neck like steel rods. "I would like an answer," he said sweetly, applying more pressure.

"It was stolen."

"By the sightless one, I know. I dreamed of him too. But he's faded now and I sense that the *Necronomicon* has moved on. No matter what you say, dear Toad, I know that you had it last. Talk about your stink fingers;

its dust still clings to you. I smell its odor on your delicate digits, dearie."

Interesting, Toad thought. Bejeezuz didn't seem to know that Moonshadow's sight had been restored, or that the Seer had been killed. More importantly, he didn't know that the *Necronomicon* no longer existed. "I-I don't know what you're talking about," Toad stammered.

The Dark Man's fingers dug deeper. "Believe me when I say that I have ways to make you talk. Jack, take these vermin to the guest room."

"Come along, scum," Jack growled. He produced a short sword from under his robe and gestured at the Freaks with it.

Toad started towards the door with his friends, but Bejeezuz's hand clamped down harder. "Not you, my pet. We still have much to discuss."

After Tambourine and Ernie were escorted from the room, the Dark Man stood silently regarding Toad for a moment. When he finally let go of Toad's shoulder he resumed playing with the rusty pendant at his throat as if he were deep in thought. His smokestick had burned down to a glowing stub in the darkness of his cowl. Its acrid fumes filled the room. "Alone at last," he said. "Now, you will tell me where The Book is. Don't try my patience, pretty one. Its smell is too strong for you to continue lying to me. Would you like to see your friends die slowly and oh-so-very painfully?"

Toad almost cried aloud as Bejeezuz's steely fingers returned to his shoulder, digging deeper than before. "You won't like the truth."

"Try me."

"Okay … I had the book, but I destroyed it!" he blurted out.

Bejeezuz looked deep into Toad's eyes. Releasing his grip on Toad's shoulder, he took a step backwards. He spit the smokestick stub from his mouth. It skittered across the floor, leaving a trail of sparks in its wake. "YOU DID WHAT?"

"I b-burned it."

"You crawling worm! You insignificant smear of dung! I ought to tear your face off right now and feed it to the dogs. What manner of stupidity caused you to do such a thing?"

"There were things, monstrously evil things. They came for the book. Destroying it drove them back to the hell they came from—the Other Place."

Shaking with rage, the Dark Man sat down on the corner of his desk. He picked up a wavy-bladed dagger from the litter on top of the desk and started to toy with it menacingly. His lidless eyes snapped fire. "Lies!" he hissed. "More lies!"

Toad fought to control his fear. This situation had to be played right. "It's the truth, I assure you. Whatever they were, your evil pales beside theirs. They would have destroyed me, you, and the whole world if I hadn't burned the book first."

Bejeezuz ran his gloved fingers along the dagger blade. In the blackness of his cowl his eyes burned fiercely. "For your sake I hope you're lying; your life depends on it."

"I wish that I was lying. The one that came for the book ... if I had looked upon him long I would have lost my mind." He shuddered.

"You'll lose more than that with me. With The Book I could have controlled him."

Though cold with fear Toad decided it was time to play the card he'd been keeping up his sleeve. "Really? I'm not sure that even you are that powerful. But—assuming you are, maybe we can still bargain."

"Dead men don't deal."

"Would you be so eager to kill me if I said that I know where there's another copy of the *Necronomicon*?"

"Another copy—more lies!"

"No, it's true. Though it is only a partial copy."

"Partial copy?" Bejeezuz laid down the dagger and picked up another smokestick, his third since the interview began. He lit it from the candle on his desk. "Quick, out with it, and I might decide to spare you."

"The manuscript is written in a strange language with letters like ours, but the words make no sense. There is the name Olaus Wormius on the title page."

Bejeezuz puffed on his smokestick reflectively. "How interesting. Is it handwritten, or printed?"

"Handwritten."

"Ah, the codex of 1228, no doubt. A wonderful find, if you really have it. It was written in Latin, a language ancient even in my day."

"Can you translate it?"

"With some difficulty, yes. How much of The Book is left?"

"Between a quarter and a half, I'd say."

The Dark Man blew out a quick series of smoke rings. "Tell me where it is and I'll be easy on you. I might even let you and your friends live."

"No, let's talk terms first."

"Terms! You must be joking. I could crush you like the insignificant bug you are."

"Then you wouldn' have the book, would you?" Toad replied flatly.

As he eyed Toad intently, a wicked grin started in the corner of Bejeezuz's mouth and spread across his face. "What could you possibly have in mind, dearie?"

"Agree to Tambourine's challenge. If he wins you let him and Ernie go. Once I'm certain of their safety I will tell you where to find the book."

"And when I win, which I surely will?" Bejeezuz asked, still smiling.

"Then I'll tell you what you want to know and you can do what you want with us."

"Surely you can't be as stupid as you sound. You must realize that I could torture you and get the information without all of the fanfare."

"You could try, but what if I died before you got what you wanted? You've waited this long. Would it be too much to wait until All Loveday?"

"You amuse me, little one. There's more to you than I had imagined, and that intrigues me. Perhaps I'll agree—on one small condition."

"What's that?"

"When your precious Freedom Rider loses you must tell me what I want to know—from my bed."

Toad paled, suddenly comprehending. "No, no, no! No way!"

"It's up to you, Babycakes. I can start torturing you and your friends immediately, if you prefer. But of course, there is always a very slim chance that your Freedom Rider might win."

Toad's throat constricted as a wave of nausea passed through him. Billy's suggestion disgusted him, but he had to buy time. At the very worst, he could hang himself in his cell at the last minute. "All right, all right, but not until after All Loveday."

"My dear Toad, I'm so glad you convinced me to agree to your plan. This worked out far better than I could have dreamed." Abruptly, Bejeezuz clapped his hands and another black-robed figure stepped into the room. He nodded at Toad. "This interview is over. Take him to his friends, but be gentle with him."

Bejeezuz's man returned the nod and guided Toad out of the room. Before the door closed behind him he took one last look over his shoulder at Bejeezuz, but the Dark Man had already returned to his desk and didn't notice him exit.

The pipesmith lay where he'd been thrown, in a dingy cell, sprawled across a pile of moldy straw. He struggled to a sitting position, gazing up at the feeble light coming in through the barred eyehole at the top of the cell door. In a moment Ernie and Tambourine were at his side helping him to his feet. There were no sounds except for the moaning of a prisoner in an adjoining cell.

"You all right?" Ernie asked.

"Yeah, I'm fine. The first step was a lulu, though."

Tambourine began to brush straw from Toad's hair and clothes. "We didn't know if we were going to see you again, man."

"Bejeezuz is not someone I'd want to party with, but he's not ready to kill us, yet."

"Yet."

"He won't kill us until after All Loveday."

The musician leaned forward; his thin face looked intense and pale in the dim light. "What do you mean? Has he reconsidered?"

"Yeah. He's going to play against you on All Loveday, unless he changes his mind again."

"How in the hell did you manage that?"

"It wasn't easy. Let's move away from the door and I'll tell you about it."

The three Freaks moved to the far end of the cell, away from prying ears. They sat down in a pile of dusty hay and made themselves as comfortable as possible.

"So, what happened?" Ernie asked.

"I was scared to death so I don't remember a lot of the details, but mostly he kept asking me about the *Necronomicon*. It took me a while but I finally convinced him that I didn't have it."

"I didn't think that was possible," Tam interjected. "He was positive you had it; he said he could smell it on you. It's obvious the dude is about as far off the deep end as you can get."

"What was it that finally convinced him, Toad?" Ernie asked.

"I told him that I burned it."

"And he bought that? I can't believe he's that gullible."

"He's not. I told him the truth." The pipesmith waited for what he said to sink in.

"What?!" Ernie and Tam shouted simultaneously, Ernie jumping to his feet.

"I burned the *Necronomicon* two nights ago. Our first night out of Hillcommune. You remember *that* night."

"How ... why'd you do that?" Ernie stammered. "What the fuck are we here for then? What were you...?"

"If you'll shut up for a minute and listen," Toad snapped, "I'll explain everything."

"Let him talk," Tam said softly as he pulled Ernie back to his seat. Toad noticed that the musician seemed remarkably calm.

Omitting the part about who first stole the book, Toad related all that had transpired since that stormy night in Hillcommune. He even told them about the growing influence the *Necronomicon* had had on him, and how Franklin's mind had been imprisoned in the Other Place. After Franklin's return, Toad's suspicions about the book had been confirmed. Indeed Franklin, with his newfound abilities, could see the disruptions in The All caused by the book, and was adamant that it should be destroyed. And in the end, it had been consumed by the campfire.

"Great Dylan, Toad, you wanted Tam and me to accompany you on this suicide mission knowing full well that Moonshadow didn't have the book?"

"*Want* is not the word I'd use. Anyway, the only person who had a choice was you; Tam and I had to come, if not now, then soon. And you're one to talk. Didn't you hoodwink me into a short road trip to Covenstead without telling me what I was getting into?"

"Come on. That was different. I didn't know that your life was going to be endangered."

"But it was—many times—including now. At least you knew what you volunteered for."

"Right ... I mean ... you know what I mean. Tell him, Tam."

"Toad's got a point," Tam stated. "For me, it makes things easier. My road led to Covenstead from the day I accepted the role of the Freedom Rider. Worrying about the book added extra pressure, but now that I know it's out of the way I can concentrate on what I came here to do. I'm sure Toad has similar feelings."

Ernie looked at the two of them and shook his head. He took off his hat, placed it in his lap, and laid his arms across its battered crown.

"Look, guys," Toad offered, "I'm sorry I couldn't let you in on it earlier, but the book had to be destroyed. If we had tried to use that accursed book against Bejeezuz, or if it fell into his hands, a worse fate, one of inconceivable magnitude, would have befallen Street-Corner Earth. I know I shouldn't have deceived you, Ernie, but if I'd told you the truth you would have come anyway."

"Shit," he said sullenly. "You're probably right. I'd definitely do something that stupid."

"What about Bejeezuz?" Tam asked. "If you convinced him that you burned the *Necronomicon*, how did you get him to agree to the All Loveday gig?"

"Good point," Ernie added.

"I offered him my great-great-grandfather's copy as part of the deal."

"You mean that old book that you keep in your desk?" Ernie commented. "The one that's handwritten in some gobbledygook no one can understand? That's another copy of the *Necronomicon*?"

Toad nodded. "Exactly. I never knew what it was until Tam mentioned what he was hunting for at Swetshop. After that it slowly dawned on me what I had. Anyway, I promised him the book if he would play against Tam. Bejeezuz thinks he can decipher it. But, I have no intention of living up to my end of the deal."

Ernie grinned. "Damn, I knew you were sneaky enough to be good Digger material."

Chapter Fifty-Two

Mizjoan looked down at the eggs on her plate and almost gagged. They were fried over-easy; one had split open, oozing a slow trickle of yellow yolk from its side like pus. To the queasy Radiclib leader the contents of her plate looked like a pair of flat, diseased eyes. She picked up a forkful, lost all courage, and set it back down. "I can't eat this," she announced.

"What?" Kentstate asked, looking up from a plate that was already half empty. "Do you have any idea what I went through to get these? Oldhips consider eggs meat, you know. I had to do some fast talking before anyone would even think of trading me these beauties."

"I appreciate your efforts."

Kentstate shrugged and greedily stuffed a forkful of egg into her mouth. "Hell, I thought you'd like a break from cheese, grain, and veggies. I cooked them myself."

Mizjoan pushed the plate away, poured herself a glass of water from the carafe at her elbow, and took a sip. It felt cold in her empty stomach, but it was the only thing she was sure she could keep down. "I don't mean to offend you, 'State. I'm sure these eggs are fine. It's just that my stomach isn't up to them. Nerves, I guess."

"You're worrying too much lately. It's not like you," Kentstate replied, pulling Mizjoan's plate towards her side of the table. "Look, if you aren't going to eat these, I am."

"Feel free. Food doesn't interest me right now."

Kentstate finished her plate and began on Mizjoan's. Looking up, she wiped her mouth delicately with a napkin. "You know, I'd like to head out tonight. I'm dying to kick some Fashie ass."

"Me too, but there's still a lot to be done. The troops that we sent out to pose as travelers need time to organize the lowland Freaks, before moving on to Covenstead. Hopefully, they can rouse every able-bodied Freak to join us against the enemy. We need all the people we can get."

"I wish a few of the Oldhips would come around. After all, we're saving their asses too. I've never seen a more apolitical group in my life."

"We've discussed this before, 'State. You know my feelings. Some of the younger Hillcommuners have approached me, but I've put them off so far. Oldhips are motivated by mystical things, and I'm sure the elders feel that by letting us stay here they've done their part in the war effort."

"Maybe so, but we could sure use their help."

"They are not warriors, 'State. Remember what Old Bob said about the chimes of freedom, 'Flashing for the warriors whose strength is not to fight.' We must do our best without them."

"Then we can only count on our own troops and the lowland Freaks that will join us."

"Don't forget Field Marshal Dillon's troops."

Hearing the general's name, Kentstate looked away from her leader.

"Oh, don't worry about that old goat," Mizjoan offered. "He and I have our differences, that's for sure; but I've never questioned his ability to lead his troops. He'll be in Covenstead on All Loveday."

"If they can get through, you mean."

Mizjoan shrugged. "We'll all be taking the same risks."

Kentstate removed the dishes from the table and put them in a basin to soak. "I hope this works. Not just for us, but for Ernie, Toad and Tambourine as well."

"I have hope that Bejeezuz won't harm them before All Loveday, but after the battle starts…" Her stomach felt like it was twisting into knots. She was more worried about the three Freaks than she cared to admit. Still, she managed to muster a weak smile. "We could be dead soon ourselves, 'State, but at least we'll die fighting on our feet, not on our knees."

"Right on, sister. But, the Fashies aren't going to like the idea of thousands of Freaks descending on Covenstead to rally around their spiritual leader."

Mizjoan nodded. "If it were me I would just pull more troops into the area and let them come. They know they have the superior numbers. But if that is their plan, it would mean fewer troops to protect the outskirts. Hopefully, that will free us to move in at night, relatively unnoticed."

"And, once the competition between Tambourine and Bejeezuz begins, we can attack," Kentstate added.

"Exactly."

"But, how do we know that the Dark Man won't let the pilgrims converge on Covenstead, then have his soldiers surround and slaughter them before the contest?"

"We have to rely on Maynard's judgement that all will go as planned. Maynard knows the Dark Man better than anyone. Bejeezuz would never turn down the opportunity to humiliate the Freedom Rider in front of his followers. It would break the spirit of the people and, as much as the Dark Man enjoys inflicting physical pain, he relishes crushing the human spirit even more. At least, that is the Beatnik's opinion. Franklin agreed with him. He says The All is full of ripples, and he can only read it up to the contest. After that, it is too confusing to make any prediction."

"Well, I hope they're right."

"Tambourine is the voice of our people. His music will have a great psychological effect. It will unite people, Freaks and Radiclibs alike. We will be as one, marching to victory."

Kentstate seemed to digest this slowly. "It's a nice romantic notion, but Bejeezuz isn't stupid; he'll know what we're doing."

"He may," Mizjoan agreed, "but that could work to our advantage. Let him think he has everything under control, going his way, and then we'll surprise him. It's the only shot we've got at liberating Covenstead."

Kentstate suddenly leaned forward and held her friend's arm. "Sometimes I think blind hope is the only real weapon we have going for us."

"Maybe it is, 'State."

Mizjoan turned and looked out the window at the teeming wharves of Hillcommune. She had often heard it said that a weapon was only as good as the one who wielded it. Hope could be such a weapon, one far stronger than the arrows and bullets of the enemy. But to be worth anything, that hope had to burn brightly in the hearts of the common people and manifest itself in the lives of Freaks and Radiclibs, Oldhips and Diggers. The Freedom Rider, not she and her army, was the avatar of that hope. As word of the Freedom Rider spread, the common people would be the ones to rise up behind him. Together they could break Bejeezuz's stranglehold on Street-Corner Earth and drive back their enemies. She sighed as her mind filled with a vision of The People marching together, tens of thousands strong, united as never before under the banners of the clenched fist and the peace symbol—at the hour of greatest need, a final gathering of the tribes. In her heart she wanted to reach out to all of them, hug them to her, be one with them as they would be one with the Freedom Rider.

Unexpectedly, a single tear slid down her cheek. "Love," she said softly.

Kentstate looked up. "Excuse me?"

"Love," Mizjoan repeated, still awash in her heroic daydream, "is all you need."

From his dingy back booth at the Sunshine Nutrition Center, which was located near Hillcommune's healery, Maynard could see everything that was going on, not only in the eatery but along the wharf as well. He allowed

449

himself a thin smile as he adjusted his reflective sunglasses and reached for one of the cheap clay pipes that the eatery provided at every table. Filling it with house weed from the box by the salt and pepper shakers, he lit it with a candle and gazed thoughtfully out the window. He could see out without being seen, which was just the way he liked it. There was too much on his mind for him to be disturbed by friends and acquaintances.

Lou, the Center's fat counter man, put down the comic almanack he'd been reading and delivered Maynard's iced tea without giving him a second glance. The Beatnik exhaled a cloud of weedsmoke that dissipated slowly, encircling him like a protective fog. Oldhips were beginning to straggle in through the front door, early arrivals for the noon meal, but none sat near him. He rested his head against the back of the booth and slipped into a meditative trance.

Dozens of conflicting thoughts hopscotched through Maynard's mind. At the rate they tumbled over one another he despaired of ever getting them straight. Chiefly, he was still upset over Moonshadow and the loss of the *Necronomicon;* but that concern gave way to a host of greater and lesser worries, each begging for his attention. Many of these were unforeseen events that had arisen lately. He felt as though he was losing control. It was not a sensation he liked—not at all, considering the influence he'd had on events over the past five centuries. Losing the book was a major bummer, but his mind had cleared somewhat after Moonshadow absconded with it.

He'd had his hands on the *Necronomicon* before, at Westcommune, and never bothered to examine it, or its spurious companion volume, more than desultorily before sending it east with the ill-fated Risen Brothers. What an egregious blunder. Both volumes had fallen into the hands of the Mansonites, only to be separated years later when the ancestors of the present-day Greasers apparently stole the true *Necronomicon* from the Charlies, during one of their infrequent intertribal raids. Thankfully, both groups were too stupid to know how to make use of the book, and Tommy Two hadn't succeeded in getting it away from Parakwat in time for it to be of any use to him either. Truly, the *Necronomicon* had a way of slipping from owner to owner in a way that seemed to suit its own needs. Maynard could only hope that this time it hadn't fallen into the Dark Man's hands. He wondered; could the book be a tool of fate sent to keep the two immortals locked in eternal combat? Maybe *that* was their destiny?

Destiny. There was a word to ponder. Maynard knew all about destiny. He knew how to shape it, how to bend it, at times how to thwart it. He knew he was a creature of destiny from the very day that he crawled out of the peat bog to greet the strange new world of Helter-Skelter centuries ago.

Maynard took another toke from the oily clay pipe, inhaling deeper this time. He let his thoughts drift back through time, allowing the images to play through his mind like the moving picture shows that he'd enjoyed as a child. He'd missed the fall of the Old Order, literally sleeping through it, but soon afterwards he learned enough to fill in the gaps in his knowledge.

Helter-Skelter wasn't as cut and dried as contemporary histories made it out to be. First came the collapse of the world economic system, and then the depletion of several key resources, which led to growing tensions between the existing world powers. A series of small but seemingly endless wars followed, which bled even those nations dry. After the wars, plagues depopulated entire regions. Plagues were followed by famines that killed off many of the remaining survivors. Cults and conflicting ideologies germinated in the ensuing chaos like maggots on rotting meat. Most died out or were consumed by the constant outbreaks of revolutionary fervor that swept the land. Those that weren't wiped out survived by consolidating under Simon Doomsayer, or others like him, bringing on the long dark night of Neo-Luddite terror. In retaliation to Doomsayer, fascism had its greatest flowering since before World War Two. In time the two movements collided in bloody all-out war, rolling over and crushing those who wouldn't or couldn't take sides. Thankfully, nobody was quite insane enough to touch off the Big One—the nuclear exchange that would have erased humanity from the picture. In the following decades of horror and technicide, people banded together into small nomadic tribes, fearful of outsiders. Within several generations civilization was gone, flushed down the toilet of history. The world Maynard awoke to was a blank slate upon which he could write anything he chose, a palimpsest of what had been and what would be.

There were attempts to build societies again; Westcommune was an example of that. Fleeing from the troubles in the east, Boswell the Lame, under Maynard's tutelage, founded an agrarian collective on the fringes of the Arizona desert, far from the madness of the 'civilized' centers. There, Boswell's people knew peace for many years until the coming of Tommy Two. Two murdered Boswell and took Westcommune for his own. It was only through the greatest effort that Maynard and Frankie Lee raised an army and took back the city, driving Two into the desert. Yet soon after that victory, Maynard and the people of Westcommune soured on the west and the great migration back east began. By then the Beatnik knew that his place was not in the forefront of history, but in the background.

There were other forces moving in the world: Mansonites, fanatical militiamen, and street punks—ancient tribes who were the ancestors of modern Fascists and Greasers. Not content to live and let live, these barbarians attacked Maynard's people whenever the opportunity arose. The hatred displayed in this current conflict had its roots buried deeply in that long-ago time. Such ancient rage would never die easily.

Maynard took a sip of the Green Zinger tea. It tasted heavily of mint and flower petals. Looking up from his glass Maynard noticed Mizjoan and Kentstate chatting with some young Oldhips in front of the eatery. It didn't take a mind reader or prophet to know what was going on. The youngsters, predominantly males who were impressed with the two warriors, were begging to be recruited, to become soldiers instead of flower children. A few might eventually overcome Mizjoan's objections and be allowed to join the cause, but there wouldn't be many. Of all the inhabitants of Street-Corner Earth, Maynard loved the Oldhips most. These gentle magical people lived closest to the ideals he'd held in his youth and were the most like the Children of Peace he and Boswell had envisioned. In them lay the last best hope of the world.

In the future, when war had outlived its usefulness, the Oldhips would be the ones who would lead the peoples of Street-Corner Earth into the Aquarian Age. Until then, like the pacifists of old, they must refrain from learning war. Ultimately they were destined to serve in other far more important ways.

After ten minutes of shaking their heads and fending off questions, Mizjoan and Kentstate left the youths and walked down the wharf. Maynard watched them until they were out of sight, and then returned to his tea. He tried his pipe again but it fumed and went out. He relit it with the candle, but toking as hard as he could, he found he was only sucking ashes. He set the grimy clay pipe on the table and sipped the last of his tea. The eatery was beginning to empty. All around Maynard patrons pushed aside their plates and ambled towards the door. Lou the counter man picked up the dishes and wiped down the tables with a rag before returning to the almanack he'd been reading. Even from across the room its lurid cover revealed it to be a back issue of *Weed Wizard Comix*. Maynard chuckled to himself. In the hands of someone like the fat counterman, the *Necronomicon* would pose no threat at all. If it didn't have pictures Lou wouldn't bother with it. Smiling, Maynard strolled past the enthralled Oldhip and out the door.

Sweet Billy Bejeezuz sat at a table in the small room next to his office. He selected a cigar from the coffin-shaped box at his elbow and lit it from the candle he kept burning for that purpose. Taking a few tentative puffs, he propped his heavily booted feet up on a trunk and sat looking out the window at the sunlit battlements of Covenstead and the hazy Purple Mountains beyond. He threw back his cowl and let the warm sunlight play over his face. The warmth felt good, but it also disturbed him. Such unseasonably mild weather could have only one source. Someone had been fucking with the *Necronomicon*, someone who knew how to use it. He took a deeper series of puffs and glanced at the scattering of clutter on the tabletop. He was willing to bet it was the one he'd come to call the Peat Bog Stinker. Well, the son of a bitch didn't have the *Necronomicon* anymore, did he? Billy grinned. He was a hatefully happy man. Things were coming together, finally. According to the news that his spies had been bringing him, his work in Street-Corner Earth was just about done. After a few loose ends were tied up here, he might amuse himself by ravaging Downeast or by backtracking and laying waste to Boston.

Billy let out a blast of smoke, his grin broadening. He felt like a fat spider sitting in the middle of the perfect web of his own creation. Jack Rabid had just been by, giving him the latest reports. Freaks from all over Street-Corner Earth were massing to come to Covenstead for their insipid All Loveday celebration, as he knew they would. Let the fools come. Let them think their precious Freedom Rider was going to play for their liberation. Let them get their hopes up. He had been careful not to let anyone see his enthusiasm when that scion of Dylan mentioned a contest. He had wanted to give these Freak scum a concert all along, but the Peat Bog Stinker ruined his plans the last time. This time Old Billy would have it his way. He'd rock them until their ears bled, just like in the old days.

The Dark Man stubbed out his cigar on the window ledge and started to look through the debris on the table—articles that were taken from the Freaks when they were captured. The contents of their pockets were of little interest—a few morsels of food, a small bag of weed and a dented harmonica. A good host would not deny them their pathetic creature comforts; as long as the Freaks were of use, they could keep their trifles.

They carried a few weapons as well: two unfired pistols, a Radiclib shortsword, and a pair of cheap, battered guitars. Billy looked at the legend 'THIS MACHINE KILLS FASCISTS' on one of the guitars, chuckled, and set the thing aside. What was in the backpacks interested him most. In the bottom of one of the packs he found a bag containing a kind of whitish weed and a small pipe. He looked at the weed with amusement. It had been a long time since he'd smoked any Marahooch, decades perhaps. Power, greed and fear were the only drugs that he ever really needed. Still, what could it hurt to have a couple of tokes? It was time for a little celebration.

Billy packed the pipe and lit it from the candle. He took a toke and nearly gagged. Sinking back in his chair, the effect was almost immediate; the fog that plagued his memory started to drift apart. He took another toke, deeper this time.

Amazingly, he remembered Westcommune in vivid detail. He remembered Parakwat, his chief poisoner, one of the few people he ever feared. He remembered his plan to kill Parakwat and steal his copy of the *Necronomicon*. He would have succeeded, if it hadn't been for the attack that took the city from him and forced him to escape into the desert. Forty days he spent in that hellish wilderness before making it back to civilization. In that time his flesh was burned raw and his mind fried by the relentless desert sun. He survived thanks to his machine half. He remembered the Stinker too, but he couldn't recall his face. All his mind could conjure up was his own visage mockingly reflected in a pair of mirrored sunglasses.

Stranger yet, Billy thought of the old, old days, before Helter-Skelter, when he and his band Ringwraith were the best known, most influential, highest-paid rock musicians in the world. Back then he was Ebeneezer Caligula Garlock, though even that was not his true given name. Ringwraith made him rich and powerful, and allowed him to have the hobbies he'd always wanted—pleasant little diversions like torture and rape, arson and murder.

The money that Ringwraith raked in from a series of sellout world tours put Billy in contact with the kind of people he needed to carry out his megalomaniacal dreams. In time he came to direct their activities as skillfully as he directed his band, an orchestral performance of death and destruction. In cities where Ringwraith played shit happened: political leaders met with untimely deaths, churches and synagogues burned, and ghettos erupted in waves of senseless violence.

After a while Billy's lust for destruction turned him from an organizer to a doer. He studied the subtle techniques of torture. He learned how to use firearms and explosives, to wield an Uzi or MAC-10 as effectively as he wielded his guitar. Then, on one of his lighthearted outings, the bombing of a Neo-Luddite meeting hall in Scranton, Pennsylvania, an accident occurred that almost cost him his life. A C-4 charge exploded prematurely, killing two of his men and leaving his body badly mangled. The Lazarus Group, a coalition of renegade scientists and engineers funded mostly by Ringwraith money, saved him. They kept him alive by building him a new body of steel, synthetic flesh and electronic circuitry. In doing so they gave him immortality.

Billy chortled warmly as the flood of memories swept over him. These Freak fools were up against God, or at the very least a damn close facsimile. It amused him to think of them flocking to Covenstead—lemmings marching to the sea to commit mass suicide. The Freaks would fight with all their souls, but in the end it would amount to Bo Diddly shit. They would be mowed down at the city gates while he watched from the comfort of his stage, but not until he humiliated their precious Freedom Rider. What was that old expression about the spider and the fly? Another one of those things he couldn't quite remember.

The destruction of Street-Corner Earth, as satisfying as it might be, was only a prelude to what Billy had in mind. To carry out his master plan, though, he still needed the *Necronomicon*. With the copy that sweet Toad would provide, incomplete though it might be, Billy could rule the planet. He laughed. That little fool thought he was so high and mighty, wheeling and dealing with the Dark Man. Well, young Toad would find out just what kind of deal he authored when Sweet Billy Bejeezuz filled his end. He smiled to think how the Freak would squeal and moan for him. Hell, he might even be good enough to keep around for a while.

Billy tapped out the pipe and lit another cigar. His smile deepened into a mask of burning hate.

Chapter Fifty-Three

Southward over Covenstead a distant thundershower was passing through. Daylight was fading fast as the sun slipped below the mountains that rose up behind the Radiclib leader. Beside her, Kentstate stood looking down the length of a small hidden pass. On the floor of the pass Mizjoan's troops were preparing for the journey ahead. Soldiers sat about in small groups talking quietly among themselves. About fifty horses, more suited to pulling wagons than serving as war mounts, were chomping patiently in their feedbags. Herded down from the pastures west of Hillcommune, where they'd ranged since the weed traffic was interrupted, these were the best horses that Hillcommune had to offer.

Mizjoan yawned and shook her head as if to clear it. As night was closing in, she was eager to be on her way.

"Dylan's Bones, I'm ready," Kentstate commented. "I've waited a long time to avenge Rudy's death."

Mizjoan nodded. The silver eye patch she wore, replacing her customary black cloth one, gleamed brightly with the last rays of daylight. "Soon, 'State, soon."

Overhead the sky blazed, red as a battle flag, slowly softening into the blues and purples of twilight. As the horizon above Covenstead flared brightly with the passing storm and thunder tolled like distant bells, she took a hit off the weedpipe that Kentstate passed her and sighed. She remembered the old song Tambourine had played at the Yule party. "Fucking underdog soldiers in the night," she said to herself. "That's all we are. And if the chimes of freedom ain't flashing for us, who do they flash for?" She exhaled, tapped the pipe out and walked down into the pass.

The noonday sun pounded down like a hammer. Beyond the river the fields of Hillcommune shimmered as if seen through a distorted glass. In the cloudless blue sky a pair of hawks circled lazily, then flew off towards the mountains. Even in the shadows of the tree in front of Wheatstraw's digs, the heat was oppressive.

Flo set aside the handful of small white mushrooms that he'd been sorting out and paused to mop his brow. He sniffed disdainfully, noticing that the armpits and back of his tie-dyed shirt were soaked with sweat. Beside him, shirtless and chewing on a weedstalk, his brother Eddie continued to lay out the tiny fungi on a cloth spread on the grass. Next to the cloth sat a bowl containing a handful of Thirdworld White.

"Far out!" Eddie suddenly exclaimed, holding up one of the mushrooms by its long pale stem.

"A real beauty, brother mine."

"How many more are we gonna need?"

"I'd say we've got enough, Eddie. The extract from a few handfuls of these little pretties should be enough to blow the minds of everyone in the valley."

Further conversation died when hurried footsteps along the wharf heralded a slender blonde Radiclib woman wearing a red kerchief. She was accompanied by Freewheelin' Franklin. Franklin nodded to them curtly as he and the Radiclib pushed through Wheatstraw's front door, letting it bang shut loudly behind them.

"What's this?" Flo wondered aloud. "Our Radiclib buddies coming back so soon?"

Eddie chomped thoughtfully on his weedstalk. "I don't think so. I don't remember seeing her."

From inside the house sounds of frantic conversation rose and fell until Wheatstraw's voice could be heard over the rest. Whatever was being discussed was obviously important, but the voices never became quite loud enough for the brothers to hear what was being said.

Flo crept to a position below the nearest open window. Holding a silencing finger to his lips, he motioned for Eddie to join him.

"Mizjoan and the rest of your people left yesterday, Comrade Tanya," Franklin could be heard saying.

"It is imperative that we reach her," the Radiclib girl insisted. "Mizjoan must be warned of the Fascist forces mustering at Indian Stream. They are walking into a trap."

"So it would seem."

The Tribechief cleared his throat loudly. "We will send a messenger, but it seems unlikely that one would reach her in time."

"Give me a horse!" Tanya shouted. "I'll go myself."

Franklin clucked paternally. "Mizjoan took all the horses that could carry a person or a pack. But calm yourself, girl. We'll think of something. Won't we, Brother Wheatstraw?"

In spite of the heat Flo and Eddie found themselves shivering. "This is bad shit," Eddie muttered. "Even one of our fastest runners couldn't get to Mizjoan on time."

"Yeah, brother mine, it doesn't look like there's anything we can do."

Eddie chewed on a bit of weedstalk thoughtfully. Suddenly his angular face brightened. "Saaay Flo, I got an idea."

"Lay it on me, bro."

"A runner couldn't get to Mizjoan in time, but a flyer could."

"Man, that's suicide. You could get shot out of the sky, or crash in the mountains, and even if you could get to Mizjoan in time, she'd still be outflanked and outnumbered."

"You got a better idea?" Eddie pouted. "We gotta do something."

Flo picked up a handful of mushrooms and regarded them thoughtfully. "I believe we have the solution right in our hands," he said, giving Eddie a sinister wink. "Remember back when our folks took us to visit our cousins in Indian Stream?"

"Just barely. We couldn't have been more than ten then."

"Eleven. Do you remember where the Streamers got their water?"

"Sure, they dammed up part of the stream and built a cistern in the market square."

Flo grinned. His small dark eyes sparkled. "Excellent, Eddie. Now where would the Fascist army in Indian Stream be likely to get its water?"

"From the same cistern, I suppose."

"Right on!"

Eddie scratched his head and looked at the pile of pale fungi. "Flo, you proposing to spike their water supply?"

"Yes, brother mine. Since you're so damn eager to fly that contraption of yours, you can fly it over their camp at night and drop a little gift into the cistern. I've got a special recipe in mind."

"I can't do it alone."

"You'll have to. That kite of yours is only big enough for one."

"I can't fly it and get the stuff into the cistern at the same time; I'll crash for sure. But I can modify her to carry two. You can drop it in the water while I keep us in the air."

"Refitting Freeblid will take too long."

"No, all I need is about half a day."

Flo grunted and fingered his pencil-line mustache, deep in thought. Then he smiled at Eddie. "Sounds like a plan, man, but let's run it by Wheatstraw and Franklin."

Chapter Fifty-four

Flo and Eddie soared. Below them the circle of stones that crowned Mount Lennon grinned like blackened teeth against the scarlet sky. In the distance, the Sludge glittered red beyond the lower hills around Ripoff Pass. It seemed that all of Street-Corner Earth was visible in the deepening twilight. Somewhere, lost among the crawling shadows, lay the towns of Indian Stream and Little Woodstock. A sprinkle of bright stars frosted the sky, winking at the rising moon.

Wheatstraw had agreed to their plan to spike the Fascists' water. The two brothers had reworked the glider, enlarging the harness to accommodate two people, increasing the wingspan, and staining the entire craft flat black to render it nearly invisible in flight. Flo held two dark-colored wineskins filled with a liquid extract of Thirdworld White—mushrooms, hashoil, wormwood, ergot and datura—a potion powerful enough to trip out anything that drank out of the Indian Stream cistern.

Once the glider was clear of the mountains and their unpredictable currents of air, its flight became steady. Twisting their bodies in tandem, Flo and Eddie banked Freebird south toward Indian Stream. In less than half an hour they spotted the Sludge, sparkling as the moon lifted itself higher above the horizon. Steering the glider slightly more to the east, they drifted along like a huge autumn leaf above the starlit current.

Within another hour the gambrel roofs of Indian Stream appeared, hunched against the snow-spotted fields. Lights burned in the upper story of the largest structure, which presumably housed the general headquarters. The rest of the encampment was dark, except for a few dying campfires burning here and there among the ruins. A horse whinnied softly as the glider swept in from the river and passed over the rows of silent tents. The brothers banked to the right. Freebird flew past a huge steamwagon parked in the market square and headed towards the squat ugly circle of the town cistern. As the craft leveled off, Flo unstopped the first wineskin and let it fall.

Corporal Krieg leaned against the doorpost of the abandoned general store, idly picking his nose. From time to time he rolled the hardened mucus between his fingers until it was perfectly round, examining it closely in the poor light, as if he were reading a crystal ball. His musket rested nearby, propped against a trash barrel and ignored by its owner. Krieg yawned, wiped his finger on his pant leg and reached into his greatcoat pocket for his flask. It was cold and lonely work guarding the deserted square, but the pint of Ragin' Redneck sourmash was making Krieg's duties less arduous. Licking his wind-chapped lips, he lifted the flask to his mouth and took a deep pull of the burning liquid.

Krieg corked the bottle and was about to return it to his pocket when something huge swooped down out of the night sky, an enormous bat, about eighteen feet from wingtip to wingtip. He blinked stupidly as it flew over the cistern. Krieg looked at the bottle and suddenly threw down it as if it had come alive in his hand. He blinked again, but the creature didn't go away. He dove for his musket and rolled behind the trash barrel, pulled back the weapon's heavy hammer and took aim at the monster as it circled back towards him.

Freebird swooped low for its final pass. Flo let go of the last wineskin, grinning as it splashed in the dark water below. "Take her up, Eddie," he said.

The two brothers shifted in the harness and Freebird banked clumsily, rising into the chilly starlit sky above the square. Suddenly there was a flash and an explosion from the shadows and something whizzed by their heads, uncomfortably close.

"Dylan's Bones!" Eddie yelped. "We're being shot at! Bank left!"

"What? Left?"

"Right!"

The brothers struggled in their harnesses, each trying to go in a different direction. Freebird wobbled drunkenly and started to roll over.

"What's with you?" Eddie screeched. "I said left!"

"No way. You said right!"

"Left! For Dylan's sake, left!"

"Make up your mind!"

Freebird, as confused as her pilots, lost her willingness to fly, and started a slow lazy dive toward the ground. While the glider curled uncontrollably down toward the center of the square, a burly figure emerged from the shadows, clutching a musket in his right hand and a shortsword in his left. The glider landed like a ruptured goose, doing a half-cartwheel as it slowly crashed to the ground. Flo and Eddie fought to extricate themselves from the twisted wreckage of Freebird. Corporal Krieg approached them warily, keeping the business end of his musket pointed in their direction. With equal caution, the two brothers struggled to their feet and stood regarding him.

"Well, I done thought I'd seen about everythin'," the soldier grunted, "until I seen hippie-faggits fly."

Flo and Eddie offered no comment.

The Fascist moved closer. "Quite a toy you got there, ladies. An' I got me a feelin' Cap'n Klerc is gonna want to see this one. In the in'erests of your good health, you best come with me."

"Our health is quite good, thank you," Flo offered.

"Well it won't be if you don't get movin', faggit!"

Corporal Krieg marched them unsteadily towards the headquarters building. A fat, balding officer carrying a book met them at the door.

"Corporal," the officer barked. "I heard a shot. What's going on?"

Krieg clicked his heels smartly and rendered a stiff-armed salute. "Sir! Corporal Krieg reporting with two prisoners, sir!"

"So, execute the sonsabitches, Krieg. You don't need my permission for that."

Krieg shuffled his feet uneasily. "I thought you would like to interrogate these prisoners personally, sir. They are ... different."

"They look like ordinary sonsabitchin' fairies to me."

"Sir, it's not so much them, as it is how they got here."

"Well, what did they do, fly in?" There was no mistaking the sarcasm in the fat captain's voice. He closed his book, a badly worn edition of the *Turner Text*, and tapped it against his leg.

"Yes, sir. That's it exactly."

"You been drinking again, corporal?"

Krieg stiffened. "Yes sir. I mean, no sir. I seen what I seen. These hippies flew into camp in some kind of flying machine. I shot it down. It's over in the square, if you want to see it."

Captain Klerc wandered back inside the building. Krieg shoved Flo and Eddie in behind him. The captain placed his book on a litter-covered desk and picked up a small bell, which he rang several times. "I want you to show me this flying machine, Krieg. Let's hope what you 'seen' didn't come from the depths of a bottle," he said. "Because, if you're lying to me, your ass is gonna be facing a court martial."

"I swear to John Birch I seen what I seen."

A side door opened and two hard-faced guards, wielding long fighting knives, entered the room and silently took up positions behind Flo and Eddie. Captain Klerc placed his wide-brimmed hat lightly on his head and grabbing his greatcoat from the hook by the door, shrugged into it. "Come on, Corporal. Show me what you've found."

As soon as Krieg and Klerc left the room the two guards moved closer to Flo and Eddie. The brothers squirmed in unison as knife points jabbed into their backs.

"What you think we oughta do with these two faggits?" the soldier guarding Flo asked his companion.

"I sure hope the cap'n lets us kill 'em, Arnie," his friend replied. "It's been a while and my knife hand's getting rusty."

"Know what you mean, Sly. We gotta warm up for Covenstead."

Arnie snickered, but he and Sly both popped to rigid attention as the door crashed open and Klerc and Krieg re-entered the room. The captain appeared agitated and removed his greatcoat with much difficulty. "Take these prisoners to the stockade, Private Drang," he barked without looking up. "They are not to be harmed by either you or Private Sturm."

"But, sir… " Arnie began.

"You heard me, Drang. Now go."

After the guards left, Captain Klerc turned to Corporal Krieg. "A wonderful new machine," he said with a fiendish grin.

Krieg coughed uneasily. "Yes, sir." Something in the way the captain's small piggy eyes sparkled disturbed him.

"A flying machine, Corporal Krieg—a machine capable of carrying the sign of the Starred Swastika to the far ends of the earth." Klerc's face burned with ecstatic vision. "With a hundred such machines … no, a thousand … the iron heel of the Great Whitelands could smash down on the face of the vermin races forever. There would be no limit to our power, no way to stop us from conquering the world."

"Blackcloak might not agree with your plan, sir," Krieg observed.

"He doesn't have to. The time of the White and Right has come around at last, just as it is foretold in the *Turner Text*. Think of it! The Thousand-Year Rule could well lie within our grasp. It's all clear to me, the future of our race writ in blood, and steel, and fire! We live in an age of destiny, Corporal, an age of destiny!"

Krieg glanced about uncomfortably. "Sir, I know you're a religious man, and you swear by the *Text* and all, but the Dark Man has ears everywhere these days."

"You are right, Corporal Krieg. Perhaps discretion is the order of the day."

Flo and Eddie sighed with relief as the door slammed shut behind them and the two guards led them across the square to a livery stable that doubled as a stockade. The Fascists' stony disappointment seemed to chill the air by several degrees.

"We'll still deal with your asses someday," Sly promised as the Oldhips were herded into a converted stall and its iron grill was slammed shut in their faces. "They belong to us."

The jailer, a fat, dull-looking private, glanced up at Sly and Arnie, grunted and returned to his game of solitaire. "Why don't you boys go home like good little troopers?" he drawled. "Their asses don't belong to anyone 'cept me right now."

"Good for you, Picklehaub," Arnie sneered. "But don't go playing with 'em, hear? We got unfinished business."

"That so? Well, life's a pisser all around, ain't it boys? Now, why don't you go rape your horses and let a man get back to work."

Chapter Fifty-Five

Captain Klerc sat at his desk, staring moodily at the papers in front of him. Absentmindedly, he took a sip from the glass at his elbow. The water was fresh from the cistern and quite cold, but somehow had acquired a funny, coppery taste. He put the glass back down and tapped on the desktop with his pen. A few drops of ink splattered on the picture of the glider that he was drawing. Grumbling, he tried to blot up the ink with his handkerchief.

The hippie glider was stored in a room behind Klerc's office. Everyone who knew of its existence was sworn to secrecy. The craft was banged up, but looked as if it could be repaired. He decided that he would go to the Oldhip prisoners in the morning and offer them his deal: build me more of these machines and you will live. Simple enough. Of course, the unspoken part of the deal was that they would live *only* as long as they were useful. Smiling, he blotted away the last of the ink drops and took another swig of water. It tasted sweeter this time, smoother. With a shrug of his beefy shoulders, Klerc tipped the glass and drained it to the bottom.

The room was suddenly close and stuffy; its contours seemed to be shifting. Tiny points of light twinkled on and off among the shadows cast by the fireplace. He mopped his sweating brow with his handkerchief and tried to concentrate on the drawing, though with every passing second that was becoming more difficult. Finally he gave up, and laying aside his pen, he gazed into the flames dancing on the hearth.

Then he heard the music.

It seemed to come from everywhere, filling the room and reverberating in the empty chambers of Klerc's mind—a haunting, eldritch sound, alien yet somehow comfortingly familiar. He began to tap his fingers to the beat. Dum-da-da-dum-dum, dum-da-da-dum-dum, dum-da-da-dum-dum, dum-da-da-dum. He blinked and images formed in his mind, black and gray moving shadows of things that had been, long ago in the glory days of the world.

Klerc watched the shadows shift and change in time to the music. A wobbly image emerged—long lines of marching men in strange, antique uniforms. Torchlight reflected from their polished coal-scuttle helmets as they goose-stepped through the streets of an ancient city, their hands raised in stiff-armed salutes. Banners emblazoned with angry black swastikas hung from the facades of the buildings. As the soldiers marched, they were joined by others pouring out of the alleys and side streets until the old city swarmed with an army of stony-faced, goose-stepping men, flowing like a river towards a huge torchlit amphitheater at the city's core. There, on a stage dominated by a huge swastika of living flame, a small man in a baggy uniform held the crowd spellbound with his fiery and passionate speech. He was odd-looking, almost comical, with his flopping forelock and silly little square mustache, but the light that burned in his eyes outshone the torches and bonfires. A chill raced through Klerc's frame as he realized that he was looking upon Hitluh the Furor, the most terrible of his people's ancient gods.

Dum-da-da-dum-dum. The beat continued as the shadows shifted again, drifting apart, then forming into Whiteriders burning a cluster of vermin shanties, then resolving themselves into images of a different kind of warrior. Row upon row of muscular uniformed men, their faces covered by strange glass-faced helmets, huge truncheons held in meaty hands, were facing off against a jeering mob of Freaks. Suddenly, with cries of rage that boomed like breakers pounding against a storm-lashed shore, the warriors waded towards their adversaries. Fists lashed out, truncheons crashed on unprotected heads and limbs, and heavy boots stomped on upraised faces. The Freaks' puny placards and banners were no match for the armed might of their attackers. Bloody and defeated, they retreated through the city, down streets lined with bright lights and mountain-high buildings. The valiant warriors pursued, driving the longhairs before them until the image dissolved into mist and fire.

Klerc's heart pulsed to the unworldly rhythm. He was sweating profusely, but he felt excited and alive. Big Brother John Birch was permitting him a vision. He, James D. Klerc, least worthy of the servants of the White and Right, was seeing what was and what would be. Mopping his streaming brow, Klerc once again turned his attention to the drawing of the glider on his desk. As he watched, the drawing began to darken and change. The dark wings lengthened and straightened, metamorphosing into a black-cloaked figure reaching out with greedy arms. The music in Klerc's head pounded against the confines of his skull ... **dum-da-da-dum-dum, dum-da-da-dum-dum**. The shape became a black cruciform figure flying through a lightning-wracked sky. The belly of the cross opened and disgorged strange dark eggs. On impact, the eggs exploded in angry plumes of fire, and the ground heaved like a wounded animal.

Suddenly the black and white images changed to brilliant color. A glaring morning sun, red as blood, was rising over a fantasy landscape of marshland and bizarre broad-leafed trees. The music swelled as black insectile forms rose out of the sun, their blade-like wings thumping and thwapping the humid air. Moving into formation, the monster insects swept in over a river, bearing down on a village of sticks and thatchwork. Between the huts small people clothed in conical hats and baggy black clothes ran about in fear. **Dum-da-da-dum-dum, Dum-da-da-dum-dum, Dum-da-da-dum-dum, DUM-DA-DA-DUM**. Lightning spurted from the sides of the insect-beasts and the little village erupted into fire and screaming death. Blood and explosions were everywhere.

The visions and music faded as Klerc leaned back, breathless. His eyes were closed, but tears of joy streamed down his face. It was clear now; these flying machines were his people's destiny, the manifestation of their blood and will. The time of the White and Right had come at last, just as the *Text* said it would, and J.D. Klerc was going to be its avatar—its apotheosis.

Corporal Krieg took a swig from his jug and spat it out immediately. It was rank beyond belief. Something must have crawled into the cistern and died to make the water taste that bad. Of course, he was no corner sewer; water rarely passed his lips. He licked his lips and peered into the jug, wishing now that he hadn't thrown away the last of his Ragin' Redneck. Still, Cap was onto his drinking on duty, and if he didn't want to end up in the slammer next to those two longhairs he'd brought in, he'd better cool his act for awhile. His crotch itched. He scratched it vigorously and sniffed at the jug again. Funny, maybe the water was foul but it had an undertaste he could get used to—kind of tingly, like good Thunderbolt beer. Jiggling his balls once again for good measure, Krieg took another pull off the jug and swallowed.

Wiping his lips, Krieg put the jug down beside his cot and stared off down the barracks into the shadows between the rows of sleeping men. Brother John, was he horny! Not being able to drink was bad enough, but going without decent poontang was sheer hell on wheels. The Freak girls that were kept prisoner to take care of the soldiers' needs didn't have the spunk for a horndog like Milo Krieg. Mostly they just lay there and cried when he was pumping them. Once or twice he punched them to get them moving, but mostly it wasn't worth the effort. Licking his lips a second time, Krieg picked up the jug again and hefted it in his hands. Almost

466

without thinking, he put it to his mouth. Yeah, it tasted lots better this time. Real sweet, like a woman's kiss.

Silvery laughter startled him. Krieg looked up suddenly, nearly dropping the jug. Walking out of the shadows between the nearest cots was one of the most striking women he had ever seen. She was nearly six feet tall with long shimmery blond hair that hung in braids to her waist and large eyes that were as blue as a glacial lake. She wore a short skirt of chain mail that barely covered her womanhood, topped by a pair of armored breastplates. On her head she wore a steel helmet ornamented with wings. A huge broadsword hung from the jeweled belt at her waist and she carried a long spear. Her feet were encased in fur boots tied about with rawhide thongs. The boots barely whispered on the floor as she glided towards him.

Krieg looked at the girl and blinked in disbelief, but she didn't fade away. When she smiled at him he rose to his feet and, giggling foolishly, he began to unbutton his fly.

Private Picklehaub set aside his water glass and made a sour face. He wondered if the water had gone stale. Stifling a yawn, he scratched his fat belly and shuffled the dog-eared deck of cards. He glanced over at the stall containing the Oldhip prisoners. They were scrunched up back to back, asleep.

As he lay the cards on the table, Picklehaub grunted softly to himself. Maybe it was only a trick of the candlelight, but the crude faces on the picture cards seemed almost real. Occasionally, they seemed to move in his hands like they were rousing from a deep sleep. Shrugging, he began to arrange the cards in neat rows.

Then he heard the voices.

Arnie threw a stick of kindling on the campfire and moved between it and the open flap of the tent he shared with Sly. Dawn was just breaking over the mountains to the east. He was hungry and thirsty, though the prospect of having another pull from Sly's canteen filled him with no joy. Arnie harbored a sneaky suspicion that Sly was too lazy to hike his ass down to the cistern for water and had filled it from the frog pond behind their tent.

Sly came out of the tent and took a seat beside his friend. He took a swig from his canteen and instinctively passed it to Arnie. "Have a slurp," he offered. "It gets better on the second swallow."

Arnie nodded. "It'd better. My throat feels drier'n pocket lint."

"Do it to it then. I left you enough to wet your whistle."

After the canteen was passed and emptied, the two Fascists set up a skillet over the fire and began cooking their breakfast of eggs and sausage.

"Strange business with the cap'n and those hippie-faggits last night," Sly commented, pushing the sizzling pieces of sausage with his belt knife.

"Damn straight, good buddy. Cap's going wacko, if you ask me. All that stuff about flying machines and all that other horseshit. He's too religious. He's always got his nose stuck in that *Turner Text*. Jumpin' John Birch, listening to him prattle on is as bad as listening to Whiteriders. I mean, who really cares about all this 'master race' bullshit anyway? Sure, White people are better than anyone else, but so what? It don't need no discussion."

Sly inserted his knife under one of the eggs and expertly flipped it over. "I hear what you're saying. Hell, vermin were put on this earth for Whitemen to stomp. That's easy enough to understand without a bunch of fancy philosophy."

Arnie leaned over and scrutinized the frying eggs with great interest. His close-set eyes glowed. "It's dumbshit officers like Cap Klerc and those snot-ass Whiteriders with their 'whiter than you' attitude dumpin' on us regular guys that screws up everything. Fuck it, I'm the right race and I don't gotta dickdance around in bedsheets to prove it."

"Yeah, and now we got ol' Brother John Blackcloak running the show. What's he done for us besides bringing in a bunch of Greasers for us to baby-sit? Swastikas and thunderbolts! What are we axising with scum like that for?"

"Brother John and his spooks, ptah! Who in the hell are they anyway? They could be anything under those robes of their—Greasers, Rowdies, maybe even Niggers."

Sly almost dropped the skillet. "Naah, that ain't possible. They're all extinct. They got rubbed out back in the old days when men was really men, before all this political bullshit."

Arnie shrugged. "You hear stories, you know? Anyway, this ain't the old days."

"Yeah, back then you had real heroes, not a bunch of pussywhips like Klaven Thinarm and Manglewurtz and that crowd. In those days men lived like men should oughta, without nobody telling them no different, guys like Dukewayne and Rambothree."

"Those guys are just old stories, Sly. They weren't never real."

"Shit! Ol' Dukewayne and Rambothree were just as real as you and me, more real than some fancy priest or politician. We could be like them if we had half a chance."

Arnie watched the muscles in his arm as he flexed them, as if he were really feeling them for the first time. He felt fully alive, like a wild beast, totally aware of all his senses. "You know, I think you're right. I'm beginning to believe I could conquer the world."

Sly nodded. "Now that you mention it, I feel pretty good too. My muscles are getting all itchy, like they are growing all of a sudden."

"I feel like stripping down and pounding on my chest or something. Ain't it weird?"

Sly didn't answer. He just grunted low in his throat and started to unbutton his heavy woolen tunic.

Chapter Fifty-Six

Sunlight streamed through the windows, transforming the stable into a checkerboard of light and shadow. In one dim corner Private Pickelhaub crouched at his desk, engaged in a lively conversation with one of his playing cards. The rest of the deck lay scattered in front of him, next to an overturned glass and a pair of flintlock pistols.

"Eddie, come over here," Flo whispered, turning away from his position by the cell door.

The lanky redhead picked himself up from his seat in the dusty straw and quietly moved next to his brother. "What's up?" he whispered back.

Flo pointed to the jailer. "See that glass of water on the desk, brother mine? Looks like our plan is working."

The slovenly private gathered up several more cards, selecting ones that appeared to be face cards, and started conversing with them as well. Before long the conversation became quite spirited and it seemed as if a full-fledged argument would soon break out.

Just then, Captain Klerc stormed through the door. His small piggish eyes were glazed heavier than Yule sweet potatoes. The wide collar of his unbuttoned greatcoat was pulled high behind his neck. A crude metal cross, threaded onto a faded ribbon, dangled on his chest and a poorly drawn swastika armband decorated one sleeve. Somewhere the captain had found an old dented coal scuttle and placed it on his head for a helmet. Ashes drifted down over his jowly face and powered his shoulders.

"Achtung!" he yelled at the jailer.

A confused Private Pickelhaub rose to attention slowly.

Flo and Eddie could not make out what was being said, but after a short time Captain Klerc started stamping one foot and repeatedly jabbed a finger in the Freaks' direction, as ashes rained down from beneath his coal scuttle helmet.

One by one, the private held up each of his cards, determined to ignore the captain until he could properly introduce them. In one quick motion, Captain Klerc knocked Pickelhuab's cards from his hand, scattering them across the desk and onto the floor.

"I vant zee prisoners in mine office, immediately," Captain Klerc shouted in a strange accent, "or you vill be sent to zee front." Then, without another word, the captain spun about-face, neatly bounced off the door, and exited.

Private Pickelhaub hurried to rescue his cards, apologizing as he carefully picked each one up and dusted them off with his shirtsleeve. When he was done, he methodically arranged the cards on his desk and saluted them. Grabbing his two pistols and shoving one under his belt, he turned his attention to Flo and Eddie. Small explosions of dust rose to mingle with their airborne brethren as he stomped across the old wooden floor. Angrily, he glared at the two Freaks.

"The cap'n must think the sun shines out of your assholes, boys. He wants to see you in his office." He pointed his pistol at the brothers and added, "I'm gonna unlock this door and we're gonna take a little stroll. Don't try anything funny." The lock clicked and, as the door swung wide, he drew his other pistol. "Get your asses movin', faggits."

As they stepped out onto the streets of Indian Stream they blinked. It was nearly noon and the town was alive with Fascists and Greasers. Most of them were exhibiting varying degrees of delirium. Two Greasers cackled mindlessly as they crawled over a monstrous steamwagon, painting it in angry swirls of orange, purple and glowing green. A few befuddled onlookers stood gawking at their handiwork. Beside the wagon a stray dog chased its tail until it dropped panting in the street; no one seemed to notice or care about its plight. Private Pickelhaub weaved back and forth slowly behind the Freaks but managed to keep his pistols pointing in their direction.

Suddenly a door burst open and Corporal Krieg ran out, naked except for a chamber pot on his head and a crockery jug hanging from his penis. He whooped loudly and ran off, screaming "Odin! Odin!" before disappearing down a side street. Eddie looked at Flo and started to giggle, but the smaller Oldhip motioned him to silence. Behind them Pickelhaub was now fully tripping. Shambling along, gibbering happily to himself, he escorted Flo and Eddie to a two-story structure that, unlike its counterparts, had an almost flat roof.

The private pushed the brothers through the front door and swore at it as if it were another soldier. At the end of a short hall was another door; without knocking Pickelhaub ushered Flo and Eddie into Captain Klerc's office. The captain was pacing nervously behind his desk, which was covered with old books and countless papers. Since his appearance at the stable, the captain had removed his ridiculous helmet and coat; his ash-encrusted hair flopped down loosely over his forehead and a smudge of black ash formed a silly square moustache under his fleshy nose. His eyes were little more than muddied slits. At first he seemed startled to see them enter, but then studied them intently as Private Pickelhaub led them across the room.

"Ah, mine vermin friends, sit down," Captain Klerc said, pointing to two oak chairs in front of his desk. "You may vait outside zee door," he continued, motioning to Pickelhaub.

Once the door closed shut, Klerc nodded and launched into a long, impassioned, and largely incoherent speech, most of which meant little to Flo and Eddie. Still, his intent was clear; the fat captain wanted them to build a fleet of gliders like Freebird for him, with which he intended to conquer the world, not in the name of the Dark Man, but for the eternal glory of the Great Whitelands. When Klerc finished his monologue he blinked stupidly and poured himself a glass of water.

"Vould you like a drink?" he said, offering the pitcher.

"No thank you," Flo replied. "We're not thirsty."

"It's very fine ... vell, it grows on you," Klerc commented. "But neffer mind, vhat do you zink of zee plan, mine vermin friends?"

"It's quite a plan," Flo offered. Eddie nodded in agreement.

"Yes, yes, quite vonderful."

Flo smoothed his mustache and sat up straight in his chair. He remembered that the building they were now in was fairly tall and had a flat roof. "And you want us to help you?"

"Yes."

"If we refuse?"

"You vill die before you leave ziss room."

"I see. A powerful argument in your favor, to be sure, Captain. If you give me a moment to confer with my brother, I believe we can come to a mutually beneficial agreement."

Captain Klerc nodded.

"Are you crazy?" Eddie whispered to Flo as he leaned closer to him. "If we help him, they will be able to fly over the mountains right into Hillcommune."

"Hold on, brother mine," Flo cautioned softly. "Here's what I have in mind... "

Flo outlined his plan as briefly and quietly as possible to Eddie. When he was finished, his brother nodded in agreement.

Turning to the captain, Flo said, "You know, this is going to take a lot of time and materials, and if you want these birds to fly, things will have to be done our way."

"I haff anticipated zat. Vat do you need to begin?"

"The very first thing we have to do is to repair our craft so we can use her as a pattern. We will need a large open space with a lot of light."

"Do you haff a place in mind?"

"Yes, I believe I do."

Within the hour Flo and Eddie were on top of the headquarters building, sitting next to Freebird, straightening the bends and dents in the craft's frame and patching the wings with material Klerc ordered sent to them. Two guards sat on the opposite side of the roof, passing a canteen between them. After every sip they leaned over the roof and attempted to spit on any one who passed by, laughing riotously each time.

"Brother mine, I think we're going to make it," Flo whispered. "Everyone is totally blitzed."

Eddie nodded. "No kidding. I just saw the two guards who brought us to our cell running down the street half-dressed, smeared with brown and green greasepaint. Holy Bob, were they out of it."

"And the fun's just beginning, Eddie. All Loveday is tomorrow and these losers are supposed to be at Covenstead. Think they'll make it?"

Eddie smiled and shook his head. Below, in the streets of Indian Stream, the party was in full swing.

Throughout the day the water-intoxication had spread through the camp. The square was in pandemonium. Many people who were still ambulatory enough to appear on the streets were naked, or very nearly so, although some had taken to wearing costumes similar to Klerc's or ones even more bizarre. As the brothers watched, Sly and Arnie ran back and forth down the street, calling out cadence to one another. The two Greasers who'd earlier been painting the steamwagon were now taking it for a wobbly joyride.

A pair of riderless horses ran in eccentric circles around the cistern, neighing wildly. Nearby, a knot of half-naked Fascists were dancing to the frantic beat of music only they could hear. On one side of the square, two Whiteriders in tie-dyed robes were watching an abandoned house they had just torched, as it burned to the ground. On the other side, Klerc stood in front of a huge starred-swastika banner haranguing a disinterested crowd in a garbled language that sounded like a cat hawking up hairballs. Behind him, Krieg was trying to extricate his penis from the jug. Flo glanced over at the guards as he tightened the last of the glider's support struts. The two were almost falling off the roof as they continued their spitting game.

Eddie stepped back to examine Freebird. "Looks good, Flo," he said, "but the wind is blowing away from the mountains. The only way we can fly out of here is south-by-east."

"So it goes, Edward, so it goes. We are children of the sun, the earth and the wind; we must have faith. Besides, I just want to get the hell out of here."

A mere half-hour later, Freebird rose gracefully from the roof of the headquarters building, banked left, and flew off into the late afternoon sunlight.

Maynard sat on a rock beneath a huge oak tree apart from the main body of the Radiclib camp. He lit his pipe with his tinderbox, toked it up to a fair boil, and gazed off towards the west. It was close to sunset and Mizjoan's troops were breaking camp for the night's journey. By morning, if their luck held, they'd be in sight of Covenstead. It would be February 14th—All Loveday—and one way or another, the day of reckoning.

The little Beatnik leaned back against the tree. Many things were in motion now. Troops under Dillon were mustering in the west while lowland Freaks, inspired by the Clear Light Society, were arming themselves for the pilgrimage to the old Fair City. Seemingly, Bejeezuz was letting all this go on without lifting a finger to stop it. It smelled like a trap, but try as he might, Maynard could think of no other strategy than to let events take their course. This had all been so neatly planned—get Tambourine to play against Bejeezuz, use the *Necronomicon*, then launch the attack. But what good was that plan now? The book was gone, maybe right into the enemy's hands for all he knew, and Tambourine and Toad could very well be dead. Sure, Wheatstraw and Franklin had both assured him that the *Necronomicon* was not a threat, and that the Oldhips would send some 'special vibes' their way, but what help was that holistic hoopla against the very real threat of Billy Bejeezuz? Could flower power stand against his black magick? He had his doubts.

Maynard blew out a gust of weedsmoke, watching it spiral up among the oak's bare branches. He tapped out his pipe on the trunk. What he needed now was instant Karma, plain old shit luck, some deus ex machina to drop out of the sky, right at his feet, and give the Radiclibs the edge they needed. He crossed his fingers, took a deep breath, and wished real hard.

Ten minutes later, he shook his head in disbelief and smiled as a big black bat-like object sailed towards him out of the setting sun.

Chapter Fifty-Seven

In the feeble light emanating from the single candle Toad could just make out the shadowy, whispering shapes of Tambourine and Ernie huddled at the far end of the dank cell. Except for their weapons and their guitars, they had been allowed to keep most of their possessions. Other than Tam's anxiety over his inability to practice, their time in the cell passed easily and rather uneventfully, and considering their situation their spirits had remained high. But over the last few days that was changing. All three friends had become increasingly somber, and any attempts at joviality ended.

Condensation from the cool stone walls soaked through the back of Toad's shirt. He moved, trying to find a better position. Bejeezuz was doing his best, in subtle ways, to make the trio uncomfortable and heighten their anxiety. The Dark Man seemed to be trying to keep them off balance, awash in time.

In the darkness the guards brought their meals, always a bowl of thick, bland oatmeal and a cup of sour tasting water. Their food was served seemingly at random, two meals close together and one much later, three closely spaced and then none for what seemed like days. Mealtime was the only time they saw the guards, who provided their only contact with the outside. The isolation and constant twilight provided by the candle produced remarkable results; after almost a week in the cell not one of them was sure what day it was. All that they knew for sure was that All Loveday had to be close—maybe one or two days away.

Toad jumped as a key rattled in the latch and the heavy cell door creaked open. Two Greaser guards hulked in the doorway, torchlight reflecting off their leather jackets and oiled hair.

"Ah ha. Company," Tambourine commented wryly.

"Can the shit, faggit," snarled the shorter, bulkier of the two Greasers. His face was little more than a lumpy shape in the flickering shadows. "Big Boss wants you."

"How about some food first?" Toad complained. "We haven't eaten in awhile."

"Eatin'd be kinda hard with no fuckin' teeth, faggit. C'mon, get your ass in gear."

The other Greaser stepped into the light, placing his hand on his companion's shoulder. Toad was surprised to see that it was Sonny Slikback. "Quit your playing around, Stripgear," the Fonzer said firmly. "We gotta get these boys upstairs pronto."

Stripgear sulked, "Oh, awright. On your feet, you fairies."

Toad and the others obeyed, following the Greasers through the torchlit corridors of the dungeon. As they walked along, a pair of hard-faced Fascist soldiers fell into step behind them, following at a slight distance.

"Bet you're surprised to see me again," Sonny whispered, just loud enough so Toad could hear him.

"Yeah, it's quite a coincidence."

"Coincidence? I had to pull a few strings and kiss a lot of butt to get this duty, but I had to see what all the fuss was about. Rumors about you guys have been flying all over the place. The Dark Man must have a big interest in you to have allowed you to live this long."

"You call this living?" Toad replied, with a dour smile.

Sonny winked. "Look at the bright side—maybe your buddy will beat this guy worse than a faggit at Overhau..." The Greaser stopped short, looking a little embarrassed. "Sorry, I didn't mean it like that. I mean ... hell, you know what I mean."

Toad nodded grimly as he looked into the Greaser's eyes; Sonny was a far different person from the one who had abducted him all those months ago.

The corridor terminated in a long flight of stone steps. The Greasers led their charges up to a huge open room on the bottom floor of the fortress. There were scores of soldiers bustling about their business, making last minute adjustments on their uniforms or cleaning their weapons. They hardly looked up as the prisoners were escorted through the room and up another flight of stairs to the second floor. There, more soldiers were milling about while a harried sergeant distributed clubs, short swords and long, agile spears with thin, gleaming blades.

"Looks like you're expecting an invasion," Toad remarked.

Sonny answered, "We are—sort of. Intelligence reports that longhairs are swarming in from everywhere, and the Dark Man's letting them come. Things could get real wild, real fast. But, by Great Fonzie's ghost, you should know better than me. This is supposed to be some kind of big Freak holiday."

"All Loveday?" Tam asked softly, a worried look crossing his face. "I thought it was still a couple of days off."

"You lose your sense of time in the slammer, pally. Take it from me, I know."

"But, so soon?" Tam murmured.

Sonny whispered to Toad, "Everybody knows the big man is playing off against your buddy today—some kind of musical rumble or something. They say that when Blackcloak starts wailin' on that guitar of his you wanna commit suicide and save him the trouble of killing ya. He's gonna play your boy off the wall, pal."

"I don't understand. Is he that bad?"

"No, that good. From what I hear his act's got real power; he's got magic in those steel-hard fingers of his. They say that where he comes from, that's how he rules."

The Freaks were led up another series of stairs to the fortress's unfinished third story. Sonny guided them through a maze of scaffolding and catwalks to a large wooden stage overhanging the battlements. The noonday sun was intense, and it took Toad's eyes several minutes to adjust to the glare. When his sight returned he stepped to the edge of the stage and looked down. What he saw there dazzled him more than the sun had.

Thousands of Freaks were gathered at the front of the fortress, and equal numbers were still swarming towards Covenstead Hill past the rows of tents and shanties. The crowd seemed unmindful of the Fascist horsemen patrolling their flanks, or of the light wheeled ballista trained on them. All of the Freaks looked pale and ragged, but Toad noticed that every one of them wore at least one piece of bright colorful clothing, even if it was only a headband or kerchief or tattered old tie-dye shirt. One man in the front of the crowd had even gone so far as to plait dried flowers in his hair and don an old peace symbol flag as a cape. Other Freaks held banners, or branches festooned with bright scraps of cloth, or homemade pennants. Two young girls in long faded flower print dresses held aloft a sign made from an old sheet proclaiming HOORAY FOR OUR SIDE! The pinched, solemn faces of the Freaks held a look of joyous expectation that didn't fade even when the gates of the fortress rolled open, spilling out line after line of heavily-armed Fascist and Greaser soldiers.

On one side stood the children of peace—all flowered shirts, headbands, black flags, red flags, peace symbols, love beads, denim and slogans. On the other side, in uniforms, leather jackets and guns, oiled swords in shiny scabbards, crossbows and heavy hobnailed boots, stood the dark, murdering armies of Sweet Billy Bejeezuz.

Tambourine stood beside Toad, looking down at the people of Street-Corner Earth. "They're beautiful," he whispered.

"Yes, they are," Toad agreed. Dimly he recalled the dream he'd had in Hillcommune of the people gathered at his feet, of the guitar and the book he'd held up to the storm-wracked sky.

Ernie joined them. His face looked set and grim in the shadows of his dented top hat. The streaks of gray in his hair had grown more noticeable; they were like lightning flashes in a night sky. "Holy Bob, look at them!" he exclaimed, pointing to the fields below Covenstead Hill where fresh streams of Freaks were being herded along by Fashie cavalrymen on huge warhorses. "They have no idea what they're walking into."

Toad shrugged. The noonday sun flashed off the spears and muskets of the soldiers massing around the base of the fortress. "I don't think they care any more. They've just come to hear the Freedom Rider play and take his children home."

Metal grated against metal behind them. The three friends turned to see four figures in black robes laboring at heavy iron winches. As they watched, a huge painting moved slowly and jerkily into view above the stage. It was as big as the side of a barn and depicted the head and shoulders of a dark cowled figure grasping a spearhead in its gloved hands. Where the figure's eyes should have been two red lanterns glowed and flickered sullenly. Once the portrait was positioned, other black-robed figures hastened about moving smudge pots, braziers and large portable bellows into place in front of it.

"If I remember my history correctly, this is how they did concerts in the old days," Tambourine remarked glumly as he gazed up at the huge portrait of the Dark Man.

"It's just stagecraft, man. You can play better than he can any day," Ernie replied.

"Let's hope so. I have to."

Looking over the throng of bedraggled Freaks, Ernie offered, "Just give it your best shot. It's really all they came for."

Toad wasn't so sure. He stared at the crowd below, thousands of them, milling about expectantly. Unless Bejeezuz was holding back some of his armies, there seemed to be more Freaks than there were Fascists and Greasers, but judging from the looks on the faces of Bejeezuz's men and the weaponry they displayed there was no doubt who'd win. Love couldn't stand against organized hate. Flowers and signs were no defense against guns and swords. He shook his head sadly. The Dark Man had planned this all out long in advance: let his enemies come to him and then destroy them like fish in a barrel.

Toad looked out past the sea of doomed faces towards the place where the fields touched the dark hem of the forest. Was it just his imagination, or an effect of the sunlight—did he see figures moving behind the tree line? For a second he thought he saw men in long gray greatcoats, armed and leading plunging warhorses. The vision faded. Where were Mizjoan and the Radiclib army? He turned back to the stage to see Sonny glaring up at the Dark Man's portrait. The Fonzer's face was a mask of fear and hate.

A horn sounded in the courtyard behind the wall, followed by another from the battlements, and the black-robed stagehands hurried faster to get the braziers and smudge pots lit and in place. When a third horn sounded colored smoke began to boil from the pots and the bellows pumped columns of flame out of the braziers. One of the stagehands walked towards Tambourine bearing items in each of his outstretched hands. In his right was the musician's guitar, now freshly cleaned and polished; it the left was Tam's dented old harmonica. Tambourine accepted the instruments and stood silently looking out over the sea of upturned faces. As the Freaks caught sight of him, a ripple of excitement passed through their ranks. Many smiled up at him, and those who carried boughs or pennants waved them enthusiastically.

"Freedom!" they chanted. "Freedom! Freedom! Freedom!"

Adjusting his harmonica in its wire holder, Tambourine smiled back at them. He stuck his hand into the pocket of his jeans, pulled out a guitar pick and gently but precisely tuned his instrument. The crowd fell silent and pushed in closer. The soldiers lowered their weapons and formed a ring around them.

The horns sounded again. As the smoke and flames belched up around his towering portrait Billy Bejeezuz appeared, shadowed by Jack Rabid. Bejeezuz's lieutenant was carrying an old guitar case, cradling it in his arms like a cherished infant. When Bejeezuz stopped several paces from Tambourine, Rabid opened the case and produced an odd-shaped black and white striped guitar. Bejeezuz took the instrument and held it over his head defiantly. Tambourine watched his rival intently, a slight frown creasing his features.

Bejeezuz's guitar flashed in the sunlight. The Dark Man seemed exultant—joyously, hideously alive—an ancient and savage beast whose time had come around at last. He laughed, a high keening sound that froze the heart. Bringing the guitar back down to his side he stood immobile for a long time, savoring the moment. Behind him, the lantern-eyes in his huge portrait glowed bright red and colored smoke boiled out over the stage.

Bejeezuz seemed to stand forever, silhouetted against the smoke and fire with Jack Rabid at his side, a looming black mass under a sunlit sky. Finally, Jack stepped forward and addressed the crowd. "My Lord Bejeezuz welcomes you," he announced in a rough muddled voice. "He extends his warmest greetings to you at his All Loveday fest. It pleases him that you have come to see honest competition between your esteemed Freedom Rider and my Lord Bejeezuz." With a clumsy swirl of his black robes, Jack stepped back and disappeared under the portrait.

Once Jack was gone Bejeezuz stepped forward, wielding his guitar like a conqueror's sword. When he reached the front of the stage, he laid his guitar down and loosened the fastenings of his robes. With a shrug of his shoulders he threw off his cloak and cowl. Freaks, Fascists and Greasers alike gasped in wonder.

The Dark Man, without his concealing garments, was both repellent and fascinating. From the waist down he was clothed in tight trousers of black leather, ornamented with silver studs and tucked into high boots with six-inch-thick soles. From the waist up his torso was crisscrossed with black and orange rags that did little to conceal the puckered and discolored flesh beneath. Bejeczuz's arms, from the shoulder down, were encased in gleaming armored metal sleeves that terminated in elbow-length black gloves. Behind the spearhead hanging around his neck, his chest was a steel plate, adorned with multicolored lights flickering on and off. His face, uncowled at last, was plain and nondescript, except for the unblinking eyes and the huge coprophagous grin that radiated a chilling, evil humor. His hair, which he wore in short orange-dyed spikes, made him appear almost comic, if you didn't look too closely into those deadly, pale eyes. The Dark Man picked up his guitar again and ran his fingers along its strings. A short-coiled cord hung from the body of the instrument. Bejeezuz plugged it into the metal plate below the blinking lights in his chest. Laughing heartily, he flexed his fingers to play.

"Okay, you sorry fuckers," Sweet Billy hissed. "Let's rock and roll."

Mizjoan picked up her telescope and looked through it at the crowd massing beneath the walls of the fortress. From her position on a low wooded hill about a half-mile from Covenstead, she could make out everything that was going on, even the bizarre drama unfolding on the stage above the highest wall. As she watched, enthralled, Billy Bejeezuz was cradling his guitar in his armored arms and touching his fingers to the strings. "This is it," she whispered as she swept the telescope across the crowd, waiting for the signal to attack.

"What's going on?" Kentstate asked, crouching nervously at Mizjoan's side.

"Bejeezuz is getting ready to play. Remind everyone not to attack until Tambourine starts."

Suddenly, both women froze in their tracks. The air was rent with a high-pitched shrieking like sheet metal being torn apart. Intensifying, it seemed to hang in the air forever, ripping at the ears and clawing the delicate cobwebbing of the brain. Mizjoan threw down the telescope and jammed her hands over her ears to cut out the hellish sound. White-faced with pain, Kentstate did the same. They stood looking at each other in awe, their mouths agape.

Behind Mizjoan and Kentstate, the Radiclib army drew back in terror, some trying hopelessly to quiet their frightened horses, others just clasping their hands to their ears to drive out the evil din. Flo and Eddie, who had joined up with Mizjoan's forces the day before, were cowering beside their glider, covering their heads. Only Maynard seemed unaffected by the hideous squalling. He stood to one side, face rigid behind his mirror-lensed glasses, glowering up at the distant figure of Bejeezuz capering on the stage high above Covenstead's walls.

Finally Kentstate recovered her voice. "What in Dylan's name is that horrible noise?" she shouted.

Mizjoan shook her head. "Dylan has precious little to do with it, 'State. Unless I miss my guess, that's what the Dark Man calls music."

"It's hideous! Nothing human could make that racket."

"You're right ... nothing human is."

Kentstate nodded grimly, the terror fading slowly from her eyes. "How in the name of The Hammer are we going to fight him?"

"The same way we fight any enemy—with guts and determination. C'mon, we'd better get the troops together."

"How? They're half crazy with fear."

"Their fear will pass, just as it has for us. We are Leftopian soldiers, 'State. This wretched noise won't keep us from our duty."

Kentstate brushed a tendril of dark hair out of her eyes and bent over to pick up the telescope Mizjoan had cast aside. When she straightened back up, the Radiclib leader was already moving back down the hill towards her soldiers. She closed up the glass and followed, pausing momentarily to inspect the black glider hidden among the trees. Joan was right, she decided. The hellish caterwauling could be endured at least long enough for them to get to the Dark Man and blow him to eternity. As she regarded the glider, Kentstate decided that she would to be the one to do it, the one to silence him forever.

Toad held his ears, feeling that his eardrums would burst, but it wasn't enough to block out the reverberating shriek of Bejeezuz's guitar. The notes doubled back on themselves, increasing in volume until they were knives slicing into the pipesmith's brain. Even so, Toad couldn't tear his eyes from the leather-and-rag-clad figure gyrating at the front of the stage. Sonny was right; Bejeezuz's act had extraordinary power.

481

PIPEDREAMS

The Dark Man's eyes smoldered with gloating, hateful rage. As he strutted and postured, the thing that called itself Sweet Billy Bejeezuz seemed more than a man and something far less than a human being. His music inflicted pain and fear, and like the Old Charlie, he clearly reveled in the agony of others, like a vampire feeding on anguish and suffering.

Sparks flew from his fingertips as the notes howled out, reverberating from the walls of the fortress. Behind Bejeezuz masonry cracked and fell to the stage. A window in one of the high towers shattered and exploded outward, spraying glittering shards of glass over the mob cowering below the wall. A section of scaffolding splintered and fell apart. Toad held his hands over his ears as tightly as he could and tore his eyes from the Dark Man, turning his attention to the crowd below, trying to pry his mind from the dizzying, insane performance.

Everywhere he looked the pipesmith saw Freaks in pain. Some were lying on the ground trembling, others were under wagons with their hands pressed to their ears, and some simply screamed. The Freak with the flowers in his hair and the peace-symbol cape lay sprawled on his stomach, unmoving. Fascists and Greasers, seemingly unmindful of the din, swaggered through the crowd. Most of them looked up at Bejeezuz as if awaiting instruction, their eyes alive with hate and bloodlust. A few kicked at the prone Freaks or jabbed at them with weapons, but most just ignored them. Above it all, gloating and boogying, the Dark Man kept wrenching out smoking, screaming chords as he orchestrated his mad dance of death.

Mizjoan moved quickly through the ranks, trying desperately to restore order. She mouthed instructions to confused officers and helped her troopers deal with frightened horses. She worked feverishly until Bejeezuz's shrieking guitar faded and everything was as it had been before.

Meanwhile, Kentstate had found a mission of her own. Hunkered down in the dirt beside Flo and Eddie, she inspected the Oldhips' glider. "So," she said, dusting pine spills from the knees of her trousers, "how long will it take you to teach me how to fly this thingamabob?"

Eddie chomped on the weedstem protruding from his mouth. He bit off one soggy end and spat it out. "That's hard to say, Sister Kentstate. I got the hang of Freebird first time out. Others, like Flo here, never seem to quite catch on."

"I'm a fast learner, Comrade Eddie."

"Once this battle's over, I could give you a few flying lessons."

"You don't understand, comrade. I intend to fly it now."

"Impossible! Not *now*," Eddie protested.

"I have to," the elegant brunette glowered, her dark eyes narrowing to slits. "Look at him!" she spat, pointing to the distant figure of Bejeezuz.

482

"Because of him my mate and a lot of my friends are dead. His ass is mine! I could fly right over him and drop a rock or something right on his ugly head."

"But … I'm sure Sister Mizjoan needs you here," Eddie answered.

Kentstate shook her head. "Let me worry about Joan, okay?"

"I-I don't know… "

Just then Maynard entered the conversation. "Dig it," he said, jamming his hands into the pockets of his threadbare jeans. "Like, the chick's gotta do what she's gotta do. I can groove on the whole riff, but, like, I have one suggestion."

Kentstate eyed Maynard suspiciously. "What it is?"

The little Beatnik dug deeper into his pockets and brought out a handful of brownish-green plant material that gave off a heavy musty odor. He handed the material to Kentstate.

"What's this?" she asked.

"Peat moss. Drop this anywhere near the Dark Cat when you fly over him, and it will freak him out far more than any bomb or bullet ever would."

"That? Come on, don't make me laugh."

Maynard laid a hand on her shoulder. "Hey, you wanna hurt the dude? This'll hurt him just fine—it's like Kryptonite, babe."

"Krypto night?" Kentstate replied, looking perplexed.

"Superman … you know … never mind. Just trust me."

On stage, Billy's playing was reaching a fevered pitch. Grinning insanely, the Dark Man hopped first on one leg, then the other. He stopped in mid-note, whipped his guitar up and over his head, then brought it back down, slamming out the last few bars of his song so loudly that the stage was in danger of crumbling. Eyes blazing, he jumped up, spun in midair, and landed with a crash on the heels of his thick-soled boots, as the last notes reverberated around him. Sneering, he made an exaggerated bow, first toward Toad and company, and then to the cringing Freaks below the fortress. "Are your ears bleeding yet?" he hissed.

Taking his hands away from his ears, Toad looked around the stage at the others. Ernie was white-faced and shaken, while Sonny looked about sadly, like one who has glimpsed the future and doesn't much care for what he sees. Only Tambourine seemed cool and under control. Unflinching through everything, he'd sat at the edge of the stage among the Greasers and Fascists, waiting for Bejeezuz's set to end. Now that it had, and the Dark Man had stepped back to gloat over the chaos he'd created, Tambourine got slowly to his feet and sauntered over to the spot Billy had vacated.

PIPEDREAMS

"A Dylan, huh? Well, you look like one sad sack of shit to me," Bejeezuz sneered as he unplugged his guitar and relinquished the stage to the Freedom Rider.

Toad's ears still rang, but he could feel his fear draining away as Tambourine slipped into the first few bars of *All Along the Watchtower*. The reaction of the crowd below wasn't as encouraging, however. Except for a few Freaks near the front who looked up attentively, straining to hear the words, nobody seemed to be aware that the Freedom Rider was even playing. In comparison to Bejeezuz's high-pitched assault that blasted out over the countryside, Tambourine's music wasn't carrying very far at all. Most of the audience was looking at each other, confused. They could see the Freedom Rider going through the motions but they couldn't hear a sound. The Fascists and Greasers had noted this as well. They grinned evilly and looked up at Tambourine with glittering, hate-filled eyes.

Tambourine noticed the lack of response, as well. He smiled weakly at Toad and finished off the song. Sweating slightly, he began re-tuning his guitar. "We'll get 'em with the next one," he told Toad without much conviction.

The pipesmith nodded as Tam took a deep rasping breath and began to play again, louder this time, *Chimes of Freedom*, the very same song that Tam had played so powerfully at the Yule gathering. The notes rang like bells and the words rolled like thunder, and they allayed Toad's fears momentarily. Tam's effort was good and clear, but Toad saw that it had no effect on the horde of Freaks below. Tam noticed it too and, wiping sweat from his brow, redoubled his effort, pouring every ounce of passion into the song. It was the best performance Toad had ever heard, but even so his heart sank as the music evaporated before it reached the ground.

Though Tambourine was pouring his entire essence into his playing, his voice still wasn't reaching the Freaks. The magick just wasn't happening. The pipesmith wracked his mind for a way to help his friend. If only there was some way to get the message across, if only there was some way to make the people hear. He glanced over and saw Bejeezuz lounging at the back of the stage. The Dark Man had put on his robes again, but had left his cowl down so that Toad could see his sinister, smirking face. The bastard's won and he knows it, Toad thought. Now he's waiting. When this is done and he's killed my friends and crushed Street-Corner Earth, he'll come for me and demand the *Necronomicon*.

Nervous and desperate, Toad started to mouth the words of the song along with Tam. Where was the help Franklin had promised? Where was Mizjoan? What were the Radiclibs waiting for? In a few short minutes the Greasers and Fascists would be slicing through the multitude of Freaks. Even with his eyes closed, he could picture the fear and hopelessness that

484

dogged their faces. As the gates of Covenstead opened and a contingent of Whiteriders rode out in front of three huge steamwagons, his mouth kept forming words. Smoke belched from the stacks of the great engines and sunlight flashed from their cruel spiked wheels as they rumbled towards the crowd.

Toad's attention was drawn abruptly back across the stage. Bejeezuz's eyes glowed as he blew the pipesmith a playful kiss. Bowing his head to avoid the Dark Man's gloating stare, Toad gradually became aware that he wasn't singing along with Tam at all. He was chanting lines from the *Necronomicon*, the same lines he'd used to raise the demons that night in the clearing:

> "Krog-gogalog Megagog
> Ia! Cthulhu-Krogalog
> Mekatoom! ..."

Toad looked up. Bejeezuz was still staring at him, eyes ablaze, lips twisted into a sneering grin, almost daring him. He seemed to know what Toad was doing. It was as if he wanted him to call the demons. Toad froze ... it was insane to think of using this evil to defeat the Dark Man. Worse yet, he knew now that this was exactly what Bejeezuz wanted him to do. "Trust," Toad told himself. "Love." Franklin had said that when the Freedom Rider was ready, all the magick of the Oldhips would be there to help him. After all, as the old song said, he could only speak with a voice that "came from me and you." Grinning back at the Dark Man, Toad turned his head and did not utter another syllable.

Suddenly, out of nowhere, a breeze rose up. Sweet and warm, it reminded him of the mountain zephyrs in Hillcommune. It carried with it the fragrance of flowers and incense, spices, peppermint and weedsmoke. It tingled with the sound of distant wind chimes and whispered with low chanting voices. Tambourine must have noticed it too. He inhaled deeply, smiled, and continued singing. Then miraculously, just as Bejeezuz's din had swept over the land bringing fear and madness, Tambourine's voice filled the air, permeating every empty space, carrying a more powerful message ... hope. Music burst from every cloud, every tree, every blade of grass, every stone, and every distant running river. It existed in every fiber of being at once, strengthened and amplified by The All. And, as the music grew louder, the scented breeze intensified, stirring something to life. The mounted Whiteriders stopped abruptly; it was their turn to be confused. Steamwagons braked to a halt, vapor hissing from their boilers, as Tambourine's voice drowned out the clamor of men and machines. A miracle was taking place, one that would pass down in folklore from one generation of Freaks to another as long as the race should endure.

Like sunlight through breaking storm clouds, a smile spread across Tam's face. He threw back his head, the breeze rippling through his mane of thick curly hair and sang, *Times They Are A-Changin'*. It was not a pretty song. It was an angry song, a threat, a declaration, a battle hymn. If any song was a Freaks' anthem, this was it. Tam's face was hard; his voice was hoarse and his eyes snapped sparks like flint on steel. Channeling his wrath, he sang of changing times and rising waters, of gathering tribes and raging battles, each note and syllable heralding new hope.

Where the Freaks once huddled cowering on the ground, they now stood erect. Where there was once fear in their eyes, hope now flamed with righteous anger. Where they had submitted to the indignities of Bejeezuz's dark armies, they now fought back. Flags that had been thrown aside were unfurled once more.

Horns sounded in the distance. Toad could see gray-clad forms approaching from the river and from the tree line half a mile away. Even at that distance he could make out the sunlight flashing from the face of one of the riders—intense points of light that could only come from a pair of mirrored spectacles. Above the forest a huge bird circled and swooped towards the fortress. Hissing with rage, Sweet Billy Bejeezuz, the Dark Man, groped for his guitar.

Chapter Fifty-Eight

Mizjoan looked up as the dark form of the brothers' glider banked and turned overhead. After a couple of short test flights on the back side of the hill, Kentstate had gotten the hang of the contraption and was maneuvering it through the sky like she was born to it. Mizjoan saw her salute before she banked left and headed straight towards the fortress, drawn towards the Freedom Rider's playing, riding the scented wind as effortlessly as a feather. Joan watched for a moment, then turned her attention back to her troops. She was so intent on assembling her men and horses that she didn't see Maynard approaching with her telescope until he was at her side.

"Hey, you dropped this back there. You might want to like, give it a whirl," he said, handing her the instrument. "You can see that Tambourine's playing now."

"Thank Dylan for that."

"Soon you'll be able to—personally."

"Right. I guess it's his show now."

"Dig it: it's everyone's show. One of your scouts just told me he saw General Dillon's army, complete with a contingent of Yipps, coming up the Gully Oven Road not a half hour ago. Seems they crossed over north of Rivertown. Had a few skirmishes along the way, so the cat told me, but nothing too heavy."

Mizjoan took the glass and put it to her eye. "Dillon's a pompous old windbag and a pain in the ass from time to time, but he's also a damn fine soldier. I knew he'd make it."

"Hey, like, it was still chancy."

"Not really, Comrade Beatnik. The bulk of Bejeezuz's troops have been concentrated locally. In itself that seems like a careless and stupid act, but there's nothing either careless or stupid about this Dark Man. Look at the way that stage is set. He knew we were coming; indeed, he planned on it.

To his monstrously egotistical mind our armies are nothing more than stage props."

"Yeah, he's playing a mean god riff. He could have stopped your advance at any point, but he had no intention to."

"Exactly. He wants a front row seat on the bloodshed. No doubt he's got a few more nasty surprises in store for us besides that foul music of his."

"Hopefully he's underestimated us. Maybe we can have a few surprises for him."

Mizjoan adjusted the telescope. "Hey, I see Tambourine standing. That's our signal to move out." She pushed the telescope shut and slipped it into her tunic pocket. "I hear music, Maynard ... not the Dark Man's music ... good music. It's faint, but it's getting louder."

"I hear it too. Tam's playing *Times They Are A-Changin.* What a day to be alive!"

"Let's concentrate on staying that way."

The Beatnik grinned. "I'm planning just that, kitty cat. There's an old saying that the whole point of war isn't to die for your country, but to make the other poor bastard die for his."

"Sounds like a good strategy, comrade, but if you really plan on staying alive, can the 'kitty cat' bullshit." She adjusted the burnished silver patch over her eye and started down the hill. "C'mon, let's round up the troops and head out."

"You don't have to ask twice, chick."

Mizjoan and Maynard weren't the only ones inspired by Tambourine's playing. At the base of the hill, soldiers gathered up weapons and calmed down horses. Instinctively they formed into small groups and moved to the top of the hill. Peering out from behind the trees, they gazed at the tiny figure standing on the distant stage. His music rolled over them, drawing them together as it swelled out of the sky above their heads and the rocks below their feet. The last fragments of doubt and fear flew from their hearts like dust in the wind. The Radiclibs didn't have to speak to one another; their eyes told the tale. The day of triumph was at hand. With Mizjoan to lead them, and the music of the Freedom Rider to guide their way, nothing could stop them. With flags unfurled and weapons drawn the People's Army rode towards Covenstead. From the south Dillon's army, flanked by hundreds of fiercely painted Yipps, galloped to join them.

The effect of Tambourine's music on the Freaks at Covenstead amazed Toad, but the reaction of Bejeezuz and his lackeys was truly startling. While the Freaks were now fighting back, eyes bright with hope, the Greasers and Fascists were becoming disoriented and confused. Trying everything to block the sound, they looked up desperately at the Dark Man, silently imploring him to do something. He responded by snatching up his guitar from the stage and moving to a position about ten feet from Tambourine. His face was animated by a dozen angry tics, and his eyes blazed brighter than those of his portrait. Scowling blackly, he flexed his fingers to play.

Oblivious to the Dark Man, Tambourine kept strumming, his feet tapping time as his guitar and harmonica howled out their rage. As he blew a particularly brilliant, high note, horns answered in the distance. Wave after wave of gray-clad figures emerged from the tree line, gathering speed as they thundered towards Covenstead.

"You're dead!" Bejeezuz screamed, brandishing his guitar like a switchblade. "All of you—you're dead!" Then, jamming the cord once again into the plate on his chest, he cut loose with a few screaming chords that caused the advancing army to falter.

Tambourine countered the Dark Man's chords with a few of his own, ending up with a long, wailing blast from his harmonica. There was a shuffle of movement in the shadowy scaffolding behind him as Fascists and Greasers slipped out and took up positions along the battlements. They were all carrying muskets or high-powered crossbows. Colored smoke swirled about them, concealing their movements from the cheering mob below.

As Tambourine poured everything into his music, playing like he'd never played before, the Freaks became wilder and more excited, harder for the enemy soldiers to contain. When he launched into a harmonica solo, howling out a battle cry, about a hundred of the celebrants threw aside their rags and stood revealed in Radiclib gray and Digger motley. Rallying the other Freaks, they fell upon the bewildered enemy, striking out at anything in a Fascist or Greaser uniform. Tambourine grinned; never had the old battle anthems sounded so sweet.

Bejeezuz fought to regain control. Again, he poked his guitar at Tambourine like a long bladed dagger. Suddenly he jumped high in the air with his free hand over his head; as he came down his hand crashed across the strings, rending out chords that ripped the atmosphere. The Fascists and Greasers recovered from their surprise and fought to close ranks, countering the Freak onslaught with violence of their own. Spears plunged indiscriminately into the crowd, guns fired, and arrows flew. Bludgeons rained down on heads and limbs as brass-knuckled fists and hobnailed boots mercilessly beat their victims. Along the battlements Bejeezuz's guards fired at the crowd, blasting away haphazardly at the churning mass of bodies.

Tam, seemingly unaffected by the din, played even harder. His concentration and expression of emotion was superhuman. No one in the history of Freakdom had ever played with such intensity. Slowly but surely, his music rose above Bejeezuz's wailing guitar. At the rear of the crowd scores of Freaks swarmed over one of the steamwagons, rocking it until it turned over on its side. The hiss of steam escaping its ruptured boiler momentarily drowned out the gunfire and warring chords of music. From the shelter of one of the huts by the main gate, a couple of Radiclib marksmen had taken up position and were lobbing fire arrows at the stage. One hit the portrait of Bejeezuz just below the eyes. The heavily painted canvas smoldered and started to burn.

Toad watched open-mouthed as the first ranks of the Radiclib army hit the Fascist line. The air was alive with the roar of the combatants and the furious clang of steel upon steel. The overturned steamwagon was burning out of control. Around it frenzied forms in colorful rags and Radiclib gray fought figures in Greaser leathers and Fascist blue. Some of the Radiclibs had seized a ballista and were fighting to wheel it into position.

For the first time, Sweet Billy Bejeezuz looked worried. In the middle of a long sustained screeching note, he reached to his chest and feverishly adjusted a few small knobs. As he struck the next note, a high-pitched reverberating shriek that sounded like a thousand dying children, he glanced over at Tambourine and spat.

The Dark Man continued playing his guitar like he was in the throes of a seizure. His lidless eyes blazed and froth flecked his lips as he hammered at the strings. Tam was still playing with all his might, but playing against a creature such as Bejeezuz was almost futile. The Dark Man was using his music like a sledgehammer.

Unseen in the midst of the battle Flo and Eddie's glider, piloted by Kentstate, swooped out of the sky and circled above the stage. Kentstate opened her hands; the powdery brown cargo slowly drifted down over Bejeezuz.

Suddenly in mid-chord, Bejeezuz stopped. Standing completely rigid, he frantically sniffed the air, glowering as dust-like particles drifted down around him. Tiny sparks flashed from his fingertips, sputtered, and went out. He sniffed again and his face contorted into a burning mask of rage. "NO!" he screamed. "Not here! Not now!"

In that instant, Tam's music triumphed and quelled every last echo of the Dark Man's evil din. Freaks everywhere picked up their heads and smiled.

Inexplicably, Bejeezuz seemed to sag and fall apart like the burning portrait behind him. Then, with obviously painful effort he fought for composure, struggling to pull himself together. Still sniffing like a hound, he threw his guitar aside. With one trembling hand he pointed at Tambourine. His eyes bulged. Spittle flew from his lips. "J-a-a-ck!" he shrieked. "Kill them! Kill them all!"

Jack Rabid strode forward eagerly. Grinning vacantly, he reached inside of his cloak and pulled out a huge brass-barreled pistol. He cocked the hammer and aimed the weapon at the middle of Tam's back. Before either Toad or Ernie could stop him the Dark Man's assistant pulled the trigger.

The blast took Tambourine off his feet. His chest exploded in a shower of blood and shredded flesh. Face frozen in a look of waxy astonishment, the musician crumpled to the floor, his guitar still clutched in his hands. Jack Rabid giggled childishly and turned to face his master, but Bejeezuz paid him no attention. The Dark Man was storming about the stage, furiously trying to brush away the brownish particles clinging to his cloak. "No!" he was screaming. "Not now! Not now!"

Below the stage the battle suddenly stopped as thousands of pale, frightened faces turned upwards. In the confusion Toad and Ernie rushed to Tambourine's side. Feebly, the stricken musician reached out to them, his eyes already taking on the cracked-ice glaze of death. He tried to speak, but could only cough and spit up blood as his fingers reached for Toad's face.

The pipesmith cried unashamed until Tambourine's hand touched Toad's cheek, wiping away the tears. Slowly, darkness spread about them like floodlights dimming on some long forgotten stage. But before the light faded completely, a soft glow appeared around the musician's body. Suddenly, a surge of energy jolted Toad. He tried to draw away from the dying man's touch, but the life force webbing out through Tambourine's fingers would not let him loose. The glowing, pulsing energy sank into Toad's skin like a penetrating balm, permeating muscle, driving all the way to the bone. Visions and fragments of dreams swirled in the pipesmith's mind. Briefly Toad had an image of himself, guitar in hand, standing high on black lightning-wracked cliffs with all the world beneath him; then the image faded and he saw only Tambourine's tortured, dying eyes. The musician gurgled deep in his throat and Toad leaned close to catch his words.

"Keep on keepin' on," Tam rasped, closing his eyes for the last time. He shuddered once as his spirit slipped away, disappearing into the foggy ruins of time.

"I will," Toad promised, leaving Ernie to cover Tam's face with a handkerchief. Then, still half in a dream, he picked up Tambourine's guitar and stepped to the front of the stage, knowing what he must do.

Sonny nodded at him grimly as he passed and gave him a thumbs-up salute. Behind them, standing in front of the burning remains of his portrait, Bejeezuz was still brushing at his clothes while Jack Rabid tried to help. Snarling, the Dark Man pushed him away. Below the walls, the battle resumed again in full fury.

Looking out on the battle below Toad began to play, carrying on for his fallen comrade. The moment his fingers touched the guitar strings power surged through his body. Whether it was his dying friend's essence, transferred, coursing through him, or his own personal connection with The All, the feeling was exhilarating, addictive. While his fingers danced up and down the neck of Tambourine's guitar, Toad's voice rose on the wings of freedom, a people's fury was unleashed and the wheel was in spin. Swords would soon become ploughshares and blunderbusses would be turned into bongs. Synchronized with the music, intoxicating energy vibrated every atom of Toad's being. It was clear that this was the way it should be; *he* was leading *his* people as they threw off their bondage and seized their freedom.

The air was suddenly rent with a horrible, high-pitched scream. Bejeezuz was clawing at his robes now, his face ashen, his eyes twin burning beacons of hate. "N-o-o-o-!" he raged. "Jack! I SAID, KILL THEM! KILL THEM! KILL THEM!"

Out of the corner of his eye Toad saw Jack Rabid advancing on him, brandishing his spent pistol like a club. There was a blur of movement as a Fonzer launched himself at the black-robed minion. It was Sonny. Not missing a note, Toad played on as the Fascist and Radiclib armies plowed into one another beneath his feet.

Though Sonny had managed to get the pistol away from Jack Rabid, the squat, black-robed man was not defeated. With a grunt he threw the Fonzer on the ground near the edge of the wall, kicking him repeatedly with his heavy boots. Sonny could do little more than cover up and try to roll away from the savage blows.

Several Greasers had abandoned their posts and rushed to Sonny's aid; in turn, Fascist soldiers jumped them. The alliance between the two groups, which had always been tenuous at best, was quickly disintegrating. As the Greasers and Fascists squared off against one another, some of Bejeezuz's black-robes tried to separate them, only to find themselves under attack from both sides.

Intent on pummeling Sonny, Jack Rabid didn't see Ernie Mungweasle move in behind him. Just as Jack was drawing back to deliver a killing kick to the Fonzer's head, Ernie sent him sprawling with a powerful punch to the kidney.

Roaring with pain, spittle flying from his mouth, Jack regained his footing. Ignoring Sonny, he lunged at Ernie. Skipping out of the way, the herbalist spun quickly and delivered a roundhouse kick that caught Jack full in the groin. Jack stumbled backwards, moaning. Before he could straighten up, Sonny recovered enough to grab his foot. Jack staggered, off balance. Ernie jumped in, throwing a series of punches that sent the big man reeling backwards. For a second, Bejeezuz's right-hand man tottered on the edge of the stage. A look of hate and amazement twisted his features as he tried to right himself. Suddenly, he toppled over the edge and fell screaming toward the ground below. The black-robed form bounced once off the rocks at the base of the wall, then lay sprawled on the ground.

"Watch out for the first step, Jacky-boy," Ernie advised, dusting off his hands. "It's a doozy." Scrabbling about for something to use as a weapon, the herbalist retrieved Jack's pistol and held it by the barrel. Beside him Sonny rose groggily to his feet. All the while, Toad kept playing.

Behind the pipesmith, the stage was in chaos. Ignoring the battle that was going on beneath the walls, the Fascists and Greasers were turning on one another and on Bejeezuz's men. Generations-old resentments flared to life as order broke down. Whiteriders stepped in, trying to quell the riot, only to find themselves under attack, sometimes by their own men. By the time Ernie waded in to help them, the outnumbered Greasers were already gaining the advantage. They were ganging on the Fascists and black-robes, driving them back along the catwalks that connected the half-built scaffolds. Throwing aside the pistol and taking a sword from one of the fallen Fascists, Ernie lunged at a nearby Whiterider. Meanwhile, having retrieved a pistol from one of his fallen buddies, Sonny took up a position near Toad, waving the weapon at anyone who came close to the pipesmith.

With a howl of rage Bejeezuz abandoned the stage. Kicking one of his own servants out of the way, he rushed along one of the narrow catwalks leading to the fortress courtyard, snarling and brushing at his clothing as if the Old Charlie was at his heels. Quickly extricating the sword from the body of the Whiterider he had just finished off, and with blood still dripping from the point of the blade, Ernie took off after the Dark Man.

A quiet voice of confusion nattered against the confidence driven by the power still crackling through the pipesmith's nervous system. Was this really his dream being fulfilled? With Tam gone did the mantle of Freedom Rider now belong to him? The quiet voice grew louder as the carnage grew around him, but Toad knew that if he stopped, he would lose the power and the tide would turn again, in the wrong direction.

Below the walls, Mizjoan's army combined with General Dillon's and the Freaks to become a tidal wave crashing over the enemy, who now was in total disarray. Another of the great steamwagons exploded in a shower of fire and ruptured metal, while Freaks armed with weapons taken from their fallen enemies tore into a line of Whiteriders and Fascist infantry. Behind them, terrified Greasers turned against the Fascists or abandoned the battle altogether, scuttling away to the fringes of the action. With the

Dark Man gone and Toad's music heavy in the air, the Whiteriders and Fascists were quickly losing heart. They fought back, but not as fiercely as before. Some threw their weapons to the ground but were cut down as they tried to surrender.

The once quiet voice in Toad's head became steady and loud. "Killing defenseless men is not the way to peace." Another, more frantic, voice shouted back, "But they are the enemy; they want to annihilate us. They are evil and must be destroyed." Conflicting emotions wrestled in Toad like a squirming knot of mating eels, but still he played, unable to stop.

Driven forward by Toad's performance, the Freaks were fearless. One of the Radiclibs stripped a Whiterider of his robe and waved it above his head like a battle flag. His comrades cheered and surged over the Fascists, breaking through their lines. Nearby Freaks and Diggers, among them the man with the peace-symbol cape, captured a Greaser driver and forced him to start up the remaining steamwagon. Slowly, ponderously, it edged its way towards the city gates below.

As the steamwagon picked up speed, Freaks and Radiclibs surged around it, driving back the last of the Fascists and Greasers. The Freak with the peace-symbol cape crawled up on the machine's boiler and attached the cape to the wagon's single stack. It snapped in the breeze defiantly as the great engine approached ramming speed.

There was a splintering crash as the steamwagon hit the heavy gates. They buckled and fell inward. From the battlefield a triumphant cheer rose, praising the Freedom Rider, shaking the fortress itself. "Freedom! Freedom! Freedom Rider!" The Freak army entered Covenstead. Muskets thundered as the occupiers of the fortress fled from the city.

As the Freaks and Radiclibs drove their enemies before them, the part of Toad that channeled the Freedom Rider pushed aside the dissenting voice. *His* playing led to victory. *He* was the savior, the legend come to life. Smiling, he surveyed the stage proudly. But when his eyes fell on Tambourine, his fallen friend and comrade, reality crashed his party. The truth lay before him and he was filled with grief. It was Tam who was the real hero. The musician had reluctantly taken the role of Freedom Rider to save his people, not for his own glory, not because he wanted to go down in history as a great and powerful leader, but because it was the only thing he could do. The meaning of the song, *Times They Are A-Changin* became clear. War was not the answer, not long-term. Times had to change and that meant people had to change. With this revelation came a new understanding of what he needed to do, for the people of Street-Corner-Earth, and himself.

Toad adjusted his guitar and began to play one last song—not a Dylan piece this time, but an ancient John Lennon ballad called *Imagine*. He sang about a better world, a world of brotherhood where people did not have to kill or die for peace, about a united world with no greed or hunger, no armies, no tyrants, no more. While he played, his grief began to subside and when he was finished, he held the guitar over his head to the accompanying roar of approval from the remaining Freaks and soldiers below. Then, taking a step backwards, he placed the instrument on Tambourine's body. After a moment of quiet reflection he turned to Sonny and nodded. The Fonzer nodded back.

"Thanks," Toad said. "Thank you for saving my life, and thank you for allowing me to mourn my friend."

Sonny smiled. "My pleasure, man. You could have ratted me out and you didn't."

"The time for old hatreds is past. There are many wounds that need to be healed."

Behind them the struggle between the Greasers and Fascists was over. As the pair watched, the Greasers busied themselves stripping Fascists and Bejeezuz's men of their weapons. "What about your friends?" Toad asked, nodding in their direction.

"They'll do what I tell them to do. You'll be okay. Like you said, the time for that shit's gone."

Toad nodded and turned back to his slain friend. Taking a deep breath of weed-and-flower scented air, he kneeled down beside Tambourine. For a long time he wept bitterly, while Sonny stood silent vigil. He cried for the fallen musician, and he cried for himself as well; like it or not he had fulfilled a prophecy. Just as in his dream, he had played for all of Street-Corner Earth and he was sure that, in their minds, he was being proclaimed their new Freedom Rider. But such things were best left for those who thirsted for fame and power. For himself, he just wanted to be left alone with Mizjoan somewhere, making his pipes and poring over his books. But as he considered that prospect, he knew it could never happen. Mizjoan was a woman of her people and her nation. With her, Toad would never know peace again. Unwittingly he had become Maynard's pawn. Was that what the Beatnik had wanted all along? Was that why Tam had to die?

He looked down at the body and sadly shook his head. "Maybe you're the one who's better off," he whispered. "Your struggle's over, friend."

Ernie moved as fast as he could through the smoke-shrouded courtyard, but it seemed the Dark Man could move faster. Bejeezuz was in and out of sight so often that Ernie was worried he'd lose him altogether. Just when he thought he was closing in, Bejeezuz would duck down an alleyway or disappear into a rolling billow of smoke. There were new alleyways in Covenstead since Ernie had last seen the Fair City. Unpainted barracks had been erected all around the courtyard, creating many places where the Dark Man could hide. The herbalist gripped his sword tightly; he'd have to be alert and quick. Bejeezuz might be laying in wait anywhere, poised and ready to strike.

The herbalist passed a Freak work-gang, choking their Fascist guards with the chains that still bound them. Spying the black-robed figure fleeing through the smoke, Ernie followed, encountering surprisingly few Greasers and Fascists. Those he did see seemed concerned only with escape. He also recognized signs showing that the two groups had warred amongst themselves. Farther along, he saw one of the black-robes—too short to be Bejeezuz—pinned to a door with a sheared-off Fascist battle lance. He had fallen victim to the anarchy that was spreading through the besieged fortress.

Out of the corner of his eye, Ernie glimpsed the Dark Man through the churning smoke. Bejeezuz was entering the stables along the east wall of the fortress, swirling through the door just as a building across the yard caught fire and exploded. Startled, Ernie looked up to see several flaming objects arcing down from the sky. Somewhere, somehow, the Radiclibs had acquired a ballista and were using it to lob bombs into the city.

One of the bombs took out a parapet just as Ernie ducked into the shadowy stables. Flaming debris rained down on the courtyard, some of it falling only a few feet from where he crouched. Alert to every sound and movement, Ernie slipped quietly through the shadows, grasping the handle of his sword so tightly that he thought that his fingerprints would be impressed on the handle. And then, the bomb-blasts ceased abruptly. Suddenly, it was so quiet that Ernie could hear the beating of his own heart thudding in his ears like a war drum. Sweat formed on his back and brow, trickling into his eyes. He wiped it away with his sleeve. Somewhere ahead of him, maybe a dozen stalls away, he could hear a low coaxing voice. Though he couldn't make out the words he knew it had to be Bejeezuz. The Dark Man's voice crooned. It was soothing, low and soft, not at all like that of the man who had just ordered Tambourine's execution. But Ernie had been there and seen it all—the evil magick of Bejeezuz's playing and the righteous power of Tambourine and Toad's. He had felt the energy and witnessed the bloodletting. Whatever the soft-voiced thing really was, no matter what its possibilities for evil, Ernie knew it was now up to him to silence it forever.

Dropping to his hands and knees the herbalist inched his way towards the voice. Shafts of grayish light shone through the narrow, grimy windows of the stable, creating pools of illumination that Ernie was careful to avoid. Keeping to the deep shadows behind a stack of hay bales, he concealed his sword beneath his coat so that no sudden glimmer would give away his location.

Suddenly the ground shook like an earthquake. A Fascist officer, hatless and terrified, ran by the nearest window followed by a rumbling steamwagon. Lurid Greaser-style flames were painted along its boiler, but Freaks and Radiclibs hung from its cab as it lurched past with a peace-symbol banner fluttering behind its stack. One of the Radiclibs fired a shot at the retreating Fascist and then the wagon was gone from sight, leaving only a pall of sooty smoke and the slowly diminishing clanging of iron-shod wheels to mark its passage. Using the noise and confusion for cover, Ernie moved closer to the voice.

He crept along behind the stalls until he came to one, larger than the others, with a side opened to the street. Hiding behind the stanchion, he watched Bejeezuz saddling his great black warhorse. Though obviously anxious, the Dark Man paused from time to time to pat the huge beast on its flanks, cooing as he cinched the saddle into place. Seeing Bejeezuz display affection to anything was obscene, a cold cynical parody of sentiment. When the Dark Man stopped to light up one of the sticklike things he habitually smoked, Ernie drew his sword and moved towards him. "Going somewhere?" he asked, positioning himself between Bejeezuz and escape.

The Dark Man turned and regarded Ernie coolly, almost as if he'd been expecting him. Finishing the final adjustments to the saddle, he puffed on his burning stick and idly fingered the spearhead at his throat. His hand strayed slowly towards the long dagger hanging from his belt. "As a matter of fact I am, Friend Freak. Did you come to see me off, or did you think you could stop me?"

"What do you think?" Ernie sneered.

"You cannot succeed."

"Maybe not, but I'm not the one who's running, not the one who's afraid."

Billy laughed as he jumped into the saddle. "Afraid? Of you? Certainly not. I have urgent business elsewhere, but I *will* be back."

Ernie moved closer. The sword twitched slightly in his hand. "Your days of power are over."

"On the contrary, my friend; they're just beginning."

Ernie looked at the hulking black form astride the huge warhorse and felt a sudden twinge of fear. Then, a vision of Tambourine's torn and bleeding body flashed through his mind and he charged at Bejeezuz, slashing wildly with his sword.

Hissing, Bejeezuz drew his dagger. As Ernie's sword swept down he deflected it with his forearm. There was a clang of metal on metal as the herbalist's weapon flew from his hand. Laughing, Bejeezuz slashed at

Ernie's face.

The herbalist jumped aside just in time. Bejeezuz's dagger ripped a hole in his coat, but missed his body entirely. As he dove for the safety of nearby hay bales, Bejeezuz spurred his mount and galloped out of the door. Cursing bitterly, Ernie retrieved his sword and ran after him.

Toad wasn't sure how long he grieved at Tambourine's side. The raging blackness that swept through him disrupted his perception of time; what seemed like hours may have only been minutes. When the last of his rage and sorrow ran from his puffy red eyes, he wiped them with his coat sleeve and looked away, momentarily distracted by the clamor of the last of Mizjoan's army entering the city. Slowly, painfully, he made his way to the edge of the stage, his breath coming out in great hitching gasps. Grief was riding him heavily as he surveyed the devastation below.

Covenstead's tents and shanties were burned or trampled flat, and rolling clouds of black smoke obscured the sun. The battle outside was over; the ground was littered with broken weapons and broken bodies. But still the sounds of gunfire and shouting raged inside the walls. As the rear guard of Dillon's army pushed through the gates, only the medics and litter-bearers were left outside to care for the wounded and mark the dead of both sides for burial. Smoke from the burning shanties and overturned steamers drifted across the battlefield. It was so thick in spots that as he watched the crews loading the death carts, Toad imagined he was standing in Strawberry Fields looking down on them.

As the burial crews harvested their grim cargo, other soldiers gathered up scattered weapons, piling them in great heaps by the walls. Two of the soldiers wheeled a ballista into position and lobbed an aerial bomb high over the city. When it detonated in the air, a fusillade of musketry and the low boom of a small cannon answered it. Like a gathering storm, clouds of thick smoke drifted together, almost completely obliterating Toad's view. The pipesmith returned to watch over Tambourine's body.

Sonny hovered nearby. Behind him the stage was a shambles of scattered Greaser and Fascist corpses rendered all the more ghastly by the light from Bejeezuz's burning portrait. Smoke still drifted out of the braziers, obscuring the carnage. The Panzer had rescued a short heavy rifle from one of the Fascists and was standing guard with it. He nodded to Toad. "Feeling any better?" he asked.

"Yeah, a little."

"Your Raddyclib buddies have taken the city, y'know. My people and the Fashies are running from 'em like rabbits."

"I know. You don't have to stick around if you don't want to."

The Greaser shrugged and looked down at his feet. "Sonny Slikback don't run from nothin'." Lifting his head, his eyes met Toad's. "Well... 'cept that one time."

The clatter of many feet coming up the stairwell kept Toad from replying. Frowning, Sonny stepped back and crouched behind an overturned smudge pot. The pipesmith stayed where he was; it didn't matter who was coming now.

When Mizjoan stepped onto the stage followed by Kentstate, Maynard, Flo and Eddie, Toad moved to meet them. Maynard's glasses were bent and sat on his face at an odd angle.

"Toad!" Mizjoan exclaimed, stepping towards him. "We saw what happened from below. Was that really you playing just now?"

"Yeah," he nodded. "But Tambourine, he's..."

"I know." She took the pipesmith in her arms, hugging him tight with her cheek pressed against his. When they broke apart they stood for awhile, looking deep into each other's eyes. "I'm so sorry about Tam," she said. "But I'm glad you're alive."

"Tam told me to keep on keeping on. Dylan knows, I'm trying."

"You're doing just fine."

"I don't feel fine."

Kentstate hurried towards them. She held a big-bored wheel lock pistol, which she leveled in Sonny's direction. Toad reached out and pushed the weapon aside. "Be cool," he said. "That man saved my life."

"A Greaser?" Mizjoan questioned, taken aback. "A Fonzer at that?"

"Yeah. He stopped Bejeezuz's man from doing to me what he did to Tam."

Kentstate lowered her pistol, but still seemed wary. "Shouldn't we take him prisoner or something?"

Mizjoan shook her head. "Let him be. Comrade Toad has spoken for him."

"But—a Greaser?"

"His name is Sonny," Toad said. "We go back a long way."

Mizjoan shook her head wonderingly. "You're full of surprises, aren't you? Greaser friends—and that playing! It was magnificent."

"I'd rather not talk about that."

"When you're ready, Toad. Comrade Sonny, you can put down your gun now."

The Fonzer stepped out from behind the smudgepot. Cautiously, he handed his weapon over to Kentstate.

"Thank you," Mizjoan said. "You're free to go."

Sonny grinned. "If it's all the same to you, ma'am, I'd like to stick around until things calm down a bit. There's no place I'm in a hurry to get to."

"As you wish."

Maynard pushed his spectacles back into place on his nose. "Where's Tambourine?" he asked.

Sudden rage overwhelmed Toad as he pointed to the covered body. "Back there, though I don't see why you care."

"Hey, man, that's not cool."

"Cool! Tam's real cool now—he's stone dead in fact. Just the way you planned."

"That *was not* the plan, daddy-o," Maynard replied bitterly.

Mizjoan grabbed Toad's arm. "Toad! That's enough!"

"No, it's not. You used him."

Maynard tensed. Under his permanent tan his face paled. "Hey, get hip, man. I didn't off the cat, you dig? I loved him as much as you did ... maybe more. No one wanted him to die, least of all me. But, the man had a duty to perform, a destiny to fulfill. Tam knew that this was one of the possible ends to the path he had to tread."

"Pretty words—that's all they are."

"Be cool. Tambourine was your friend, mine too, but above all he was a hero to his people, same as you."

"Not me. I'm no hero."

"Oh, but you are, man. No false humility riff can change that."

Toad took a step towards Maynard, but Mizjoan restrained him. Gently, he tried to push her away. "That's your rap," he snapped. "Everything that's happened to me ... all of this ... has been your doing. I wouldn't have been able to do a damn thing if you hadn't zapped me with blue fire and magick from the *Necronomicon*. You're trying to use me like you did poor Tam, but I'm not buying it."

The Beatnik shook his head. "You were already a hero, long before you got to Hillcommune, Toad. I've done nothing but guide you; I nudged you in the direction you were going anyway."

"C'mon, you molded Tambourine to your purposes, and now you're trying to mold me."

"I do not mold, Brother Toad. A potter can only serve the clay."

"Fuck your riddles. What are you trying to tell me?" Something like lightning flashed behind Maynard's spectacles. A slight smile played over his face. "Obviously nothing that you are ready to hear. Let me pay my respects to Tambourine."

Maynard shuffled past the pipesmith to where the musician's body lay. Slowly he lowered himself to the musician's side. Putting a trembling hand on Tam's shoulder he hung his head. Sad and bent he appeared even older—ancient.

There was a sound of hurried footsteps on the stairs. Flo and Eddie, who'd been staying out of the way, stepped to one side, as Ernie Mungweasle emerged from beneath the scaffolding. The herbalist's long coat was ragged and dusty, and his top hat was bent over at a ridiculous angle. His face was smeared with grime and he was nearly out of breath. Taking a step forward he stumbled and almost fell. Toad and Mizjoan caught him and held him upright, noticing that his arm was wrapped in a bloody white bandage.

"You're hurt," Mizjoan said.

"It's no problem," Ernie gasped. "I'm all right, really."

Mizjoan was unconvinced. "Sit down over here. That's an order."

Grumbling, Ernie obeyed.

"What happened?" Toad asked.

"I went after Bejeezuz. Caught up with him just as he was mounting his horse. I tried to stop him, but he wasn't very cooperative."

"He got away?"

"Unfortunately."

"Looks like he got the better of you."

"Hell, he would have killed me if he'd had the time. But I got this little keepsake from a big Whiterider I tangled with on the way back. He came after me with an ax. I took care of him, but not before he nicked me good."

"You better let me take a look at that cut," Mizjoan offered.

"It's not as bad as it looks," Ernie grunted, "though it could probably use a clean dressing. If Skulk's around he could do it. He's a good hand at doctoring."

"Theo's not here at the moment," Mizjoan replied, tearing up the shirt of one of the fallen Fascists to use as a bandage. "The last I saw of him he was with Dillon, Lurchkin, and a couple of Yipps. I don't expect him back for a while."

While Mizjoan attended to Ernie's wound, Toad walked over to Sonny and led him aside, leaving a mumbling Maynard to look after Tambourine's body. "I want to thank you again for saving me," the pipesmith said, shaking the Fonzer's hand. "I wish I knew how to repay you."

"No sweat. A lot has changed since we first met. Maybe I've learned something since then."

Just then, gunshots erupted from within the courtyard and an explosion rocked the stage. Sonny shook his head and wiped a greasy forelock out of his eyes. "I've changed my mind about staying, if I can get safe passage out of this zoo. It ain't that I don't trust your Radiclib buddies, but I feel like a flea-bitten mutt around them. An' things are just too fucked up around here for my taste. It's not that I'm running away or nothin'. Know what I mean?"

"I do."

Sonny shook his head. "I guess the whole world's gonna be fucked up for a while. You know, after today. All I know is, I just gotta haul ass outta here."

Below them a troop of Radiclib cavalry stormed out of the gate, furiously riding away on some unknown mission. Unmindful of their passing, the crews of the death carts went about their grisly business. "I think I can arrange something," Toad said.

"Suits me. I need a change of scenery."

"Heading home?"

"Naaah, not just yet. Gotta get off by myself for a while. Got some thinking to do."

"Sure, let me see what I can do."

Toad conferred with Mizjoan for a few moments. When he returned he was smiling. The Radiclib leader offered to provide Sonny a horse and provisions, and an armed escort as far as Ripoff Pass.

"I won't forget this," Sonny said as a pair of Radiclib guards arrived to lead him away.

"Me neither," Toad promised. "Good traveling and good luck."

After Sonny's departure, Toad returned to the spot where Maynard and Ernie were holding vigil over Tambourine's remains.

Mizjoan was taking care of preparations, overseeing two soldiers who were wrapping Tam's body in a long winding sheet. "Place him with the others," she said, "but be sure to mark him well. When the funeral pyres are lit, his shall burn the highest and brightest. He was a hero and shall be sent away as one. He shall occupy the highest bier. His guitar and pipe shall be laid on his chest, and a sword and bag of weed at his feet. When we honor him, we will honor a great warrior."

Mizjoan left the soldiers to their task and led her friends down to the fortress courtyard. Yes, a hero was to be honored, but there was still a long hard battle ahead for all of them. Though her troops had penetrated the city and many of the enemy had fled, others had barricaded themselves into the southern end of the fortress. It might be days before they could be flushed out and destroyed.

Chapter Fifty-Nine

As twilight faded, crowds of people gathered at the site of the old Concert Hall, while the Radiclib army stood in somber formation nearby. Some came to help with the preparations, others just to gaze at the line of pyres in silent reverence.

Ernie fought the urge to scratch himself. The dressing on his arm, though fresh this morning, was made of coarse cloth that itched unmercifully. And as if the itching wasn't bad enough, the wound throbbed, hurting worse than when he'd received it two days before, making it almost impossible for him to remain still. Turning his head slightly he glanced at the people lined up beside him. Like Ernie they were standing rigidly at attention. Even the normally antsy Flo and Eddie stood relatively motionless, though they were talking quietly to each other. Fine, he decided. If they could talk, he could scratch.

Skulk, Maynard, and the two Oldhips were closest to Ernie. A little way off were Mizjoan, Kentstate, and Field Marshal Dillon, standing as stiff as statues, looking straight ahead at the towering pile of logs and old timbers occupying the space where the Concert Hall once stood.

Mizjoan and Dillon seemed to be getting along very well. For all his brash and arrogant behavior, the old soldier had come through when it counted. In Mizjoan's absence he'd rallied all the available Radiclib forces at Froggy Bottom and kept up a series of raids on enemy strong points that had severely hampered the Fascist incursion west of the Sludge. Then, when the time had come, he'd relinquished his command to Mizjoan without so much as a petulant look. The old boy had character after all. Now that Covenstead was liberated and the enemy forces scattered or dead, Dillon could stand proudly by his leader's side.

The itchiness under his bandage nagged; Ernie strove to ignore it. He craned his head and perused the entire assemblage hoping to catch sight of Toad, of whom he'd seen little since the All Loveday battle. The pipesmith was nowhere to be seen. Where was he? It would be dark soon and the memorial service for Leftopia's fallen heroes would begin. Breaking formation he walked over to Mizjoan and asked quietly, "Where's Toad?"

Mizjoan shrugged. "I haven't seen him all day. I just sent two of my guards over to check on him. They should be back any time. But Toad worries me, Ernie. He's been acting strangely."

"He's been through a lot."

She nodded, watching as some of her soldiers were arranging the last tier of the highest pyre. They too were tired and worn from so much fighting and so little sleep.

"We all have," she said, "but we're not through yet. Fashies are nothing if not tenacious fighters. Though we've retaken Covenstead, we've still spent the better part of two days rousting them out of the ruins at the south side of town, and they'll no doubt be raiding up and down the Sludge for a while to come. There'll be skirmishes until all the Fascists are subdued, or a formal peace can be worked out. There's a lot more to do here too, what with rebuilding the city and all."

"It's not enough just to rout their armies and destroy their steamwagons," Kentstate interjected angrily. "We should take the war to the very gates of Himmlerburg and Moloch and Krakkerton. We should burn their country to the ground and piss on the ashes."

Mizjoan shook her head wearily. "Enough, 'State; it's over. Klaven Thinarm is dead, along with most of his Whiterider command. Overhed Kham is in prison."

"With due respect, Comrade Leader," 'State continued, "it just doesn't feel like a victory. We have lost so very many good people."

"So did they, Comrade Kentstate … so did they. Still, we've won, Bejeezuz is gone, and if he doesn't run all the way back to where he came from we'll catch him."

Two soldiers approached Mizjoan and saluted. They seemed nervous.

"Where is Comrade Toad?" she asked.

The taller of the two handed her a folded scrap of paper with her name on it. "All we found was this note."

Mizjoan nodded, recognizing Toad's handwriting. She unfolded the paper and read it. Frowning, she refolded it and slipped it into her tunic pocket. She glowered at the soldiers.

"It's done, then. You're dismissed."

Once the soldiers were gone the others gathered around Mizjoan. "What'd the note say?" Ernie asked.

"It said that Comrade Toad won't be joining us this evening."

"Why? What's wrong?"

"It was a private note, Ernie, but I will say that Toad feels strongly that he needs to be alone right now."

"He just thinks he wants to be alone. I'm going looking for him."

"Don't bother. You won't find him in Covenstead. Respect his wishes and let him be. He really wants to be left alone."

"I'll bet I know where he's headed. Doesn't he realize that it's still not safe to travel? Hell, I can't let anything happen to him now—not after all we've been through."

"Like, I'll go with you," Maynard offered. "Two can travel as fast as one."

Ernie stroked his long mustaches thoughtfully and shook his head. "No thanks, I think I'll go by myself."

"As you said, the roads are still dangerous," Skulk interjected, laying a hand on Ernie's shoulder. "Perhaps it's best if Maynard and I both accompany you."

"You maybe, Theo, but not Maynard. You know the way Toad feels about him ... perhaps with good reason."

"Whoa!" Maynard said, holding up his hands, palms out. "Mellow out, daddy-o. I just want Toad to dig the whole picture. What he does after that is his own gig."

"I think he's already seen the 'whole picture', Maynard, and he's made his decision."

"Look, man, I..." Maynard's protest died on his lips as muffled drums sounded in the distance, slowly pounding out a dirge.

A line of soldiers appeared, marching half-step towards the line of pyres. In their midst was a black stallion, a pair of boots turned backwards in its stirrups and a guitar lashed to its saddle. Behind the riderless horse eight uniformed pallbearers carried Tambourine's body on a simple oaken bier. The musician was dressed as Ernie had last seen him, in jeans and a leather jacket, but now his head was wreathed with strawberry leaves and several strands of dried flowers were hung around his neck. He was barefoot, as was Freak custom for one about to tread in Strawberry Fields. Tam's remains were reverently removed from the bier and gently lifted to the summit of the highest pyre. Fighting back tears, Ernie thought how pathetically thin and pale Tam's bare feet looked in the guttering light of the pallbearer's torches. When the musician's guitar was removed from the saddle and placed on his chest along with his pipe, Ernie finally gave in to his grief. Tears ran in rivulets down his cheeks as the sword and ceremonial sack of weed were placed below Tambourine's feet. The drums increased their funeral beat.

Mizjoan raised her arm in a power salute and the drumming ceased. She spoke in a soft, gentle voice, but loud enough so everyone could hear. She spoke of Tambourine and the others who had fallen in battle. She spoke of sacrifice. She spoke of duty, and honor, and love. When she was finished she lowered her arm and bowed her head. The drummers again took up their low, sorrowful beat as the torchbearers stepped forward.

The drumming died away and there was only silence as the torches were hurled up at the pyre, like a flurry of meteors arching their way across the night sky. Their passage was brief, and as they hit the dried lumber and pitch-soaked timbers the pyre erupted into a pillar of flame that would transport Tambourine to paradise—to Strawberry Fields forever. Sparks swirled up to dance between the stars, each spark carrying the soul of a dead comrade. Lesser funeral fires were lit around the great pyre, producing tongues of flame that coiled together, making it seem as if the very sky itself was part of the great burning.

Later, when the fire finally burned down and the evening breezes rose to scatter the ashes, Ernie turned away and headed toward the stables. Alone, or with companions, he was going to search for Toad, even if that search was to take him all the way to the very ends of the earth. Somehow, though, he didn't think he'd have to go that far.

Chapter Sixty

The low dark headland of Smuttynose Island loomed out of the moonlit sea. Seeing it for the first time in so many months, Toad's heart raced. In the two days since leaving Covenstead he'd dreamed of it often, dreams as vivid as the ones he used to have of the Dark Man. Toad stroked the neck of his guitar and eyed the tiny sparkle of steel that peeked out of the roll tied to the top of his backpack. Except for the guitar and the Radiclib sword rolled up in his blanket, everything he had been through might have been a dream as well. Even now, the sight of the island rising higher to greet him seemed like a fantasy. It was more intoxicating than Oldhip wine.

Taking a deep breath of salt air, Toad fumbled in his pocket for his pipe. Pulling out the faithful cherrywood that he'd carried since Hillcommune, Toad packed it with weed and lit it from the boat's cabin lantern. Satisfied that it was stoking properly, he passed it to Ishmael, the cross-eyed old lobsterman who was manning the wheel.

"Thanks to ye, son," Ishmael said in his thick Downeast accent. "These here smokeables of yourn be a damn sight better'n the frickin' local homegrown we been makin' do with these past few months."

"There's plenty more where that came from," Toad replied, glancing towards the still, dark waters of Islington Harbor.

The old lobsterman flashed a gap-toothed grin. "Glad to hear it son, glad to hear it. Since them Fashies been raisin' a ruckus up no'th, times has been hard."

Hard times, Toad thought. Ishmael was a hardy lobsterman, seasoned to making a living off the sea and tough in his own right, but the pipesmith doubted that the kindly old man had any idea what really hard times were.

Toad stifled a yawn. Even with a horse to ride, he'd spent more time off the road than on, and hadn't made it to Rivertown until after dark. Not only had there been rag-tag groups of fleeing enemy soldiers to worry about, there were Radiclib patrols he wished to avoid as well. By the time he'd reached Rivertown the entire community was celebrating liberation. Bands were playing in every tavern and all Freaks of age, along with some younger ones, were drunk and dancing in the streets. Happily, no one paid any attention to him.

The Fascists had held Rivertown until this very morning. However, many had been called to Covenstead several days before, leaving only men enough to keep the locals in check. That was, until a troop of Radiclib cavalry entered town in hot pursuit of escaping Whiteriders. Together the Radiclibs and the townsfreaks easily dispatched the remaining enemy forces.

With a free Rivertown, its citizens were celebrating like never before. In the chaos of the festivities, Toad had made his way to the waterfront where he hoped to catch Captain Chives' late ferry to Smuttynose. However, Chives was nowhere to be seen. While inquiring about the ferryman, he learned two things. The first was that he had missed the late ferry. The second was that the war had hardly touched Smuttynose at all. The Fashies, it seemed, didn't see any value in the offshore islands and having their hands full on the mainland, did not see fit to waste their efforts on them.

Having missed the ferry, Toad searched for fishermen who might be coerced bring him to the island, for a price. He was almost ready to give up when he encountered an old half-Freak, half-Downeaster named Ishmael. Ishmael informed him that ferry service had been irregular for some time, but that local fishermen like himself often made trips over to the islands delivering goods the islanders needed, for a price. Toad dangled a sack of Hillcommune Red under the lobsterman's nose and a deal was struck.

"Welp, looks like we'll be makin' port soon," Ishmael said. "Ye oughta be thinkin' 'bout gettin' your gear together."

A strong breeze filled the little lobster boat's sail. Toad watched as the darkened houses of Islington loomed closer. It was nearly midnight, he judged, but the sky was clear and the half-full moon bathed the town in a soft silvery light. It amused him to think how surprised Gary would be when he woke up to find his master home. He imagined the joyous reception he'd get from Chives and Poetryman and the others at Toker Jones' when he walked in casually for his customary pint of beer.

He yawned again as he looked at the lengthy dark shadows covering the town. The moon was already halfway down the western sky; its silvery light reflected off the many-paned windows of Toker's store like coins shining in a wishing well. Brighter than the rest, a stable window behind Toker's glowed with lamplight; that seemed very unusual to Toad. Islanders were notorious for their early-to-bed-early-to-rise nature.

Toad slung his pack on his shoulder and gathered up his guitar as the old lobsterman trimmed sail and brought the little craft neatly into place beside Islington's main wharf. "End o' the line," Ishmael grunted. "All ashore that's goin' ashore."

Reaching inside his cloak, Toad produced an ounce weedsack, which he passed to the grizzled mariner. Ishmael hefted it; then opening the small bag, sniffed its contents carefully. A smile crept over his craggy features. Centering his knapsack on his back, Toad started up the short ladder to the top of the wharf. He turned and looked back at the old man with his nose buried in the weedsack. "You know, Ishmael, if you'd prefer money… "

"Daow, son. What good's money in times like these? Like the fella sez, 'weed'll get ye through times of no money better'n money'll get ye through times of no weed'. So good night to ye, sir, and good luck." Then, grabbing a long pole, Ishmael began pushing away from the dock and out into open water.

Toad waved goodbye and followed the wharf into town. Islington had never looked quite so lovely. The large open square shone almost as bright as day, except where it was cut by the stark, elongated shadows of trees and houses. Homes and businesses were all shut up for the night. Only the stables behind Toker's store showed signs of activity. Harsh lantern light shone through the grimy windows and raucous laughter spilled from the half-open door. Suspicious, Toad moved to the shadows beneath a sprawling elm on the far side of the street. There was something in the laughter that made him uneasy.

Suddenly the stable door flew all the way open and a woman came running out, laughing wildly, with four drunken Rowdies close behind her. Toad stayed to the shadows hoping they would pass him by, but at the last moment the girl veered abruptly and crashed into him. He grabbed her to keep her from falling. Holding her close, his breath was almost taken away by the reek of cheap liquor swirling about her.

"Hey! Suzie's got a new friend," one of the Rowdies boomed.

"Don't sweat it, Gumma," another replied. "There's enough of her for all of us."

Toad's head reeled. He took a close look at the heavily made-up woman clinging to his chest. Her hair was bleached an unconvincing blond and her mascaraed eyes were bloodshot and out of focus, but he still recognized Suzie Creamjeans. She and Gumma Lout were the last two people Toad wanted to see.

"Heeey, I know you," Suzie slurred, blasting liquor fumes in Toad's face. "You're Josie."

Toad stiffened. "I told you to never call me that."

"Oh, honey, why-y not? You *are* my Josie. Where you been, sweetie?"

"Jeesh, man, I know you too. You're Toad, ain't you?" Gumma marveled, lurching closer.

There was no sense in denying it. "Yeah."

Gumma's pockmarked face twisted into an ugly sneer. "Now, ain't that somethin'? I heard you ran away like a pussy, but here you are, back home and all duded up like some fancy git-fiddle player. You're really somethin', ain't you, boy? Got you a pretty little cloak, an' a guitar, an' everything."

"Gumma, it's late, and I've really got to be going."

"Not so fast," Gumma insisted, shoving Toad with one ham-like hand. "I ain't done talkin' to you yet."

"Well, I'm done talking to you."

"Tough boy, huh? Maybe we should ask Suzie how tough you are. She knows you real well, right?"

Toad shrugged. "Suzie knows all the guys."

Gumma seemed to find this hilariously funny. He smacked Toad on the shoulder hard and laughed until he hiccupped. If anything, his breath smelled worse than Suzie's. "Hear that, boys? An' she told us we was the first!"

The other Rowdies hooted with glee. One gaunt creature, with heavily tattooed arms and no front teeth, guffawed until he fell to the ground and rolled around in the dust. When the fit passed, he let out a long, gross belch and passed out cold.

Suzie staggered up to Gumma Lout and started to fondle the crotch of his tight jeans. "I know him real well, Gumma honey," she cooed, blowing in the Rowdie's ear. "Josie and I use ta live together before I met you."

She leered mockingly at Toad and rubbed up against Gumma's leg. "He wasn't any fun at all, hon. He ain't a real man like you."

"I can see that, Sugar-Tits. Still, a buddy of yours oughta be good for somethin'. Maybe he can play a tune for us on his git-fiddle. Whatcha say, faggit," Gumma said, thrusting a jug at Toad, "play us a tune? If you're really good maybe we'll let you have sloppy fifths with Suzie here."

"No thanks."

Gumma wiggled the jug in Toad's face. It smelled as if a rat had crawled into it and died, adding its putrefying essence to the cheap booze. Toad wrinkled his nose and shook his head.

"Hey, could you possibly be sayin' no, here?"

"I'm afraid so."

"That ain't polite, pussyboy, an' def'nat'ly not healthy. You think maybe you're better'n us or somethin'?"

Toad shuffled nervously. There was no way to answer that question. Either way, at this point in their dialogue Gumma would twist it around to something he didn't like.

Suzie seemed tired of the game. She eyed the jug hungrily and rubbed up closer to Gumma, running her fingers through his long stringy hair.

"Let him go, Gum. Maybe he's gotta get home to his company."
Toad felt an eerie chill creep up his spine. "Company?"
"Sure, Josie. Some weird guy in a black cloak. I seen him in Toker's
around sunset asking after you. He seemed in an awful hurry to find out
where you lived. He sure was creepy."

The wind left the pipesmith's lungs with an audible whoosh; the effect
was the same as if Gumma had jumped on his chest. Great Dylan's Ghost!
He couldn't be here. Suddenly, an image of his unsuspecting apprentice
opening the door for Sweet Billy Bejeezuz flashed in his mind. It blinded
him to his current predicament, and pushing past the Rowdies, he started
up the road.

Gumma brought his hand down hard on Toad's shoulder before he'd
gone three steps. "Not so fast, asshole. We're havin' a homecoming for
you, an' that's that. Now, start pickin' on that git-box or I'll break your
face."

"Get your grubby paws off me!" Toad snapped, pushing Lout's hand
aside. "My apprentice is in danger."

The Rowdie shoved Toad in the chest, hard. "You don't unnerstand
nothin', faggit. It's you that's in danger. Now you start wailin' on that box
or I start wailin' on you. Am I right, boys?"

"Right, Boss!" the other Rowdies hooted, slapping their thighs in
malicious glee.

Toad wished that the sword wasn't packed away in his bedroll. "Okay,
I'll play you something you'll never forget."

"That's more like it."

He took his guitar from his back, methodically removed its protective
sack and, violently swung the instrument at Gumma's head.

Before the Rowdie could move to protect himself the guitar hit him full
in the face, splintering into pieces. He staggered backwards and collapsed
in a sprawl beneath the elm tree. Without a second's hesitation, Toad
jammed the broken guitar neck into the groin of the nearest Rowdie, who
screamed and dropped to the ground, clutching his injury. The remaining
tough gawked at Toad for a second, and ran away when the pipesmith
brandished the guitar neck at him. Suzie sat down in the middle of the
road, laughing and hiccupping uncontrollably. Toad tossed the shattered
remnant of his instrument aside and ran as fast as he could up Toad Hill.

By the time he'd reached the top of the hill the pipesmith was gasping
and nearly out of breath. He could see his house through the trees; it was
luminescent in the pale moonlight, and ghostly silent. Bejeezuz can't be
here, Toad tried to tell himself. Lights were burning in the living room and
study windows, and smoke was curling up from the center chimney. The
kitchen door was open a crack and a long finger of light shone through it,

beckoning. But months on the road had sharpened the pipesmith's senses, and he kept well into the shadows of the maples in the front yard as he crept towards the door.

The sliver of light, with its promise of rest in familiar well-loved surroundings, enticed Toad. Part of him wanted to run for the door, throw it open and yell, 'I'm home.' Another part, the road weary, world wise part, held him in check. Taking a deep breath to quiet his nerves, Toad slipped across the moon-dappled yard and through the threshold. He applied pressure gently, so that the old paneled door didn't squeak on its hinges as he eased it open.

A single candle guttered on the kitchen table casting long, dancing shadows. In the living room, beyond the kitchen, a fire burned cheerily on the fieldstone hearth and tapers flickered in their holders on top of the bookcases and end tables. A pipe and a variety of books lay on the slate-top coffee table, right where he and Ernie had left them months ago. Toad could even see the marks where they'd been dusted around. With a slight sigh, he eased out of his backpack and set it on one of the overstuffed chairs. Except for the crackle of the logs on the fire the house was utterly silent.

Gary was nowhere to be seen. Toad considered calling out to him, but thought better of it. In the past Toad had several times come home to similar situations—lights on and the fire not banked for the night—only to find Gary crashed out in the study with a pipe in his hand and an unread book in his lap. Quietly, nervously, he crept towards the study, his heart beating furiously against his ribcage.

The study light was turned down low. It was a curious antique oil lamp with an adjustable wick that could be set for whatever degree of light the user desired. It filled the study with long, menacing shadows, but still cast enough light so that Toad could see the figure of his apprentice. He gasped in horror, his guts churning, full of ice. Gary was slumped face down across the desk. His head was cocked at an impossible angle, and his tongue protruded limply from his mouth, which was stretched wide in a silent scream. Already cracked and glazed with death, his eyes bulged with terror. His pants lay torn and tangled around his ankles.

"Gary!" Toad gasped.

"I assure you he died at the moment of greatest pleasure," said a cold, familiar voice. "My pleasure, that is."

Toad whirled about to see Sweet Billy Bejeezuz sitting in a chair in the corner. His cowl was up, shadowing his face, but lamplight reflected from his pale, unblinking eyes. A burning stick protruded from a mouth that had far too many teeth. Bejeezuz smiled, but his flat icy eyes regarded Toad with cockroach-like contempt.

"H-how did you find this place?" Toad asked, turning his head so that he wouldn't have to look at Gary's pitiful corpse. He was fighting for time, trying to think of some way to retrieve his sword from his knapsack in the living room.

The Dark Man snickered. "There's a link between us, remember? That's changed somewhat since my little—uh—setback in Covenstead, but all I really needed to do was to ask a few discreet questions as to the residence of one Josiah Toad, Pipesmith. Believe it or not your reputation is quite well known. It was a simple matter to pinpoint your origin to one of the off-shore islands and then to this smudge on the face of the world that you so aptly call Smuttynose."

"Why did you come here? You no longer hold any power in Street-Corner Earth."

"Au contraire, Sweetcheeks. Once I've collected what is rightfully mine—what you promised me—nothing will be able to stop me."

Toad shook his head. "You'll get nothing from me. And you're going to pay for what you've done to Gary."

"Wrong on both counts, dear Toad," Bejeezuz replied, playing with the rusty spearhead hanging at his throat. "These little setbacks only make me stronger. They make the game more interesting. Besides, your little friend here wasn't that good, you know, particularly after he started to get cold. I prefer my meat a little livelier ... like you."

"No!" Toad screamed, slamming his fist down hard on the desk. "You'll get nothing from me!"

The Dark Man laughed and blew out a series of smoke rings. "I already have," Bejeezuz stated, producing a sheath of crumbling yellow pages from under his robe. "Your apprentice showed me where you kept it. He was very talkative, once he got to know me."

The ice in Toad's stomach turned to ground glass. For a moment the room seemed to swim in front of his eyes. Gary's blood-smeared corpse, the light, and Bejeezuz's mocking eyes all congealed into a blur. Fear rose up in him but it was kept at bay by hatred, rage, and a strange resurgence of the power that he'd felt when he was playing at Covenstead. Toad's breath escaped in a harsh rasp. He looked about frantically for a weapon. Just as Bejeezuz loomed out of his chair, Toad grabbed at the base of the heavy oil lamp. He'd hardly raised it a foot before the Dark Man's hand was clenched over his, squeezing. White-hot needles of agony raced through Toad's hand. His arm bent back at an awkward angle, and he stifled a scream as the lamp returned to the desk.

"Naughty, naughty," Bejeezuz taunted, his breath hot and foul on Toad's face. He threw the *Necronomicon* down on the desk, and gripping Toad with both hands, forced him down next to Gary's corpse. Eagerly, his gloved hands roved along his victim's body, caressing here, brutally tweaking and pinching there. His breath, almost as hot as the tip of his burning smokestick, came in hitching gasps. "But that's all right, my pretty-pretty," Bejeezuz wheezed. "I love naughty boys; they're so exciting." Slowly, his voice softened until it was like the cooing of a dove. "We dream of each other at night," he gushed. "It is our destiny to be together."

Toad tried to struggle free, but Bejeezuz's weight bore down on him, making movement difficult. The Dark Man's breathing became more ragged again, coming in short excited bursts as one of his hands worked at the fastenings of Toad's cloak. Closing his eyes to fight back the horror of what was happening, Toad's fingers reached out instinctively, searching for anything to grab. They closed on a long brass letter opener lying near the corner of the desk. Mustering all his strength he seized the opener and, ripping his arm free, drove the blade savagely into Bejeezuz's side, sinking it to the hilt just below the right armpit.

The Dark Man screamed and jerked upright. His right hand convulsed and lost its grip. He clawed at the letter opener with his left; his right arm now hung at his side, jerking and nearly useless. Slowly, agonizingly, he extricated the implement from his body. It came out in a sizzle of smoke and leaping blue sparks, as Toad rolled out of the way. Bejeezuz approached him slowly, weakly flexing his damaged arm as he stumbled forward. "You little worm!" he hissed. "You think this will stop me?"

"We'll see," Toad replied as he picked up the *Necronomicon* and bolted out the door. The letter opener slammed into the doorjamb beside Toad's head, as Bejeezuz let out a howl of rage and ran after him.

Toad ran through a tapestry of moonlight and long, twisting shadows toward the cliffs west of his house where he could scatter the pages to the wind and sea. He heard the door bang on its hinges and knew the Dark Man was not far behind. As the black form closed in, Toad could feel Bejeezuz's cold eyes burning holes in his back. He thought that any second those gnarled claw-like hands would start tearing into his flesh.

The path to the cliffs wended slightly uphill through a rocky field long overgrown with juniper and thistles that snagged at his cloak as he ran. In the moonlight the old clamshell path shone softly among the weeds. Overgrown piles of clutter marked generations of his family's occupancy: pieces of abandoned wagons, piles of rotting lumber and shattered crockery, remnants of furniture and farm tools. There were a thousand pitfalls and snags that could turn an ankle or send him sprawling if he was foolish enough to leave the path for a moment. Creepers curled across the path in places, lying in wait for a careless foot. Still, Toad didn't dare to slow down. Behind him he heard harsh breathing and the crunch of heavy boots on broken clamshells.

Nearing the edge of the cliff, Toad suddenly tripped, crashing down hard on the path, his head barely missing a large jagged rock. Pain shot through his leg where shards of broken shell penetrated his jeans, cutting into his knee and shin. He turned over just as the black form swirled down on him, blotting out the moon. Instinctively, Toad rolled to one side as a dagger flashed by his face and snapped in two as it clanged into a rock beside his head. Dazed, Toad scrambled to his feet and hurried toward the edge of the cliff. Heavy, ominous surf pounded on the rocks hundreds of feet below.

When he reached the edge of the cliff, Toad turned. His breath was coming in racking gasps. Bejeezuz swooped toward him. The Dark Man's hands were outstretched, hooked talons; his eyes and teeth, even shadowed in his cowl, shone with reflected moonlight. Smiling grimly, Toad held the sheath of pages out over the edge of the cliff. But before he could let go, Bejeezuz launched himself, clawing at Toad's outstretched hand. One gloved talon crunched down on Toad's wrist, twisting it forward, and the pile of papers fell to the ground several feet from the edge. Pinning Toad with his left hand, Bejeezuz scrabbled for the *Necronomicon* with his impaired right. Toad kicked at the pages, scattering them across the ground. Several, stirred by the night breezes, fluttered over the cliff like sea birds. Slowly they drifted into the booming darkness below.

"I was hoping to enjoy you—fully," Bejeezuz hissed, "but it's too late for that. Time to die." Snarling, he grabbed Toad with both hands and shoved him towards the precipice.

The pipesmith fought back valiantly, though the Dark Man's hands held his throat like a vise. His vision blurred; pinpricks of light danced before his eyes, but still he resisted. Even in his fear and desperation, Toad could smell the salt air and hear the surf pounding far below him. He was home, and hadn't traveled endless miles and endured terrible hardships to be slain like a dog in his own dooryard. In the pale moonlight, they were mad dancers circling close to the cliff edge, then away, then back again. Beneath their feet, remnants of the *Necronomicon* were torn to shreds by their boots. A dole of torn pages escaped the frenzy, spun into the air and drifted peacefully into the blackness beyond the edge of the cliff.

As their death waltz continued, the Dark Man's robe opened, revealing the spearhead pendant leaping and swaying before Toad's eyes. Bejeezuz's grip on Toad's throat tightened, making it impossible for the pipesmith to breathe. His vision faded into darkness until all he could see was the spearhead in front of him and the moon over Bejeezuz's shoulder. Suddenly he felt calm, in control, as if time had slowed. The moon was behind the Dark Man now. That meant it was now Bejeezuz who had his back to the sea. One push and they'd both plunge to their deaths. Since

Toad's fate was inevitable he braced himself and prepared to shove. Then, Bejeezuz froze. His grip loosened and he began sniffing the air wildly like he had at Covenstead. Reflexively, Toad sniffed too. He couldn't be sure, but he thought he caught a faint whiff of something musty, a scent neither of field or sea.

"NO!" the Dark Man howled. "It can't be! Not again!" He took a slight step back, still maintaining his grip on Toad, and glanced fearfully at the creeping shadows beneath the tall pines at the edge of the field.

In spite of his peril Toad almost laughed when one of the shadows moved and a soft voice called out, "Hello Darkness, my old friend."

Like a man in a trance, Bejeezuz let go of Toad with his right hand while doubling his grip with the left. "Show yourself!" he screamed, shaking his fist. "You've haunted me long enough. Show yourself now!"

"Your wish is, like, my command," the voice replied. A small shadow moved towards him, while behind it a larger one kept pace. Moonlight flashed, reflecting from something in the shadows.

Bejeezuz gurgled deep in his throat as the shadow approached. "Yesss," he said, trembling slightly. "I remember you now. You were at Westcommune!" Looking behind Maynard, he sneered. "And you're the one from the stable."

In the instant that Bejeezuz was distracted, Toad grabbed at the rusty spearhead dangling from his adversary's throat. With a violent tug, it broke free of its chain, and he slammed the point into Billy's chest. A flash of searing blue fire coursed up Toad's arm. He cried out and jerked back, letting go of the spearhead as the Dark Man lurched backward towards the rim of the cliff. For a moment Billy stood silhouetted against the moon like a great black bat, clawing frantically at his smoking chest. He staggered, but at the last second his arm snaked out, seizing the pipesmith's cloak in his claws, pulling him toward the edge of the cliff. Toad gasped in horror. With glowing, hate-filled red eyes and his chest a crackling mass of blue flame, the Dark Man hissed, trying to speak, but no words sounded. Instead, acrid-smelling smoke curled out of his mouth. Sputtering and twitching, Sweet Billy Bejeezuz continued to drag Toad toward him, into the darkness beyond.

Suddenly, Toad felt Ernie's arms around him, fighting the Dark Man's fearsome strength. Bejeezuz lurched backwards, and for a moment it seemed he would take both Toad and Ernie into the abyss with him. Then with a loud RRIIPP, the fabric of Toad's cloak let go. With the torn cloth clutched in his hands, Bejeezuz fought to right himself. Silently, he plunged over the edge of the precipice.

For a long moment Toad could only stand and gape as Bejeezuz spun out of sight. With all of his energy spent, the pipesmith slipped from

Ernie's grasp. He fell to his hands and knees and crawled to the edge of the cliff. As Ernie and Maynard stood beside him, he peered into the darkness. Far below a black shape lay sprawled across the rocks, sparking and burning with blue fire as the waves washed over its lifeless form.

Breathing a long sigh of relief, Toad whispered, "Sweet dreams, asshole."

"He's gone for good this time," Ernie commented reassuringly, as he slipped a protective arm over his friend's shoulder. "It's over now."

Toad let Ernie and Maynard lead him away from the edge of the cliff.

"What are you guys doing here?" he rasped.

"There'll be time enough for questions later," Ernie answered.

Maynard came and stood beside him. "Like, let us help you get back to the house. You need to get those injuries taken care of. "

Toad shook his head. "I don't think I can."

Trembling, he shrugged off Ernie's arm and walked back toward the cliff's edge. "I-I don't think I can ever go there again," he choked, knowing what was waiting back in his study.

"It's all over," Ernie soothed. "A bottle and pipe will calm you."

"No ... G-Gary's back there. He's dead. Bejeezuz t-tortured ... murdered him."

The herbalist's shoulders sagged. "We will take care of him," he promised, his voice cracking. "Come back with us. Skulk should be there by now."

Assisted by his friends, Toad stopped short. In his excitement he'd forgotten about the *Necronomicon*. He glanced about, hoping to spot any remaining pages.

"Looking for something?" Maynard asked.

"Uh ... no. Nothing important."

The Beatnik smiled. "Then it can wait till daylight."

Toad started slowly back across the field towards his house.

Chapter Sixty-One

Silhouetted by the warm light filling the doorway, Skulk waited to greet them. He slipped an arm around Toad and led him through the kitchen into the living room, where he guided the pipesmith to a chair by the fire.

"I found your apprentice," the old Digger said sorrowfully. "I cleaned him up and wrapped him in a sheet. There wasn't much more that I could do for the poor lad."

"Thanks. I couldn't have done it myself," Toad replied with a weak nod.

"Yes ... well ... in the morning we can notify his parents and arrange for the burial."

"Gary was an orphan, like me. He had no family."

"Sad, very sad. Still, it makes things a little easier."

Ernie rummaged through his pack for medicinal herbs and bandages, while Skulk poured everyone a small cup of heavy, fruited brandy from a flask that seemed to have materialized out of thin air. Skulk passed the cups around and then filled a pipe with weed from his belt pouch.

"I can't help thinking," Toad said, "that if I was here earlier, Gary might still be alive."

Maynard shook his head. "Don't guilt-trip yourself, man. It's not your fault. Bejeezuz was an evil cat. You rid the world of an ancient horror. Dig it; if the timing was different, Bejeezuz might have killed you both and survived to menace Street-Corner Earth again, when his power returned."

Toad winced as Ernie removed broken bits of clamshell from his knee and applied a poultice to his singed hand.

Skulk lit the pipe he was holding with a few quick tokes and handed it to Toad. "I'm just glad it's all finally over," he said exhaling a huge cloud of smoke.

"Everyone is," Maynard added. "That Bejeezuz was one tenacious cat. Centuries ago we thought we had him at Westcommune. I was sure he'd died in the desert; only within the last century did I start to believe that he'd escaped."

"I know you told us everything you knew about him," Ernie interjected, "but after seeing him on stage, with all those lights and everything, I wonder if we'll ever really know what he was."

"Hold on, daddy-o, I never said I told you *everything*... "

Somehow that didn't surprise Toad.

"I told you everything that I was absolutely sure of. The hearsay and conjecture I saved for the proper time and, considering the events of this evening, it appears as though that time has come. Pull your chairs closer to the fire and I'll tell you a story, the likes of which you will never hear again."

They formed a semi-circle around the fireplace with their chairs. Maynard sat in the middle next to Toad, with Skulk and Ernie taking the end positions. The Beatnik settled deep into his wingback chair and gazed into the flames. Swirls of firelight reflected from his glasses.

"As you know," he started solemnly, "the cat went back a long way— almost as far back as me. In the early twenty-first century there was a musician named Garlock—E.C. Garlock if I remember correctly. I suspect that wasn't his real name, but it is the earliest reference I know of. This Garlock cat was a heavy talent. Just before Helter-Skelter, he and his band Ringwraith were the biggest thing in rock music. From what I've heard and read the man was pure evil, evil enough so that his name was permanently stricken from the Roster of Musicians. He was connected with some really fanatic, radical dudes—Fashie types, only worse. Terrorists, they were called in those days. Story had it that he was almost killed when a bomb he was planting exploded prematurely. Lucky for him, the people he ran with were scientists, wizards of a sort, who were delving into a kind of physical immortality. They rebuilt his body, replacing much of it with machinery designed never to wear out. What you killed tonight was more a soulless mechanism than a human being."

"It's all so hard to believe," Toad muttered.

"The world's full of unbelievable things. Take a look at me, a fossilized old beatnik. Anyway, the story is mainly conjecture. Most of it came to me at Westcommune, from a dying confidant of Tommy Two's. Maybe he told us the story because we cared for him, tended his wounds and made the remainder of his life a bit easier. Or, for all I know, he could have made it all up."

"But you don't think he did?" Skulk offered.

"No, I don't. But after we ran Tommy Two into the desert I thought that was the end of it. Then, maybe seventy years ago, I began to hear disquieting rumors about an ageless, faceless Dark Man building a great empire in what used to be the state of Utah. I didn't think much of the stories at first, but as he extended his power further east, accounts of the Dark Man increased in frequency and detail. It wasn't long before I became convinced that this Dark Man was a new incarnation of Tommy Two. Since my last reawakening I've had him watched. Until tonight he was only dimly aware of me, as a faint peat bog odor that caused him fear. I suspect he didn't even know why. Like, it's wild, but for the past few years I've been the Dark Man's dark man. Thanks to you, Toad, that job's over now."

Toad smiled weakly. "Glad I could help."

"Yes ... still, I need a little help to tie up some loose ends, if you don't mind. I'd like to hear everything you know about Bejeezuz. Like, what happened between you two, things he might have said, even if they didn't make much sense."

Toad nodded, waiting until the pipe passed his way again. He took a couple of tokes before beginning his story. The pipesmith stayed as close to the truth as possible but omitted any references to his copy of the *Necronomicon*. The sky outside the window was turning from black to gray by the time his tale wound to a close.

" ...and he would have finished me off for good if you guys hadn't shown up when you did," Toad finally concluded. "That look he got on his face when he was sniffing the air ... damn!"

"Probably the only time in history that body odor won a war," Maynard laughed, pouring himself a shot. During the course of Toad's narration they'd killed off one flask of brandy and were well into their second. "The cat could probably smell me a mile off."

Ernie left his seat and stretched out beside the fire, pillowing his head with a birch log. "There's one thing I can't figure, Maynard," he said. "We all knew Toad would head home to Smuttynose, but why were you so sure Bejeezuz would follow him?"

"You'd know that if you gave it some thought, Ernie. But, like, maybe Brother Toad can shed some light on the issue."

Toad fiddled nervously with his bandages. "Uh, maybe he wanted revenge. Then again, he was kind of queer for me."

"How'd he know where you'd be?"

"Dreams, I guess. He dreamed about me, just as I did about him."

Maynard pounded down his drink and poured another. It didn't seem to affect him in the least. "Like, it doesn't really wash that the Dark Cat'd go so far out of his way simply for revenge or to satisfy his twisted desires; he wasn't *that* reckless. Maybe there is another possibility?"

"Such as?" Ernie asked.

"Remember what you told me about the deal Toad made with Bejeezuz to buy time?"

"You mean that shit about the *Necronomicon*? Yeah, now I see; he kills

Gary while looking for it, then when Toad arrives he tries to kill him too."

"Right. But what hasn't been laid on the table is that he found what he came for—didn't he, Toad?"

The pipesmith trembled as he reached for his glass of brandy and polished it off in one gulp. It was strong stuff that made his eyes water. "If you know that much, then you must know I dropped it by the cliff."

"You're in the groove, daddy-o; that I do."

"Well, it's gone now. Blowin' in the wind."

Maynard laughed and reached inside his ratty turtleneck. With a flourish he produced a handful of soiled and tattered pages. "Don't be so sure, man."

Toad's drink had warmed his stomach, but now it felt like it wanted out. "S-so, what do you intend to do with them?"

"Nothing, man. They're, like, yours. As old as I am, I hope that I'm never too old to learn from my mistakes. I was wrong about the book. I couldn't handle its powers, and I doubt that I could ever learn to. These pages belong to you. You decide their fate. They're no longer of any interest to me. Besides, they're written in Latin; I flunked Latin in school."

Toad took the crumbling pages from Maynard and held them in his hand. In them were sealed the fate of peoples and nations. Men had killed to possess them. Touching the pages, he remembered their power and the omnipotent feeling of Freaks chanting his name in adoration. Then he thought of Maynard on Mount Lennon, Hillcommune and Foreseein' Franklin. But in the end, he remembered Moonshadow and Tambourine. With a strained smile he turned the tattered remains over in his hands, then casually tossed them into the fireplace. The ancient paper exploded into flames immediately and flew up the chimney in a swirl of sparks.

Maynard nodded his approval. "Like, what's done is done, man. Now, what about you, Toad? What are you going to do?"

"When I came back here tonight I thought I'd stay and settle back into my old life. I don't want to be a hero, and I don't want to be a legend. Here I was going to be neither. But after tonight, I know there'll be no peace for me here either."

"What about Joannie?" Ernie suggested.

Toad ran his fingers through his rumpled hair. "I love her, and in her way I'm sure she loves me. But, I can't change her life, or undo what's happened to me. She's got her troubles; I got mine. Living my life in Leftopia just wouldn't work."

Maynard refilled Skulk's pipe and lit it with a splint from the fire. Once it was properly stoked he passed it to Toad. "I can dig what you're saying."

"Can you? It seems to me that the only thing you can 'dig' is what *you're* saying. Ever since I met you, you've done nothing but manipulate and use people. You used Tambourine. And, though I'm not quite sure how, I'm sure you've been using me."

"Hey, man, like, before you make any hasty assessments, let me finish the whole story."

Toad shook his head. "I already know what I need to know."

"If you've been used, Toad, it's because Fate used you, History used you, as they do all of us. I didn't cause those prophetic dreams of yours. That link was already there. Perhaps it was a coincidence, perhaps it wasn't, but to me it just proves that your fate was as I originally perceived it. Who really knows what powers run the universe? Not me, man, and I've been groovin' it a long, long, time."

"Say what you want, Maynard. But from my viewpoint it seems that you've caused everything that's happened to me. Except the dreams. Maybe, somehow, they were Bejeezuz's doing."

Maynard shook his head. Reflected firelight flashed from his spectacles. "I doubt that even Bejeezuz had that power, and you vastly overrate mine."

"I find that hard to believe. I suspect that you two have been running the world for a long time."

"This is getting heavy," Ernie interjected. "Mellow out, Toad."

Toad took a toke off the pipe and passed it to Skulk, who had been sitting quietly to one side. "This *is* heavy, Ernie. Haven't you ever wondered how we really got where we are—the true story of our culture, I mean?"

"Of course I have. And I've read about it the same as you. Maynard freely admits he had a lot to do with it. Hell, he was the one who initially gave Boswell the Lame the idea of how to structure the whole thing."

"My point exactly. He manipulated Boswell, and now he's manipulating us."

Maynard spread his arms wide, forcing a grin. "Hey, whoa! Not so fast. Give an eyewitness to history a chance to tell it like it was."

"Why bother? It would probably be a lie."

"Dig it. I could lie, and you wouldn't know the difference, but I have no need to hide anything. You all deserve the truth.

"You've got good deductive powers, Toad," the beatnik continued, "and a passion for truth. You'll make a good historian someday. But first, hear the tale of one who's truly been there."

"The truth? The whole truth? And, nothing but the truth?"

"Just so, big daddy, just so." Maynard paused and poured himself another shot. "Let me begin at the beginning. After I awoke from the peat bog and joined Boswell and his people, I soon came to realize that the world needed a long range plan for its future. After all, we couldn't afford to repeat the mistakes of the past. Society's growth needed to be regulated, invisibly—a clandestine oligarchy if you will—so that nature and technology could advance together, not separately and at odds with one another.

"Having grown up in the Hippie Era, I believed that a peaceful farming and craft-oriented society would provide the best chance for success. Early on, I knew that my place in any new world order would be off-stage, so to speak. I made it look like all the planning and structuring were Boswell's ideas. Indeed, some of it was, so I guess it wasn't a total fabrication.

"There were those who violently disagreed with our way of life: the wandering tribes of what were then called 'militias', who wanted military rule, and the remnants of urban street gangs who were primarily interested in violence for its own sake. In time these two groups developed into the ancestors of the Fascists and Greasers of today. We battled these groups from time to time, but mostly we learned to avoid them.

"I became hip that, to hold our new society together, we needed something like religion, but without all its ritual trappings and dogma. Something more mythological, based on folklore.

"I dug heavily on the music of the sixties musicians, particularly Ol' Bob Dylan, who I'd been pretty friendly with when we both lived in a place called Greenwich Village, back in the old days. Like it wasn't a perfect plan, but I realized that his writings, and the writings of other musicians of the times, already possessed the nucleus of our new folklore. Man it was crazy, but it made more sense than pre-Helter-Skelter religions. And still, I knew, it would not be enough to keep technology from reaching dangerous levels. I was hep that advances would come in time, but they couldn't be allowed to happen too fast. If they did, the ecology of the planet would be in peril again and there'd be another outburst of Ludditeism. To keep everything in the groove I founded the Clear Light Society—The Diggers. Their primary directive was to regulate scientific growth, by studying and preserving what should be preserved and killing dangerous technology, keeping it buried."

"Was Tambourine 'dangerous technology'?" Toad snorted.

Maynard set his glass down hard, spilling some of his drink. Something like heat lightning flashed behind his shades. "Totally uncool, man!"

"Don't try to deny it. In Hillcommune I overheard you and Skulk talking about Tambourine 'outliving his usefulness.' Sounded pretty cold-blooded to me."

"You're way off base, cat. I dug Tam a lot. All I was saying was that his house, the house of Dylan, was coming to the end of its power."

"Then you weren't planning his death?"

"Of course not, but he *was* the last of his line. Another clan needed to rise up. One that would, in time, wield greater influence than the House of Dylan."

Toad shook his head. "I guess I owe you an apology. But, why do you place all this importance on family names?"

"Mythology, folklore. People need real heroes, Toad. The old religions tried to satisfy that with talk of messiahs and prophets who had some mystical connection to a supreme being. But in those pre-Helter-Skelter days the old faiths were slowly dying—dying because nothing they offered related to peoples' lives. A hero: now there's a symbol the whole world can embrace. And what better choice than the greatest of the sixties musician-poets? The happy discovery of living Dylan descendants, like Frankie Lee, was pure serendipity, man. Everything came together as if it were destined to happen. I believe it was."

"You better pass that pipe this way," Toad remarked. "This is way too heavy."

"If you think it's heavy now, daddy-o, you should have been in my sandals then. Here I was, for all intents and purposes immortal, trying to help get the world back on its feet. If it wasn't for this Dylan gig, I don't know what I would have done."

"But the old religions, they must have had something to offer?" Toad asked.

"Rules, daddy-o. Supposedly God, the Creator, put people on this earth with free will, the ability to choose right from wrong. And to guide them, he gave them rules to follow. But, people don't follow rules for long, not on their own. Watch kids. Kids don't really follow rules, unless they think someone's looking. When it counts, they follow what they learn from role models, mostly their parents. You know the old saw: 'The apple does not fall far from the tree.' If the father's a douche bag, then the kid's probably stocking up on vinegar and water."

"What's that got to do with it?"

"Well, when God saw that people weren't following his rules, he sent them a preacher, a prophet—his son Jesus."

"So, Jesus was a role model, and people followed him?" Toad offered.

"He was a role model for people who really wanted to follow. For the rest, he was a preacher. Unfortunately, most people have the attention span of a Rowdie reading a mathematics book when they're hearing about rules, and how they should act in society, an' such. When they got tired of listening, they nailed the kid up on a tree."

Skulk and Ernie sat quietly incredulous at what Maynard was saying.

"So the religion just ended?" Toad asked.

"Heck no. With Jesus safely out of the way religion thrived. Without a living role model, people were free to interpret his teachings any damn way they wanted. New cults popped up everywhere. Before long, subtle differences between them led to disagreements, arguments, religious schisms and war.

"After a time the Old-Timers' wizard technology grew to such an extent that they began to worship science instead of God, though they still gave Him plenty of lip service when it served their purpose. Soon there was greater confusion, higher technology, and more effective means of warfare. As time went on, not only did people lose faith in God, but in technology as well. Hungering for answers, any answers, people were prone to listen to any old idiot that came along. Enter Simon Doomsayer and his Neo-Luddites, exit civilization. This was the mess I woke up to inherit."

"I don't get it. What's the difference between the old religions and what you did?"

"The difference? The difference was that we built a myth *and* a culture, one matching the other, relating spirituality with daily life. But, we also planned to have a symbol for each generation, in the form of a living person. That is where the Clear Light Society came in. Whenever times got tough, the Society would know where to find a Dylan descendant and would groom him to be a spiritual leader. During peaceful times the Dylans lived out their lives in quiet anonymity. But even if they weren't needed, all people knew that a hero lived somewhere among them, ready to lead when the time was right. Society changed slowly and, for a long time, that knowledge was enough to keep people content."

Toad nodded solemnly as the pipe came his way. The weight of history itself seemed to be settling in on the room.

Maynard took a sip from his drink, sat deep in his chair, and sighed heavily. "All of you know how Skulk found me," he continued, "but what you don't know is that it was no accident. When I 'sleep' it can be for decades, sometimes long enough that Head Diggers come and go, and I never know who they are. But when times get really weird and they need some assistance getting society back on track, then dig it, they know where to find help. In the Clear Light Society, the Head Digger alone is entrusted with the knowledge. In a society of secrets, I'm their biggest one.

"This time, when trouble started and it appeared to be more than mere Greaser brigandry or some border dispute between Fascists and Radiclibs, Skulk had the Diggers do some investigating. And when the center of the hubbub turned out to be Bahston, Skulk did what he was destined to do. Using the directions left for him, Skulk found my resting place and dug me out. After hearing what Skulk had to say, we both agreed that Brother Mungweasle should go to Beantown and scope it out. I had friends in the Thirdworld that I knew would help him. In the meantime the Clear Light Society helped locate the latest Dylan descendant.

"It turned out some heavy crap was in the wind, and it smelled *bad*. Ernie came back with tales of a faceless Dark Man, an immortal like myself, who was rediscovering dangerous lost knowledge. Seeming to desire nothing less than the total conquest of Street-Corner Earth, he was arming our enemies with deadly weapons—firearms, steamwagons, and other lethal innovations.

"I already suspected that Tommy Two had survived Westcommune centuries before, and had returned as the Dark Man. This was a critical time for all of Street-Corner Earth. Important steps had to be taken, not only to rid the world of him once and for all, but also to help society assimilate the changes he was bringing with him."

Ernie tugged at his mustache thoughtfully. "You mean the weapons?"

"Dig it. But more, too. Since the beginning, Freaks have been involved in a never-ending cycle of hostility with their neighbors. The roots go back five hundred years, to pre-Helter-Skelter street corners. Fascist and Greasers hated Hippies for their long hair and free-thinking ways, and Hippies hated them back for their intolerance and blind adherence to dogma. Little has changed. The cycle has to end. It is essential that we find ways to heal those old wounds. Freaks and Radiclibs have to grow closer to their enemies and show them the long and winding road to lasting peace."

"It's way too early for that, Maynard," Ernie stated.

"No, man, the time is *now*. The endless cycle of war, like, has to end with us, with this generation. All peoples, regardless of ideology, must learn to live with one another or we're all doomed. It's time for a new perspective, a new line, a new hero."

Toad toyed with the glass in his hand. The room grew silent and he felt Maynard's eyes boring into him. "Me??"

The Beatnik nodded.

"Why?! I have no outstanding gifts, no special lineage."

"Not true. One of your forefathers was a pretty heavy dude."

"C'mon. More of your stories." Toad squirmed uncomfortably in his chair.

"Hah! Think about it. Do you recall the night on Mount Lennon and how you felt? And, how about your, uh, natural ability with the guitar?"

"That was just an effect of the *Necronomicon*, wasn't it?"

"In part. But, remember those glasses I gave you?"

"Yeah. So?"

"They once belonged to an ancestor of yours ... John Lennon."

Toad looked around the room, first at Ernie, whose chin seemed to have fallen past the ends of his long drooping mustache, then at Skulk, who smiled knowingly, and then back at Maynard. "Whaaa? No way. This is the most absurd thing you've said so far. I was just starting to believe you, too."

"Oh, believe me. It's the truth, daddy-o. It's no coincidence you played

Imagine at Covenstead, a song that presages our future." The Beatnik smiled as he adjusted his dusty beret. "You can't cheat history, Toad."

"Maybe not, but it seems you excel in making up history to suit your purposes."

"Hey, I *could* lie about this shit, but I'd still know the difference. A cat's gotta play straight with history—real history."

"But how can you say I'm a Lennon? That's impossible."

"All things are possible, man. Let me tune you in to the poem of life."

The room seemed suddenly too close, too warm. Toad felt himself beginning to sweat. He said in a small voice, "Go on."

The Beatnik leaned back, grinning. "I've never told anyone this, not even Boswell, or Frankie Lee, or Skulk, but back in the old, old days I had a younger sister. Her name was Rachel. Rach' was quite a bit like me, only a hell of a lot better looking. We were both into the same things: art, music, the hip scene. I went to all the important events and met all the big Beatnik and Hippie idols, as did she. But, whereas my heroes were mostly folksingers and poets, Rachel was more interested in the big rock bands of the era, like the Beatles, and the Rolling Stones and The Who. Somehow she managed to meet Lennon at one of his concerts. She was a real groupie. Nine months later she had a son named Adrien. His dad, as far as I know, was never aware of his existence.

"Adrien was just a young boy when I fell in the peat bog. After I awoke, I went in search of any relatives that might still be alive. When I found the old homestead it was a wreck. The roof was sagging and the walls were in sore need of paint and repairs, but it was still recognizable. There was an old man sitting on the porch whittling on a stick.

"I approached the coot and, like, rapped with him awhile. He me told me his name was Adrien, and that the house had belonged to his mother and his grandparents before what he termed the 'Great Going-Backwards'. I didn't tell him who I was, of course, but he sure looked enough like his mom, old and half-senile though he was, for me to know that he was my nephew. Later on, when I went west with Boswell and his people, I persuaded nephew Adrien to go with me."

"That's all very interesting," Toad said, crossing his arms, "but what has all this got to do with me?"

"Have patience. During my wanderings with Boswell I began to plan and formulate goals for the future, not just for myself, but for all our people. Adrien, in the meantime, became a favorite of the tribe, particularly among some of the younger and more impressionable girls. He fathered a daughter by one of them. This daughter, whose name was Melody, later married a pipesmith by the name of Whatley Toad, your great, great, ever-so-great grandfather."

Toad felt dizzy. It took him several moments to absorb what he was being told. "T-then what you're saying is, that not only am I related to Lennon, but you as well?"

"You're in the groove, daddy-o. Since Adrien's time I've been keeping a close watch on my relatives. It's been easy; there's never been that many."

"And you've chosen me to begin your new ruling line?"

"No. History chose you. Sheer poetry, I tell you."

"I don't want any part of this," Toad said angrily. "I don't want to be a hero, and I sure as hell don't want to be your great-great-grandnephew or whatever you'd call it."

"Hey, like, both things have been done and can't be undone. Besides, you're more a hero by your own deeds than by my say-so."

The pipesmith shook his head. He was beginning to perspire heavily. "I have no control over the past, but I can control my future. I'm sure you mean well, but I refuse to be manipulated into being part of your fantasies. I've got my own life to live."

"You, like, misunderstand what we want, man, the Society and me. You can write your own history of things. Like, there's tons of books in the Clear Light Society library and the University Library at Shambullah for you to pore over. Hell, maybe you could even work things out with Mizjoan and have a few kids, if that was agreeable to her. You won't be on display to the world, if that's what bothers you."

Toad laughed, a bitter, drawn-out laugh. "What version of history do you want me to write—mine or yours?"

Maynard said nothing, but his grin deepened.

"Hah! Just as I thought. Didn't you say that one couldn't cheat history? It seems to me that that's exactly what you're asking me to do."

The Beatnik shrugged. "Whoever said that real history is what you read in books?"

Toad gestured at his crowded bookshelves. "Are you saying that Badmoon, Pedanticus, and these others are liars?"

"No, but how often do any of them agree? Hell, some of these books right here I wrote myself, under assumed names of course, and I know they aren't a hundred percent accurate."

"What are you trying to tell me?"

"That 'truth' and 'history' are very subjective things. The past is as changeable, if not more changeable, than the future. Like, your view of past events is colored by your personal biases and, intentionally or not, by the effect you want your writing to have on future generations. Contrived history can have an effect on real history, and vice-versa. It's that way today just as surely as it was before people even wrote things down."

Toad shook his head. "This is all leaving me numb. Are you telling me that you want me to deliberately miswrite history?"

"Certainly. If that's the proper way to get things done. In a generation or two it won't matter what was real and what wasn't. Think about it; what makes your interpretation more 'true' than another? It's a matter of perspective. Go ahead, write your own version of events. What the hell, they're as valid as mine or anyone else's."

"Now I know I'm confused. If what I say totally contradicts something you say, you won't censor it?"

"Of course not. Obviously you didn't dig what I just said about the subjectivity of reality. *Everything* is a matter of interpretation. Man can't grasp the larger workings of history because he can't see the subtle patterns, the whole picture. Even if he could, he couldn't deal with it objectively. Centuries ago, when I was in school, a teacher of mine said that history helped us learn from our mistakes. That was unmitigated bullshit; mankind has made the same mistakes over and over again. The chronicling of the events of history is one thing, and we owe it a certain reverence; the way we interpret and use that information is another."

"You're being about as clear as mud, Maynard."

"Am I, daddy-o? Well, dig this then: history has always been modified to influence events for good or ill. If enough people believe something for long enough it becomes fact. Way back when, long before I was on the scene, bards and musicians embellished stories to flatter their patrons and to keep their audiences entertained. Later, after records started to be written down, scribes did the same thing, honoring some leaders while the names of others were stricken from the records, extolling the virtue of one group while vilifying another. Who was right depended on what side you were on. In time who the hell was to know the difference? History books often confused wishful thinking with reality. Leaders, or presidents as they were called, were often endowed with better morals than they actually possessed, or had feats attributed to them that they never actually performed. I think the idea was to set up ideals that the common people could follow. At least that's what Boswell and I attempted at Westcommune. It's good; people need ideals. All I want is for Street-Corner Earth to survive, and for its people to live peacefully and to mature ahead of their technology."

Toad nodded numbly, trying to absorb all he was being told. He was beginning to understand, and maybe that frightened him a little. Maynard seemed like a shape-changer to him: talking about truth one minute, then explaining the necessity for lying the next, expounding like a scholar, then lapsing into his strange jivey dialect.

"The Hippies of my own era were the closest to what I'd call the social ideal," Maynard continued, "though they were far from perfect. They

529

moved out of the cities and into the country to live in peace and commune with nature. Respect for the land and the judicious use of natural resources is a holy thing, but unfortunately most of these early pioneers didn't persist. Except for the people who were to eventually become the ancestors of the Oldhips, most abandoned their new way of life and reverted to the old, often with a vengeance. That's why I love the Oldhips so much, and why they'll always be my favorite people. I fear that if man is ever allowed complete free will, his curiosity about technology and gadgetry will condemn him to failure and self-destruction time and time again."

"That still doesn't justify your meddling with people's lives."

Maynard threw up his hands in gentle exasperation. "Is trying to keep mankind from destroying itself, and the world, such a bad thing, Brother Toad?"

"No. But, why does it have to be *your* way? What about what other people want? What about creativity—like Eddie? He was made to feel inferior for having new thoughts. You say that you want us to progress materially and spiritually, but only, it seems, if it's in the direction you want. You put your goals above trust and friendship. Maybe I can't stop what you're doing ... and, who knows, maybe you're right. You'll use my name, I'm sure. I can't prevent that. But, you *won't* use me."

Toad glanced at Ernie and Skulk, then got up and started towards the door. Halfway across the room he stopped and turned to regard Maynard coolly. "I can't live here, and I can't live in Leftopia with Mizjoan. Tomorrow I'm putting this place up for sale. After that, I intend to see what's beyond Street-Corner Earth. Maybe I'll find something out there for me—something I can live with."

He went to the door and pulled it open. Before he could walk through, Ernie Mungweasle was at his side.

"You won't be traveling alone," the herbalist said.

Chapter Sixty-Two

Except for an occasional hardcore partier stumbling home and the faint random echoes of drunken voices bumping down alleyways and spilling out into the street, the town was as still as a graveyard. Here and there solitary lamps glowed in upstairs windows, but for the most part the celebration had burned itself out after a few days.

The wayfarer, pulling his cowl deeper over his face, hunched down in the saddle of his sturdy black pony as he made his way through the cobbled streets. The hooded cape felt strange on his body, as did the patched jeans and the heavy Oldhip moccasins. These new clothes would take some getting used to, but he needed a disguise in these strange and perilous times. Running his hand over his stubbled chin, he wished for more familiar clothing, but he had left his leather jacket far behind—in many ways.

After riding north for most of a day, he had come to a decision and turned southeast, following the river towards the sea, to Rivertown. When he arrived at the waterfront area the traveler dismounted, tied up his pony, and headed down to the wharves. There'd be boats there, hopefully one he could borrow. He would be well on his way before it was missed. Sighing, he drew his cloak around his shoulders. Dawn was hours away yet, but still he hurried. As he neared the wharf, he saw a number of small boats tied there, unattended. The traveler smiled deep within his cowl, as he untied the mooring rope of a small, open skiff. Moving with surprising speed, he began rowing out to sea, leaving the dark headlands of Rivertown behind.

Toad stretched and yawned as he walked out of the front door of the Rusty Roachclip Tavern. It was a bright, clear day and he relished the feel of the sun on his face. The air was cool and clean and carried a heavy scent of sea and pine. Above him gulls circled and cried in the nearly cloudless sky. He stretched again and felt the backpack shift on his shoulders. Even this small sensation seemed good and right.

The old canvas pack contained everything that the pipesmith now owned. All of his possessions, his house and lands included, had been sold to Toker Jones several days ago for a tidy sum. The sale had been consummated not more than an hour after Gary was laid to rest in the Island burying ground. Skulk and Maynard had departed soon afterward, leaving on Captain Chives' ferry for the first leg of their journey back to Hillcommune. To be honest, Toad wasn't overly sorry to see them go. As he and Ernie had stood on the dock watching the ferry unfurl its sail to the sea breezes, Toad reflected on how much older he'd felt before the start of his adventures, and how much younger he felt now. Today, short on possessions but long on freedom, he felt even younger still.

Toad and Ernie had paid fifteen Rubins apiece for a night in one of the small rooms over the Rusty Roachclip. Breakfast was five more. Exorbitant prices, Toad felt, but he hardly cared. As soon as he and the older Freak picked up a few supplies they'd be on the road, with no particular direction in mind, other than away from Street-Corner Earth. Who knows, maybe their path would take them to Bahston, or west to the ruins of Westcommune, or even to the birthplace of Freaks and Oldhips, Haight-Ashbury. The possibilities were, as they say, endless.

Glancing down Rivertown's main street towards the waterfront Toad spied Ernie's brightly painted caravan wagon parked in front of the Penny Lane General Store. The wagon had arrived in town just yesterday, driven by two Radiclib teamsters who kept it on the road all night, driving from Camp Hoffman to Rivertown in record time. At Mizjoan's request it had been greased, repaired and painted, and equipped with extra grain for Ernie's horse and a blunderbuss and brace of pistols as gifts for Toad and Ernie. Hitching his pack higher on his shoulders, Toad headed down the long boardwalk to meet his friend.

It was still early and there were few people on the street. Inside the store the clerk, a young Freak with a long black beard and a stained apron, was tallying up Ernie's purchases while the herbalist laboriously counted out his coins.

"Mornin', Toad," Ernie said, glancing up. "Can you think of anything else we'll need for our trip?"

Toad looked over the pile of gear and foodstuffs on the counter and shook his head. His attention was drawn to a dusty guitar hanging behind the counter.

Ernie smiled when he noticed Toad eyeing the old instrument. "You oughta buy it, Toad. We'll need music on our journey."

Toad almost said no, but the guitar fascinated him. "How much is it?" he found himself asking the clerk.

"That's a custom Wackenbacker Concert Model, sir," the young man replied. "We took it in trade several years ago. It'd normally go for a hundred twenty-five Rubins. I can let you have it for, say, ninety."

The pipesmith nodded. It was a beautiful instrument, and Ernie was right about the need for music on the road. "Usually, I would try to dicker you down a bit more," Toad said, carefully counting out a number of heavy silver coins, "but today I seem to have more money than I will need for a while. If you'll put it into a nice sack for me, I'll take it."

While Ernie began gathering up his purchases, the clerk popped the guitar into an oilcloth sack and handed it to Toad. With the guitar in one hand and an armload of their provisions in the other, the pipesmith followed his friend out to the street. After loading the wagon, they climbed in and headed south down Penny Lane.

The town was almost fully awake now. Shopkeepers were sweeping off the stoops in front of their stores, fishermen were wandering out of the street's small cafés on their way to the docks and townsfreaks, seemingly unaffected by the recent trouble, were starting about their daily errands. As Toad and Ernie passed the livery stable the town blacksmith, shirtless in spite of the coolness of the day, was already sweating heavily, cursing a steady stream as he tried to shoe an uncooperative draft horse. At the lower end of Penny Lane, where it ran into Harbor Road, nets were being spread out to dry along the wharves. In the harbor boats, with crews mostly hungover, were hoisting sail and setting out to sea in search of a fresh catch of lobster or cod.

As Toad watched, squinting into the sun, a fishing boat docked at the wharf and let off a single cloaked figure. The stranger paid the boatman, looked about nervously, and walked over to a small black pony hitched to the railing in front of Ferndoc's Chandlery. Toad squinted harder, watching the figure intently. Something about him seemed familiar. Recognition dawned at last. Toad reached out and grabbed Ernie's sleeve. "Check this out," he said. "Look who's over there."

Ernie glanced and did a double take. The stranger, dressed as he was in dusty cloak and patched jeans, was still recognizable as Sonny Slikback, the Fonzer who'd aided them at Covenstead.

Waving, Sonny got onto his pony and rode over to greet them. "Hey, I been lookin' for you two," he announced. "I went over to that island of yours last night, but the guy that runs the store said you'd left. I was afraid I was gonna miss you altogether."

"How in hell did you find out where I lived?" Toad asked. To his surprise he realized he was actually glad to see the Fonzer.

"That redheaded Raddyclib lady friend of yours. She sends her love, by the way."

"I thought you left Covenstead the day of the battle."

"I did, but after I got halfway to Lubejob I turned back. There ain't nothin' for me there now. Kham let that Dark Man walk all over him, and my people just went right along with it. Things ain't the same no more, ya know?"

"I know exactly how you feel."

Sonny shifted nervously in his saddle. "Yeah? Well ... uh ... it all made me think, maybe I oughta go on the road for awhile. Kinda blow the dust outa my head. But a guy needs buddies to do somethin' like that with."

"As you can see, we're leaving Street-Corner Earth ourselves—maybe forever. What do you think, Ernie?"

"Bring a Greaser along? I don't know, Toad," Ernie replied, smiling.

"Hey, I ain't that bad, ya know," Sonny declared, stiffening. "Besides, I'm good company. I know a lot of jokes, an' I'm good at fixin' things, like that wagon for instance. What da ya say?"

Ernie stroked his mustache like he was deep in thought, though the twinkle in his eyes showed that he'd already made up his mind. "What the hell?" he said, sticking out his hand to shake Sonny's. "Welcome aboard."

The pipesmith grinned as the Fonzer tied his pony to the back of the wagon and climbed up to sit between him and Ernie. Toad looked off across the water towards Smuttynose; the island seemed blurry in the distance. Almost without thinking about it he reached into his jacket pocket and took out the glasses that Maynard had given him at Hillcommune. When he slipped them on the island leapt into focus. Pushing the old, comfortable wire rims up on his nose, he leaned back and fumbled in his jacket for his pipe. Ernie snapped the reins and the wagon lurched forward, churning up dust on the road that led south and west, far away from the Freaklands.

Epilogue

Dusk was rapidly approaching, as it seemed to do more quickly during the holiday season. Snow sifted down over Camp Hoffman, dusting the wide expanse of Aquarius Square with fine white powder. Lights were going on in the barracks and houses close to the Square, while uniformed work crews were hurrying to get the last of the Yule decorations up before the light failed completely.

Mizjoan sat in an overstuffed chair by the window, watching a pair of Weathermen struggle to mount a giant red star on the crown of the tall pine across the street. Her thoughts ran back to last year's Yule party in Hillcommune—of old friends and new, some here, some departed—too many of them, like Tam, having passed from this world. But mostly she thought of Toad. Soon after the Battle of Covenstead, he'd left Street-Corner Earth with Ernie Mungweasle. Except for rumors brought by traders from far south, there had been no news of them since.

A baby cried in the next room. Slowly Mizjoan got to her feet. She loved little Justin dearly, but between caring for him and running her country she had hardly any time to herself. Would Toad have stayed if he'd known she was pregnant with his child, she wondered? No ... she was confident that he would have stayed.

Maynard and Kentstate entered the room. Kentstate was carrying Justin, who was swaddled in a red blanket; the dark-haired girl always beamed when she got to baby-sit. With a grin Kentstate handed the chubby, gurgling infant to Mizjoan and stepped back.

"Has Comrade Kid been giving you a hard time?" Mizjoan asked, attempting to hug the struggling, mewling baby.

Kentstate shook her head, smiling. "He just missed his Comrade Mommy."

"I can understand that. At this time of year, especially this year, I stop and think about family and friends, especially ones far away, and I miss them too. This little guy's dad is not the least among them."

Maynard pulled up a chair next to Mizjoan's. "Perhaps it's just as well," he said. "It wouldn't have been right to keep Toad here just for the sake of a child."

"I know," Mizjoan replied; her eyes held a faraway look. "But it seems to me that you and the Diggers took full advantage of his disappearance, Maynard. Without Toad around you're free to build his legend as you see fit. And it's disgusting, the way your Diggers shamelessly hint that he may return some day, when the need is great. What is going on in your devious little mind, Beatnik?"

"Not to worry, MJ. Your son is part Lennon and part Berkeley. He'll be well looked after. The Society will see to his education, and all of Street-Corner Earth will honor him. He's Toad's son, and I *am* confident that Toad will return someday."

Mizjoan shook her head. "Don't try to push your legends on me, comrade. That's just another one of your pipedreams."

The Beatnik turned and looked out the window. The snow was falling faster now, filling the streets. He smiled slyly, checking his reflection in the glass.

THE END

About the Authors

Stephen Hartford was born in 1948 in South Lebanon, Maine (Leb'nin if you were from there) and enjoyed a Huck Finn childhood. He attended local schools and joined the Air Force in 1967, serving eighteen months in Vietnam.

Steve has worked as a security guard, mill rat, printer's devil, salesman, assistant toy designer, gravestone installer, arcade attendant, resort caretaker and motel night clerk.

An avid amateur historian and folklorist, his interests include hiking, model building, photography, restoring old steamer trunks, anything Renfaireish or Steampunky and collecting and shooting antique firearms.

Other than a few cranky Letters to the Editor, *Pipedreams* is his first published work.

Michael Harmon was born and raised in Rochester, New Hampshire. He enjoyed the stereotypical boy's life in the early sixties—neighborhood sports, riding bikes, and exploring the woods behind his house with his dog. He attended the University of New Hampshire and has worked with the same company for 39 years.

In the tradition of one of his favorite literary characters, Ebenezer Cooke, Mike is interested in just about everything. He is a devoted family man and community volunteer, donating much of his free time to soccer leagues, school music booster clubs, and scouting groups. He is happily married with three wonderful children and his American Eskimo dog, Jack.

Mike has dabbled in short stories, poetry, and amusing characters for his kids, such as *TIMpathy and EMpathy* and the irrepressible *Bunnygungamog*. *Pipedreams* is also his first published work.

26189887R00310

Made in the USA
Charleston, SC
27 January 2014